The
Professor

Mi'Chelle Dodson

DEDICATION

The Professor is dedicated to two of my faithful reader friends -
Paula Thomas and **Bambi Mac** (aka Mạc Bích Cổ Trúc).
Both were very helpful with my V.I. (Paula) and Vietnamese
(Bambi) research, which is just one reason I named two of
my characters after them. Thanks again, ladies!

Other published eBooks/books by this author

Big Girlz Won't Cry

Bittersweet Interruptions

Changing Gene

Colors of Love

Hump Day

Misguided Reunion

My Lover, My Friend

Pretty Packages

Pulling Him Back

Side Dishes

Sweet Lips

Treachery Among Diamonds

Mr. Mrs. & Miss Trilogy

Enticing Mr. Wrong

Pursuing Mrs. Regrets

Miss Opportunity

* * *

Contact Info

Email:

mochainterlude@yahoo.com

Main Website:

http://suprinafrazier.webs.com/

ACKNOWLEDGMENTS

Special Thanks to God – He's a Way-Maker.

PROLOGUE

May

    Despite the grating presence of Cain Laker, her soon-to-be ex- boyfriend, Aurelia Bunting continued to throw clothes in the two black suitcases on the bedroom floor. Her clothes.

    She was leaving behind all the garments Cain bought her over the year that she'd been here, taking only what she'd gotten for herself. So what if the things he purchased were nicer and more expensive. There was a statement to be made here.

    That statement – I don't need you or anything from you!

    "Roxy's lying on me," Cain contended, sticking with his story as he sat on the edge of the large oak bed in the middle of the room.

    "You're the liar here, Cain!" Aurelia snapped, glaring at the wavy- haired man across from her.

    Once upon a time she deemed him so handsome. Now Cain was the ugliest thing she'd ever seen. And that expensive cologne she once thought smelled so delicious on him, now stank to the point of nausea. She couldn't wait to get away from it and him.

    "No, I'm not—"

    "Yes, you are," Aurelia interrupted, cutting off yet another lie. "Cheating on me wid meh own best friend. Ex-best friend, dat is, since I don't want nuttin else to do wid you or Roxy," she added as her Virgin Island accent grew thicker the way it usually did whenever her ire rose.

    "She's lying I tell you," Cain insisted. His bronze cheeks deepened in color.

1

Aurelia scoffed. "And I guess she lying 'bout you being de father of her unborn child, too, huh?" She flung more clothes into the suitcases. Who cares that she'd strayed from her usual neatness? She'd deal with organizational issues later. Leaving her cheating boyfriend was at the top of Aurelia's to-do list right now.

Cain scowled. "That girl is not pregnant by me! How could she be? I always use protection during sex," he denied. "Besides, my previous medical condition makes it next to impossible for me to conceive."

Aurelia abruptly stopped packing. She placed her hands on her hips and just laughed…at him! Did the man not have any sense at all? Did he not realize what he just said?

"I don't know what I ever saw in you," Aurelia replied, her accent loosening back up as her ire decreased considerably. What was the point of wasting anger on a fool?

"You're too stupid to even realize that you just told on yourself," Aurelia continued. "The correct answer should have been, 'Roxy's not pregnant by me because I never had sex with her', not because you always use protection or have some previous medical condition. It's a good thing you're set for life financially, because you simply wouldn't make it in the working world acting dumber than a block of cheese."

Cain's eyes bucked at his blunder, further confirming his guilt and dumb jock persona. He never could hold his own with Aurelia on an intellectual level no matter how much he tried. And he had tried over the last year…hard.

Cain even went so far as to secretly partake of classical music and literary classics to increase his intelligence and try to catch up with hers. So what if he listened to the audio versions of Jane Austen. Everybody weren't strong readers, some people never would be, at least that's what he'd been told by all of his teachers.

Pushing past his inadequacies, Cain focused on his strengths instead. "You saw what all your friends saw in me, good looks, financial security and a man capable of hitting all the right spots in a woman," he said, telling on himself even more as he bragged about his attractiveness, sizable music store inheritance, and sexual prowess.

Aurelia bristled at that cheap, yet true stab in the gut. She had stayed with Cain so long because of the great sex…and of course the free room and board. Don't forget the frequent trips to hair and nail salons.

Although he also bought her plenty of clothes, shoes, and accessories, they were all purchased with selfish motives. How else could Aurelia explain having so much formal wear when she felt more comfortable in jeans and t-shirts? It was Cain that wanted her dressed to the nines for the countless social functions he was invited to in the music industry. It was that same formal wear that Aurelia was gladly leaving behind today.

There had been no help with her college tuition or books. Cain outright refused to assist with her educational expenses. He wouldn't even put gas in her car so that she could get to school. And he always changed the subject whenever she brought up her educational or career goals.

"Besides, you and I both know you have no place to go," Cain continued, sounding more arrogant by the minute. "You have no family here in the states. The few relatives you have back home are just as broke as you. Even if they pool all their money together, I seriously doubt it would still be enough to get you all the way from Alcove, California to the Virgin Islands. You can't send yourself since all the money you make at your part-time job goes to that high-priced college you insist on attending and to help your mother and little brother. If it wasn't for me, you wouldn't even have food to eat. Face it, girl, you need me," he concluded smugly, leaning back on the bed with his hands folded behind his head.

"I'll manage." Aurelia returned to her packing with a vengeance. No hands had been quicker. "I did all right before I met you," she reminded him.

"Oh, so you're going back to stripping, huh?" Cain smirked, alluding to how he'd met her. "Now I know you're going to come running back to me. Probably by the weekend since I know how much you hate dancing for money."

"I hate cheating men more!" Aurelia retorted, zipping her suitcases with relish. She clenched their handles tight as she lifted them from the floor. Inwardly she commended herself for keeping her P.O. Box as her mailing address. Now she wouldn't have to worry about returning here for missing and lost mail. Or worse, mail held hostage by her ex.

"When you try to come back, don't be surprised if Roxy's here taking your place in every way, you Catherine Willows wannabe," Cain spat out, putting up no protest as she stalked towards the bedroom door. He was too proud to beg. Didn't

3

think he had to. Not with his looks and money.

"I won't be surprised at all." Aurelia smirked, actually flattered by his comparison to her favorite CSI character. "Unlike you, I am smart enough to realize that Roxy's whole purpose for telling me about the baby and the affair is to get me to move out so she can move in." She paused at the door. "Hold on to your inheritance tight, Cain, because she's about to take you for everything you got."

Cain's eyes bucked again as he suddenly realized just what he'd gotten himself into with Roxy. Whereas Aurelia was hardworking and had clear career goals, Roxy was lazy, a lackluster exotic dancer at best, and wanted to marry out of the hood instead of work her way out. Marry a rich man, that is, which Cain definitely was.

Frustrated with this vexing turn of events, he polluted the airwaves with a loud expletive.

Halfway down the hall, Aurelia's ears picked up that harsh curse. She smiled and chuckled to herself.

I see dumb-dumb finally got it, she mused, convinced that Cain deserved whatever Roxy had in mind for him.

As for Aurelia, she'd learned a hard lesson behind this situation. The next guy she dated would need to have more than just sex appeal and money to snag her. He would also need honor and character. Don't forget about intelligence. Aurelia's next man would definitely need lots of that. The more, the better.

CHAPTER ONE

Three Months Later – Early August

Aurelia was almost at her wit's end on that starlit Monday night. Another semester of tuition was due in two weeks and she simply did not have it. She knew where to get it though – Dingo's, a strip club in the next town to the north.

Had Aurelia returned to exotic dancing before now, she might have been able to come up with the money in enough time. More than enough money considering her talents. Yet Aurelia had delayed going back to that profession until she'd completely run out of all other viable options. She ran out of those options sooner than expected.

After working a slew of part-time jobs over the summer, Aurelia found herself still three grand short of her tuition. Those jobs barely kept her fed and in the one bedroom apartment she rented on the poor side of Alcove, much less provided excess money for college savings.

On top of all that, she'd had to send more money home than usual this month to help her struggling mother and little brother out of a new financial fix that arose due to a leaky roof. Even maxing out her school loans weren't going to be enough to pay for her remaining matriculation.

Getting help from a wealthy new boyfriend was out of the question. Aurelia was still too traumatized from that Cain experience to even go on a date with another man. Just today she'd turned down five date requests from five different men, despite the fact that her hormones had never raged louder.

Aurelia didn't want or need the added aggravation of a

man right now. She wasn't into one-night-stands, so her hormone driven libido would just have to wait for satisfaction.

Since Aurelia wasn't a prostitute and never would be, she decided to earn the money she needed through exotic dancing. Although her primary job as a switchboard operator in the Alcove Mall was more respectable, it paid chicken scratch compared to her night job.

I have to score big for the next two weeks, Aurelia mused, parking her '68 white Volkswagen Beetle in the back of the strip club. Either that or sit out this next semester. She really didn't want to do the latter.

As a new senior, the twenty-two-year-old only had one more year to finish college. Aurelia didn't want to delay her chemistry degree for one day longer, much less a whole semester. That college degree was going to be her and her family's ticket out of poverty once and for all. It was also the key to unlock the door to Aurelia's dream career, which was to one day become a forensic scientist and work in a real crime lab.

Maybe I can hook up with Crystal and them on that bachelor's party in Cabo, Aurelia thought, hoping it wasn't too late to join in. After all, that party was this Friday.

Already a club favorite in the month that she'd been here, Aurelia was asked by Crystal a week ago to join the traveling crew to the upcoming event in Cabo San Lucas, Mexico. Out of pure hatred for her second job, she promptly and yet politely declined the head dancer's invitation.

Aurelia didn't want to do any more exotic dancing than was absolutely necessary. Especially since every time she danced for money it was like dishonoring her father's memory. For it was he that bartered three years of lawn care service to a top dance studio in St. Thomas just so she could enjoy free dance classes there.

Now Aurelia realized how important it was to put her hatred aside for the greater good – her degree from a university with a top-notch forensics program. Now she wished she'd been wiser…sooner.

"Hello, Six-Eight," Aurelia said, pleasantly greeting the burly bouncer by his nickname and actual height as she approached the back entrance. A black garment bag with tonight's outfits was draped over her right forearm. A black leather purse with matching accessories inside hung from her left shoulder.

"Hey, lady." Six-Eight gave her a gap-toothed smile as he held the door open for her. "Ready to make that paper tonight?"

"You know it." Aurelia grinned, mindful to always be nice to him. Not only was Six-Eight the brother of the owner, he was always respectful to the dancers, kept the occasional unruly customer from attacking them on or off stage, and he always made sure they got safely to and from their cars. Who wouldn't be nice to a great guy like that?

"Here, I brought a little something for you," Aurelia added, reaching into her purse for a king-sized pack of Now and Laters, Six-Eight's favorite sweet treat.

"Ahhhhh…snap! You got the grape kind and everything." He grinned. "You all right, lady, you know that?" Six-Eight said, receiving his candy with a grateful nod as she passed by him.

"I try to be," Aurelia replied over her left shoulder as she continued down the back hallway of the club.

* * *

In the dressing room, Aurelia quickly changed into one of her other outfits. Around here a girl had to be able to get in and out of her clothes quick. She also couldn't be bashful. Shyness had no place in a strip club.

Even so, Aurelia was glad that she had the dressing room all to herself for once. That didn't happen very often around here, which meant most of the girls were working the crowd for lap dances while another one performed on stage.

Suddenly Crystal entered the dressing room. She'd just finished her set. Her glistening olive skin was proof of how much effort she'd put into her performance.

Aurelia smiled. Crystal was just the person she wanted to see. "Hey, can I tag along on that Cabo trip with you guys after all?" She opened her combination locker and place her belongings inside.

"Sure." Crystal smiled, sitting down at the long mirrored vanity to remove the money from her person. As usual, the pretty redhead had a thong and a garter full of large bills. And this was despite the presence of other dancers during her set.

Crystal was the highest paid dancer at the club due to her agility and many on-stage tricks. She was the owner/manager's favorite and also his steady girlfriend. And yet she never used her position to slack off, but instead remained one of the hardest working dancers there.

"Dingo asked me about you again just today," Crystal continued. "He says he wants to take the best the club has to offer on this trip. Said these guys are high rollers and ready to spend big money for their entertainment. An exotic island beauty like yourself could get paid real well at an event like this."

"What kind of high rollers?" Aurelia asked cautiously. Although she hated dancing for money period, she really hated dancing for high rollers of the illegal kind. Those kinds of guys usually tried to dope the girls up with drugs and/or alcohol and always expected the dancing to lead to sex afterwards.

Aurelia never had sex with customers. The one time she agreed to even date a customer turned out bad. Real bad. That customer was Cain, who was currently hiding from Roxy overseas because she wasn't classy enough for him to marry and because he wasn't ready to be a father yet. If ever.

"The doctor, lawyer, white collar kind of high rollers will be there," Crystal explained, laughing at Aurelia's question. "You really are a prude, aren't you?" she said, echoing what some of the other girls had said about the V.I. native. "Money is money with me. I'll dance for anybody. Now when it comes to sleeping around, you know only one man has what I need – Dingo." Crystal smiled, looking totally in love now.

"I guess I am a prude." Aurelia chuckled as she closed her locker and gave the combination dial a final swirl for the road. "Sign me up for that trip anyway though," she said, adjusting the revealing green top over her full bosom.

"Will do," Crystal replied just as Aurelia's unique stage name was called. "Have a good set, Miss Prude," she teased.

"Will do, Miss Brown-noser," Aurelia teased in return, letting Crystal know what the other girls were saying behind her back, too.

Crystal pealed with laughter. "They can call me what they want, but they can't deny that I'm also Miss Paid." She waved a stack of fifties in the air.

Aurelia laughed. As she walked down the hall towards the stage area, she thought more about Crystal's prude comment. She wasn't surprised that the other girls called her that behind her back.

Aurelia was a prude when it came to drinking, drugging, and sleeping with customers. Yes, she took off her clothes and danced for money just like the rest of the girls, but that's where the similarities ended. She'd never taken drugs and her alcohol consumption amounted to a glass of wine once or twice a year, and then only for special occasions.

Aurelia was also a recluse. At least she was now. Though friendly to everyone she encountered, she pretty much stayed to herself these days. She learned a hard lesson from that Roxy situation. Aurelia wouldn't complain if she never had another best friend in her life. If only she didn't have the type of personality that made other people want to befriend her, including the jealous ones like Roxy.

Right before she went on stage, Aurelia closed her eyes, took a deep breath, and allowed the Aurora in her to emerge. She took on that particular stage name due to her strong interest in science and her fascination with the natural colored light displays often seen at night in the polar regions of the world.

To perfect her Aurora stage persona and to highlight her light milk chocolate skin, Aurelia always wore either bright or neon-colored outfits. Tonight was no different.

Tonight Aurelia was clad in a neon green lingerie set that fit her like a second skin. The tight outfit would be taken off piece by piece until all she wore were pasties and a thong on her voluptuous 34D-22-36 frame. She never got fully nude for any customer on or off stage.

All right, Aurora. Go out there and make no less than five hundred tonight, Aurelia coached her inner sex kitten, aiming high as usual.

Such ambition and determination is what got her stateside and into the college of her choice in the first place. She planned to ride those traits right into her destiny.

You might make over five tonight, girl. Willy's in the house, Aurelia thought, immediately spotting the big spender who hardly ever missed her shows. *If only he didn't want so many lap dances in exchange.*

CHAPTER TWO

Friday Night

"I'm really not up for this," Baron Weaver told his fourth older brother as they waited in the largest suite of the two adjoining rooms that were reserved for tonight's entertainment.

"You're my best man, Professor. You have to be here," Count replied, calling the twenty-nine-year-old by his nickname.

Extremely smart and studious, Baron earned that nickname early in life. That same childhood name turned out to be a self-fulfilling prophecy because that's exactly what he became in adulthood.

"Besides, I need you here to help keep Duke in line, remember?" Count continued, referring to their oldest brother of all.

Duke was in mid-life crisis mode these days. Thus he was prone to cheat on his wife Sasha just to feel young again. He'd already been unfaithful once this year.

Duke was almost uninvited when Sasha learned there would be strippers at tonight's bachelor's party. Yet when Baron and Count promised to watch out for him, she reluctantly agreed to allow Duke to attend.

Though the youngest out of the five Weaver brothers, Count and Baron were the most responsible, levelheaded and sensible. Their other older brothers, Marquess and Earl, were no help since they were just as likely to be unfaithful to their wives. Which is why one of them was currently going through a nasty divorce and the other only had a marriage of convenience for appearances sakes.

"You're right. I'll stay…for Sasha's sake," Baron consented, pushing pass his own disappointing love life, which included being dumped three weeks before his own wedding.

Megan Griswold, Baron's social-climbing ex-fiancée, found someone with a larger net worth and a higher social status than him back in May. She left him high and dry with a Dear John text message.

A text message!

Megan hadn't even taken the time to craft a handwritten letter. Nor had she lingered over the word count. All Baron received was a simple text message that consisted of six measly words: 'Found someone new. Sorry. Toodles! Megan'.

How heartless and callus is that?!

What happened to the girl who'd had a crush on him since she was seventeen? The same girl who'd followed Baron around like a lovesick puppy for eight years until he finally surrendered to her pursuits and saw her as a serious love interest.

Now Baron wished he had followed his first instincts and never dated Megan at all. For one thing, her valley girl mannerisms had repelled him from the start, despite her great beauty. She'd reeked of airhead and blonde bimbo. So much so that he'd been concerned about her ability to hold an intelligent conversation.

Baron would later learn that Megan was quite capable of holding her own in a conversation, though she only knew trivial things about any given subject. Never any in-depth information.

Secondly, Megan had been entirely too shallow for his tastes. Most of her thoughts were about herself…or him since he was her heart's desire. Beyond that it was as if nothing or no one else in the world mattered.

Having been raised to be mindful of the people around him and their needs, Baron had found that type of shallowness highly irritating. But then when Megan started to do volunteer work with senior citizens, his irritation had lessened. She suddenly became considerably more tolerable. However, that irritation always returned in full force whenever she wanted to receive accolades for her volunteerism, which was often.

Thirdly, Megan had always been too quick to grow tired

of things once she acquired them. The fact that she had dresses in her closet that had only been worn once should have told Baron that she would eventually tire of him also after he finally gave into her.

Megan's refusal to give her barely worn dresses away to charity unless there was an audience was a red flag to the depth of her shallowness and revealed how insincere her benevolence truly was. Her refusal to finish her college degree, despite the fact that all she had to do was study harder and re-take her exit exams, indicated that she would abandon ship if things got too rocky. Especially if she saw no benefit to staying on board.

Megan had never seen any real benefit to having a higher education for herself. She'd only wanted to be a wife. His wife.

Even though Baron knew all those things about Megan, he still consented to date her anyway. He did so for two seemingly happy years. He even consented to marry her, thinking that they could stretch their happiness out over a lifetime. They'd certainly been compatible enough in the bedroom.

I was a first-class fool for ever getting involved with her, Baron now realized, wishing he could rewind time. If so, he would have made sure to spend the last two years of his life doing something more constructive with his time besides being in love with a shallow, disloyal woman.

Ready to push all thoughts of Megan aside for now, Baron mentally prepared himself to pretend to be happy for one brother while babysitting another. Truthfully, he'd much rather be home grading papers like the studious professor that he was. But since he'd just had a long summer break from teaching there weren't currently any papers to grade.

Bummer.

No worries though. Baron would be back in the classroom soon enough with papers up to his neck to grade since he was such a big homework giver.

* * *

At a much cheaper hotel in Cabo, Crystal had all the girls line up for their regular inspection before heading out to the bachelor's party. Hair, nails, makeup, clothes, and especially hygiene had to be on point. Dingo didn't half-step at his club when it came to things like that. He had a reputation to maintain for having the finest, sexiest, and the cleanest ladies on roster.

Like other facets of the adult entertainment industry, Dingo's dancers also had to be tested every thirty days for STDs. As usual, Aurelia made the cut. Not only had she submitted her latest test results just yesterday, she made a habit of keeping her outside just as immaculate as her inside.

Aurelia's outer adornment used to be even more impeccable when she was with Cain. But ever since that relationship went sour, she'd taken to dressing all the way down so as not to draw any extra attention to herself, especially at school where there were two men to every one woman.

Aurelia's school wardrobe now consisted solely of jeans or sweatpants, jerseys or t-shirts, and sneakers. Her hair was usually worn in a ponytail or loose under a baseball cap. Her new personal school motto was: 'I'm here to learn, not to impress anyone with my beauty.' And yet men still flocked to her on a daily basis.

While Aurelia passed today's inspection with a breeze, blonde-haired Raven almost didn't make the cut. Her last test results were almost expired and the cold sore she had under her lip earlier in the week was still slightly visible. However, after a bit of camouflaging with makeup and a lot of pleading from Raven, Dingo allowed her to go with everyone else.

Once they made it to the more expensive hotel, Aurelia took stock of the high rollers that were present at the bachelor party. One of the lawyers in the bunch was the groom. Everyone called him Count.

A handsome Hispanic looking fellow, Count had a diverse group of relatives and peers. They included lawyers, doctors, various businessmen, and a man they called Professor.

Professor was the best man and also one of the brothers of the groom. Aurelia learned that bit of information after each man introduced himself using first names only. Some also shared their occupations, most likely to impress the beautiful women in their midst and gain a certain amount of special attention from them.

After each girl had a chance to present herself individually in dance to the cheering men, the time for lap dances came into play. This was where some girls garnered their biggest tips as they gave the men personalized attention.

Crystal stopped issuing lap dances when she became

Dingo's girl. Now she remained at his side during working parties and helped with the sound system, the aromatherapy candles, and the fancy lighting equipment he brought along for extra effect.

As expected, Raven and the other girls immediately went for the lawyers, doctors, and a few of the young businessmen. Since Aurelia had just concluded her first solo dance in front of everyone, she was slightly delayed in snagging a man from the first group. Now she was left with a few gray-haired businessmen and the one they called Professor.

Was he really a professor? When he introduced himself earlier, he'd been very brief and had failed to share his occupation.

If the man was a professor, he didn't look like any Aurelia had ever seen before. What kind of professor had muscles from head to toe and looked like he just strutted off of a magazine cover? And where were his nerd glasses? His pocket protectors?

All the male professors that Aurelia encountered at Alcove University looked like professors. This man looked like a Hunk-of-the- Month. This professor would probably qualify for a Hunk-of-the-Year award if he would only smile.

And just like that Aurelia knew why the professor's countenance was so glum. Why he had the saddest blue-brown eyes she'd ever seen.

He was heartbroken.

Discerning their similar pain was enough to make Aurelia pick the professor over the businessmen. Older businessmen at that, who would have surely given her a big tip just for choosing them over a young buck any day.

This was new.

Aurelia usually went for the big bucks in her personal and professional life. As someone that was trying to get as far away from poverty as she could, she tended to gravitate towards those who were already financially established. And yet she didn't regret choosing the professor at all.

"Would you like a lap dance, Professor?" Aurelia asked the gorgeous Latino. "By the way, I'm Aurora in case you weren't listening before," she said, automatically using her stage name again.

Baron shook his head 'no', but what came out of his mouth instead was, "Yes."

This had to be the most beautiful black woman he'd ever seen in his life. Light milk chocolate from head to toe like a candy bar dipped in cream, she had large caramel eyes, dimples, and a full mouth. Her hair was in fresh micro-braids that reached down to her mid-back. She had curves so full and luscious that even men who already had female attention wished they had waited for hers. And her slight Virgin Island accent was simply adorable, especially when she emphasized the 'sor' part of his nickname.

Aurelia chuckled. "Which is it, Professor? Yes or no?" she asked, yanking him from his daze with her sweet voice just as one of the club's most popular songs came on. She began to sensually sway in front of him to the tune of Chris Brown's Take U Down.

After that Rihanna incident many radio stations pulled all of Chris' music from their playlists. But not the strip clubs. Even to this day, they continued to have that song in heavy rotation because of its hypnotic-like beat. Plus, it was a bit hypocritical for strip club owners/operators to judge anyone for their actions, good or bad.

Baron swallowed hard before speaking again. Those hips. Those beautiful island hips had him absolutely mesmerized.

"Yes," Baron echoed, feeling his body stir in a way that it hadn't in months.

He thought Megan had gelded him, too, when she broke his heart due to its adverse effect on his libido. Now Baron saw that he was definitely on the mend. Totally healed, in fact, ready to be put back in service.

Megan who? It was like she never existed now.

"Good choice, Professor." Aurelia danced closer to him to the disappointment of several men to their right and left.

With the no-touching rule in effect for as long as she willed, Aurelia went to work, using her body to drain all sadness from the professor's eyes and deposit potent desire in its place. It gave her a huge sense of accomplishment to be able to bring this man some type of reprieve from his troubles, even if it was only temporary.

By the end of that song, Baron was breathing hard and looking like a totally different man. "Mind if I have another lap dance, Aurora?" he asked huskily, slipping a large bill into her garter.

Briefly noting which dead president was on that bill, Aurelia nodded. If this man was going to be shelling out hundreds all night, she would give him as many lap dances as he wished. Not even Willy tipped this good right off the bat. He usually started with tens and worked his way up to fifties.

Aurelia ended up giving the professor a total of ten lap dances, making a cool thousand off of just one customer. Combine that money with the funds she had at home from earlier this week, now she only needed nine hundred dollars more and she'd have the rest of her tuition.

Fortunately, Dingo had already been paid for tonight's live entertainment – half at the time of booking the event, the other half when he actually walked through the door with the girls. That meant that Aurelia and the other dancers got to keep all of their earnings tonight.

But first she needed to take a break. All that dancing and nonstop grinding, coupled with her sheer attraction to her handsome customer had Aurelia sweating more than usual. In short, dancing for the professor had truly gotten her hot and bothered. This was the first time her libido had stirred since Cain. The first time it had stirred at work, period.

Thankfully it was time for another costume change, giving Aurelia the perfect excuse to cool off and pull herself back together. The first half of girls prepared for more solo shows while the latter half continued the lap dances. They would switch again when it was time for the second half to perform.

* * *

"Dang, girl. You sure latched onto a Mr. Money Bags tonight," Crystal said after closing the door to the adjoining room where they would freshen up and change.

"Yeah, I had to dance for nearly every man in the room just to get the four hundred I did get this last hour," Raven inserted, eyeing Aurelia's cash, too, but for a different reason.

"It's all going towards school," Aurelia replied, stating what her priorities were.

"School or not, I'm heading straight for the professor when I go back out there. I got mouths to feed," Raven said, letting Aurelia know upfront that she now had some competition.

"You don't have any kids." Crystal sent Raven a disapproving frown. The short blonde was always starting trouble among the girls with her competitive nature. If Dingo ever gave Crystal hiring and firing power, Raven would definitely be the first to go, despite how much money she made for the club with her Nordic facial beauty and alluring figure. A figure that suggested that she had a few ethnic roots in America's melting pot.

"My boyfriend has six kids," Raven replied, revealing just how young and stupid she was. No sensible mature woman would take care of a trifling man's responsibilities. No wonder Raven's boyfriend couldn't keep a steady job. He didn't have to with an enabler like her.

Paying haters like Raven no mind as usual, Aurelia secured her money in her portable combination lockbox, stuffed it deep into her rolling suitcase and then went to the bathroom to freshen up. Instead of just washing up, she took a quick shower.

The professor had really gotten to Aurelia with his handsome face, hard body, and gorgeous eyes that haunted her even now. A slow orgasm had been building while she danced for him. Had he moved his hips at all instead of just pressing upwards; she would have surely gone over the edge.

I hope he likes my next outfit and my new wig, Aurelia found herself thinking, though she knew better than to get too fond of any customer. Yet somehow this particular customer seemed special. Real special.

CHAPTER THREE

"What are you trying to do? Hog the best one all night?" Duke whispered to Baron as the second shift of ladies continued to give lap dances to all who wanted them. Only the older men opted for lap dances at this time. All the hottest chicks were on the first shift.

"Don't hate," Baron teased his oldest brother. "Just be glad you're here at all to enjoy any of this, you cheater."

"Don't you hate on me for having a woman that wants to stick by my side no matter what," Duke countered with a scowl, highly defensive about his recent infidelity.

Would the family ever let him live that mistake down? And why weren't they just as diligent about nagging Earl and Marquess concerning their indiscretions? They'd cheated far more than him. Far more than Duke ever intended to cheat on his wife.

Baron's gaze grew hard and somewhat sad again at that reminder of Megan's disloyalty. She hadn't stuck around long enough for him to be in crisis. At least not in any real crisis.

After two years of togetherness, which included exclusive dating, a large engagement party, and a slew of wedding plans, Megan had simply moved on to a richer man. Or so she thought since Baron had never revealed to her how much he made from outside investments and business dealings. He'd only shared what his teaching salary was.

Unable to watch Megan parade around Los Angeles on the arm of her much older new beau, whom he heard she had married by now, Baron made plans to relocate immediately following their breakup. After finding an even better teaching position and a great home in Alcove – a city of Orange County, his relocation was now complete.

Who cares that Megan had also relocated soon after their breakup? Her relatives and associates still lived in Los Angeles, which meant that she would surely return for their parties and other social events…with her new husband. If it wasn't for his parents and siblings, Baron would never return to the L.A. area again.

"Count your blessings, big brother. Sasha may grow tired one day. They all eventually do, you know. Need I bring up our brothers or even your very own father?" Baron told Duke, reminding him of what could happen if he continued down the dangerous road he was on.

Duke instantly grew quiet. Like Baron, he knew how their mother had grown tired of her first husband's infidelities after three sons and seven years of marriage. Upon divorcing Duke, Earl, and Marquess' father, Ana Maria moved from Mexico and later married the son of a wealthy American businessman whom she'd been a maid for.

That second husband was Count and Baron's father, Nicolas Weaver. Nicolas adopted Ana Maria's three oldest boys as his own. He put all of their sons through law, medical, or business schools.

Meanwhile, Ana Maria's first husband died a broken man in poverty two years ago in Tijuana. It didn't have to end like that, but he stubbornly refused to take money or assistance from the sons who'd disappointed him by becoming too Americanized and downright ashamed of their Mexican heritage at times.

Refusing all lap dances after that, Duke began to conduct himself more like a married man that didn't want to lose his wife. Less like a man going through a mid-life crisis.

Baron smiled, glad to see his first oldest brother thinking logically again. If only his third oldest brother was so easily swayed to do right, so willing to see the error of his ways.

These days, Marquess just didn't seem to have the do-right gene in him. He was almost as reprobate as Earl now, which was why the family stopped nagging them both about their behavior. Only their praying mother still got on them about their wicked ways.

Wicked was the most fitting word right now. What other term could be used to describe what Marquess was currently doing?

Waving big bills in the air for Aurora to see while she performed a two-minute solo routine to Alison Hinds' Roll It Gal, Marquess deliberately pitted himself against Baron. Yes, he knew his youngest brother wanted that delicious piece of chocolate cake, had even seen their mutual attraction, but he didn't care. Marquess stopped caring about a lot of things when his wife filed for divorce. He hadn't been too happy even before then.

Fortunately, Baron's second oldest brother didn't start competing for Aurora's favor, too. Although Earl usually cheated on his blue-eyed blonde wife with women of the darker hues, he had settled for an olive- skinned dancer from India tonight.

Not usually competitive against his brothers, Baron just couldn't sit back and allow Aurora to give Marquess or any other man here a lap dance. In his mind, she was his...at least for the night.

Baron opened his thick black wallet and looked inside. He smiled down at all the greenery. Suddenly he was glad to be single, childless, and a wise businessman like their father. Less debt and minimum responsibilities meant more disposable income. More disposable income gave Baron an edge over his brothers. Especially the brother that was currently going through a costly divorce.

It was time to make it rain up in here.

Come get under this shower, baby, Baron willed to a dancing Aurora as he looked up and smiled at her with determination in his eyes.

* * *

Aurelia kept looking the professor's way the whole time she performed her routine. In her mind, there were no other men in the room. In her mind, she was dancing just for him.

The more Aurelia watched the professor watching her, the hotter she got. The hotter she got, the more sensual her moves became.

When the professor held up a stack of bills that were sure to pay the rest of her college tuition, her rent, and put food in her fridge, Aurelia gave him a wink and a smile. He winked back and nodded her over. That's the cue she'd been waiting for. She was his...for tonight.

Aurelia concluded her routine and started towards the professor. With swaying hips, she made every step count. This sexy strut was her very own walk of fame. She wanted him to remember it well.

Seemingly out of nowhere, Raven rushed to stand in front of the professor, immediately blocking his view of Aurelia. "Do you want a lap dance, Professor?"

Slanderous heifer, Aurelia thought with flashing eyes.

"Yes, I do," Baron replied.

Raven smiled triumphantly.

"From Aurora," Baron added smoothly, leaning to the left to smile at the woman he really wanted. The same woman that had sparked life into him again after months of walking around like the living dead. The fact that Raven was a blonde like Megan made her even less appealing to him.

Thoroughly rejected, Raven's smile fell to the ground and broke into a thousand little pieces.

Meanwhile, liquid lava coursed through Aurelia's veins to hear the professor prefer her over Raven. Her!

Maybe some gentlemen still preferred blondes, but not this one. This one preferred hot chocolate.

Aurelia was officially on cloud nine. She didn't realize until just now how much she needed to feel preferred by someone. How much she needed to feel special. The professor was going to get the best lap dance he ever had for sure now.

"Excuse me, girlfriend," Aurelia purred super-sweetly to her rival. On the word 'girlfriend', she used her left hip to help the competitive woman on her trifling little way. In the background Ciara's So Hard cued up.

Barely catching herself from falling on her face at that helpful shove, Raven huffed and reluctantly moved on to the next man. That man happened to be Marquess, who welcomed a lap dance from her. He looked ready to receive anything else she wanted to offer him. too.

Across the room, Count laughed at his competing brothers and the two rival strippers. He found the whole thing hilarious. Despite the fact that he was the guest of honor tonight, he was too in love with his fiancée to receive any lap dances for himself. However, Count didn't mind watching other men enjoy themselves with the girls while he sipped champagne and smoked his favorite Cuban cigar.

"Can I have my dance over there in the corner?" Baron nodded towards a semi-secluded spot near a large potted plant.

"Sure." Aurelia preferred a bit of privacy, as well. Sexually charged to the max, she'd gladly follow the professor anywhere right about now.

Allowing him to sit down first, Aurelia settled into his lap with a seductive smile. Draping her arms about his neck, she sensually moved her lower body upon him in time to the slow tune. It was her normal routine, but this time something felt different about it. She felt different this time.

Baron moaned as his body instantly responded to her presence again. His whole body was at attention, nerve endings and all as desire skyrocketed through his veins.

"Aurora," Baron whispered her stage name with fervor.

Oh, it felt so good to be a man right now. The fresh floral scent of this woman intoxicated him. That peek-a-boo neon pink outfit had his mind dizzy, and the way she worked her hips had him thinking about much more than a lap dance.

Baron also liked that straight wig Aurora had on now. It not only gave her a completely different look than before, but increased her level of gorgeousness tenfold. Not every woman had the kind of face that dramatically changed in degrees of beauty based on her hairstyles and facial expressions. That could only mean that this woman was truly special.

Aurelia could see the thick desire forming in his eyes. She could feel the thickness in his body, the way he trembled as he fought for restraint. "You can touch me if you want, Professor," she whispered. Around them, other couples were starting to get friskier as well.

As if he'd been given a get out-of-jail-free card, Baron's hands moved upwards to stroke her elegant neck, unaware that he'd just caught her off guard by that action.

Aurelia thought for sure he would go to her lower curves or even to her breasts first. But no, this unique man went to her neck instead, tracing it with gentle strokes as if she was a treasure to behold, not a stripper. That unexpected act caused Aurelia to behave just as unexpectedly.

Placing one hand on his shoulder for balance as she continued to slowly grind upon him, she used her other hand to untie her halter top. Soon her pasties were seen.

Baron inhaled sharply at the sight of her full brown swells. A breast man, he licked his pink lips, greedy to taste her. Yet because he knew that was against the rules, he used his hands instead since she'd only given him permission to touch so far.

Curious to see what was behind those pink floral-shaped pasties, Baron slowly peeled them away. He licked his lips again as two beautiful dark-brown peaks entered his eyesight. Still restricted to only touch, he rubbed the tips of his fingers across those rigid peaks before kneading the heavy globes attached. They felt better than the ripest melons. Looked better, too.

Scrumptious. Just scrumptious. Baron licked his lips once more.

Aurelia shuddered and moaned at that action. She arched closer to him. "I like your hands on me, Professor," she said, amazed that they were so deliciously manly based on her assumption that he worked indoors.

But maybe he didn't work indoors. Maybe he worked outside or at least spent a large portion of his free time engaged in outdoor activities like hiking and camping. There had to be some reasonable explanation for his masculine hands and chiseled body.

"I like touching you, Aurora." Baron looked up into her eyes as he continued to knead her in circular rotations.

"Well, you can touch me for the rest of the night if you want to." Aurelia arched towards him even more. "And as of right now, I officially designate all of my remaining lap dances to you."

Moaning at those words of exclusivity, Baron sent both hands to her round bottom, squeezed and began to grind heatedly beneath her. He didn't know if lap dances were all he was ever going to get from her tonight, but if they were, he wanted the full effect of them.

Aurelia sucked air in through her teeth as he squeezed her closer to him, grabbing even bigger handfuls of her bottom. She liked that eagerness. That fervor.

Aurelia also appreciated the natural rhythm of the professor's hips. How he met each and every thrust of her hips in perfect unison. The man had her moaning and groaning as if she was the one receiving the lap dance instead of him. He made her glad to be a woman. Made her want to see what he was working with as a man.

Aurelia hadn't been this turned on in a long time. Ever, to be perfectly honest, because what she felt right now was different from anything she had ever felt in her life. Therefore, when the professor sent his exploring fingers for a covert little dip in her pond, she didn't complain. Instead

Aurelia made up her mind once and for all to sleep with him tonight.

Forget her rules. She wanted this man. She needed this man!

It had been a long time since Aurelia had been with any man. Cain had been her last one, so her hormones were definitely jumping tonight. No wonder she embraced the professor's neck tighter, moved closer still, and placed her bosom right at the door of his gorgeous pink lips.

Seeing that as an invitation to feast, Baron prepared to do just that. But first he needed to fulfill an impromptu fantasy.

Leaning closer, Baron used the nearest rigid tip to slowly trace the circumference of his soft lips. He repeated the same action with the other peak, just as slowly.

Aurelia let out a low elongated moan that continued from the first lip outline to the last. No man had ever done that to her before. Was he trying to set her thong on fire?

Surely she would be putty in a minute. Silly Putty at that, ready for him to mold at will.

And then he did it. Baron opened his mouth wide and feasted. He moaned as his taste buds came in contact with her sweetness.

Aurelia moaned, too. She grinded faster as scorching desire pumped through her veins. Forget about keeping on beat to the song playing in the background. She was on fire for this man!

Only the professor could put her fire out.

Just then, Dingo walked up, causing everything to abruptly end like a scratched record on a DJ's turntable. In other words, this lap dance was officially over.

* * *

"Everything all right over here?" Dingo looked pointedly at the position of the professor's hands.

It didn't take a genius to know what Baron's fingers were doing beneath that thong. And anyone at close range could see how greedily he'd stuffed his mouth with Aurelia's treats. Even now Baron was reluctant to release any part of her, though he slowly did due to the awkward circumstances.

Aurelia and Baron had Crystal to thank for Dingo's intervention. Thinking that Aurelia had gotten in over her head with the professor, the head dancer had sent her burly boyfriend over to investigate the situation. To thoroughly investigate it.

It just wasn't like Aurelia to go off in a corner to be alone with any man. It definitely wasn't like her to let a customer touch her so intimately. Even her pasties were gone!

Had Six-Eight not been left at the club this time around, he would have snatched Baron up and flung him away from Aurelia by now. Probably even broken a few bones, particularly the professor's offending fingers. All ten upper phalanges. The whole bachelor's party would have come to an abrupt stop then.

"Everything's fine," Aurelia assured her mahogany-skinned boss as she looked back at him over one shoulder, careful to keep the rest of her body still. If only she didn't sound so breathless. "The professor and I were just getting to know each other better. Matter of fact, we're probably going to go to one of the other rooms for a little bit more privacy," she added, letting Dingo and Baron know what her new intent was.

"You sure about this, Aurora?" Dingo looked just as surprised as Baron.

A lenient boss when it came to things like this, Dingo didn't stop the girls from making whatever money they wanted to on the side. Since he was not a pimp, any additional funds they earned outside of dancing were out of his jurisdiction and he deliberately looked the other way. All Dingo required in these matters was confirmed consent, a follow-up call to make sure the girls arrived home safely if they were in town, or a face-to-face check-in if they were out of town.

"Am I sure about this, Professor?" Aurelia looked at the man beneath her, who'd released his various holds on her body by now.

"Yes." Baron smiled with a nod, behaving just as spontaneous tonight. He looked just as eager to be alone with her. Just as ready to explore this overwhelming attraction between them. "She'll be in my private room next door. Room 938," he told Dingo, speaking of the room that wasn't joined to the double suite. "No harm will come to her," he promised, actually looking protective of her already.

"All right." Dingo gave the professor a 'you-better-not-hurt-her' look. "Just remember we head out noon tomorrow," he added to Aurelia.

"Noon. I got it." Aurelia re-tied her top for the trip next door to wonderland. She made a brief stop in the adjoining room for her suitcase and to whisper a word of thanks to Crystal for her concern.

Baron knew he was the envy of most of the men in the room as he and one of the finest women on the planet strolled out hand in hand a few minutes later.

As for the women, only Raven fumed with jealousy. Crystal, Dingo, Duke, and Count just looked on in wonder at the couple who were behaving completely out of character tonight.

CHAPTER FOUR

Baron knew this was going to be a night to remember when he saw the woman known to him as Aurora fully undressed. A woman this fine ought to have her own theme music. A special song needed to play every time she walked into a room.

As if on cue, So Beautiful by Musiq Soulchild started to play in the next room. From now on Baron would think of Aurora every time he heard that song.

He paused from his own undressing just to stare at her gorgeous 5'9 frame in wonder. She'd gotten undressed in record time. But then again, she hadn't had much on to begin with.

"You're even more beautiful than I thought," Baron said in a husky voice that had been dipped deep in a bucket of desire.

"So are you." Aurelia licked her lips as her eyes roamed over his muscular frame as he stood across from her in nothing but a pair of black boxer briefs. The 6'1 man had a chiseled hairy torso, rippled arms, and strong thighs and legs. His abs were impeccable. Lickable.

When did he find the time to work out?

"Thanks." Baron quickly closed the distance between them.

The moment had finally come for them to share their first kiss. Would it be awkward? Clumsy? Explosive?

And our survey says…

Explosive was the winning answer.

As soon as Baron's lips touched hers, a bomb went off,

hurling hot spikes of passion into every cell of their bodies. A strong need to be closer attacked them. Their frames lined up immediately in a desperate attempt to satisfy that need.

Female arms went around a strong masculine neck. Male arms went around a small feminine waist. Hips began to grind once more.

Aurelia melted into that kiss, finding it better than any she'd ever had. She relished the professor's long tongue, savored the delectable champagne taste of him, and marveled at his seemingly unquenchable thirst for her. Such eagerness was a great ego booster for her damaged self-esteem. Oh yes, she needed this man.

Baron found her lips just as soft as he imagined they would be. She tasted as sweet as a reddish-purple plum. A plum so juicy it made his mouth water just thinking about it and was ideal for fresh eating, cooking, and canning. No wonder he couldn't seem to get enough of kissing her.

Baron's hands also couldn't seem to get enough of touching her. And when his mouth met up with those hands at her bosom, he found himself heady with desire. His whole body shuddered in response. Never in his life had he wanted a woman this badly before.

Had three months of abstinence done this to him? Or was all this excitement because this was going to be his first sexual experience with a black woman?

Baron didn't know. All he knew was that he liked feeling this way…a lot.

Now fully undressed with the help of her eager hands, Baron laid her down on the large poster bed against the wall. Then he kissed her from her forehead downward. He lingered at her dimples, lips and especially at her lovely breasts. He laved them thoroughly, tasting every brown inch of them before going lower.

Baron wanted to taste all of Aurora. But since they were still virtual strangers, he exercised extreme caution by going no farther than her belly. Though her navel was used as a substitute for something more intimate, his mouth gave it superior service nevertheless.

Aurelia writhed beneath the professor's ministrations on the bed. Her eyes were wide, watching everything he did to her. Fear entered her caramel pools initially, but quickly subsided when he stopped at her stomach. For a minute there she thought he was going to…to…

Go beyond her personal boundaries.

Aurelia wasn't ready for that level of intimacy with any man. Relief flooded her soul when he demonstrated boundaries of his own. Then and only then did she close her eyes to relish the moment to the full.

"Yes," Aurelia whispered when he began to lap at her navel like a hungry puppy. Her hips instantly moved just as hungrily.

Baron moaned at her heated response. He sent one of his hands down to press the hidden button of her desire. Doing so caused her secret compartment to slide open, giving additional fingers access to all kinds of precious treasures inside.

Aurelia's eyes fluttered open at his intimate touch. Her hips lifted off the bed. Her thighs moved in a snatching motion that caused two of his digits to be yanked farther into her sultry portal.

Baron inhaled sharply, sucking air through his teeth. If that wasn't a sign that she was ready for the rest of him, he didn't know what was. He quickly removed his hands from her body long enough to don adequate protection.

Aurelia watched him be responsible with swift fingers. She liked how his eyes kept returning to her body while his hands moved, as if he couldn't wait to return to her in every way.

The professor hovered above her a few seconds later.

Aurelia moaned out her pleasure as he finally entered her woman's gate. She liked how he slow walked through it, not racing full speed ahead. Such consideration gave her body a chance to adjust to his extraordinary presence.

Were all Latino men this impressive?

Aurelia didn't know since this was her first one. What she did know was that he felt so good to her. So right.

"Aurora," Baron whispered, relishing her blissful expression as he continued to travel deep within her snug cavern, searching out all her hidden places. The contrasts of their skin tones against each other turned him on even more.

"Professor," Aurelia purred, keeping in line with their anonymity as she moved her hips in a different kind of dance now.

Baron joined in, following her rhythm, though he had the position of power. From childhood he'd been taught that a strong leader had to first know how to follow. And follow he did tonight.

Aurelia found the professor to be the gentlest lover she'd ever had in her life. He knew exactly how to work his width for a woman's ultimate pleasure. There was no premature macho banging just to prove his prowess like Cain had done.

No, this man was confident enough to just let his sexual prowess naturally unveil itself during intimacy. Aurelia literally felt massaged from the inside out with each advance and retreat. Her fingers and toes tingled, even her scalp, at the professor's lovemaking. At the way he kept leaning in to lick her dimples. And when she went over the edge, her toes curled, and a long squeal bubbled up from deep within her throat.

On fire now for sure, Baron once again did the unexpected. He disengaged them.

"Is that all you want, Professor?" Aurelia panted out, missing his presence already.

She'd been apart from Cain for months and hadn't missed him once. Not even for a second. This proved that she'd never really been in love with him in the first place. There hadn't even been enough lust to keep her holding on to that man.

"All I want? Hardly." Baron smiled. "This is just a brief intermission so that we can switch things up a bit. You know, go to the top another way," he said, lying on his back beside her.

"I get it," Aurelia replied excitedly, promptly moving to rise above him.

"Yes, that's exactly what I want you to do. Get it," he flirted, playing on words.

"Oh, I will." Aurelia chuckled. "Without this," she added, snatching her wig off and flinging it across the room. Rising passion had her scalp sweltering beneath all that extra hair.

Baron lifted his left brow at her wig-slinging act. He grinned. His eyes twinkled with mirth.

This woman was simply adorable!

Then just like her lap dance, Aurora begin to work her hips like a pro, making Baron glad to be a man all over again. He followed her lead once more, letting her set the tempo.

The pace soon became frenzied as she bucked above him, prompting him to respond in kind. He did…with unbridled passion and untamed hips.

The headboard of the bed banged noisily against the wall,

alerting those in the next room that there was some serious activity going on in here. Sweat spilled from their pores in droves. What a way to get in some meaningful cardio. What a fun way to lose a few pounds.

Even after Baron went over the edge with her trailing closely behind him, their passion still didn't abate. The positions kept changing, but the level of passion didn't. It was like they literally couldn't get enough of one another.

Truthfully, they didn't want to get enough of each other. Didn't feel the need to. Not tonight.

* * *

Concerned that Baron was going to kill Aurelia in there, especially when they heard her scream over the loud upbeat tune of Claudette Peters' Flaunt It, Crystal asked Dingo and one of Baron's brothers to go check on their missing dancer. All the other girls were accounted for. They were either packing up to leave or else having sex in other suites as well. Raven and Marquess were in a suite of their own, too, but there was no riotous sounds coming from their room.

Using the extra key to Baron's room, Count and Dingo found Aurelia unharmed. It was the professor they needed to be concerned about.

With eyes bucked one minute, rolling in the back of his head the next, the man looked like he was about to lose his mind as Aurelia hovered above him in a sensual squat, rotated her hips upon his royal crown, and then literally slammed down upon him. Each time she repeated those actions, Baron shouted out his pleasure and begged her for more.

His exact words were, "Baby, please don't stop. Don't ever stop."

Count and Dingo looked at each other in wonder and quietly left the room unnoticed, closing the door securely behind them.

"Is your brother the stalker type?" Dingo asked once they were in the hallway.

"No, why?" Count replied, still trying to process what he'd just seen. He was going to suggest that fantastic trick to his new bride tomorrow on their honeymoon.

"Based on what we just saw, he might not want to let Aurora go in the morning. Shoot, even I might be tempted to stalk a woman with those kinds of tricks up her sleeve. Even my girl Crystal doesn't have that particular trick in her repetoire...yet. She will after tonight though," Dingo said, revealing his eagerness to share what he'd seen with his own woman. "Which is why I need to know if there's going to be trouble at my club later," he continued, getting back to what he really wanted to talk about.

"There won't be any trouble," Count replied, convinced that his brother cared too much about his personal and professional reputation to allow himself to become a stalker.

"All right." Dingo didn't looked or sound convinced. "In any case, Crystal and I will be coming to get our girl around 9am just to make sure she leaves without any problems."

"I'll let my brother know what time you'll be back when things finally quiet down in there." Even now they could still hear Baron yelling out his pleasure.

With each new shout, Count became increasingly less convinced about Baron's ability to let the island beauty go when this was all over. The fact that his youngest brother had a tendency to hold onto things longer than most people invoked even more concern for him.

Maybe it was a bad idea to bring strippers to my bachelor's party after all, Count thought, starting to dread the decision he'd made with Earl and Marquess in each ear. If only he had listened to Baron, who had been against hiring exotic dancers from the start.

* * *

Back inside Room 938, Baron found himself rapidly reaching his breaking point again. He couldn't help it. Aurora just kept sending him over the edge with her hips, her lips, her everything.

Yet before he would allow himself to surrender to ecstasy this time, Baron shifted their positions yet again. He didn't want to go over the edge this way. He had something else in mind.

Determined to have Aurora in every position he could while he could, Baron soon had her glistening brown frame hedged in between him and the wall at the head of the bed. Reentering her hot core soon thereafter, he literally went for broke.

Her squeals of pleasure, heavy pants, and the way her nails tried to dig into the wall ahead told him that she was still enjoying herself just as much as he was. Those gyrating hips of hers confirmed that assessment.

Tingling from head to toe, Aurelia arched her back for

32

more, more, and yet more. When the professor gave her more, she matched his aggression beat for beat. Inside her mind swirled with questions, despite the fact that it was also cloudy with passion.

Who was this man that had her so zoned out? So dazed that she actually thought she was Aurora instead of Aurelia. Where did he live? What were his parents' names? What was his favorite food? And by the way, what was his real name?

Aurelia suddenly wanted to know everything about the professor now. All the non-sexual stuff. The stuff that made for a real relationship.

But how could she? Sex had come first for them. Never mind the obstacles of their polar opposite professions.

Realizing that this might be all she'd ever have of the professor, all she'd ever know about him, Aurelia began to thrust against him even harder. Faster. She was desperate for him now.

Misinterpreting that desperation as passionate fervor, Baron responded in kind, matching her pace and fervency. His mind twirled with questions at the same time.

What manner of woman had he come across tonight? Was she this giving, this much of a team player in other areas of her life? More importantly, would she allow him to get to know her better beyond tonight?

When the pleasure got to be too much for Baron, he threw his head back and roared out his passion as he went sailing over the edge once again.

Aurelia trailed behind him a few seconds later with a deep shudder and a loud scream of ecstasy. And that's when she knew that one night with him would never be enough for her.

* * *

Things finally quieted down next door around 3am. Soon thereafter Baron received a call from Count. He picked up his cell phone on the sixth ring. He sounded groggy and tired to his own ears. He ought to be after four straight hours of sex. It was a good thing the wedding wasn't until 2pm.

"I just wanted to let you know that they'll be back to pick Aurora up at 9am," Count reminded him. "So in case you sleep in late, make sure you have her fee laid out so she won't have to wake you up for it."

Baron was suddenly wide awake now. He forgot this was a business arrangement just that fast. It had felt so real. Like

Aurora was really into it. Even now she slept with a smile on her face as she dozed beside him.

"Will do." Baron frowned, now wondering how much to pay her. No money had been discussed between them concerning this tryst. Having never done anything like this before, he had no price references to pull from.

"And, Baron?" Count said, interrupting his thoughts by calling him by his given name.

"Yes?"

"You're not going to stalk this woman, are you? Because everybody heard how much you were enjoying her. Some of us saw it, too," Count confessed.

"Saw? Who did? When?" Baron hissed, feeling territorial over the precious time he and Aurora had spent together.

"Just me and Dingo. Crystal asked us to check on Aurora to make sure you weren't killing her in there. Oh yes, you all were just that loud."

Baron relaxed a little when he learned that their peeping toms had actually been two concerned, trustworthy people. "We couldn't help ourselves. We were very compatible." He smiled at the memory of their long fervent encounter.

"I understand that. But I'm really going to need you to answer my question, Professor. Are you going to stalk this woman?" Count persisted.

"No. I understand it was just business," Baron replied, telling himself that as well despite the fact that it had felt so personal.

"Good." Count let out a breath of relief.

When Baron hung up, he eased out of the bed and got more cash from his suitcase. Still unsure about the price, he decided to give Aurora a grand for each hour of pleasure he received from her. Even then he wondered if that was enough to pay someone for restoring a precious commodity like his libido.

After laying the funds on the nightstand with a note that said, 'Yours', Baron did not return to the bed. Instead he went to take a long shower. He needed some time alone to think. Time to figure out why this sexual encounter was so powerful. More powerful than any he had ever known before.

Baron also needed time to mentally prepare himself for the moment that Aurora would leave him and go back to her real life. For the moment when he would have to say goodbye…forever. Why did that suddenly grieve him more than losing Megan?

* * *

Aurelia stirred from her slumber around 3:30am. It took her a few seconds to realize that she was not at home, but instead in a fancy hotel room…with a man. Or rather she was with a man. There was no sign of the professor anywhere now.

Oh wait. Was that the shower running in the bathroom?

Aurelia immediately relaxed when she realized that he hadn't left her high and dry. That he was just getting his hygiene back on point.

Maybe I'll join him. She moved out of the disheveled bed.

Suddenly she froze. Was that money on the nightstand? And was that accompanying note actually declaring that those hefty funds were hers?

All hers?!

Aurelia instantly felt ashamed, not flattered by the large stack of bills. She certainly felt no greed.

Yes, Aurelia had danced for the professor's money tonight, but the sex had been free. She'd wanted to give herself to him. For free!

Now all that fantastic lovemaking they'd done tonight had been reduced to a filthy transaction. As a result, the memory of tonight would be forever tainted in her mind.

Unable to face the professor in light of this awkward and highly embarrassing misunderstanding, Aurelia quickly and quietly gathered her things and left. She'd take another shower once she got back to the hotel where the rest of the girls were.

Yet just like the fairytale Cinderella, Aurelia left something of hers behind in her haste. Not a glass slipper or even a piece of lingerie. No, she left behind a wig. One of her best wigs at that —made of 100% human hair.

* * *

When Baron finally emerged from that shower, he found Aurora gone and the money still where he'd left it. She hadn't touched the stack at all. Not a dollar was missing.

Why? Had tonight meant just as much to her as it had to him?

Baron would never know since he didn't even know her real name. And he was pretty sure Aurora wasn't it.

But I do know where she works, Baron thought, recalling

35

that Dingo's club was in Friendly, California. That's not too far from where I live now, he deduced, glad that he'd relocated to Alcove.

He even had a legitimate excuse to see Aurora again – the wig he just spotted underneath the beige cushioned chair by the window. Surely all black women valued their hair, real or not. Surely Aurora would want her wig returned as soon as possible. Right?

Baron found it ironic that he'd found the wig beneath a dancing lady chair of all things. Poetic, too.

No, I said I wasn't going to stalk her and I meant it, he promptly reminded himself before things went too far. If Aurora, or whatever her real name is, wants to make this one a freebie, then so be it, Baron decided, ready to let the whole thing go, no matter how much it grieved him inside.

CHAPTER FIVE

The Wednesday after Count's bachelor's party, Baron received a disturbing call from his brother Marquess. A call that tilted both of their worlds on their axes.

Marquess had gone to the doctor and discovered that he had not one, but two STDs – gonorrhea and herpes. He'd gotten both from Raven at the party due to a broken condom.

Although none of Baron's condoms had broken, he still went to get checked out. Fortunately, all of his tests turned out clean. Even so, that whole experience scared him straight. No more strippers for Baron, even though he couldn't help but think about Aurora every other hour it seemed.

As for Duke, who'd tested both of his brothers for everything under the sun after Marquess' diagnosis, he was scared all the way straight now. Sasha didn't know it yet, but she never had to worry about him straying ever again.

Realizing that someone had to act responsibly since Marquess was too bitter to do so; Baron went to the club to inform Dingo of Raven's condition on the Friday before school started at Alcove University. But that wasn't the only reason he showed up at the club. Baron was there to see Aurora, too. Why else would he have her wig in the trunk of his car?

The minute Dingo saw the professor walk through the club doors that night, he shook his head. He was surprised it took the man this long to search Aurelia out.

Making a beeline for Baron, Dingo quickly escorted the

man to his private office in the back. On the way there, he gave Six-Eight a nod across the room, letting him know to mind the store until he got back. The nod he got in return indicated his brother's agreement of that assignment. The club couldn't have been left in better hands.

"Before you ask, Aurora no longer works here. She quit right after Cabo," Dingo said before the professor could even have a seat or get the first word out.

"Aurora quit? Why?" Baron asked, suddenly looking like the absentminded professor as he took the empty seat in front of Dingo's cherry wood desk.

"Because somebody made her realize that this life just wasn't for her," Dingo accused, settling his large frame into his black swivel desk chair. "What did you do, promise her the moon and then take it back?"

"No. I didn't promise her anything. And the extra four grand I tried to pay her was left on the nightstand," Baron replied with a puzzled expression on his face. "We had such a great time that night. I honestly don't know what went wrong to make her slip out of the room while I was in the shower and leave her hard-earned money behind."

Dingo winced. "What went wrong is the fact that you tried to pay her for sleeping with you, man. Aurora's not like some of the other girls around here. Like my Crystal, she was just here to dance and get paid."

"Which means she slept with me that night because she wanted to," Baron deduced, looking thrilled by that news.

"Exactly."

"Which also means I blew it with her big time." Baron raked a frustrated hand through his thick dark hair as his body tensed up in the chair.

"Yep. You blew it for me, too. Aurora brought in a lot of new customers in the short time she was here. High paying customers," Dingo replied, speaking from a business point of view. "Some of them quickly became regulars because of her and now they're gone just like she is."

"Sorry to hear that. I didn't mean to offend you and especially not her. Do you have Aurora's phone number? I owe her a huge apology," Baron said with penitent eyes.

"I have all of Aurora's personal information, but I'm not giving any of it to you," Dingo said matter-of-factly. "The fact that you're here at all tells me that you have stalker tendencies. I can't unleash you on that girl like that no matter how sorry you seem."

"Maybe you'll change your mind after I tell you the other reason I'm here," Baron said with hope in his eyes. Then he quickly disclosed his suspicions about Raven based on his brother's recent diagnosis.

"So now I'm about to lose another big money-maker?!" Dingo raged after hearing the man out. "And for the record, I'm not about to change my mind about anything except my club policy."

One of Dingo's club policies mandated that if a dancer was infected with any kind of STD, she had to be cleared by a licensed physician before returning to work. If what she had was incurable, she was fired to keep from putting the clientele at risk. He would stand by that policy even now, but his look-the-other-way policy was about to be revamped. Tonight!

"Out with you, Professor! Out and never come back!" Dingo stood to his feet now. "For all I know your brother might have been the carrier of those STDs."

"He might have, but I seriously doubt it," Baron said, looking angry and highly disappointed as he stood to his feet as well. "In any case, you can't say that you weren't told about Raven. Don't blame me if there's an outbreak and you lose everything you've built here instead of some dancers and a few customers. As for Aurora, I would never stalk her or any other woman. But if that island beauty ever comes across my path again, you better believe I'm going to do everything I can to make her mine...the right way."

I believe you, Dingo thought, secretly admiring the man that stood up to him without fear in his own establishment. Even so, he still wasn't going to give out Aurelia's contact information just in case the professor turned out to be less than the honorable man he seemed.

* * *

In an upscale Bel Air home Jacuzzi; Sasha Weaver listened quietly as her husband Duke unexpectedly declared that he wanted them to renew their marital vows. He made that declaration after apologizing to her yet again for being unfaithful earlier this year.

"What brought all this on? Residue guilt from your illicit affair?" Sasha pierced him with dark eyes that she knew contained lingering ire and pain stemming from that same illicit affair. She still felt that same anger and pain in her heart.

"Part of it is from residue guilt," Duke admitted, easing closer to her red bikini clad figure in the Jacuzzi. "The other part is because of the major wakeup call I recently had when one of my married patients ended up with two STDs from an affair he had. One of which he will never be cured of," he explained, bound by doctor/patient confidentiality agreements that kept him from revealing that patient's name.

"I see," Sasha replied, not letting on that she knew exactly who he was referring to. She made it her business to know all of her husband's secrets and a few that belonged to others. "And so now you're going to be 100% faithful to me?"

"Yes."

"Til death do us part?"

"Yes, that's why I want us to renew our vows. I want us to start over fresh. With a clean slate," Duke said, gently tucking wet strands of her long black locks behind her ears.

"If we're truly going to start over with a clean slate, I guess I should tell you that I've been unfaithful, too," Sasha confessed, holding his gaze.

Duke's eyes bucked. His ruggedly handsome face paled in shock. "You...cheated?!" he shouted, recoiling from her as if she'd just grown two heads. "When?!" he demanded in that same loud tone. Thankfully, their two children were already in bed, weren't light sleepers, and so wouldn't hear them arguing tonight. There had been too many loud arguments in their home this year.

"Yes, I cheated. Right after I discovered your infidelity with that shapely waitress at the club," Sasha shared as he moved clear across the Jacuzzi to the other side. "Although I felt vindicated at the time, I'm not proud of myself or of what I did. I now know that two wrongs don't make a right. I haven't cheated since. Nor will I ever stray again."

"Who did you cheat with?" Duke demanded to know, looking murderous in his jealousy.

"With one of the busboys at the club," Sasha said, amazed by his jealousy since he'd been the first to cheat. How hypocritical. Deeper inside she got a secret little thrill out of Duke's heated reaction. It showed that he still cared.

"I'll have his head on a platter! He'll never work in this town again," Duke roared, continuing to show more fire than he had in years.

"He doesn't even live in this town. He was only working

at the club for spring break anyway. That's the main reason I chose him to get back at you. As for the girl you cheated with, I'm the one that had her fired," Sasha said calmly, careful to avoid mentioning any names as she made yet another confession.

"I knew that last part. Fran told me that." Duke still looked upset about his wife's infidelity though his tone was normal again.

Sasha frowned. So Fran was telling secrets now, huh? How would she feel if her secrets were revealed? Sasha was personally aware of a few secrets that could keep Fran from getting that big divorce settlement she wanted from Marquess.

And yet Sasha endeavored to keep her mouth shut. Fran was entirely too close to Meadow Griswold-Weaver to betray. And everyone knew that Earl's wife wielded the real power around Bel Air. Especially at the club that the Griswold family had been a member of for years.

Sasha was just coming into a certain level of societal power in this town. Because she thirsted for more, she had to tread lightly about certain things and around certain people.

"The way I see it, Duke, we have two choices here," Sasha propositioned. "We can, one, continue to be upset about past indiscretions and likely end up in divorce court like Fran and Marquess. Or we can, two, forgive each other and move forward into a happier, more faithful marriage in the future."

Duke grew quiet. Thoughtful. After a full minute of silence had passed, he finally said, "I say we move forward."

A smile graced Sasha's face, highlighting her exotic beauty, which was a unique blend of her Greek, Caucasian, and Hispanic heritages. "I concur." She moved closer to him this time. "Does this mean that we still get to have a second wedding?" She draped her arms about his strong neck. "If so, I'd like to get started on our second honeymoon right now."

Duke smiled. "Oh yes, my sexy senora. We get to have a second everything." He let out a low moan as she pressed her generous bosom against his chest and offered him her full pouty lips.

* * *

After registering on Monday, Aurelia took the whole night off from work to rest up for school tomorrow. Since she no longer worked at the club, the time she took off was from her switchboard job in the main office of the local mall.

There just has to be another way to earn an honest living at night, Aurelia thought, ready to abandon the exotic dancer background of her favorite CSI character without abandoning the dream of having that character's current on-screen job.

Although Aurelia was off tonight, she didn't head straight home after registration. Instead she made her way over to the student center to check the employment board again. First things first.

Perusing her schedule once more, Aurelia noted the dates and times of her classes. She also noticed that she had a new science professor on the roster, an instructor by the name of Dr. Baron Weaver. That class was at 9am sharp, making it her very first class of the day.

Oh goody, my last class ends at 3pm. Aurelia read further down the list. She was pleased that her new class schedule still left room for her 4pm–9pm switchboard shift. This meant that she wouldn't have to get her hours reduced at the mall.

Now if I can just find a job at a 24-hour supermarket, I'll be set, Aurelia thought.

With a job like that, she could work from 10pm-2am and still get enough sleep in time for her first class. She'd probably still be able to squeeze in her Saturday volunteerism at a local soup kitchen.

Furthermore, if Aurelia actually got a cashier's job at an all-night grocer, she would be eligible for food discounts. Which meant she wouldn't have to go back to eating Ramen noodles and hot dogs. Nor would she have to depend on those free meals at the soup kitchen, but instead let someone needier have that food. But most importantly, she'd finally be able to hold her head up high again.

The whole time Aurelia had worked in the adult entertainment industry, she'd kept her gaze averted as much as possible in public. She'd been so afraid of someone from school or work recognizing her. That's why she'd chosen to work at Dingo's. It was in another city and mostly frequented by older men, who had solid bank accounts specifically set aside for that kind of entertainment.

College students in Alcove tended to camp out at local strip clubs where the patrons were just as young as the girls on stage. Not at places where they might run into their fathers and uncles. Even a few grandpas. Most of the people Aurelia worked with at the mall were women and thus less likely to have visited Dingo's anyway.

Even though she was completely out of the adult entertainment industry now, she couldn't help thinking about some of the things she'd done there. Particularly the things she'd done with him...the professor.

Aurelia thought about him even now as she pleasantly greeted one of her real professors from last year as they passed each other on the student center stairs. The professor in passing was a wrinkled face, gray-haired man that was old enough to be her grandfather. The professor from the hotel was a young tenderoni with a chiseled body, a soft touch, sizzling lips, and powerful hips.

Aurelia's body tingled at the memory of that heated hotel encounter. An encounter that she would very much like to repeat, despite how badly it turned out.

That'll never happen, she thought, convinced that some good things only came around once.

* * *

The next day, Aurelia found herself running severely behind schedule. She mentally kicked herself all the way down the hall for being late on the first day of class. And for a new professor at that, somebody she wasn't familiar with.

Would this new professor view her tardiness harshly? Casually? Would he be quick to forgive once she apologized? Or would he be like a former professor of Aurelia's that still resented her for something she did in her freshmen year?

I guess I'll see when I get there, she thought, forging ahead.

This forensics class was too important to her future career to miss or mess up. And based on the brief bio she'd been given of her new professor in her registration packet, Dr. Weaver was just the man to teach her everything she needed to know about her profession of choice.

According to the bio, Dr. Weaver had an extensive background in science, forensic and otherwise. Academically, he had several degrees, most of which were in medicine and one in engineering. Professionally, he had worked as a forensic engineer, crime scene examiner, crime lab analyst, and medical examiner. He'd been teaching part-time for the last three years, opting to teach full-time this year.

Dr. Weaver was also a huge CSI fan. That little tidbit had

been added to the bio to give it a touch of humor and to make him seem more personable to his students. It worked. Aurelia liked him already, sight unseen.

By now it was obvious that she was a fan of CSI, too. She'd gotten the idea to work as an exotic dancer from that television show. CSI was also part of the reason she was running late today, or rather was on island time right now, if you will.

Now Aurelia wished she hadn't stayed up late last night looking at that CSI marathon. Now she wished she'd just recorded the marathon and watched it later when she had more time.

Hearing a man's authoritative voice coming from the room designated for her 9am class, Aurelia increased her steps. She was nearly jogging down the long hallway at this point. Just outside the classroom door, she suddenly stopped short.

That voice!

It sounded so familiar. Too familiar.

Could it be? Aurelia asked herself, almost afraid to peek around the corner of the door to find out as delicious tingles attacked her body. And yet she had to.

Leaning to the left, Aurelia saw...

The professor!

And worst of all, he saw her, too.

Baron couldn't miss her, considering the fact that he'd been just about to close the door and officially began his instruction.

Who's the dumb-dumb now? Aurelia mused, feeling like a straight fool as she forced her legs towards the door and mentally prepared herself to face the consequences of yet another bad decision.

CHAPTER SIX

Baron's lower body twitched the instant he saw Aurora. His pulse sped up. His heart started to pound against his ribs. Blood thundered in his ears as his body chemistry changed to that of a male specimen in heat.

Though it was a bit hard to distinguish her shapely figure in those baggy gray sweats she wore, he'd know her beautiful face anywhere. And those full lips were undeniably familiar. He'd dreamed about those.

Thinking quickly, Baron smoothly blocked the classroom entrance and entered the empty hallway more fully, causing her to back up in the process. He closed the door behind him for more privacy.

"Aurora," Baron breathed out in a discreet whisper. Desire had his voice huskier than usual. "What are you doing here?"

Had she hunted him down the way he'd wanted to do her? How did she find out where he worked? More importantly, how did his body get so granite so fast? If not for the confines of his tight jeans, he would be saluting her in a most unique way right now. Thankfully Baron's jacket was long and loose enough to hide the evidence of his desire...for the moment.

"It's..." Aurelia paused to swallow over the nervous lump that had formed in her throat. "It's Aurelia, Professor Weaver," she clarified breathlessly, making the most obvious assumption about him as well. He had to be Dr. Baron Weaver. There was no other way to explain his presence here today or the voice of authority by which she'd heard him speak just a few minutes ago.

"I'm here for class. I apologize for being late this morning. It won't happen again," Aurelia continued, speaking just as discreetly as him in the quiet hall. It took everything in her to keep her head up when all she wanted to do was bow it in shame.

She felt like such a skank right now. Did he think she was one? Aurelia couldn't blame him if he did. If only she could take back that night. It was a mistake. One of her biggest mistakes to date, despite how enjoyable it was.

"Oh, so you're Aurelia Bunting," Baron said, matching the name she'd given him with the full name of the only student marked absent on today's attendance roster. All the other students had showed up on time. And yet knowing that she was also one of his students did nothing to abate his passion.

"Yes, sir. That's me," Aurelia replied as politely and respectfully as she could in this extremely awkward moment. "May I enter the classroom now, Professor?"

Once again, Baron became conflicted inside. It showed on the outside when he shook his head no, but his mouth said, "Yes."

Aurelia suppressed a dimpled smile in memory of another time he'd been at odds with himself. "Which is it, Professor? Yes or no?" she couldn't help but ask, inwardly pleased that he was just as unsettled as she was. It evened the playing field between them. It also made her relax and feel considerably less like a skank.

"Y…yes," Baron stammered out, suddenly wishing his libido was dormant again. Aurelia had his hormones in an absolute uproar. His jeans were getting tighter and tighter around the pelvic area, making him even more uncomfortable.

"And please tell the rest of your classmates that I'll be right back. I need to get something from my office," Baron added, before quickly moving to the side so that she could access the door.

Liar, Aurelia mused humorously, doubtful that Baron was about to retrieve anything from his office as he hurried down the hallway in the opposite direction. She'd seen that flare of desire in his eyes. She knew what memories her questions had conjured up.

Aurelia also knew about lying for convenience sake. She'd

told a few convenient lies of her own over the years. Couldn't promise not to tell a few more if the situation required it.

One thing Aurelia couldn't lie about was how good Baron looked in those black jeans. The fact that he was so untraditional in his teaching attire impressed her tremendously. It turned her on.

Although he wore a business-like thigh-length black jacket, white dress shirt, and a black and white patterned tie, it was those jeans that screamed how much of a free thinker he was…and a lover of comfort. When those kinds of traits could be found in a professor, students always seemed to be able to connect with him/her so much better.

In Aurelia's case, she had connected with Baron on a level that no student should with a professor. And yet it had felt so right.

* * *

Actually, Baron hadn't lied to Aurelia at all. He did need to retrieve something from his office – his sanity. Because he honestly didn't know how he was going to teach a class with her in it.

Even now Baron wanted to throw caution to the wind and just take her home with him. Not tonight. Right now. There he would…he most definitely would…

Finish what they started in that hotel room. And then he'd start all over again.

Ten minutes was how long it took for Baron to get his body back in check and his mind focused on school again. In that amount of time, he pulled up student records from his office computer. Aurelia's was the first reviewed, despite the fact that her last name wasn't at the top of his alphabetical student roster. There were two other people before her.

From that brief review, Baron learned that Aurelia was from St. Croix in the U.S. Virgin Islands, had one younger sibling – a brother, and was from a single-parent home due to a deceased father. He also saw her transcript, detailing what she was majoring in, her high GPA, future career choice, and the fact that she was due to graduate in the spring magna cum laude if she kept up her momentum.

As a result of what Baron now knew about Aurelia, he was even more impressed by her. He was also determined to help her any way he could. He had to do something, anything to keep her from returning to exotic dancing, from having to give lap dances to men other than him.

Aurelia Bunting, Baron recited, wrapping his mind around her real name again as he reached for the phone and made a pivotal call before heading back to his classroom.

* * *

"Sorry it took me so long to return, class. But you'll be happy to know that I spent my time away from you wisely," Baron began after reentering the classroom in full professor mode. "I have good news for those who are senior chemistry majors. I just got off the phone with a good friend of mine in Alcove's crime lab. As it turns out, they are offering a paid internship for their weekend shift."

Aurelia's ears instantly perked up, matching the rest of her body, which had perked up as soon as Baron reentered the room. The detailed syllabus she picked up from the stack on his desk earlier was all but forgotten. Now all she could focus on was this golden opportunity he'd just presented to the class...and the way those jeans fit him.

Okay, back to our regular scheduled program, Aurelia thought, forcing her mind to return to the business at hand, if only for a moment.

Could it be true? Did she really have a chance to work in a real crime lab before graduation?

"The pay isn't all that great, but it's steady," Baron continued, slowly scanning the sea of student faces, looking everywhere but at Aurelia. "This job will also give whomever gets it a foot in the door to a crime lab career, which could lead to so many other great career choices."

"What type of work will be involved, Professor?" Aurelia asked.

Baron smiled, pleased down to his bones that she had shown such prompt interest in the position. He could only hope that she applied for it. Even though she wasn't the only chemistry major among his students, she did have the highest GPA. That would help her tremendously since his friend at the lab believed in only hiring the best and brightest.

"Mostly indoor work such as analyzing crime scene evidence and testing blood samples and the like. In short, routine stuff. So for those seeking adventure, this might not be the position for you." Baron chuckled, causing a slew of female students to sigh with infatuation. A few male students rolled their eyes in envy.

Aurelia didn't sigh or roll her eyes when he smiled. But

48

she did tingle…all the way down to her toes and back up again. Baron was just that gorgeous. If the Spanish actor/singer JenCarlos Canela had a twin, Professor Weaver would definitely be it.

Even now Aurelia could recall how Baron's gorgeous factor increased in the throes of passion. How slick the hairs on his chest got when the sweat of exertion streamed from his pores. How those same hairs felt against her glistening…

Stop!

I can't do this, Aurelia lamented, convinced that there was no way she could endure four months of this kind of torture. The likelihood of her being able to fully concentrate for one minute of a two-hour class with Baron was slim to none at this point.

But I must do this. Aurelia couldn't drop this class. It was part one of two required courses in her degree plan. Since Baron was the only teacher assigned to the first half, she wouldn't be able to avoid him. Nor would she be able to graduate on time if she decided to take this class at a later date. A timely graduation was crucial to her family's prosperity. Thus she had no choice but to stay in this class.

"For those interested in this position, please see me in my office before the day is out. My office hours are listed on your syllabus. Now without further ado, let's talk forensics," Baron continued, breaking through Aurelia's thoughts and tingles as he finally began his instructional time.

Despite her tingles, heated memories, and internal conflict about taking this class, Aurelia found that she actually enjoyed Baron's teaching. She could actually concentrate on the lesson, soaking up every word that was said as if she was SpongeBob Squarepants.

Baron made forensic medicine sound even more interesting than it already was to her. His command of the subject matter impressed her more than his looks, more than his lovemaking. Well…not more than that. But Aurelia was definitely impressed with her new professor on a different level today.

* * *

Since she didn't have another class until noon, Aurelia decided to follow Baron to his office and inquire more about the crime lab job. Yes, she felt awkward about being in his presence again, but she wanted that job. She needed that job.

Pride and shame be gone!

Even more pleased to find Aurelia so prompt about the job announcement, Baron closed the door behind them and quickly gave her the contact information she required. He also explained a few more details about the position to make sure she knew exactly what she was getting into.

"Thanks so much, Professor. I really appreciate this opportunity," Aurelia replied, upon hearing him out.

"You're welcome, Miss Bunting. Make the most of it."

"I will." Aurelia gave him a dimpled smile as she rose to her feet.

"If you could just linger a few minutes longer, I'd like to discuss a few other things with you," Baron said, halting her departure as he broached a new subject. He didn't have another class until noon, too, and so was in no rush to conclude their meeting. Besides, there was the matter of that apology he owed her.

Aurelia immediately stiffened at his words. Her smile flew away like a bird seeking shelter from a storm. "Discuss what, Professor?" she asked cautiously, sitting back down again.

"Discuss the grave mistake I made with you." Baron clasped his large hands together on top of the desk.

"M…mistake?" Aurelia's ears grew hot. Although she labeled what happened between them a mistake, too, it still grieved her to know that he felt the same way.

"Yes. I made the mistake of thinking that you were something you weren't," Baron clarified, talking discreetly even though the door was closed. "Dingo explained the situation to me when I went to the club. Therefore, I apologize for any discomfort or embarrassment I caused you as a result of that incident. It was certainly not my intent."

A different kind of heat shot through Aurelia's body now. The fact that he had searched her out at Dingo's had her feeling hot and bothered again. The fact that he now knew the truth about her put her mind at ease. It was comforting to know that he didn't think badly of her.

"All is forgiven, Professor. I can't really blame you for the misunderstanding given the…um…circumstances," Aurelia assured him, finally relaxing in her seat.

"Even so, I'm truly sorry that I misjudged you. I also want to reassure you that I will maintain and respect all student/teacher boundaries."

Aurelia let out a loud sigh of relief. That had been another concern of hers.

"For as long as you are in my class," Baron added, finally allowing the desire he'd been holding at bay since she entered his office to surface in his eyes. There was a plethora of it, too.

Another wave of heat shot through Aurelia's body. She swallowed over the thick lump in her throat before speaking. "Wh...what is going to happen after I get out of your class, Professor?" she forced out, involuntarily licking her lips.

At the sight of her tongue, Baron inhaled sharply and semi-rose from his seat. Had he not quickly remembered where they were, he would have gone over and kissed her socks off...on school property.

"Anything you want to happen, Au-rel-ia," Baron whispered huskily, forcing his body back down in his chair.

Aurelia let out a low moan at that open invitation to have something more permanent with him. The peaks of her bosom strained against her shirt at the sexy way he rolled her name off his Latin tongue. A pulsating began in her valley.

Even still, Aurelia had to exercise caution. "A lot can happen between now and then, Professor. By the time I'm out of your class, you might not be conducive for such a thing."

"I will be," Baron said without hesitation, without even blinking an eye.

"How can you be so sure?"

Baron leaned forward and gave her an intense stare. "Because after talking to Dingo and after replaying that night over again in my head for the umpteenth time, I realized that that night was just as special to you as it was to me. That although it was a bad way to start off a relationship, our compatibility was undeniable and certainly worth exploring further. The fact that you single-handedly pulled me out of the depths of heartbreak and opened my world back up to happiness makes me want to wait on you forever if I have to."

At those heartfelt words, Aurelia snatched her gaze away, lest she climb across that desk and kiss him until the cows came home. Since there weren't too many cows in the whole state of California that kiss would last a long time.

"Wow, Professor. You sure have a way with words." Aurelia looked down at her hands just to keep from looking at him. She'd never met a man that was so upfront with his feelings. It was highly stimulating.

"And you sure have a way with me as I recall," Baron replied huskily, before clearing his throat. "So do I have permission to pursue you once the coast is clear?" he asked, looking for consent now as he spoke in his normal voice again.

"Yes," Aurelia whispered, lifting her gaze to his again. She was flattered that the gorgeous, accomplished man even wanted to pursue her further. A man like him could have his pick of available women.

"Great." Baron smiled. "And Aurelia?"

"Yes, Professor?"

"Work hard in my class, because the only free ride you will ever get from me will be in the bedroom."

Aurelia smiled, showing off those adorable dimples again. "That's the only free ride I want." She stood to her feet, ready to prove to this gorgeous man that she could hold her own in every way. "See you in class, Professor," she concluded as she headed for the door.

"Yes, and don't be late again," Baron teased her about today's tardiness.

"I won't." Aurelia chuckled at the door. Upon opening it, she found Professor Rhoda Griffey on the other side just about to knock. "Hello, Professor Griffey," Aurelia said in greeting on her way out the door.

"Aurelia," Rhoda replied curtly, remembering this particular student from her freshman year, though she didn't want to.

How could the slender blonde woman forget the V.I. native? Aurelia was the only student that ever earned a perfect score on all of Rhoda's chemistry exams, passing each one with flying colors. To this day, she wondered if Aurelia had somehow stolen her tests and gotten the answers in advance.

But what caused Rhoda to literally start hating the V.I. native was when Aurelia pulled an innocent prank in her class. A prank which the other students readily joined in on, making it even more nerve grating for the female professor. Who cares that the prank was harmless and also justifiable because it was done on April Fool's Day? Now Rhoda fought not to scowl every time Aurelia was around.

Pushing those thoughts aside the same way she'd stepped aside and let Aurelia exit the office a few seconds ago, Rhoda focused on the man at the desk instead. "Professor Weaver, do you have time to chit-chat with a colleague?" she asked, entering the office uninvited.

"I can give you five minutes." Baron pasted a neutral expression on his face. He might have given Rhoda more time if he hadn't noticed how disrespectfully she treated Aurelia just then.

"She gets forty minutes and I only get five?" Rhoda looked peeved…and jealous as she boldly sat down in the empty visitor's chair and made herself comfortable.

"She is a student. As I recall, she's the very reason we were hired to teach here. Why would I not give her more of my time?" Baron replied, incensed that the nosy woman had actually counted how long Aurelia was in his office.

Was Rhoda some kind of stalker chick? Megan had been a borderline stalker, so he knew exactly what signs to look for. In the short time he'd known Rhoda she'd already displayed several of those signs. The most irritating one of all was constantly trying to start a romantic relationship he clearly didn't want.

Rhoda's pale skin turned crimson with embarrassment at his blunt rebuke. "I'm sorry. I was just hoping you and I could go grab a bite of lunch together, that's all. My hunger caused me to grow impatient and irritable in my wait. I apologize."

Baron nodded, although he didn't believe a word she said. "In any case, I always bring my lunch to work with me. I try not to put fast food in my body and I seldom eat out at even the most upscale of restaurants."

"Really?" Rhoda's eyes roamed over his muscular body. "Are you a vegan? You don't look lean enough to be a vegetarian."

"No, just very health conscious. I like to know what goes into my food before I eat it. In order to do that, I have to be very familiar with the chef or else prepare the food myself."

"How ever do you manage at dinner parties?" Rhoda asked, thoroughly intrigued by him now.

"To be polite to my host or hostess, I partake of the meals they offer, yet in small quantities. I also eat before I arrive, so that I won't be tempted to overindulge in the wrong things," Baron replied, ready to bring this particular Spanish Inquisition to an end. "Now if that's all, I have some things to attend to."

"Right. We'll finish where we left off later," Rhoda said,

practically begging for an invitation to return to his office later.

Baron suppressed a frown. He also refrained from nodding in reply, refusing to give her any kind of encouragement. He never wanted Rhoda to return to his office. Ever!

Now Aurelia was another story. That sexy brown woman could come as often as she liked. Stay as long as she liked, too.

Although this conversation was far from over with Rhoda, she decided not to push her luck with Baron today. Thus she rose to her feet instead of lingering longer. Rhoda knew that if she wanted this man as her own, which she did, she was going to have to practice some patience. If only that wasn't such a weak point in her character.

CHAPTER SEVEN

September

Aurelia quickly realized that Baron wasn't playing when he told her to work hard in his class. He gave a hundred and ten percent and expected the same effort from his students. No one was given a free ride, male or female.

The females that thought they would pass this class based on their looks alone quickly got a rude awakening. Many of them dropped the class by mid-September, unable to keep up with the barrage of assignments, unable to use their beauty to gain Baron's favor or his leniency, unable to entice the handsome professor in any way. Dr. Baron Weaver was all about business.

Aurelia wouldn't think of dropping this class. Besides the fact that she needed it to graduate, she seriously doubted if she would have learned as much from another instructor. Baron was a wealth of information on any given topic it seemed, especially forensics. He welcomed student questions and always answered them thoroughly.

Baron also liked asking questions. Many of which he directed at Aurelia just to see if she was up on her game. Or so it seemed to her. That only made her study harder. Aurelia even put in extra study time during her breaks at both jobs, one of which was the weekend position at the crime lab. Oh yes, she'd gotten that coveted job after interviewing better than all of her peers put together.

There was no time to study at the soup kitchen. It stayed busy the whole two hours she was there on Saturdays.

This past Saturday, one of Aurelia's Vietnamese-

American classmates was involved in a very bad car accident. That accident totaled Bambi Mac's vehicle and sent her to the intensive care unit at a local hospital. Incidentally, everyone called the injured woman Bambi Mac because they couldn't pronounce her Vietnamese name.

That extraordinary name was Mạc Yên Cổ Trúc (in order from last name, middle name, with Cổ Trúc as the two-part first name). The meaning of Bambi's Vietnamese name was ancient or old (Cổ),bamboo (Trúc), and peace (Yên). In short, peaceful old bamboo.

Although Bambi was anything but old right now, she was definitely peaceful and an outright peacemaker at times. She was also as versatile as the bamboo plant, which was used for all kinds of things, including food, medicine, and construction.

Bambi would need some of that versatility to help her through this trying time in her life. For even though she miraculously survived her accident, she broke both of her hips in the process. Now she would miss a few weeks of vital class time due to her injuries.

Wanting to do something to help her injured classmate, Aurelia came to class extra early today and asked Baron for all of Bambi's assignments upon informing him of that unfortunate weekend accident. She stuttered over her words a time or two while she talked as her emotions ran higher than usual. Her island accent had never been thicker.

Yes, Aurelia was upset about Bambi's accident. Yet it was Baron that made her emotions spike so significantly. That made her accent thicken so considerably in his presence.

The whole time Aurelia talked, Baron remained completely silent in his chair with his hands clasped tightly together upon the desk. His eyes kept going from her eyes to her mouth in a slow sweeping motion. He kept licking his lips every so often, stirring up volcanic memories in the process.

By the time Aurelia finished, she was almost breathless with desire, despite her somber news. It was a good thing no one else was in the room. Otherwise they would know that there was something personal going on between her and the professor, despite the fact that his hot gaze never went any lower than her chin.

"I'm really sorry to hear about Bambi," Baron finally replied, sounding a bit breathless himself and also concerned for his injured student. However, he looked impressed…by Aurelia.

"What's wrong with Bambi?" Claude Greenman asked, suddenly appearing at the door. The gifted biology major, who was heading straight for medical school to be an oncologist when he graduated, had heard the tail end of their conversation. Now his interest was thoroughly piqued.

Aurelia took a deep breath and repeated the sad news she gotten via text message last night from Bambi's mother. That message had been sent to all of Bambi's close friends and study buddies. Aurelia was still in the study buddy group. Though she and Bambi were friends, they hadn't hung out long enough to be in the close friends' category yet.

"Wow. I'm sorry to hear that. But Bambi's a trooper. I'm sure she'll pull through just fine," Claude said, once he'd heard a much quicker summary of the accident than Baron had gotten.

"I certainly hope so. She be such ah tiny little ting," Aurelia replied, her eyes shiny with fresh emotion. Her accent still just as thick.

Moved by her concern for others, Baron sprung to his feet, ready to comfort her in his arms. But after quickly remembering where they were, he refrained from all physical contact and instead offered Aurelia time and space to pull herself back together.

"Miss Bunting, why don't you have a seat now and leave it up to me to tell the rest of the class about Bambi. If there's anything you want to add afterwards, please do so."

"Thanks, Professor." Aurelia blinked her eyes free and turned to give him a grateful smile before moving to her usual seat on the third row.

An emotional lump formed in Baron's throat at that dimpled smile. Amazement filled his heart that something as simple as a smile could affect him so deeply.

Returning to his desk, Baron waited for the rest of his students to arrive so that he could keep his word to Aurelia. Wisdom dictated that he tell them all at one time to eliminate the need to repeat himself.

At the end of his solemn disclosure, Baron turned to address Aurelia. "Before I give you the floor, Miss Bunting, just know that you're welcome to come to my office after class today to receive the next two weeks' worth of assignments for Bambi," he said, maintaining his habit of addressing his students formally when talking to them directly, but referring to them informally when discussing them with others. "Then if she's still unable to return to school after that, I'll give you another two weeks' worth."

"Thanks again, Professor." Aurelia blessed him with another grateful smile. Then she turned to address her fellow classmates. "As for the rest of you old chaps," she said, now speaking in an Australian accent to help lighten the heavy mood that had settled in the room. "I'll be taking up the usual donations after class, so dig deep in your pockets," she concluded, making sure to elongate her vowels and end her sentences an octave higher so that they all sounded like questions.

Everyone burst out laughing, including Baron.

"Will you be getting the usual card, flowers, and fruit basket, milady?" a grinning Claude replied, speaking in an Australian accent of his own, except his sounded a bit more British. Though best known for his intelligence and overall good looks, his easy wit was also renowned. Thus it was no surprise when he was the first to link up with Aurelia's Aussie Express.

"You know it, mate." Aurelia chuckled.

Soon more classmates join in on the animated conversation, all speaking with their own versions of Australian accents. The rest laughed.

They were used to Aurelia's witty antics, although this particular prank usually only occurred on her April 1st birthday.

Baron continued to roar with laughter as the unique banter persisted among his students, getting even funnier with each new comment. His reaction was much different from Rhoda's. She'd wanted to suspend the whole class for talking with a Swedish accent when Aurelia initiated the same prank during their freshman year.

Interesting enough, Rhoda was the only AU professor to ever get offended by that prank. All the others found it funny.

Baron found Aurelia's playful side downright hilarious. Adorable, too. Deeper inside, more than just laughter swirled in his heart. There was now love there, too.

Seeing the other students' reaction to Aurelia made Baron even more impressed by her, even more conducive to loving her. The fact that they were readily pulling money from their wallets and purses and passing it to her already proved to him that she'd not only led the way in charitable acts before, but that she could also be trusted to carry out such acts.

Megan had been almost the exact opposite. Any acts of charity always had to have an audience. None of them were ever done just from the heart.

Discovering that Aurelia was genuinely a trustworthy and benevolent person made Baron's lower body stir to life, as well. He recalled another time when she had been just as giving of herself. As a lover, she'd been the epitome of unselfishness.

Realizing he was going to have to spend the next thirty minutes or so teaching from his desk, forgoing his usual walk-about method of instruction, Baron respectfully closed the Aussie Express by asking the class to open their textbooks to the review questions at the end of the chapter. He garnered smiles from them by making that request in an Australian accent of his own.

Aurelia smiled at his playfulness, too. She also tingled…a lot.

* * *

Upon collecting the rest of the donations for Bambi, Aurelia went to Baron's neat office. The door was open when she got there, yet she did not enter. She also didn't make a sound to alert him of her presence.

Aurelia was too busy staring at Baron as he stood with his back turned to the door while sorting through some files in a large file cabinet behind his oak wood desk. Starting from his thick head of black hair, her eyes went downward…

Past those broad shoulders that kept his navy-blue jacket from ever needing shoulder pads.

Past that muscular torso that strained against his white dress shirt every time he moved.

Aurelia's gaze suddenly slammed to a halt and parked at Baron's magnificent tush. Those formfitting blue jeans he wore today framed each cheek just right. Not too tight. Not too loose.

Mmm…just right.

Memories of that night in the hotel instantly revisited Aurelia. Heat washed over her as she recalled how she'd squeezed that same outstanding tush with both hands, drawing him closer and so much deeper…

"Aurelia!" Baron said, using her first name after turning

around and catching her staring at him. He addressed her more formally two times prior, but to no avail. She'd been in some kind of trance as she stared at his lower body.

"Yes?" Aurelia blinked rapidly to refocus as she forced her gaze upwards.

"Don't do that," Baron replied huskily, walking over to his desk chair even as his body swelled with desire. If this kept up, he was going to have to start buying his jeans a size larger for better cloaking purposes.

"Don't do what?" Aurelia asked, pretending she didn't know what he was talking about as she entered the room more fully.

Baron gave her a knowing look as he sat down. "Don't be...distracting." He licked his lips as his eyes settled upon her swaying hips in those peek-a-boo jeans she wore. Delicious brown skin showed through every slit from her lower thighs to her ankles.

Did Aurelia have any idea how much he wanted her right now? How much he would love to lift her upon this desk and just...just...

Wrong time for that, Professor, Baron scolded himself, forcing his mind back on track as he glanced pointedly at the open door behind her.

Aurelia cleared her throat, suddenly mindful of the open door as well as she took the empty seat in front of his desk. "Yes, Professor," she replied humbly, consenting to his gentle rebuke. She bowed her head and took a deep breath.

Baron took a deep breath of his own. And then another, because the lingering heat in his body called for more ventilation. Quick!

To further quench his desires, Baron forced his mind upon business by reaching into his lower right desk drawer for the folder that held all of his printed assignment sheets. Taking out two weeks' worth, he passed the documents across the desk. "I think this is a great thing that you're doing for Bambi."

"As my father would say, 'Dis ah God ting," Aurelia replied with a deliberately thicker island accent. She chuckled. "Daddy believed heavily in the whole 'do unto others' principle."

Baron laughed, too. "He sounds just like my mother, who taught me to live by that same principle." He reached into his inner jacket pocket for his wallet. "Give Bambi my regards and also this," he added, passing a stack of twenties across the desk and laying it upon the assignment sheets.

"Th...thanks, Professor," Aurelia replied a bit on the husky side, completely turned on by his generosity. The stack he slid across the desk totaled a cool three hundred dollars. That was more than what she'd collected from the whole class. In addition to the other gifts already predetermined, Bambi was going to get a nice robe and a pair of slippers behind this act of benevolence.

Baron's ears soaked up the desire oozing from Aurelia's voice like a sponge to water. It made him more rigid than ever. It also made him ravenous for her.

"You're welcome," he finally said, after clearing his throat, which did little to remove the huskiness from his own voice. "Well, I won't keep you. I know you have a few errands to run for your classmate," Baron concluded, trying to put some distance between them now. He needed to get Aurelia out of his office before he said the wrong thing. Did the wrong thing.

"Yes, I do have a few errands to run for Bambi. I also have to mail off my little brother's birthday present so that it will get there in time." Aurelia stood to her feet and headed to the office door. "Thanks again, Professor," she said, pausing in the doorway a few seconds later.

Baron simply nodded, not trusting himself to say anything more right now. Inwardly, he was counting down the days to when they could be together again. On that day, he would tell her his newest revelation – that he loved her!

CHAPTER EIGHT

When Bambi returned to school, Baron found one more reason to love Aurelia. The way she went out of her way to cater to her temporarily wheelchair bound classmate was endearing. He found it downright adorable like the rest of her.

There was no need for Bambi to sharpen her pencils, take her turn writing her assigned problem on the board, or even open the door to exit the room when class was over. Aurelia gladly did all of that for her.

She would make an excellent nurse. Baron smiled as he watched his beloved chat it up with Bambi on the way out. An excellent mother, too.

Baron's body stirred at just the thought of impregnating Aurelia with his seed. In his mind's eye, he could see her writhing beneath him. Her eyes open, looking up into his as he pumped his seed deep into her fertile womb, making sure she conceived.

Because of heated thoughts like that, Baron now had to wait an extra fifteen minutes at his desk. He couldn't enter the hallway in his current condition.

When Baron's body was finally calmer, he exited the classroom with his leather briefcase in hand. The hallways of the science building had quieted down again now that most of the students had made it to their various destinations.

Suddenly his eyes bucked in wonder. Was it a bird? A plane?

No, it was Aurelia riding on the back of Bambi's wheelchair.

A chuckle bubbled in Baron's throat. More love stirred in his heart as he watched the electric transport coming full speed ahead up the hallway en route to the elevators. Both women wore smiles and their eyes sparkled with animation. Their long black tresses flapped on their shoulders from the breeze created by their joyous ride.

Bambi's olive cheeks were rosy with the vibrancy of life. Aurelia's dimples had never been deeper.

When they passed by Baron, Bambi grinned and threw up a peace sign. Aurelia grinned, too, and winked at him. Chuckling even more, he saluted the mischievous women, and proceeded to his office.

Making a mental note of Aurelia's adventurous side, Baron now looked forward to taking her for a ride on his motorcycle – a Harley Davidson of the Street Glide edition. Until then, he was taking his bike for a run up to Bel Air this weekend to watch Duke and Sasha renew their vows.

Since Baron didn't have a date for the wedding and since the weather reports indicated sunny weather all weekend, he was going alone on a vehicle that would allow him to partake of nature even more. He could hardly wait.

But first he had to make it through the rest of the day. There were not only more classes to teach, but also staff meetings to attend. Such was a regular workday in the life of a college professor. This particular professor loved every segment of his job.

All Baron needed now was a good wife to come home to at night. He needed Aurelia.

* * *

After school, Aurelia went with Bambi to an orthopedic doctor's appointment in Friendly. Usually she steered clear of the city where Dingo's club was, but since Bambi volunteered to take her to dinner afterwards, she saw no just cause to refuse.

The less Aurelia had to pay for her own food, the better off her budget was. The better off her budget was, the more money she could send home to help her family.

"Can my friend come to the back with me, Aunt Mai Ly?" Bambi asked the pleasant receptionist when her name was called. Incidentally, that receptionist really was her biological aunt on her mother's side.

"Sure thing," Mai Ly replied with a smile. "Dr. Johansson won't mind since it's just a routine consult."

"Great." Bambi grinned, showing pearly white teeth that had been straightened with braces as a child. "Are you riding this chariot to the back? Or are you Ike and Miking it?" she turned to ask her classmate, careful not to bump either of her thoroughly signed leg casts against anything.

"Who wants to walk when they can ride in style?" Aurelia chuckled, immediately positioning herself on the back of Bambi's wheelchair for the second time that day.

Mai Ly simply laughed at them and buzzed the automatic doors open to allow them entry to the back examination rooms. She waved goodbye to the jovial friends as they passed by.

Although Aurelia didn't seek out a close friendship with anyone in light of the Roxy situation, Bambi was so personable that it was hard not to get attached to her once you spent any significant amount of time in her presence. They might have been close friends sooner had Aurelia been more of a party animal like Bambi was…or rather used to be before her accident. The fact that Aurelia had a contagious smile and was very personable herself caused their previous casual friendship to deepen very fast over the last few weeks.

The old Bambi would have fit right in on the Virgin Islands, despite the fact that she was from a different cultural background. Islanders loved to party and knew how to do it well. Aurelia liked a good party as well as the next islander, but when she went off to college, she curtailed her partying ways and became a serious student. She barely attended social functions around campus these days.

Aurelia and Bambi's mirth continued well into the examining room they were shown to by a white uniformed nurse. They even had the nurse laughing before she left to retrieve the doctor.

Aurelia's laughter abruptly ended when Dr. William Johansson walked into the room a few minutes later. Instant recognition bounced between them.

See that's why I stay out of this city, Aurelia mused, having come face to face with one of her regulars from the club – Willy as he liked to be called.

* * *

"Good afternoon, Bambi. How are you today?" William sounded casual, but looked anything but that as he sat down opposite his patient on a stainless steel stool.

"I'm feeling fine, Dr. Johansson. Are you well? Your face

64

is all red," Bambi replied, staring at his fair complexion with concern.

"I'm well, just a little hot right now. Thanks for asking." William sent a hand through his thick dark tresses that contained only a few streaks of gray. Then he turned to look at Aurelia, who was sitting in the blue cushioned chair by the unused hospital bed. "And who may I ask is this?"

Like you don't know, big spender, Aurelia mused, recalling how much money Willy used to put in her G-strings and thongs on a regular basis. How many lap dances he usually requested on a given night.

"That's my friend and fellow classmate, Aurelia Bunting," Bambi shared, turning to her classmate with a warm smile. "We're both chemistry majors at AU. She's been very instrumental in keeping my spirits up during this whole ordeal."

"I see. Nice to meet you, Aurelia. We all need people like you around to help brighten up our lives." William's gaze lingered a little bit too long upon his favorite exotic dancer.

"Nice to meet you, too, doctor," Aurelia replied with a cordial nod and a smile that she had to force across her lips.

Why oh why did Bambi have to volunteer so much of her personal information? And what was Willy going to do with that information? Aurelia could only hope that the distinguished doctor wasn't some kind of stalker, but rather a relatively decent man that just needed to get his libido stroked every now and then.

Unaware of the dilemma she just put her friend in, Bambi grinned knowingly at the smitten look on her widowed doctor's face. Who would have thought that Dr. Johansson would develop an instant crush on Aurelia? But then again, a lot of men developed crushes on the V.I. native, including the man Bambi had a crush on – Claude Greenman.

Actually Bambi was secretly in love with Claude. Had been since sophomore year. He was the same guy that she was working extra hard to fully recover for so that she could actively pursue.

Although many of her traditional Vietnamese elders might frown upon a woman pursuing a man, Bambi did not hold to those ideals. She didn't want to be submissive and delicate like her mother, letting the man take the more dominant role. As a Vietnamese American woman, she wanted to be strong and able to vocalize her feelings to the man of her choosing.

Plus, that car accident taught Bambi a very important lesson. It taught her that life really was short, subject to end at any moment. That she had to seize all the happiness she could get out of life while she could. She wanted to seize that happiness with Claude. That's if Aurelia hadn't submitted to his charms by then.

Maybe I can hook her up with Dr. Johansson instead. He's not too much older than her, Bambi thought, estimating the handsome Patrick Dempsey look- alike to be in his mid-forties.

At the first opportunity she would ask her aunt about Dr. Johansson's likes and dislikes. Then she'd use that knowledge to help nudge Aurelia along a different romantic path. A path that was far, far away from Claude.

* * *

After getting her aunt to tell her personal things about Dr. Johansson, albeit reluctantly for some reason, Bambi sang the doctor's praises to Aurelia from the time they left his office all the way to the restaurant. They were now in her family's home lab/garage experimenting with original perfume formulas and she was still talking about the man.

"I bet Dr. Johansson would love this scent on you," Bambi said after taking a long whiff of the perfume her friend just created. She twirled the long wooden handle of the cotton swab in the air a few times and smelled the tip again. "Yep, he'll definitely love this on you."

Aurelia chuckled. "I'm not interested in your doctor, Bambi, so you can just stop matchmaking right now," she replied, using another cotton swab to dab the fragrance on her left wrist so that she could smell it on her actual skin. "As for this scent…mmm…the more I smell it, the more I like it," she said after another deep whiff.

"Why don't you package it and sell it? It could make you a lot of money, if you marketed it right." Bambi spoke with confidence as she put her swab down and started lining up empty perfume bottles on the stainless steel countertop.

Though formally educated as a chemist at AU, Bambi had been introduced to the basic elements of chemistry as a child. Her maternal grandmother taught her perfumery when she was ten, detailing how to combine the right ingredients in the proper measurements in order to make outstanding fragrances.

Bambi became so good at perfumery that she could now mimic any designer brand on the market. Her enlightened sense of smell could also accurately identify the main ingredients in any fragrance just from a single whiff. That little trick went over well at parties where she usually blindfolded herself and engaged in random sniff tests.

Over the years, Bambi developed her own line of scented soaps, perfumes, and colognes. Her Peaceful Bamboo line was currently being sold in the chain of beauty supply stores her family owned in predominantly black neighborhoods. She also knew how to make wigs and hairpieces having garnered that expertise from her father's side.

As a result of her considerable talents, Bambi has earned enough money to pay for her own college education. She certainly didn't need to live at home with her parents, grandmother, and four siblings. Yet she continued to do so because she liked having family around her and because she actually liked the tradition of a girl waiting until she was married to move out of her parents' home.

"Do you really think someone would want to buy my perfume?" Aurelia sniffed her wrist again and smiled with pleasure. The concoction of jasmine, lily of the valley, orange blossoms, vanilla, and various spices was undeniably appealing. Maybe someone other than her would like it enough to buy it after all.

"Trust me. I've been making perfumes since I was a tween. I know a hit when I smell one. Your perfume is refreshing like flowers, seductive like a woman, and hot like passion burning in the veins. It enters the nostrils like a strong wind and then softens like a whisper. Women are going to love wearing it. Men are going to love smelling it on women." Bambi chuckled and added, "I just wish I'd thought of it."

Aurelia laughed. "If you show me how to mass produce and market it, I'll split a fair share of the profits with you. After all, I made the prototype in your lab with your ingredients," she said with sincere eyes.

Bambi paused from her task and smiled, pleased by her friend's sense of integrity and equality. If Aurelia kept this up, she was going to be reassigned to the BFF - best friend forever category. "Agreed. I'll draw up some tentative business plans by next week. I'll also show you how to patent your formula for your own protection."

Aurelia's eyes shined with emotion as she moved towards the wheelchair to give Bambi a hug. "Thanks a lot, girl. I really appreciate this." Inside she could feel the shackles of poverty falling off her and her family already.

Come prosperity come. Run fast!

"You're welcome," Bambi replied, receiving that warm hug of gratitude with a smile. "Now back to your love life," she said, smoothly changing the subject as they released each other. "If Dr. Johansson is not your type, what man is?" She involuntarily held her breath as she waited for the answer to her question.

Please don't let it be Claude. Please don't let it be Claude, Bambi recited inwardly to the rhythm of Dorothy's 'There's no place like home. There's no place like home' recital in The Wizard of Oz.

Aurelia smiled. "I got my sights on a handsome Latino right about now." She returned to the wooden stool at her workstation. "He's not quite thirty yet, highly intelligent, and seems to know all the right things to say and do to me."

Bambi sighed in relief. Based on that detailed description, Aurelia's love interest wasn't Claude. It wasn't Claude! Her smile was wide and gleeful now.

"What is this mystery man's name? Where is he from? Does he live in town?" Bambi asked, returning to her previous task of lining up small glass bottles for Aurelia to pour her new perfume into. They would be taken home for personal use or utilized as free samples to help drum up business.

"Because we still have a few things to work out, all I can say right now is that his first name is Barry, he's from California, and yes, he does live in town," Aurelia said, mixing one of her convenient lies in with the truth. She didn't like lying, but sometimes felt the need to when trying to protect someone or something precious.

"You still have a few things to work out? Things like what, a wife? Barry's not married, is he?" Bambi frowned.

Aurelia chuckled at her stern motherly look. "No, he is definitely not married, unless you count his job as a spouse. It's his job that's standing in our way of being together. Once Barry gets his business issues under control, it'll be smooth sailing for us in every way. I can hardly wait." She giggled.

"In that case, I wish you and Barry well." Bambi's gleeful smile returned.

"Thanks." Aurelia returned her left wrist to her nose and inhaled. "Now if you're done with all the matchmaking, let's get back to the subject of my new perfume. I'd like to call it Aurora, because it's exotic and catchy enough to be remembered."

"Uh-uh, try again." Bambi shook her head. "Disney already has a scent called Aurora."

"Awww, man." Aurelia pouted, folding her arms across her chest. "Really?"

"Yes, really," Bambi confirmed with a chuckle.

"Now stop pouting." Aurelia grinned. "Yes, Mommy," she playfully endeared in a little girl's voice, twirling a finger in her right dimple for extra effect.

Bambi burst out laughing, thereby setting off a laughing spree among them.

When their mirth finally calmed down, the two women bottled Aurelia's perfume and packed them into a medium-sized box. The whole time they worked, they brainstormed about possible names for the fragrance. Name after name was checked on Internet databases from Bambi's laptop. Name after name was crossed off their list when discovered that they were already taken by someone else.

Finally the women settled on the name Aurora's Whispers. That name stayed in line with Aurelia's original idea and incorporated a bit of the description Bambi had assigned to the fragrance earlier.

So excited about the new name, they even designed and printed out computerized labels for the bottles. Now Aurora's Whispers actually looked like a professionally made product.

Later, in the wheelchair equipped vehicle that Bambi used to drive Aurelia back to campus to retrieve her own car, they discussed the business side of the perfume industry. That conversation ended up with them agreeing to become 60/40 partners with Aurelia garnering the largest portion. Now all she needed was her part of the required capital to successfully launch the fragrance to the buying public.

* * *

After his last meeting, Baron gathered a few things from his office and finally trudged to his car. Though his mind was drooping with fatigue from the long day he'd had, his heart was light and upbeat. He was in love. Love made everything better.

Even the dank, overcast night didn't really bother him. In Baron's eyes, the sky was starry and clear. Better yet, it was as if the sun was shining brighter than the well-lit parking lot behind the science building.

Suddenly Baron's mood darkened. Adrenaline rushed through his veins. His feet seemed to speed up instinctively and head towards that sound.

What sound?

The sound of a woman being abused by a man in the dark alley in between the buildings.

"Please don't hit me anymore," the woman whimpered, sounding like a helpless child.

"Do as I say and I won't," the man growled out. "Now get on the ground, trick, before I have to school your face with my other hand. On second thought, let me give you a little motivation to obey." He smacked her again, causing the woman to cry out in pain. "Shut up, trick!" he hissed.

Baron's legs moved faster. He had to get around that corner before the woman was assaulted even worse.

Take long strides, Professor. Long strides, he coached himself as he sprinted with briefcase in hand. His high school track coach would be so proud of his current time. But would that time be fast enough to save a life tonight?

The sound of wet pavement connecting with the soles of Baron's boots made it around the building before him and echoed in the alley, causing a chain reaction.

Hearing rapid footsteps approaching, the assailant released his hold on the woman and ran away. By the time Baron made it into the alley, all that was left was a crying female humbled and humiliated on her knees.

"It's going to be all right," he soothed, bending to comfort the mystery woman. When she looked up at him with tears streaming down both cheeks, he instantly recognized who she was.

Oh no! Why did it have to be her of all people?

* * *

News of Rhoda's attack spread around the school like a wildfire. People's sympathy for her soon rose above their previous dislike of her. Extreme dislike in some cases.

People even excused the fact that Rhoda had called the man to meet her after work that day, skipping out early on a departmental meeting just to see him. That she'd even planned on sleeping with him that night, just not at that location. This was excusable because any previous romantic dealings a woman had with a man or intended to have with him in the future didn't give that man the right to abuse or force himself upon her.

Admiration for Baron rose as well, though he was already highly esteemed around campus because of his teaching style alone. He won cool points from the men. The women hailed him as a hero. A local TV reporter even called him in for a televised interview.

Aurelia watched that interview on the big screen television in the student center along with a lot of other students. With each new question Baron answered superbly, she became even more impressed by him. Pride swelled in her heart.

Who knew that myman would turn out to be such a knight in shining armor? Aurelia thought.

Hold the presses! Her man? Was she already claiming him?

Well, he'll be my man come December, Aurelia mused with a secret smile from her place at the end of a long sectional couch.

Unfortunately for her, Jordin Summerville, the extremely beautiful female reporter, looked like she wanted Baron to be her man. The sultry looks she kept giving him during the interview and the way her hand lingered during their opening handshake were all flirtatious.

"She is so feeling him," Bambi said from her wheelchair, which was parked next to the brown sectional couch.

"Definitely," Aurelia agreed without turning from the TV screen. "I wonder if he's feeling her," she pondered aloud, biting nervously on her bottom lip.

"It doesn't look like it to me," Claude said from behind them with a soft drink in one hand, a bag of popcorn in the other. "Which means he's either gay, just not attracted to that kind of woman, or else deeply in love with someone else."

"Professor Weaver ain't gay!" a chorus of angry females protested from around the room.

"Stop hating, dawg," said some of the men.

Claude held his hands up in surrender. "All right. All right. Don't start a riot up in this piece."

"Yes, please let's keep it civilized in here, good people," Bambi said, forever the peacemaker.

"Listen to the girl," Claude advocated, sending the pretty

Vietnamese woman a grateful grin. "All I was doing was stating possibilities for why the man wasn't feeling that Kim Kardashian look-alike," he went on to explain.

Aurelia, who'd remained silent while the other women protested, looked at Claude and said, "I think it is possibility number two. Professor Weaver is probably just not attracted to that kind of woman." She had to pick the second possibility. It made more sense to her and held the least amount of emotional turmoil for her than possibilities one and three.

"I personally think he's in love," Bambi said, revealing which possibility she favored.

Aurelia felt heat bathe her from head to toe. She clenched her leather purse tighter in her lap. Forced herself to breathe, just breathe.

Could Baron be in love...with her? If so, when did that happen? How did that happen? They'd only had that one night together. Hadn't kissed or even held hands since.

Not ready to deal with that possibility, Aurelia returned her attention to the interview, leaving Bambi and a few others to speculate about what kind of woman Baron might likely be in love with. Not surprisingly, an ex-stripper was not named among the choices.

"Professor Weaver, I'm sure you've been keeping up with the latest details of this assault case," Jordin said, continuing her interview. "So by now you know that the alleged assailant claims that he is innocent, that it was his twin brother who committed that horrendous act against your colleague. A brother, who also maintains his own innocence. And that as a result, the police are having a hard time trying to decipher who the real guilty party is."

"Yes, I am very much aware of the complex nature of this case." Baron sounded as somber as he looked. "With identical DNA as a factor, no fingerprints to lift off of a purse or even an earring, what could have been an open and shut case has become unduly difficult. However, I have every confidence in our local police department and crime lab's ability to solve this case."

"With your level of expertise, Professor, I'm sure you could probably help them solve the case even sooner." Jordin gave Baron another one of those sultry looks.

Aurelia bristled in her seat at that look.

"I'll certainly do what I can," Baron replied, looking

unaffected by the flirting reporter.

Aurelia let out a low sigh of relief at his reaction. Maybe the man is in love. She was starting to warm to the idea herself.

CHAPTER NINE

October

It was mid-term now and Aurelia had done what she set out to do in Baron's class - ace all his tests and assignments. As a result, she currently had an A average in his class. At least that's what it said on the bulletin board outside Professor Weaver's classroom. The same bulletin board that Aurelia and her classmates were standing in front of right now on that bright autumn morning.

An A. What a way to start the day off. Aurelia smiled at the high mid-term grade beside her assigned student number.

Baron assigned them all personalized student numbers during the first week of class. This way they could access their grades at any time via computer and could maintain their anonymity when he posted grades via bulletin board.

"You must have a good grade," Claude said as he stood beside Aurelia.

"Yes." Aurelia turned to him with a grin. "That big smile on your face must mean that you got a good grade, too."

"Yep!" Claude's smile turned into a full grin now.

"Nuff respect," Aurelia said, using island lingo that reflected her accolades of his accomplishment. An equivalent stateside lingo of praise would be, 'You go, boy!'

Claude chuckled at her reply. "Want to go celebrate our good fortune together over lunch today? I got two coupons to an all-you-can-eat buffet and I'm not afraid to use them."

Aurelia laughed, appreciating Claude's humor like always as they walked away from the bulletin board towards the door of their classroom. Inwardly she was amazed that he hadn't given up trying to date her by now. He'd been trying since their freshmen year.

Aurelia might have considered dating Claude once upon a time, if he wasn't so promiscuous. Smart, witty and handsome as all get out with that smooth mocha skin and those gorgeous chestnut eyes, the tall man had women falling all over him. Claude gladly caught them all.

Instead of falling all over him, too, Aurelia resisted his charms. It wasn't very hard to do since she was naturally repelled by even the thought of becoming part of a harem. Plus, she liked her men a tad more muscular, though not freakishly packed with muscles like some overachieving bodybuilders.

Another reason Aurelia wasn't interested in dating Claude was because he was just as broke as her. Although she didn't consider herself a gold-digger since she enjoyed making her own money, too, and actively tried to do so, Aurelia was convinced that she could do bad all by herself. She'd seen enough of poverty to last a lifetime.

Her parents were poor, their parents before them, and their parents before them. It was poverty that contributed to the death of her father. Trenton Bunting died prematurely due to overwork, poor diet, and no healthcare to adequately manage his Type 1 diabetes.

Nine months after her father died, Aurelia appointed herself as the person to break the cycle of poverty over her family's life once and for all. She worked odd jobs, studied hard, and only dated guys that were financially secure. If love blossomed within those relationships, fine, but it was not a requirement like financial stability was.

Although Claude would be financially secure one day, the fact that he wasn't right now was another solid deterrent. Aurelia needed someone that could help her and her family out today or at least in the very near future.

Baron was that man.

Besides being wealthy, Aurelia was genuinely attracted to many other notable things about the professor. Things like his kind heart, understanding nature, and those adorable pink lips of his. She also liked his easy sense of humor. Don't forget about how great he was in bed.

Aurelia wasn't going to blow what she could have with Baron to accept a lunch date with Claude no matter how cute he was. No way. No how.

"Before you try to give me another rain check, just remember that we can talk over our upcoming lab project while we eat, knocking two birds out with one stone," Claude added, as if he knew she was about to let him down easy again.

Aurelia paused for a moment to weigh her options. As long as she kept things platonic, there was no real harm in having a free meal with her new lab partner. Was there?

"All right. I'll have lunch with you today," Aurelia told Claude, unaware that Baron was a mere ten feet behind them now as she headed to her usual seat on the third row. That he'd just heard her seemingly agree to a lunch date with another man.

"Finally!" Claude's grin returned in full force. "I may even leave the waitress a big tip behind this monumental event," he said, oblivious to Baron's frown.

That frown signified that the professor had jumped to the wrong conclusion about Aurelia yet again. But would he foolishly act on that wrong conclusion like before, despite the fact that he still loved her with all his heart?

Unfortunately, Bambi happened to enter the room right behind Baron. Like him, she only heard the very end of Aurelia and Claude's conversation. Like Baron, she'd come to the same wrong conclusion. Suddenly she didn't want to be Aurelia's partner in business. Suddenly she didn't even want to be her friend anymore.

* * *

"Whew!" Claude said as they settled into his black pickup truck two hours later. "Professor Weaver was brutal today. He just wouldn't stop with the questions. You seem to get the brunt of them. Are you all right?"

"I'm fine," Aurelia lied, forcing a smile upon her face. She was anything but fine after that two-hour class. She'd felt almost interrogated by Baron's barrage of questions.

What in the world had gotten into him today? Aurelia hadn't seen Baron's face that flushed since the night they...well, since that night.

And Bambi. What was up with her today? She seemed so distant. She'd barely made eye contact with Aurelia during class, had left before it ended and never returned. And she wasn't even answering her cell phone.

"Yes, you are very fine," Claude flirted, spring boarding off Aurelia's last statement.

She genuinely smiled this time. "Stop flirting and start driving, mon. We only have an hour before our next class. We need to use that time to eat and discuss whose going to be responsible for what in our lab project."

"Still just as focused as ever," Claude noted, looking impressed by the woman who hadn't bothered to join any sororities or clubs in her quest to just focus solely on her education.

"Focused is the only way I know to be," Aurelia replied, although she was having a harder time of it today with all these distracting thoughts of Baron and Bambi. Mostly Baron.

"Even so, there's nothing wrong with letting your hair down every now and then." Claude finally started up his truck.

Let my hair down, Aurelia echoed internally, squeezing her eyes closed as those words triggered a memory. A very sensual memory concerning a certain wig.

She'd forgotten all about that wig until now. It had been her favorite, too. How could something like that have slipped her mind? And for so long?

Blame Aurelia's wig faux pas on the fact that she'd only used it for dance performances, hadn't needed it lately because she'd switched professions, thus causing the wig to slip from her mind. Dig a little deeper and an even greater truth will be found.

That truth: Aurelia found it hard to remember anything beyond Baron from that night.

She remembered how he kissed her, touched her, and especially how he made love to her. She also recalled how enthralled he was when she did the same things to him.

"You all right over there?" Claude asked with concern, interrupting Aurelia's trip down memory lane.

"I'm fine," she lied again, opening her eyes. "Just having a bit of a hunger headache."

"In that case, let me take the shortcut to the restaurant."

Aurelia simply nodded, unwilling to pour more lies into her friend's ears. She'd lied enough as it was today. Inwardly her mind returned to the case of the missing wig. Did a member of the hotel's custodial staff find it and throw it away? Or did Baron find it and keep it as a souvenir?

* * *

Back at Alcove University, Baron sat in his office with the

door closed. There were papers to grade in front of him, but he was too distracted to concentrate on any of them. All he could focus on was Aurelia and the fact that she hadn't waited on him. That she was out with another man right now. He'd personally seen her get in Claude's truck through the blinds of his office window.

Baron could kick himself for not asking Aurelia to wait on him. For just assuming that she would because he made it clear that he would wait on her. She'd said that a lot could happen between now and the time he'd have the all-clear to date her.

I guess Claude happened, Baron deduced, continuing along that path of erroneous thinking as he officially put himself back on the dating market as of now. As of right now!

Baron would not allow the type of depression that seized him post-Megan reclaim him again. Last time Duke had wanted to prescribe anti-depressants for him because Baron had been such a mess. He'd let his hair and beard grow out, stopped cleaning his house, and had lost a lot of weight.

Despite all that, Baron had refused to take any medication during his depression, almost preferring to dwell in his misery. This time he would not allow misery to even touch his soul…well, at least not for very long.

* * *

Bambi finally dried her eyes after crying for almost an hour straight. After going through a whole box of tissue, she had an epiphany.

Bambi realized that it was wrong of her to be upset with the V.I. native. It wasn't Aurelia's fault that Claude liked her better. How can you blame someone for something like that?

Deciding not to lay blame where it didn't belong, Bambi took a deep breath, squared her shoulders, and pulled out her cell phone. Then she typed a pivotal text message.

That message read: "Aurelia, I'll put up all $ to launch Aurora's Whispers. But it'll hav 2 B a soft launch, cuz more kin is due from old country soon and need relocation $. Lots of it. If U want 2 do soft launch now, all U have 2 do is sign agreement to pay me back outta your share of future profits. Luv Bambi."

After pressing send, Bambi started to feel a whole lot better. Doing the right thing always lifted a person's spirit. If only that righteous act could have healed her broken heart, too.

Fortunately for Bambi, that kind deed towards Aurelia did at least start the healing process.

CHAPTER TEN

November

Aurelia didn't realize Baron had given up on her until she saw him at AU's annual charity carnival. He had a sultry brunette on his arm as they toured the various booths on the school's large football field. A very familiar looking brunette...

Jordin Summerville.

Aurelia might have missed them altogether if Claude hadn't pointed them out from their place on the bleachers. They'd just finished their lab project today and had journeyed across campus to celebrate with cotton candy and candy apples.

Now Aurelia wished she had gone to work instead of taking off this weekend to complete the project, type the results, and email them to the professor's electronic dropbox before Monday's deadline. Now she wished she was at her forensics job or even at the soup kitchen serving the homeless.

"I see them, Claude. I didn't know Professor Weaver and Jordin Summerville were dating," Aurelia forced out, trying to sound casual after this unfortunate discovery.

"Me either. I guess she was his type after all," Claude said, bringing to mind a previous conversation they'd had about the local TV reporter and their professor.

"Apparently so." Aurelia seethed inside.

"The professor obviously likes 'em full at the top and the bottom. Me, too," Claude said, diverting his attention to the shapely woman next to him on the bleachers.

"There are quite a few women around here that fit that description." Aurelia dragged her gaze from Baron to the man beside her. "Need any help pointing them out?" She chuckled to mask the current pain of rejection she felt.

Claude laughed. "No thanks. I see all I need to see right here. By the way, now that our lab project is over, can I take you out on a real date?"

Aurelia started to say yes just to ease some of the hurt she felt about Baron. But after quickly realizing that Claude deserved better than second-choice status, she stayed in do-right lane. Plus, she was starting to pick up on Bambi's attraction to Claude. It was hard not to when the woman's eyes grew starry every time he walked into a room.

Don't forget about Bambi's sudden interest in Aurelia's love life and that matchmaking she tried to do back in September. Now Aurelia understood that her new friend had simply been trying to assess the competition and peacefully eliminate it.

But why hadn't Claude picked up on Bambi's feelings by now? He was a smart man in every other way. In fact, his brilliant contribution to their project was likely going to earn them both A's.

Aurelia wondered if she should redirect Claude's attention to her friend instead of just letting him down easy the regular way. Before she could do that, she needed to make sure it was okay with Bambi first. Especially since each starry-eyed look her friend gave Claude was usually followed by one of pain. There was a good chance that Bambi couldn't be with him for cultural reasons.

Although the Macs treated Aurelia well whenever she visited their home and seemed to approve of her friendship with Bambi, it was possible that they might not take too kindly to their Vietnamese relative actually dating a black person. After all, interracial friendships and interracial romantic relationships were two entirely different things.

"No thanks. I'm not ready to start anything new with anybody just yet," Aurelia said, feeling grieved in her heart.

He nodded in understanding, noting the pain in her eyes as she let him down easy once again. "Let me know when you're ready, okay? Some relationships are harder to get over than others," Claude said gently, naturally assuming that she was still heartbroken over Cain, whom he'd disliked upon sight.

Aurelia's response was a quiet nod. Although she knew she should probably clarify things on the Cain front, she suddenly didn't have the strength to. Doing so would surely start a discussion about what new man had broken her heart. She just wasn't ready for that conversation right now. If ever.

Blinking back tears she didn't understand, Aurelia couldn't believe that she was so emotional over a man that she barely even knew. A man that she only had sex with once.

At any moment now she expected to hear a Heather Headley song. Particularly In My Mind, where Heather talks about feeling like she would always be a certain man's lady even though they were no longer together. And like the song, was Baron standing with Jordin, yet had his soul calling out Aurelia's name?

"Now with that out the way, how 'bout I help you chow down that mountain of cotton candy you got there," Claude suggested with a smile, smoothly changing the subject.

Aurelia chuckled. "Only if you give me some of your candy apple in return," she countered, holding her treat to the opposite side during her negotiation. She was starting to feel better already, but only just a little bit.

Would the medicine of laughter help ease the pain even faster? Aurelia hoped so.

Claude threw his head back and laughed loudly at her actions, causing attention to come their way, some of which came from Baron. "All right. But we hand off at the same time," he said in between chuckles.

"On three," Aurelia said, appreciating his friendship. She realized at that very moment that that was all they'd ever have between them - friendship. She had peace about that.

Aurelia couldn't wait to share some of that peace with Bambi when she told her that she was absolutely not interested in Claude romantically. But first there were a couple of bites of candy apple to attend to.

"One, two, three," the two classmates chimed together before handing over their treats to share.

* * *

Baron frowned at the sight of Aurelia and Claude having so much fun together on that sun drenched Saturday afternoon. It irked him. A lot.

"Do you know those students?" Jordin observed where his attention had gone and that deep frown upon his face.

"Yes, they're in one of my classes." Baron continued to glare at the couple on the bleachers.

"Are they bad students? You're practically scowling at them." Jordin touched his bare left arm to regain his attention. They'd both worn short sleeves on that warm day. Hers were part of a red sheath dress. His belonged to a gray polo shirt that complimented the blue jeans he wore.

"No, they're both actually quite brilliant," Baron replied honestly, returning his gaze to the woman that he wouldn't have even given the time of day to before Aurelia's rejection. Or rather what he perceived to be her rejection.

Jordin had given Baron her business card complete with her personal contact information months ago after their first meeting. He had promptly thrown that card away because of his feelings for Aurelia. When his hopes for that relationship were dashed, he phoned Jordin at work and asked her out on a date. They have been dating intermittently ever since.

Baron deliberately rationed his time with Jordin for two reasons. One, he didn't want to get too serious with anyone too fast considering his lingering feelings for Aurelia. Two, he wanted to keep his options open just in case…well, in case Aurelia's relationship with Claude didn't work out.

"I was just thinking they should be at the lab working on their project instead of goofing around out here. After all, the deadline is Monday," Baron continued, trying to cover up his jealousy with a more politically correct explanation.

Jordin chuckled. "Calm down, Professor." She ran a manicured hand up his muscular arm. "If those two are as brilliant as you say, I'm sure they're probably finished with their project by now or either just taking a short break to let off some steam."

"You're probably right." Baron took a deep breath and blew out some of his frustration. It sucked not having the woman he really wanted. It sucked the sourest of lemons.

"Let's go play a round of miniature golf," he suggested, trying to force himself to move on in every way.

I have to stop holding on to things so long. Stop always assuming the worst of women, Baron thought, referring to what had become the Achilles heel of his personality ever since Megan deserted him.

* * *

Underneath the bleachers where Aurelia and Claude sat was a gray- haired Caucasian man with blue eyes. He was dressed in all black. In his hands was a key chain voice recorder. That was just one of many tools of the trade for the discreet private investigator.

Bringing the mini digital recorder up to his mouth, the P.I. whispered into it. "She's still not dating anyone." After concluding his short message, he put the key chain in the front left pocket of his jeans and proceeded to his car.

With each step he took, he marveled at the irony of this case. What were the odds of four different people hiring him to gather information on the same young woman? Four wealthy people at that, two stateside and two not. All men.

Client #1 required quarterly updates on Aurelia, which had been going on steadily for years. Client #2 required semi-annual updates, which were as sporadic as his payments. Clients #3 and #4 were new additions and both wanted weekly updates on Aurelia. They'd been willing to pay through the tooth for such a fast turnaround.

This woman must be pretty special, the private investigator deduced, having no problem getting paid four times for the same job. He almost wanted to thank Aurelia for being so special. He needed the money to continue caring for another special woman – his sick wife, who was suffering from Alzheimer's.

* * *

Marquess headed to his Bel Air home after leaving the condo of yet another very special woman. That woman was Paula Jackson, a fellow lawyer that he not only admired on a professional level, but who stirred his loins more than any woman he'd ever met.

Marquess met the Hispanic/African-American beauty back in law school. There was an instant attraction between them. Sparks flew every time they were in the same room. Most onlookers deemed it only a matter of time before they sealed the deal.

Unfortunately for Marquess, Paula wouldn't give him the time of day on a romantic level. He was too much of a ladies man even then. Too much of a heartbreak risk.

Paula was too serious about her life goals to ever hook up with a playboy. She had too many righteous missions to complete in the Hispanic and African-American communities of Los Angeles, unlike her older cousin Sasha, who was and still is a socialite to the bone.

Sasha is the same cousin that went on to marry Marquess'

oldest brother Duke...twice. The women's kinship stemmed from their Puerto Rican mothers.

Yet for all of Paula's seriousness, for all of her aversion to Marquess' hedonistic ways, she finally gave herself to him the night they graduated. Boy did she ever.

It all started with a drink.

Paula arrived at Marquess' graduation party late that night. He was surprised she'd come at all considering the fact that she hadn't attended any of his previous parties, though she'd been invited to each and every one of them. Had it not been for Sasha's crush on Duke, which prompted her to beg her cousin to take her to that party, Paula might have blown Marquess off again.

Deciding to seize the moment while he could, Marquess greeted Paula at the door and promptly offered her a glass of champagne in celebration of their accomplishment. After all, she'd graduated earlier that day, too.

One drink led to another. Soon a whole bottle of champagne had been consumed and they were halfway through another.

With the kind of false courage that only alcohol can give, Marquess leaned in to kiss Paula in the middle of a lively discussion on torts. When she did not pull away and/or slap his face in protest, he deepened the kiss. Soon they were openly trying to devour each other.

Many were astonished to see Paula so uninhibited. She was usually so reserved. But in light of the mutual attraction that had been brewing for years between the two lawyers, no one made a big deal of that kissing fest. Plus, everyone was too busy enjoying themselves to really care what anyone else was doing or not doing.

When kisses ceased to be enough to satisfy them, Marquess led Paula to his private bedroom. Locking the door behind him, he thought he was about to deflower a virgin or at least teach an inexperienced woman a few things about making love.

Wrong.

The second that door locked, Paula literally attacked him. Marquess didn't know if he was coming or going as she taught him a few things about making love. More than a few things.

Keeping her stiletto boots on the whole time, Paula showed Marquess how serious she could be in the bedroom, too. Even now he moaned from the memory of all the things she did to him that night. Things that no other woman had been able to match since.

That blissful night, Marquess went to sleep with a big smile on his face and the love of his life in his arms. Unfortunately for him, he woke up alone. Paula had left some time during the early morning hours.

When Marquess sought her out in hopes that they could turn last night into the beginnings of a real romantic relationship, she turned him down flat. Said that she could never get serious with a guy like him. Said that he should consider their time together as one of his regular one-nighters.

Marquess was devastated. Yet his arrogance wouldn't allow it to show on the outside. To prove how quickly he could bounce back from Paula's rejection, he started dating a paralegal named Fran the very next week.

The two women were almost the exact opposite in every way.

Paula was outgoing and feisty with black hair, brown eyes, olive skin and a voluptuous figure. Fran was a timid beauty with red hair, green eyes, fair skin, and a shapely slender frame that was neither too big nor too small. Fran was also comfortable being a housewife whereas Paula wanted to be out there on the frontlines doing her part to right grievous wrongs in society.

And yet it was Paula that Marquess craved every night, even on his honeymoon. It was the pain of not having her that drove him to eventually start cheating on Fran, though he vowed to be a faithful husband. It was Paula that he sought out when his divorce became final yesterday.

Although Marquess knew he was wrong for cheating on Fran and even felt guilty about it, he deemed her greedy for attaching such a high dollar figure to her pain. A figure that was in direct violation of the pre-nup she'd willingly signed while they were engaged.

Yet when Fran told their lawyers about Marquess' double diagnosis and about how she thought she should be compensated for the years his cheating put her health in jeopardy, there was little he could do but grant her request. Not even his counter argument that he contracted those STDs months after they stopped being intimate was effective.

To this day Marquess still didn't know how Fran found out about his diagnosis. Duke, his primary care physician, was bound by law not to reveal such things. Baron claimed to have only told the owner of the strip club in an attempt to act responsibly. And yet one of them must have slipped up with Fran. But which one?

Last night, Paula offered Marquess a listening ear and all the Mexican food he could eat as he expressed his guilt about Fran, his anger and frustration at his ex-wife's greed, and his ire towards his brothers for inadvertently betraying him. He didn't want anything more than that from Paula. Or rather wouldn't allow himself to want anything else. Not with his diagnosis, which he watered down to include just the disease he'd long since been cured of. He said nothing about the disease that remained.

Marquess valued Paula's opinion too much to tell her about his lingering diagnosis. Why open himself up for that kind of rejection? He hadn't fully gotten over her last rejection yet.

Marquess also cared too much for Paula to put her at even the slightest risk. Even when his instincts told him that she was prime pickings for another tryst, he didn't act on that gut feeling no matter how many times it arose last night. When you love someone you protect them. And he definitely loved Paula.

Marquess came to that realization the moment she opened her front door, saw his grief stricken face, and invited him inside without a question asked. Instead Paula had offered him a comforting hug, some of the tasty dinner she'd just finished cooking, and silence when he was finally ready to share some of his grief.

I need a drink, Marquess suddenly decided, unaware that he'd just gone a full twenty-four hours without one.

Around Paula he hadn't needed alcohol. Her stimulating presence and lively conversation had kept the blues away. Had made him forget all about his pain, disappointments, and guilt. He'd even forgotten about his herpes diagnosis for a while as they talked all night and well into the morning. They slept fully clothed in each other's arms until this afternoon.

Unfortunately, that brief smack on the cheek Paula had given him before he left today had stirred his libido to distraction again. Now Marquess craved real kisses and so much more.

I need more, he thought miserably as that familiar glove of loneliness surrounded him and squeezed. And yet I can't have more...with any woman...especially Perfect Paula, Marquess thought, deciding to keep his distance from her for both their sakes.

Pressing down harder on the gas pedal, the despondent man couldn't get to his favorite bar fast enough.

* * *

Back at Paula's condo, she finally went upstairs to her bedroom after her platonic all-nighter with Marquess. A time or two she thought that he was going to kiss her, but he never did. She was relieved and disappointed about that.

Interestingly enough, Paula was in no way regretful about opening her door to Marquess last night. She'd wanted to be there for him. They'd talked for hours about any and everything. Any and everything except for their deepest darkest secrets.

Paula suspected that Marquess had held something back last night when he was talking about his health. He kept pausing and stuttering while discussing his diagnosis, which was so unlike the highly articulate man. As for her, she could never build up the nerve to tell him that she was less than the perfect female specimen he deemed her to be. That she would never be that epitome of perfection.

It's better to just let him keep thinking that I'm Perfect Paula, she mused, making the hard decision to return to her post-graduation-tryst vow.

That vow: Stay as far away from Marquess Weaver as she could get.

CHAPTER ELEVEN

On Sunday, Aurelia decided to treat herself to some live jazz at an amphitheater on the affluent side of town. Tickets to the event were a hundred dollars a head, but thankfully she didn't have to pay a cent to get in.

Liam Thornton, her boss, had given Aurelia two tickets to the jazz event for a job well done last week. He often gave top performing employees boons like this. And she was definitely a top performer at the crime lab. Had been ever since she started.

Since Aurelia was still single, she only needed one ticket. Thus she gave the other ticket to Claude yesterday as a gift for being such a great lab partner.

Going over to her small closet, Aurelia took out a hazelnut-colored cocktail dress that would be excellent for the evening. She discovered the designer dress among the donated items in the thrift shop of the same church that hosted the soup kitchen. When Aurelia saw Carmen Marc Valvo's name on the dress label, she knew she'd found a treasure. Even celebrities like Oprah Winfrey, Queen Latifah, Vanessa Williams, and Mary J. Blige wore this designer.

Aurelia used to wear CMV designs all the time when she was with Cain. She loved them because they seldom needed the help of accessories. Even the dress she was about to wear tonight had its own personality which consisted of a beaded embellishment right underneath the bustline, elegant pleats along that same bustline, and a bra-friendly V-neck that was sure to accent her ample bosom.

The designer dress cost Aurelia all of $6 at the thrift shop, though it was well worth $600 even in its used state. Barely used at that. To set the dress off perfectly, she retrieved a shoe box from the bottom of her closet that contained a pair of transparent stilettos with a studded center strap and hazelnut-colored trimmings. They'd been found on a 75% off clearance rack in the Alcove Mall.

I just might snag another rich guy tonight with this outfit, Aurelia thought as she went to take a shower.

Why not put herself back on the dating market? Why not follow Baron's lead? He didn't want her anymore.

* * *

"Did I tell you how nice you look in that dress?" Baron said to his date for the evening.

Jordin smiled. "Three times already and it's still not enough, considering how much I paid for it."

Baron chuckled. "Well, let me say it again. You look nice in that dress. Very nice," he complimented, once again admiring her shapely form in that hazelnut Carmen Marc Valvo dress. On her feet was a pair of elegant brown and gold pumps.

"Thank you." Jordin grinned and leaned over to give him a light peck on the cheek. Suddenly she frowned as her eyes came in contact with something offensive over his left shoulder. "Unfortunately, it looks like someone else decided to wear the same dress tonight," she added, glaring at a woman who was taking a seat ten people away from them in the midsection of the amphitheater. "Wait a minute. Isn't that one of your students? The same female student you were scowling at during the carnival yesterday?"

Baron's head snapped to the left. Sure enough there was Aurelia in the exact same dress as Jordin. His heart instantly pounded in his chest. His lower body instantly stirred.

Baron thought Jordin looked good in that CMV dress, but she didn't have anything on Aurelia. Matter of fact, that dress looked like it was specifically made for the V.I. native and her alone. It hugged every curve just right and showed off more leg since she was at least four inches taller than 5'5 Jordin.

And those sexy heels Aurelia wore. They reminded Baron of the whole glass slipper theme in Cinderella.

Would Aurelia like him to be her Prince Charming? Oh wait, he was already obligated to be that guy for Jordin tonight.

Dang.

Then as if she'd felt his hot gaze upon her, Aurelia turned

and met Baron's eyes. That's when he knew that she wasn't into Claude as much as he originally thought. If so, why would her nostrils flare and her eyes momentarily flash with jealousy before she gave him the stiffest of nods and looked away?

"Yes, that is the same student. Her name is Aurelia Bunting," Baron finally replied, forcing his gaze forward. "I must say I'm very surprised to see her here tonight."

"Why? Because you think she should be home typing up the results of her lab project?" Jordin asked, looking at him now as she settled comfortably on her embroidered seat cushion.

Baron's cheeks were flushed with color. His nostrils flared. His voice sounded huskier, especially when he said Aurelia's name.

Baron took a deep breath and cleared his throat before speaking again. "No, she emailed those lab results to me yesterday," he replied, recalling how he'd gone over those results with a fine tooth comb before finally giving her and Claude A's for their team project. "I'm surprised to see Aurelia here for economic reasons. Last time I checked, her budget was too tight to splurge on big ticket items like that dress and a concert of this caliber. Last time I checked, she needed every dime she made to pay for her education."

"You sure know a lot about your students," Jordin noted, not looking too pleased about that at all.

"It's my job to know as much as I can about them, so that I can do everything I can to help them reach their goals," he said as the audience lighting lowered and the stage lights brightened. It was almost time for the show to begin.

"Spoken like a true educator." Jordin chuckled, lightening up again after that satisfactory response. "As for Aurelia's presence here tonight, that's a no-brainer. A woman with looks like that doesn't have to pay for stuff like this unless she wants to. I'm pretty sure her very rich date will be sitting down beside her shortly. He probably just went to retrieve a jazzy basket like you did for us when we first got here." She looked down at the wicker basket at her feet. "Speaking of jazzy baskets, let's see what we have inside ours."

Aurelia with a rich date?! Baron chose that opportune time to look her way again.

What happened to her and Claude? Was she not dating exclusively right now? Just playing the field for a while? That would certainly explain the absence of Claude, who couldn't afford a concert like this either on his waiter wages.

Baron didn't know whether to be happy about Aurelia not dating exclusively or angry. On one hand, he could throw his hat in the ring and vie for her heart now, too. On the other hand, he would have to share her with other men. Baron knew he would not be able to handle the latter. If he dated Aurelia, she would have to be his, all his, and no one else's.

Straining his eyes to see if there was an unattached man anywhere in close proximity to Aurelia, Baron was relieved to find not a one. The person she was currently talking to wasn't even a man at all. It was a salt and pepper-haired black woman.

"You pour the wine while I serve us up some goodies, okay?" Jordin suddenly requested from beside him. An expensive bottle of red wine was in her left hand. Two fluted glasses were in her right. Packaged crackers and wafers, exotic cheeses, various nuts, and fresh organic fruit still remained in the basket.

Baron's gaze snapped back to his date. "Of course." He smiled, receiving the fancy bottle and glasses from her. Inwardly he wondered who would be the man to pour Aurelia's wine tonight. He would watch carefully to see.

* * *

Baron barely watched the show or listened to the music. He was too busy trying to keep tabs on Aurelia without his date knowing it. Too busy trying not to be jealous of all the men with the liberty to openly pursue her. And there were a lot of them, too.

Baron counted a total of twelve men that propositioned Aurelia so far. Were any available men watching the show? Or were they all trying to get with this one woman?

Some of the men sent roses over to Aurelia with their phone numbers. Others came to deliver their numbers personally and to hopefully get hers in return. One bold fellow even bought her a jazzy basket from the amphitheater's attached gift shop.

Aurelia politely turned all of them down. Every last one. She was clearly skilled at turning men down easy because not one of them went away mad. Disappointed, yes, but not angry. All the gift-givers left their presents behind, perhaps wanting her to have something to remember them by.

Those multiple rejections would have done Baron's heart good if they hadn't led him to assume that she was turning down men out of her loyalty to Claude. How else could he explain her refusal to receive a single man's phone number tonight?

Maybe she won her ticket through a local radio station contest, Baron thought, still trying to figure out Aurelia's presence here in light of what he knew about her finances and had seen tonight.

One thing Baron was grateful for tonight was the darkness. He'd been able to cloak his I-Spy routine quite well in the night shadows. Having mastered the art of nodding in all the right places during his days of only half-listening to shallow Megan, he was able to keep Jordin clueless about where his real attention was tonight.

Suddenly Baron saw something that threatened to blow his whole cover. By the light of the moon, he saw Aurelia close her eyes and sway slowly in her seat as the current songstress sang Cassandra Wilson's version of Time After Time. She looked so at peace. So at one with herself.

Baron wanted to be one with her, too. Or rather one with her again. He could still remember the blissful expression Aurelia wore the first time he entered her. He closed his eyes and moaned at the memory of how good her sugar walls had felt around him. Too good.

Aurelia, baby, why didn't you just wait for me? Baron lamented, right before Jordin leaned over to whisper in his ear.

"I like Cyndi Lauper's version better."

"I'm kinda partial to this one myself," Baron replied, not sure if he was bias because Aurelia enjoyed this version or if he truly preferred it over the original because it was slower and more sensual.

Sensual. That word described Aurelia to a tee and yet didn't describe her enough. She was so much more.

So much more, Baron echoed silently, chancing a look at Aurelia again. I wonder if she's as loyal as she appears to be or just hasn't had the right man to tempt her yet, he thought, recalling the jealous look she'd given him earlier. Maybe I'm that man.

Whoa!

Baron snatched his eyes away. He couldn't believe what just entered his mind. Was he actually starting to think like most of his older brothers who cared nothing for relationship boundaries? Where was his sense of honor? His sense of integrity?

Did Baron really want Aurelia this badly to go against his most fundamental principles? The same principles that allowed him to look at himself in the mirror each day without guilt?

The saddest part of all was the fact that Baron truly didn't know the answer to those questions right now. What he did know was that his heart, body, and soul wouldn't stop sending him the same message.

That message: Aurelia was supposed to be his. His!

CHAPTER TWELVE

When the jazz concert was over, Aurelia quickly headed for the parking lot. She didn't want to take the risk of running into Baron and Jordin. She also didn't want to linger around and be accosted by any more men. She'd barely been able to enjoy tonight's show for all the male attention she received.

Although Aurelia had come with the partial intention of catching the eye of another rich man, once she got that attention from several rich men, she realized she didn't want it. Man after man just didn't measure up to what she really wanted. Who she really wanted.

After seeing who she wanted with someone else again, the same someone else as yesterday, Aurelia had to fight to enjoy her night out. Claude's mother, who had been given her extra concert ticket, helped with Aurelia's enjoyment by engaging her in animated conversation during intermissions and by helping her to consume the jazzy basket an admirer had left behind.

Keeping her gaze straight ahead or shutting her eyes altogether throughout the concert helped Aurelia to enjoy tonight's music. She had enough sense than to torment herself with frequent glances at Baron. It was going to be hard enough looking at him in class five days a week now that she knew for certain that he was seeing someone else.

I can't wait for this semester to be over, Aurelia thought, wishing a quick end to her time in Baron's class for a different reason now.

* * *

Baron wanted to leave right after the concert to avoid running into Aurelia and creating any additional awkwardness between them. It was awkward enough being in the same classroom with her and Claude ten hours every week.

Baron got no farther than the bottom level of the amphitheater. Jordin was to blame for the delay. She wanted to say hello to some of the other jazz lovers before they left. Many of whom were her friends, colleagues, and associates.

After Jordin introduced him to the first person as her boyfriend, Baron realized that she wasn't making her rounds just to be sociable. Nor was she just trying to show her handsome date off in that black designer suit he wore. No, Jordin was staking claim, trying to let everyone know that they were an item.

But they weren't an item. Not yet anyway. Nothing had been officially declared by either of them, especially not by Baron. Matter of fact, this was the first week he'd gone out with her two nights in a row.

Somewhere around the fifteenth introduction Baron's head begin to throb. Blame it on the tense night he'd had watching Aurelia and all this shallow conversation. Did no one in Jordin's circle of friends have a deep bone in their bodies? Weren't they concerned about the Middle East? The current status of the economy? The effects of global warming?

All Baron heard Jordin and her friends talk about were the latest social events that they had either attended already or planned to attend in the very near future. Fluff, fluff, and more fluff.

"I feel a headache coming on. I'd like to leave now if you don't mind," Baron leaned in to whisper in Jordin's ear. Relief flooded his soul when she nodded, quickly wrapped up her current conversation, and then allowed him to escort her out to his car.

Jordin might not be Aurelia, but she sure knows how to honor a man's wishes, Baron thought.

Megan had been just as cooperative. She'd also been a whiner, which meant that whenever she left an event early at his request, she would whine about that early departure all the way home. It got to the point that Baron would stay at a party until Megan called it quits just to avoid her whining later on.

Would Jordin prove to be a whiner as well?

* * *

As Aurelia walked determinedly to a bus stop a block

away from the amphitheater, she released expletive after expletive. She wasn't a cuss-bucket by nature, but after what happened to her tonight, she let as many as came to mind slip off her tongue.

Why would anyone want to steal 'my' car when there were so many more expensive cars to choose from in that parking lot? Aurelia wondered bitterly, plopping down on the wooden bench at the bus stop. Because the owners of those cars can afford alarms and I can't, she mused, answering her own question a few seconds later.

Although Aurelia had promptly reported the theft to the amphitheater's security unit and to the city police, she seriously doubted if anything positive would ever come of it. The two security guards on duty had acted like she'd been done a favor when they discovered what kind of car she had. The city police officer that arrived shortly thereafter had spent more time flirting with her than taking down her information.

Aurelia ended up writing down her vehicle details on a napkin and handing it over for him to transfer to his official paperwork later. Then she'd left, refusing the ride home the kind officer had offered her.

Aurelia would rather walk home than be in the back seat of a car driven by a man that had the ability to rape her at gunpoint if he so chose. She'd already had a similar traumatizing experience back in St. Croix. She didn't want or need another in California or anywhere else.

"Where are the good men?" Aurelia mumbled to herself, oblivious to anyone or anything but her own misery as she searched her purse for her favorite can of mace. "Are there even any left?"

"Aurelia?"

Her body instantly stiffened. Her hands stopped moving. Please don't let it be him. Aurelia was afraid to look up from her purse at the driver of the black Porsche at the intersection.

But who else could it be? She knew that voice from anywhere. Would never forget it as long as she lived.

Maybe if I just ignore him, the light will change and he'll be forced to go on about his business, Aurelia lied to herself.

"Aurelia!"

Taking a deep breath of resignation at that insistent tone, Aurelia finally looked up and met the eyes of none other than…

Professor Baron Weaver.

"Hello, Professor," Aurelia forced out, fighting down jealousy that Jordin was in the car with him instead of her. The same Jordin that didn't even bother to look Aurelia's way. She was too busy fixing her makeup in a mirrored compact.

"Why are you at a bus stop?" Baron asked, continuing to peer at her through the lowered passenger side window. His left arm was out of the driver's side window, motioning for the cars behind him to go around now that the light had changed to green.

"I'm waiting on a bus," Aurelia quipped, unable to keep the trace of bitterness out of her voice.

Baron frowned.

One of Jordin's brows rose. She gave Aurelia her full attention now.

"I know the purpose of a bus stop, Aurelia. I was just wondering if you were here because you had car trouble tonight," Baron said in an even tone.

Aurelia took a deep breath, blew it out, and quickly apologized. "Sorry about my bad attitude, Professor. Just because I'm having a horrible night is no excuse to take my frustrations out on you. To address your previous inquiry, yes, I am having car trouble tonight. The worst kind of all. My car was stolen from the amphitheater's parking lot."

Baron's eyes bucked. "Your car was stolen?!"

"Yep." Aurelia nodded as her eyes glossed over with emotion. Blinking rapidly, she immediately averted her gaze to her purse, unable to keep looking at him.

Baron looked so handsome tonight, so prosperous, so with another woman. Whereas Aurelia was down and out yet again. When were things going to truly turn around for her?

At the sight of her tears, Baron quickly and skillfully glided his car out of traffic and into the parking lot of the gas station that sat directly behind the bus stop. "I'll be right back," he told his date before swiftly exiting the vehicle.

"But I thought you had a headache…," Jordin began in protest, only to have the rest of her words cut off with the slam of his door.

"Now tell me everything that happened," Baron requested of Aurelia once he was beside her on the heavily advertised bench.

"There's really nothing to tell. While I was busy listening to a little jazz tonight, someone was busy stealing my car," Aurelia replied.

"Did you inform the amphitheater's security?"

"Yes, but dey no give ah flying…" She paused, took a deep breath, and curtailed her angry tongue before she lapsed into too thick of an accent or started cussing all over again. "They could care less about my troubles. In fact, they laughed when I told them the make and model of my car. Sight unseen, they condemned my '68 VW Beetle to the junk pile, having no idea how much work I put into it. How I rebuilt that engine with my own two hands, using every trick my daddy taught me. How long and hard I saved to redo the upholstery, get a quality paint job, and some decent tires." Tears sprung to her eyes again as her emotions steeped once more. "De city policeman twas no betta. All he cared 'bout was gettin' me into his bed."

Baron immediately pulled her into his arms and just held her as she cried. "It's going to be all right, baby," he soothed gently, stroking her back just as soothingly. "You don't have to take the bus home tonight. I'll drive you. I'll make everything all right, baby. I promise."

Baby? Aurelia echoed silently as her ears picked up that repeated endearment and gave it to her heart to hold dear. It had been said with such fervor. Such sincerity. It was like he'd meant it from his heart.

* * *

Back in the car, Jordin frowned at the hugging couple on the bench. Her frown deepened when she learned that they would be taking Aurelia home tonight instead of the bus.

"I'm not going anywhere near that neighborhood. Can't she catch a cab or something?" Jordin protested within seconds of learning where Aurelia lived.

"Cabs don't like going to my neighborhood either," Aurelia replied matter-of-factly. "Professor, if you could just drop me off at the next bus stop, I'll take it from there." Had she known Jordin was going to act this way, she never would have gotten in the back seat of Baron's car, must less allowed him to merge back into traffic with her inside.

"No!" Baron said almost vehemently from the driver's seat. "I'm taking you all the way home and that's that," he told Aurelia, looking at her in the rearview mirror. He turned to Jordin and added, "After I take my date home first, of course, since she's a little skittish about certain areas of town."

"I…" Jordin began.

"It's settled," Baron interrupted with finality, facing forward again.

I guess he told you, Aurelia mused, smiling to herself in the back seat.

Unfortunately, Jordin saw that smile through the mirrored compact she still had in her hands. As a result, she turned around and gave Aurelia a menacing look.

Aurelia gave her a 'If you mess with me, I'll take your man' look in return that would have made old school Salt n' Pepa proud.

* * *

On the way to Jordin's luxury home, Baron and Aurelia monopolized the conversation. It didn't start out that way. It started out with Jordin leading the way as she discussed an upcoming party she wanted him to escort her to next week.

After quickly telling her that he'd think about attending that event, Baron engaged Aurelia in conversation about her stolen car. He wanted to know things like the size of her engine, how much horsepower it had, and how well it handled on the road.

Aurelia proved to be a wealth of information about German cars as a whole. She was particularly knowledgeable about Volkswagens and Porsches, who were both designed by the same person – Ferdinand Porsche.

"I don't talk about this much, but my brother Count and I used to own a fire engine red convertible '67 Beetle," Baron said, finding it so easy to open up to Aurelia. Had it just been Jordin in the car, this subject would have never come up. "We spent a whole summer working on that car, trying to get it just right. It was going to be our teenage love bug. Yet another way for us to get girls."

Aurelia and Jordin chuckled.

"I would have dated you in that car." Jordin put a possessive hand on his right arm.

"I would have wanted to see what was under the hood of that car," Aurelia said. "Especially since around '67 the VW engine was upsized to 1493-cc and the horsepower was raised to a solid 53." She chuckled. "Then I would have wanted to drive that car."

"I would have let you." Baron met her gaze in the

rearview mirror.

Jordin instantly frowned and smoothly removed her hand from his arm. It wasn't like he had paid attention to it anyway.

Aurelia simply smiled. "Whatever happened to that car? Seems like I remember you saying that you and Count used to own it. Did you sell it? It didn't get stolen, too, did it?"

"We sold it, but not willingly." Sadness crept into Baron's eyes. "My father made us sell the car after his Jewish grandfather came for a visit, saw it, and got deeply offended by it."

"The whole Hitler thing got to him, huh?" Aurelia asked, fully aware of the Volkswagen's controversial history. A history that included the car being commissioned by Adolf Hitler to ensure that every German was mobile and equipped with an affordable vehicle. In fact, Volkswagen actually meant 'people's car' in German.

"Yes, the Hitler thing got to my great-granddad in a major way. We thought he was going to have a heart attack right there on the spot," Baron replied. "He thought it blasphemous for any of his offspring, even those who weren't fully Jewish like Count and I, to have a car associated with a man that had caused his people so much pain and suffering."

"Didn't he know that the Volkswagen had been in the works years before Hitler ever got involved? That Porsche was simply the designer of the vehicle, not the one slaughtering innocent people? That under the circumstances it wasn't like he could refuse Hitler's request anyway. If you want to even call it a request." Aurelia scoffed. "It was more like he'd been made 'an offer he couldn't refuse'," she added with a faux mobster's accent.

Baron smiled, despite the painful memory this topic had stirred up. He actually found it therapeutic to finally talk about a subject that had long been taboo in the Weaver family. "I tried to tell my great-granddad all of that, but he was beyond listening to reason on the subject. He insisted that Porsche could have still found some way to refuse instead of profiting from the suffering of so many. In the end, the car had to go just to keep peace in the family. To make up for the loss of our beloved vehicle, my father bought us two brand new American made cars."

"Let me guess, two Lincolns, right? Because they are so

American that they're even used by U.S. presidents," Aurelia deduced with a chuckle.

Baron laughed. "Right. A month after my great-grandfather died, Count and I traded those Lincolns in for Porsches."

"Smart move. Less controversy with those models." Aurelia laughed.

"Right again." Baron looked downright impressed by her keen perception, by her remarkable intelligence.

"I didn't know you were part Jewish?" Jordin interjected, clearly trying to end the laugh fest between the other two people in the car.

"Yes, but only a quarter since both my paternal great-grandfather and grandfather married Caucasian women and my mother has deep Mexican roots," Baron replied in a more somber tone.

Great! Just when the conversation was getting deep and interesting, she had to go and drag us back to the boring shallow end of the pool, he mused with resentment towards Jordin. It would be a long time before he went out on another date with her.

As Baron pressed down harder on the gas, anxious to get Jordin home sooner, Aurelia smiled knowingly from the back seat. That smile disappeared a few minutes later when she saw Jordin give Baron a goodnight kiss at her front door. A deep French kiss at that.

CHAPTER THIRTEEN

After watching Baron share that kiss with Jordin, Aurelia grew extremely silent in the car. Angry, too. If flames could shoot from her hot ears, they would.

When Baron reentered the Porsche and requested that Aurelia sit up front now, she almost refused. Yet refusing would have alerted him to just how upset she was about that kiss, about his relationship with Jordin as a whole. Since she didn't want to do that, she consented to leave the back seat as requested.

Now in the front passenger seat, Aurelia sat with her arms folded across her chest, her body stiff in her seat, and her gaze straight ahead. Her face was devoid of emotion, expressionless. Her mouth was a straight line, wordless. She didn't want to say a thing to him. And he better not say anything to her!

Meanwhile, Baron put on his seatbelt and started up the car. As he drove with one hand, he kept stuffing sticks of gum into his mouth with the other. Unexplainable guilt propelled him to do something to remove Jordin's flavor from his taste buds. Plus, the gum gave him a convenient excuse not to strike up an awkward conversation with Aurelia.

What could he say in this embarrassing moment anyway? What should he say? I'm sorry I kissed Jordin?

Why should Baron apologize for doing something that he'd done at the end of every date with Jordin? Especially since Aurelia was probably kissing Claude every day at school and on the weekends.

Aaugh!

Why did things have to be this way? Especially when in

Baron's heart of hearts he knew that he and Aurelia were supposed to be a duet in the song of life. Not him and Jordin. Not Aurelia and Claude.

In an attempt to reduce the thick tension in the car, Baron turned on the radio. Instead of listening to his favorite Latin station, he turned to an R&B station that he overheard Aurelia and some of her peers talking about before class one day. Maybe, just maybe that would appease her. Or at least help them both relax some.

For the first three miles, they rode in silence, allowing the radio to do the talking for them. They listened to crooners like Eric Benet singing songs like Chocolate Legs.

Baron suppressed a moan as he thought about Aurelia's legs. He glanced at them now out of the corner of his eye, using the light from the traffic signal above to get a real good look at them. He licked his lips upon noticing that her legs were devoid of stockings, smooth and freely shaven.

What Baron wouldn't do to have those milk chocolate legs wrapped around him again right now. He suppressed another moan before forcing his gaze back on the road.

Aurelia rolled her eyes and looked out the passenger window. She'd felt his hot gaze on her. She'd seen him lusting over her out of the corner of his eye. That only increased her ire. Stirred up disturbing questions.

Was Baron like Cain? The kind of man that deemed himself too attractive to be with just one woman? Or was he just plain greedy, wanting more than one woman at a time regardless of his looks? It would certainly explain why Baron's eyes were already roaming after just kissing a perfectly beautiful woman who was clearly smitten by him.

Although Aurelia couldn't make all such men pay for being so disrespectful and unfaithful, she could definitely make Baron pay. Pay for not waiting on her. Pay for rubbing his new relationship in her face tonight.

And so the payback begins…

"Oh, I love that song," Aurelia said, referring to the Ginuwine tune that was just cueing up on the radio. "Mind if I turn it up a little louder?"

"Let me do it for you," Baron offered, reaching for the volume button. Soon When We Make Love was saturating the airwaves.

Aurelia closed her eyes, raised her hands in the air and sensually swayed in her seat. As she lowered her hands, she ran them provocatively down the sides of her body from head to hips.

The low moan Aurelia heard coming from the driver's seat told her that Baron was watching her little performance like a hawk. She'd counted on him doing so. She wanted to give him a vivid reminder of what he was missing out on by being so impatient, of what he would never get again.

Aurelia didn't count on Baron being distracted to the point of actually swerving in the road, putting both of their lives in danger.

"Whoa!" Aurelia clenched the dashboard with both hands. Her eyes were wide with the fear of crashing into one of the trees or light posts aligning the street. Thankfully there were no other cars on this lonely road.

"I got it, baby," Baron reassured with confidence, smoothly handling the vehicle with expert hands. Soon they were safely back in their own lane. Yet instead of staying in that lane, he pulled over to the side of the road and parked.

To catch his breath?

No.

To calm his nerves? Her nerves?

Double no.

Baron parked the car to undo his seatbelt, discard his wad of gum, and capture Aurelia's lips with his. Although he knew that he should respect their relationships with other people and also school policy, and had originally intended to do so, his good intentions flew out the window when she started moving those sexy island hips of hers. When she started touching herself.

Although Aurelia should have been repelled by Baron kissing her so soon after kissing Jordin, she was not. Her own needs, her own desires temporarily blinded her to the ramifications of her actions. Aurelia would probably hate herself in the morning for acting just like slanderous Roxy, but right now...right now...she was consumed by her passion for Baron.

Willingly parting her lips for his probing tongue, Aurelia allowed Baron to taste freely of her. She freely tasted of him, showing him what it really meant to be kissed by a woman.

They kissed long and deep. Loudly, too. Ravenous slurping and sucking sounds filled the air. Moans and groans, too.

Aurelia undid her seatbelt, giving herself more mobility.

She used that newfound freedom to ease her hands into his jacket…

Underneath his shirt.

Up his muscular torso.

It was still so hard and rippled. Another moan bubbled up from Aurelia's throat at the thrill of touching Baron again. It had been so long since she'd touched him like this. Too long.

Eager to touch more of her, too, Baron sent a hand on an unhurried journey starting at her lower left calf…

Up her thigh.

Underneath that dress.

Right to her field of dreams, where he promptly found her secret windlass and used it to gently pump water from her hidden well.

"Yes," Aurelia purred against his lips, loving a man with a slow hand and an easy touch. A man like that usually made sure a woman enjoyed herself to the max during intimacy. Her body couldn't help but respond to him.

Baron actually whimpered when her hips immediately moved with the rhythm of his hand. No other woman could break him down so low. So fast. His body was granite and on fire at the same time.

Baron abandoned Aurelia's lips for the moment, used his free hand to lower the straps of her dress and bra, licked her sweet gumdrops and then stuffed his mouth full of supple chocolate. His other hand removed her lacy thong and pocketed it before returning to its former task.

Aurelia couldn't stop Baron even if she wanted to, which she didn't. She was too far gone from the things he'd done to her thus far. She wanted more. Needed more. In fact, her clenching core demanded more.

Just then, Baron's cell phone went off. Had it just rang and stopped, he might have ignored it and proceeded to the next stage of lovemaking with Aurelia. But when it continuously rang, he had no choice but to at least see who the persistent caller was.

"Who is it?" Aurelia panted out, watching him frown down at the lighted panel of the black phone in his hands.

"Jordin." Baron looked and sounded apologetic.

That's when the realization of what she'd done tonight hit her. Hard. Realizing that her plan to tease and reject him had backfired on her big time, Aurelia snatched her gaze away, now too embarrassed to even look at him. Her hands swiftly fixed her clothing.

"You might want to answer that. If she's like most women, she's not going to stop calling until you do," Aurelia said when his cell phone rang for the tenth time.

Baron took a deep breath, turned the radio completely off, and reluctantly answered Jordin's call.

* * *

"Sorry about that," Baron said upon ending his brief call with Jordin. A call that mainly consisted of, "No, I haven't made it home yet. And yes, I'll be sure to call you when I do."

"No need to apologize." Aurelia secured her seatbelt now that her clothing was back in order. Well, most of it. "I was just as wrong for disrespecting clear relationship boundaries. You would think I'd be the last person to do something like that considering the fact that I've been cheated on before and know how awful it feels to be done that way," she continued, referring to the relationship boundaries he had with Jordin. "Rest assured it won't happen again."

Baron frowned, assuming that she was referring to the relationship boundaries she had with Claude. He didn't consider himself in a committed relationship with Jordin, no matter how much she tried to pretend otherwise.

Switching the subject, Baron asked, "How are you going to get to school tomorrow? By bus?"

"I could, but I would have to get up at the crack of dawn just to make all the right transfers and get to school on time. I had enough of that tedious routine my freshmen year," Aurelia replied, grateful for this subject change. "No, I'll just call Claude. He and his mother only live four blocks from me. I'm sure he won't mind letting me catch a ride back and forth to school with him. I'll still have to use the buses to go to work though." If Aurelia had known she'd be having car trouble tonight, she would have requested a ride from Claude's mother before they went their separate ways after the concert.

"I see." Baron's jawline tightened. He didn't want Aurelia to call Claude for anything. He didn't want her to need Claude for anything.

For such a brilliant man, Baron was acting really dumb right now. It hadn't dawned on him yet that Aurelia hadn't called Claude once tonight. That a woman in a committed relationship would have had her boyfriend at the top of her call list if her vehicle was stolen. That if Claude was indeed Aurelia's boyfriend, he would have gotten off work early tonight and taken her home himself. She definitely wouldn't have been at a bus stop or catching a ride with Baron.

Determined to forfeit her dependence on any man outside of him, Baron started up the car, drove a few more miles down the road, and stopped at a 24-hour check cashing place. Inside he bought a prepaid credit card.

"Here." He dropped the plastic card and receipt in Aurelia's lap upon his return to the car.

Aurelia's eyes bucked. "What's this for?" She picked up the card and stared at it.

"It's for you to rent a car so that you won't have to depend on anyone for transportation. At least for the next week or so. If your car isn't found by then, let me know and I'll increase the balance on the card."

"Professor, I...don't know what to say," Aurelia stammered out, overwhelmed by his generosity once again. Especially when she saw the accompanying receipt and noted how much he'd put on the credit card. What kind of car did he expect her to rent for the week? A Mercedes?

"Thank you would be sufficient." Baron smiled as he restarted the car.

"Thank you a thousand times, Professor." Her eyes shimmered with tears. "I'll pay you back as soon as I can."

"That card is a gift, not a loan."

"And yet I'm going to pay you back anyway," Aurelia replied firmly. "You're not my man, so I can't be accepting gifts like this from you. It could...complicate things too much for the both of us."

"I see." Baron's jaw locked with tension again. "Consider it a loan then," he said as he guided the car out of the check cashing center's parking lot and into the night traffic.

The rest of the ride was cloaked once again in silence. Not even the radio was turned on this time.

In front of Aurelia's building, she finally broke the silence. She had to. There was a most sensitive topic left to discuss.

"Thanks again for driving me home tonight, Professor, and for the card." Aurelia forced her voice to sound casual.

"You're welcome." Baron unlocked the automatic doors. "Do you want me to walk you to your door?"

Aurelia smiled at his chivalry. "No, but you can…" She paused, took a deep breath of courage and just came out with the rest of it. "…you can return my thong."

Baron winced. "Sorry about that." He dug into his left jacket pocket for the missing item and handed it over. "If you want your wig back, too, I have that in the trunk of my car."

Aurelia gasped as the case of the missing wig was finally solved. "Yes, please." She kept her gaze averted as she quickly stashed her black lacy underwear in her purse.

How embarrassing can one night get?

* * *

Fortunately for Aurelia, the private investigator that had been hired to trail her neglected to follow her and Baron tonight. He'd been too busy following the teenagers that stole her car.

Doing his good deed of the day, the P.I. not only followed the wayward youths for several miles, but he also called in the stolen vehicle to the local police. He gave them detailed descriptions of the teenagers and the exact direction they were headed in.

By the time Aurelia went to bed that night, her car had been impounded and the teens involved had been arrested. She received a call early the next morning telling her when and where she could retrieve her vehicle with proper ID.

Aurelia immediately emailed Baron with the happy news of her car's return, of her need to be excused from class that day to deal with the situation, and of her intentions to return the unused prepaid credit card he'd loaned her.

CHAPTER FOURTEEN

December

Aurelia fought not to moan as Baron walked to the chalkboard to illustrate one of his lesson points on bloodstain pattern analysis. His long-legged walk was so confident and sure like a cowboy's. Just sexy.

With every sexy stride, Baron's hips whispered promises of pleasure. Promises that he would never keep to Aurelia. Pleasure that she would never receive again.

Dang.

Why couldn't she just let it go? Why must she constantly torment herself by continuing to long for a man that had moved on with his life?

Baron hadn't looked at Aurelia with desire once since that night in his car. He'd been all business when she came to his office the next day and returned the credit card he loaned her. He'd been the epitome of professionalism ever since.

"Miss Bunting, can you come up here and draw three patterns representing dripped blood, spilled blood, and projected blood from the same distance to target?" Baron asked, interrupting Aurelia's lustful musings.

She cleared her throat before answering, lest her husky tone give her away. "Yes, Professor," she said in her normal tone, getting up from her desk to walk to the board.

As Aurelia proceeded to draw and label each pattern Baron requested, she noticed that he only moved to the side, failing to return to his desk as usual. Now she really found it hard to concentrate.

And his spicy masculine scent. It was driving Aurelia to distraction. She wondered if Bambi could duplicate that fragrance in her lab. If so, Aurelia would keep a gallon-sized bottle of it beside her bed. That way she could reach for it in the middle of the night, inhale deeply, and pretend like Baron was there.

"You're doing good, Miss Bunting. But that last pattern needs a little bit of work. Here, let me help you." Baron moved closer to assist her with his own chalk in hand.

As he stood behind her and modified the last blood pattern to show the distinctive spikes that projected blood left on a target, Aurelia suddenly had a déjà vu moment. Baron had been behind her like this in that hotel room. Except she'd been wedged in between him and the wall while he'd pleasured her to the point of almost losing her mind.

Rational thoughts were leaving Aurelia's mind in droves now because of those hot memories. She licked her lips just thinking about the delicious time they had that night.

Baron stifled a moan at the sight of Aurelia's tongue sliding over those beautiful full lips of hers. He promptly stepped away from her. Far, far away, all the way back over to his desk.

And yet that was still not far enough to remove her delectable vanilla scent from his nostrils. That was the same scent she'd left on his Armani suit the night of the jazz concert. A suit that he refused to have dry cleaned for that very sentimental reason.

"Well, that is all for today. After copying the patterns Miss Bunting drew on the board, you may be dismissed," Baron said, quickly bringing today's session to an end for his own sake. Who cares that there were at least ten more minutes of class left.

"See you tomorrow, Professor," student after student said to him as they exited the classroom a few short minutes later.

"See you tomorrow," Baron said in reply. Though a pleasant smile was on his face, a frown was in his heart.

How could his smile go any deeper when he was tormented every day and night with thoughts of Aurelia? When every time he saw her he had to fight to keep things professional between them.

Getting over Megan had been easier than this. Much easier. Matter of fact, Baron hadn't thought about her in months.

As for Jordin, she was basically old news to him. Had been ever since that night Baron drove Aurelia home and got another succulent taste of her. Though Jordin still called him at least four times a week, he had yet to go out with her again. Didn't want to.

Quite frankly, Baron wasn't really trying to get over Aurelia. He was in waiting mode. He was waiting for this semester to end. Waiting for Aurelia to show any sign that she was available again. Once those two things happened, he was going for the gold.

When the time is right, you're going to be mine again. All mine, Baron thought determinedly as he watched Aurelia walk to the back of the room where Bambi was.

When he saw Claude fast on Aurelia's heels, he frowned. That was Baron's cue to leave, lest his jealousy show. Lest he got himself fired by displaying inappropriate behavior towards his students.

Quickly retrieving his assignment folder from his desk, Baron rose from his seat and made his way to his office.

* * *

"Thanks for reviewing that video I emailed you," Bambi told Aurelia now that it was just them and Claude in the classroom. "I really appreciate you helping my girls out like this."

With her sorority's regular choreographer pregnant and going through morning, noon, and night sickness, Bambi's sorors were struggling with their dance routine for an upcoming Christmas talent show. At the rate they were going, they might not even place; much less win the grand prize.

If winning was just about the prize money, Bambi would have donated the extra cash the sorority needed to buy more Christmas presents for local disadvantaged kids. But since this was also about winning the privilege to compete in a national dance competition, she volunteered to recruit a new choreographer for them instead.

"You're welcome, Bambi." Aurelia stretched out her arms. "I don't mind doing whatever I can to help the poor. However, I do regret ever telling you that I took formal dance lessons. Especially after my additions to your routine worked muscles I haven't used in months." She chuckled.

"Sure they did even though we haven't seen you wince one time since you started stretching," Claude countered with a playful grin, taking a seat beside Bambi, who also sat in a regular desk. Her wheelchair was long gone. She now walked with a cane.

"So true," Bambi seconded, laughing as well. "Even so, will lunch at your favorite restaurant today make your little boo-boos all better?" she asked, speaking in a playful mothering tone. Her ebony eyes twinkled with mirth.

"Yes, Mommy," Aurelia replied in a babyish tone, sticking out her tongue mischievously at the end. "Or shall I say Lil Mama since you're so short and petite?" She chuckled again.

"Lil Mama will do just fine." Bambi grinned, making her beautiful slanted eyes even more pronounced.

"Lil Mama it is then." Aurelia reached over to playfully tug on her friend's long silky black locks. "Now if we can just get Claude to make himself useful by moving some chairs back instead of sitting there like a bump on a log, I'll show you how I tweaked your routine," she continued, returning her arms out to her sides for more stretching.

"Get busy, homeboy," Bambi playfully ordered, snapping her fingers impatiently at him.

Claude rose to his feet. "You're lucky I like bossy women." He picked up four chairs nearby, two in each large hand.

Bambi blushed with stars in her eyes. "Thank you, Claude," she practically purred.

"You're welcome." He gave her a flirtatious wink.

At the realization that Claude actually liked petite Asian women enough to flirt back, Bambi blushed even more. She was so relieved. For a while there she thought he only liked voluptuous black women since they were all she ever seen him date before.

Although Bambi had been exposed to African-American females all of her life via her family's stores and thus had adopted a lot of their mannerisms, dance moves, and musical tastes through association, she knew that she could never actually be a black woman. Plus, no matter how much she ate, her super-fast metabolism simply would not allow too much weight to stick to her.

There was the option of surgical enhancements, but Bambi wasn't that desperate to get any man. Not even Claude. Now it appeared that she no longer had to try to be anything or anyone but herself to get his attention. How refreshing!

Aurelia noticed the flirtatious exchange between Claude and Bambi and smiled. Claude was finally starting to come around. Good. About time!

Aurelia wanted to help him come around faster by just telling him about her friend's crush. But after the heart-to-heart talk she recently had with Bambi, she agreed to just let nature take its course.

Bambi wanted it to be Claude's idea to be with her. She didn't want to be his second choice girl, the woman he settled for simply because he couldn't have Aurelia. That was the main reason Bambi decided to postpone her aggressive pursuit of Claude. She wanted to make sure his infatuation with Aurelia was long gone first.

While her classmates continued to interact flirtatiously, Aurelia continued to stretch out her limbs. She paused briefly to remove her bulky sweatshirt to have more agility and freedom of movement. Thankfully, there was enough heat in the room for her to wear her black tank shirt that looked more like a long sports bra.

Claude's brows rose at that sudden appearance of brown feminine flesh. He instantly became distracted, completely forgetting all about Bambi for the moment.

"Did you remember to bring your camera, Bambi? As you know my work schedule prevents me from showing your whole sorority the routine in person," Aurelia said, oblivious to Claude's attention as she stretched some more. This time with her eyes closed.

"Yes, and the music, too," Bambi replied, very much aware of Claude's redirected attention. Fighting a frown of disappointment, she searched through her book bag for her camera and iPod.

When the music was cued up, Aurelia went to work demonstrating a revised routine that was sure to make Bambi's sorority a winner in the talent show. So preoccupied with her performance, Aurelia failed to see Baron reenter the room for the briefcase that he'd left behind in his earlier haste.

Bambi didn't notice the additional person in the room either as she focused on keeping the camera steady.

Claude noticed. He'd seen the other man's red shirt out of the corner of his eye. It was through his peripheral vision that he saw Baron licking his lips at Aurelia's dancing frame.

Claude also saw that longing look in the professor's eyes before he blinked it away. He saw the deep breath Baron took to quickly get himself back in check before he was really noticed.

Claude didn't blame the man for looking at or longing after Aurelia. She had the kind of body that appealed to men of all ages. A wrinkled old man in a wheelchair would probably still lust after her.

"Bravo, girlfriend." Bambi stopped the camera and clapped after the end of Aurelia's performance. "I think you might have just put my girls over the top with that routine." She pressed stop on the iPod, causing Flo Rida's Low to instantly cease playing.

"I would vote for you, sweetheart," Claude said encouragingly. "What about you, Professor?" he prompted, addressing the quiet man with the briefcase. "Would you vote for Aurelia's routine in a talent show?"

Aurelia gasped and snapped around to face the front of the room. When did Baron return? And how much of her routine did he see?

"Yes, definitely," Baron replied, shoving his eyes away from Aurelia's sexy frame. "See you guys in class tomorrow." Then he left without another word.

As for Aurelia, she quickly redressed and got out of there, too. Her lunch with Bambi had been postponed, moved to another more convenient time.

Right now Aurelia needed some time alone to think about a few things. Things like which category did Baron actually belong in – cheater, greedy-guy, or easily-excitable? How else could she explain him lusting over her when he was probably still dating Jordin?

Maybe they broke up, Aurelia thought with hope dancing in her soul. After all, this was the first time Baron had ever let any of his other students see his attraction to her. Maybe he was starting to loosen up, because he knew the semester was almost over, bringing him that much closer to freedom.

Freedom to do what though? Aurelia mused, hoping that the semester's end would finally bring them the freedom to be together. But only if Baron was truly done with Jordin.

* * *

I need to get laid, Baron decided, closing his office door behind him, fighting the urge to be insanely jealous over that endearment Claude called Aurelia.

The pressure of not having her, of not being able to make love to her, to even kiss her, had finally become too much for him. He was almost willing to pay for sex right about now. But then again, why should he pay for something that he could get for free?

Baron was a handsome man. Women flocked to him every day. And there was no bar that he couldn't go into and come out with a suitable one-night-stand if he wanted to.

But why go to a bar when there was a willing woman right in the next office?

Baron quickly crossed Rhoda off the list when he remembered how stalker-ish she was.

Jordin, he thought, referencing yet another willing female as he put his briefcase down on the floor beside his desk and settled into his chair.

Jordin didn't have stalker tendencies. She was simply shallow, which didn't necessarily mean that she was a washout in bed. Megan had been shallow, too, and she'd been great in bed. Plus, just last night Jordin called and expressed her desire to see him again. All of him.

Baron smiled, got on his cell phone and called Jordin. Within a few short minutes he had set up a romantic date with her. Jordin would come to Baron's house tonight where he would cook dinner for her, entertain her with his charm, and then hopefully make love to her. Maybe then he could forget about Aurelia.

I hope, Baron thought, yearning for her even now as quick flashes of that dance routine bombarded his mind. Like a Texas oil rig, he wanted to drill as deep as he could get within Aurelia's field. Instead Jordin would get that level of fervent loving tonight.

Suddenly Baron's office phone rang. It was Liam Thornton, the head of Alcove's crime lab and also a childhood friend of his. Liam was also Aurelia's boss. It was she that he was calling about today.

Baron promptly ended his cell phone call, bidding Jordin a quick and yet warm goodbye. Then he took a deep breath and blew it out slowly before returning to his office phone. "Now what was it you wanted to say about Aurelia?" he asked of his friend.

"I just wanted to call and tell you thanks again for recommending her to me. That girl is sharp as a tack and she works hard," Liam praised, unaware of his poor timing.

"I'm glad she's working out so well." Baron's heart swelled with pride, causing the pain of not having Aurelia to lessen for the moment.

"She's working out better than well," Liam replied. "Since

Aurelia came on board we're solving more cases than ever and employee morale is at an all-time high. Everybody likes her. And those are just a few of the reasons I don't mind giving her time off when she needs it."

"Does Aurelia ask for a lot of time off?" Baron asked for more reasons than one. "With her being young, single, and attractive, I imagine she wants the occasional Friday or Saturday night off to date."

"So far Aurelia has only asked for a couple of hours off on Saturdays. And even then, it's to work at a local soup kitchen," Liam shared.

Baron's eyes bucked. "Aurelia works at a soup kitchen?" How special can this woman be?

"Yes, faithfully every Saturday, usually from noon to 2pm. Every now and then she'll come in two hours late after helping the soup kitchen with their breakfast rush. I can only hope my own daughter grows up to be as hardworking and unselfish as Aurelia." Liam sighed with exasperation and added, "Right now Miley is in her gimme stage. Gimme this and gimme that. She wants everything she sees."

Baron chuckled. "She's only five, Liam. Miley will probably grow out of her selfish stage soon enough."

"Did Earl ever grow out of his?" Liam asked, having grown up right next door to the Weaver boys in Bel Air. One of his older sisters had even dated Earl for all of two weeks before his arrogance drove her away.

"Unfortunately, no." Baron laughed harder. "So start praying now and never stop. My mother is still praying for Earl. Uncle Miguel is, too, and not just because he's a priest either."

Liam roared with laughter.

The two men spent the rest of the conversation catching up on each other's families after that. It was only after Baron hung up the phone that his depression about Aurelia returned. It returned with a vengeance, too, causing him to lose his appetite for the rest of the day. All of his appetites.

CHAPTER FIFTEEN

The next day, Aurelia received the worst news of her life. Her little brother suddenly took ill and had to be rushed to the hospital. Thankfully it wasn't Trent's diabetes. But the fact that it was appendicitis ravished her nerves in an equally bad way.

Like any other science geek, Aurelia was quite aware of the risk of leaving appendicitis untreated. She knew that her brother had to have emergency surgery lest he die.

Since her family had no medical insurance, Aurelia emptied her savings and wired the money home to help out. Although it still wasn't enough to pay for everything, it would convince the right doctors to perform the necessary surgery and be more conducive to put them on a payment plan for the rest.

The next morning, Aurelia made her way to school after getting only three hours of sleep. She'd spent most of the night on the phone with her mother, checking on Trent every other hour. Now she was tired, sleepy, depressed on multiple levels, and in no mood for two hours of interrogatory questions from Baron.

Had it not been so close to finals, Aurelia would have simply stayed home today and rested. But she needed to be here. She needed to take as many notes as she could to pass the whopper of an exam that Baron prepared for them. An exam that would show whether or not they'd truly grasped the material he presented to them in great detail throughout the semester.

If only Aurelia could have stayed awake long enough to take those notes.

"Miss Bunting, if you nod off one more time, I'm going

to ask you to leave my class," Baron said, incensed that she wasn't paying attention today. Only an hour of class had passed and she'd dozed off at least three times. The last time she even released a loud snore.

Aurelia stirred awake again. "I apologize, Professor. I didn't get much sleep last night." She held her head upright again. Her right palm and elbow had been supporting her head.

"Tell your boyfriend to go home a little earlier next time," Baron replied sternly, his cheeks flushed with emotion that he wouldn't allow his eyes to show. He made himself not look in Claude's direction, whom he suspected had kept her up so late last night…having sex.

Aurelia's eyes bucked. She was wide awake now. Had she just detected a bit of jealousy in Baron's voice?

Oh, yes.

How dare he be jealous, when he was the one that gave up on them first?!

"I don't have ah boyfriend, Professor. Wha I have is ah sick brotha who gone hospital yesterday and had surgery last night," Aurelia retorted. "As for remaining in yur class, I tink eh be ah good idea dat I leave befor I seh someting we both will regret." She gathered her things as she talked.

Aurelia knew herself. She knew how blunt and brutally honest she could get when angry or in high emotion. How not even a convenient lie could slip through at times like these. How the wrong word spoken to her in this moment could cause her to tell Baron off, possibly even question him openly about why he was really giving her a hard time today. Which made leaving all the more wise now.

"Everyone else is dismissed, too. The rest of today's lecture will be put in bulleted note form and emailed to you later," Baron said, immediately taking control of the situation. When he heard Aurelia's island accent kick in, he knew he'd pushed her too far. Now he had to make things right. "Miss Bunting, I need to see you in my office ASAP," he added in a curt tone that broached no argument as she stomped towards the door.

Aurelia glared at him, biting back another sharp retort. Then after quickly reminding herself that Baron held the power to fail her and prolong her graduation, she nodded her consent. Exiting the classroom seconds later, she reluctantly turned right instead of left.

Did she just say that she didn't have a boyfriend?! Baron thought with hope leaping in his heart. If he heard right, he was going to do a little bit more than apologize for his insensitivity today. He was finally going to make everything right between them.

* * *

"First of all, let me just say that I had no idea your little brother was ill," Baron began once they were alone in his office with the door closed. "Had I known, I would have understood, excused you from class today, and sent study notes to your student email account."

"Well, now you know. Can I leave now?" Aurelia retorted, ready to go home and crash into bed until it was time to go to her evening job. She didn't have time to waste on a jealous man. Not today. Maybe not ever with all the stuff going on in her life. Aurelia had enough problems to contend with.

"Not yet. I also want to apologize for that boyfriend comment. I was jealous and totally out of line back there," Baron admitted, once again setting precedence for open and honest discussion between them.

"What right do you have to be jealous, Professor? You changed yur mind 'bout me first, remember?" Aurelia's eyes flashed fire. She was too emotional right now to hide any of her feelings. Too angry to appreciate how quickly he was to admit when he was in the wrong.

Baron shook his head. "No, I didn't." Even now he still wanted her, still loved her.

"Well, explain Jordin den," Aurelia demanded, revealing a touch of jealousy of her own.

Baron instantly detected that jealousy and was highly pleased by it. Where jealousy dwelled there was hope of reconciliation, however slight.

"I only went out with Jordin because I thought you were dating Claude," Baron confessed; ready to set the whole record straight.

"Dating Claude? Wha in de world would make you tink dat, mon?" Aurelia frowned.

"I heard you agree to go on a lunch date with him back in October. Ever since then I've seen you two around campus together."

"Any time I eva spent wid Claude has always been 95% school- related and 5% social. Dat October lunch meeting was no different. We had ah lot to discuss 'bout dat big lab project you assigned us." She paused to take a deep calming breath before continuing. "As for me dating Claude, he knows friendship is all I have to offer him. All I will eva have to offer him. I made dat very clear on numerous occasions."

Baron's eyes widened. "So all this time we've been functioning under yet another misunderstanding?" Hope continued to grow in his heart.

"It would seem so," Aurelia replied, coming to the same conclusion as her accent lightened in direct response to her falling ire. "But unlike you, I'm still available."

Baron closed his eyes, took a deep breath, and exhaled. She was still available.

Available!

Opening his eyes a few seconds later, Baron whispered, "I'm still available, too, baby."

Aurelia's eyes bucked. Did she just hear correctly? Did Baron just say that he was available?

Double yes.

"Wh…what happened to Jordin?" Aurelia stammered out, forgetting all about the rest of her troubles in this heated moment. "Did you recently break up with her or something?" It just made sense to her that Baron would be the one to call it quits. Not only was Jordin too shallow for him, she was also too enthralled by him to cut ties without the help of a major offense.

"Jordin and I were never really together," Baron replied from his place at his desk. "We only dated sporadically and I never once agreed to exclusivity with her. We haven't even slept together."

Aurelia's eyes bucked again. "You really haven't slept with her after all this time?"

"Baby, I haven't slept with anyone since you," Baron confessed. "Every time I headed in that direction, memories of you popped in my head and I couldn't go through with it. I even cancelled a date with Jordin just last night because of you."

Tingles went through Aurelia's body at his words, at his delicious candor. "I've been celibate since our night together, too, baby."

Baron moaned. "That pleases me more than you could ever know," he whispered huskily, his eyes ablaze with hot desire and a heavy dose of something else - love.

Leaning forward in his chair with his hands clasped tightly on the desk, Baron said, "Aurelia, I know this might not be the best time to say this, but I love you. I want to be with you in every way. I want you to be mine. All mine, starting today in word. Starting at semester's end in deed because of that rule in AU's school policy."

The rule Baron referred to was simply this: No student/teacher dating during the semester in which they share a class.

Although the practice of student/teacher dating was heavily frowned upon at Alcove University as a whole, the powers that be recognized that love often blossomed in less than ideal places. Combine that with the fact that both parties are usually of consensual age when they meet in college. Thus the current ban on such dating only covered the semester in which the teacher and student shared a class. This meant that Baron and Aurelia could date without fear of administrative consequences when the current semester was over.

"You...you love me?" Tears pricked Aurelia's eyes, making it hard to see clearly.

"Yes." Baron got up from his seat and walked around to the front of his desk where she sat. "I have loved you for quite some time now."

"I...I love you, too," Aurelia replied, realizing at this very moment that she really was in love with him. Somehow her feelings had turned from lust to love. But when?

It happened the night of the jazz concert. That's when Baron had held her while she cried, willingly drove her home in his expensive car to a crime ridden part of town, and given her a credit card all without asking for a thing in return. Had Aurelia not tried to entice him in the car, he might have acted even more chivalrously that night.

"I love you so much, Baron," she reiterated, calling him by his first name for the first time. Happy tears streamed down her face in droves. They were so welcome after all the anxious tears she'd shed last night and well into the morning hours on her brother's behalf.

Baron moaned with pleasure at the sound of his real name on her lips. He dropped to his knees in front of her, humbled by her heartfelt declaration twice spoken.

Could this be true? Could the woman of his heart's desire already share the depth of his affection?

Oh, yes.

"I want to kiss you so badly right now that it hurts." Baron reached up to wipe her tears away with both hands. "If it wasn't for that school rule and if we weren't on school property, I would."

"Blak dat rule. I need dis kiss…now!" Aurelia said right before she threw her arms about his neck and attacked his lips.

* * *

Thankfully Baron had thought to lock his office door after closing it, because when Aurelia's lips touched his, a dam of passion broke within him and he forgot all about the school's rule. He temporarily forgot that he was even at school as he dove into that kiss with fervor. At the same time, he eased the top half of his body between her legs to close any remaining distance between them. Now they could really have a kissing fest.

Baron soon discovered that Aurelia meant what she said about needing this kiss. She literally latched onto his tongue and wouldn't let go. He didn't want her to. He willingly gave her the full length to suckle at will, putting her in command of his taste buds.

After Aurelia got a good taste of him, she made the kiss mobile by licking a trail from his mouth, past his chin, and down to his neck.

Baron moaned as she slid her tongue along his Adam's apple before stopping at his collarbone. There she inhaled deeply. So deeply…and then moaned, causing him to moan again, too, at that provocative sound. His body grew achingly rigid with need.

"Take your shirt off, baby. I want to lick your chest," Aurelia whispered against his neck where she proceeded to plant the lightest of kisses.

Those words were all the wake-up call Baron needed. "No, baby," he said, promptly withdrawing from her.

"No?" She panted out. Rejection singed her eyes, her very soul.

"No, as in not here, not yet," Baron clarified as he rose to his feet. "You and I both know that even if one piece of clothing comes off you or me, we're going to make love again. Right here and right now. And if our would-be union today is anything like it was in that Cabo hotel room, there's going to be trouble for the both of us."

Aurelia chuckled. Joy was in her eyes now, understanding in her soul. "We were pretty loud that night, huh?"

"Very. People thought I was killing you in that room." He chuckled. "Now up on your feet, beautiful. I need to hold you something awful." He pulled her up from her seat.

Aurelia willingly entered his embrace, convinced that she would get more than a hug. Oh, how she wanted another one of his toe-curling kisses even if she couldn't have anything else right now.

Instead of getting a kiss like she thought, all Aurelia got was a warm comforting hug. How deliciously unpredictable was that? What a show of restraint!

Aurelia was even more impressed by Baron now.

"I'm sorry about your little brother," he said compassionately, continuing to hold her tenderly against him.

"Thanks for saying that. It means a lot." Aurelia snuggled against him. She didn't feel so alone, so stressed and depressed, or so hopeless now. For the moment, she forgot all about the fact that she had no more money left over for next semester's tuition after giving everything she had to her family.

"Do you need to take your finals early in order to go see the little tyke?" Baron asked, soothingly stroking her back in an up and down motion.

"What's the point?" Aurelia stiffened in his embrace as a few harsh realities slapped her on both sides of her face. "I have no money for plane fare." She withdrew from him and returned to her seat. "And all the money I had saved for next semester's tuition had to be sent home for my brother's medical expenses, which includes the surgery and his monthly supply of pills for his Type 2 diabetes. So, no, I don't need to take my finals early. I need to stay in California now more than ever to work and try to recoup my losses before next term."

Baron frowned. "Aurelia, you only have four weeks before the new semester begins. How are you going to come up with that kind of money in so little time?" Like her, he knew how high Alcove University's tuition was. That was one of the reasons the institution could afford to pay professors like him so well.

"I'll find a way. I always do." Aurelia looked down at her hands. She was suddenly too ashamed to look at him right now.

Baron's frown deepened. "You're going back to dancing, aren't you?" he asked in a painful half-whisper.

"I'm too close to graduating to let anything stop me now, not even my dignity." Aurelia forced her gaze upwards. "Dingo said I could always come back to his club if I ever needed to."

Baron's nostrils flared. His mind instantly calculated how many lap dances she'd have to do to make tuition in time. And that's if her customers were as generous as him when he was Aurelia's lap dance recipient.

"Before you leave school today, make arrangements to take all of your finals early. I'll stop by your apartment later tonight with a round-trip plane ticket and the necessary funds for next semester's tuition," Baron replied decisively, thinking that one lap dance was one too many for his woman to give to another man.

Aurelia's eyes bucked, though she should have been used to his generous nature by now. "I can't deny that I need the help, Baron, but don't you think that's too much too soon? I mean, we've only been a quasi-couple for fifteen minutes and already you're playing the role of sugar daddy. I don't want you to think that money is all our relationship will be about. I don't want our love tainted by dollar signs."

"First of all, I'm still too young to be anybody's sugar daddy." Baron chuckled. "Second of all, I'm willing to turn this gift into a loan, if it'll make you feel better. Matter of fact, consider this a loan to a hardworking student in dire circumstances."

"A loan?" Aurelia's left brow rose in interest at that prospect.

"Yes." Baron smiled. "A zero-interest loan at that. This way, you can still be there for your family, pay for school, and maintain your dignity." He left out that this loan would enable him to maintain his sanity, because if she went back to Dingo's, Baron was going to lose his mind with jealousy. Probably even act out of character and literally stalk the club every night and run the risk of angering Dingo and Six-Eight.

"As for your jobs, if you work as hard for them as you do in your classes, I'm sure your bosses will understand your need to make this trip and thus oblige you the time off that you need. I know for a fact that Liam will," he added just to sweeten the deal.

Aurelia remained silent. Her gaze drifted around the

office as she mulled things over in her head.

First of all, her two jobs weren't going to cut it in this situation. Not with the limited amount of time she was working with. Secondly, the excess profits from her perfume were minimal after finally paying Bambi off. What little remained had been sent home, too.

Thirdly, more financial aid was out of the question. Aurelia had applied for every grant and scholarship she could before having to take out so many student loans. Loans which still hadn't covered the high cost of AU's tuition.

Now Baron was proposing another loan, one with no interest and no strings attached. Meaning, she would just owe him the principle of the loan and nothing else, not even sex. Which also meant that she'd get to accomplish her goals, keep her dignity, and her man.

Aurelia would be a fool not to take this loan!

"I accept your offer, Baron," she finally replied, looking at him through glossy eyes full of emotion. "And thanks for always being there for me in my times of need."

"You're..." Baron stopped to clear his throat after an unexpected wave of deep emotion washed over his own soul. Oh, how he loved this woman! "You're welcome," he continued, upon regaining his composure. "As for my class, just check your inbox for study notes. I can give you the final on Thursday if you're ready by then."

"I'll be ready by then," Aurelia said determinedly.

"Great." Baron smiled at her fortitude. Outside of his mother and Paula Jackson, he'd never met a more determined woman. "What time should I drop everything by tonight?"

"Any time after 10pm. I should be home from work by then. Do you remember my address or do I need to write it down for you? I also need to give you my phone number." Needing writing utensils, she reached down beside the chair for her backpack.

"I remember your address. As for your phone number, I've had that since the first day of class," Baron confessed. Then he quoted it by memory just to prove it.

Another woman might have been scared by this new revelation, but not Aurelia. Tingles attacked her body all over to know that Baron was interested in her enough to go digging for her personal information. Besides, the fact that he hadn't used that information once to harass her proved that he was harmless.

Most stalkers had violent tendencies and would have acted upon any personal data they had on their victims by now. They certainly wouldn't have waited for permission to call like Baron had.

"Well, I guess I'll see you after 10pm then." Aurelia used her hands to brush any wayward hairs back into her ponytail before standing to leave.

Baron simply nodded, unable to trust himself to even speak right now as thick desire coursed through his veins. Her casual acceptance of his knowledge of her personal information had him on fire. For it meant that she didn't mind him knowing that information. That she wasn't afraid of him. That she had a level of trust in him already.

A solid relationship could be built off of such trust. Baron planned to do just that...all the way to the altar.

"There's just one more thing I need from you before I go," Aurelia said at the closed door.

"What is it?" he forced out after swallowing over the emotional lump in his throat.

"I need you to officially break off all social contact with Jordin and any other woman you've been dating lately."

"Done. Will you do the same with Claude?"

"I'm willing to try, even though it's going to be extremely hard with him being in so many of my classes, including yours. Plus, we're only just friends like I stated before. Claude and I never dated. Not even once."

"In that case, just keep a reasonable distance from him and I'll be happy," Baron compromised.

"I can definitely do that." Aurelia smiled.

Baron smiled in return. "By the way, when are you due to check on your brother again?"

Aurelia's eyes watered again as his concern touched her heart. "In another two hours or so," she said, looking down at her black-faced wrist watch. "I'm trying to let my mother get in a few more Z's before I phone her again for another update."

"That's considerate. I look forward to hearing all about that update when I come over later, okay?"

"Okay." Aurelia blinked her eyes free. "Times like these make me love you even more, you know that?"

"I love you, too, baby." Baron forced himself to remain in his seat after those words. Though he stayed put, his eyes roamed. They roamed over Aurelia's departing frame, zoomed in on her shapely bottom that not even her baggy black sweat suit could hide.

Beautiful. Just beautiful, Baron thought, looking forward to making love to her again.

CHAPTER SIXTEEN

Claude and Bambi were waiting in the reception area outside of Baron's office for Aurelia when she came out. There was concern upon their faces.

"Are you all right?" Bambi asked.

"Yeah, you were in there a long time," Claude said, just as Professor Griffey sauntered by without even bothering to speak. But then again, Rhoda seldom spoke to students outside of the classroom unless she absolutely had to.

Aurelia smiled at their concern. "I'm fine. Never better, in fact. Professor Weaver agreed to let me take his final early so I can go home and be there for my family."

"Cool. I'm glad the Professor was so accommodating. For a minute there I thought he was going to kick you out of class or something. You made him pretty mad today," Bambi replied.

"The Professor and I worked everything out," Aurelia said with fresh tingles coursing through her body. She glanced back at Baron's open office door and smiled. "We're fine now."

"That's good," Claude replied, unaware of just how much had been worked out between Baron and Aurelia today.

"Yes, that is good," Bambi agreed. "In any case, do you want to go grab an early lunch? I still owe you a meal for helping us with that routine, remember?"

"No, thanks," Aurelia declined. "I have to talk to my other professors to see about taking early finals from them, too."

"Want us to come with?" Claude offered.

Aurelia shook her head. "No, but thanks. I can handle that alone. I'll see you both in class tomorrow."

"You'll hear from me before then. I plan to call and check on you tonight when you get off from work," Claude said, inadvertently causing Bambi's eyes to cloud with pain beside him. "By the way, I'm really sorry to hear about your little brother."

"Thanks for your concern, Claude. As for calling me tonight, I don't think that would be a good idea. I plan on doing a lot of studying. Plus, a guy that I've been seriously interested in for quite some time is finally available to date. He's coming over tonight to keep me company and in comfort on account of my brother's illness. I'm sure he wouldn't appreciate another man calling me while he's there or at all for that matter. Not even males who are just friends," Aurelia replied, letting him down as easy as she could. She also lingered in the reception area so that Baron could 'overhear' her break social ties with Claude. She hoped that her words made Bambi's day, too.

Although disappointment shrouded Claude's face, those words brightened Bambi's eyes. Yet she contained the full extent of her joy for obvious reasons. "Is it that gorgeous Latino you told me about? Barry something or other?" Bambi prompted.

"Yes, him." Aurelia smiled, still refusing to give up Baron's real name. "I really hope our relationship turns into something special. I can't wait to see him tonight, to kiss him again, to just be in his arms again. And if I get a good report about my brother, there might even be a bit of etcetera, etcetera tonight." She chuckled, finally heading towards the exterior door that led to the hallway. She'd done what she needed to do here.

"And etcetera." Bambi giggled, egging Aurelia on as she followed her out of the reception area with the help of her handy cane. "Don't forget to wear your new perfume, girl."

"Good idea," Aurelia replied.

Claude remained silent as he followed the ladies into the hallway and prepared to go his own separate way. It wasn't until that very moment that his remaining hopes of ever being with Aurelia were thoroughly and finally dashed. It was time to go his separate way in every way.

* * *

In Baron's office sat one happy man. He'd been listening hard to Aurelia's conversation with her classmates and was pleased about it. He loved what she told Claude and was physically stirred by what she told Bambi. Yet Baron knew that he had to keep things non-sexual between them until Aurelia was safely out of his class for their respective academic and employment sakes.

But how?

He didn't know. Aurelia was pretty hard to resist when she wasn't trying to seduce him. When she laid the charm on thick, it took everything in him to resist her.

While Baron figured out how to do that, he proceeded to dial Jordin's cell phone number again. He'd already made one call to that number with no answer, which meant that she was probably still tied up in business meetings.

Suddenly recalling how Megan had broken things off with him, Baron replaced the receiver and decided to do what needed to be done in person. No callus phone call from him. Jordin would learn that he was no longer interested in her face to face.

Fortunately for Baron, he didn't have to be bothered with Rhoda today. Having the phone up to his ear for so long caused her to walk past his open door and go to the office she occupied next to his.

Baron's only regret in rescuing Rhoda that fateful night was the fact that it made her want to get even closer to him. Whereas he had rejected the very thought of being with her even in his weakest hour.

* * *

After getting approval from the rest of her professors, Aurelia went home, called her mother, and then took a much needed nap. She was able to sleep very soundly because the update about Trent was such a positive one. The robust little boy was going to be just fine.

Hallelujah!

At 3pm, Aurelia arose, showered and changed, and then went to her job at the mall. When she arrived home at 9:30pm, she scrubbed her apartment clean.

Fortunately, there wasn't much to clean. Though her building was massive, Aurelia lived in a first floor efficiency apartment, which meant the kitchen, living room, and bedroom were all in the same room. Only the bathroom was separate and not easily seen.

With the apartment being so small, there wasn't room for much furniture. Aurelia only had a sofa bed, a chair, a radio alarm clock, and a hand-me-down desk. Upon that study desk was her lap top computer. Her backpack was on the floor in a corner by the desk.

After that quick tidying up, Aurelia went to take another shower.

Shave, shave.

Trim, trim.

Everything had to be neat and in order.

Upon drying off, Aurelia applied lotion to her body and then strategic dashes of Aurora's Whispers in all the right places. She dressed in a white tube top with a satin-like frontal bow and a pair of white Daisy Dukes with a front zipper and studded designs running diagonally from her hips to her thighs. She left all underwear out of the equation, convinced that she wouldn't need those tonight anyway.

When she was done primping in the mirror and had put enough finishing touches on her hair, Aurelia made her way over to her desk. There she engaged in some much needed study time while she waited for Baron's arrival.

* * *

Baron met Jordin at The Crowne, an upscale restaurant with high prices, high ratings, and high sanitation. It was the perfect place for a health conscious person like him to dine. It was also the perfect place for him to break things off with Jordin.

Baron opted for a public setting over a private one to keep any potential emotional outbursts at a minimum. Meeting at a restaurant also reduced Jordin's ability to make a convincing false claim later about tonight consisting of a romantic rendezvous at either of their places.

If only Aurelia could have been nearby to witness Baron's handling of the Jordin issue like he'd been able to witness her dealings with Claude earlier. Speaking of Claude, he was also here tonight. He was their assigned waiter. A very diligent waiter at that, which would warrant him a big tip from Baron tonight.

"I appreciate you being so honest with me tonight," Jordin said after hearing Baron out over dessert. "And you're right; chemistry is an important element to have between two people. I had hoped you would develop some for me by this time." She chuckled and added, "Or at least allowed the amount of chemistry that I had for you to cover the both of us."

Baron laughed, too, grateful that she was taking things so

well. "I'm sure you'll run across a man with enough chemistry to match your own."

"Yes, but will he be as handsome and as financially stable as you, Professor?" Jordin flirted, licking cream off the edge of her fork for extra effect. "So far I've come across handsome men with no money and financially stable guys with no looks."

"I'm sure there are more men like me around. I have a brother that's recently divorced, but he's too much of a player for a nice woman like you," Baron replied, omitting some of Marquess' other flaws. He also ignored Jordin's flirtation, inwardly wishing that Aurelia was the one doing that trick with her fork. Better yet, doing that to him.

Jordin scrunched up her perky nose. "No players allowed on board this train."

Baron laughed. "Well said, lady. I don't blame you. I also prefer monogamous relationships."

Jordin frowned. "Are you sure about that, Professor? As I recall, there was a very attractive female student that caught your eye a couple of times while we were dating. I hope she's not the one you're replacing me with," she said, revealing her disbelief that lack of chemistry was the only reason he was breaking ties with her. "You could lose your job behind a taboo relationship like that. Imagine the kind of negative publicity such a thing could create for Alcove University," she added with a bit of wicked glee in her eyes.

Baron fought not to outright scowl at her. Did Jordin just issue a veiled threat to him? If so, now he and Aurelia really had to be careful with their relationship. Baron also had to be careful with his next comments. Careful about a lot of things if Jordin proved to be vindictive simply because she couldn't have what she wanted – him.

"I'm not replacing you with anyone, Jordin," Baron said evenly, not considering Aurelia anybody's replacement. She was already in his life before he ever met Jordin. If anyone was a replacement, it was the TV reporter. A poor replacement at that.

"My decision to call it quits with you was largely based on our lack of chemistry," he continued. "I also didn't want either of us to waste any more time on a relationship that wasn't meant to go anywhere behind that initial interview." Then throwing a hand up in Claude's direction, Baron said, "Check please!"

* * *

Baron showed up at 10:30pm, looking handsome as ever in garments that cost more than Aurelia's monthly rent and utilities. Her breath hitched when she opened the door and found him on the other side of it in a black designer suit that matched his ebony hair, smelling like expensive cologne, and giving her a smile that made up for months of misunderstanding and frustration.

Oh how she loved this man. Oh how she wanted him. Needed him. Baron's breath also hitched when he saw Aurelia in that white outfit and with bare toes painted fire engine red. Hot desire flared in his loins, stroking his libido like a firebrand. His mind jogged with a musical memory from the 90's era.

Look at that girl with those Daisy Dukes on, Baron thought, borrowing from a catchy tune that traveled all the way from Augusta, Georgia to Bel Air, an affluent community in Los Angeles, California.

"Did you have any trouble finding the place again?" Aurelia asked breathlessly, smiling as she reached for one of his hands to escort him into her humble abode.

"No, I remembered the way from last time. Plus, I have a GPS system in my car as backup." Baron refused to budge from his position in the hallway. There was no way he could enter her apartment with her dressed like that. A man can only take so much temptation.

Aurelia released her hold on his hand and frowned. "What's the matter, Baron? You think my apartment is too poor for you?"

Baron shook his head vigorously. "No." He quickly cleared up any misunderstanding. "I just don't think it's a good idea for me to come inside, that's all. Not with you wearing that," he clarified as his eyes roamed over her sexy frame yet again.

Aurelia's smile returned. "Come on inside, Professor. I'm not going to bite you." She reached for his right hand again. "Unless you want me to, of course," she added seductively, tugging on him in more ways than one.

Baron suppressed a moan and followed her inside against his better judgment.

CHAPTER SEVENTEEN

Baron's eyes scanned Aurelia's sexy frame again as she led the way inside her apartment. His gaze settled upon her bottom, appreciating how nicely those shorts hugged it. The way they allowed her lower swells to peek out from under them as she walked.

Just sexy for no reason at all.

Up until Aurelia, Baron was a bonafide breast man. But after that night in Cabo, he started to notice a woman's lower body more, particularly the derriere section. Now he was a top and bottom man.

Aurelia turned around just in time to catch him admiring her bottom. She smiled as tingles attacked her body, making her taut in certain places, tropical in others. "Can I offer you anything to drink? I only have non-alcoholic drinks though. Cola and orange juice."

"No, thanks. I didn't come to stay long. I just wanted to drop off this." Baron pulled a brown envelope from his interior jacket pocket.

"We'll get to business a little later." Aurelia waved the envelope away. "Right now I want to play hostess to my man. So tell me which beverage you prefer and then have a seat on the couch while I fix it."

"Orange juice please," Baron consented with a smile as he returned the envelope to his pocket.

He liked being called her man. He liked being her man, even if that meant no sex for a little while longer. All he had to do now was keep her talking and maybe, just maybe he'd be able to leave here tonight without sleeping with her. He couldn't make any promises.

"So tell me the latest about your little brother," Baron

said, forging ahead with Operation Keep-Her-Talking.

Aurelia's eyes lit up at that talk prompt. Then as she fixed their drinks, she gave him updates about her little brother, about her dealings with other professors on taking their finals early, and about the responses of her bosses.

Baron was pleased to hear so much positive news. In between conversations, he took the time to peruse Aurelia's tiny, yet extremely clean apartment. He couldn't help but notice how sparsely it was decorated. The lack of frills made Baron want to hand over the keys to one of the condos he owned in Alcove. He had at least one unit still available for occupation.

Yet Baron refrained from making that offer. Yes, he wanted to raise Aurelia's standard of living, but not in a condo. He wanted her living at his house with him...in matrimony. He realized that just tonight. Planned to do something about it real soon.

Baron also realized that Aurelia's humble dwelling confirmed that she really was putting everything she earned into her educational and living expenses. Based on her extremely casual school wardrobe, it was also clear that she wasn't spending a lot on her attire either. That impressed Baron even more.

But wait. What about that expensive dress she'd worn to the jazz concert? How could she have afforded that on her budget?

Maybe she didn't buy it for herself at all, Baron mused, recalling something that Jordin once said about Aurelia. Maybe some wealthy man bought the dress for her and paid for that ticket, too.

Instead of jumping to conclusions again, Baron swallowed the juice in his mouth, opened his lips and initiated dialogue on the issue. "Do you own many dresses, Aurelia? I've only seen you in one since I've known you."

"I used to have a whole closet full of dresses," she replied from her place beside him on the couch. "Expensive dresses, all with designer labels." She paused to take a sip from her own glass of juice.

"What happened to them? Did you give most of them away?"

"I probably should have donated them. But at the time I was too focused on making a symbolic statement to my ex-boyfriend Cain the day I left him to think about the less fortunate."

"You didn't do an Angela Bassett, did you? Except burn up your own clothes in his car," Baron inquired, referring to a scene from Waiting To Exhale, a movie that his sister-in-law Sasha loved and watched often.

Aurelia burst out laughing. "No, I didn't do that. I simply left everything he ever bought me behind, including those dresses. Everything I have now was bought with my own money, including that CMV design you saw me in at the jazz concert. I found that hazelnut treasure at a local thrift shop and was just waiting for a special occasion to wear it. That special occasion arrived when Liam gave me two free concert tickets for a job well done."

"Who did you give your other ticket to? As I recall, you were alone that night."

"I gave it to Claude for being such a good lab partner. He, in turn, gave it to his mother since he had to work that night and wasn't a jazz fan anyway. She and I sat next to each other at the concert and shared a jazzy basket."

"I saw you sharing that basket with Claude's mother. I saw who gave it to you, too," Baron replied with a flash of jealousy in his eyes.

"Don't you dare get jealous, Mr. Sharing-His-Basket-With-Jordin!" Aurelia countered with the green-eyed monster creeping across her face as well. "Speaking of Jordin, did you break things off with her today?" she asked in a much calmer tone.

"Yes," Baron said, grateful for the slight subject change as his jealousy also subsided. "I did it in person tonight over dinner."

"At your place or hers?" Aurelia frowned as the green-eyed monster returned for a brief encore.

"Neither. I took her to a restaurant that I trusted."

"Oh." She chuckled, immediately calming down again. "I put some distance between me and Claude today, too, you know," Aurelia shared.

Baron grinned. "I know. I heard. I liked."

She smiled. "I hoped you did."

"Claude took it well. I was impressed. That's yet another reason I gave him a big tip tonight at the restaurant he works at."

"How did Jordin take your rejection?"

"I thought she took it relatively well until she started

sprouting her suspicions about us," Baron replied. "Wow! There were a lot of 'S's in that last statement, weren't there?"

"Too many." Aurelia chuckled, clearly loving their easy rapport just as much as he was.

"Anyway, after I set her straight about a few things, I paid the check and left. Speaking of checks." He put his glass on the folding dinner tray table Aurelia sat near the sofa and reached into his jacket again for the envelope he'd tucked there earlier. "Or rather speaking of credit cards since I find them easier to manage than checks. I have two for you."

"Two?"

"Yes, I had to get two because the limit was too small to put the full amount on just one card." Baron handed over the envelope. "I've also taken the liberty of drafting up a proposed repayment schedule which I hope will suffice. That's also inside the envelope, along with your plane ticket."

"I'm sure you were fair with the schedule." Aurelia put her drink on the table before receiving the envelope with semi-shaky hands.

Suddenly her hands shook in full force. Inside that brown envelope was a typed repayment schedule, which didn't begin until after her graduation; a first-class round-trip plane ticket, and two prepaid credit cards totaling $10,000 each.

What did Baron think AU was? An Ivy League school? The private four-year institution's costs were a little over $27,000 for the whole year. He'd just given her $20,000 for one semester.

One semester!

Aurelia now had more than enough to cover her tuition, books, supplies, and graduation fees. With the leftovers, she could send more money home and even get the steering wheel column on her car fixed from the damage the teenagers had done to it.

"Baron, this is too much." Aurelia turned glossy eyes to him. "I could have flown coach. And I only needed enough for tuition since I usually swap books with other students. Plus, my graduation fees don't need to be paid right away."

"I didn't want you to have any financial worries your last semester at AU," Baron replied. "I also wanted you to be comfortable on your flight home and back."

"Oh, Baron," Aurelia purred as silent tears streamed down her cheeks.

Baron moved closer and put comforting arms around her.

His intent was just to hug her. But when she embraced his neck and actually put her lips upon his, he knew he was lost…to passion.

* * *

With a needy groan, Baron surrendered to Aurelia's kiss as she smoothly straddled him. With fervor, he poured deep passion into that kiss as his greedy hands reached down and grabbed hearty handfuls of her bottom.

This was a full contact sport. All manner of touching was allowed in this game.

Her eyes now dry and the brown envelope a forgotten entity on the floor, Aurelia worked her sensual hips upon Baron, prompting him to do the same. He did.

Rhythmic was their grind. Slow and erotic, too.

"I've been waiting for this for a long time, baby," Aurelia whispered against his mouth.

"So have I," Baron replied.

They dove into another kiss.

"You've been tormenting me for months in that class, you know," she said, briefly pausing from the kiss. She continued to move her hips slowly upon him.

"How so?" He matched her pace in every way.

"By walking your sexy frame back and forth in those fitting jeans of yours," Aurelia replied, beginning a unique sequence of kiss-confession- kiss.

Kiss.

"Flexing your hard biceps in those short-sleeved shirts while writing on the board."

Kiss.

"Constantly licking those gorgeous pink lips of yours while reading at your desk."

Kiss.

"And when you stood behind me at the board yesterday, I thought I was going to explode right then and there."

Baron moaned and deepened the latest kiss even more. Just knowing she'd been paying that kind of attention to him in class had him ablaze, rigid and throbbing to the point of distraction.

"But the worst torment of all was believing that you were giving all that body to someone else," Aurelia concluded, bringing her string of confessions to an end.

"How could I settle for Jordin, when the woman I really wanted to be inside of was you?" Baron replied in a hoarse whisper, speaking again after a long silence. The aching in his body had him in literal pain now. "Only you," he said, plunging a hand inside the back of her shorts, his fingers traveling until he reached the hottest vacation spot of all.

Aurelia gasped at his delicious invasion and moaned aloud.

"Baby, you're so ready for me," he said upon finding her beyond tropical. She was drenched.

Drenched!

"Always." Aurelia rocked her hips forward to communicate with his hand. Her own hands tugged down her top, placing her melons right at the door of his mouth.

Baron knew exactly what to do with that silent invitation. He opened his lips and feasted.

Aurelia moaned aloud again and anchored her hands on the back of the sofa for leverage. It was time to go to work. Soon she began to move her hips at lightning speed as the clenching inside her body tripled.

"Slow it down, baby. At least long enough for me to really get inside," Baron said against her bosom, using his free hand to reach between them to unzip his pants.

"I can't wait, baby," Aurelia panted out, too impatient and too far gone to wait for the real connection.

Discerning the truth of that statement, Baron continued to prime her pump with his hand tool.

Within seconds Aurelia went over the edge with a violent shudder and a loud scream. And just as suddenly everything went...

Black.

CHAPTER EIGHTEEN

"What...what happened to me?" Aurelia asked when she finally came to. She looked down to find herself completely naked, on her back, and lying full length on the sofa now. Her legs were elevated eight inches on a pillow to help the blood flow back to her brain. A cool compress was on her forehead.

Baron held one of Aurelia's wrists, measuring her pulse rate from the artery on the thumb side. He looked like a regular medical doctor right now instead of a doctor of pathology. All he had to do was complete another residency and he could very well be a regular medical doctor.

"What happened to me, baby?" Aurelia reiterated, wondering if she should be concerned. Baron was extremely quiet right now. Too quiet. Plus, she'd never fainted during sex before.

Sex? That wasn't sex. That was just foreplay. What kind of man made a woman faint during foreplay?

"You fainted while having one whopper of an orgasm," Baron replied after silently checking her pulse for the required full fifteen seconds. "By the way, are you diabetic like your brother?"

"No. Fortunately, that ailment skipped me for some reason."

"Good. Now when was the last time you ate?" Baron asked, having noticed how often her stomach growled while she was out for that excruciatingly long minute. He'd never done so much praying in his life. Had it not been for his medical training, which had kicked in at just the right moment, he would have called 911.

Aurelia's eyes bucked as she recalled that her last meal

had been twenty-four hours ago. "Yesterday around this time," she confessed with a sheepish grin.

"Yesterday?!"

"Yes." She winced at his loud tone. "I was so worried about Trent that I completely lost my appetite. It never came back even after the worst was over."

"You didn't have any snacks at work? Not even a granola bar?"

"Nothing. All I've had in the last twenty-four hours is juice and water."

Baron shook his head with disapproval. "You have to take better care of yourself, Aurelia. Do you have any soup in the cupboard?"

"I have Ramen noodles. With enough water, they make a great soup."

"That'll work. I'll be right back." Baron got up and headed for her kitchen.

"But you don't know where everything is." Aurelia removed the wet compress from her forehead and sat up.

"Don't you dare get up from that couch, young lady!" Baron ordered, swinging around to face her upon hearing too much movement from the sofa. "Just tell me what I need to do from there."

"Yes, sir." She chuckled, settling back down again and reapplying the compress. It felt so good to be taken care of for a change. "By the way, why am I naked? Before I passed out, I still had on clothes, barely, but nevertheless still somewhat clothed."

Baron laughed. "I had to take those tight clothes off you just to make sure you could breathe with ease. If you tell me where your nightgowns or pajamas are, I'll get something looser for you to wear."

Aurelia promptly gave him the information he requested. Soon she was in a pair of black cotton pajamas and resting comfortably again.

* * *

Baron and Aurelia continued to talk as he prepared the makeshift soup in her small kitchen. One of the things they talked about was her new perfume.

"So that's why I've smelled delicious vanilla every time I've been near you these days," Baron said, after he'd heard how Aurelia's new perfume was developed, where, and when.

"Wow, your sense of smell is almost superior to Bambi's. There is vanilla in my fragrance." She looked at him in amazement.

"I thought so." Baron chuckled and then spoon fed her another helping of soup from the large blue plastic bowl in his left hand.

Aurelia chewed the noodles in her mouth, swallowed, and then shared even more details about her fragrance. "With product placements in Bambi's family stores and a few local boutiques, we've already made enough to recoup all of our original investment. We hope the upcoming Christmas season will help us to really turn a profit," she said with a proud smile. "I could sure use that boost in income in light of everything that's happened recently."

"I'm sure you'll do just fine," Baron said, determined to make sure of that. "Matter of fact, I'd personally like to order some of Aurora's Whispers for the adult females in my family. Especially my mother. She's a perfume-aholic." He chuckled.

Aurelia laughed, too. "I'll make sure you get all that you need for free. Just email me with the quantity."

Baron shook his head. "I'd rather pay for my order."

"No, baby. You have to allow me to give to you sometimes," she insisted, reaching up to stroke his left cheek.

He closed his eyes at her soft touch. "Okay, and thank you in advance." Baron smiled, opening his eyes again. "Now open wide."

"You're welcome." Aurelia parted her lips for another spoonful of soup.

"By the way, what made you pick the name Aurora's Whispers?" he asked after she'd had a chance to swallow.

"Necessity. When I learned that the name Aurora was already taken by Disney, I had to come up with something else. To keep the Aurora part, which I loved for scientific purposes, I simply made it possessive and added the word 'Whispers' since the scent becomes extremely soft-spoken after a few minutes. Our current ad slogan plays on the whole whisper theme. It goes like this: 'Aurora's Whispers are "Yes" and "More" – words that you and your lover will say after just one whiff."

Baron moaned. "A provocative slogan like that will help your fragrance fly off the shelves," he replied a bit on the husky side. "I remember when you first whispered those two words to me." He fed her more soup.

"I remember that night, too," Aurelia replied after chewing and swallowing. "I said yes, because you were doing something I liked. I said more, because I wanted you to repeat that special something over and over again."

Baron moaned again. Then he quickly shook his head to clear away the cloud of passion that threatened to besiege him. "I'm starting to think that your fainting spell might have actually been a blessing in disguise. We really shouldn't have sex while you're officially still in my class. Plus, I want the next time we make love to be without restriction. I want us to be completely free to enjoy each other…in every pleasurable way." He licked his lips at just the thought of tasting all of her one day soon.

Aurelia moaned this time. "Maybe it was for the best," she agreed. "But know this, Dr. Baron Weaver, when we do make love again, I'm going to be well-fed, well-rested, and ready to put our first time to shame," she said, determined to pull out all the stops in this relationship. Well, as many as she could without drudging up another painful part of her past. Either way, Cain would be the last man to ever cheat on her.

Slamming his eyes shut, Baron took deep breaths to calm down. His mind continued to swirl with Aurelia's words and the implications thereof. If what he got that night in the hotel was just the tip of the iceberg, then he was really going to lose his mind the next time they made love.

"Okay, no more sex talk for the remainder of my visit," Baron announced, upon opening his eyes again. "I can only handle so much temptation in one night." He spooned up another helping of soup. "Now open wide again. The sooner I make sure you've eaten everything in this bowl, the sooner I can leave for both our sakes."

Aurelia chuckled and then opened her mouth wide for another spoonful of noodles and flavored broth.

* * *

"Goodnight, beautiful. I'll call and check on you when I get home." Baron leaned in to give her a brief kiss on the forehead before standing to his feet.

"Goodnight, Professor," Aurelia replied with drowsy eyes and an equally drowsy voice. It was a good thing he'd pulled out her sofa bed after cleaning up behind himself in the kitchen, because she was sle-ee-py.

"No." Baron shook his head at her farewell. "From now

on I want you to call me Baron whenever we're alone, okay? There's something about the way you say it that really turns me on."

"Goodnight, Baron," Aurelia amended. "And thanks again." She pointed to the brown envelope on her desk with emphasis.

"That's better." He smiled. "And you're welcome again." Baron headed for the door. Five steps away, he paused, and turned to face her again. "Aurelia?"

"Yes, Baron?" She smiled sweetly at him .

"Can you make your exam day a special occasion and wear another dress?" Baron whispered huskily.

"Yes." Aurelia smiled, knowing exactly which one to wear, too. "Don't forget to lock the door behind yourself."

"Yes, ma'am." He grinned, loving the easy flow of their new relationship. It was about time their love became less complicated.

* * *

As Baron exited Aurelia's building and headed to his car, the P.I. in the black jeep down the street proceeded to snap several pictures of him, his vehicle, and his license tag. After doing that, he pulled out a notepad to write down the time of Baron's departure alongside the time of his arrival.

Underneath that the P.I. wrote: She is definitely seeing someone now…looks like one of her professors from school…not good news for Clients 3 & 4…simply more interesting facts for Clients 1 & 2.

CHAPTER NINETEEN

Baron prided himself on successfully avoiding temptation Tuesday night. Yet when Aurelia showed up to take his final on Thursday afternoon dressed in black stilettos and a formfitting double V-neck black dress that was both sexy and elegant, he seriously thought about taking her before she took that exam.

There was no one else in the classroom besides them. If they closed the blinds and locked the door, no one else had to know what happened in there. It could be their own little secret. It would also be a great birthday present for him since today was his 30th birthday.

However, because Baron was committed to playing by the rules, he did the right thing. He put business before pleasure...again.

Twenty aching minutes later, Baron lived to regret that decision. He thought about exiting the classroom several times just to collect himself, but when he recalled that he didn't do that with any other test-taking student, he stayed put at his desk and just suffered in silence.

When Aurelia finally turned her test in, Baron met her gaze. Heat resonated between them. "I'll have your final graded before I leave work today. Your grade will be turned into the registrar's office soon thereafter."

"That soon, huh?" One of Aurelia's arched brows rose.

"Yes, it's imperative that I conclude this particular school business, so I can get on to other things." Baron spoke discreetly since the door to the classroom was still open.

"I completely understand." Aurelia smiled with a knowing look. "I'm very pleased to have yet another obstacle removed in my life as well."

"Yes." Baron licked his lips with anticipation, wishing he could lick her dimples instead. "Well, it was nice having you in my class, Aurelia. You've been one of my brightest students to date. I wish you the best in your future endeavors."

"Thanks, Professor. I learned a lot in your class. You're definitely one of the best instructors I've had at AU. Although you interrogated us like a lawyer…" She paused to chuckle. "…you made the material easy to grasp and gave excellent notes. I couldn't help but learn a lot in your class."

"I appreciate that, Aurelia." Baron smiled. "Make sure you put all that on the teacher evaluation survey. It might help to extend my contract here." He let out a husky laugh.

"I already did." Aurelia grinned, patting her backpack. It contained the survey form that she would turn into the dean's office before leaving school today.

"Very good. Here's one of my cards. Stay in touch." Baron slid a business card across the desk.

"Thanks, Professor, I will." Aurelia received the card. After briefly perusing the gold calligraphy on the front that contained his work number, email address, and work address, she flipped over to the back and saw where he'd handwritten his home address. There was no need to put his home or cell phone numbers on the card. They were both given to her Tuesday night when he called her from home.

"Thanks again…for everything," Aurelia reiterated, giving him a sensual smile this time. She planned on using that handwritten information tonight.

"Y…you're welcome." Baron watched her as she started towards the door. He suppressed a moan at the way that dress hugged her bottom and at the sight of all that sexy brown calf action.

Snatching his gaze away, Baron looked down at Aurelia's completed test. Her handwriting was just as neat as always. Everything was legible. All answers were coherent and well thought out.

Picking up his red pen, Baron began to grade that test with vigor. The sooner he got this done, the sooner he could pursue Aurelia more openly.

* * *

Aurelia called Baron around 9pm that night. It was right after she checked her student grades online and learned that she'd gotten a high score on the final, giving her an 'A' in his class.

An A!

That final grade also meant that Aurelia was technically and officially out of Baron's class. That they were finally free to be together…in every way.

Baron answered on the second ring. "Hola, baby," he said, speaking a bit of Spanish to her.

"Hola." Aurelia understood that term though she was more fluent in French. "I just called to see if you felt like having some company tonight. My flight doesn't leave until 9am tomorrow and with all of my tests behind me and my bags packed, I find myself with some extra time on my hands."

"I would love some company tonight," Baron replied, unable to keep the huskiness or the excitement out of his voice. "Do you need me to pick you up? Or can you find my place on your own?" Inwardly, he was so glad that he'd given his place a good cleaning yesterday. He'd been slipping in that department lately in direct response to his unpleasant moods.

"I may not have GPS in my car, but I'm pretty sure I can find your place on my own." Aurelia chuckled. "Expect me in the next hour, okay?"

"Okay, beautiful," Baron replied.

"And, Baron?"

"Yes, Aurelia?"

"Your medical tests are still up to date, right?" Aurelia asked, posing the question that she should have asked the first time they had sex. Or even Tuesday night for that matter.

"Yes, and they all say that I'm still just as healthy as I was the first time we were together." Baron confirmed what she suspected all along.

"Good. I am still healthy as well. Plus my birth control is sufficient, so you don't have to worry about that either," Aurelia said, letting him know what he already suspected and a little bit more. "By the way, I'm glad that you didn't sleep with anyone else. That you kept saving it all for me. I'll make the wait so worth it, baby. I promise you that."

Baron moaned, amazed by how excited she could make him with just words.

"Now don't forget to do a few stretches before I arrive. You're about to get quite a workout tonight," she concluded in a sensual whisper.

He moaned again. "You just make sure you've eaten today and taken your vitamins. I don't want you fainting on me again."

Aurelia chuckled. "All of that is covered, too."

Baron also laughed. Hanging up a few seconds later, he shouted, "Finally!" in his lonely bedroom. Then he proceeded to prepare the master suite and a few other areas of the house for his pivotal night with the woman he loved.

Maybe I'm going to get that special birthday present after all, Baron thought. He could hardly wait.

* * *

Aurelia showed up at Baron's house within thirty minutes of their phone call. When he opened his front door, he discovered that she had on yet another dress. This one was just as formfitting as the last one she'd worn, but much shorter. It barely reached down to her mid-thighs.

The mustard-colored garment was sleeveless with a V-neck front and a draped hood in the back. On Aurelia's feet was a pair of white thigh high boots that laced up in the back.

Tell the judge that the verdict was now in. That verdict: This woman knew exactly how to dress to tantalize a man!

Baron moaned and swelled with desire at the very sight of Aurelia. "You look beautiful in that dress. Just beautiful." His voice was a husky whisper saturated with need.

"I'm glad you like it." Aurelia smiled at his reaction. "I dressed with you in mind."

"Oh, I like it. I like it a lot. Come inside," Baron said, ushering her into his home on that calm December night.

When Aurelia crossed that threshold, she just knew he was going to take her in his arms, kiss her passionately and make love to her on the spot. Instead Baron captured one of her hands, kissed it chivalrously, and then announced that he was going to take her on a tour of his six-bedroom, seven-bath Spanish styled home.

Submitting to his wishes, despite her raging hormones, Aurelia made herself concentrate on the things he shared along that tour. She found herself actually enjoying the personal tidbits he shared and the fact that he seemed to want her to get to know him better on a non-physical level first tonight.

So far Aurelia learned that Baron was the youngest of five

boys. His mother was a full-blooded Mexican. His father was two-thirds white/one-third Jewish. His mother was responsible for naming him and his siblings after English peerages. Those titles went in order according to rank and the chronological age of each son. There was Duke, Earl, Marquess, Viscount aka Count, and Baron.

"I'm closer to Count than any of my other brothers. I don't know if it's because we share the same father as well as mother. Or if it's because we're so close in age. Whatever the reason is, we just click," Baron shared as they ascended his staircase. "Count is married to Jenny, a Hispanic/Caucasian woman with light brown hair, gray eyes, and a figure like J-Lo." He chuckled. "Come to think of it, she kinda looks like J-Lo in the face, too."

Aurelia laughed. "A face and figure like J-Lo, huh? No wonder Count didn't cheat at his bachelor's party."

"That might have been a large part of it. The other part is that just like our father, Count and I are faithful through and through. We wouldn't dream of cheating on the women we love," Baron replied, thereby confirming that he'd had no love for Jordin.

"That's good to know," Aurelia replied, glad that she was someone he loved. But then again, Cain claimed to love her and he still cheated. She hoped this time would be different.

"Speaking of cheaters, there's Marquess." Baron looked a bit more somber now as they walked into yet another well-furnished bedroom. They'd already visited two downstairs. "We share a love for the great outdoors. He's my primary camping and hiking buddy. Marquess was married to red-headed Fran, but they recently got divorced due to his cheating ways. No kids were produced from that marriage."

"Perhaps that was a blessing in disguise," Aurelia said, equally somber. "Raising children with no father in the house is tough."

Baron noted her sad tone and assumed she was remembering her own father. "I imagine so."

"Tell me about Duke and Earl," Aurelia prompted, pushing past all feelings of melancholy before they lingered and caused depression.

"Well, I consider Duke to be my intellectual equal due to our bookwormish sides. He's married to Sasha, who is a mixture of cultures. I think she's part Greek, Caucasian, and Hispanic, but don't quote me on that." He chuckled. "Either way, she's a stunning beauty with black hair, dark eyes, and a figure that one would call voluptuous. Much like yours," Baron flirted at the end.

Aurelia chuckled. "You just had to slide that in there, huh?"

"You know it." Baron laughed. "Except Sasha's more top-heavy than you. Whereas you…" He paused and licked his lips. "…you are definitely more endowed in the bottom area."

"Anyway." Aurelia rolled her eyes, though inwardly thrilled by his words. "By the way, I love everything you've shown me thus far. You have a beautiful home."

"I'm glad you like it." He smiled, looking outwardly thrilled by her words.

Aurelia briefly touched a hand to his cheek. "It's hard not to love anything connected to you," she replied, before getting back to their original subject. "So how many kids do Sasha and Duke have?"

"Two. A boy and a girl. They were the ringbearer and flower girl at their parents' recent marriage renewal." Baron took a deep breath and continued. "Last, but not least is my brother Earl, who is the king of habitual cheaters. I used to look up to him when I was younger because he was such a chick magnet. Actually all of us did, including Duke, who is the oldest and the most rugged-looking among the brotherhood. These days, we can barely tolerate Earl due to his snobbish ways. He's even starting to rub off on Marquess, who used to be one of the most down-to-earth people you'd ever want to know before he became such a hotshot attorney."

"Is it a social status thing with Earl and Marquess? Is that why they're so snobbish?" Aurelia recalled how snobbish Marshall's uncle was. Marshall Jean-Baptiste was her first real love in the V.I. She'd willingly given him her virginity at sixteen.

"It's a social status thing for Marquess since the more big cases he wins, the bigger his ego gets. For Earl it's a social status thing, a racial thing, a some of everything. Every year he seems to find some new reason to dislike new groups of people," Baron shared, leading the way to bedroom number four. "I blame it on his extreme need to fit in with what he deems to be the 'right' people. Thus it wasn't a big surprise to any of us when he married Meadow. Not only does she come from a very socially connected family, but she's blonde, blue-eyed, and whiter than white in complexion. They have three kids, one dark-haired little boy and two blonde little girls."

"I don't know whether to feel sad for Earl or be mad at him," Aurelia replied. "While I deal with my confusion, why don't you tell me what your other brothers do for a living. You already told me about Marquess being a lawyer."

"Count is a lawyer, too, but he's into family law, not environmental law like Marquess," Baron said. "Duke and Earl are doctors. The first practices general and family medicine. The latter and definitely vainer brother is a plastic surgeon." He chuckled and added, "I'm the oddball by going into education. I can't tell you how much teasing I've gotten for that choice over the years. Especially after I went to medical school, completed my residency, and could have had a long and very successful career as a pathologist. People didn't understand that just having knowledge wasn't enough for me. That I was most happy, most fulfilled, when I was sharing that knowledge with others."

"Good for you for taking that stand. For the record, I don't think there's anything wrong with being different. I'm the oddball in my family, too," Aurelia shared. "My mother and most of my other St. Croix relatives are domestics for rich folks on St. John and the surrounding islands. I'm the one that dared to rise above those occupations by going to college. My mother and aunt could have elevated their statuses in life as well with their excellent basket weaving abilities. However, there never seemed to be enough money to take care of their families and buy perpetual basketry supplies."

"Hopefully your mother and aunt will be able to realize their basket-weaving dreams in the near future. As for you, I commend you for going your own way. For setting such a great example for your little brother." Baron looked even more impressed by her as they now exited bedroom number five, which had been turned into an upstairs exercise room.

At that reference to Trent, Aurelia's eyes grew glossy for more reasons than one. The main reason was the fact that Baron was the first person that she ever wanted to tell the whole truth about her little brother.

But she couldn't. Not yet anyway. Aurelia needed to be sure that Baron was going to stick around for a while before she let that deep, dark secret run free between them.

"Yes, I do what I can to look out for Trent in every way. I also look forward to helping my mother and aunt realize their dreams," Aurelia said as he led the way to the flat landing that contained his rooftop garden, forgoing a trip to the last bedroom – the master suite.

Suddenly she gasped. "Oh my. It's so…so…beautiful. Peaceful and serene, too." She looked around with pleasure at her surroundings.

There were plants galore in this special garden. Some were tall, some wide, all added to a person's privacy and serenity. A cement and cobblestone sidewalk surrounded a grass square center. Along that sidewalk were a couple of lounge chairs on the south wall and a two-seater bench near the north railing. The south wall contained a sliding glass door that led to the master suite.

At the very center of the solarium's grassy square was a beautiful eagle fountain. East and west stairs led down to the water that flowed out of that fountain. Beside each pair of stairs were two-seater chaise lounges with comfortable weatherproof cushions, wide umbrellas overhead to block out any unwanted sunlight, and round tables to sit a favorite book and beverage upon.

Combine all those elements and Baron's rooftop garden really was a place of serenity. The flameless scented candles positioned on the various tables gave the area a romantic feel as well.

"I'm glad you're so pleased with my private sanctuary." Baron smiled, clearly pleased with Aurelia's reaction as she followed the sidewalk around the whole area of the rooftop solarium in exploration. "This is the one place I thought about making love to you the most on the whole property." He walked over to one of the wide chaises and sat down. "Many a night I sat in this very spot and thought about all the things I wanted to do to you."

Aurelia turned away from a tall plant and smiled at him. "Oh really?"

"Yes, really." Baron patted the space beside him in invitation.

"Is that why you have yet to give me a real kiss?" Aurelia asked, walking in a sexy strut towards him. "Were you waiting to bring me up here before the fireworks began?"

"Yes and no," Baron admitted. "A part of me really

wanted to share my home with you before things turned physical between us again. The other part knew that if I had given you a real kiss downstairs or anywhere else on this property, I would have taken you right there on the spot. Since I wanted our first time at my home to be in the garden and since tonight's mild weather was so perfect for such a thing, I decided to wait a little longer."

"There's no need to wait now, baby." Aurelia settled into his lap. Her hands went about his neck.

"No, there isn't," Baron agreed, cupping her face gently before descending upon her lips for a long awaited ravenous kiss.

That mild California night suddenly got blazing hot as Baron and Aurelia's kiss caused desire to instantly sizzle in their veins. They couldn't get enough of tasting one another, touching one another, just loving one another.

Her hands found their way underneath his black polo shirt and roamed that hairy chest of his. His hands couldn't seem to stop squeezing her supple bottom.

When Baron couldn't find a panty or thong line, his hands roamed upwards. Finding no evidence of a bra strap either, he abruptly broke the kiss.

"Are you completely naked underneath this dress?" Baron asked with passion aflame in his blue-brown pools.

"Yes," Aurelia panted out, pulling his head back towards her for another kiss.

"Happy, happy birthday to me," Baron whispered huskily, before lowering ravenous lips to hers again. His hands pulled her dress up to her waist, eager to remove all hindrances to the flesh-to-flesh squeeze he desired.

Aurelia moaned when he filled his large hands with her bottom again and gently squeezed. "Is today really your birthday?" she asked against his mouth.

"Oh, yes. And as a present to my eyes, I'm going to watch myself take you tonight…inch by inch," he said, withdrawing a bit to give her an intense stare with that promise.

Aurelia gasped at his provocative words, shuddered at that heated look. Then with a hungry groan, she literally attacked his mouth.

That kiss led to many more. Deep kisses. Suckling kisses. Kisses that traveled.

Aurelia gasped when Baron lowered the V-neck of her dress, descended with his kisses, licked her gumdrops, and then took turns feasting upon her chocolate boom-shocka-locka-booms. Moaning out her pleasure, she instinctively arched towards him, encouraging him to feast even more. Her eyes, though barely seen under her long hooded lashes, took in the view of Baron's pink lips working overtime.

Was the man trying to swallow her melons whole?

And his hands. The left one supported her back while the right one cascaded downward for a time of deep sea diving and exploration.

As if the command 'open sesame' had been given to them, Aurelia's legs moved farther apart, giving Baron even greater access to her hidden treasures. She moaned loudly as his right hand took full advantage of that access. "Yes," she whispered breathlessly.

"That word is music to my ears, baby," Baron muttered against her bosom. "Let me see if I can press replay." He licked a trail from one rigid peak to the other.

Aurelia shuddered, moaned again, and repeated the same whisper. "Yes." She ran her tongue slowly over her lips even as her hips communicated with his hand.

Seeing her tongue, Baron leaned up to capture it between his lips. He pulled it deep into his mouth for a long suckle. His right hand continued to prime her for what was to come.

Aurelia didn't need any priming. She was already ready. Had been for months. As a result, she went over the edge quickly.

Baron continued to kiss her the whole time, swallowing her screams of ecstasy in his mouth. When most of her internal clenching had calmed, he broke the long kiss, and laid her on her back on the chaise. Then he removed his shirt, lowered his black jeans and underwear, and quickly donned their protection.

When everything was in place, Baron positioned Aurelia's right leg upon his left shoulder, and slowly joined with her under the starry sky. Like he promised earlier, he watched himself take her inch by satisfying inch, moaning the whole time.

Finally they were completely reunited again and it felt so good. Too good.

The journey to ecstasy began slow and steady. Baron continued to watch their coupling, licking his lips constantly. Every now and then he'd look up into Aurelia's eyes to make sure she was enjoying herself, too.

She was. Immensely. That much was evident by the naughty looks she kept giving him. The husky whispers of "Yes" and "More".

Ready to add to their enjoyment in every way, Aurelia pulled her leg from his shoulder and tucked it behind her head.

What?!

Baron's eyes bucked at that unexpected action. A surge of adrenaline whipped through his body.

Ready, set, go!

Fueled by months of hunger, Baron leaped into the fast lane with both feet. Like a track star running the 50-yard dash, he went at Aurelia hard and fast. His hips were programmed to lightning speed. Yet every stroke was smooth and fluent, revealing his proficiency in yet another area of his life.

Eager to run the same race, Aurelia lowered her leg and matched his brisk pace. She didn't miss a beat as her hips surged up to meet his time and time again. She wanted Baron to know that she could keep up with him in every way. Was thrilled to do so. Not even Cain had gotten this level of enthusiasm from her.

Soon they were both going over the edge, together this time. Forgetting where they were, they cried out loudly in ecstasy. A neighbor's backyard dog barked in protest, quickly reminding them that they were outside. Unseen, but still outside.

"I think that's a sign that we need to take this inside now." Baron chuckled, panting against her neck as he endeavored to catch his breath.

"Me, too. I wouldn't want your neighbors to call the police on us." Aurelia laughed, just as breathless as him.

Soon they were making their way towards the master suite for round two.

CHAPTER TWENTY

Aurelia entered the master suite through the door that led from the solarium. She barely got a chance to peruse her surroundings before Baron took her fast and furious again. This time up against the bedroom wall. The man was relentless and she loved every second of it.

After round two, Baron suggested a soothing bath for them. Not only didn't he want to wear Aurelia out too soon, he wanted them both to stay in top form for the long night of loving he had planned.

When Baron was done running their bath, he let Aurelia enter first while he doubled back to the bedroom to check on the solarium door. He'd been in such haste before that he wasn't sure if the door had been properly secured. Upon tending to the lock, he then made a trip downstairs to the kitchen for a bowl of fruit. They had to keep their strength up.

"Enjoying your bath so far, baby?" Baron asked, easing into the large Jacuzzi tub beside her after putting the fruit on a silver tray nearby.

"Yes, I'm enjoying it a lot." She opened her eyes to smile over at him before closing them again. The soothing waters were hitting all the right spots on her body. It was almost like getting a spa treatment.

"Good. By the way, what you said about my neighbors possibly calling the police on us tonight couldn't be truer."

"Really?" Aurelia opened her eyes again to look at him.

"Yes. Mrs. Applegate, my neighbor to the left, would be the first to dial 911." He chuckled. "Not used to nonwhites living in this area, she called the cops the first night she saw me on the property alone. She thought I was one of the movers and had come back to rob the place while the owner was away."

Aurelia laughed, too, but she shook her head nevertheless. "It's amazing that America can join together to elect a black president, but some of us still can't seem to dwell together in peace."

"Sad, but true," Baron agreed. "But to Mrs. Applegate's credit, she appears to have accepted my presence in the neighborhood now. She even gives me fresh produce from her garden every week."

"That's nice." Aurelia closed her eyes again; oblivious to how gorgeous she looked right now. To how sexy her melons looked bobbing up and down in the water.

"Yes, that is nice," he agreed, not just talking about his neighbor's benevolence, either.

* * *

After their bath, Baron and Aurelia took turns drying each other off. Minutes later, she curled up in the bed while he put on some music. The first song of choice was Musiq Soulchild's So Beautiful – the theme song that he personally assigned to Aurelia's life.

"Mmm...I love that song." She instinctively moved her hips on the bed.

Baron moaned at that sight and licked his lips. "And I love the way you're moving on that song. Your body seems to take to music like a fish to water. Just fluid all over and so graceful. You're the sexiest woman I've ever met in my life."

"And I've never met a more rhythmic man. Your hips always seem to know just how to move with mine," Aurelia replied. "Matter of fact, how about you do a little dance for me. Show me just how rhythmic you can be on the solo tip."

Baron's left brow rose at that request. This was different. No woman had ever asked him to dance for her before. With her, yes. For her, no.

Would he do it? Would Baron honor Aurelia's special request?

"Sure. Let me just switch to something closer to my speed and style of dancing." He quickly switched the CD to a Latin recording artist named JenCarlos Canela. The same artist that many people thought he favored.

When the upbeat music began to play, Baron began to dance.

Aurelia watched from the bed as he showed off fantastic

moves from his rich culture. Moves that soon had her panting for more of his love. Every inch. Every centimeter.

"Enough!" Aurelia semi-shouted over the music. "Drop dat towel, mon, and come ova here…quick!" she added, deliberately using a thick island accent this time.

Baron chuckled, switched the stereo back to Musiq's tune and then took long strides over to the bed.

Aurelia welcomed him with outstretched arms.

Baron quickly entered her embrace. His lips quickly found hers again. This kiss was just as hungry as all the others. Just as hot.

The ravenous man didn't stop there. No, Baron went…

Low.

Lower.

"No, baby. I can't let you do that." Aurelia gently pushed his head away from her candy shop before he proceeded to sample every treat she had in the store.

Baron lifted his gaze to her. "You don't want me to taste every part of you?"

"Yes. No." She let out an exasperated breath. "I don't know."

With puzzled eyes, Baron sat upright. "Why are you so conflicted on this issue?"

"Because of a bad experience I once had," Aurelia confessed with shiny eyes. She sat upright, too, angry that the past could still affect her so deeply.

Baron frowned. "Were you raped?"

Aurelia shook her head. "No, mon. But I was sexually assaulted nevertheless. Had he not had dat gun pointed to my head, I neva would've gotten on meh knees no matter how much bigger den me he was," she replied, careful not to call the man's name. It was bad enough that she remembered Oliver Jean-Baptiste at all, who was Marshall's extremely wicked uncle.

Aurelia swallowed hard before continuing. "Even den he had to push me down and literally pry meh lips apart." Tears spilled upon her cheeks. "I thought I gon' choke to death." She nearly choked on a sob now.

"Oh, baby." Baron immediately pulled her to him in gentle comfort. "I'm so sorry that happened to you."

"Me, too," Aurelia said through her tears. "Ever since den, I swore off dat kinda sex. I figured dere was no need to ask or expect somebody to do to me what I'm not willing to do to dem. Tis not fair."

"I understand," Baron said, inwardly cursing the mystery man that traumatized Aurelia this way. "We don't have to do that or anything else you feel uncomfortable with," he continued, though it pained him to say those words. Baron was used to total freedom in the bedroom. Yet for love he would deny himself even that level of pleasure.

Sniffing back her tears, Aurelia lifted her gaze to him. "Thanks, Baron." She smiled and wiped her cheeks free.

"You're welcome, baby." He gave her an affectionate squeeze.

"Now can we please get back to the business of making love?" Aurelia withdrew from him after giving him a return squeeze. "I don't want that part of my past to ruin this special moment. Especially when there are so many other things that I do engage in. Things that I can't wait to show you." She repositioned her body on the bed in a sexy split.

"Yes, we can," Baron said, sounding like President Obama in his famous speech.

Aurelia chuckled, feeling better already. Soon round three had begun.

* * *

Once protection was in place again, Baron and Aurelia couldn't get enough of each other as she pulled trick after trick from her extensive bag of knowledge. He became her willing student as she introduced him to new ways of making love that he had never known before. They rocked this bed harder than the one in the hotel room.

By the time they finally concluded tonight's lovemaking out of sheer exhaustion, Baron knew that he was whipped. Aurelia knew that she would love him for the rest of her life.

"I've never loved a man as deeply as I do you, Baron," she said, making that startling confession as she snuggled in his arms on the disheveled bed. Covers were everywhere. Some of the pillows were on the floor. The music on the stereo had long since stopped.

"I feel the same way about you, beautiful," Baron replied. "In fact, I remember the exact day my lust for you turned into love. It was the day you took up that collection for Bambi. Seeing how benevolent you were or rather still are made my heart want to love you. It has ever since."

Aurelia smiled up into his eyes. "I fell in love with you the night you gave me a ride home from the jazz concert. I didn't realize it was actually love until that day in your office when you declared your feelings first. During the home tour tonight my love was confirmed yet again."

"How so?"

"You were telling me about your family and suddenly I found myself wanting to tell you everything about my family, as well. Share all my secrets with you. I realized then that you had become extremely special to me. So much so that I'm starting to regret having to take this trip home tomorrow. If it wasn't an emergency, I'd probably be trying to sleep over tonight and on as many nights as I can after that." She chuckled.

Baron beamed with happiness at her words. Having learned from past mistakes about procrastinating in his love life, he opened his mouth and prepared to ask Aurelia to marry him on the spot. "You can sleep over tonight. Matter of fact, I'd like you to sleep over for—"

The sound of the doorbell interrupted his spontaneous proposal. Baron groaned in protest and exited the bed.

"Who can it be at this hour?" Aurelia looked over at the clock on the nightstand. It read 3:27am.

"Probably my brother Marquess. He said he was coming up to hike with me this weekend. I guess he came a day earlier." Baron retrieved his bathrobe from the back of the bedroom door and put it on. "I'll let him in and be right back, okay, beautiful?"

"Okay." Aurelia gave him a sweet dimpled smile as she snuggled against the pillow he abandoned.

As soon as the door closed behind Baron, she started to feel awkward as memories of how competitive Marquess behaved from the bachelor's party suddenly flooded her mind. Was he like that in everyday life? Or was that an isolated incident in Cabo?

Aurelia would soon find out.

* * *

"What took you so long to answer the door?" Marquess asked as he staggered into his brother's hilltop house.

"Never mind that. What are you doing driving drunk?" Baron countered, frowning at his inebriated sibling.

Ever since that herpes diagnosis ushered in a costly divorce settlement and no hope of a future with Paula, Marquess had been drinking even heavier. Now he was drinking and driving, putting the lives of others at stake, too.

"I got here safe, didn't I?" Marquess insisted from a drunkard's mentality. Alcoholics never thought about the consequences of their actions. They just acted.

"Barely," Baron replied. "And you practically parked on my lawn." He frowned out at the gray Mercedes parked halfway on the curb where a row of shrubs aligned the driveway.

Closing the front door and locking it behind them, Baron was inwardly glad that Aurelia's car was parked safely in the detached four-car garage near the back of the house. It gave them more privacy and also kept her vehicle out of harm's way yet again in light of his brother's unexpected arrival.

"I'll move my car in the morning." Marquess headed for the stairs where his favorite guest bedroom was.

Although there were two bedrooms downstairs in the large house, one of them had been turned into Baron's home office/study. The other only had a daybed, which was entirely too short for Marquess' long legs.

"Give me your keys and I'll move it tonight," Baron said.

"Suit yourself." Marquess reached into his jacket pocket for the keys to his Mercedes. When he swirled around to hand them to his brother, he stumbled. Ironically, his mind could remain steady with alcohol on the brain, but not his body.

As usual, Baron was right there to catch Marquess and hold him up. He'd held him up in a different way when Paula broke his heart all those years ago. Back then their camping trips had been inundated with long conversations about the female lawyer. Sometimes Paula's name still came up in conversation.

"You smell like sex," Marquess said, having gotten close enough to get a good whiff of his brother. "Is that what took you so long to answer the door tonight? Were you knocking boots with someone?"

"Yes." Baron neglected to say anything beyond that as he pocketed Marquess' keys in his black bathrobe with one hand and continued to hold his brother upright with the other.

Baron didn't want to take his new relationship with Aurelia public until she gave him the official okay to do so. If she said yes to his pending marriage proposal, they would go all the way public, lavish wedding and all if that's what she so desired.

Marquess grinned. "It's about time you gave Jordin

something to write home about. How was she? Good, I bet."
He withdrew from his brother and headed for the stairs again.

"Jordin and I broke up," Baron informed, following him upstairs after he stumbled yet again. "I'm with someone else now."

Marquess chuckled. "You dawg! Does this one have a plump rump, too? I bet she does. Ever since you got a sample of that black chick in Cabo you've been stuck on bodacious buns. What was her name? Aurora. Yes, that's it," he rambled, not even pausing to get a response from his brother. "I can't tell you how many times I wish I'd hooked up with her instead of that disease ridden chick that gave me gonorrhea and herpes."

"Aurora was mine," Baron replied possessively, determined to make that true in every way soon enough. But first he had to get his brother safely upstairs, down the hallway, and into a guest bedroom before he fell flat on his face. He'd put the Mercedes in the garage later.

"Aurora was never yours, Professor." Marquess scoffed. "You just borrowed her for the evening. Matter of fact, none of those women at that party could ever belong to a Weaver man. Their occupation is the main strike against them. I mean, do you really think a woman like Aurora would fit into our social circle?" He scoffed again. Hardly." He chuckled.

"You sound like Earl now – stupid. Real stupid," Baron countered.

"Even so, on that particular issue Earl does have a valid point. People really do judge you by your profession or lack thereof. People also judge you by your ethnicity, which would have proven to be yet another strike against Aurora. Not with me, mind you since I could care less about anybody's complexion, but definitely with our brother Earl. You know how big he is on appearances. Those expensive skin bleaching treatments he gets on the regular ought to tell you that. Earl would probably blow a gasket if he had a black sister-in-law. I can see him shaking in his boots now, afraid that all of his country club friends were going to shun him for having a relative with a year round tan." Marquess chuckled again. "Shoot, he can barely stand for Paula to come to the club with Sasha while he's there. And Sasha is Duke's wife."

"Keep your voice down!" Baron hissed, looking back at

the closed door to the master suite they just passed. He hoped against hope that Aurelia had fallen asleep in his absence and missed Marquess' comments. Especially the last few.

* * *

Unfortunately for Baron, Aurelia heard every single word his loud talking brother said from beginning to end. Even now, she hastily dressed. Having kept her garments to a minimum tonight and with her experience as a stripper, she was dressed and ready to go in under five minutes.

Then while Baron proceeded to help his brother get undressed and settled into bed, Aurelia snuck downstairs with her boots in hand, opened the front door, and left. She would put her shoes on in the car or else simply drive barefoot tonight. It wouldn't be the first time she'd driven barefoot. She used to do it all the time in the Virgin Islands.

Aurelia could handle social class issues in her private life, had even gone through them before with Marshall and his uncle. But racism? No. She refused to align herself with a man whose family looked down on others to that degree for things that simply couldn't be helped.

Wealth was no respecter of persons. Anyone could attain it and usually did. But skin color was genetic. One simply had no choice in the matter, though some may argue that point considering sunbathers and, of course, Michael Jackson and Earl Weaver.

I wonder if Dingo knows about Raven, Aurelia mused, recalling those two unfortunate pieces of Marquess' medical history that had dropped into her lap tonight. I'll call Crystal and put her on the alert before I leave tomorrow, she decided, running quietly towards the garage area.

* * *

Baron didn't hear the front door open and close, but he sure heard Aurelia's car start up and zoom away from his house. The sound of a Volkswagen's engine was pretty hard to miss.

She heard my stupid brother! Baron realized, quickly running downstairs. He flung the front door open in hopes of catching Aurelia before she left. But it was too late. She was gone. He could hear the engine on full throttle from here.

Closing the door and locking it, Baron ran back upstairs to his bedroom where his cell phone was. Using speeddial, he called Aurelia's cell phone only to find out that she had turned it off. He quickly sent her a text message even though he knew she wouldn't receive it until she actually turned the phone back on.

That message read: Can't we talk about it?

Tempted to get dressed and drive over to her place, Baron nevertheless refrained. The sound of Marquess puking out his guts down the hall swayed him. He had to make sure his brother was all right first, even though it was he that caused all this trouble tonight.

On top of that, Baron had class in the morning and a 7am breakfast meeting with the dean and the other instructors in the science department. With it being almost 4am now, he was already going to be functioning on very little sleep after his long night with Aurelia.

Baron's night suddenly got longer when he walked into the guest bedroom Marquess occupied and saw vomit almost everywhere. Even on the headboard.

"Don't you dare go in my closet!" Baron scolded loudly, stopping his brother before he relieved himself among the hangers again. "I barely got the smell out from the last time you mistook this closet for a bathroom."

"Ain't my fault you got a closet where a bathroom should be." Marquess staggered towards the real bathroom in the adjoining room.

"Nothing's ever your fault," Baron grumbled, snatching soiled sheets from the bed.

As he went about the task of cleaning up behind his brother, he made plans to call Aurelia after his morning meeting. He just hoped she'd turned her cell phone back on by then and would be more conducive to taking his calls.

* * *

As Aurelia continued to speed away, she failed to see the black jeep following her. The driver of the second vehicle drove with one hand. He held a mini-recorder up to his mouth with the other.

"Subject and her beau looks like they just had a big fight. Probably caused by his late night guest. They might make up considering the loud night of passion they just had. It's still too soon to tell," the P.I. said, determined to wait outside Aurelia's apartment building just in case Baron showed up later to reconcile.

After freeing his hands of the recorder, the P.I. picked up

his cell phone and dialed the number to a local private duty nurse. It was time to check on his beloved sick wife.

* * *

An hour later, Baron finally got a return text message from Aurelia.

It read: Nope!

Please, he typed, starting to feel desperate inside.

Nope! Now leave this 'black chick' alone. 4 good! Aurelia replied in her final text message before turning her phone off again.

Baron became dumbfounded. He couldn't believe she was dumping him after the wonderful night they just had, after all those declarations of love, and after all the trouble they'd gone through to be together.

No! Baron lamented inside. This just cannot be happening!

CHAPTER TWENTY-ONE

A Week Later

Once Aurelia returned to the Virgin Islands, she kept her cell phone constantly turned off for seven days straight. She only turned it on when she needed to make a call. It was promptly turned back off soon thereafter.

Aurelia practiced this new phone habit to avoid Baron's calls, which were many. She outright refused to read any more of his text messages. All of them were deleted as soon as she saw the name of the sender.

The person that Aurelia did continue to communicate with in California was Bambi. As business partners they needed to stay in touch. Especially with this new website they were trying to develop for Aurora's Whispers. For that task, they enlisted the help of one of Bambi's sorority sisters, Flora Torrey.

Flora was a computer technology major who free-lanced as a website designer on the side. She was also the twin sister of Fletcher Torrey, a very popular AU basketball star.

After talking with Bambi about the progress of the website on Thursday afternoon, Aurelia turned her phone off again and went to check on her brother. Trent had been released from the hospital three days after his appendix was removed. He was expected to make a full recovery between two to three weeks.

Eager to do her part to assist in his recovery, Aurelia made sure that Trent got lots of bed rest, ate a high-fiber diet, and drank lots of water to keep his digestive system properly flushed. She also checked his incisions often to monitor any signs of infection. So far there were none.

The hardest part of all was getting Trent to remain in bed

for any long period of time. With it being only a week after his surgery, he was already itching to get back outside and play like he'd done before.

Aurelia wasn't having that. However, she did let Trent outside for walks around the property and non-strenuous games when the weather was nice. Today the temperature was seventy-five degrees as it had been almost every day this week. Thus Trent was in the front yard playing marbles with a neighbor's grandchild.

Upon making sure that her brother was fine, Aurelia returned to the house to do a load of laundry. Her mother was busy cooking dinner in the kitchen. They were having roti, a West Indian type burrito usually made with curry spiced chicken, shrimp or conch, potatoes, vegetables, and hot sauce wrapped in a tortilla.

The Buntings were not eating roti with conch tonight. Aurelia and Trent were not partial to snails no matter how edible they were. However, chicken and shrimp were definitely among tonight's menu items.

As a whole, the Buntings had been eating a lot heartier this past week, although they still had hot dogs and Ramen noodles in the house. This surplus was largely due to the excess funds Aurelia still had on her credit cards after prepaying next semester's educational expenses before leaving California. She also used some of those funds to pay her apartment rent and a trusted neighbor to watch out for her car.

The rest of the money Baron loaned Aurelia had been spent on other Bunting family members. Unable to stomach the consequences of her aunt, sickly uncle, and six young cousins being in the dark, she paid their overdue electric bill, bringing the balance down to a satisfied zero.

In the dark.

Aurelia suppressed a moan as she recalled a few things she and Baron had done in the dark at his place. Or rather in the semi-darkness of his candlelit bedroom.

The man had been so good to her in every way that night. She'd felt so loved, so desired, so downright adored in his presence.

And yet they couldn't be together. There was no room for a black person in the Weaver family.

Suddenly curious about the number of times Baron had tried to contact her in the last thirty minutes since she'd been outside, Aurelia went to the wicker end table in the living room and retrieved her cell phone.

Turning the phone back on, she saw that Baron had tried to contact her twice in the last half hour. She also saw an urgent text message from Bambi, telling her to call her immediately. She quickly phoned her in return.

"What's wrong? Did Flora run into some problems with the website designs?" Aurelia asked in a rush, automatically assuming the worst. One couldn't really blame her considering how gloomy her life had been recently.

"Nothing's wrong. Everything's right!" Bambi exclaimed in an excited tone.

Then she began to tell Aurelia about the latest sales figures and reports that all pointed to the same phenomenon – Aurora's Whispers had sold off the shelves in every store it was located. Boutiques that wouldn't have stocked an unknown fragrance like hers even if she'd paid them to a month ago were now calling in orders. Some of those boutiques were even from the Platinum Triangle – a trio of adjoining high income areas that included Bel Air, Beverly Hills, and Holmby Hills.

"Girl, I just got off the phone with yet another boutique from Rodeo Drive. Rodeo Drive!" Bambi giggled. "They want three whole cases of Aurora's Whispers."

Aurelia's eyes couldn't stretch any wider in their sockets. They'd been bucked for minutes now. She'd even had to sit down on the nearby sofa, because her legs simply couldn't bear up under this kind of news.

"H…how did they find out about my fragrance? We've haven't even gotten the website up and running yet," Aurelia stammered out.

"Word of mouth, girl. Boutique managers are calling by customer request. Meaning, people are coming in and calling in for your fragrance. The calls have been most dominant in the Bel Air area," Bambi informed.

Baron has relatives in Bel Air. Lots of relatives. All wealthy and influential, Aurelia recalled silently as tears welled up in her eyes. That man. That wonderful, wonderful man.

Convinced that Baron was somehow connected to this sudden blessing caused Aurelia's love for him to grow. Like a chain reaction, the pain of not being able to have him grew as well.

Aurelia swallowed over the emotional lump of misery in her throat and forced herself to return to the main focus of her call.

* * *

"Do you need me to come back to California and help fill orders?" Aurelia asked.

"I thought about that, but I hesitate to take you away from your family so soon after your brother's illness," Bambi replied. She smiled fondly at Claude as he took a seat beside her at the lunchroom table. He winked in return, causing her heart to flutter with renewed love.

After a long morning of grueling finals, they were both eating a late lunch in the near empty cafeteria. Almost everyone else had taken their exams and gone home.

"So if it's all right with you, I suggest you let me and my sorors fill the orders instead," Bambi continued, dragging her attention back to Aurelia, despite the butterfly wings flapping in her stomach from Claude's presence as he ate silently beside her. "I can mix the fragrance privately to keep anyone from learning your formula. Then my sisters can come in and help bottle, label, pack, and ship it. It's the least they can do considering how you helped them out with the talent show. They won the grand prize, you know."

"I'm glad they won. However, I insist on paying for their labor out of the sales budget," Aurelia replied firmly. "It'll be my way of helping them earn some money for personal Christmas presents since their prize money was already slated for underprivileged kids."

"You're the best, Aurelia. I'll let the girls know as soon as I get off the phone with you," Bambi said with admiration in her voice.

"When you're done talking to Aurelia, let me holler at her for a minute," Claude inserted, looking entirely too excited to speak to the V.I. native.

Bambi frowned. Rage attacked her soul. Before she knew it a rush of Vietnamese had come out of her mouth. "Đầu ngu! Khi nào anh sẽ ngưng chạy theo một người cô gái không thương anh để theo một người dã yêu anh?!"*

Claude's eyes bucked. As realization set in, a knowing smile graced his lips. "No need to call me stupid, Cổ Trúc," he replied, fluently using her Vietnamese name.

Bambi gasped. The cell phone in her right hand dropped into the hill of mashed potatoes on her plate below. "Y...you understood what I said?" she asked in English. Aurelia was a forgotten entity for the moment...by both of them.

"Yes, thanks to the teenage years I spent bagging groceries in a neighborhood store owned by another set of Vietnamese people," Claude replied in English. Then he leaned closer to her and added in a more discreet tone, "Had I known you were in love with me, I would have definitely paid more attention to you. You would have had all of my attention a long time ago, Bambi. But since I thought all Vietnamese people were like the ones I used to work for, who didn't approve of interracial unions and actually fired me for taking their daughter on a date, I didn't dare go after you. Why set myself up for another disappointment like that? Thus I went back to dating among my own people."

"You wouldn't have been disappointed with me," Bambi whispered with glossy eyes.

In response, Claude leaned even closer and captured her lips.

With three and a half years of pent-up desire fueling that kiss, it was no surprise that the kiss was fervent, deep, and long. At the end of it they both issued the same four-letter word...

"Good."

Applause came from the five cafeteria occupants that remained at various tables.

"Bambi? Bambi? Bambi!" Aurelia's loud voice could be heard coming from the mashed potato area. She'd been calling her friend's name for at least a minute now.

Bambi and Claude broke all the way apart at that sound and laughed. "Better answer your mashed potatoes," he teased, no longer wanting or needing to talk to Aurelia about anything.

"Sorry about that, girl," Bambi said once she'd retrieved the phone and wiped most of the potatoes off of it. "Me and Claude..."

"You and your man," Claude quickly corrected with a sensual smile.

"Me and my man were kinda busy for a couple of minutes there," Bambi amended, getting a nod of approval from her official new boyfriend before he returned to his meal.

"Try three whole minutes exactly." Aurelia chuckled, despite the twinge of envy that attacked her soul simply because it had not been her and Baron kissing for those succulent minutes. "By the way, congratulations on finally getting your man. I wish you and Claude much happiness," she said, quickly counterattacking and annihilating that envy with heartfelt best wishes for her friend.

"Thanks, Aurelia. Now while my man cleans his plate, let's clear up any lingering business between us. I have a feeling I'm going to be very busy tonight...in more ways than one," Bambi said.

"Very busy," Claude echoed, giving her a hungry look that had nothing to do with the food on his plate.

Returning that heated look, Bambi nodded her consent of any unspecified romantic plans that he might have for their first night as a couple. Then she forced her attention back on the call she needed to complete with her business partner. After that, more kissing!

The exact translation of Bambi's Vietnamese words in English: "Stupid! When are you going to stop pursuing a woman that clearly doesn't want you and pay attention to the one that is secretly in love with you?!"

CHAPTER TWENTY-TWO

Around 7:30am the next morning, Baron made his way from a luxury resort in Christiansted on the east side of the island and headed towards Aurelia's house, which was located on the west side in Frederiksted. Had he stayed at the Divi Carina Bay Beach Resort, located on the farthest east coast of the island, his journey would have been even longer.

Baron chose The Buccaneer not only because the resort was closer to Aurelia, but also because it was an excellent place to spend a luxurious honeymoon. In fact, the resort was just as highly recommended as its easternmost island rival.

Baron's vehicle of choice for this excursion was a red jeep Wrangler from a local car rental agency. The jeep handled well as he navigated his way through the winding, sometimes hilly, and often very narrow roads of St. Croix. The whole time Baron had to keep telling himself to stay on the correct side of the road since the people of the Virgin Islands drove on the left side, not the right.

Baron also had to remember to look for key landmarks per the written instructions he received from a hotel clerk since the roads were often unmarked. When that same clerk found out he was going to the west side of the island, he issued a few verbal warnings about the people there.

"People from the central and west areas are more likely to start trouble. Unlike those from the east side, who are more subdued with their tempers and know how to stay away from trouble," the Caucasian clerk had said. "And you know Frederiksted is the spot where that unsavory slave revolt took place."

Baron knew all about that successful slave revolt led by

General Buddhoe, a fellow slave. He actually agreed with Buddhoe for doing what was necessary to gain his freedom and the freedoms of others in the town that was aptly called 'Freedom City' by locals.

These days, Baron was determined to do what was necessary to liberate another Frederiksted resident – Aurelia, who had the calm temperate of an east-sider, but was vicious like a pit-bull when stirred up. Except the oppressive master he was trying to liberate her from was poverty.

One way in which Baron sought to accomplish his noble goal was by helping to spread the word about Aurelia's new perfume. After shipping Aurora's Whispers to his female relatives via next-day mail and discovering how much they loved it, he suggested that they call their favorite boutiques and make formal requests for it. In this way, the fragrance would be easily accessible to them all the time and the creator of the scent would experience a little bit more financial freedom in her life.

That one suggestion was all it took to get the ball rolling for Aurelia's perfume. Baron's mother, in particular, called every boutique she knew. His sisters-in-law quickly followed suit and even got some of their friends involved.

I wish I'd been there to see Aurelia's face when she got the news about her spike in sales, Baron thought, finally starting to get the hang of left-sided driving as he got even closer to his destination. He still wasn't used to all the potholes yet.

Ten minutes later and after more beautiful scenic views of the island, Baron was finally at the road that led to Aurelia's home. The top of the road was steep and semi-paved with gravel. The road changed from gravel to dirt the farther down it went, eventually leading to a cul-de-sac where a circle of picket-fenced houses were aligned.

The Bunting home was the one on the far left end. At least that's what the neatly painted address on the white fence of the small sky-blue home indicated.

Baron smiled. So this is where my future wife grew up, he thought confidently, parking the jeep directly in front of the Bunting house.

He couldn't wait to see Aurelia again. Couldn't wait to propose to her, to beg her to accept that proposal if necessary. One way or the other, Baron wasn't leaving this island without his chosen bride.

And suddenly he did see Aurelia. Or rather a brief glimpse of her as she rounded the side portion of the backyard with a push lawnmower in hand.

Baron moaned with need. His heart swelled with even more love for her.

Aurelia looked so good to him despite her colorful head scarf, which was slightly askew; baggy green sweat suit, and worn black sneakers. He could easily overlook those things because he knew what treasures lay beyond them.

Boy, do I know. Baron licked his lips as he prepared to make his presence known.

* * *

Aurelia gasped loudly when she saw Baron round the corner of the backyard. Her shaky hands instantly loosened on the mower handles, thereby turning it off. Now nothing but the slight morning breeze caressing nearby tree leaves could be heard in the backyard.

What is he doing here? Aurelia's heart hammered against her ribs.

Had she sexed Baron up too much and turned him into a real stalker? Or had he come in the name of love?

There was only one way to find out the answers to her questions. After taking a deep breath, Aurelia flung open the door of her mouth with words this time.

"What are you doing here, Professor?" She put her hands defiantly on her hips. Her eyes flashed with fire even as her hidden valley pulsated with need.

Instead of being offended by her fiery response to his presence, Baron moaned and licked his lips. Now he wished he had come sooner. He would have been here sooner had he not had final exams to administer all week and then taken a brief, yet extremely necessary business trip to Vegas.

"You know why I'm here, Aurelia," Baron replied impassioned, moving closer to her. "Why I had to come as soon as my work schedule allowed."

"I'm not going to have sex with you again, Baron." Aurelia frowned, folding her arms across her stimulated bosom, lest he see just how turned on she was from the mere sight of him in that white polo shirt and those khaki trousers. "Besides, don't you think this is a little too far to travel for a booty call?"

"Is that how you're labeling what we did that night? Mere sex? A booty call? I made love to you, Aurelia. Love!" Baron countered fervently, pushing his sunglasses up and past his hairline so that she could see his eyes as he stood directly in front of her now. "I thought you made love to me, too, based on your heartfelt words and the delicious way you responded to me." He licked his lips again. "In fact, the last I heard, you had fallen just as deeply in love with me as I had you."

"The last I heard, your family was extremely opposed to interracial dating," Aurelia quipped, fighting against the potent memories he invoked with his fervent words. And the sincere affection shimmering in his eyes proved that he was no obsessed stalker, but rather a man deeply in love.

In love!

"My brother Earl isn't open to such dating. I am," Baron replied firmly. "In fact, I'm open to interracial marriage, which is why I was about to ask you to marry me that night before Marquess interrupted us. Why after turning in the final grades of all my classes and handling some unexpected business in Vegas, I caught another plane and flew all the way here late last night just so I could ask you to marry me today," he added, laying all his cards on the table as usual.

Aurelia inhaled sharply. "Y…you want to m…marry me?" she stammered out.

"Yes." Baron pulled a ring out of his pocket to prove his intentions. "I love you, Aurelia Bunting. I don't ever want to be without you again. Please marry me, baby." He dropped down to one knee on the freshly cut lawn.

Who cares that he was ruining the knee of an expensive pair of trousers? Only one thing mattered in this pivotal life-changing moment – Aurelia's answer.

Aurelia's eyes watered at Baron's heartfelt proposal. Her mouth watered at the sight of all those carats in his hand. And not the kind you eat either.

What did he do, go directly to Africa for that rock? Surely no store in America sold diamonds that big.

"Marry em, gal," said a voice from behind them.

It was Emile Bunting, Aurelia's mother. She'd been in the kitchen cooking breakfast when Baron arrived. After hearing the mower turn off for too long, she'd turned off the food and come to the back door to investigate.

"I don't even know em yet and even I kin see de love dropping from him eyes," Emile continued through the screen door.

"Mrs. Bunting, I presume." Baron rose to his feet again. He turned to face her, prepared to make the proper introductions and whatever else was required to win Aurelia's hand in marriage. "My name is Dr. Baron Weaver. And yes, I do love your daughter very much. If it's all right with you, I'd like to marry her as soon as possible."

"'Tis fine wid me," Emile said, noting his expensive clothing, shoes, and that large ring in his hand.

Baron's obvious love for her daughter was enough for Emile to give her complete approval of the union. Yet it was his ability to take care of Aurelia financially is what really put him over the top. Finally her daughter wouldn't have to struggle so hard to make ends meet. Finally she'd have an easy life like her father always wanted.

"I need to think about this," Aurelia said, heading for the house, leaving Baron and the lawn mower in the yard.

Emile motioned for Baron to follow her daughter inside as she held the screen door open for them both.

He quickly obeyed that non-verbal gesture, following Aurelia all the way into the Bunting living room, which was inundated with unique wicker furnishings handcrafted by Emile and her sister. The same living room that doubled as a bedroom for Aurelia because she wanted her mother and brother to have the only two real bedrooms in the house.

"What's dere to tink 'bout, Ree-Ree?" Emile asked her daughter upon entering the living room right after Baron. "De man loves you. Do you not love em?" She already knew the answer to her question since Aurelia had done nothing but talk about the man all week, especially last night. However, Emile deemed it necessary for her daughter to openly admit her feelings now.

Aurelia twirled around from her place near the large picture window. "Yes, but I wish I didn't." She kept her gaze averted from Baron's.

"Why?" he asked in an anguished tone, clearly pained by her admission.

"Cause it hurts too much to love you, Baron," Aurelia squeezed out in a semi-whisper as she forced glossy eyes his way. "I been heartsick all week 'cause of you. I may have been born on April Fool's Day, but I'm not foolish enough to sign up for dat kinda pain ova ah lifetime," she concluded with tears rolling down her cheeks.

Baron moved towards her in comfort. He stopped short

in his tracks when Aurelia put up a hand and shook her head, signifying that she couldn't handle his touch right now. She could barely handle being in the same room with him.

"Eh sounds to me like you bin heartsick 'cause you won't let yourself love em. Not 'cause you love em as ah whole," Emile spoke up, quickly getting to the heart of the matter.

Aurelia broke gaze with Baron and looked at her mother. "So you're saying I should let myself love him, despite our obvious differences and de pain it may cause?" She blinked rapidly to clear her vision.

"Yes," Emile advised. "Sharing de same culture, background, and complexion is no guarantee for happiness or pain-free living. Nor should deh be requirements for ah serious relationship. Sometimes tis de differences demselves dat add spice to ah great love."

"I agree, Mrs. Bunting. My parents are living proof of how great love can be between people from different backgrounds. And whatever pain they suffered was considerably lessened by and paled in comparison to their great love," Baron said, looking grateful to have such a worthy and an unexpected advocate in Aurelia's mother.

"But yur mutha is one of de lighter-skinned Mexicans, Baron. Which means she's around de same complexion as yur daddy and so could pass for an exotic brunette, thereby producing less painful racial situations," Aurelia replied, recalling the pictures of them that she'd seen hanging on the walls of his home. "I may look light brown now, though I'm still not as light as meh mutha and little brotha. But I can get deep brown like meh daddy, especially if I spend a lot of time outside in the summer. Which means I could neva pass for anyting but black."

Baron moved closer to tenderly cup her face in his hands, one of which contained the ring he bought her. "I don't want you to pass for anything but who you are, Aurelia. I love your beautiful brown skin. That's not going to change even if the whole world hates your complexion."

Aurelia's eyes shimmered with fresh tears. "Oh, Baron," she whispered, truly unable to resist any longer in the face of such unconditional love. "Since you put everyting dat way, of course I'll marry you. But only under one condition."

"Name it." Baron rubbed his thumb across her bottom lip. He couldn't wait to kiss her.

"Dat you get to know meh…meh little brotha first. If

Trent likes you by de end of de week, I'll marry you without hesitation," Aurelia insisted.

Although Baron had not made his brothers' approval mandatory for her, he nodded in consent anyway. At this point, and after the miserable week he'd had without her, he would have agreed to anything. The fact that he'd already greased the palms of so many to cut down on the island's eight-day waiting period and a few other red tape items were added incentives.

Across the room, Emile smiled as Baron finally slipped the ring upon Aurelia's left hand. She discreetly headed back to the kitchen when her future son-in-law proceeded to seal that moment with a loving kiss.

I'm gonna make sho' Trent loves Baron, Emile mused, determined that no one and nothing messed up her daughter's happiness this time. Aurelia deserved to be happy after all the pain she'd gone through in her young life. Emile would do whatever she could to make it so.

* * *

"Who dat man out back wid de dark eyes?" Trent asked upon entering the kitchen where Emile was just finishing up breakfast. "And why he got on Daddy's overalls?"

Upon awakening, the lad had looked out his rear bedroom window expecting to find his sister engaged in her usual outdoor tasks whenever she was home for an extended stay. Except this time there was a sunglass wearing man helping her in a familiar pair of blue jean overalls.

"That's Dr. Baron Weaver from California." Emile smiled warmly at Trent. "He gonna marry yur sister. As for why he got on yur daddy's old work clothes, I let em wear dem after he insisted on helping Ree-Ree out back. De clothes he came here in twas too nice to ruin wid yard work."

Trent nodded in acceptance of that explanation. He walked to the open back door and looked through the screen at the two people hard at work in the backyard. Aurelia was still pushing the mower, though she was now on the last row. Baron had the cordless hedge trimmer, diligently turning the remaining unruly shrub into a neat masterpiece like the others before it.

"Dey just 'bout finished. It usually takes Ree-Ree lots longer to get done by herself," Trent noted.

"When folks wuk together tings get done faster," Emile replied. "Now how 'bout wukkin wid me to set de table for breakfast. I gotta feeling dem gone be mighty hungry when dey come back inside."

"Yes, ma'am." Trent obediently moved towards the small round table and four hand-woven wicker chairs.

* * *

As breakfast got underway, Emile discovered that she had to do very little to convince Trent to like Baron. The lad liked the Latino man almost from the start.

Favor was planted in Trent's heart the moment he saw Baron pitching in to help Aurelia with the yard work. That seed grew when he learned that the man was an avid outdoorsman and even knew a lot about scuba diving, one of the main sports of choice in the Virgin Islands.

After breakfast, Trent gave Baron a lesson in how to get 360 waves. What Emile found so adorable about that was the fact that the professor was actually enjoying being tutored on the finer points of male hair grooming. His smile was wide. His questions and comments were frequent.

"Okay, go over the steps one more time just to make sure I have them down correctly," Baron prompted the child as they sat across from each other in the small, yet very tidy living room.

Aurelia sat beside him on the couch, snuggling against his left side. They were both fresh from individual showers after their sweaty yard work. Her braids were in a ponytail. His hair was slick, combed straight back, and already starting to wave up. That is what prompted this hair discussion in the first place.

"One, wet de waves," Trent said from his place on the floor near the wicker coffee table. "Two, brush de waves. Three, put yur favorite grease on de waves. Four, brush de waves again. And just to make sho' you do it right, mon, dis is how you brush de waves," he concluded, illustrating his last point with a brown hairbrush.

"This is how you brush the waves," Aurelia corrected, once again trying to help Trent tone down his thick dialect.

From personal experience she learned that too thick of an accent put up a language barrier even among English-speaking people. That hard lesson was learned while they briefly lived in Florida. After too many people from all walks of life complained about not being able to clearly understand her and her mother, Aurelia deliberately set out to loosen her accent and keep it loose as often as she could. However, she has long since resigned herself to it thickening back up automatically whenever her emotions were high.

In contrast, Emile stubbornly refused to change her speech. She was proud of her V.I. accent and wasn't going to change it for anyone. Plus, a lot of men still found it very attractive. According to Emile, if she was ever going to remarry, she needed more going for her than just her looks, which were fading faster than she expected due to too many years of stress and hard work.

"I understood his lingo just fine. I think it's great," Baron intervened, causing Trent and Emile to smile with gratitude and approval. "I wish you spoke your native tongue more often," he told Aurelia.

"Just get her mad enough and it'll come out all on tis own." Emile chuckled from her place in the wicker chair near the exit that led to the kitchen.

"Like now?" Aurelia teased and then uttered a tirade of thick island lingo. "Did you understand all dat, mon?" she concluded when her tirade was over.

"Most of it, yes." Baron laughed. "Shall I speak a few things in my native tongue to you?" He gave her a heated gaze.

"Later." Aurelia blushed, uttering her reply in a husky tone. "I'm hot…I mean, thirsty. Anybody else thirsty?" She quickly rose to her feet, though no one had given her a reply yet.

"I'm thirsty, mami," Baron endeared, though he did not say what he was thirsty for.

"Me, too, mami," Trent replied, mimicking that Spanish endearment.

Aurelia's eyes welled up with emotion at her brother's words. She abruptly turned around and headed to the kitchen, too choked up to say anything else.

"I help wid de drinks," Emile volunteered with a wide grin on her face as she followed her daughter out of the room.

* * *

"You like her, don't you?" Trent asked Baron when they were alone.

"Yes, very much so. In fact, I love your sister," Baron shared. "Are you okay with that?"

Trent nodded. "Yeah. I want her happy."

"Me, too." Baron smiled, liking the young lad a little bit

more with each passing second.

"I wanna be happy, too. Maybe you kin talk meh mutha and sista into letting me go regular school," Trent shared.

"You don't like being homeschooled?"

"No, 'cause eh keeps me from kids meh own age."

"I'll see what I can do," Baron promised. "Although I think homeschooling is one of the best ways a kid can learn in his early years, I do understand your need to be around your peers."

"Is peers ah fancy word for gals?" Trent asked. "'Cause dat's who I really wanna be 'round. Gals like meh waves." He smiled, brushing his hair again. "I like dat dey like meh waves."

Baron grinned, now fully aware of the real reason Trent wanted out of homeschooling. "I tell you what. In case I'm unable to convince your womenfolk about this regular school thing, how about I ask them about letting you join a few teams. When a boy is on a team, there are usually girls cheering on the sidelines in cute uniforms, all shouting your name on account of how good you're playing."

Trent's eyes lit up. "Deal!" he exclaimed, extending his free hand to shake on it island style.

"Deal," Baron confirmed, careful to hold his fist out and gently bump his knuckles with Trent's the way he'd been taught to earlier by the lad.

"You two seem to be gettin long good," Emile noted with an approving smile as she and Aurelia reentered the room with beverages in hand.

"Yeah. Baron de best! I like em even betta den meh favorite rap group. Rock City, mon," Trent replied excitedly.

His response gave Aurelia all the incentive she needed to finally marry the man of her heart's desire. And the conditional week had barely even started.

Unknowingly, Trent also gave Aurelia a reason to investigate how he'd come to listen to a seasoned V.I. hip-hop group whose catchy tunes she even liked, but whose lyrics were too mature for a boy his age. And did him listening to this group mean that he was now into girls? After all, that was one of the main things Rock City rapped about in some of their more popular songs.

Aurelia wasn't ready for Trent to grow up just yet. She wanted him to remain a kid just a little bit longer. Especially since she'd already missed so much of his everyday childhood because of her educational endeavors.

CHAPTER TWENTY-THREE

Aurelia waited until the following Wednesday to tell Baron that he'd passed the brotherhood test. She procrastinated because she wanted to be extra sure that Trent really did like her future husband. After five days of watching them grow even closer, she realized that she had nothing to worry about. The two males were well on their way to being the best of friends.

As expected, Baron was overjoyed to hear that he'd passed the brotherhood test. That joyous smile literally wouldn't leave his face. He smiled all during the dinner that Emile prepared for them from the groceries he brought to the house today. He was still smiling now as he helped Aurelia with the dinner dishes tonight.

They were hand washing the dishes since Aurelia's family didn't own a dishwasher. Matter of fact, the Bunting kitchen only contained the most necessary appliances like a refrigerator, an electric stove, and a washing machine. All were outdated models. Clean, but ancient nevertheless.

Baron made a mental note to buy up-to-date appliances for Aurelia's family. He also made a note to go back to the grocer and purchase more fresh produce, whole grain breads, and other nutritious items for the Buntings. Anything to keep them from consuming so many processed foods. The latter is what he decided to discuss right now.

"How often does Trent eat hot dogs?" Baron asked as he rinsed the sudsy plates she handed him from the left, then stacked them in the brown dish rack to his right.

"Almost every day, why?" Aurelia asked.

Baron frowned. "I thought so," he said, unable to recall a day when he hadn't seen Trent with a hot dog in his hand.

184

"You do know that hot dogs should be eaten in moderation, right? Especially if you are a growing kid. It's also not the best way to properly manage his diabetes."

"Of course I know dat, Professor," Aurelia snapped, sending angry eyes his way. "But when you poor, can't seem to grow enough healthy food to sustain yourself, and all yur local stores have to charge higher prices 'cause dey import most of dere goods, you buy what you kin. Since hot dogs and Ramen noodles be two of de cheapest tings on de market, dey go in de shopping cart first." She snatched her hands from the dishwater, not even bothering to dry them on her apron before she reached into the cupboard on the left and pulled out a large pickle jar that was filled with various condiments from restaurants.

"I…" Baron began only to be interrupted.

"When you poor, you also save ketchup, mustard, and even packets of salt and pepa from restaurants dat you happen to visit," an angry Aurelia continued with glossy eyes. "Not to buy dere food. No, you too poor for dat. But to buy ah cup of water so dat you won't feel like you stealing when you load up on all de condiments yur purse kin hold." She pushed the jar back inside and slammed the cupboard door closed.

"And don't forget 'bout de napkins," she continued, snatching a drawer open to reveal stacks of restaurant napkins. "As ah poor person, you neva know when you might have to choose between bathroom tissue and food 'cause de food stamps done run out, yur neighbors are too jealous-hearted or selfish to help, and yur relatives be barely able to help demselves." She slammed the drawer shut again. "Sometimes ah good newspaper will simply have to do. I even taught Trent how to crumble it up just right so not to scratch himself. But I'm sure you know nuttin 'bout dat, huh, Professor? I'm sure yur mutha neva fed you hot dogs five times ah week or made you wipe yur bum wid newspaper," Aurelia concluded, sobbing by this time.

Baron snatched her to him. "I'm so sorry," he lamented, squeezing her closer with wet hands.

"I don't want yur pity, you trust fund baby!" Aurelia jerked away from him.

"You don't have it. What you do have is my apology for coming across as a condescending rich kid a few minutes ago," Baron replied. "And you're right. I don't know what poverty is like. I was raised in Bel Air, went to private schools, and the best colleges. Even when I go camping, I have everything I need. So I'm never really roughing it in the great wild even though I was taught how to as a boy scout."

He moved closer to Aurelia, causing her to back up against the fridge. "As of today, you and your family will have everything you need, too. I will personally see to it. I may have been raised rich, but I was not raised stingy. Both of my parents are big givers and so am I, especially to those I love. Surely you know that about me by now."

"Yes, you are a very generous man," Aurelia admitted softly as her ire plummeted to the floor. "I'm sorry for overreacting just then, for taking my frustrations about poverty out on you, and for calling you a trust fund baby. You deserve better treatment than that," she continued, issuing a necessary and heartfelt apology of her own.

"You're forgiven," Baron replied with an equally forgiving smile. "And I am a trust fund baby." He chuckled. "All of our kids will be also." He cupped her tear-stained face in his hands. "I love you, beautiful."

Aurelia smiled through her tears. "I love you, too."

With a moan, Baron dipped down to her mouth for a kiss. A hot kiss at that, because as soon as their lips touched things started to sizzle between them. His arms went about her body even as her arms when about his neck.

Soon their hips got in on the deal. Had there been a piece of peppercorn between them now it would have been grinded to bits.

* * *

"Everyting right in dere?" Trent asked from his place on the living room floor where he'd been putting a 100-piece puzzle together. Worry shrouded his features. He didn't know whether to be worried about the angry voices he'd heard in the next room or the sudden silence in there now.

Emile smiled reassuringly. "Oh yes. Ree-Ree and Baron just had to iron out ah little wrinkle in dere relationship. Everyting good now…for everybody," she said, having heard Baron's promises to Aurelia from her place in the wicker chair near the kitchen door.

* * *

Back in the kitchen, Aurelia abruptly broke the heated kiss. "We got to stop before things go too far," she panted out in a whisper as she moved back towards the double sink.

"Things need to go too far, if you ask me. We haven't been together-together in almost two weeks," Baron whispered back, equally breathless. "Come back to the hotel with me tonight." He followed her to the sink, stood behind her, and pressed his body closer in all the right places.

Aurelia moaned at that provocative contact. "As much as I want to, I can't." She wisely moved to the side before turning around to face him. "Not only did I promise to let my mother teach me how to cook Trent's newest favorite breakfast in the morning, I kinda want to wait until we're married before engaging in anymore sexual activity. You know, allow our passion to build up just a little bit more so that our honeymoon will be explosive."

Baron groaned out his disappointment. He sighed. "All right, even though our honeymoon is going to be explosive either way." He put more distance between them for both their sakes. "It's a good thing I completed all the necessary paperwork before I left California. Now all we have to do is appear before the proper authorities to have the completed paperwork notarized, posted for public inspection, and filed. I've already greased enough palms and paid enough fees to reduce the waiting period, which means we can get married before the week is out if we want to."

Aurelia smirked. "You were that confident I'd marry you, huh?" She returned to her dishwashing.

"That hopeful." Baron grinned, also returning to his previous task at her side. "I even went to Mass and applied prayer to the situation."

Her eyes widened. "I can't believe you brought God in on the deal," Aurelia said, truly amazed by this new development. No other man had ever mentioned God or anything remotely religious to her before.

Correction, they'd called out God's name in the throes of passion, but Aurelia really didn't think they wanted Him to show up then...especially not at those times.

"Hey, desperate times call for desperate measures." Baron chuckled. "Plus, I got tired of my mother interrogating me about when was the last time I'd been to church."

"So you figured why not kill two birds with one stone, huh?" She handed him another plate.

"Yes, although I prefer the phrase, 'solve two problems with one deed' since it sounds considerably less harmful to our little animal friends," Baron said, revealing how much of a nature lover he truly was as he rinsed the plate he'd been given.

Suddenly overwhelmed with even more love for this brilliant, strong, and yet sensitive man, Aurelia flung her arms about his neck and attacked his mouth this time. Once again, no thought was taken to drying her hands first.

Baron welcomed that kiss, sizzled with desire therein as he responded with equal fervor. The plate in his right hand was clumsily put in the dish rack as the kiss deepened even more. His wet hands wrapped around her body again, causing her shirt to get just as saturated as his.

"Marry me tomorrow," Baron moaned against her lips when they finally came up for air two minutes later.

"Friday," Aurelia decided, although the gumdrops straining against her wet t-shirt screamed for his attention now. "That'll give me a couple more days to spend with my family before I'm whisked away into marital bliss."

"Friday it is then," Baron agreed reluctantly. Then he dipped down for one more kiss before they had to get back to the business of kitchen cleanup.

* * *

Once the Bunting house was back in order, Aurelia put Trent to bed. She read to him while he performed his nightly hair routine under Baron's watchful eye.

Emile retired to her room and proceeded to do some basket weaving from the large box of supplies Baron had blessed her with earlier today. Another box of supplies had been taken to her sister Gladys, who was also a master weaver. That trip gave Baron yet another chance to ingratiate himself with Aurelia's other relatives.

Gladys and her husband Samuel, who was also the brother of Aurelia's father, welcomed Baron back into their home with open arms. All six of their children did, too. But then again, who wouldn't welcome someone bearing gifts? There had been something for everyone in that large box.

As Aurelia walked Baron out to his car in farewell later that night, she noticed how reluctant he looked to leave. She wasn't particularly ready for him to go either.

"Do you want to check out some nighttime festival events?" Aurelia asked, referring to the Crucian Christmas Festival, which began the first Saturday in December and ended the first Saturday in January. Some festival events didn't start until nightfall. Those were the ones she had in mind now.

"If you're up for it, it wouldn't take me very long to go back inside and get dressed," Aurelia added as they came to a stop outside the driver's side door of his rented jeep.

"I'd rather spend some time alone with you instead…in my hotel room." Baron gave her a hungry look as he pulled her close.

Aurelia took in a shaky breath. "Be a little bit more patient, baby. Please," she whispered, mindful of her neighbors who were going to and fro in lively festival attire behind her.

One of those neighbors was her childhood rival Jewell Miller. Jewell had been jealous of Aurelia ever since she could remember. She especially hated the fact that Trenton Bunting Sr. wanted great things for Aurelia and tried to give them to her while he was alive. Whereas Jewell and her four older brothers were raised by a single mother across the street from the Buntings. She still lived with her mother in that same house along with her three kids, by three different men, and no husband.

"Hey, Ree-Ree!" Jewell shouted, clearly trying to get Aurelia's attention and the attention of the handsome man with her.

"Love your enemies. Love your enemies," Aurelia muttered, reminding herself of yet another life principle that she'd been taught by her father. Then after taking a deep breath, she turned around and faced the brash woman in the skimpy yellow outfit.

"Hello, Jewell," Aurelia said in a polite tone.

"Who be yur gorgeous friend dere?" Jewell inquired, posing provocatively by her own car as Baron's eyes took in her voluptuous bronze frame from top to bottom in the yellow-feathered outfit. Disappointment soon rolled across her face when he simply nodded in greeting and remained unaffected by what he'd seen.

"This is Dr. Baron Weaver, my fiancé." Aurelia put a possessive arm about his waist.

Jewell's eyes expanded in their sockets. "Y…yur gettin' married?"

"Yes," Aurelia replied.

"Wh…when?" Jewell sputtered out. "Surely I'm invited to de wedding?"

"Soon and it's a family only affair. Now have fun at the

festival tonight, girl," Aurelia concluded super-sweetly before turning the whole of her attention back to a quiet Baron. "Now what were we talking about, baby?"

Baron chuckled. "Smooth. Real smooth," he said as the jealous woman in yellow got in her car and sped away.

Aurelia laughed. "Call me Miss Parkay," she replied, sprouting the name of her favorite brand of butter.

"I'd rather call you Mrs. Weaver." Baron pulled her fully into his arms. "So what's the deal with you and Jewell?"

"In a nutshell, because I always wanted a sister, I decided to befriend the closest female neighbor in my age group and make her my pretend-sister. Big Bird over there decided to be my pretend-friend instead, primarily because she was unwilling to deal with her not-so-secret jealousies of me."

"Big bird?" Baron laughed at her wit.

"Yes. At least that's what she looks like to me tonight." Aurelia chuckled, then she became extremely serious. "Anyway, I finally realized what Jewell really was the day she came up to me after my father's funeral, smirked, and said, 'Looks like we both fatherless now'."

"That was just cruel." Baron frowned, starting to dislike Jewell himself.

"It was beyond cruel, which is why I smacked her around a bit that day. Dragged her across a few floors. And it felt so good, too." Aurelia grinned.

"I bet it did." He chuckled.

"Anyway, our mothers made us apologize to each other. We did, but I never tried to be Jewell's friend again after that, only a polite neighbor. However, since I'm not the kind of person to extend adult animosity to innocent children, I am especially nice to her kids and even let them play with Trent."

"Good for you." Baron looked downright proud of her for being the better woman. "Speaking of Trent, while he was brushing his waves tonight, I had a light bulb moment. It made me think about something Rhoda told the police about her attacker. Particularly about the man's hair."

"About the fact that it was wavy like Trent's?" Aurelia asked, familiar with the case details as well. Not only had her job at the crime lab given her familiarity with Rhoda's assault case, but her participation in AU's forensics club had done so as well.

Aurelia and her fellow students had taken it upon

themselves as a pet project to help solve the crime of the innocent/guilty twins. They also wanted to do their part to bring justice to one of their professors, despite Rhoda's continual moodiness and drooping approval ratings around campus.

"No, about the fact that the man's hair was not naturally wavy like Trent's or his brother's." Baron looked almost gleeful now. "If you recall, the assailant mentioned to Rhoda that he'd been to a salon earlier that day to get a permanent wave in his hair because he was too lazy and impatient to build his waves naturally like his twin."

"Which means the collected hair samples we have on file from each brother will reveal which of them is the guilty party due to the ammonium thioglycolate within the strands," Aurelia deduced, starting to feel gleeful herself.

"Exactly." Baron grinned. "I predict that the perm salt in those hair strands will lead the police right to Rhoda's attacker," he said, referring to the layman's term for ammonium thioglycolate. "I'm calling my hunch in to Liam when I get back to the hotel."

"Nuff respect, Baron. You're brilliant, mon! Just brilliant!" Aurelia exclaimed, excitedly jumping up and down in his arms.

At the first bounce, Baron moaned and squeezed her close to prevent another. "I can't handle you bouncing against me like that," he whispered in her right ear. "Either you send me away right now or I'm going to kidnap you, take you back to my hotel room, and—"

"Consider yourself sent," Aurelia interrupted, smoothly withdrawing from his tight embrace. Then after giving him a brief smack on the lips, she waved goodnight, and quickly headed back to the house.

"Come on Friday." Baron licked his lips as he got into the red jeep.

CHAPTER TWENTY-FOUR

On Thursday night, Aurelia played with Trent for a while, read him a bedtime story, and then put him to bed. When she turned out the light and walked out of his blue painted room, it suddenly dawned on her that this was actually her last night living and sleeping at her family home. As a married woman, she would be expected to live and sleep where her husband was.

Although Aurelia wanted to be where Baron was, a part of her was going to miss staying with her family. She was particularly going to miss putting Trent to bed at night. She had hoped to do more of that after she graduated and returned home to work in the Virgin Islands.

Now Baron was going to want her to stay in California with him after graduation. That's where his very expensive home and high-paying job were. That's where a very lucrative future career was waiting for Aurelia. All she had to do was accept it.

Right before Aurelia left for the V.I., Liam outright stated that if she kept doing well at the crime lab, she could turn her part-time gig there into a full-time career after graduation. It was a very profitable career given all the experience she had acquired in the short time she'd been there. Which meant she'd have even less reasons to return home on a permanent basis. Which also meant that she'd miss out on even more of Trent's childhood.

Grieved deep in her heart about even the thought of Trent growing up without her presence, Aurelia forfeited going to the living room where a sofa bed awaited her. Instead she made her way to her mother's room. She needed another one of their heart-to-heart talks and some timely advice.

"Mama, do you think I should tell Baron the truth about Trent before we get married?" Aurelia asked after closing the door to Emile's room.

That truth: Aurelia's brother was actually her son!

At the age of sixteen, Aurelia lost her father due to complications stemming from his improperly managed diabetes. Overwhelmed with grief, she found comfort in the arms of Marshall Pierre Jean-Baptiste, the nineteen-year-old nephew of her mother's wealthy St. John employer.

Marshall had been secretly in love with Aurelia for years. He never approached her because of their age differences, social class differences, and his general lack of self-esteem due to his weight issues. Had it not been for Aurelia making the first move by kissing him after he finished tutoring her in French one day, Marshall might have secretly pined for her for the rest of his life. He definitely wouldn't have taken that kiss and ran with it all the way to his bedroom.

When Aurelia later told Marshall that she was pregnant, he was overjoyed. He immediately saw the pregnancy as a sign that they were meant to be together forever. A marriage proposal soon followed.

Since Marshall had lost both of his parents at an early age and since Aurelia had lost her father a month prior, he asked his uncle and her mother for their blessings of the union. Only one of them gave it.

Marshall's uncle outright refused to bless the union. In fact, Oliver Jean-Baptiste flew into a rage about those pending nuptials. He called his nephew stupid and careless. He had more degrading names for Aurelia.

After having it out with Marshall, Oliver paid a visit to Aurelia at her St. Croix home. During that visit, which took place while her mother was at work, Oliver accused her of being a gold-digger, who had used sex to ingratiate herself into the pockets of his rich nephew. He even tried to pay her off.

When Aurelia declared her love for Marshall and refused the money offered her, Oliver balked at her claims. Then to add insult to injury, the man actually tried to sexually assault her at gunpoint. Had it not been for a neighbor's teenage son persistently knocking on the door to inquire about buying one of her father's five lawn mowers, things would have gotten even uglier in the Bunting house that day.

Unwilling to marry into a family that contained the likes of Oliver, Aurelia decided to call the wedding off. The threat that the older man gave her before he left that day, which hinted at his ties to organized crime, gave her even more incentive to break the engagement and to also maintain her silence about his visit.

Unfortunately, Marshall refused to accept Aurelia's abrupt change of heart or her excuse about not wanting to get married without his uncle's blessing. Determined to make her his wife, the young man insisted that he would do whatever it took to make Oliver accept their union. That he would make sure their child lacked nothing before and after it was born. That he would continue to woo her until his dying day.

That dying day came a week later.

Marshall drowned at sea on one of his uncle's boats, causing many to wonder if the Jean-Baptiste family was cursed. Especially since his parents had also died at sea.

Needless to say, Aurelia was crushed to hear the news about Marshall. She'd lost two very dear men in such a short span of time and thus couldn't be anything but devastated. Plus, she was pregnant and had yet to finish high school.

Aurelia was further devastated when Marshall's uncle paid her yet another visit. This time her mother was at home. During that meeting, Oliver revealed even more of his wickedness and made Aurelia wonder if Marshall's death truly was accidental. If even his parents' death was accidental.

With his big girth taking up almost half the sofa he sat on, Oliver outright demanded that Aurelia terminate the pregnancy. He claimed that he didn't want such an unfortunate situation to malign his nephew's memory or the Jean-Baptiste's esteemed reputation.

Aurelia countered by insinuating that Oliver likely didn't want another heir to the Jean-Baptiste fortune. Marshall had told her all about how the totality of his parents' assets would belong to him on his twenty- first birthday, officially ending his uncle's custodial tenure. About how one day those assets would belong to their child.

Oliver looked like he was either going to have a stroke at Aurelia's words or else pull out his gun and kill her and the baby on the spot. Instead he quickly composed himself, told her that she was going to get that abortion or else suffer dire consequences, and then gave her a large sum of money to take care of the situation. Those funds were also a one-time payoff for Aurelia's continual silence.

As for Emile, Oliver fired her during that visit. That was all fine and good since she no longer wanted to work for the evil man anyway.

Terrified of the man for sure now, Aurelia took the money and promised to abort the child. But she couldn't. She couldn't kill the only part of Marshall she had left.

Aurelia found her mother equally supportive of her decision to keep the baby, despite Oliver's threats. After putting their heads together, the two women decided to relocate to Florida and rent their V.I. house out.

Stateside, Aurelia laid low and awaited Trent's birth, not even leaving the house to check the mailbox. That act was necessary in order for Emile to claim the child as her own. Emile also deliberately gained weight and wore maternity clothes to appear pregnant to the outside world.

In preparation for the baby's delivery, they hired a midwife to deliver the baby at home. A midwife who agreed to certify that Emile was the birthmother and not Aurelia…for the right price, of course.

That plan might have worked perfectly if Aurelia hadn't changed her mind at the last minute. All it took was one look into Trent's amber eyes, which were exactly like Marshall's, and she knew that she could never legally disown him. Not even at the risk of her own life. Besides, since they had no intentions of ever returning to the Virgin Islands anyway, she figured it wouldn't matter as much.

However, as a special precaution, Aurelia left the father's name blank on the birth certificate. She also named Trent after her own father, but left the junior part off since he was not actually her father's son.

Six weeks after Trent was born, Aurelia went to get a long overdue checkup. She'd skipped prenatal care altogether, relying on the prayers of her mother to avoid exposure. To throw the doctors off at the clinic, she lied about having a recent abortion to explain the obvious signs of childbirth that had been left in and outside of her body. Either the doctors didn't care enough to investigate or they were just lazy, because they simply took Aurelia at her word about the faux abortion.

After getting a clean bill of health, Aurelia enrolled in a local night school. She finished her high school diploma in a matter of three short months. She nursed and took care of

Trent during the day while her mother worked freelance housekeeping jobs. They saved every penny they could and lived very modestly, banishing pride as they subsisted off of Ramen noodles, hot dogs, and day old bread.

Although the money Oliver gave them was long gone within two years' time, neither of them ever thought of asking him for another dime, not even this last time when Trent needed an operation. Quite frankly, they were still scared of the wicked man, downright terrified of what he might do to them if he ever found out the truth about Trent.

Had Oliver not left the V.I. completely and moved to France soon after Marshall's death to pursue business interests overseas, and had Gladys not reported how bad their renters had trashed the house, Aurelia and Emile would have stayed in Florida. Yet it didn't make sense to continue to pay rent stateside while rowdy tenants destroyed the only thing they owned. The fact that those same tenants were often delinquent with their rent payments was another deciding factor.

And so Aurelia and her mother returned home. With Trent, yes. But also with a well-crafted lie – Trent was to be the son of Emile and Trenton. Not even Gladys and Samuel questioned them about it...at least not for very long. It helped that Trent bore a lot of Bunting features, despite his unique eyes.

Aurelia and Emile also crafted a long-term plan of prosperity upon their return to St. Croix. That plan consisted of Emile taking care of Trent while Aurelia went off to college, which is what Mr. Bunting always wanted for their daughter. Then after she graduated, she would return home and use her degree to help prosper the family.

That plan successfully stayed on track until...until Aurelia fell in love with Baron.

* * *

"I don't tink you should tell Baron 'bout Trent 'til after yur married. Why put yet anotha roadblock in yur way?" Emile pushed aside her latest weaving project to make room for her daughter on the full-sized bed. "Are you tryna sabotage yur own happiness, Ree-Ree? Yet anotha chance at instant financial stability?"

"No, Mama, I'm not trying to sabotage my happiness at all," Aurelia replied, settling down beside her mother on the peach-colored comforter. "I just feel like I'm defrauding

Baron by continuing to withhold the truth about Trent. Especially after he came all this way to ask me to marry him. I keep thinking about how if I was in his shoes, I'd want to know if my future spouse had a secret child somewhere before we got married. That's why I have to tell Baron the truth." She said nothing about telling Trent the truth since they still both agreed that he should be told when he was old enough to handle it.

"I understand," Emile said, even though she still wished her daughter would wait until after the I-do's. "Answer me dis though. How come you never felt de need to share de truth 'bout Trent with Cain? And you were wid em ah whole year."

"I never truly loved Cain," Aurelia admitted with all sincerity. "I thought I did, but I realized later on that I was mainly there for the financial benefits of the relationship. To be honest, I was more hurt about Roxy betraying me than I was about Cain doing so. I guess that's because a sense of sisterhood still meant more to me than a man back then. It doesn't now though. Now I'd rather have a good man over a lousy sister-friend any day."

"Well, I kin seh one ting for you. You sho' know how to pick 'em. Every man you eva been in love wid or thought you were in love wid was rich. Mind telling me yur secret now dat I'm finally ready to lay aside meh widowhood?" Emile chuckled, having married just for love before.

Emile's sister Gladys had also married just for love. In fact, they married two brothers. Both Bunting men were poor when they met them.

One died in poverty. The other was still in it and having health problems to boot.

Fortunately, Samuel kept his diabetes better maintained than his older brother had done. It certainly had not affected his ability to produce more children like it had Trenton, who had suffered from severe erectile dysfunction for years.

"It's all about associations, Mama," Aurelia shared, ready to move on to another subject now that her mind was made up about Baron. "At least that's what Marshall taught me long ago. He said that the reason his parents grew so rich so fast was due to the people they associated with. That as they were building up their scuba diving and boating empire, they simply hung around people with money. As a result of what Marshall taught me, I learned to place myself in the presence of wealthy people so that I could glean even more from them. I wanted to learn how they got to the place of prosperity they were in. How to stay there once I got to my own place of prosperity. Hanging around such places naturally caused me to meet wealthy men. Men who found me attractive and wanted to date me."

Emile frowned with disapproval. "Okay, I know we talked 'bout how important it was to find ah wealthy man, but I neva told you to slide into gold-digger shoes, Ree-Ree."

"I haven't, Mama," Aurelia reassured her. "All a gold-digger thinks about is money when she meets a man. Looks, age, and background seldom matter. A gold-digger definitely doesn't care about a man's character or even if he got his money the wrong way. I care about all those things and so much more. Especially after my relationship with Cain."

"I guess I kin tek comfort in dat." Emile sighed in relief. "By de way, how did you and Baron meet?" she asked, still unaware of her daughter's career as an exotic dancer. All this time Emile thought Aurelia was being paid to choreograph dance videos, thereby putting those years of dance instruction to good use. At least that's what she'd been told.

Aurelia's face took on the look of shame as she suddenly realized how many secrets she had been keeping from everybody. When did all of this secrecy begin?

With Marshall.

After that kiss they shared, Aurelia and Marshall kept their relationship a secret for a whole month. She didn't tell her mother that she had become sexually active. If Marshall hadn't been a man and stepped up to the plate of responsibility after the pregnancy was discovered, she wouldn't have even shared whom she'd been sexually active with.

After Marshall died, those secrets had led to so many more. Each one had seemed so necessary to keep at the time. Now Aurelia was tired of them all.

Ready to purge to her mother, Aurelia told Emile all about her secret profession as an exotic dancer, including how she met Cain at an upscale strip club and Baron at a wealthy bachelor's party.

Emile was stunned to say the least. She had no idea that her daughter had used her dancing abilities to make money that way. Or that that money had been used to not only help pay for Aurelia's education, but to also help Emile and Trent out back home.

"Say something, Mama," Aurelia urged when her mother remained silent for two whole open-mouthed minutes after hearing her out.

"Wha I 'posed to seh? Dat I'm proud of what you did? 'Cause I'm not!" Emile fumed. "And in no way would yur daddy have approved of dat occupation no matter how hard tings got for dis family. In fact, he'd be furious to know dat all dat lawn care he traded for yur dance lessons was in vain. Dis is de kinda ting we would expect from ah gal like Jewell, not you!"

"I know." A glossy-eyed Aurelia hung her head. "I'm sorry for disappointing de both of you."

"You should be!" Emile snapped. At the sight of her daughter's tears, a level of guilt pricked her heart. How could she stay angry with someone who had sacrificed her own dignity for the greater good of others? Aurelia's sacrifice had been misguided, but still done from a good heart.

"I still love you, baby," Emile said soothingly, wrapping her arms around her silently weeping daughter. "And I'm way more proud of you den disappointed."

"Thanks, Mama." Aurelia sniffed back tears.

"Dis Baron must really love you, huh? Knowing what he does already," Emile said in a lighter tone.

"Yes, he does. Which is why I know I have to tell him the truth about Trent. Tonight." Aurelia blinked away her tears as she sprung to her feet. "I just hope he loves me enough to overlook yet another offense."

"Maybe he won't see eh as ah bad ting at all. Maybe he'll see eh as anotha chance to give you even more unconditional love." Emile hoped for the best as well. "And, Ree-Ree?"

"Yes, Mama?" Aurelia paused at the door.

"If dis man do forgive you dis other ting, you betta rock dat honeymoon on Friday."

"Yes, Mama." Aurelia chuckled and then headed for the bathroom to shower. It was time to get real spiffy. She knew exactly which dress to wear, too.

If showing some leg can help me get the man. Then maybe showing some leg can help me keep the man, Aurelia reasoned desperately, determined to give herself every possible advantage tonight.

CHAPTER TWENTY-FIVE

Fresh from a shower, Baron dried off and climbed into bed with nothing on the way he usually slept at night. Using the black remote from the glass topped nightstand nearby, he prepared to spend his last night as a single man alone watching a boxing match on television.

Before his shower, Baron placed a call to his brother Count to let him know that the wedding was still on for tomorrow. This was the same brother that he'd used as a sounding board about Aurelia for months now.

Count had been just as encouraging as ever tonight. He knew how much Baron loved Aurelia. How long he'd waited to have her again. Count also knew how their other brothers, namely Earl and Marquess, had almost blown things for Baron and his ladylove. That's why he advised his baby brother to wait until the last minute to tell their parents.

Baron heeded that wise advice. Like Count, he knew that his mother would go shouting to the world about his nuptials once she found out. When he finally called her an hour ago, that's exactly what Ana Maria proposed to do.

So excited about Baron being in love again and especially to the point of actually getting married, Ana Maria told him to expect a big congratulations party in Bel Air when he and Aurelia returned to the states. After they had settled back into their work and school schedules first, of course.

Nicolas, his father, enthusiastically seconded that motion. Like Ana Maria, he thought Baron would remain a bachelor for the rest of his life after that Megan situation. To hear their baby boy genuinely happy about plunging headfirst into matrimony again was a clear sign that his heart had truly healed.

Baron was definitely that – healed.

After that call with his parents, there was no need to call the rest of his family with the news of his pending nuptials. Ana Maria would do that, the same way she'd helped to spread the word about Aurelia's perfume.

To keep any naysayers out of his ears, namely Earl and Marquess, Baron turned his cell phone off for the remainder of the night. No one and nothing would change his mind about marrying Aurelia. She was going to be his wife and that was that.

Aurelia.

Baron smiled just thinking about her now. His body stirred in anticipation of making love to her again. The boxing match on TV soon became a forgotten entity.

I wish she was here right now. Oh the things I would do to that woman, Baron thought, moaning aloud. Just as his mind began to go wild with sensual possibilities, there was a knock on his hotel room door.

Leaving his comfortable bed, Baron put on a robe and went to answer the door. When he opened it a few seconds later, saw Aurelia in a short white dress with a plunging neckline that reached almost down to her navel, all he could say was…

"Wow!"

"Baron, I came to—" Aurelia never got to finish her statement.

At the sight of her in that dress, Baron yanked her into the room, slammed the door, and ravished her mouth right up against the wall.

* * *

Aurelia instantly melted into Baron's kiss, momentarily forgetting what she'd come here for tonight. All she could think about right now was how good it felt kissing him without limitations. Without the fear of someone walking in on them at any moment. Without having to remain respectful of others when all she wanted to do was get wet and wild with her man.

Wild was the key word tonight.

Their kisses were untamed and feral, producing loud sucking sounds that drowned out the television.

Their hands were wildly roaming each other's frames, kneading and squeezing everywhere they touched down.

It suddenly became a nudist colony up in there. No

clothes allowed! Fortunately for them, there was very little to take off.

"I was just thinking about how much I needed you, baby," Baron said in between kisses as his hands undid the crisscrossed straps in the back of her dress. "About how much I wanted to make love to you tonight." He peeled that tight dress off her frame like a banana and then allowed it to drop to the floor at her feet. "About all the things I would do to you if you were actually here."

"Things like what?" Aurelia panted out, stepping out of her fallen dress and then kicking it aside where his white hotel robe was. Her black thong had been the first thing to go with those quick hands of his.

"Things like this." Baron tucked his right hand under her left knee to lift her leg before smoothly creating a pivotal first for them.

Their eyes met as they moaned in unison from the delicious sensations attacking their bodies. Everything instantly slowed all the way down as they both realized the significance of this moment.

This was Baron and Aurelia's first time without any physical barriers between them. The first time he had ever taken her raw. It was sublime.

"I love you," they said simultaneously.

Smiling at their unity on even that front, Baron leaned in to kiss Aurelia again. His lips moved just as slowly as his hips.

Though standing on just one leg now, Aurelia responded in kind with her lips and her hips. There was no fear of losing her balance. What support the sturdy wall behind her didn't provide, the gorgeous man in front of her did.

"I have no idea what brought you here tonight, but I am so glad you came," Baron whispered against her mouth. Then he licked a trail down to the hollow of her neck.

The question, 'What brought you here?' suddenly echoed in Aurelia's soul, causing her to instantly remember her purpose for being here.

"I came here to talk." Aurelia stilled her hips completely before moving her leg from its resting place on his right forearm.

"We'll talk about whatever you want, beautiful." Baron smoothly put her leg back in place. "...after we finish what we started here." He slammed into her on the word 'after'.

Aurelia squealed with delight, sucked air through her teeth, and moaned at that aggression. "But it's important, Baron," she persisted, removing her leg again.

"This is important, too." He put her leg back in place yet again. "Besides, until I release some of this pent-up passion, I won't be able to concentrate on a thing you're saying anyway. Can't you feel how much I need this?" He slammed into her again on the word 'feel'.

She squealed and moaned again. "I—"

"Let me have this, baby. Let me have you," Baron interrupted, continuing to use his mouth and hips to emphasize certain words.

"O…kay," Aurelia finally consented in a husky whisper. Then she did what she wanted to do all along – get wet and wild with him until they both screamed with ecstasy.

* * *

After they were both sated and resting on the bed, Aurelia finally had a chance to tell Baron the secret about Trent. She told him everything, leaving nothing out.

Baron listened quietly as he heard all about Aurelia's first love, Marshall's suspicious scuba-diving death, and the man's wicked uncle. How Oliver was not only the one to sexually assault her, but was also the reason there was so much secrecy surrounding Trent and why there continued to be a need for secrecy on that issue.

"To this day, none of my relatives, outside of my mother, of course, ever knew that I was romantically involved with Marshall or had ever been pregnant," Aurelia continued from her comfortable place in the crook of Baron's left arm. "My belly was flat when we moved to Florida. When we returned to the islands, I made sure my belly was still flat, although I clearly had more curves than before. Thus everybody naturally assumed that my mother had conceived before my father passed since he died only a short time before Marshall and I became lovers."

"So that's why it was so important that Trent and I get along. That's also probably why you got all teary-eyed when he innocently called you mami the other day," Baron said, finally speaking after his long silence.

"Yes." Aurelia got teary-eyed all over again. "Dat's also why I came here tonight. I couldn't marry you without telling you de truth 'bout meh son." She grew quiet herself as the shock of finally claiming Trent as her son took some adjusting in her ears.

"I'm glad you told me." Baron exited the bed. "But I have to admit, it's a lot to ask any man to go from being a potential brother-in-law to a potential stepfather. One carries way more responsibility than the other."

At those words, at the clear physical distance he was putting between them now, Aurelia's eyes welled up with even more tears. Was Baron rejecting this new role she had imposed upon him? Should she have kept her mouth closed about Trent until after the I-do's?

"Y…you're absolutely right, Baron. Stepfatherhood is a lot to ask any man to take on," Aurelia got up from the disheveled bed. She could take a hint. Clearly the wedding was off. It was time to go home and live in the real world again.

"Thanks for de wonderful memories. It was fun while it lasted," Aurelia concluded, wiping tears from her cheeks as she bent to pick up her dress from the floor. She had no idea where her underwear was. Didn't really care at the moment.

"Wonderful memories? Fun while it lasted?" Baron repeated, pausing in his tracks near the table and two chairs of the sitting area. "What are you talking about, woman?" He frowned. "And why are you crying?"

Standing upright now, Aurelia cocked her head to the side and just gawked at him for a few silent seconds. Why did he look just as confused as her? Could she have misunderstood Baron yet again?

Aurelia was more than ready to find out. In fact, the fate of her future happiness depended upon it. "Didn't you just break up with me because of the whole stepfather thing?" She blinked her eyes free to look at him more clearly.

Baron's eyes bucked this time. "Absolutely not!" He forgot about the bottled water he wanted from the stainless steel champagne bucket on the table and stalked towards what he wanted a thousand times more.

"You d…didn't?" Those words sputtered from Aurelia's trembling lips even as fresh tears entered the windows of her eyes. The dress in her shaky hands slipped back to the floor unnoticed.

"No," he said firmly. "All I did was state the obvious - stepfatherhood is a lot to ask any man to sign up for. However, I'm not just any man as you should very well know by now. I don't shrink from challenges or responsibilities.

Some would even say that I run towards them, regardless of the risk to myself. Didn't my intervention in Rhoda's assault teach you anything about my character? And I don't even like her."

Baron cupped Aurelia's face tenderly in his large hands. "But I love you, baby. And because of that love, I'll gladly be Trent's big brother figure until you decide that it's time for me to be his stepfather figure. Neither of you will have to fear the likes of Oliver Jean-Baptiste ever again, even after the truth finally comes out to the world," he reassured her.

Wonder danced in Aurelia's glossy eyes. She swallowed hard before speaking. "You really do love me, don't you?" Happy tears rolled down her cheeks now.

"Yes, I do." Baron smiled and gently wiped her tears away with his long fingers. "So will you still be my wife tomorrow?"

"Oh, yes!" Aurelia grinned. "Now let me show you how much I love you, too." She led him by the hand over to a nearby chair. It was time for a new round of lovemaking to begin.

Aurelia wasted no time straddling Baron once he sat down. Not chest to chest, mind you. But rather back to chest to switch things up a bit from the norm.

Poised to make them one again, Aurelia proceeded to move her hips counterclockwise...

Down.

Down.

Down.

Then they went clockwise...

Up.

Up.

Up.

The constant repetition of that unique rhythm had Baron's eyes rolling in the back of his head, his teeth biting down hard on his bottom lip, and his tongue wagging out of his mouth. He looked about ready to lose his mind.

He really lost it when Aurelia started a new rhythm. This one was even better than the last. With short twists of her hips to each side followed by hard thrusts downward, she popped, locked, and dropped it upon his lap...over and over again. Those dancing girls in that Huey rap video had nothing on Aurelia.

Oh, the howls. The screams...coming from the both of

them.

Ready to give back in a big way, Baron held Aurelia's hips still against him, immediately placing her on the receiving end. Then with lightning fast hips, he…

Gave.

Gave.

Gave.

With squeals of delight, she…

Received.

Received.

Received.

When Baron relaxed his hold on Aurelia, they both became as untamed as some of the animals he studied on his nature hikes. Sweat poured from their slick bodies. Unbridled ecstasy couldn't help but unfold in the presence of these fervent lovers.

Aurelia went over the edge first with another loud scream. As Baron followed closely behind her, he actually started to moo like a cow.

Moo!

Blame it on Aurelia and the way she kept using her clenching canal to milk him for all she was worth.

When it was over and they could breathe normally again, Baron whispered that they were getting married in the morning instead of in the evening as planned.

"Why the sudden change?" Aurelia asked as she continued to lounge in his lap sideways this time, snuggling against his glistening hairy chest. "I'm not protesting the change. I'm just curious as to why it exists," she clarified, wanting there to be no further misunderstandings between them.

"After what you just did to me, I need to take you off the market quicker." Baron blew out a satisfied breath. "Because there's no way I'm going to risk losing you to some other guy so he can get that kind of royal treatment. No way. No how."

Aurelia chuckled. "There's no other man on this earth that I want more than you."

"That's certainly good to know. Even so, I'm still marrying you come daylight," Baron said decisively. "Now let's get you into a nice hot soothing bath. I want everything to be in prime working order again for our real honeymoon."

* * *

Thirty minutes later, Baron and Aurelia lounged chest to

back in the large whirlpool bathtub. Before entering the tub, they'd taken a quick shower where he gently washed her body and she returned the favor. Now they were just relaxing among soothing botanical bubbles.

"Do you regret putting your name on Trent's birth certificate, seeing as how it hinders him from attending regular school on the island?" Baron stroked her flat belly as he held her close in the tub.

"Yes. Especially since he is such a social being," Aurelia replied. "But if I send him to regular school, it's going to lead to unwanted questions about the other half of his paternity. I'm not ready for that yet. I don't think Trent is either."

"If we bring him to California with us, he can just enroll in regular school there. I seriously doubt if anyone will care about the other half of his paternity there."

Aurelia turned excited eyes towards Baron. Suddenly she frowned with disappointment. "That would be a great idea if I wasn't in school all day, at work during the night hours and on weekends. Not to forget all the studying I have to do to keep my GPA up for my scholarships and the extra time I now have to give to my budding perfume business. A business that I can't thank you enough for supporting, by the way." She paused to plant a brief kiss of gratitude upon his lips.

"You're welcome, baby."

Aurelia gave him a brief smile before turning serious again. "Anyway, with a hectic schedule like mine, when would I ever have any quality time to spend with Trent? I'm still trying to figure out how I'm going to spend enough quality time with you once we get back to California."

"You could quit your job at the mall, which would instantly free up your evening hours," Baron suggested. "As my wife, it's not like you will need that extra income anyway."

"True, but there's still the issue of whether or not Trent is ready to know the truth. Which is what we'll definitely have to tell him if we abruptly take him back with us. In case you haven't noticed, Trent's really attached to Mama. What if he resents me for uprooting him from the only mother and the only home he's ever known? I don't tink I could handle meh son hating me." Her eyes grew glossy and her accent thickened just thinking about that possibility.

Realizing how upset Aurelia was becoming, Baron

squeezed her closer and offered a less emotionally taxing suggestion. "How about we put this particular conversation on hold for now. At least until after you graduate. Then you'll have more time for me, Trent, and more time to figure out how to deal with the adjustments everyone will have to make once the truth is finally out."

Aurelia instantly relaxed and faced completely forward again. "I like that idea much better, although I think I'm still going to incorporate that 'quitting-my-job-at-the-mall' thing. I would love to have my evenings free even before Trent comes to live with us."

"Free to do what?" Baron leaned in to lick the left side of her neck.

She moaned. "Free to do you." Aurelia turned her head to the left and captured his tongue between her lips, soon pulling it deep into her mouth for a hard suckle.

Baron moaned at that act of aggression. His hands separated, leaving her belly to move up and down in exploration. He squeezed in both places of settlement. So much for his promise not to make love to her again tonight.

Aurelia moaned again, this time at his intimate touch. "Yes," she purred out upon releasing his instrument of speech to utilize her own.

"Don't tempt me, woman. I said I wasn't going to have you again tonight. That I was going to let you rest up for the honeymoon. I mean to keep that vow," Baron reminded them both as he moved his hands back to a neutral place on her body – her belly.

Aurelia chuckled. "I'll believe that when I see it, horny toad." She faced forward again, causing ripples in the warm water.

He laughed. "Do that," he challenged and then changed the conversation altogether for both their sakes. "I'm curious about Marshall's last name. Jean-Baptiste is a French name, right? If so, does that mean that Trent's father was French, too? It would certainly explain the boy's wavy hair and fair skin, which is even lighter than your mother's."

"Jean-Baptiste is a French surname. Marshall was French and West Indian," Aurelia replied. "His uncle called him Frenchie. I called him Marshall because I liked it much better and because I just didn't want to have anything in common with evil Oliver. Sometimes I called Marshall 'Brainiac' because he was so smart. At nineteen, he already knew six languages."

"Wow! That's impressive. I only know three and a half languages myself. English and Spanish were necessities in my largely bilingual family. My third language is Italian, most of which my college roommate Gino taught me while we were in school. I only know a little Hebrew, which is why I call it my half language. I learned most of that for the bar mitzvah that my great-granddad insisted I have."

"Knowing three and a half languages is nothing to frown at either." Aurelia looped her fingers through his at her waist. "As for Marshall, I was more impressed with his brilliant mind than anything else. It was the thing that initially drew me to him. The main reason I fell in love with him in the first place. Such brilliance made me completely overlook the fact that Marshall was a bit on the chubby side," she shared, inadvertently revealing the depth of her character in those statements.

Baron smiled, glad that his future wife cared about more than just a man's wallet or his outward appearance.

"As for Trent's fair skin, most folks excuse that away because my mother and aunt are so light. But that wavy hair and those amber eyes of his still bring a lot of speculation even to this day," Aurelia continued. "Some people, namely Aunt Gladys and Uncle Sam, originally thought that my mother had an affair with Oliver after my father died because of those eyes. And also because they were among the few to know about Daddy's reproduction issues."

"Emile and Oliver would seem like a logical paternity match if you just considered Trent's complexion, eye color, and hair texture. Yet one look at the boy's nose, mouth, and bone structure and it's clear to see that he's a Bunting man all the way."

Aurelia chuckled. "Yes, Trent does look a lot like my father and uncle. The fact that he also has diabetes like them keeps a lot of the speculation down as well."

"Earlier you mentioned falling in love with Marshall's mind first. What are some of the things you love the most about your son?" Baron asked, enjoying their ability to talk about any subject.

"I love Trent's brilliant little mind, as well. In fact, I think he's going to be just as smart as Marshall was one day. But what I love most of all about our son, at least for right now, is the fact that he's such a lover of the outdoors."

"Why is that, baby?"

"Because it reminds me so much of my father. Daddy was a great outdoorsman. He made me one, too." Aurelia smiled. "I loved camping in the backyard with him on warm nights. I also love the fact that he taught me enough about engines to keep any car or lawnmower running." She chuckled. "Daddy had to make me take dance lessons when Mama complained that I was becoming too much of a tomboy. And she absolutely hated the fact that I was so resistant to cooking. I'm still only a so-so cook to this day just to remind you of what you're really getting into tomorrow."

Baron laughed. "It's a good thing that I'm practically a chef then," he replied, fully aware of her culinary deficiencies. He learned about those last Sunday when Aurelia burned the jerk chicken they were to have for lunch that day. An impatient cook, she had the fire turned up way too high. Out of his love for her, Baron had eaten every agonizing bite of that meal.

"You can cook that good?"

"I had to learn in order to have home-cooked meals that were not only tasty, but healthy. Plus, the fiancée that I had before you couldn't cook a lick and didn't even want to try," Baron replied, clearly referring to Megan since there had been no other fiancées. "By the way, I am sooooo grateful for those dance lessons your mother insisted upon."

"You would be." Aurelia rolled her eyes and chuckled.

Baron laughed again. "Anyway, I like that you and Trent enjoy the outdoors so much. I do, too. I can see us having so much fun camping together when he visits the states. By the way, before we leave, I want to set him and your mother up in another location while the house is being renovated. Because there's no way I could rest at night in our comfortable California home knowing that Trent and Emile were back here living far below the poverty level, even if it is on family owned land. I felt guilty enough coming back to this luxury hotel every night."

Aurelia's eyes grew glossy yet again on this emotionally charge night. "And that right there is yet another reason I love you so much." She turned sideways and draped her wet arms about his neck.

"Exactly what reason is that?" He smiled, encircling her waist a different way now.

"Your generosity. The guy in my last serious relationship could care less about my family's well-being. Cain thought I should be grateful that he was doing so much for me and so shouldn't expect him to do anything for my family." Aurelia frowned. "Although when I think about it, all he was really giving me was free room and board. Room and board that I actually worked off by playing his maid. Matter of fact, a cook was Cain's only in-house expense while I was there because I kept his house and his laundry clean. He even stopped taking his designer suits to the cleaners because I took care of them so much better."

Baron frowned now. "Cain should have been grateful he even had you. I know I am. Which is why I want to do everything in my power to make you and yours happy. I gave you my word on that, Aurelia, and I plan to keep it."

"Oh, Baron," Aurelia purred, before literally attacking his lips.

It took everything in Baron not to break his word after that heated kiss. Yet he remained strong even after they returned to the bed to cuddle until sleep claimed them.

CHAPTER TWENTY-SIX

Baron did right to marry Aurelia on Friday morning instead of that afternoon. Had he stuck with his original plans, they might not have gotten married at all that day. An unexpected storm threatened the area, causing all evening weddings and scheduled Crucian festivities to be canceled until further notice.

That winter storm also caused Aurelia's mother and brother to have to temporarily relocate due to flooding issues in their low-lying neighborhood. Usually they went to Gladys and Samuel's house to wait out the storm since they lived on a more elevated part of the island. But not tonight.

Tonight Emile and Trent were staying in one of the best hotels on the island per Baron's firm request. It just didn't sit right within his soul for him and Aurelia to be living in the lap of luxury while her closest relatives were residing in a crowded three-bedroom house with eight other people.

Unfortunately for the newlyweds, there were no available rooms at the hotel due to the surge of tourists that had flown in for the Christmas festival from all over the world. Thus Baron and Aurelia had to share their honeymoon suite with her family.

Fortunately, it was a two-bedroom suite. The master bedroom contained a king-sized bed, sitting area, and full bath. The second bedroom contained two queen-sized beds and a full bath, which is where Emile and Trent would sleep tonight.

After making sure their guests had eaten to their heart's delight and were comfortably watching television in the next room, Aurelia and Baron retired to the master suite. As soon as the door was closed and locked behind them, Baron became frisky. He pulled Aurelia into his arms, captured her lips in a fervent kiss, and roamed over her curves with his hands.

Coming up for air a few minutes later, Aurelia was amazed at how quickly Baron could distract her. She'd completely forgotten all about her family in the next room just that fast. "Let's tone it down a bit tonight," she said breathlessly, withdrawing from him to remove the brown satin robe that he bought for her earlier today. Underneath was a matching gown that accented her curves to perfection.

"I don't think I'm going to be able to do that," Baron replied, looking ravenously at her as he removed his robe as well. His robe belonged to the hotel. Underneath it was a pair of black satin pajamas, which had been purchased at the same time as his wife's brown honeymoon gear.

"We have to, Baron. My family is in the next room," Aurelia whispered, draping her robe over the back of a nearby chair before heading for the bed. "And you know how loud we get. I would be so embarrassed if they heard the wrong kind of squeaking coming from this bed tonight."

Amusement and amazement saturated Baron's eyes. He couldn't believe how shy and modest she was behaving right now, considering what she used to do for a living. Considering some of the things they'd done in front of a whole room full of people.

Had Aurelia been bolder then because most of those people had been strangers? People she never intended to see again? Was this sudden shyness because the people in close vicinity now were her family members? After all, she certainly hadn't seemed to mind his family being around that night in Cabo.

"First of all, outside of physical abuse situations, there is no wrong kind of squeaking from the bed of a married couple." Baron spoke just as discreetly low as she had. "Secondly, if you recall, practically all of my brothers were in the next room during our first time. They and everybody else in that room got a full earful of our rowdiness. Crystal got so worried about all the shouting and yelling that she sent Count and Dingo to check on you." He draped his robe over a different chair in the sitting area.

Aurelia gasped. Her eyes bucked. "I forgot dey were even in de next room dat night. Did Count and Dingo..." She paused to swallow. "...check on me?"

"Yes, with the extra key my brother had. But they didn't stay long," Baron assured her. He could tell she was getting upset by her change in accent and facial expressions. "According to Count, they quickly realized that we both were fine and closed the door again."

"So dey actually saw us, too?" Aurelia looked horrified now. "Dat's it. I'm not doing anyting tonight." She plopped down on the side of the bed with the heat of embarrassment flaming in her cheeks. It was one thing to dance half-naked in front of others, but to actually be caught in the act of sex was downright humiliating for her.

"Nothing at all?" Baron's eyes grew wide now.

"Zilch," Aurelia replied firmly, folding her arms across her chest. "Last night and dat quickie we had over breakfast dis morning will just have to hold us both 'til tomorrow."

Baron's lips went into a straight line. Cloaked in silence now, he looked down at his aroused body and then at the beautiful woman sitting on the bed. He quickly came to one conclusion – something had to happen in this room…tonight!

Somehow Baron had to get Aurelia's need for consummation to match his own. Suddenly he knew exactly how to do it, too.

"All right, Aurelia. We'll wait to consummate our marriage tomorrow." Baron walked towards the television to manually turn it on. Outside the rain continued to fall heavily to the ground, though all the thunder and lightning had ceased.

"Thanks for being so understanding, baby." Aurelia turned to pull the covers back on the bed.

"No problem, beautiful," Baron replied matter-of-factly as he removed his pajamas. "By the way, I was thinking about making an offer on the temporary place we selected today for Emile and Trent while the Bunting house is undergoing renovations and upgrades. That way, we'll have a permanent island home to reside in whenever we return to visit and won't have to censor our behavior like we're doing tonight," he continued, stripping down to his silk boxers and beyond.

"I'd like that." Aurelia smiled, turning to face him again. Suddenly she gasped as her eyes drank in his chiseled nudity, every hard inch of it. "Ooo…mmm." She moaned.

"What's wrong, baby?" Baron behaved as if his body

wasn't at full attention as he calmly walked across the room to the closet.

"N…nothing," Aurelia replied breathlessly. "D…don't you wear anything to bed at night?" She licked her lips at his muscular frame even as she spoke.

"Not usually, no." Baron slid the closet door open to place his used garments into the wicker hamper therein. "Wearing clothes to bed ended when I moved out of my parents' home."

"Don't you think you ought to tonight?" Aurelia greedily watched his biceps and triceps flex as he slid that heavy wooden door open and closed as if it was nothing. "You know, considering the fact that we're not really alone."

"I locked the bedroom door, so everything should be fine." On his way to bed, Baron turned off the nightstand lamp, allowing the TV to provide the only illumination in the room. Then he entered the bed from the left side. "Now if it's all right with you, I'd like to hold my wife until we nod off to sleep." He opened his arms in invitation.

Aurelia hesitated, torn about entering his embrace. Yes, she wanted to be close to all that fineness. But she was scared to be so close at the same time, especialy with desire blazing through her veins, making even her fingertips sizzle with heat.

Aurelia didn't trust herself not to forget about her mother and son again while in Baron's arms. After all, they were in the very next room…wide awake!

"Can I at least hold you?" Baron asked, breaking into her freeze frame moment.

"Sure." Aurelia finally entered his embrace. Another moan bubbled up from her throat when she came up against his hairy chest and all that hardness. She had to fight to keep her legs closed, lest literal flames start shooting out from her valley. If she'd worn any underwear tonight, they would have been burnt like toast by now.

"You all right, beautiful?" Baron acted like he didn't know what was wrong with her. As if he couldn't tell that she was just as turned on as him.

"Yes, I'm fine." Aurelia took in a deep breath and blew it out.

"Good, just relax. Sleep will come soon enough for the both of us. In the meantime, let's watch a bit of TV." He picked up the remote from the nightstand and casually flipped through the channels.

"Any idea when you might relax?" Aurelia referred to the part of his body that was most distracting right now. The man even had the covers tented. All of them, including the thick comforter.

Baron looked down at himself and chuckled. "Don't mind that, baby. My body's just protesting the way our honeymoon night is going, that's all. If you want, I can go to the bathroom and negotiate a peace agreement with it."

Despite the aching status of her own body, Aurelia chuckled at his colorful description of how he intended to handle his own pulsating ache. "Would you like for me to be in on those talks?" She felt bad about denying him sexually on their honeymoon night and wanted to do something to bring him some kind of relief.

"No," Baron said, though his body screamed for him to say 'yes'. "With you involved I might make too much noise. Wouldn't want to embarrass you in front of your family." He put down the remote and exited the bed. "I'll be right back." He chuckled and added, "Okay, maybe not right back, but eventually I'll return." Then he gave her a wink and headed for the bathroom.

Aurelia really felt bad now. "Wait, Baron!"

Stopping instantly in his tracks at her words, Baron grinned knowingly in the semi-dark room. "Yes, baby?" he prompted, smoothly wiping that grin off his face before turning around.

"This isn't right. I'm your wife. There's no reason for you to be talking to yourself when I'm around. Surely there has to be a way for us to enjoy our honeymoon and not disturb my family." Aurelia looked downright guilty now.

"There's been a way for us to do both, baby. I just needed for you to be all the way on board before I suggested it," Baron shared, allowing his grin to return.

"Wait a minute! I know you're not over there grinning." Aurelia quickly leaned over and flicked the lamp back on.

* * *

"You little Cheshire cat," Aurelia teased upon seeing Baron's grin in better light. "Why do I suddenly feel like I'm in your class again, Professor?" She couldn't help but smile herself now.

He chuckled. "Because you just learned another important lesson, that's why. This time about marriage." He headed towards the nightstand area.

"And that lesson is?" she prompted, no longer looking at his face. Something else had her attention now.

Is all that mine? Aurelia thought, watching Baron swing that baseball bat like a major leaguer as he strutted his sexy frame across the room. She couldn't wait for him to hit a homerun with her.

"That lesson involves us doing what we can to put each other's needs first." Baron picked up the remote from the nightstand.

"I get it. You put my need not to be embarrassed before your need to make love to me tonight," Aurelia said as he turned the TV to a music channel that played slow tunes from all over the Caribbean. Soon Alaine's Deeper played in the background. "I, in turn, put my need aside for yours when I realized just how important it was to you. Now we're both about to get what we need," she concluded, amazed by his ability to teach her more than she ever expected to learn on so many levels.

"Excellent. Brilliant as always," Baron replied, heaping praise upon her as he often did in the classroom. Fortunately, in this particular classroom he could give her so much more than accolades and high marks. "Come here, Mrs. Weaver. I haven't had the opportunity to enjoy a first dance with my wife yet." He extended a hand and a smile to her.

"Certainly, Mr. Weaver." Aurelia smiled in return and rose to her feet with his assistance.

As the newlyweds danced slowly together, moving sensually as one, they kissed just as slowly. With each new kiss, they fell deeper in love.

Aurelia's gown fell as well. Thanks to Baron's hands, that brown material fell all the way to the floor. When she stepped out of it, he kicked it aside, despite how much it had cost him.

With no barriers whatsoever between them now, Baron's lips began a slow descent. From Aurelia's mouth, he traveled past her chin, her neck, and her collarbone until finally settling at a ripe melon. His tongue swirled around the rigid peak he found there twice before his mouth opened wider and engulfed as much of that delicious fruit as it could. A hand tended to her other melon, making sure it was not neglected.

Aurelia moaned and arched towards him. Thankfully the

music had been turned up loud enough to muffle any lovemaking sounds, but not loud enough to disturb other guests, including Emile and Trent.

All regular dancing came to a halt. The dance of love had begun in earnest.

Supporting Aurelia's back with one hand while he sent the other to her valley, Baron once again demonstrated his sexual prowess, his ability to send her over the edge from foreplay alone. Moving to the other melon and feasting just as voraciously, his ministrations soon had her whole body trembling with release. Her knees grew too weak to stand as violent shudders wreaked her frame.

But why stand when one can lie down?

Quickly snatching fluffy pillows from the bed, Baron lowered Aurelia gently to the thick carpet, placing her head comfortably on one of the pillows. Just as Alaine's Sincerely In Love started to play in the background, he joined his wife in pure wedded bliss. Their corresponding moans mingled with the ravenous kiss they shared to seal that pivotal moment.

"I love you," Baron whispered seconds later, supporting his weight on his arms as he sunk even deeper into her clenching canal. What an amazing place for a husband to be when his wife was still in the throes of ecstasy.

"I love you, too," Aurelia whispered back, digging her heels into the carpet as she arched her hips for even more of him. She never wanted to come down from this mountaintop.

Withdrawing just enough, Baron drove home again, giving her more of what she wanted. More of what she needed.

Aurelia sucked air through her teeth and moaned softly. She rolled her hips in a slow counterclockwise motion, urging him on in his possession.

"Aye," Baron moaned out in Spanish, withdrew and drove home yet again. Harder and faster this time.

Aurelia shuddered again and clenched around him even stronger. Her eyes closed in ecstasy. Her tongue licked the circumference of her top lip before biting down on the bottom one.

Baron almost lost it then and there at her intense reaction to his loving. But it was too soon. He'd waited too long for this night to pop so fast. Biting down on his own bottom lip just to keep focus, he slowed the pace all the way down.

At the new tempo, Aurelia's eyes fluttered open. She smiled knowingly up at him. A mischievous gleam entered her eyes right before she pulled not one, but both legs up behind her head.

Baron's eyes bucked at all the access she'd just given him. A longtime fantasy that had been spurred from a Shakira video that he once saw leaped to the forefront of his mind.

Was Aurelia about to make that fantasy come true tonight? Baron's body grew even more rigid at just the possibility of that fantasy finally becoming a reality in his life. There was no way he was going to be able to hold on now.

"Take what you need of me, baby. Get it all," Aurelia urged in a whisper, prompting him not to resist the inevitable.

A primal grunt surged up from his throat as a fresh dose of adrenaline shot through his body. Shifting his position until he was on both knees and hovering slightly above her with strong arms on either side of her body, Baron did as his wife requested. He took what he needed of her. Fast, feral, and oh so fervently.

From the onset of all that passion, it was easier for Aurelia to keep her flexible legs in place than it was to keep her eyes open. Every few seconds they wanted to close in bliss from the delectable sensations alone that her husband's incredible lovemaking produced. Did the man operate in excellence in every area of his life?

Through sheer willpower Aurelia kept her eyes open. She refused to miss those deep plunges, rapid pistons, and all that drilling. It was intoxicating to watch such love and passion in action. She almost felt drunk with desire.

Unable to hold on for much longer, Baron stretched himself over the entire length of Aurelia's body again, lowered her legs and tucked them about his waist. Then driving deep one last time, he captured her lips and muffled his shout of ecstasy as he went soaring over the edge of reason.

Aurelia went right over the edge behind him, clinging to his glistening frame with her arms and legs as she did.

"I'm in this for life. I will never leave you. Nor will I ever cheat on you. You and you alone will be the only woman to have my heart and body until the day I die," Baron vowed impassionedly when he had enough breath to speak again.

"There will be no one else for me either," Aurelia replied, more than ready to spend the rest of her natural life with the man who had restored her faith in love. True love.

* * *

In another suite across town at a cheaper hotel, Murray Underwood, the private investigator who'd followed Aurelia from the states hung up the phone with a tired sigh. He'd just had the last of four intense conversations with his current clientele.

Client #1 was overjoyed about Aurelia's nuptials. Client #2 was relieved because as the wife of a wealthy man, Aurelia now posed no financial threat to him. Thus he could devote his remaining funds to his physical and financial recoveries.

Client #3 was sad and disappointed that Aurelia was off the dating market. Yet he saw her marriage as a clear sign for him to just step aside. Client #4 was piping hot mad about those nuptials. He even planned to physically stop the wedding, but was delayed in London due to the bad weather currently swirling in the Atlantic Ocean.

The end result was the same for Murray – loss of income. Only Client #1 felt the need to keep the P.I. on retainer for future updates about Aurelia's life, but still only on a quarterly basis. Client #4 wanted to pay him a one-time fee to investigate Baron's background now. Clients #2 & 3 released Murray from his assignment altogether.

How did the blue-eyed private investigator feel about this sudden drop in income?

Not good.

Murray still had a sickly wife to provide around the clock care for. He almost wanted to invent something new about Aurelia just to keep the defecting clients on board. Surely Dr. William Johansson, aka Client #3, and Oliver Jean-Baptiste, aka Client #2, could be persuaded to put him back on retainer somehow.

No, Murray couldn't do that. That would go against his number one P.I. principle – be honest with all clients.

The only alternative was to look up his illegitimate daughter and ask for help. She had money now. Lots of money. The fact that her mother was dead meant that Murray wouldn't have any resistance to revealing his daughter's true paternity. The fact that his wife could barely remember his name, much less her own, meant that she wouldn't be hurt by the knowledge that he'd cheated on her twenty-eight years and nine months ago. That he actually had a child in this world. A living child!

But would Murray's long lost daughter be grateful for his sudden appearance in her life? Especially since it was primarily motivated by his need for money. Or would she reject him for taking so long to look her up, spew venom because of his wrong motives, and resent him for snatching her from under the protective umbrella of her high society Bel Air family?

"Hmmm…" Murray uttered aloud. "This is going to require a lot more thinking than I expected." He reached for the phone again. It was time to check on his beloved wife.

CHAPTER TWENTY-SEVEN

Around 5:30am the next morning, Baron awakened to the most unexpected sounds. Familiar sounds, yet unexpected nevertheless since they were coming from a very unlikely source - Aurelia, who'd gotten up before him today.

Click, click, click. Snort.

Cough, cough. Spit.

That interesting sequence of sounds used to be a normal part of Baron's morning routine. For years it had been his way of trying to scratch the back of his irritated throat with his tongue and then clear his sinuses.

Knowing exactly what Aurelia was doing and what was causing her irritation, Baron got out of bed and located the smallest of his suitcases from the closet. Pulling out a pill bottle marked 'C', he walked over to the closed bathroom door and knocked.

The human noises inside the bathroom instantly stopped. All Baron could hear now was water running in the tub. Even that stopped within seconds of his knocks.

Aurelia's eyes widened in horror at the sound of her husband's voice. Had she awakened him with her highly unattractive morning sounds?

"Is that you, Baron?" she asked gingerly, though she knew it couldn't be anyone else. Their bedroom door was still locked when she entered the bathroom.

"Yes. Open up," he replied, his voice still husky from sleep.

"No, I'm not decent yet. My face isn't washed and my teeth are not brushed," Aurelia protested, even more horrified that he would want to see her this way. She hadn't even let Cain see her before the completion of her morning routine.

Baron smiled. Women. He rolled his eyes and shook his head.

"My face isn't washed either and I'm pretty sure I have dragon breath right about now." He chuckled. "However, I also have a solution to your sinus issues. But you have to open the door to get it."

"Oh." Even so, Aurelia didn't unlock the door and open it until after hasting to splash a bit of water on her face and after taking a swig of mouthwash.

"Baby, all of that really wasn't necessary." Baron casually leaning up against the wall as she inched the door open a full minute later.

"Yes, it was," she countered with a grin, readjusting the black plastic shower cap on her head. "Now where is this miracle solution?" Aurelia opened the door wider, revealing a body that was wrapped in a white towel and waiting to get in the soothing hot bath behind her. She'd been given quite a workout last night and well into this morning. Thus her body was in serious need of some pampering.

"It's right here." Baron handed the pill bottle to her.

"Vitamin C?" Aurelia quickly read the label on the bottle she received.

"Yes. I used to have bad sinus problems as a child. Back then my morning routine was much like yours, which used to drive my teenage brother Duke up the wall. He liked to study before going off to school each day, but all my coughing, snorting, and spitting distracted him. Tired of my annoying habit, Duke put in extensive hours of study on the subject. After finding a connection between sinus problems and a Vitamin C deficiency, he begged our mother to increase my intake of that particular vitamin. To further persuade Mama, Duke even got a signed statement from several doctors stating that they agreed with his research findings." Baron chuckled at that memory. "Dad said that that's when he knew that Duke was going to be a prime candidate for medical school. He immediately arranged visits to Ivy League schools. By the time Duke graduated from high school, he had those same Ivy Leaguers begging him to come through their doors and stay awhile."

Aurelia laughed. "Good move by your father."

"I agree. Anyway, long story short, my immune system greatly improved and my sinus problems gradually disappeared after my mother increased my Vitamin C intake. I've been following the same regiment ever since, though my doses go up and down as needed."

"Is this prescribed C? Although I believe in what you say, I'm a little leery about taking other people's medication," she stated, wisely exercising caution.

"As you should be," Baron commended with a smile of approval. "No, that right there is an over the counter product just like your common cold medicine. Except I get my supply from a local health food store that specializes in buying products from companies that use purer ingredients and sterilized production processes."

"In that case, how much should I take, Dr. Weaver?" Aurelia finally twisted the cap off the bottle.

"I usually take a 500mg capsule every morning and then again two hours before bedtime with a full glass of water. I suggest you start with just one capsule daily. The fact that Vitamin C is water soluble means that it will be out of your system in no time after doing its job. You'll know when you've had too much because like a horse, you'll have 'the trots'." He chuckled.

"Got it." Aurelia snickered. She quickly cupped her hand over her mouth to keep from outright guffawing out of consideration for the people still sleeping in the next room. "You definitely have a way with words," she said in between chuckles as she took a capsule from the bottle, replaced the cap, and then handed the bottle off to him. "Thanks, baby." She returned to the bathroom for a glass of water.

"You're welcome." Baron smiled. "And by the way, I've already seen you with crust in your eyes and I still thought you looked beautiful."

"When?" Aurelia's gaze snapped back to his.

"Yesterday when I woke up before you. And I stared for a lonnnnng time, too. Even saw a little slobber line trailing down the right side of your mouth." Baron chuckled at her embarrassed expression. "Now hurry up in there. You're not the only one with a morning routine."

"Said the man with the dragon breath." Aurelia gave him a playful evil eye look.

"Ouch." Baron winced at her quick comeback before surrendering to a husky chuckle. "Finally, a woman that can match my intelligence and my wit," he muttered jovially as he headed back to bed for another thirty minutes of sleep.

* * *

Now fully up and dressed, Baron used his cell phone to make calls from the master bedroom while his lingerie clad wife used the hotel phone to order room service. She ordered blueberry pancakes, a mushroom omelet, milk, and fresh fruit for her son. For the grownups, she ordered hot cereal, eggs, fresh bread, fruit, and bush tea. The latter was a traditional beverage enjoyed among islanders for it was not only delicious, but could also be used for medicinal purposes.

Done with her call, Aurelia finished dressing under Baron's watchful eyes. He licked his lips from the time she slipped the royal-blue drop waist dress over her red lacy lingerie to the time she slipped her pedicured feet in a pair of red and royal-blue stilettos. This was just one of many outfits that he handpicked for her during his week on the island.

So enchanted with Aurelia's grooming habits, Baron could barely concentrate on his call. After asking the realtor to repeat something twice, he politely concluded the call until a more convenient time. Preferably a time when he was less distracted.

"Come here, baby," Baron whispered, putting his cell phone down on the nightstand.

Aurelia shook her head. "No," she replied huskily from her place in front of the mirrored closet doors.

Baron lifted his left brow. "No?" His mind immediately raced with possible reasons for her refusal, despite the fact that she was shaking like a leaf with desire from all the ardent attention he'd shown her over the last few minutes. "Is it the my-mother-and-son-are-in-the-next-room-thing again?" He frowned, coming up with the most logical conclusion.

"No." Aurelia briefly turned back to the mirrors to fix her fresh micro-braided tresses. "It's the I-don't-think-you're-ready-for-this-jelly thing," she challenged, smiling sensually over her left shoulder as she heartily jiggled her bottom in the short dress.

Baron moaned and sprung to his feet. "I'm ready for whatever you got on the menu." He grinned, taking long strides towards her. He turned on the TV en route.

Within seconds, the back of Aurelia's dress was promptly pushed up. Other clothing was maneuvered around. Whatever it took to unite them, Baron's hands were quick to get the job done.

The pace started off steady and strong. Power thrusts

225

went both ways. You-take-this - I'll-take-that was the name of this game.

The up-against-the-closet-doors quickie soon turned into an actual game. Baron and Aurelia joked with one another while their hips communicated more serious matters for their ultimate pleasure.

"Am I ready now?" he asked, sounding like the guy from the Verizon Wireless commercial. He followed up his question with a power move.

"What?" she replied, mimicking Dave Chappelle trying to sound like Lil Jon, even as she returned that power move and added a sensual grind at the end.

Baron moaned. "Am I ready now?" He issued another power move, a grind, and then an unexpected roll of the hips.

Aurelia moaned this time. "What?" she panted out in her own voice, continuing to look back at him as she arched her lower body for more of his unique brand of loving.

"Am...I...ready...for...this...jelly...now, baby?" Baron reiterated, dragging out his words in the same slow way he dragged his pelvic across her bottom before slamming into her.

"Ye-ah," she moaned out, closing her eyes as the trembles in her body intensified. Her hands curled into fists on the doors ahead. Her toes curled in her shoes.

"Okayyy," Baron replied, mimicking Lil Jon now, thereby proving that hip-hop had truly made its way into Bel Air homes.

Then sensing the urgency of the moment, he captured Aurelia's lips in a heated kiss. Had he not covered her mouth at that exact moment, she would have screamed out her pleasure at the top of her lungs. The intense clenching, the violent shudder, and the strong muffled sounds she made as she went over the edge confirmed that fact.

Going over the edge soon thereafter, Baron continued to hold her trembling frame close as the long kiss ended and their breathing patterns tried to return to normal. One hand supported her pliable frame. The other caressed her torso in a soothing manner, squeezing and kneading along the way.

When they could breathe normally again, Aurelia thought for sure Baron was going to disengage them to freshen up before breakfast arrived. No, the unpredictable man disengaged them only to turn her around, place her hands above her head on the closet doors, release her ripe melons, and then lower his mouth to feast.

Aurelia let out a contented sigh and arched her body closer to him. A woman didn't find too many men who practiced after-play. Baron not only practiced it, he was a master at it.

Letting out a low moan, Aurelia watched his gorgeous pink lips engulf one brown sugar treat after the other. The fire of passion kindled within her again, within both of them as she looked farther down and saw the current state of Baron's body.

Suddenly there was a knock on the outer door. "Room service!"

* * *

Baron quickly got his clothing back in order and headed for the door while Aurelia escaped into the bathroom to freshen up. Once the hotel employee was generously tipped and sent away, he knocked on the bathroom door.

"When you finish in there, take the meals next door while I freshen up and make a few more calls. Don't feel bad about starting without me," Baron said.

"Okayyy," Aurelia teased, flinging the door open, looking fresher than ever.

Baron's eyes bucked in amazement. If not for the sated look in her caramel pools, one wouldn't have been able to tell that she'd just been ravished. There wasn't even a hint of passion's scent on her.

"Wow! You work fast." He stepped aside to let her pass.

"It comes with the job." She paused, looked back at him and amended with a smile, "Ex-job, that is, since I'm never going back to that particular occupation ever again."

Baron smiled and nodded with approval. "Now that's what a man likes to hear."

Leaving him to handle his business in the master suite, Aurelia pushed the mobile breakfast cart next door to where her mother and son were. Emile and Trent were up and about by now, fully dressed as well.

After making sure her family had their meals, Aurelia settled down on the bed her mother occupied and proceeded to enjoy her own breakfast. Trent sat at the small desk on the east side of the room eating his meal and sneaking longing looks at the handheld video game beside him. Baron purchased that game for him yesterday. Trent had been playing it almost nonstop ever since.

"Ree-Ree, I'm worried 'bout cha." Emile spoke in a low tone as they sat side by side on the bed.

"Worried? Whatever for? I'm happier than I've ever been in my life," Aurelia replied just as discreetly, looking puzzled by her mother's statements.

"But is Baron happy? I heard no honeymoon sounds coming from dat room last night. None at all. Not even de slightest squeak of ah bed, just music," Emile said. "I knew we should've stayed wid Gladys and Sam." Regret shrouded her features.

Aurelia chuckled. "Mama, trust me, a lot of honeymooning went on in that bedroom last night," she said, omitting what happened this morning. A few minutes ago, in fact. "We just didn't use a noisy bed, that's all. We kept the volume of our love turned down and the music turned up out of respect for you and Trent."

Emile's eyes brightened like the shining sun outside. "I see." She grinned. "So den all well?"

"All is great!" Aurelia shared her mother's grin.

"What are you two cheesing about?" Baron asked good-naturedly, suddenly appearing in the doorway.

"About how thrilled I am to be your wife, dear husband." Aurelia beamed with happiness at the sight of him.

"Likewise, dear wife." Baron gave her a secret smile.

Emile smiled at them both and relaxed all the more.

"Want me to get your breakfast for you?" Aurelia was ready to personally feed him that breakfast if he wanted her to. Especially after what he just did to her in the next bedroom.

"No, thanks, baby. I'll get it." Baron retrieved his own meal where she'd left it covered up on the cart. "Good morning, Mama Emile," he said, calling his mother-in-law by the name she requested, which was the same name that Trent referred to her by. "Good morning to you, too, Trent.'

"Morning," Emile and Trent said in unison.

"Mama Emile, I will be needing your input about a few things today." Baron uncovered his meal for full inspection. When everything met with his approval, he smiled.

"Wha tings?" Emile asked.

"Things like, what type of car do you want for Christmas. It is in a few days, you know." Baron carried his tray of food to the bed opposite the two women and sat down.

Emile's eyes bucked. "I…I gettin' ah new car?" she stammered out, forgetting all about her meal.

Had her daughter really found a man this generous? Baron had already pledged to have the Bunting house renovated and to put Emile and Trent up in a temporary residence while the work was being done. Now he was about to buy her a new car?

"Yes." Baron grinned. "We'll take you to pick out the one you want today after we show you the temporary home that you and Trent will be staying in soon," he said, before starting with his meal.

"I already know you're going to like the place we picked out, Mama," Aurelia gushed, too excited to eat now. "It's the same house that I used to dream about staying in as a child."

Emile's eyes bucked wider. "De one wid de cathedral ceilings, sea views, fruit trees, and is located close to de hospital and dat great park?"

"One and the same," Aurelia replied. "Baron made an offer on it today so that we can actually make it a permanent place for us to reside when we're on the island. I hope we get it."

"I hope so, too." Emile turned glossy eyes to her son-in-law. "Tank you for making meh daughter so happy."

"I want to make all of you happy, Mama Emile," Baron replied. "Which is why we're also going to hire Trent a private tutor as well as sign him up for some sports teams when he is physically able," he added, keeping his secret promise to his stepson.

"Yay!" Trent shouted from across the room.

The adults laughed at that reaction. Only Baron knew why the lad was really cheering so hard – sports teams = access to girls!

Emile secretly sighed in relief as she returned to her meal. Finally her grandson was going to get a real teacher. She barely passed high school. Thus she never thought she was the best person to educate Trent. Although Aurelia called often to help with school assignments and homework over the phone, Emile was still overwhelmed by the whole process. Now just like that, the problem was solved.

"As for any clothing that you and Trent might need, Aurelia has all the necessary credit cards to take care of that later today while I meet with a local contractor about all the repairs you said the Bunting house needed."

Emile's eyes grew glossy again. "Tanks ah heap."

"You're welcome a heap." Baron smiled affectionately at her. "You and Trent are part of my family now. Since I was raised to always take care of family, this is really the least I could do to make sure you guys are provided for before and after we return to the states."

Then he told Emile about yet another way he intended to take care of them, namely by obtaining independent health and life insurance for her and Trent. As his spouse, Aurelia would naturally go on Baron's policies at work and the multi-purpose group policy that all of the Weavers enjoyed as a family.

Emile found herself literally tongue-tied by his generosity. She honestly didn't know what to say as happy tears filled her eyes again.

Before Emile could say anything, Aurelia spoke up in a rather sharp tone. "Put the game down now, Trent, or get it took," she warned him sternly after she'd seen him pick it up and play yet again in between bites of food.

"Aww...Ree-Ree, do I have to?" Trent whined, still holding the game.

"Yes, now put de game down," Aurelia said firmly with flashing eyes.

"Do as she sehs, Trent," Emile inserted, no longer tongue-tied as she backed up her daughter's disciplinary methods.

Baron smiled, pleased to see his mother-in-law so supportive of Aurelia's true role in Trent's life. Such support was going to make the inevitable transition of parental care that much smoother for everyone involved.

Baron's smile widened when Trent actually obeyed the women in spades. Not only did the lad put the game down, he turned it over on its face to keep himself from further temptation.

"There's one last thing I needed to talk to you about, Mama Emile." Baron got back to the business at hand. "And that's your basket-making business," he continued, ready to shock his mother-in-law and his wife, who had no idea what he was about to say next because he had not discussed it with her like all the other stuff.

"But I don't have ah basket-making business," Emile replied.

"You will, if you let me provide the capital for you to start one. Feel free to partner with your sister if you like and make it a real family business." Baron grinned.

Emile and Aurelia gasped in shock. Yet it was Aurelia that looked at him with volcanic heat in her eyes.

At that look, Baron's lower body swelled beneath his breakfast tray. He was going to get another night of hot passion behind this unexpected act of benevolence. He just knew it. Baron could hardly wait. But for now, he had to take in a deep calming breath to keep himself in check until then.

"Mama Emile, you 'bout to cry again?" Trent looked worried. All the tears he'd seen in her eyes during his brief hospital stay had made him extra sensitive to her emotional state.

"Yes, but for happy reasons dis time," Emile replied with tears already rolling down her cheeks.

"Same ting for you, too, Ree-Ree?" Trent noted Aurelia's tears as well.

"Yes," Aurelia replied over the emotional lump in her throat.

As the two women got up to hug Baron, they continued to cry happy tears. Neither could believe their good fortune. And to think, Aurelia met this wonderful benevolent man while working as an exotic dancer!

Love truly could be found in the strangest places.

CHAPTER TWENTY-EIGHT

The day after Christmas, which was yet another long day of shopping, Aurelia called a halt to all the spending. "Baron, you're spoiling us rotten. It's too much. I don't want Trent to start thinking of you as some kind of Santa Claus or worse becoming ungrateful," she said, putting the designer luggage in her hands near the closet.

"But everything I bought you and your family was needed," Baron countered, kicking their hotel room door closed behind him. "The house, food, clothes, furniture, insurance, Mama Emile's new car, Trent's new tutor, and your new luggage were all necessities." He put the larger baggage pieces in his hands on the floor beside the door. He'd make room in the closet for them later.

"I know, but even then you went overboard." Aurelia sat down on the side of the bed to remove her shoes and rub her tired feet. "I mean, you packed out every corner of our new kitchen and pantries with food, the utilities for both houses are paid six months in advance, and Mama and Trent have enough clothes for all seasons, not just the one we're currently in. And that new tutor that my son loves so much didn't have to be a retired professor from the local university. It could have been a competent stay-at-home mother who is already home-schooling her own children." She pointed to the navy-blue designer luggage and added, "And I could have gotten new luggage from a regular department store, not some fancy boutique that didn't even have price tags on its wares."

"Only the best for my family," Baron replied, showing no remorse for his purchases. "Tomorrow your uncle and I are going to trade in the truck your mother gave him and get a minivan. Which Sam and Gladys desperately need for all those children they have. As for you and me, we still have more furniture to buy for our first island home. If you recall, every room is furnished except for our bedroom, which is the second reason you and I are still in this hotel room." The primary reason the newlyweds hadn't joined Emile and Trent at the new house yet was out of a need for nighttime privacy during the rest of their honeymoon.

"Aaugh!" Aurelia threw her hands up in exasperation and headed for the bathroom. It was time to relax in the tub and soak her aching feet.

Baron just chuckled, loving the fact that she wasn't so materialistic. It made him want to give to her even more.

Hmmm...that bracelet I saw earlier would be perfect for her pretty little wrists, Baron thought, recalling a piece of jewelry from the hotel gift shop. He quickly scribbled a note to his wife and left.

* * *

As Baron headed back upstairs with his latest purchase, he overheard the hotel manager address a man by the last name of Jean- Baptiste. His ears immediately perked up.

Could this particular Jean-Baptiste be Trent's great-uncle? Had Oliver finally come back to the islands?

Pausing by the elevator, Baron casually glanced in the direction of the gray-haired man in question. Sure enough the stranger had distinct amber eyes just like Trent. Yet instead of being tall and burly like Aurelia described him, he was tall and gaunt-looking.

Sickness has attached itself to him, Baron quickly surmised.

Yet despite the man's clear battle with some unknown illness, rage instantly attacked his soul. All he could think about was what Oliver had done to Aurelia. What he had probably done to Marshall. What he had robbed Trent of on so many levels.

As if he felt the heat of Baron's displeasure upon him, Oliver suddenly turned towards him. Their eyes met and held like cowboys poised for a showdown in an old western.

It was at that moment that Baron decided to wage war on the older man. Not openly. No, subtly and on a level that only a man like Oliver would ever feel any real pain - financially.

I'm going to get your rightful inheritance,Trent, Baron

vowed concerning his stepson as the elevator dinged its availability behind him.

* * *

"Who is that young man? He looks very familiar," Oliver asked the hotel manager when the Latino stranger entered the elevator after that potent stare down.

"That's Dr. Baron Weaver, sir. He recently married one of our own beautiful island birds," the manager replied, looking proud of the fact that he could remember every wealthy individual he encountered, islander or not.

"I see," Oliver replied through a tight mouth, finally recalling where he'd seen Baron's face before and where he'd heard that name from. He'd heard that name from the P.I.'s mouth and seen that face from the pictures the P.I. had taken of Baron and Aurelia together.

I wonder why an insider like him didn't stay at the hotel with the casino, Oliver mused, having done his own research into Baron's past. He hadn't needed a private investigator for that task. Just a few well-placed friends in high and extremely low places.

Unwilling to dwell on how another man made his money, Oliver quickly switched the subject back to the topic they'd been discussing previously. A topic that involved the hotel putting up a few stateside dignitaries, who might help salvage his faltering island business holdings.

After this, Oliver was going to his St. John estate to rest up. He had another round of chemo in the morning.

* * *

Upon returning to his suite, Baron found Aurelia out of the shower, attitude free, and ready for some loving. When she threw the covers back and revealed all that delicious bare chocolate, he literally drooled and completely forgot about his brief encounter with Oliver Jean-Baptiste.

Baron also forgot to give Aurelia the diamond bracelet. The black box it was in fell to the floor along with the pants it had been nestled in.

After they'd made love twice, Baron finally remembered the bracelet, retrieved it from his black trousers and presented it to his wife. "I thought this would look good on your wrist. It goes well with that big rock on your finger," he said, handing over the box as he settled back upon the bed again.

"No, Baron." Aurelia shook her head, putting the

expensive gift on the nightstand without even opening it. "If you really want to give me something else, give me something priceless." She moved to lie on top of him with her elbows and knees on either side of his body.

"Priceless like what?" Baron reached down to give her bottom a firm squeeze.

"Like a goatee." She reached up to trace his lips with her right index finger. "For the longest time, I've wondered how your gorgeous lips would look framed by a goatee. Will you grow one for me?"

Baron smiled. "Yes. I actually used to wear one during my college days. I cut it off before I started teaching, hoping that the clean cut look would help me land my dream job."

"Did it?"

"Yes. I got a couple of dream jobs with this look, including the one that I have now."

"Will re-growing your goatee cause you to lose your current dream job?" Aurelia's finger stilled on his bottom lip as she waited for his answer.

"I seriously doubt it. If I lose my job behind anything it will be because I married you, not because of some hair on my face, which I am going to grow back, by the way."

Aurelia shot completely upright. "Oh, Baron, I don't want you to lose your job! You're a great teacher. The students at AU need a professor like you."

"I don't want to lose my job either, but I'd rather lose that than you." He didn't look too concerned as he pulled her back down upon him again.

"I'm going to pray that you don't lose either." Aurelia willingly returned to her former position and snuggled against his hairy chest.

"Please do. Heavenly help is always welcome," Baron answered, showing respect for all things spiritual. "Now I need you to do something else for me."

"Name it," Aurelia said, ready to travel to the moon and back for her wonderful husband.

"I want you to join a sorority when we get back to California."

"A sorority?!"

Baron laughed at her shocked tone and expression. She clearly hadn't expected him to say what he did. "Yes, a sorority. Not only do I want you to start enjoying your college days for a change, especially now that they're almost over, I think that a Greek affiliation would be great for networking purposes and also allow you to look more well-rounded on your resume. I'm a Sigma myself. Purple and gold all the way, baby." He chuckled.

Aurelia laughed, too. "Bambi has been after me to join the pink and reds for a while, especially after my routine helped them win that Christmas talent show," she shared. "Plus, I've always secretly wanted sisters. Most of my cousins are boys and the ones that are female aren't even past five years old yet. My attempts to turn friends into sisters have all failed thus far. Maybe joining a sorority is an instant way to get sisters without having to put in so many years of hard work."

"The Kappas are a great group. Very community oriented at every college I've known for them to have a presence at. They certainly have a rich history, being among the first Greek sororities that were established and incorporated by black college women," Baron cited.

"True. Unfortunately, they don't hold a candle to the Deltas at our school when it comes to winning the annual Greek step show." Aurelia chuckled.

"Maybe you can help them win it this year. You definitely have the talent for dancing and choreography. I can personally attest to that." He squeezed her bottom again and pressed her closer to his hardened desire.

Aurelia moaned at that intimate contact. "I'll pledge Greek as soon as we get back. Right now, I want to pledge more love to the handsome Latino beneath me," she said, joining them again.

"Yes," Baron agreed huskily, offering his all as he rolled his hips upwards to meet hers.

CHAPTER TWENTY-NINE

January

Aurelia got a huge kick out of being carried over the threshold of her new Alcove home. The kick fell short once she saw the state of the living room. There were clothes strewn across sofas. End table drawers were opened with some of their contents spilling out. A lamp was broken. One chair had been turned over on its side.

"What in the world happened in here? Were you robbed?" Aurelia asked as Baron gently put her down. "I hope this is not an act of revenge from the twins. Do you think the innocent twin forgave his brother for lying on him and then wanted to make you pay for getting his guilty sibling locked up? After all, it was your perm salt tip that landed Professor Griffey's attacker in jail. Possibly for a long time to come."

"No, on all accounts," Baron replied, closing the door behind them.

"No?"

"I was not robbed and the innocent twin is not on some revenge spree. Last I heard, he was grateful for getting his name cleared and being reinstated at his government job after his brother's guilty verdict."

"Don't tell me you live like this." Her eyes bucked. "The last time I was over here the place was spotless. You could have eaten off the hardwood floors."

"The last time you were here I wasn't in a rush to pack and I wasn't depressed." Baron picked up the toppled chair.

"Okay, is that a nice way of telling me that you become a slob when you're depressed or in a rush?"

Baron paused in his tracks. "Unfortunately, yes." He

237

winced. "Are you going to hold that against me?" he asked gingerly.

"No, since everyone deals with depression differently. I personally become a bit of a neat freak whenever I'm stressed in my need to work off all that nervous energy. However, so that we won't bump heads over cleanliness issues, I propose we draw up a rotating chore list. For example, while you cook one week, I'll do the dishes. The next week, I'll cook and you do the dishes. Or we could each stick to our strengths. You do all the cooking for the family while I do all the cleaning."

"I like your first idea better." Baron returned the chair to its rightful position. "After all, if we both just stick to our strengths, how will we ever improve in our weak areas?"

"Okay, but don't complain when you're staring at a plate of burnt, I mean, Cajun chicken." Aurelia laughed, moving to gather his scattered clothes.

"Cajun chicken?" Baron burst out laughing. "I suddenly have all the extra incentive I need to teach you how to cook delicious and healthy meals."

"I'll be your willing student as always, Professor," Aurelia consented. "By the way, what did that chair ever do to you?"

"It stole my keys." Baron laughed.

"Stole your keys?" She paused in her tasks.

"Yes. Right before I had to leave for the airport in December, I sat in this chair to tie my shoes. My keys dropped out of my pocket into the left side cushion. Since my hands were too big to pry it out with the chair in an upright position, I turned it onto its side and used gravity to help me."

Aurelia burst out laughing this time. "Makes perfect sense to me," she said, looking forward to a lifetime of laughs with her semi-eccentric husband.

* * *

Awaking in the master suite of her new home early the next day, Aurelia sighed with contentment. All was well in her world.

Her husband was downstairs cooking breakfast for them by the smell of turkey bacon in the air, her family was happy in the V.I., her new car - a gold mist-colored Cadillac Escalade, was being delivered today, and their stateside jobs were still secure.

Although Aurelia let her job at the mall go as planned, she

was pleased that they had held her position despite her long absence. Thus she sent her ex-supervisor and the whole evening staff gift baskets of appreciation.

Baron's job security had been touch and go for a moment. Having called Dean Paterson while they were still in St. Croix with the news of their elopement, he'd gotten an initial response of extreme disapproval from his supervisor.

However, since Baron had proven to be an excellent teacher in so short a time and had at least waited until after the semester was over to marry Aurelia, Dean Paterson was able to push past his disapproval rather quickly. He seemed particularly pleased about Baron marrying Aurelia instead of just dating her. Marriage between a student and teacher indicated true love while simply dating pointed more towards lust.

All Dean Paterson asked of Baron and Aurelia was that they be discreet about things until after she graduated. This was to deter any speculation that Aurelia hadn't earned her grades the right way. Nor did the Dean want to spark any copycat behavior among other students and teachers. It just wasn't good for business.

Aurelia agreed with the dean's decision and willingly consented to cooperate with his request once Baron informed her about it. Her respect level for Dean Paterson also grew. She had no idea that the reserved bow-tie wearing administrator could be so open-minded about such things.

* * *

Unfortunately, not everyone was so accepting of Aurelia and Baron's union. Two of his brothers saw fit to drop by unannounced today to personally voice their displeasure.

"He's in love with a stripper," Marquess said, singing his rendition of T-Pain's popular tune, which sounded more like the Chipmunks' version. He'd been singing it off and on ever since he entered the house.

"Exotic dancer," Baron amended, feeling blissfully happy as he removed a tray of turkey bacon from the oven and sat it on a rack to cool in the spacious kitchen of his home. "And can you please stop singing that song? Better yet, stop singing altogether because you suck at it. You always did know how to mess up a good rap song. Ruined It's Tricky for me forever," he said, referring to a famous Run-DMC tune that they once performed in a school talent show.

Marquess abruptly stopped singing. "Hey, I told you to let

239

me be Run on that song. DMC's part was way too short."

Baron shook his head. "No, it wasn't. Those dudes shared every verse equally. Unlike you, Mr. Hog-The-Spotlight." He freed his hands of the brown oven towel before moving to the carton of eggs on the countertop nearby. "It was a wonder we didn't get booed or snatched off the stage that night behind that lousy performance. Had Earl not been sleeping with our principal, we probably would have," Baron continued, referring to the taboo relationship their older brother had had with one of their young, extremely hot female principals.

"And I still haven't been thanked properly for that little favor," Earl inserted from his place at the kitchen island where fresh orange juice had already been squeezed. There was a basket of freshly baked croissants to his left. He helped himself to some of each.

"I believe Principal Fuller thanked you quite enough for everybody," Baron countered.

Marquess chuckled, despite the fact that he didn't want to. "Now back to this wife of yours." He forced himself to become serious again as he sat on the wooden stool beside Earl. "You can call her profession what you want, but either way you never should have fallen in love with, much less married a stripper," he said, revealing what he was most concerned with. Aurelia's race and cultural differences didn't bother him at all. After all, Paula got very dark in the summer time and he liked the look of her just fine. "And for all we know she could be after your money," Marquess suggested.

"First of all, exotic dancing is my wife's ex-profession," Baron corrected. "Secondly, if Aurelia wanted me just for my money, she would have taken the cash I tried to give her the first night we were together. She definitely wouldn't fight me so hard when I try to spoil her now. Just yesterday I had to argue her down just to get her to accept the new car I bought her."

"Never mind the stripper and gold-digger part. How could you marry a black girl?" Earl stated what he was most concerned about.

"By signing on the dotted line and saying I do," Baron replied, totally unruffled by their questions as he cracked organic egg after egg in a stainless steel bowl. He was just too happy to let anyone rain on his parade right now.

"Do you care nothing about your reputation?" Earl

turned red in the face with ire.

"Obviously not as much as you do. Feel free to disown me, if you like," Baron replied nonchalantly, cracking yet another egg. "I feel like disowning both of you right now myself. None of us were raised to be snobs on any level and yet you two take the cake these days."

"Have you thought about your professional career?" Marquess inquired, ignoring his younger brother's comments as he headed for the metal wine rack in the corner. "Count told us that Aurora is a student at the same college you work for. Aren't you afraid of getting fired? What will your peers think? Your superiors?"

"Her real name is Aurelia," Baron corrected, starting to wonder what else Count had told them. "And I could care less what my peers think. As for my main supervisor, I've already placed a call to him and explained the situation. Dean Paterson supports me one hundred percent, only requiring that we don't overtly publicize our marriage in Alcove until after Aurelia graduates."

Earl let out a frustrated breath. "Did you ever stop to think how your decisions will affect others, Professor? As a full-blooded Mexican, I had to work hard enough to be accepted in certain social circles. Even had to alter my complexion. Those same people are not going to like being vicariously associated with someone even darker than I used to be. I have a hard enough time trying to get them to accept Duke during the summer months." He left out any references to Marquess' complexion, because their middle brother never got very dark due to his genetic makeup leaning more to their mother's light complexion.

"Have you stopped to think about how your decisions affect others? Particularly your beautiful blonde wife whom you continually cheat on," Baron countered, once again showing that he could hold his own with his older brothers. Such fortitude had come from years of practice. "And why do you still cheat on Meadow? Is it because you secretly crave darker women? Which incidentally are the only mistresses I've ever seen you with."

Earl felt his face get hotter. "Mistress is the only station a black woman should have in a man's life!" he raged. Although he'd cheated with a blonde woman before and had even loved her more than his wife, he wasn't about to mention that to his brothers. They might ask who that mystery blonde woman was. The answer might cause an irreparable rift in the family instead of just a temporary disagreement like this argument was.

"That might be where you want to relegate all the black women in your life. But the black woman in my life will get the place of prominence that she deserves. Furthermore, I'm starting to think that maybe you're not so concerned about the family's reputation at all by coming here today. That maybe you're simply jealous because I had the guts to marry the woman I really wanted instead of what certain segments of society thought I should have," Baron said, using a long whisk from the counter to finally scramble the eggs he'd cracked.

"I'm leaving!" Earl stood to his feet, unwilling to discuss the matter further. He had to leave before his little brother picked up on even more truths about him.

"About time," Baron retorted. "And take your alcoholic partner-in-crime, too." He pointed to Marquess, who seemed to have forgotten all about the argument and was silently enjoying a full glass of wine from his corner hub.

"Hey, I'm just a social drinker," Marquess protested, even though it wasn't even noon yet and no one else in the room was drinking alcohol.

"And Rome was built in a day." Baron scoffed. "Adias, amigos." He smirked, waving goodbye to his scowling brothers as they exited the kitchen one by one. "And, Marquess."

"What?!" Marquess snapped, pausing to look back over his left shoulder.

"Let me know when you're ready to go into rehab, okay? I'll gladly be your sponsor. Be there for every AA meeting, too." Baron spoke with brotherly concern now.

"Bite me!" Marquess retorted as he exited the kitchen.

"You're too bitter and sour for my tastes," Baron countered, having the last word. When the front door finally closed behind his brothers, he heaved a loud sigh of relief. "I'm glad they're gone. Now maybe I can finally finish breakfast."

"I'm glad they're gone, too," Aurelia suddenly said from behind him.

Baron swung around to face his wife, who was standing in the kitchen's second entrance that led from the rear staircase. "How much of that did you hear?"

"Nearly all of it. I didn't know Mexicans could get just as loud as black folks when arguing." Aurelia chuckled, entering the room more fully in one of her many new satin robes and matching gowns. This one was golden.

"And that was just our regular disagreement volume. Wait until we get really angry." Baron smiled, pleased that she wasn't overly upset about what she overheard. "I'm just glad my brothers didn't cause you to sneak out the back way and leave me again," he said, turning serious again. The memory of her leaving him the night of Marquess' last visit was still very vivid in his mind.

"No more running away for me." Aurelia approached him with a loving smile. "Although I don't like what Marquess and Earl said about me, until their opinions become yours, I'm staying right by your side where I belong."

Baron's smile returned. He heaved another loud sigh of relief. "That's good to know, because those particular brothers may never change. To know that you're willing to hang in there with me despite opposition is very important to me, Aurelia. Very, very important." His eyes clouded over with pain. To hide that pain, he blinked rapidly and turned to the sink to wash his hands.

Aurelia frowned. She'd seen that flash of pain in Baron's eyes. She knew Megan had just crossed his mind, particularly how she abandoned him.

"I took our vows seriously, Baron." Aurelia embraced his waist from behind. She relished the feel of his hard bare torso, wished he didn't have on those blue pajama bottoms. "As long as you treat me right and remain faithful, I'm going to remain your faithful wife through sickness, health, riches, poverty, and despite racism and cultural differences. I'm even willing to put up with you being such a health nut."

Baron chuckled at her teasing as he dried his hands with a paper towel. "Well, I guess you're going to remain my faithful wife until I die then." He discarded the towel and turned around to face her. "Because I'm never going to cheat on all this goodness." He cupped her bottom and squeezed even as he spoke. "And I wouldn't dream of mistreating such a beautiful treasure." He squeezed in an even more intimate place.

"Oh, Baron," Aurelia purred right before his mouth lowered to hers.

No more words were exchanged as the newlyweds had a post-honeymoon honeymoon right there at the kitchen sink. Breakfast didn't get eaten until much, much later.

CHAPTER THIRTY

"Okay, where is it?" Aurelia panted out from the doorway of Baron's home office. After practically tearing their bedroom apart, she'd run downstairs to satisfy her curiosity once and for all.

"Where's what?" Baron replied, noting her akimbo stance and her shortness of breath.

What had gotten Aurelia's dander up on this quiet Saturday evening? After only living here for three days, had she found their Alcove home lacking in some way? Misplaced something? If so, what could it be?

"Where's your hidden porn collection?" Aurelia revealed what had her so perplexed.

Baron's eyes bucked. "My what?!" He chuckled.

"Your porn collection," Aurelia reiterated, after taking a deep breath to get her second wind. "I've cleaned this house from top to bottom since I've been here, organized every room, and still found no signs of a girlie magazine anywhere. Is your porn collection underground? In a secret compartment somewhere?"

"You won't find any girlie magazines on this property, because there are none." Baron laughed again, finding the whole thing extremely funny. "Matter of fact, I haven't looked at one of those since I was a teenager."

"Oh, so you watch porn on your computer. Is that why you spend so much time in here?" Aurelia came farther into his office, looking at his computer with narrowed eyes.

Baron's laughter grew louder. "No. What is with you and this porn thing?"

"I'm just finding it a little hard to believe that any man, particularly a man that likes sex as much as you do, doesn't

245

own some kind of porn. Or at least watch it regularly online."

"All men aren't porn-noisseurs, baby," he said in between chuckles.

Aurelia couldn't help but laugh now herself, at the new word he just created, and at the delicious sound of his laughter. "All of my other men were porn-noisseurs, including Marshall," she said, approaching his desk chair.

"Well, this man isn't." Baron pulled her into his lap. "And why should I settle for fantasy, when I can have the real thing?"

"As I recall, you didn't seem to mind the fantasy at Count's bachelor's party." Aurelia draped her arms about his neck as she settled into his lap.

Baron let out a husky chuckle this time. "If you also recall, I got the real thing that night, too."

"Yes, you did. Many times." Aurelia moaned.

"Can I have the real thing now?" His hips moved suggestively beneath hers.

Aurelia moaned again as her core became spastic with need. "Yes." She readily offered her lips and everything else to him.

And they were off again. At this rate their honeymoon was never going to end.

* * *

Thirty minutes later, during their joint shower, Baron decided to ask Aurelia about something that she continued to keep secret from him. Something that he'd known about for quite a while now, but had waited on her to bring up first.

Since she hadn't said a thing yet, he decided to broach the subject. Especially after Aurelia had gone missing for two and a half hours earlier today when she was supposed to be at the grocery store. No way did it take that long to pick up a loaf of bread and a gallon of milk.

"Liam told me about your volunteerism at the soup kitchen, so no need to go MIA on me next Saturday, okay? What I want to know is, when were you going to tell me about this recurring act of kindness?" Baron used a red loofa to lather up her back as she stood in front of him in the large shower stall.

Aurelia looked back over her left shoulder. "Probably never."

"Never? Why not? Don't you think this is something I'd

want to know about my wife?"

"I guess so now that you mention it." Aurelia turned fully around now, allowing the shower spray to rinse her back free of scented soap suds from her favorite bath gel. "But you see, my parents taught me never to call attention to my good deeds. For one thing, doing so forfeits a greater reward from our Maker and only brings the briefest of recognition from people, which sucks all the way around. On the other hand, keeping quiet about my alms not only reveals where my heart truly is, but it makes me eligible for the Master's reward, which I'd much rather have over mankind's puny reward any day."

Baron looked at her in awe. Within seconds he had kissed her breathless.

"Wow! What was that for?" Aurelia panted out two minutes later.

"For being you." He smiled, reaching up to tenderly stroke her left cheek. "Now while you wash my back, why don't you tell me how you came to volunteer at the soup kitchen." He turned around so that she could return his earlier favor.

After Aurelia got Baron's favorite soap on a rope and his sky-blue loofa, she proceeded to lather up his back and honor his information request. She talked about how when she first left Cain she had very little start-over money. How there was barely enough to keep a roof over her head, much less buy food. Thus she had to go to the soup kitchen for meals just to get by.

During one of her visits there, Aurelia decided to make herself useful. "Too often people come to places like that with their hands out, not bothering to give back even when they can. I didn't want to be like them, so I went to the director of the soup kitchen and signed up to volunteer. I emptied trash, cleaned tables, washed dishes, and mopped floors. I still do those things now since I'm not the world's best cook."

"Yet," Baron inserted. "You're a lot better already. Today's pancake breakfast was delicious."

"Thanks, baby." She smiled and tapped him on his sudsy bottom. "Now turn around, so I can do your chest."

Baron readily obliged her. "Furthermore, Liam tells me you do a little bit more than that for the soup kitchen. Said you got his department to sponsor new chafers and appliances for the church that oversees the soup kitchen ministry."

Aurelia blushed. "Okay, what hasn't your little workplace spy told you about me?" Wanting to feel his hairy chest skin to skin, she lathered it up with her hands and not the loofa like she'd done on his back. "More importantly, did you tell him about us?"

Baron chuckled. "I plead the fifth on the first question."

"Anyway." She rolled her eyes.

"The answer to your second question is yes," he continued. "Liam knows we're married and how important it is to keep things a secret for now. He can also be trusted with that information."

"Good," Aurelia replied, pleased to know that her boss really was as trustworthy as he seemed. "As for the crime lab's sponsorship, I only petitioned for that out of necessity. I got tired of seeing the homeless and downtrodden eat grit and egg cookies for breakfast, and then glacier mashed potatoes for lunch due to faulty heating units that couldn't keep the food hot enough for satisfactory consumption."

"Did you just say grits and egg cookies?" Baron threw his head back and roared with laughter at her vivid word pictures.

Aurelia couldn't help but laugh, too. By the end of their shower, she had another sponsor for the new dishwasher the church needed for its soup kitchen ministry.

* * *

With his stomach now full and his body thoroughly sated, Baron turned on a boxing match and then reclined on his bed to watch it. His hands were folded comfortably behind his head. A contented smile was upon his face. He looked euphoric as he lounged there.

He was. What man wouldn't be happy with a wife like Aurelia?

In the adjoining bathroom, Aurelia also had a euphoric look upon her face. She'd never been happier. In fact, she kept smiling at her reflection as she stood in front of the large vanity mirror redoing a few braids that had loosened during her steamy tryst downstairs and subsequent shower.

On Aurelia's body was a black charmeuse robe made of the most lightweight silk available to man. It stopped right at her thighs and had a plunging back panel of lace. This was yet another piece of lingerie that Baron picked out for her.

On the long wide countertop in front of Aurelia were various hair care products needed to keep her braids properly maintained. A universal remote to the flat screen television in the bathroom also sat nearby. That was the thing she reached for once she was done with the current braid.

As Aurelia changed the channel to another CSI episode, she suddenly realized that all of the televisions in the house used the same type of remote control. And just as suddenly the prankster side of her stirred to life.

Smiling mischievously, Aurelia tiptoed to the bathroom door and pointed the remote to the TV in the bedroom.

Click!

"What?!" Baron exclaimed from the bed, having just missed a great uppercut. He immediately reached for his remote and changed the channel back to the boxing match.

Aurelia stifled a giggle with her free hand. She counted a full ten seconds before turning the channel again.

Click!

"What in the world is going on with this TV tonight?" Baron changed the channel back to the boxing match yet again.

Tears sprung to Aurelia's eyes as she clasped her mouth tighter, trying to restrain the giggles. She sagged against the wall as merriment weakened her ability to stand upright on her own.

After waiting ten more seconds, Aurelia changed the channel in the next room once again. When she heard Baron utter what sounded like a Spanish expletive, one of few that she ever heard him speak, she had to clasp both hands over her mouth to keep from laughing out loud. Even still a few snickers escaped.

"Had enough fun tormenting me tonight?" Baron stood in the doorway a few seconds later with a knowing smirk on his face.

When Aurelia removed her hands from her mouth, a string of laughter spilled out instead of words. "I...I'm sorry," she said in between guffaws.

"No, you're not." Baron chuckled good-naturedly.

"I would have been sorry if you were mad. But since you're not, then I guess I'm not sorry after all," she said even as her laughter continued on a lesser level.

"No apologies necessary." He grinned before suddenly turning serious. "But know this, my little prankster, my brother Count and I were kings of practical jokes. Kings! We had to be in order to even the odds with our older brothers. So unless you want to find red food dye in your showerhead or green dye in your toothpaste one unsuspecting day, I suggest you make me a prank ally instead of a rival. Otherwise we're both going to constantly be looking over our shoulders in this house and I don't want that. Do you?"

Aurelia abruptly stopped laughing. "No, I don't want that at all."

Baron's smile returned. "Good. Then we're partners in every way from now on?"

"Yes." She draped her arms about his neck, which was just as bare as the rest of him. "From now on, it's us against the world, baby." She offered her lips to him as she snuggled against all that fineness.

With a deep guttural moan, Baron captured her mouth and ravished it. His hands went about her body and then started a downward squeezing and kneading trail. Televisions, remotes, and everything else were quickly forgotten as another heated tryst began.

Afterwards, the newlyweds washed up and talked about the party Baron's parents were throwing for them in two weeks, particularly about what Aurelia should expect once she got there. They also planned a little surprise for his mother. Just as they were finalizing the details of that surprise, someone rang their doorbell.

Aurelia stayed upstairs while Baron went to answer the front door. She looked at the clock on the nightstand. It read 11:40pm. Who could it be at this hour?

I hope it's not Marquess again. She immediately put her guard up in case her pesky new brother-in-law came to ruin another relaxing night with one of his drunken benders.

Muting the television so that she could find out exactly who their late night visitor was, Aurelia stiffened when she heard Baron say, "Jordin? What are you doing here?"

Jordin?! Aurelia sprung upright in bed.

"De gal gon mad! De man seh go way. She no listen," she muttered aloud.

I'll make her listen, Aurelia decided, exiting the bed with a determined look upon her face.

* * *

"I'm sorry about the late hour, Baron," Jordin apologized, smiling up into his eyes as she eased closer to him in the doorway.

"I'm not merely protesting the time of your visit, Jordin. I'm protesting your visit as a whole. You shouldn't be here at all. We're over, remember?" Baron frowned. He took a few steps back to put some much needed distance between them.

Bad move.

Jordin used that occasion to cross the threshold of the Weaver home. "Why are you playing so hard to get, Baron? You haven't answered any of my calls. Not even the professional ones about the follow-up interview that I want to do with you for helping the police finally crack Professor Griffey's case."

"That dress and the late hour suggest that you came here to do more than just interview me tonight." Baron looked pointedly at her short black halter dress with its bare sides and pin striped collar.

Jordin chuckled huskily. "I came so late to make sure you were home. This dress was to make sure I got in the door," she flirted, moving even closer to him. "Now that I'm inside, what are you going to do about it?"

"Nothing at all," Aurelia said from behind them.

Baron winced, took a deep breath, and shook his head as he slowly exhaled. Could things get any worse?!

"Now, baby," Baron began soothingly as he turned around to face his...

Super-calm wife?

"Baby?!" Jordin exclaimed, looking from him to Aurelia's barely clad frame in that short black robe she wore. "I knew something was going on between you two."

"Yes, something like marriage." Aurelia held up her left hand, revealing her sparkling diamond wedding band and engagement ring set.

"M...marriage?!" Jordin choked out, staring at Baron's left hand now. "You married her, Baron?"

"Yes. That's what you do when you love someone." He wisely closed the front door to keep whatever else this awkward conversation would hold between the three of them.

"You're really in love with one of your students?" Jordin asked incredulously.

"Aurelia's no longer my student," Baron replied, amazed by how calm his wife was. Usually she would be talking fast and in thick island lingo by now. What gives?

Baron didn't know that Aurelia had made up her mind on the staircase not to lose her cool in front of her rival. That she was determined to deprive Jordin of any victories tonight, great or small. Since he was ignorant of those decisions and since he was determined to avoid any catfights, Baron went to stand beside Aurelia just in case things turned physical between the women. No blows would pass either way if he had anything to say about it.

"I would bet every dollar I have in the bank that she was your student when you two first started fooling around," Jordin surmised angrily. Her cheeks looked like red candy apples.

"Then you would go broke, because Baron and I didn't sleep together once while I was in his class," Aurelia replied in that same calm tone.

"The way I see it, I'm not the one with the most to lose here." Jordin scowled. "All it would take was one exposé about college professors who date their students and both of you would lose everything you hold dear. Your jobs, the respect of your peers and neighbors."

"We wouldn't lose each other." Aurelia smiled at Baron with confidence. "Besides, don't you have to run all of your story ideas by your boss first?" she turned to ask her rival.

"Yes, but I know he'll approve of this one. Mr. Richardson loves sensational pieces." Jordin smirked with equal confidence.

"Yes, Cordell does love sensational pieces," Aurelia agreed, calling her rival's boss by his first name. "But I seriously doubt if he's going to approve this one, especially when he learns that I'm involved."

Jordin gasped.

Baron frowned. His body stiffened with tension.

"H…how do you know my boss? Have you had a secret affair with him, too?" Jordin inquired, asking the same things Baron wanted to know.

"My dealings with Cordell were strictly platonic and served to help his marriage, not hurt it," Aurelia replied honestly, giving her husband a look that immediately put him at ease. "It would be pretty disloyal of him, don't you think, to approve a story that was going to harm someone that helped him in his time of need."

"I'll take my story to another network then. Maybe even to one of California's many newspaper outlets," Jordin

THE PROFESSOR

threatened.

"Then I'll have to take my side of the story public as well," Aurelia replied, calling her bluff. "I'll tell people all about how you showed up here wearing next to nothing on a late Saturday night with some flimsy excuse about a follow-up interview with my husband. Not boyfriend, husband. About how you threatened to expose our relationship simply because you couldn't have Baron for yourself. Imagine how pathetic and bitter you're going to look to your fans. Imagine how you're going to repel other men when they learn how vindictive you've been to Baron."

Jordin bristled. "You have no way of proving I was even here. It'll be your word against mine," she said, making one last attempt to bluff her way into the upper hand.

"The cameras posted outside our home will have all the proof I need," Aurelia countered with a smirk. "They're not just good for catching burglars on tape, you know. They're also good for recording late night visitors to one's house. Unwelcome visitors at that."

Jordin's cheeks flamed even redder. Recognizing her defeat, she turned to leave.

"One last thing before you go, little Miss Reporter," Aurelia said, causing her rival to pause in her tracks. "This is how you really kiss a man." Then she turned and gave Baron one whopper of a kiss, a kiss that he immediately sizzled into.

Jordin huffed and left, slamming the door behind her. Yet before her departure, she got enough of an eyeful of that kiss to know that Baron was lost to her forever. He had never kissed her like that. Ever!

There was no doubt in Jordin's mind that that kiss was about to lead to something more intense in just a few short minutes. The dejected reporter was right on that tip.

Back inside the Weaver home, Aurelia and Baron had kissed their way over to the sofa by now. There she straddled him and proceeded to give him a stark reminder of just one of the reasons he chose her over Jordin.

After that heated encounter, they made their way back upstairs to their bedroom. It was time to get some much needed sleep.

"By the way, how did you help Cordell Richardson's marriage?" Baron asked as they ascended the stairs together.

"By going to his house twice a week to teach his wife how to use that stripper pole he bought for their bedroom."

Aurelia chuckled. "Kate was a little round and pretty stiff at first, but after I got through with her, she was fit, toned, and ready to put on quite a show for her man. Cordell enjoyed the results so much that he sent me a huge bonus. I used it to pay for my entire sophomore year at AU."

"Wow!" Baron replied. "I had no idea that exotic dancers could reach so many people on so many levels."

"I reached you, didn't I?"

Baron smiled at her. "Yes, you did. And now I'm never letting you go." He squeezed her close as they completed their ascent.

CHAPTER THIRTY-ONE

Two days later, Count and Jenny came to visit their Alcove relatives. They were in the area on business and wanted to stop in for dinner and a few hours of fellowship before heading back to Bel Air. Count also wanted a good look at and a good drive in Aurelia's VW that Baron paid to have restored while they were still in the V.I.

While Count and Jenny took the car for a spin around town, Baron cooked dinner for them all. Aurelia acted as his sous chef. She chopped, diced, and organized all the raw ingredients that went into the meal. Together they made a perfect culinary team. As a result, the meal was ready and waiting for their relatives by the time they returned from their drive.

"Aurelia, I noticed that the house and even the furniture is still the same as it was before," Jenny said over dessert, finally changing the subject from cars. That former subject had dominated the first part of mealtime thanks to Count's infatuation with their sister-in-law's classic vehicle. "Although it might be a bit premature to ask this, do you have any future plans to redecorate?"

"I plan to do more reorganizing than redecorating since I really like the layout of the house and the furniture placements," Aurelia replied from her place at the end of the oval-shaped mahogany table.

Jenny smiled proudly. "I can't tell you how glad I am to hear that," she said, forsaking her delicious strawberry shortcake for the moment.

Baron chuckled from the head of the table. "You would be glad. Especially since you're the one that decorated the house in the first place." He turned to the right and grinned at his interior decorator of a sister-in-law.

"Did you really?" Aurelia learned something new today.

"Yes." Jenny nodded.

"You did an excellent job," Aurelia complimented.

"As always," Count added to that compliment before returning to his half-finished dessert.

"Thank you both." Jenny smiled at her sister-in-law and husband in turn. "I tried to put my interior decorating skills to work in the master bedroom, too, but your stubborn husband wouldn't let me near that room," she turned to inform Aurelia.

Aurelia chuckled, making light of that reference to her husband being a bit of a control freak at times. "I hope I don't meet any resistance when I move your upstairs gym to the downstairs guestroom. That way you can go from working in your office to working in your gym right next door," she said, now addressing her husband.

"Sounds like a great idea to me. It would definitely be more convenient." Baron smiled.

"Then I want to turn your former gym into a private dance studio for me. I want to put mirrors on one whole wall, take the carpet up, and then buff and shine the hardwood floors underneath. Maybe add in some free standing ballet barres," Aurelia continued.

"Another good idea." Baron nodded his approval.

"As for the master suite—"

"No! The master suite stays the same," Baron interrupted firmly, cutting Aurelia off mid-sentence. "I love every piece of furniture in that room. Had it all custom made to my specifications from trees that I chopped down myself."

"Don't be too hasty with your no's, Professor," Count cautioned evenly, noting the dark thunder clouds forming over Aurelia's head. "After all, that is your wife's bedroom now, too."

"Exactly!" Aurelia agreed with her brother-in-law. Then she turned flashing eyes of ire to her husband. "Had you simply waited to hear what else I had to seh 'bout de matter, you would've learned dat de color scheme was de only ting I wanted changed, not de furnishings demselves. You would have also learned dat I love dat furniture and have no desire to eva change eh, particularly 'cause you put so much time and energy into having eh made."

"Aurelia," Baron began apologetically.

"Save eh, you…you…control freak!" Aurelia retorted, rising to leave the room before she said even worse things to him in front of company.

* * *

"Way to go, Professor," Count said sarcastically as Jenny left the table to console their sister-in-law. "Way to make your new wife feel real comfortable in her new home."

Baron hung his head in guilt and shame. "Sometimes I really put my foot in my mouth around her." Then he briefly shared how he'd upset Aurelia in the Bunting kitchen in his zeal to change the bad eating habits of her family.

"Yes, you have definitely been putting your foot in your mouth lately. Both feet," Count agreed after hearing that short account of the St. Croix incident. "But why? Are you anxious over your marriage? Feeling insecure?" He sounded like the psychologist that he'd almost been before changing his major to law.

Baron took a deep breath and blew it out. "Yes, I'm very anxious and insecure," he admitted. "I'm so afraid of this marriage not working out. Of Aurelia leaving me just like…"

"Megan did," Count finished for him, nodding in understanding. "That's why you keep tripping over your own feet, putting said feet in your mouth, and also going out of your way to spoil Aurelia."

"Wait a minute now. You know I'm a generous man by nature," Baron protested.

"Of course you are. Yet based on the things I've heard Aurelia gushing about to Jenny during today's visit, you've gone beyond your usual generosity with her," Count replied. "I mean, you actually reversed poverty in the whole Bunting family. Had her grandparents still been alive, you probably would have spoiled them rotten, too."

"Probably," Baron acknowledged. "But as you know, I could certainly afford to do what I did several times over."

"Don't remind me." Count rolled his eyes. He was one of the few people that knew his brother's true net worth. "Now although being generous with your wife and in-laws is not a bad thing, going overboard out of fear is. You have to understand that fear is a monster, Professor. A monster that seeks to control everyone, particularly the people that submit to it. Fear is also usually at the root of every control issue."

"What do you advise?" Baron asked, needing to gain a different perspective of the situation.

"I advise you to face your insecurities head-on and then share them with your wife. Trust her to understand. Invite her to help you get over them. If I remember correctly what you told me about Aurelia, she has a few trust issues of her own. Something to do with a cheating ex-boyfriend?"

Baron nodded. "You're exactly right...about everything." He took a deep breath and blew it out. "Thanks for the sound advice. Now I need your advice about something else. Something that I may need to help Aurelia get over."

Count listened quietly as Baron shared the specifics about Aurelia's encounter with Oliver. The frown in his forehead grew deeper and deeper with each new piece of information. When the candid disclosure was over, he said, "I have but one question for you."

"Shoot," Baron prompted.

"If for some reason Aurelia is unable to get over that painful part of her past, can you be satisfied with what she is willing to do in the bedroom? Not just now, but for the rest of your married lives? Because if not, this thing is going to be like the forbidden fruit in the Garden of Eden all over again. You're going to want it to the point of utter distraction and cause even more damage to your marriage."

"Okay, that's technically two questions," Baron teased before turning very serious again. "However, the answer to both questions is yes. I can be satisfied with what Aurelia is willing to do...forever." I have to be, he added to himself.

Count smiled. "Good." Then he issued some tips on how Baron could gently help Aurelia get over the sexual abuse in her painful past.

Those tips were simple: Be understanding, be loving, be patient, and lastly, be a motivator for change.

"Prayer wouldn't hurt either," Count concluded.

Baron grinned. "Mama and Uncle Miguel would love that last thing for sure," he said, referring to their devout Christian mother and Catholic priest of an uncle.

"Most definitely." Count chuckled. "One last piece of advice," he said, about to bring this impromptu counseling session to an end.

"I'm all ears." Baron leaned closer.

"Go find your wife, apologize for being a control freak, tell her that she can change anything she wants in this house, and I mean anything. Then give her the biggest kiss you can muster."

Baron smiled. "I was going to do that anyway." He rose to his feet even as he spoke.

"Well, be quick about it then. One minute of unresolved conflict in a marriage is a minute too long," Count said, quoting their wise mother.

Baron was out of the room before that quote was done. He took the stairs two at a time upon hearing female voices on the upper level of the house.

After following Count's last piece of advice to the letter, Baron found Aurelia quite forgiving. She even escorted him to their bedroom so that they could make up in style.

Meanwhile, Jenny slipped back downstairs unnoticed. "I don't know what you told Professor, but he's up there practically ramming his tongue down that girl's throat," she said, entering the dining room where her husband was wiping down the table he just finished clearing.

Count grinned. "Is she liking it?"

Jenny chuckled. "Very much so. Matter of fact, they might be a while, if you know what I mean." She walked over to her husband.

"I know exactly what you mean." Count pulled her close. "Open wide, lady. It's time you got a little tongue lashing of your own."

Jenny's subsequent chuckles were swallowed up in a heated kiss.

Still on the newlywed side themselves, they ended up going upstairs to one of the guest rooms to satisfy another type of appetite. They stayed there all night.

Baron and Aurelia didn't mind. They were too busy making love in their own bedroom to care one way or the other. It would be much later when they discovered that they had overnight guests.

* * *

Count and Jenny hit the road early the next morning. The sun hadn't even come up yet. It was still dark outside.

Because Jenny could barely keep her eyes open after their long night of passion and then early rising, Count volunteered to cover the whole journey even though they usually shared the driving on road trips. Her soft snores and a national news radio station kept him awake.

Halfway home, Count received a call from Earl on his cell phone. It was not good news.

"Megan is coming back in town today. To stay this time,"

Earl informed rather gleefully. "She thinks Professor is going to divorce Aurora as soon as he finds out she's back and now single again," he said not so gleefully.

"Our new sister-in-law's name is Aurelia," Count corrected. "Megan's single again?" He frowned. "That was quick. Did she divorce her husband?"

"No. The old coot up and died on her." Earl chuckled, ignoring the fact that he would one day be an old man if he lived that long.

"Sorry to hear that for more reasons than one. Either way, Megan's singleness is no longer Professor's concern. Besides, he really loves his wife. I can personally attest to that," Count replied.

"He loved Megan, too, for an even longer period of time," Earl reminded him. "Because of their extensive history, Megan thinks that all Professor has to do is see her again and those old feelings are going to come rushing back in."

"Even if they do, he is going to overcome them. Hey, if Professor can push past the sexual hang-up Aurelia has and still want a future with her, he can definitely push past any lingering feelings he has for Megan."

"Sexual hang-up? What sexual hang-up could a stripper possibly have?" Earl inquired with his previous gleefulness firmly intact again.

Count winced, instantly wishing that he had kept his mouth closed on that particular matter. He really had to break that bad habit of speaking too soon about things best left unsaid. Since he had already opened that door, he quickly shared the sexual hang-up Aurelia had and why. Before hanging up the phone, he made Earl promise not to say anything to anyone.

"Bad move, Viscount Weaver," a drowsy Jenny said from the passenger seat. "Earl is the last person you should have told that kind of information to. He's going to use it against baby brother at the first opportunity."

"If he knows what's good for him, he'll keep his mouth closed as promised. Otherwise there's going to be a nice knuckle sandwich waiting for him," Count replied, more than willing to put his considerable boxing skills to use on Earl if he betrayed his confidence.

"All I ask is that I get a ringside seat to the main event. Because somebody needs to pop that particular brother in the mouth…hard," Jenny replied, thinking that Earl should have been popped in the mouth a long time ago. She almost did it the night he tried to come on to her. It was the same night she met the Weaver family for the first time.

Had Ana Maria not entered the room at that exact moment, Jenny probably would have slugged Earl. Thankfully, he has kept a respectable distance from her ever since. Had he persisted, she might have had to tell Count about that encounter. Or worse refused to marry into the Weaver family altogether, thereby forfeiting all the happiness that she has since enjoyed with her wonderful husband and his less dysfunctional relatives.

CHAPTER THIRTY-TWO

Exiting the LAX terminal on that bright morning, Megan Griswold entered the waiting limo and headed to her new luxury estate in Bel Air. Yet despite her plush surroundings, she was not fulfilled. She could never be fulfilled without Baron.

Once upon a time Megan knew exactly what she wanted to do with her life. Marry Baron, start a family with Baron, and use her marriage to Baron to climb higher on the social ladder than her first cousin Meadow.

All of Megan's plans drastically changed when she allowed her competitive spirit and her disdain for her cousin to overshadow good judgment. One bad decision made in anger cost her the man she loved.

If only she hadn't...hadn't...slept with Meadow's husband in vengeance. Unfortunately, that man just so happened to be Baron's second oldest brother Earl.

Earl had been secretly in love with Megan for years. In fact, he claimed to have fallen in love from the moment he laid eyes on her at the age of seventeen. Megan had just lost both of her parents and had come to Bel Air to live with her widowed Uncle Ford and female cousin – Meadow.

At the time, Earl was engaged to Meadow and thus not available to pursue Megan, even if she had been old enough. If that wasn't frustrating enough for Earl, Megan had fallen madly in love with his brother Baron upon first sight, who was visiting Meadow's home with him that same day. Combine all those obstacles with the fact that Meadow was just a better fit for Earl socially and it was easy to see why he chose to go through with his intended marriage to the older cousin.

262

Megan suspected Earl's feelings all along, even subtly encouraged them whenever Baron wasn't around. Yet she didn't take full advantage of his affections until after yet another horrific argument with her cousin. The same cousin whom she had never gotten along with.

From the start, Megan and Meadow developed an almost instant distaste for each other. Megan thought her cousin hated her because she was younger and prettier. She refused to believe that she was hated because she milked her parents' deaths to get years of sympathetic gifts from Meadow's father. That she was to blame for starting out their relationship wrong from the jump by boldly asking Uncle Ford for a bigger bedroom, namely the one that belonged to the real daughter of the Griswold house.

Megan added to her cousin's hatred by trying to best her at being a social darling. Thanks to those expensive etiquette classes Uncle Ford paid for, she transformed herself from a typical middleclass valley girl to a well-bred lady of the elite class. Because Megan conducted herself in a more down-to-earth manner than her snooty older cousin, she was generally better liked in their social circle.

To add insult to injury, Megan was always overly kind to Earl during his courtship of Meadow. Even more so after they finally got married. As a result of that constant provocation, Meadow sought every occasion to make Megan feel bad about any and everything.

That particular day of bad judgment, Meadow chided Megan about her pending nuptials to a teacher of all things. She told her that the real reason Baron ever suggested that they elope wasn't because he was being romantic, but because he was simply being cheap. That Baron would never be able to ascend to Earl's social status or net worth. That Baron would never be able to afford to keep Megan in the lifestyle to which she'd grown accustomed to over the last few years. That she would always be dependent upon the truly elite like Meadow and her father.

Then Meadow arrogantly concluded with, "As soon as my father dies, I'm cutting you off in every way, particularly socially and financially."

Incensed by that bleak assessment of her future, a bitter Megan decided to be spiteful and hit Meadow where it would hurt the most – her marriage. Seducing Earl only required one kiss. The man instantly became an open flower, welcoming her kisses, her everything as he ravished her body over and over again that day in his office. That was also the day he confessed his secret love for her.

Unfortunately for Megan, what she thought was going to be a one-time thing, turned into three long months of secret trysts. Earl simply refused to end the affair once he finally had her. He even threatened to tell his brother about them if Megan tried to end it without his consent.

Telling Meadow was out of the question since they both had much to lose by that disclosure. Earl would lose all the social benefits that had come along with his marriage. Megan would lose all her family's financial support, which did not include a large trust fund to fall back on because she'd already spent most of that trying to keep up with her cousin.

With the guilt of cheating on Baron piling up on her conscience and with the realization that Earl was never going to let her go, Megan sought another way out of her dilemma. Reasoning with Earl had proven futile time and time again.

The only way to freedom Megan could find involved giving Baron up completely, at least for a while. Although it pained her to do so and she wept bitterly for days before putting her plan into action, she eventually did what needed to be done.

What did Megan do to get out of her dilemma?

She secretly courted a new man. A man richer than her own family. A man unrelated to the Weaver family. A man that could free her from the prison she allowed herself to be put in.

As expected, Megan's actions devastated Baron. Earl was devastated, too, although he kept a lid on his feelings for obvious reasons. Baron became practically a hermit. Earl began to cheat on his wife even more, having been robbed of the woman he really loved.

Although Megan's new husband was old enough to be her grandfather and was very sickly, she didn't mind. Those very reasons had much to do with why she'd chosen Scottsdale in the first place. It would definitely explain why she suddenly wanted to volunteer more hours with the country club's senior citizens program so close to her intended nuptials with Baron.

Megan figured that she could play the doting wife for at least five years, which was the amount of time the doctors had given Scottsdale to live; get her husband to change his will, and then soon after he died, find Baron and marry him. It never crossed her mind that Baron would eventually move on with his life. And so fast.

Megan erroneously thought that she was that indispensable to him. What other woman would cater so much to his needs like she had? She even learned Spanish and how to dance like Shakira just to please Baron.

Megan also enrolled in college for him. However, she secretly paid others to do her homework and to let her copy off their tests, which were the same things she did in high school.

Unlike high school, Megan never did finish that business degree. The college she attended was strict about their exit exams. Each student had to schedule an appointment to take his/her exam since it was not given in group sessions. A watchful moderator was present at all times.

As a result of those procedures, Megan failed all of her exams. The fact that she failed them by a mile proved that she was unworthy of any college degree. It also caused her professors to wonder if and question whether she had ever learned a thing in their classes or had indeed cheated as they suspected all along.

Baron lovingly offered to help Megan study for the retests, but she was too embarrassed to let him. She didn't want him to know just how dumb she was. She definitely didn't want him to make the right connection between her extremely high grades and excessively low test scores.

Instead Megan claimed that she was just a poor test-taker and would probably always be the kind of person that got overly anxious during tests. Then she used those claims as excuses to give up trying to finish her degree altogether.

Though Baron continued to try to motivate Megan to complete her college degree, he eventually let it go. He eventually let her go, too. Especially after she broke his heart.

For a long time, Megan hoped that Baron would get over his broken heart and pursue her. Yet when she recalled how principled he was, she should have known better than to expect that.

Baron would never pursue a married woman, no matter how much he loved her. He respected the sanctity of marriage unlike most of his older brothers. That had been one of the reasons she loved him so much.

As fate would have it, Megan wasn't married for long.

Scottsdale died within ten months of their marriage, leaving her a very wealthy woman since he had no other family surviving him. Now she was back in town to reclaim what she'd lost – Baron.

Earl couldn't stop her either. Not after Megan just used a large portion of her newfound wealth to rescue him and Meadow out of the enormous debt they'd accumulated over the years trying to live the high life. Debt that Earl was too ashamed to ask his family for assistance with because it would confirm what they all suspected anyway – that he was terrible with money. That his wife wasn't much better with it either.

Incidentally, Megan found out about Earl and Meadow's financial problems from her uncle. She happened to call Uncle Ford on a day when he was very upset with Meadow.

During that call Uncle Ford ranted about how he was tired of seeing his money being poured down the drain by his spoiled daughter and irresponsible son-in-law. About how they weren't even grateful for the help they received from him thus far. About how cowardice he deemed Earl to be because he wouldn't even ask for the money himself, but rather continued to send Meadow to ask for it instead. About how if it wasn't for his grandchildren, the promise Uncle Ford had made to his wife to look after their daughter, and the Griswold family's reputation in the community, he would have cut Earl and Meadow off a long time ago.

When Megan decided to return to Bel Air, she called Earl with a proposition. In exchange for helping him out of his financial hole, she would gain his eternal silence about their affair and his assistance in helping her get Baron back.

Earl immediately balked at that proposition. Yes, he wanted and needed Megan's financial support. But he did not want to help her reconcile with his brother under any circumstances. Not when he still wanted her for himself.

That's when Megan decided to play hard ball.

She mocked Earl about his inability to take care of his wife in the manner Meadow had been accustomed to. She told him about how cowardly his father-in-law deemed him to be behind his back. About how shameful it would be to him if others, especially his brothers, were to find out just how broke he was.

Then Megan painted a rosier picture for Earl. She told him how responsible and manly he would now appear in his wife, father-in-law, and brothers' eyes if he came up with alternative means to take care of his responsibilities. She promised him that no one would ever have to know that she was his private financial backer. Not even Meadow.

Megan was waiting for Earl's response to her proposition even now. It had already been a full week since she made that offer. He'd needed that much time to think about it.

Megan hoped that the large deposit she wired to a secret account that she'd set up for Earl showed just how serious she was about this deal. More importantly, she hoped it served to finally sway him over to her side.

As if she'd somehow conjured him up, Earl suddenly called Megan on her cell phone.

Although she wanted to snatch the phone to her ear, she let it ring three times before answering. She didn't want to appear too eager, though she needed this alliance with Earl like she needed to breathe.

"What's your decision?" Megan cut to the chase as soon as she answered the phone.

"Count me in," Earl replied, formally accepting her proposition. "However, I'd like to make a slight addendum to our deal."

"What kind of addendum?" Megan frowned.

"I'd like us to resume our affair until you and Professor get back together."

"What?!" Megan exclaimed incredulously, causing her limo driver to lower the glass partition to check on her.

"Is every-ting a'ight, ma'am?" the dreadlock-wearing, mahogany-skinned man asked in a thick island accent.

"Yes, everything is fine, Kingston," Megan told her driver, prompting him to raise the partition again. "Now back to you, Earl. I know you didn't just say what I think you said," she stated angrily upon returning to her phone call.

"I certainly did," Earl replied, revealing no remorse about betraying his brother again. Not on a romantic level. Not on any level.

Earl had always been jealous of Baron. He was jealous that his youngest brother was half-white and thus carried around less social stigma, grew up to be more handsome than him, and had won Megan's heart without even trying to.

Earl was even jealous of Baron's name. Yes, all of the brothers had been named after English peerages, but it was Baron's name that garnered the most female attention over the years. Not even Marquess held that honor.

"I will call this whole deal off right now and demand prompt repayment of that loan I just sent you if you ever and I mean, ever proposition me that way again," Megan told him through tight lips. "What you and I had is over, Earl. Over! Do you hear me?"

"Don't make me tell my brother about us." Earl quickly returned to his old way of trying to control her – through blackmail.

"Then we'll both forfeit what we want. Except your losses will be greater. Yes, I will likely lose your brother forever, but you will lose the opportunity to finally get out of debt, you'll lose your wife, kids, close family ties, and the respect of your peers," Megan replied. "Matter of fact, how about I tell Professor myself and just get it on over with," she bluffed, knowing full well that that was the last thing she wanted to do. But Earl didn't have to know that.

"No!" Earl shouted into the phone, inadvertently startling his receptionist in the next room. "I'll do what you ask," he added in a much quieter and humbler tone.

"Everything I asked?" Megan prompted with a triumphant smile.

"Everything," Earl agreed, sounding like a defeated foe. He was. And it was his own fault.

"Good. Now tell me everything you know about Baron's so-called wife." Megan frowned at the memory of how maliciously Meadow had delivered Baron's wedding announcement to her – through an animated email full of laughing hyenas.

Pushing that painful memory aside, she forced herself to listen very attentively as Earl shared basic facts about Aurelia. Things like the fact that she was black, from the Virgin Islands, a student, a former exotic dancer, and part owner of a budding perfume company.

"An exotic dancer, huh?" Megan focused on the part that interested her the most. The frown in her forehead was so deep that she was sure to need Botox treatments soon. The kind that Earl specialized in at his office.

"Yes, that's how they met. She danced for him at Count's bachelor's party. She was really good at it, too. Made a lot of money that night from Professor alone. He was so impressed by her that he took her to the next room and…" Earl paused to chuckle. "Well, let's just say that whatever she did to him in that room was enough to make him want to marry her."

Megan cringed. "Do you have any idea what she did to him in that room?"

"I know what she didn't do." Then Earl revealed that there were certain things that Aurelia refused to do in the bedroom based on the conversation he had with Count just one phone call ago. Things that Baron enjoyed doing…thoroughly.

A calculated smile slithered across Megan's lips at that news. She'd just garnered her first piece of ammunition against Aurelia. She planned to use it at the first available opportunity.

Concluding her call with Earl after promising to wire more money to his secret account, Megan leaned back against the limo's black leather seat with a satisfied smirk on her face.

Keep denying him the kind of pleasure he deserves, island girl. That will make it even easier for me to get what I was always intended to have, she mused.

"Baron," Megan whispered aloud.

Then as her luxury vehicle continued to cruise through the streets of Bel Air, she closed her eyes and recalled happier times with the man of her heart's desire. Sexual times. Times when Baron had looked into her sparkling blue eyes and declared how much he loved and adored her.

Oh how Megan wished she had just eloped with him like he wanted. But no, she just had to prolong the engagement to plan a wedding that would have put her cousin's elaborate ceremony to shame.

Megan wouldn't make the same mistake twice.

CHAPTER THIRTY-THREE

The very next day was the first day of a whole new set of classes at Alcove University. Aurelia didn't have any classes with Baron since he was only teaching the first sections of AU science courses, leaving the latter sections for the professors that had had more tenure.

As agreed upon, Aurelia and Baron left their wedding bands at home today. However, to represent their committed relationship in some way, she switched her engagement ring to her right hand. As of now, Baron would be known among her friends and associates as Barry her fiancé. A fiancé that they would never officially meet until after Aurelia graduated.

The Weavers also rode in separate cars today, despite the fact that they were going to the same place. Neither liked these inconveniences or their attached lies, but those things were necessary evils right now as it pertained to Aurelia's matriculation and Baron's job security at Alcove University.

What was also necessary in light of the sensitive nature of their marriage was the postponement of Aurelia being added to Baron's work insurance policies. Instead of insuring her at his job, he opted to insure her through the Weaver family group policy, which was just as effective.

Another plus was the fact that although Aurelia had to drive to school separately from her husband, she drove in comfort in the new Cadillac Escalade Baron bought her as a wedding gift. He put in the order for it while they were still honeymooning in St. Croix.

Baron originally wanted to get Aurelia a Porsche like his, except in a different color. But after she protested that purchase, he settled for a Cadillac instead. When Aurelia protested that purchase, too, it fell on deaf ears. Or rather it garnered counterarguments. Counterarguments that eventually wore her down to agreement.

When Aurelia said that she didn't want to draw too much attention to herself with such an expensive car, Baron countered with the fact that a beautiful woman like her was going to draw extra attention anyway. That people were going to look at her no matter what kind of car she drove. He then brought up the fact that the Cadillac was also roomy enough for her to make deliveries to local boutiques since her perfume operations were still relatively small and her budget not yet large enough to hire a delivery person.

When Aurelia then told Baron that inquiring minds would want to know how a struggling student like her was suddenly able to afford a Cadillac and an expensive wardrobe to boot, he countered with the fact that she was already known for dating wealthy men. That many would simply assume that she was involved with yet another wealthy man. A more generous one, at that. Cain never bought Aurelia a new car or even tried to fix her old one. He simply rode her around in his BMW whenever he wanted to show them both off.

When Aurelia finally suggested that they just get her VW restored, Baron deemed that an excellent idea. Not so the car could be driven on the regular, but rather used as a trophy car that they only drove on special occasions. He even suggested that they enter the VW in a few classic vehicle competitions.

At that point, Aurelia gave up the fight. Then she spent the rest of that night thanking Baron for her new vehicle in the most primal of ways. They'd had even more nights of fantastic lovemaking since then. Days, too. Aurelia thought about a few of them now as she rushed down the hall to her first class.

Her thoughts stayed on Baron from that point on. By noon, she'd made up her mind to go to his office for a midday quickie.

I just hope his office is soundproof, Aurelia thought, heading over to the science building.

* * *

Alone in his office, Baron thought about the horrible day he'd had thus far. He'd just completed another two-hour class filled with gawking female students. All wearing sexy outfits. Many of whom weren't even science majors.

Baron couldn't prove it, but he was convinced that those

particular students only signed up for his class in hopes of enticing him. The same thing happened at his last teaching job. Unfortunately, the female attention was worse at AU because of his hero-like status after rescuing Rhoda.

Because he'd been down this road before, Baron knew that a month of grueling assignments would cause most of those females to drop out of his class. Some probably wouldn't even last that long.

Aurelia lasted the whole semester, he recalled, even though she wasn't in the category of females seeking his attention. She already had it before ever entering his class. She never lost it even when he became temporarily distracted by Jordin.

I wonder what my baby is doing right now, Baron thought, missing his wife terribly. He'd grown very attached to Aurelia in just a short period of time. Blame it on all the time they spent together in the Virgin Islands and over the past few days at home.

Mindful of Aurelia's school and work schedules, Baron naturally assumed that she was in the cafeteria eating lunch with her friends right now. That's when he suddenly remembered his own lunch.

Retrieving the turkey on rye sandwich and a bottle of spring water from the mini-refrigerator behind his desk, he settled into his seat again to eat and read. Hopefully this time of peace would relax him enough to deal with the new barrage of female admirers that were sure to populate his evening classes.

Just then, someone knocked on his office door.

"This better not be Rhoda," Baron grumbled underneath his breath as he stood to his feet. That one woman was the main reason he kept his office door closed and locked these days.

It wasn't Rhoda at the door this time. It was Aurelia.

Baron's eyes immediately roamed over her shapely frame in that midnight blue V-neck sweater dress she wore. He loved how it hugged her curves in a sexy, yet sophisticated way. He licked his lips upon seeing that gold belt about her narrow waist. It reminded him of the gold lingerie that he knew she was wearing underneath.

Baron handpicked that gold bra and thong set in St. Croix. He watched Aurelia put each piece on after her shower just this morning. Now he wanted to rip them off of her.

Would he?

"May I speak with you for a moment, Professor?" Aurelia asked in an innocent tone, breaking the knowing silence between them. She could pick up on his desire just as much as he could pick up on hers.

"Yes." Baron paused briefly to clear some of the huskiness out of his throat before speaking again. "Come on in," he continued in a semi-normal voice as he opened the door wider and moved to the side to allow her entry into his office.

"Thanks, Professor." Aurelia crossed the threshold with swaying hips. "I really appreciate you making time for me like this."

"It's no problem at all. In fact, it's my pleasure." Baron promptly closed the door and locked it again. He quickly became distracted by Aurelia's swaying bottom as she switched all the way to the black visitor's chair in front of his desk.

What an invitation. He licked his lips as his body swelled with need.

Baron knew Aurelia was trying to seduce him. If they weren't on school property, he'd surrender to that seduction wholeheartedly. But since they were at his workplace, he couldn't run the risk of them being exposed. Thus he had to stay strong and keep things strictly on the flirtatious level only.

"What did you need to speak to me about?" Baron sat directly in front of her on the edge of his desk. His black jacket was on the wooden coat rack near the door. His matching silk tie was hanging on a wooden hook beside it.

"I needed to talk to you about an ache I have." Aurelia pulled the hem of her dress up just a bit as she spoke.

"An ache?" Baron licked his lips again as more gorgeous brown thighs entered his eyesight. His black jeans grew even tighter as a pulsating ache began in his body as well. "You do know I'm not a regular MD, don't you?"

"Yes, but that's only because you don't want to be one. Complete a second residency and you could have that, too, you brilliant man." Aurelia smiled seductively, tugging her dress up a little bit higher. "In fact, you probably know more about the human body than both of your doctor brothers put together."

Baron licked his lips yet again. "I don't know about that last part, but in any case, tell me more about this ache of yours," he said, enjoying the sweet torture. It would add even more fuel to the fire that he planned on rekindling when they got home tonight.

"Well, it started soon after I left the house this morning." Aurelia continued to inch her dress up her thighs. "I thought it would go away by now, but it's only gotten worse. I need to get some relief soon or I don't know how I'm going to make it through the rest of the day."

"Where is this ache?" His words came out in a husky whisper.

"It's in a private place." She pulled her dress up even higher. "A private place?"

"Yes, a very private place." Aurelia yanked her dress clear up to her waist and propped her legs on each arm of the chair, showing all her business.

Baron moaned at the sight of that shimmering gold thong nestled among all that hot chocolate. He immediately dropped to his knees before her. Bump the flirting. A little foreplay was in order now.

Foreplay is as far as I'm going to let it go, Baron promised himself as he licked a trail all the way up one of Aurelia's pretty brown legs, which she shaved smooth every morning because he liked to touch them so much. He stopped at an inner thigh.

"Is the ache here?" He sent a hand to her special place even as he spoke.

"Yesssss…" Aurelia moaned and arched towards him.

Baron's mouth literally watered at her response. At the way her body instantly clenched around his privileged digits. Her intoxicating scent compelled him to inhale deeply. He did.

"Mmm…you smell delicious," Baron whispered before tasting each inner thigh. He ended with suckles each time, leaving passion marks behind in places only he was privy to.

"That's my perfume," Aurelia panted out as stronger spasms attacked her body.

Baron shook his head. "No, that's all you, baby." He leaned in to taste her thighs again, restraining himself from doing what he really wanted to do. He felt grieved about that.

"Come join me on this ride, baby," Aurelia petitioned as her hips rolled with primal rhythms. Rhythms meant to allure. Rhythms meant to persuade him to change his mind about waiting until they were at home for full consummation.

"I can't...we can't..." Baron forgot what he was about to say when he looked up and saw Aurelia releasing the twins. Liquid lava flowed through his veins.

This woman was playing to win!

Drooling now for sure, Baron greedily descended upon those identical brown sugar swells. While his right hand stayed busy with one thing, his left hand discarded the necessary items from both of their bodies. Soon they were as close as any two people could be.

The second Baron entered that hot-blooded woman he went for broke. He took Aurelia two times in that chair and once again upon his desk. Each time was fast and furious. Each time the only noises in the room were the sounds of their bodies slapping happily against one another in fervent passion.

Thankfully, they had practiced how to make non-verbal love back in St. Croix. Otherwise, all of Baron's neighboring colleagues would have heard him making loud, steamy love to a student that fortunately happened to be his wife.

When their midday tryst was over, Baron and Aurelia cleaned up as best they could. Then they shared a loving kiss, a secret smile, and temporarily went their separate ways. They would pick things back up where they left off later at home.

After that sultry encounter, Baron was completely relaxed for the rest of the day. However, he proved to be no less informative in his afternoon classes, giving those students the same level of instruction as he'd given the morning crew, just with a few more smiles.

As for Aurelia, she kept getting compliments about how radiant she looked today. Many thought it was because of that big engagement ring upon her right hand. She knew it was because of the handsome man who had given her that ring and so much more.

CHAPTER THIRTY-FOUR

A Week & A Half Later

That sunny afternoon, all Baron wanted to do was get off from work, go home, and make love to his beautiful wife. But he couldn't.

Today was the day of the first forensics club meeting of the semester. Baron couldn't miss that. Especially since he was the one to spearhead it for students that wanted to specialize in forensic medicine as a career. Students like Aurelia.

Other students like Claude and Bambi deemed such a club an extra boost to their resumes and so joined as well. The fact that this club gave its members an inside track to the world of forensic medicine, complete with field trips and part-time employment opportunities was an added boon.

As usual, Baron and the other advisors present sat at a long table at the front of the science building's mid-sized meeting room. The student members of the club sat in the audience. The elected student vice-president of the club was on the third row along with the secretary. They were Claude and Bambi, respectively. The president of the club, which was Aurelia, had not arrived yet.

I'm going to have to buy her a watch with an alarm, Baron mused, disapproving of his wife's tendency to run late at times.

Aurelia didn't run late all the time. But it was often enough for him to want to put a stop to it. He didn't want her to get a reputation for tardiness, professional or otherwise.

Today Aurelia was running late due to the hair appointment she had after her last class. That appointment had been set up by Bambi, a senior member of the sorority that his wife recently pledged to. Because Bambi's stylist was a Kappa alumnus, she willingly squeezed Aurelia's appointment in despite how busy her Fridays usually were. The fact that she was well-versed with all types of hair textures was an added bonus.

Baron recalled how grateful his wife had been for that appointment. He knew how much she wanted her micro-braids freshly done for the big shindig at his parents' house in Bel Air tomorrow.

I can't wait to see how her hair looks, Baron mused, recalling that she was getting tree braids this time. Although Aurelia explained that tree braids were the most natural and undetectable braids a person could get, he had never seen any. He looked forward to seeing them up close and personal tonight.

To be honest, Baron couldn't wait to see his wife as a whole. Although they still shared the same house and the same bed, they hadn't been intimate in almost a full week because of her women's days.

The sensitive side of Baron knew to be understanding of such times in a woman's life. Yet the hot-blooded side of him was growing weary of just snuggling with his wife every night. He was ready for some action now. Thankfully he was due to get some action tonight now that Aurelia's private boutique was finally open for business again.

I can hardly wait, Baron thought, determined to possess everything in that specialty shop once he got back inside. All the way inside.

Just then, Aurelia walked into the room.

Musiq's So Beautiful instantly played in Baron's mind. She's gorgeous! He licked his lips as he took in the sight of his wife in yet another classy dress and with a beautiful head of curls that reached all the way down to her shoulders. Wow!

Smiling at her husband as she passed by the advisors' table, Aurelia took a seat on the front row. She just had to be near him in some small way. She wished she was sitting in his lap.

So enthralled with Baron, Aurelia was oblivious to the fact that Claude had reserved the usual seat for her on the third row where he and Bambi sat. Unfortunately for the Weavers, their undeniable attraction to each other was noticed by several students and all of the professors present. Most of the females and a few of the males felt a mixture of surprise and jealousy by what they saw.

Claude was not surprised about Baron's attraction to Aurelia at all. He'd known about it ever since that dance routine in December. However, he was surprised that Aurelia returned that attraction considering the fact that she was supposed to be engaged to another man these days.

As for being jealous, Claude didn't feel an ounce of that emotion. Not with things going so well between him and Bambi. He'd even met and been accepted by her parents.

Bambi simply smiled at Aurelia and Baron's attraction as a theory formed in her mind. Professor Weaver was about the same age and the same ethnicity as her friend's mystery fiancé. Plus, Barry could very well be a nickname for Baron.

Could Aurelia's fiancé and Professor Weaver actually be the same man?

It was possible. But then again the two men were in different lines of work. Baron was a teacher. Aurelia's fiancé was a traveling business man...or so they'd been told. Clearly Bambi's theory required a lot more thought. Some evidence would be nice, too.

"Take heed, Professor," Rhoda suddenly leaned over to whisper in Baron's ear. "Although that one certainly appears more studious than all the others, I wouldn't be surprised if half of Aurelia's grades were earned in other ways," she slandered without an ounce of conscience.

* * *

Baron stiffened and frowned at Rhoda's low opinion of his wife. How dare she act like Aurelia was a woman on the prowl for a passing grade!

If anyone was on the prowl, it was Rhoda. Convinced that all Latino men had a thing for blondes, she'd been trying to get a date with Baron ever since he started working at AU. Her attempts increased after he rescued her and helped the police solve her assault case.

Although Baron had been nice about rejecting Rhoda and had done his best to let her down easy, what she just said about his wife was enough to provoke a different kind of response from him. From now on, Baron would be blunt and to the point with his rejections.

"First of all, I resent your low opinion of the female students at this school. Secondly, Aurelia's beauty didn't earn her that A in my class no more than yours will earn you a date with me," Baron whispered back in his wife's defense.

Rhoda stiffened in her seat this time. "I was just trying to help you avoid some trouble in your life. Trying to repay the huge debt I owe you in some small way."

"Are you sure you weren't trying to help yourself to me instead? In any case, consider any debt you feel you owe me paid in full as of this moment," Baron replied, concluding their whispered conversation before turning to face forward again.

Rhoda sat upright and faced forward again, too. Her face was flushed with color. Her eyes were daggered with ire as they stared straight ahead. She grew even angrier when she saw Aurelia's dress.

Rhoda would know a Shani design from anywhere. That red dress with its modest high neck, embroidered eyelet detailing, and scalloped hemline was from her very own wish list.

Where did a college student get enough money to buy an expensive Shani dress like that? As a college professor, Rhoda had to save up to buy one of those designs. Had Aurelia found another wealthy boyfriend? If so, who was he?

While Rhoda continued to ponder about things that weren't any of her business, Baron's irritation level rose even higher. It went up a big notch when he saw Aurelia get up and move to a seat beside Claude. He paid no mind to the fact that Bambi was on the other side of Claude.

Baron was too busy counting down the days until he and his wife could proudly wear their wedding rings. Oh what a happy day it will be to finally proclaim to the world that they belonged to each other. To finally let everyone know that Aurelia was Mrs. Weaver, not Miss Bunting.

As Baron and his colleagues opened the floor for discussion, it took everything in him to remain focused. By the end of that meeting, tension was in every muscle in his back and his jaws were tight with repressed anger. His hands actually clenched at his sides when he later saw Claude walk Aurelia out to her car.

Once again, Baron's jealousy blinded him to the fact that Bambi was also with them. Now he was counting down the minutes to when he could go home and confront Aurelia about her lingering attachment to Claude.

* * *

Baron found Aurelia in the shower when he arrived home. He would have been home long before now, if he hadn't gotten held up by two talkative colleagues and a few students who needed his input about the field of forensics.

"Why did you do it, Aurelia?!" Baron roared, shoving the sliding shower door open with one forceful thrust. His voice was even louder than the radio playing in the background.

A startled Aurelia jumped at his sudden appearance, dropping the loofa and soap in her hands. "You almost scared the life out of me." She paused briefly to take in a deep breath of serenity. "And why did I do what?" she continued seconds later as she turned the shower radio off.

"Why did you sit by Claude tonight? You know I don't want you around him. In fact, I forbid it as of today." Baron seethed, still talking way too loud.

"First of all, lower yur voice when you talk to me!" Aurelia snapped back, mirroring his ire. "I'm right here, mon. There's no need to yell at ah gal. Secondly, I may've been one of yur students, but I've neva been yur child. You can't forbid me to do nuttin. Thirdly, you not dealing wid one of dose timid little white girls here, so understand dat if you keep raising yur voice at me, you gonna get de same treatment in return."

Baron's mouth opened and closed without a sound. Although he wanted to rebuke that erroneous stereotypical comment about white women as a whole, he remained silent. Especially since Aurelia did have a point about at least one white woman.

Had this been Megan, Baron would have gotten quick submission and an apology. He wouldn't have gotten ire and a fiery attitude that matched his own.

And yet it was Megan who cheated on him, despite her passivity and tendency to behave like a bobblehead, nodding in agreement at everything he said or did. It was Megan that made him think he was secure in their relationship only to suddenly pull the rug out from under his ego and self-esteem. Megan, not Aurelia.

With that reminder at the forefront of his mind, Baron took a deep breath and blew it out before speaking again. Whatever he said next, he knew it had to begin with an apology.

"I'm sorry for yelling, baby. Please forgive me," Baron said in a much calmer and humbler tone.

"You're forgiven," Aurelia gruffed out, though her tone and frown seemed anything but forgiving as she readjusted the shower cap on her head to protect her new hairdo.

Baron smiled nevertheless. He knew her ire had decreased considerably in light of her less concentrated accent. Hopefully all of her anger would be gone very soon and they could get on with the process of making up...properly.

"As for the situation with Claude, I sat by him and Bambi tonight. The same Bambi that Claude just so happen to be dating now," Aurelia continued, turning the shower head to rinse the suds off her body before the soap dried in certain places on account of the open shower door. "I relocated to throw everybody off you and me, Baron. People saw the way we were looking at each other tonight. They're starting to suspect something's up, which means no more midday quickies in your office for us. Bambi even asked if I had dumped my fiancé because of my obvious interest in you now. If I hadn't sat by them, I would have confirmed what they were all thinking anyway."

"Oh," Baron replied thoughtfully. "That makes sense."

"Whether it does or not, it's the truth."

"I had no idea Bambi was interested in Claude even a little bit." Baron wondered how he could have missed that.

"Of course you didn't. Men are stupid like that. They usually pay attention to all the wrong things. In Claude's case, he'd been paying attention to the wrong woman for years until Bambi finally spoke up for herself. In your case, you were paying attention to the wrong issue. Instead of focusing on my friendship with Claude, you should have been focusing on getting that stalker chick off your back."

"You mean Rhoda?" Baron suppressed a moan when Aurelia bent to pick up her loofa and soap. His lower body swelled with desire in direct response to that live centerfold spread his eyes were just privy to.

"Yes, Rhoda," Aurelia confirmed, standing upright again. "Or as we students like to call her, the nuttiest professor on the planet because she acts like a mad scientist, doesn't bother to remember any of our names, and lives with a bunch of cats in a big haunted-looking house on a hill," she added, revealing her own jealousy issues as she put her hands on her wet hips. "Now what was she whispering in your ear tonight?"

"She was whispering about you." Baron smiled, loving

that she was just as jealous as he was tonight. That he wasn't the only one with insecurity issues, thereby making her just as human and imperfect as him.

"About me?" Aurelia started soaping up her body again.

"Yes, she was trying to warn me about female students who try to get good grades with their bodies instead of their brains."

Aurelia frowned. "She has some nerve badmouthing me like that. And she wonders why nobody around campus feels sorry for her anymore. Why some folks almost wish you hadn't saved her that night."

"Although I'm glad Rhoda was spared further abuse, I kinda wish someone other than me had been her rescuer. She's been extra clingy ever since," Baron acknowledged.

"You got that right." Aurelia scowled. "Anyway, what did you say to her in return tonight?"

"I told her that you earned the grade you got in my class and then rejected her in a very blunt way." As Baron talked, he kicked out of his shoes and shed his tie and jacket.

Aurelia gasped in shock as he suddenly entered the shower stall seconds later. "Baby, what are you doing?" She giggled as the rest of her ire and jealousy melted clear away.

"Mmm...nothing," he lied, reaching for her soapy swells.

"You still have clothes on." Even so she made room for him in the large enclosure.

"Not for long." He unbuttoned his shirt even as the water proceeded to soak it through and through.

"Let me give you a helping hand." Aurelia used her hands to unfasten his wet jeans.

"I'd like a kiss, too." Baron pulled her to him for a ravenous smooch.

A minute later, his clothes were in a pile at one end of the shower stall. As for the Weavers, they were intimately at the other end of the stall making up in a major way.

Baron took his time stroking Aurelia slowly and oh so tenderly up against that wet wall. Her arms clung about his neck. One of her legs stood on the floor while the other wrapped around his waist.

"This right here is yet another reason why I get so jealous at times," Baron confessed, continuing to act like Mr. Love-Me-Long-Time. "I've never loved anyone this deeply before. Never been this attracted to anyone before in my life. The thought of you giving all this to someone else is enough to drive me—"

"Shh…" Aurelia put a finger up to his lips to silence that negative confession. "You will never lose that brilliant mind of yours behind me or anyone else. As for me giving my body to another, that will never happen as long as I'm married to you. And we will stay married as long as you remember to treat me right and stay faithful."

"I'll treat you right, baby." Baron put more power behind his strokes.

Aurelia squealed and moaned in response.

"I'll stay faithful." He picked up the pace.

Aurelia squealed again and jumped upon him, linking both legs about his waist as things quickly got out of control in that shower stall. Soon they were going over the edge together.

When it was all over, Baron did a most considerate thing. He gently washed Aurelia's body from head to toe. After a thorough rinsing, she returned the favor. Oh yes, the Weavers had officially made up tonight.

* * *

Later, as Baron and Aurelia moved about their bedroom in the buff, sex was the last thing on their minds. That particular appetite was sated for the moment. Right now they had more packing to do for the trip they were scheduled to take first thing in the morning.

Baron chose that time to address a very important subject. A subject that he should have addressed a long time ago.

"Aurelia, since we've been prone to misunderstandings from day one of our relationship, I was thinking that we needed to deal with something that could possibly open the door to even more misunderstandings," Baron said, careful not to come across as demanding or controlling in his statements. A quick learner, he now realized that those methods of communication just did not work with his wife.

"Something like what?" Aurelia prompted from her place near her bedroom vanity table where she was packing makeup into a traveling case.

"Primarily my trust issues," Baron replied, ready to follow another piece of Count's brotherly advice as he left the closet area and went to sit on the edge of the bed beside his large black suitcase. "Or rather our trust issues."

Aurelia turned around on her cushioned stool to face

him. "Our trust issues?"

"Yes, I'll start with mine first," he replied. "You see, before Megan ran off and left me for another man, I was extremely confident in my ability to keep a woman. I had looks, intelligence, sexual prowess, and a bank account to be envied. After she abandoned me, my confidence was deeply shaken. I started second-guessing myself in almost every way. I started thinking that every new woman would do the same thing that Megan did to me. Maybe for different reasons, but always with the same result – abandonment."

"So most of the jealousy you've been exhibiting lately is because of what Megan put you through?" Aurelia deduced.

"Exactly. And I suspect that your return jealousy is because of what Cain put you through."

"I think you're right. So what do we do about these trust issues of ours?" Aurelia asked.

"I suggest that we stay open and honest with each other in order to build up trust in our new relationship," Baron replied. "That we also stop assuming the worst of each other based solely on past experiences. Which means I have to start trusting you around your male friends, namely Claude. All I ask is that such friendships don't include lone meals or private meetings with these men. Agreed?"

"Agreed," Aurelia consented with a nod. "As for you and Professor Griffey, all I ask is that you limit the amount of time she spends in your office. I mean, what could she possibly have to talk to you about after every class?"

"Nothing at all, which is why I keep my office door closed and locked these days," Baron revealed. "Only 10% of what Rhoda ever talks about with me is school related."

"Which means the other 90% is flirtatious banter." Aurelia seethed with ire. Her hands balled into fists at her sides. "Fire bun dat heifer!"

"Relax, beautiful." Baron chuckled, rising from the bed. "No need to start a catfight." He paused to kiss her on the forehead as he passed by en route to his closet. "I will keep Rhoda in her place from now on. That's if she ever decides to flirt with me again, which I seriously doubt after the harsh brush off I gave her tonight."

Aurelia instantly relaxed. "Catfight officially averted." She chuckled.

Baron laughed, too. "One last serious item up for discussion tonight and then I'm done. It's about that timid little white girl comment you made earlier." He took a suit from his closet and headed for the suitcase on the bed.

"What about that comment?" Aurelia frowned, clearly not in the mood for another argument.

"I don't think it's accurate. In fact, I believe that timid women come in all colors. You just so happened to be strong and black, not strong simply because you're black. I've personally seen strong Latinas, strong white, Greek, and strong Asian women. And the list goes on and on. I've also seen weak black women who will let a man treat them any kind of way. You get the point I'm trying to make here, baby?" Baron folded his suit neatly into the suitcase as he talked.

"Yes, Professor. I get the point that I shouldn't buy into stereotypes," Aurelia replied. "I also get the point that I'm never really going to be out of your classroom." She chuckled.

Baron laughed. "Sorry. I'm a teacher everywhere I go."

"I can live with that." Aurelia had lived with worse.

"That's good to hear." Baron smiled, heading for the closet again. "By the way, I love your new hairdo. Keep it like that for a while, okay? It turns me on more than any of your other hairstyles." He paused to finger a curly ringlet that had fallen from the silk scarf she had her tresses wrapped in.

"As you wish, my husband. As you wish." Aurelia smiled up at him. "I try to do my best to please you in every way." She turned back around to finish packing her makeup .

Your best? Are you sure about that, baby? Baron mused, keeping that riotous thought to himself, lest it spark another argument. An argument that could literally destroy the current peace they had and so much more.

CHAPTER THIRTY-FIVE

Early the next morning, Aurelia and Baron set out for Bel Air. Riding in the same car again was sublime for the both of them. They hadn't been able to do that since St. Croix. The last time they'd been in the same car stateside was the day they rode home from the airport together.

"Relax, beautiful," Baron told Aurelia as she fidgeted in her seat for the umpteenth time since they left home.

"I can't," Aurelia replied with anxious eyes. Although she met his parents over the phone, this would be her first time meeting them in person. And that was just one reason to be nervous. "What if Earl and Marquess have turned your parents against me by now?" Aurelia continued, revealing what else she was nervous about. "What if they've turned everybody against me by now?"

"I seriously doubt that. My family is a pretty strong-minded bunch. They will either like or dislike you for their own reasons. They usually don't take on other people's offences," Baron informed from the driver's seat. "You already know Count and Jenny like you. As for my parents, I called them before we left and they sounded just as excited to finally meet you in person as they ever were."

"Really?" Hope shimmered in Aurelia's eyes. She desired the favor of her parents-in-law above anyone else in the family. She already loved her long-winded father-in-law. Nicolas reminded her so much of her own father with his long tales about anything under the sun.

And his laugh. Nicolas Weaver's laugh was downright contagious and so unique. It reminded Aurelia of another unique laugh that actually brought down the house on a show called Comedy Barn. She looked forward to hearing her father-in-law's laugh in person.

"Yes, really," Baron assured her. "Duke and Sasha sounded excited when I talked to them this morning, too. Does that make you feel better?"

"Only slightly better since the last time Duke saw me I was wearing next to nothing. And I don't even want to talk about what Count saw." Aurelia stiffened even more in her seat.

"I don't like the fact that my brothers saw so much of my future wife either, but it is what it is, Aurelia. We have to move past it. That's one of the reasons I suggested we do this surprise dance routine for my mother. I wanted to use some of the things she taught my brothers and I as children to get everyone to see you in a different light. I want Earl and Marquess in particular to see that you have dancing abilities that transcend what they saw at that bachelor's party."

"Okay, now that does make me feel better." Aurelia smiled and finally relaxed in her seat. "And you watch, baby, I'm going to make you so proud of me on that dance floor."

Baron smiled over at her. "I'm already proud of you, on and off the dance floor."

Grinning at his words, Aurelia relaxed all the way now. Soon she was dozing quietly beside him.

Baron chuckled softly at how fast she'd fallen asleep. He was surprised she'd stayed up this long after getting up super-early this morning to cook breakfast for them – a good pancake breakfast, at that, and to make love to him until he screamed with ecstasy.

Although Baron loved his meal and that early morning tryst, he did not love the fact that no more loving would take place until they returned home. Aurelia made it clear that she would not feel comfortable having sex under his parents' roof, despite the fact that they were married now and knew how to be quiet during times of intimacy.

She's such a woman of contrasts. Baron reflected upon his wife's personality as he drove in silence.

For such a sexual being, Aurelia had some very clear hangups in the sex department. Having enjoyed a very liberating sex life with all the other women he'd been intimate with, Baron had to keep making adjustments in his mind concerning his wife's growing list of 'sexual don'ts'. He had to keep reminding himself that the things Aurelia chose to do with him were more plentiful than the things she wasn't. That they were enough to satisfy him for the rest of his life.

For the most part, they were. After all, some men never got a smidgen of quality loving over their lifetimes. And quality loving was Aurelia's trademark. Everything she did in the bedroom was first-rate.

Even still, there were times that Baron felt restricted. Times like these when he just wanted to pull over on the side of the road and just drink from Aurelia's fountain. Blame it on that large expanse of inner thigh showing from the rising of her skirt as she shifted positions in slumber.

I will respect her wishes, Baron told himself. Even so he couldn't help but lick his lips at what might have been without Aurelia's restrictions, without that traumatic experience she suffered at the hands of Oliver Jean-Baptiste.

Feeling himself getting angry now, Baron turned the radio on low. He needed something to distract him as he drove the rest of the way to Bel Air.

* * *

From the second Aurelia walked into her parents-in-law's home, she fought against being overwhelmed. First of all, Baron never told her that he'd grown up in a bonafide mansion. The main Weaver home was huge, boasting at least ten bedrooms and twelve baths. There was also a pool, tennis and basketball courts, a bowling alley, theater room, and a commercial-sized kitchen.

On the walls were paintings by famous artists, some dead and some alive. The floors had carpet flown in from overseas. The ceilings all had chandeliers in various shapes and sizes. And the bedroom Baron and Aurelia would occupy during their visit was fancier than their honeymoon suite had been.

Who lives like this? Aurelia followed her husband back downstairs so that he could introduce her to the rest of his family who had arrived and were now waiting in the great room.

Did Aurelia and Baron walk back downstairs?

No, an elegant elevator took them back to the first floor. The only reason they walked upstairs was because Ana Maria had wanted to give Aurelia a brief tour of the place while Baron and the Weavers' butler had tended to their luggage.

That's right, the Weavers had a real live butler to assist them around the house. A maid came in twice a week to help keep the place maintained and to help with certain social events.

"Try to relax, baby," Baron said soothingly in the elevator.

Aurelia nodded, but she really didn't see how that was possible. She felt so out of her league here.

That feeling intensified when the elevator doors opened and Baron began introducing Aurelia to a barrage of close relatives from both sides of his family. Relatives who, despite some of their deep tans, were still several shades lighter than her.

Aurelia suddenly knew exactly how it felt to be the only black person at an event. It didn't feel good. Maybe she would have felt better had she not seen Earl's smirking face in the crowd.

Earl didn't come alone today. Beside him was his wife Meadow and…

Megan?

What was she doing here?

Tall, blonde, blue-eyed, and thin, Megan looked almost exactly like the socialite Paris Hilton, except with much bigger breasts from the boob job she had in her early twenties. Her cousin Meadow looked like the actress Gwyneth Paltrow. Both women were dressed to the nines although the actual party would not start for several hours and most everyone else was dressed very casually for this family only event.

Aurelia instantly felt dowdy in their presence in her white silk blouse, black skirt, and stiletto boots, despite the designer labels and hefty price tags of each item. She also felt fat compared to Megan and Meadow. The two women couldn't weigh over two hundred and twenty pounds between them, with Meadow weighing the most.

"Megan, what are you doing here?" a frowning Baron said, asking the exact question that was on Aurelia's heart.

"I came to meet your new wife like the rest of the family," Megan replied with a smile, though she had yet to even look Aurelia's way.

Baron's frowned deepened. "I don't consider you a part of this family."

"Oh, Professor, stop being such a boar." Megan chuckled lightheartedly as she placed a manicured hand on his right arm. "You know I'll always be a part of the Weaver family through my cousins. By the way, I'm back in town to stay after my husband's untimely death."

Aurelia's nails dug into Baron's left arm to keep from snatching Megan bald. She bit her bottom lip to keep from erupting into an angry tirade.

As if he knew how close his wife was to blowing her stack, Baron immediately took control of the situation. "Sorry for your loss, Megan. Now if you'll excuse us. My wife and I have more relatives to greet," he said and then promptly whisked Aurelia away to the other side of the room.

* * *

After Baron and Aurelia walked away, Megan said, "How could he be with that fat cow? And she's not even that pretty. I thought Professor would at least marry a black woman that looked like Halle Berry."

Meadow scoffed. "Aurelia is nowhere near fat, Megan. She's voluptuous. There's a difference you know. And she looks absolutely stunning in even the simplest of outfits," she replied, coming to her new sister-in-law's defense for two main reasons. One, to aggravate her cousin. Two, because Aurelia really wasn't fat or unattractive. She was gorgeous!

"Plus, a black woman doesn't have to look mixed with something to be beautiful. Baron's wife has that Nona Gaye kind of beauty – flawless skin, great bone structure, and natural poise. In fact, the way her hair is today, Aurelia looks like a slightly lighter version of Nona in that November 2003 issue of People magazine," Meadow continued, enjoying the spots of red appearing in her cousin's cheeks from being slapped hard with the truth.

Earl's cheeks also colored. "I personally don't find her attractive in the least," he said, his nostrils flaring erratically the way they always did when he was lying.

"Well, Baron certainly does," Meadow countered. "Look at the proud way he's introducing her to everyone. One would think she was royalty or something."

"As if." Megan scoffed, sounding like the valley-girl she used to be.

"Perhaps she is royalty to him." Meadow smiled, unable to resist taking another not-so-subtle dig at her cousin. "The fact that Baron does esteem Aurelia so highly makes me want to get to know her even better. Maybe I'll find out how she was able to snag Baron so fast when it took other women years to get him to even look at them a certain way."

"Earl, you better restrain your wife," Megan hissed after Meadow strutted away towards the newlyweds.

"How can I without alerting her to things best left in the dark?" Earl spoke just as discreetly. "Besides, if Meadow suddenly starts being cordial to you, people are going to become suspicious. Everybody knows she hates you with a passion."

"Is jealous of me is more like it. And although you might be right on that front, I still didn't appreciate her comments today." Megan sent a daggered look her cousin's way. She hated Meadow far more than she hated Aurelia. If it wasn't for the Griswold name, she wouldn't even claim Meadow as kin.

"What I don't appreciate is being made to help you ruin my brother's marriage." Earl looked around with a faux smile as he spoke under his breath.

"What do you care?" Megan asked, amazed by his sudden case of brotherly loyalty. What happened to that loyalty a year ago? "Besides, you want Aurelia gone just as much as I do anyway."

"But not to be replaced by you. Never you," Earl replied impassioned.

Megan frowned. "You better restrain yourself now, Earl Weaver. Because the only repeat of the past will be between me and Baron." Then she walked away, leaving him to stew on that as she went to mingle among so many familiar faces.

* * *

Aurelia felt better by the time she and Baron went up to their room to shower and change before the official wedding party got underway. The fact that she was now adored by her parents-in-law, all three of her sisters-in-law, and two of her brothers-in-law went a long way towards changing her mood.

Even Marquess was cordial to Aurelia. He was also sober since he never drank around his mother. Come to think of it, the only people Aurelia hadn't won over yet were Earl and Megan. Yet she wasn't too particularly interested in winning them over anyway. No one could expect to be liked by everyone.

"It's good to see you so relaxed again," Baron told his wife as she stood in front of the mirrored dresser pinning up portions of her curls.

The bejeweled custom-made white dress Aurelia wore

looked almost like a wedding gown except for the pretty pink accents along the hem. Baron had on a black tuxedo-looking costume with the traditional plunging V neckline that most male Latin dancers wore. Both outfits were perfect for the dance routine they planned to do in honor of Ana Maria and her Latin roots.

Aurelia smiled at Baron in the mirror. "It's good to be relaxed again. It was rough for a while there. But your family really went out of their way to make me feel welcome." She chuckled and added, "Most of them anyway."

"Never mind Earl." Baron came up behind her and hugged her about the waist. "Or anyone else who wants to hate on our love," he added, refusing to mention Megan by name.

"That's what we have, don't we, baby? Love." Aurelia turned around to face him.

"And lots of it, too." Baron gently traced the left side of her face. "I want to kiss you so bad right now. Can I? Or will you be mad about me messing up your lipstick?" he asked, recalling such things from his days with vain Megan.

"Lipstick can be reapplied, baby." Aurelia offered her lips to him even as she draped her arms about his neck.

Baron smiled. He couldn't have chosen a better wife.

* * *

The same love that Baron and Aurelia displayed upstairs in their bedroom was continuously displayed downstairs in the great room as they danced the Paso Doble. No one could deny the depth of that love, not even Earl and Megan. It practically oozed from the newlyweds' pores and spilled from their eyes whenever they looked at each other, which was often.

When Aurelia and Baron danced the Bachata, their abundance of passion was also displayed. It was in the way they stared at each other, touched each other. It was especially in the way Baron's hands always ended up somewhere on or near Aurelia's derriere, although he kept that action G-rated for the general audience observing their dance.

Ana Maria cried with joy throughout the lively dance routine. She led the way in clapping with encouragement at various intervals. It was the first time any of her sons had ever willingly performed the dances from her rich culture. It had been like pulling teeth trying to teach those dances to her boys. Back then, it hadn't been cool to even learn them. Now Baron displayed a finesse that Ana Maria always suspected he possessed.

As for Aurelia, she was superb as she glided effortlessly across the dance floor. Simply superb.

"She moves so beautifully," Ana Maria said, speaking highly of her new daughter-in-law from her place across the large room.

"Yes, she does. Both of them do," Nicolas agreed from beside her.

"Watching them is like watching art in motion," Jenny whispered from her place in back of her parents-in-law.

"Yes, it is," Count replied, sitting beside his own wife. He could recall another time when he'd seen Baron and Aurelia moving so flawlessly together. "They really do belong together."

"Like us?" Jenny smiled.

Count nodded. "Yes, exactly like us." He leaned in to give her a kiss.

Ana Maria smiled back at them. She'd overheard Count and Jenny's comments and approved of them. She was also pleased to find three out of her five sons happily married now. Ana Maria would just have to keep praying for Earl and Marquess, because they showed no signs of changing any time soon.

* * *

At the end of the dance, Baron requested his mother's hand while Aurelia requested the hand of his father. Together they led the rest of the family in a time of even greater fellowship as they all practiced a few Latin dances of their own. They even got Ana Maria's brother the priest to dance with them. Uncle Miguel could really cut a rug, too.

Earl reluctantly danced the salsa with his wife. Not only would he have preferred dancing with Megan instead, but he absolutely hated the dances of his heritage. Hated almost everything about his heritage because it limited him in the social circles he still craved to be a part of. Social circles that Aurelia was going to make even harder for him to be included in since a lot of his associates judged a man by his bank account and his family connections.

As for Megan, she got up from her seat and danced along with everyone else. Not sans partner, mind you. No, she made sure to dance with one of Baron's attractive cousins on his father's side in hopes of making him jealous.

Unfortunately for Megan, Baron didn't even look her way. Hadn't since that awkward greeting. Baron only seemed to have eyes for his wife. Even now he changed partners with his father so that he could dance with Aurelia again.

And the way Baron took her in his arms again and held her. It was like Aurelia was precious to him.

But how could she be precious to him? She can't even satisfy him completely, Megan mused, starting to wonder if Baron no longer cared about full sexual pleasure.

He used to be so uninhibited in the bedroom. If there was something to be done to a woman to bring her pleasure, Baron was the kind of man to seek it out and do it. Several times over.

Megan's body tingled just thinking about Baron's sexual prowess. It had been so easy to submit to his control because he'd made each and every submissive act worth her while.

Baron had also been the greatest teacher. He taught Megan so many things about making love to a man. So many ways to bring a man pleasure. Some of those things she wished she had never used on Earl because it had been so hard to break free of him afterwards.

Thinking about Earl caused Megan's tingles to instantly cease. Making love…correction, having sex with him had only been pleasurable one time – that first time. And that was only because it had the thrill of vengeance fueling it. Every time after that had contained one-sided pleasure. Meaning, Earl was the only one receiving pleasure from the act.

Ironically, that didn't seem to bother Earl at all. He'd simply kept on going even after Megan stopped responding favorably. Had that been Baron, he would have paused, made some inquiries and even gotten some suggestions, and then started again with new tricks. He would have made sure Megan enjoyed herself, too, even if it took him all night.

I really miss you, Baron, Megan lamented, grieving inside that this wasn't their wedding party instead. She grieved even deeper when she looked over and saw that Baron's hands had found their way down to Aurelia's bottom once again.

* * *

Across the room, Baron leaned in to whisper in Aurelia's ear. "Let me make love to you tonight, beautiful." He squeezed her closer.

"Baron—"

"I'll be real quiet about it," he interrupted her protest. "It'll be just like our honeymoon night or that time in my office. I'll take you on the floor, up against the wall, even in a chair. Anywhere you like. Just please let me inside again, baby. Tonight." He squeezed her even closer, taking full advantage of their semi-private place by one of his mother's large plants.

Hearing the need in his voice and feeling the pulsating need in his body, Aurelia surrendered to the need in her own body. "Okay."

Baron moaned with pleasure at her words, at her willingness to relax that rule. He hoped she would eventually relax them all when it came to their sex life. "I can hardly wait for this party to end now." He moved his hips slowly against hers.

Aurelia let out a return moan. "Me, too." She instinctively followed the rhythm of his hips, adding a suggestive grind at the end.

Baron inhaled sharply and moaned again as his body swelled and ached to distraction. "Okay, the party officially ends right now for us," he said determinedly, leading her towards the staircase.

"But Baron, we're the guests of honor. We can't leave our own party early," Aurelia protested, although she liked when he took control at times like these.

"Consider this an intermission then. We'll slip up for a quickie and come back down when we're done," he persisted, continuing to lead her out of the great room. It was time to let off some of the steam they had created on the dance floor.

CHAPTER THIRTY-SIX

Upon noticing that Baron had been gone for ten whole minutes with his wife, Megan went to investigate his whereabouts. Since she knew the Weaver home like the back of her hand, she was able to make her way up to Baron's old bedroom unnoticed.

Megan hadn't come within five feet of that closed bedroom door when she heard heavy breathing coming from the floor area. *They're making love on the carpet?!* She couldn't recall a single time that she and Baron had gotten busy on the floor.

Megan tiptoed closer to the door. She told herself that this was just a fact-finding mission. That she could handle anything she heard coming from the other side of that door. Ten seconds later, she wasn't so sure about that.

"I see you want to be my little cowgirl tonight," Baron whispered hoarsely.

Aurelia moaned. "Just call me Miss Lone Ranger, baby."

"Well, giddy up then." Baron chuckled huskily, giving her bottom a playful smack.

"Hi-yo, Silver. Away!" Aurelia chuckled, ending the last of their words as things quickly spun out of control on the floor.

Outside the door, Megan's eyes glossed over with pain. Baron sounded so happy in there. So fulfilled. So downright...playful and carefree.

He'd never been playful and carefree with Megan. Never!

Their bedroom time had always been a serious occasion, pleasurable, but serious nevertheless. Baron hadn't even been playful with Megan outside the bedroom. Yet just now he acted as if he and Aurelia were the best of friends as well as

296

lovers.

Staggering away from that door as if someone had just stabbed her in the gut, Megan made her way back downstairs. She immediately sought out Earl. He had some serious explaining to do.

* * *

By the time Megan finally got Earl alone, the smiling newlyweds had returned to the party and everyone had transitioned outside to the Weavers' lighted patio to eat. The sun had set and the whole area had taken on a romantic glow.

Baron and Aurelia sat at the head table with Ana Maria and Nicolas. The rest of their relatives populated other tables. Those standing in the buffet lines did some of the same things as those seated at tables – happily chatted, laughed, and enjoyed each other's company on that warm starry night.

Megan and Earl were two exceptions to the rules. There was no happy chatter between them. No laughter. And they definitely weren't enjoying each other's company as they sat at a half-empty table in the back.

"Are you sure she denies Baron certain pleasures in the bedroom?" Megan whispered when Meadow finally got up to check on her children at one of the kiddie tables.

Before replying, Earl made sure his wife was well out of hearing distance. "Yes, I'm sure," he whispered back once the coast was clear.

"Well, that look of pure satisfaction on Professor's face says otherwise." Megan remembered that look well from her intimate times with Baron. "I mean, he's like totally relaxed right now, so their little quickie must have been extremely gratifying," she added, once again sounding a bit valley-girlish.

"Look, I basically told you what Count told me," Earl replied discreetly, looking towards that very brother right now.

Hot-headed as a child, Count used to be the one to hit first, ask questions later. Only their parents and Baron used to be able to calm his temper down. Jenny was added to that list when she came on the scene. Now Count was the calmest brother among them. Earl hoped he stayed that way, because that particular little brother had a left hook out of this world.

"Well, she must have relented to his wishes by now then,"

Megan persisted, drawing Earl's attention back to her. "As I recall, Baron can be very convincing in the bedroom."

Earl frowned. He hated even thinking about Megan with his brother...or any other man. Life suddenly seemed very unfair.

"Yes, she could have relented by now. If not, then the other thing that Count said about them must be true, as well," Earl suggested.

"What other thing?" Megan scowled, looking highly displeased that any information about Baron had been withheld from her. After all, wasn't she paying to know every little tidbit about him? Paying generously at that.

"The thing about Professor not making a big deal of his wife's sexual restrictions because he's content with all the other things they do together," Earl replied, taking great pleasure in dashing her hopes.

"What things?" Megan's blue eyes followed Baron as he made his way back inside the house alone.

"Things like positions and techniques. From what I've seen and been told, my new sister-in-law is quite skilled with her hips. The fact that she's so curvy is another plus. As you know, Professor is quite the breast man. Now he seems to be hooked on that plump rump of hers, too." Earl suppressed a grin. This was the most fun he'd had all night.

"Perhaps Baron needs a little reminder of what I'm good at," Megan hissed under her breath.

"She might be good at that by now, too, if he's gotten through to her," Earl countered.

"Yes, but not good enough. Remember, I have years of experience under my belt in that department. Perhaps my little reminder is just what your brother needs to bring him back to his senses, to get him to finally realize that he and I belong together instead." Then Megan rose from her seat and walked determinedly in the direction that Baron had just taken.

Earl scowled now. Did the woman have no shame? Baron barely just finished making love to his wife less than thirty minutes ago and already Megan was ready to drop to her knees for him?

Earl had to do something to keep her from degrading herself like that. Hopefully that same something would ensure that Megan and Baron never hooked up again. Unfortunately for Earl, this meant becoming an unexpected ally to Aurelia now.

* * *

"Aurora," Earl said, addressing his newest sister-in-law in a hushed whisper as he stood behind her at the long buffet table where a variety of seafood could be found.

"It's Aurelia," she corrected, not even bothering to turn around. Why put forth any amount of effort for someone that didn't like her?

"Whatever." Earl showed his disdain for Aurelia even now. "If you want to keep your husband, you shouldn't let him be alone with Megan, whom I just saw follow him back inside the house."

Aurelia's head snapped around to look at Earl now. Her eyes narrowed in suspicion at him. She didn't trust Earl no more than she could throw him. The fact that he walked away smirking gave her even more reason to distrust him.

But what if Earl had spoken some truth? What if what he just said had some merit?

Baron had definitely gone back inside the house to get the extra disposable cameras they'd brought along for their visit. And Megan was nowhere to be seen right now. Were they together?

Remembering that she'd left Cain and Roxy alone too many times to count and also recalling how badly that turned out, Aurelia abandoned her half-fixed plate of seafood and discreetly made her way back inside the house. She just hoped history wasn't about to repeat itself tonight.

* * *

"We have nothing to discuss, Megan," Baron told his ex-fiancée as she stood in the doorway of his bedroom. "You said everything that needed to be said in your text message, remember?"

"I had to marry Scottsdale to gain my freedom…financial and otherwise," Megan replied as truthfully as she could without revealing her deepest, darkest secret.

"You would have had financial freedom with me if you had only waited a little while longer," Baron informed her, reaching into the closet for his largest suitcase.

Megan scoffed in disbelief. "What kind of financial freedom would we have had on your teacher's salary?" She entered the room more fully.

Baron shook his head at her. "That goes to show how much you really knew about me. For your information, I was

299

a millionaire before I ever finished undergrad school. I gained multi-millionaire status by the time I finished my residency." As he talked, he unzipped a side compartment of his suitcase and retrieved a brown bag of disposable cameras from inside.

"What? How?" Megan's eyes were wide. This was the first she'd heard of him being a millionaire, much less a multi-millionaire.

"I gained my current wealth mostly from investments. Unlike my brothers, I listen carefully to our father's long ramblings. Particularly when he talks about how to watch for the best stocks and bonds and when to sell those holdings. I also know when to seize a business opportunity," Baron replied, thinking of the lucrative business he and his college roommate started in Vegas, though he wasn't too keen on continuing that partnership these days.

"Why didn't you tell me this before?"

"Because my father also told me never to discuss the whole of my finances with anyone except for my wife, accountant, and a trusted lawyer. The only reason I'm telling you this now is because I want you to know exactly what you walked out on." Baron zipped his suitcase and returned it to the closet.

Megan's eyes grew sad. "I will always regret walking out on you, Professor. I'd like a second chance to make all that up to you."

"Second chance?" Baron's eyes were wide now. "Are you crazy?! I'm married now. Or did you miss the whole point of tonight's party?" With the bag of disposable cameras firmly in one hand, he shut the closet door with the other.

"Marriages end all the time just like jobs." Megan moved closer still. "We can send Aurelia home with a nice severance package for her trouble. Then we can go back to building our lives together, the way it was always meant to be."

Baron shook his head. "I'm not sending Aurelia anywhere. I love her. I plan to be with her for the rest of my life."

"Do you also plan to be sexually frustrated for the rest of your life, too?" Megan retorted. "Yes, I heard all about how uptight your wife is in the bedroom," she continued at his shocked look. "As you know, I will do any and everything when it comes to sex." Her voice lowered as she moved even closer to him. "I'm willing to do any and everything tonight, if you want me to." She licked her lips in invitation. "Don't you miss being my Popsicle, Professor?" Megan purred out his nickname.

If only Aurelia had just said that to me, Baron mused. His lower body twitched to life again at that very thought. The tight pants he had on showed that life growing in leaps and bounds.

"I see you do miss being my Popsicle." Megan chuckled, looking down at him with satisfaction before dropping to her knees before him.

"I kin see dat, too," said a curt female voice from the doorway.

Baron and Megan's attention snapped to the right from where that familiar thick island accent had resonated from. As expected, it was…

Aurelia!

CHAPTER THIRTY-SEVEN

Megan grinned at the sight of her rival in the bedroom doorway. Baron winced and shook his head in disbelief. Surely this could not be happening!

This is bad. Real bad, he thought, quickly deducing that Aurelia had heard enough of his conversation with Megan to come to the wrong conclusion. That she'd seen enough with her eyes to confirm that wrong conclusion.

Things got considerably worse when Megan opened her mouth to speak before him. "Well, hello there, Aurelia." She smugly rose to her feet again.

"Don't you dare say another word, Megan!" Baron ordered, quickly trying to take control of the situation. His body was nowhere near stimulated with desire now. Only fear coursed through his veins now. The fear of losing his wife.

"Baby, regardless of what you saw or heard just now, it's not what you think," Baron continued in a humbler tone as he addressed his wife.

Aurelia looked both of them up and down in disgust and just shook her head. Instead of answering either of them, instead of surrendering to the angry outburst and the physical violence that were itching to get out of her, she calmly walked over to the dresser and retrieved her purse.

Forget the clothes Baron had bought her for this trip. Forget him. Forget everything. Aurelia didn't want any of them now.

So much for thinking that all she had to do was keep her man sexed up to prevent him from cheating. That theory had been proven wrong tonight. Now it was time to leave all of this pain and misery behind.

"Aurelia?" Baron asked with concern when she turned around and walked out without saying anything. Without so much as looking at him. Dropping the bag of cameras in his hand, he followed her out into the hall. "Aurelia!" he semi-shouted. "Baby, please let's talk this thing out."

Aurelia continued to ignore him all the way down the long hall. The more he called her name, the faster she walked. When she neared the staircase, she actually broke out into a run.

A run!

Momentarily shocked by her unexpected flight, Baron quickly recovered and took off running behind her. "Aurelia!" he shouted in earnest now.

Behind them, Megan entered the hallway with a satisfied smirk on her face. She could almost taste the victory now.

* * *

Aurelia made it safely inside Baron's Porsche before he could catch up with her. She even had time to lock all the doors to keep him from getting inside. All those years of dancing in heels had made her agile on her feet. Combine that with her natural speed and that good head start she'd had and it was easy to see how she left Baron in the dust a few minutes ago.

Mentally blocking out her husband's pleas as he banged on the car windows, Aurelia swiftly started up the Porsche, put it in reverse and backed all the way out of the five-car garage at top speed. Driving on St. Croix's narrow roads really came in handy tonight. Aurelia didn't sideswipe a single car as she made a quick getaway down the long Weaver driveway.

Entering the main road a few seconds later, she put the car in drive and headed home.

Home?

Where was that now?

Home definitely wasn't with Baron anymore. Maybe home was the small efficiency apartment that was still in her name until May.

Aurelia had originally thought about subleasing the place. She even advertised her intentions in the newspaper upon returning to Alcove.

Unfortunately, no one wanted to take the apartment because of the neighborhood it was in. Fortunately, Aurelia had no problem with that particular neighborhood. If she had problems with any neighborhood it was this one – the one where nothing but rich folks lived.

Aurelia couldn't seem to find her way out of Bel Air. She'd been asleep when they arrived earlier and the pretzel-like roads around here were confusing her. She must have passed the same blue house twice already.

"I'll find my way out of here somehow," Aurelia said determinedly. "I'll find my way out of everything that's got me twisted up."

* * *

Back at the Weaver mansion, a furious Baron stalked his way to the patio, ready to confront his fourth oldest brother. He wasn't afraid of Count's mean left hook. They'd been sparring partners for years. He knew how to avoid it. Knew how to get in a few power blows of his own.

Halfway to Count's table, Baron was sidetracked by his mother. She piled more guacamole upon her plate at one of the buffet tables he attempted to pass by.

"There you are, my precious baby boy," Ana Maria said cheerfully, gently patting him on the right cheek. "Where is your beautiful wife? Did you two sneak away for another rendezvous?" She smiled knowingly and with complete approval upon her face.

"No, Mama. Aurelia left," Baron forced out, glaring straight ahead at Count.

Ana Maria frowned with puzzlement at his words. "She left? Why would Aurelia leave so early and without you? Without saying goodbye to anyone?"

Originally the newlyweds were supposed to remain until Sunday evening after they'd attended Mass and had an early dinner with Ana Maria and Nicolas. Now it appears that those plans had changed.

"She left because Count opened his big mouth and told Megan something that I told him in confidence," Baron shouted loud enough for that particular brother to hear.

Unfortunately, everybody else heard what he said, too. The music was instantly turned off so that everyone could hear that much better.

"I didn't tell Megan a thing," Count replied with sincere eyes. "And what I did say, I said by mistake to that village idiot over there." He pointed accusingly to a red-faced Earl on the opposite side of the patio. "He probably told Megan on purpose."

"What is going on here?" Nicolas demanded to know, frowning as he stood to his feet. His frown deepened when he looked over and saw Megan smirking in a corner. He never liked the reformed valley girl. Thought she was an airhead for life, certainly not intellectually challenging enough or even principled enough for his youngest son.

"I'll explain everything later, Dad," Baron told his father, cutting off all further questions. "Right now, I need a set of car keys so I can go find my wife and bring her back."

"Here. Take mine," Marquess volunteered from a nearby table and then threw a silver key ring his brother's way.

Catching the keys with a grateful nod, Baron took off for the garage. At the last minute, he made a brief detour upstairs to retrieve his cell phone. He had a feeling he might need that particular item of convenience.

* * *

"I knew we shouldn't have brought you here tonight. What did you do in that house?" Meadow scowled at her cousin.

"I simply reminded Baron of what he was missing out on with me, that's all." Megan smirked. "I doubt if his marriage will last another night now, much less another month."

"You...home-wrecker!" Meadow raged, secretly inundated with suspicions about her cousin's involvement with her own husband. Did Megan have no boundaries?

"Call me what you will, but Baron and I belong together," Megan said defiantly. "Now that my work is done here, I will retire to my own house and let the rest of the chips fall where they may. A house that is much bigger than yours, I might add."

"Coward!" Meadow hissed as her cousin made a quick escape after causing so much destruction tonight.

Beside Meadow, Earl seethed with jealousy. He actually thought Baron's love for Aurelia was strong enough to withstand his lust for Megan. But then as he recalled that Megan could even put that scandalous rap video vixen to shame, he realized that he'd basically been hoping that Baron's love was strong enough to resist that kind of temptation. That way Earl could be free to pursue Megan...once he discovered a new way to do so, of course.

Earl suddenly saw Count rise to his feet across the patio. He instantly stiffened in his seat. Dread and trepidation filled his heart, weakening his knees.

Should he run and show people what a coward he really was? People that included his wife and children. Or should he stay and at least attempt to fight his more muscular, stronger, and quicker younger brother?

"I'm coming for that jaw, Earl, so you might as well stand up and take your punishment like a man," Count said in a menacing tone as he quickly closed the distance between them. He steadfastly ignored the attempts by Duke and others to get him to calm down. Others that did not include his wife Jenny.

Earl forced himself upon his feet. Twelve seconds later, he was on the ground unconscious.

* * *

"Great! Just great!" Aurelia threw her hands up in exasperation as the not-so-helpful red-haired police officer refused to give her directions yet again. He also refused to let her drive off without showing proof of ownership for the expensive car she drove.

It seems that being black in an expensive vehicle was still a crime in certain parts of America. Or at least it was still reason enough to be treated as a suspect.

"Ma'am, just produce the proper identification and documentation and I'll let you go. I'll even give you the directions you seek to boot," the freckled-faced officer said, looking doubtful that she had any such proof.

"I told you dat meh driver's license still in meh maiden name. I ain't got it switched ova to meh married name yet," Aurelia replied, so close to losing her temper that she could feel the sizzle between her hot ears.

"Then I need for you to call your husband and tell him to come with proof," the officer replied sternly.

Thoroughly frustrated now, Aurelia opened her mouth and let out a tirade of thick island lingo.

"Speak English, ma'am. This is America, you know."

Rolling her eyes at that uncalled for rebuke, Aurelia took a deep breath, and calmly said, "You call him." Then she recited Baron's cell phone number very, very slowly as if she was talking to someone who was mentally challenged.

Racist people were mentally challenged in her book. No one in their right mind could seriously believe that the color of a person's skin automatically made him/her inferior or superior to others.

The officer's subsequent call to Baron was very short.

Whatever was said between them was enough to change the policeman's whole attitude towards Aurelia. He suddenly became very friendly. More respectful. He even offered to give her a container of bottled water from his vehicle while they waited on that humid night.

"No thanks," Aurelia replied through a tight mouth. She didn't want anything from the likes of him after the way he just treated her. She definitely didn't want to be tempted to speed away if he walked back to his car for the water.

Within ten minutes, Baron was there. He would have been there sooner had he not doubled back to get his own identification. He invited Marquess along, so that he could drive the Mercedes back to the house while Baron rode with Aurelia in the Porsche. Marquess was in the driver's seat when they pulled up, still just as sober as ever.

After presenting the proper documentation to the officer, Baron thanked both men and then waved goodbye to Marquess as he drove off. The same Marquess that had so much pull in the local police department that as soon as Baron said their last name over the phone, the officer was suddenly willing to be at their beck and call.

After taking a deep breath, Baron opened the driver's side door of his Porsche and addressed his wife, who had not uttered a word to anyone since he arrived. "Move over, baby. I'll drive," he said in a humble tone.

Aurelia rolled her eyes at him before doing as he requested. Sitting in the passenger seat a few seconds later, she folded her arms across her chest and stared straight ahead as he started the car and drove away from the police vehicle.

When Aurelia realized Baron was taking her back to his parents' house, she immediately protested. "Please take me to the airport, because I'm not setting foot back inside your parents' home. Matter of fact, I'm not setting foot back inside any Weaver home."

Baron's hands instantly tightened on the steering wheel. He slammed on the brakes as the gravity of the situation slammed to the forefront of his mind.

Aurelia's words and particularly her lack of accent in this highly emotional moment told him two important things. One, that she intended on leaving him tonight, not just his parents' house. Two, that she was settled in her mind about doing so.

The last time he'd seen Aurelia this calm at a highly emotional moment had been during her confrontation with Jordin. His wife's mind had been made up about her course of action that night, too. She had not strayed from that course, not even a little bit.

Taking another deep breath, Baron turned glossy eyes Aurelia's way. "Please…don't leave me, Ree-Ree," he said in a painful whisper, using her island nickname as his own emotions rose to an all-time high.

CHAPTER THIRTY-EIGHT

Aurelia squeezed her eyes closed upon hearing Baron's potent words. Did he have to call her Ree-Ree? Did he have to say it so tenderly? Why oh why did she still love this man so much? What kind of fool loved a man with a cheating heart?

"You're not worthy to call me by my island name. Now drive the car, freak boy!" Aurelia said, using anger to shield her vulnerable emotions.

"No." Baron ignored her dig as he glided the car closer to the curb and parked. "You promised you wouldn't leave me again. No more running away, remember?"

"If you recall, that promise was largely based on you being faithful to me." She turned to glare at him in the dark car. "Judging from what I heard and saw tonight, you were mere seconds away from cheating on me. And less than thirty minutes after I rocked your world. Now how greedy is that?"

"I was not about to cheat. Think, Aurelia. The facts just don't add up," Baron said, attempting to tug on her intellect and not her emotions right now. "For one thing, that bedroom door was wide open. If I was a cheater, do you think I'd be stupid enough to have any kind of sex with the door open in my parents' house? Mama could have easily walked past that door tonight and you know that I would never disrespect her like that, or you for that matter. The fact that Megan followed me up to that room and chose that occasion to drop to her knees should tell you that she was trying to set me up. Trying to set our very marriage up for failure."

"I don't doubt that Megan and Earl were trying to set our

marriage up for failure tonight," Aurelia replied, remembering her brother-in-law's little message. "However, your response to Megan's seduction is what has me most concerned. It clearly tells me that I'm not enough for you. That it's just a matter of time before you do cheat on me with a woman that's willing to drop to her knees in front of you. Why waste my time or yours waiting for the inevitable infidelity to occur? Let's just end this now so you can get back to who and what you really want."

"I want you, Aurelia. You! Only you," Baron said impassioned. His eyes glistened with emotion in the darkness.

"It didn't look like that to me a little while ago," Aurelia retorted as her own eyes grew shiny. "A little while ago, you wanted Megan or at least what she could do for you."

"That was just my body reacting to verbal stimuli," Baron said, sounding like a true science professor now. "It meant nothing."

"Oh, I beg to differ, Professor," Aurelia replied sarcastically as her accent temporarily thickened in places. "The fact dat yur body reacted to yur ex-fiancée on any level means ah lotta tings. One of which is de fact dat you have unfinished business with Megan. Cain could strip down naked in front of me right now and I wouldn't be moved by his humongous muscles or dat third leg of his. Why? Because I love you, Baron. You! My heart, my body only wants you. At least it did until now," she concluded, trembling with high emotion as tears ran down her cheeks.

"I love you, too, baby. Please believe me," Baron said, stung by her rejection and by her unexpected testament to Cain's physical superiority over him. Yet he unbuckled his seatbelt and embraced her in comfort anyway.

"No!" Aurelia jerked away from him. "I'm not falling for yur nice guy persona again. A genuine nice guy would've had de decency to at least tell his wife dat he had ah problem wid dere sex life 'stead of his ex-fiancée and whoever else you told." She wiped her tears away as she struggled to regain her composure in totality.

"I didn't tell Megan anything about us. I only told Count, who I'm used to sharing all of my secrets with. I didn't know he was going to blab that secret to Earl, intentionally or unintentionally. He never did before." Baron returned his hands to the steering wheel.

"I've never been married before, but based on what I've heard and read on the topic, you're supposed to tell your wife all your secrets." Aurelia used sheer willpower to regain the rest of her composure. "Anyway, can you please drive me to the airport now? Otherwise I'll be forced to walk that long distance in these heels and I really don't want to do that."

"Aurelia, please!" Baron remained immobile, refusing to budge in his desperation. His eyes swam with unshed dew. "Baby, don't give up on us over yet another misunderstanding," he said in an anguished whisper. Inwardly he couldn't understand how she could act so casually about leaving him when his heart was breaking into a thousand pieces.

"Call it what you want, freak boy. I got a plane to catch." Aurelia unlocked the passenger side door. She would show him that this Crucian didn't issue idle threats. That her word was her bond.

"You don't have to walk, Aurelia," Baron quickly conceded. "I'll drive you to the airport," he lied, mentally reminding himself to go to confessional soon.

Surely God would forgive him this one little sin compared to the big sins his brothers committed on a regular basis. Marquess and Earl usually were absolved from their sins via Uncle Miguel, though he hated to see them coming at times due to their habitually corrupt behavior.

"Just let me go say goodbye to my parents and let them see that you're okay," Baron added as he finally restarted the car.

"I suggest you call them on the phone instead, because I'm not going anywhere near that house." Aurelia wasn't ready to face his family again after everything that occurred tonight.

"At least let me go pack your things," Baron petitioned.

"I don't care about those clothes, man! Didn't you learn anything from my dealings with Cain? When I leave a man, I travel light," Aurelia replied without a hint of accent in her voice. "As for all the great things you've done for me and my family, just know that we'll find some way to pay you back. I'll personally make sure you get back every brown penny."

Baron was about to say, 'I don't want any of the money back. I just want you!' but he wisely refrained. Instead he took in a deep breath and then counted to ten as he slowly exhaled through his mouth.

If you think you're leaving me tonight or any other night, you are sadly mistaken, baby. Baron kept his thoughts to himself as he prepared to take Aurelia somewhere other than the airport.

* * *

Using his wife's ignorance of the area to his advantage, Baron got on the highway and headed home to Alcove. Not to Aurelia's apartment. To the house that they shared together.

During that long drive, Baron practiced a lot of deep breathing to keep himself under control and his mind clear. The phone call that he received from Jenny midway helped him to calm down a lot.

His sister-in-law basically called to explain that Count hadn't intentionally betrayed his trust to Earl. Jenny even shared the context in which her husband had shared Baron's info, confirming that it had been an innocent mistake.

Now Baron was mad with just one of his brothers. That ire increased at the memory of who brought Megan to the party anyway - Earl.

He's trying to ruin my marriage, but I'm not going to let him, Baron thought, determined to keep his wife.

He had a good mind to retaliate against his brother, but doing so would only upset their parents. Based on Jenny's call, Nicolas and Ana Maria was upset enough as it was.

It seems that right after Baron left, Count walked up to Earl and decked him right there in front of everyone. Soon after Earl regained consciousness, their father sent everyone home while their mother escorted their brother to the hospital to get checked out. As usual, Meadow was right there by Earl's side the whole time.

Sharp as a tack, Aurelia quickly picked up on Baron's intentions by noting the highway signs. "Don't think I'm not on to you, man. I know this is not the way to the airport." She didn't even look his way when she spoke.

"Still smart as ever I see," Baron replied, speaking to her for the first time since leaving Bel Air.

"Obviously not smart enough," Aurelia quipped. "Otherwise, I would've realized that I was just a bed warmer until Megan came back."

"You're not a bed warmer, Aurelia." Baron deliberately kept his voice calm. "In fact, you are all I could ever want in a wife. You're intelligent, caring, witty, benevolent, and my equal in the bedroom."

Aurelia scoffed in disbelief. "Nice try, Professor. But you and I both know that last thing is an outright lie."

"I beg to differ this time. As a lover, you are my perfect match in terms of passion, stamina, and creativity. Your only shortcoming is in the area of variety, but that's only because of that traumatic experience you had with Oliver. I only shared that experience with my closest brother because I hoped Count could shed some light on how I could help you through it. After all, he almost became a psychologist before switching to law."

Aurelia finally looked over at him. "If you only told Count, how did Megan know our business?"

"All signs point to Earl telling her." Then Baron disclosed how that conversation with Count and Earl went according to Jenny's testimony.

"I see," Aurelia replied when he was done with his recitation. "That still doesn't let you off the hook, you know. I saw what Megan's words did to you with my very own eyes."

"If the truth be known, when she mentioned that Popsicle thing, I immediately thought about you," Baron shared, telling Aurelia what he should have told her a long time ago. It would have helped clear up this misunderstanding once and for all. But then again, sometimes even the smartest people can act dumb, especially when their emotions are involved.

"You thought about me?"

"Yes, about the fact that I wanted you to be saying those words to me, not her. About how much I want to be your Popsicle. About how much I want to make you my full meal deal." Baron licked those gorgeous pink lips of his. "Sometimes I even dream about tasting you, Aurelia. About laying you across the dining room table and just having you for breakfast, lunch, and dinner. About—"

"Enough!" Aurelia interrupted as a violent shudder wreaked her body. No doubt about it – the man still had a way with words. She quickly turned back to the window to pull herself together again, lest she give Baron permission to pull over to the side of the road and just…feast.

"What do you want from me?" Aurelia whispered after an elongated silence.

"I want you to forgive me for unintentionally violating

your trust. For being stupid enough to even hold a conversation with Megan again," Baron replied, just beginning with his list. "I also want you to stay with me and help make our marriage work. I want you to be willing to let me teach you a few things in the bedroom, the same way you allowed me to do so in the classroom. I want to show you everything I like, baby. Things that you might even like, too, if you just give them a chance. If you just allowed yourself to stop associating those things with bad experiences of the past."

"And if I still don't like these things?" Aurelia turned to face him again.

"I'll never ask you to do them again."

Aurelia remained quiet for a few moments, pondering what she should do. Finally she said, "All right. I'll do what you want. But not tonight. Not even this week or next week for that matter since I'm still mad at you for sharing our intimate business with anyone."

"Whenever you're ready, beautiful," Baron replied in a husky whisper. He was thrilled that her heart was so willing to correct their marital woes. Proud that she was so willing to finally face another painful part of her past.

Baron was also deeply relieved. Aurelia's cooperation meant that she still wanted this marriage just as much as he did. She had him scared for a moment there. Real scared.

As for Cain's physical superiority over him, Baron was about to increase his muscle mass…all over.

CHAPTER THIRTY-NINE

When the Weavers finally made it back to Alcove, it was almost 4am. Although Baron was tired and cramped from all that driving, they were both emotionally drained. Too much had happened to them over the last twenty-four hours. Now it was time to get some much needed rest.

"I'm sleeping in one of the guestrooms tonight," Aurelia said once they were inside their quiet home. "I think that's wise under the circumstances."

Too tired to argue, Baron simply nodded. He was just glad that she was sleeping in the house at all after all they'd gone through. Closing the front door and locking it, he took a deep breath and blew it out as he watched her ascend the staircase alone.

Alone.

That's exactly how Baron felt as he lay in the master suite's bed by himself a few minutes later. He missed his wife already and they hadn't been home an hour yet. What would he do if Aurelia really left him?

I don't want to be alone, Baron thought, suddenly reminded of a heartrending verse from Phyllis Hyman's classic hit Living All Alone. And just as suddenly, he got out of bed, grabbed one of his sleeping bags from the closet and made his way to the guestroom where his wife was.

* * *

Aurelia woke up at 10am to the sound of loud snoring coming from the floor. Was a grizzly bear hibernating in the room?

Peering over the left side of the bed, she found Baron enclosed in one of his sleeping bags on the floor just a few feet away. A smile graced her lips.

That man. That wonderful, wonderful man. Aurelia started to understand how her husband thought more and more each day.

Sleeping on the floor was Baron's way of respecting her decision not to sleep in the same bed with him. It was also his way of satisfying his desire to be near her. In short, the man had created another win/win situation for them.

Though touched by his sentiments, Aurelia fought not to give in to their influence. What if Baron was trying to use his nice guy routine to win her favor in the same way that Cain had used expensive gifts and sex?

Either way, she refused to be manipulated by another man. Favors, gifts, and sex with strings attached just weren't worth a person's peace of mind.

If only just looking at Baron right now didn't make Aurelia weak in the knees. Why did he have to be so handsome? So sexy? So...utterly adorable even in slumber?

Stay strong, girl, Aurelia told herself as she renewed her resolve.

Forcing her gaze away from the sleeping man on the floor, she quietly exited the bed on the other side and tiptoed to the bathroom. Today she was going to do something she hadn't done in a long time, something that she would have done anyway had she stayed in Bel Air – go to church.

* * *

Baron woke up around noon to a definite chill in the house. It was one of those rare winter days in lower California where the temperature refused to climb to its usual mid 60's. Even the sound of the wind could be heard dancing against the window panes.

Getting up from his sleeping bag on the floor to adjust the thermostat, Baron quickly became anxious when he discovered that Aurelia was not only gone from her bed, but also gone from the house itself. Attempts to reach her via phone were fruitless. She had her cell phone turned off.

Don't jump to conclusions. Don't start assuming the worst, Baron told himself as he fought the urge to go to Aurelia's old apartment and then comb the city if she wasn't there. He couldn't call any of her friends because no one was supposed to know they were even together.

Instead of going off the deep end, Baron went to take a hot shower. After forcing a sandwich and a glass of juice down his throat, he went to his home gym to work off some of his nervous energy. If only he could stop watching the wooden clock on the wall.

* * *

Around 1:30pm, Aurelia arrived home. The instant she crossed the threshold she remembered that she forgot to leave a note for Baron telling him where she'd gone today.

How could you be so careless?! Aurelia scolded herself. The man probably thinks you went back on your word to stay and work things out.

Retrieving her cell phone from her purse, she promptly checked her messages. Seven of them were from Baron. He didn't leave any audio or text messages, but their house phone number was definitely listed seven times in a row on her display panel.

That poor man, Aurelia thought as she went in search of her husband. First she would apologize for not leaving a note like usual. Then as an olive branch, she would offer to fix lunch for them, despite the fact that it wasn't her week to cook.

Aurelia found Baron in his gym giving his punching bag quite a workout. At the sight of his shirtless torso and those glistening muscles, she suddenly wanted him to give her a workout, too. A long one.

In her lustful thoughts, Aurelia forgot all about the Bible in her right hand. But wait, it wasn't a sin to lust after one's own husband. Or was it? Now she wished she'd listened better in church over the years, gone to a few more Bible studies.

"Baron," Aurelia called out with a voice dipped deep in huskiness. When he didn't turn around right away, she didn't take offense.

Those earphones in his ears signified that he was exercising to one of his favorite Latin tunes again. The fact that he didn't hear her meant that the volume on that tune was turned up very high.

Aurelia cleared her throat and called his name even louder. "Baron!" That did the trick.

Baron's head snapped to the doorway at the same time that he backed up from the swinging punching bag to avoid getting hit in the face. Love and desire instantly filled his eyes at the sight of her in that gorgeous three-piece beige suit with its detachable cape and cuffs that were made from faux animal print fur. The matching animal print trimmed hat really set her outfit off just right.

The black Bible in Aurelia's hand added understanding to Baron's eyes. It told him all he needed to know about her whereabouts this morning. She'd gone to church.

To church! Hallelujah!

Out of respect for that sacred book in her hand, Baron instantly forced his mind out of the gutter. "I see somebody went to church today." He lowered the earphones from his ears.

"Yes. I'm sorry for not leaving a note. I meant to, but I forgot in my haste to make it in time for the 11 o'clock service at the church that sponsors the soup kitchen," Aurelia explained, taking a deep breath to force out the lingering desire in her own body just in case it landed her in trouble in other ways. She deemed it entirely too soon to be jumping back into bed with her husband after what happened yesterday.

"I wish you'd awakened me. I would have liked to have gone with you." Baron walked over to the mini-refrigerator in the room for a bottle of spring water.

"I didn't think you'd like going to a Baptist church. They tend to be a little bit more...emotional and demonstrative. Whereas Catholic churches tend to be more...ritualistic and reserved," she replied, trying to use all the right words so as not to offend anyone's religion.

He chuckled. "As long as they believe in the risen Lord, I'll go to any church at least once." He unscrewed the top off the water bottle and took a long swig.

"I'll remember that next time," Aurelia replied. "By the way, I'm open to fixing lunch today if you want to continue your workout. Nothing fancy, just soup and sandwiches for this chilly day."

"I'd like that. Thanks." Baron smiled at that olive branch she just handed him. It indicated that they were well on their way to restoration, to 'starting their love over' like Miles Jaye sang in his popular tune. And they were. Baron could just feel it.

Aurelia could feel restoration brewing, as well. Yet it was the speed of that restoration that had her worried. If they reconciled too fast, would Baron have really learned his lesson? If they moved too slowly, would it drive another wedge between them?

So much to think about, Aurelia mused as she headed

upstairs to change into something more casual.

* * *

After lunch, Aurelia kept out of Baron's way for the rest of the day. She even ate the dinner he cooked in the guestroom. No use tempting herself unnecessarily. That was one of the reasons she decided to go back to wearing pants. No use tempting Baron unnecessarily either.

Around 8pm that Sunday evening, Aurelia received a call from her mother-in-law. Not on the house phone, but on her cell phone.

"I'm just checking to make sure you're okay," Ana Maria said at the beginning of the call.

"Overall, I'm fine, Mother Weaver. However, I am more than a bit embarrassed to have my first visit to your house turn out so badly," Aurelia replied as she continued to iron the remaining wrinkles out of the denim pantsuit she selected for school tomorrow.

"It wasn't your fault, sweetie," Ana Maria reassured her. "I blame it on my sons and that awful, awful chica Megan. The same chica who is forever banned from my house, by the way, never to return!" she added with a flash of Latin temper.

Aurelia smiled. She was glad to know that her mother-in-law wasn't the type of parent to uphold her children in their wrong. She was also glad that Ana Maria didn't like Megan either.

"Are you blaming all your sons, Mother Weaver? Because from my understanding, Duke and Marquess are innocent in all this. And even Count didn't mean to participate in my pain and suffering," Aurelia said, trying to be fair, too, as she flipped her pants over on the ironing board.

"Duke and Marquess are excused…this time. I had to blast Count out for returning to his old way of dealing with problems. And although I'm still mad with Earl for ever teaming up with Megan in the first place, I didn't want him physically knocked out because of it."

I did. Aurelia smiled, keeping that thought to herself. After all, had this been Trent they were talking about, she might not have wanted him knocked out either, but rather reprimanded in other nonviolent ways. She might have even begged someone to have mercy on her son, despite his wrongdoing. Such was the plight of any caring mother whose child had turned rebellious.

319

"I have since told all of my sons that I will not tolerate any more sabotage in this family," Ana Maria continued in a stern tone. "And that's exactly what you are, Aurelia. Family! I knew it from the moment I met you over the phone. Then after I saw you in person, I said to my husband, why she could be from my father's side with that beautiful brown skin and that thick curly hair. As you know, Latinos come in all different skin tones just like black people. In fact, mestizos make up the majority of Mexico's population. And many modern Mexicans, such as myself, don't subscribe to the old caste system and its beliefs."

"I appreciate you being so welcoming of me," Aurelia replied, deeply touched by her sentiments. "However, I have to confess that most of my curls were created and added at a beauty salon. My natural hair is not that thick or wavy."

Ana Maria chuckled at her honesty. "Who cares if all of your hair is fake. All I care about is making sure you know that I accept you and so does my husband."

Aurelia's eyes welled up with tears. "Thank you for saying that, Mother Weaver." She paused from her ironing to blink her eyes clear.

"Anytime," Ana Maria replied and then smoothly switched the subject. "Now the last time I spoke to my youngest, which was two hours ago, he was terrified to even leave the house to put gas in his car. He was fearful that you would be gone by the time he got back. Do you intend to leave my son, Aurelia? And if so, will you ever return to him?"

Aurelia lifted her left brow. Now she understood why her mother-in-law called her cell phone instead of the house phone. It also explained why Baron had been inside all day. Usually he was outside in the garden, washing the cars, doing yard work, running errands, anything to enjoy the great outdoors even on a cold day like today.

Right now Baron was in his office down the hall preparing for his classes tomorrow. He'd been in there so long that he probably had the next two weeks of lesson plans mapped out. Had their marriage been on better terms, he would have gone upstairs to watch TV in the master bedroom by now.

"Mother Weaver, I've decided to stay and try to work things out with my husband." Aurelia returned to her ironing. "In fact, I'm in our laundry room right now."

Ana Maria let out a loud sigh of relief. "Gracias a Dios!"

Aurelia smiled as her mother-in-law thanked God in Spanish. Those words were comforting somehow. "When we're done here, I'll go tell Baron that it's okay to gas up his car. I wouldn't want him stranded on the side of the road tomorrow," she said, recalling how they'd driven straight from Bel Air without stopping last night.

"So thoughtful. I knew you would be an excellent wife to my son." Ana Maria's tone was saturated with approval. Then after a bit more conversation on lighter topics, the two women bid each other goodbye for now.

Done with her ironing, Aurelia put everything back in its place in the laundry room and then went to her husband's office. The door was open as usual. "I just wanted to tell you that I'm going up to take a long soak in the tub now. That's where I'll be when you come back from getting gas, okay?"

Baron gave her a knowing smile. "You've been talking to my mother, haven't you?"

"Yes." Aurelia smiled, too. "Now go fill your tank up, man. I don't want you stranded on the highway tomorrow." Then without another word, she turned and walked away.

She still cares! Baron grinned, feeling considerably less anxious now. Even so, he still didn't leave the house until he heard Aurelia actually run water in the tub.

Aurelia is not Megan, Baron reminded himself as he turned the key in the ignition a few minutes later. She won't leave without just cause, he thought, determined to never again give her a reason to leave him, not even unintentionally.

CHAPTER FORTY

With Baron working late for the second time this week, Aurelia saw to the cleanup of the house and to their dinner tonight. She'd gotten pretty handy at using the wok. Pretty handy at cooking and eating healthier as a whole thanks to Baron's culinary tutelage.

As a result of eating better, Aurelia found herself feeling better and more energized. She even lost the seven extra pounds she'd put on after leaving the club. Not having to practice dance routines all the time had allowed those pounds to settle upon her body.

Baron didn't seem to mind Aurelia's extra pounds at all. She didn't mind them at first either. Yet after meeting his skinny ex-girlfriend, she started to feel very self-conscious about her weight. Started to wonder if Baron secretly preferred a thinner woman as well as a freakier woman.

Thinking about Megan now caused Aurelia to frown.

Just then, the house phone rang. Since it was in the living room, Aurelia turned off the stove and moved the wok to a cold rack before going to answer it.

"Weaver residence," she said pleasantly into the black phone receiver.

"Aurelia?" a female voice said, sounding surprised to find her on the other end of the line.

Aurelia frowned as she immediately recognized the distinct sound of Megan's voice. "Dat's Mrs. Weaver to you, heifer!" she spat out, instantly putting her guard up.

"Oh, so you do have a backbone," Megan quipped, recovering quickly from her shock. "I wasn't sure based on how quickly you fled the scene the last time I saw you. And your little accent is so...cute!" She chuckled wickedly.

Aurelia bristled. "Consider yourself lucky I left when I did," she said, forcing calmness into her voice and deliberately loosening her accent. "Otherwise you might be missing a few patches of hair right now. Or perhaps you would've preferred being punched purple. Tell you what, next time I see you, I'll fill both of those orders. Really give you something to remember me by."

"How primitive," Megan replied in a condescending tone. "Does Professor know how violent you are?"

"Does he know how desperate you are?" Aurelia countered. "Why else would you be running this hard behind a married man?"

"He won't be married for long...at least not to you," Megan said. "Professor needs a woman that can satisfy him in every way. Face it, Aurelia. You're just not that woman. The fact that you're so fat makes it even worse. Baron must gag every time he sees the cellulite on your thighs." She released another wicked chuckle.

"Says the woman with the fake boobs and the flat behind. Butt so flat you can use it as an ironing board," Aurelia quipped, showing that she could hold her own in a war of words.

Megan gasped at that fiery retort. It cut deep. She knew now that she'd seriously underestimated her opponent. She didn't know Aurelia could think so fast on her feet or was so quick-witted.

"What a hot little tongue you have there. Too bad you don't know how to use it for your husband's good," Megan said with forced calmness of her own now. "Now be a good little girl and bow out gracefully. If you do, I'll make it worth your while. You won't even miss Baron's money."

Aurelia scoffed. "You're even more desperate than I thought. The fact that you're trying to pay me to leave my husband proves that. Any rival worth her salt would have tried to seduce him away at least one more time before trying to strike a deal with the wife."

"Well, I never—"

Bang!

Aurelia slammed the phone down before Megan could say anything else. Right then and there she decided to learn everything there was to know about cunnilingus and fellatio sex. She knew exactly who to seek out for advice, too – Crystal.

I'll make a trip to the club after school tomorrow, she thought determinedly as she headed back to the kitchen.

* * *

After that call with Aurelia, Megan got on her computer and logged onto the internet. Then she proceeded to do what she did most nights when she was feeling particularly miserable and lonely – engage in flaming. In other words, she anonymously left nasty comments all over the internet.

Megan left such comments in hopes that someone would get offended enough to engage her in written combat. Not only did this bring attention her way, it allowed her to let off some steam and helped with the loneliness.

No website was exempt.

Megan left nasty comments on news and entertainment sites, literary blogs, and even porn sites. She was especially nasty on porn sites that featured interracial couples where the woman was black and the man was Latino. Those sites got her most potent venom.

As expected, Megan's comments were constantly flagged. Her user profiles have even been blocked on certain websites. Still she returned to spew her vile comments under yet another alias.

Lately, flaming had become Megan's favorite new pastime. She fed off all that negative energy more than she ate real food. Tonight she planned on attacking a site that featured nothing but black women with ba-dunk-a-dunks.

Somebody needs to tell them how fat and nasty that looks, Megan thought, ready to type her fingers off as they hovered over the keyboard.

If only she had a delete key for her heart. Then maybe she could remove the pocket of jealousy she felt towards such well-endowed women, particularly Aurelia Weaver.

* * *

Around 3pm the next afternoon, Aurelia pulled up in back of Dingo's club and parked. Before exiting the car, she reached into her purse for her wedding band. After putting the gold band on her left hand, she switched her engagement ring to that hand as well.

I can do this, Aurelia coached herself as she took in a deep breath of courage. Then after retrieving a case of Now and Laters for Six-Eight and a box of Aurora's Whispers for Crystal from the backseat, she prepared to face one of her biggest fears once and for all.

* * *

"So tell me. What really brings you this way, stranger?" Crystal asked after gratefully receiving the box of perfume Aurelia had given her. "Are you ready to be put on the roster again? If so, I'll gladly make a space for you. I do have hiring and firing abilities now, you know." She grinned from her seat in Dingo's newly renovated office – a clear sign of the club's increasing prosperity.

"I figured you'd get them eventually, girl." Aurelia chuckled from the comfortable high-back visitor's chair. "But no thanks. Fortunately, my financial worries are all over. Been over ever since I started my own perfume line and got married." She held up her left hand.

Crystal's eyes bucked. "You're married now? To whom? And, girl, that's some serious bling you got going on there."

"I know, right?" Aurelia chuckled, briefly admiring all the diamonds on her left hand, as well. "As for who I'm married to, you're never going to believe who my husband is." She returned her hand to her lap. Holding it up any longer would be bragging and she just wasn't that kind of person.

"Who, girl? Tell me," Crystal urged, leaning forward in her seat.

"The professor from that bachelor's party we did in Cabo," Aurelia revealed.

"What?!" Crystal's eye sockets widened even more. "How? Did he stalk you down and then finally win you over with his loot? Dingo told me he came looking for you at the club one time."

"I heard all about Baron's visit here. But believe me, there was no stalking involved. Baron was just as surprised as I was to learn that he was one of my new professors at school last semester. Since our strong attraction was still there, we waited until after the semester was over to officially hook up. When that wasn't enough to satisfy, we got married over the Christmas break. I'm now Mrs. Dr. Baron Weaver."

"Ahhhhh...snap!" Crystal sounded like her boyfriend's brother for a moment there. "Do you love this man, Aurelia? Or is this a financial security and lust thing? If so, I completely understand," she said, being as open-minded as she always was as she leaned back in Dingo's desk chair.

"I love him, girl. Very much," Aurelia acknowledged with glossy eyes. "Anything else that comes along with Baron is a bonus to that love. And because I love him so much and want to keep him satisfied in the bedroom, I sought you out for sexual advice. I'm even willing to pay you for that advice." She patted the gold silk purse in her lap.

Crystal's arched brows knitted together in confusion. "As I recall, you didn't have a problem satisfying the professor in Cabo. Has something changed since then?"

"Yes, the return of his ex-fiancée. The same ex-fiancée that wants him back with a vengeance and who, from what I heard, is quite good with a few things." Aurelia pointed to her mouth with emphasis. "Things that Baron likes a lot more than I thought he would. Things that I was turned off from because of some gun-toting fool in my past. Things that I need to now work into my repertoire unless I want to give this woman an even greater competitive edge over me."

"Oh, those things." Crystal nodded in understanding. "Anything else?"

"Yes. I'm also tripping over the fact that my rival is white, a well-bred society chick, and much slimmer than me. As you know, there's nothing I can do about the race thing. Nor do I want to," Aurelia said, revealing pride in her black heritage. "However, I did buy a slew of etiquette books and videos in an effort to step up my game in that area. Plus, I've been thinking about dropping another ten pounds or so. I've already dropped the seven that I gained after leaving the club."

"Well, you definitely came to the right person for sexual advice. I know too many tricks to count and I'm more than ready to help my favorite ex-dancer overthrow any competitor." Crystal grinned mischievously. "As for paying me for my advice, I'll put this one on the house. After all, it's not every day one of us snags a professional man whose not ashamed of our pasts and who is willing to go the distance with us. A man that clearly loves the size that you are, as I recall, so don't even think about losing any more weight, Aurelia," she added, very adamant about that last thing.

"You really don't think I should drop a few more pounds?" Aurelia looked down at herself in the beautiful golden raw silk pantsuit that she ordered from overseas. The outfit was elegant, but it did hide most of her curves, which was the main reason she bought it from a company in a country that specialized in female modesty.

"Not even one pound. Besides, there's something very un-sexy about a woman whose ribs are showing through her skin. At least it is for most men, although there are some exceptions to that rule. Why do you think Dingo has a weight requirement for each girl's height?"

"I thought that rule was there to keep us from gaining too much weight," Aurelia replied.

"Yes, but it's also there to keep us from losing too much weight, too. Very few men want to pay top dollar to see skin and bones dancing on stage. Most men want to see something that jiggles, even in the bedroom. So promise me you won't go a size lower."

"I promise." Aurelia smiled, raising her right hand as if taking an oath. "Now when can my lessons start?"

"Right now if you want to since the club won't be jumping for another seven hours or so," Crystal said, looking at the platinum watch on her left wrist, which was yet another sign of the club's prosperity. "Just go to the store up the block and get some bananas, whipped cream, cinnamon, and a bottle of honey. We already got more than enough scotch around here." She leaned forward in her chair and added, "Girl, when I'm through schooling you, the professor ain't gonna know what hit him."

"That's what I'm counting on." Aurelia grinned, her eyes sparkling with excitement.

It was time to submit to another type of instruction now. It was time to finally be free from Oliver's trauma!

* * *

Later that day, Aurelia was put in a position to teach someone a few things herself. That someone was Mrs. Applegate, the Weavers' next door neighbor.

Mrs. Applegate was in her eastside garden when Aurelia arrived home. The gray-haired woman had a peeved look upon her face. Her lips moved in rapid succession as she stood among her vegetables, which, for the most part, were still producing in winter thanks to the warm California weather.

Is she talking to herself or to her vegetables? Aurelia wondered, unwilling to believe that their sharp-minded seventy-year-old neighbor had suddenly surrendered to dementia or some other kind of mental illness since they last spoke this morning.

As a result, she went over to chat with Mrs. Applegate instead of heading straight into the house where Baron awaited. He had gotten off from work at the regular time today and was likely in the kitchen starting dinner by now.

"What seems to be the problem, Mrs. Applegate?" Aurelia approached the chain linked fence that divided their properties.

"Oh, hello, Aurelia." Mrs. Applegate looked upwards with a smile. Though raised to believe that her culture was superior to others, she'd actually taken to Aurelia quicker than she had to Baron, proving that no one was too old to change. "It's these doggone jalapeno pepper plants that's giving me problems. No matter what I do, I can't seem to get them to grow!"

"We grew jalapenos just fine at my childhood home in St. Croix. If you tell me what you've done so far, maybe I can help you find a solution to your problem," Aurelia offered, resting her arms upon the top of the fence.

"Well, when I started growing them last year in early April, I put them in their own pots and gave them the proper amount of water during the right times - mornings and evenings, complete with plant food. No peppers came. Then I tried leaving them in the shade for a while, before taking them out of the pots altogether and putting them into the ground in direct sunlight. Still no peppers. All they do is form little white flowers and those usually fall off within three days. Meanwhile my daughter-in-law neglects her garden terribly and yields peppers all year round." Mrs. Applegate sighed out her frustration after that long recitation. "I don't know what to do next except rip them out the ground and toss them into the fireplace," she said, revealing just how deep her anger was.

"No need to start a bonfire just yet, Mrs. Applegate," Aurelia said soothingly. "Especially when I'm pretty sure I know what the root of your problem is."

"Do tell," Mrs. Applegate prompted with eager green eyes.

"Your problem lies in that bag over there." Aurelia pointed to the green and yellow plant food container. "Although plant food is great when the plants are just starting out, because it not only keeps them healthy, but also makes the leaves all lush and green. However, that same plant food will keep your plants in a vegetative state as they mature. To get your blooms to stay long enough to actually produce peppers, you need a little less nitrogen in the mix." Then she told Mrs. Applegate exactly what to try and in what doses.

"Okay, let me get this straight in my head," Mrs. Applegate said after hearing Aurelia out. "Because nitrogen puts plants in a vegetative state and causes them to prematurely abort flower blossoms, I should stop fertilizing for a while and just use plain water."

"Right."

"And when I do start re-fertilizing, I should use less plant food this time around and only dose my peppers once every two weeks or so," Mrs. Applegate continued to recite.

"Right." Aurelia smiled, impressed by the elderly woman's sharp mind once again. "You do all that and you should have peppers year round in this part of the world."

Mrs. Applegate smiled wide. "Thanks, Aurelia. I really appreciate your help. And in case you haven't figured it out yet, I'm so glad you're my neighbor," she said with sudden tears in her eyes.

Aurelia's eyes welled up as well. "I'm glad you're my neighbor, too. I always wanted a living grandparent."

"Oh, you dear girl. I think you've just given me the vapors with that one," Mrs. Applegate replied as tears ran down her wrinkled cheeks. "Now let me see if I can give you a grandmotherly hug over this here fence."

After that warm hug over the top of the fence, the two women parted ways with satisfied smiles upon their faces. Aurelia hadn't gotten five steps away before her cell phone rang.

* * *

Inside the Weaver home, the kitchen curtain closed. It was Baron. A smile rested upon his face, too, after hearing and seeing Aurelia use her knowledge of science to help someone in need.

Times like these made him proud to be a teacher. Times like these made him so proud to be Aurelia's husband. Such times also made Baron really want to kiss his wife. Badly.

Yet there would be no kiss tonight. Aurelia was still keeping an emotional distance from him. Still sleeping in a guestroom after almost a week since their trip to Bel Air.

At least she's still coming home every day, Baron thought, finding something to be grateful about in this sticky situation.

CHAPTER FORTY-ONE

Aurelia was still on her cell phone when she entered the kitchen where Baron was. Instead of kissing him hello like she used to pre-Bel Air trip, she simply waved to him and continued to chat with Bambi.

Baron nodded in greeting, hiding his disappointment well. He really missed those hello and goodbye kisses. To ward off depression about the current state of his marriage, he returned his attention to the stir-fry he was making for tonight's dinner.

"What do you mean it looks like we are going to be more than just friends and business partners soon?" Aurelia asked, repeating what she'd heard just a few seconds earlier. "Are you trying to tell me that I made it into the Kappas? That we are going to be sisters now?"

Baron's ears perked up at those words.

Aurelia suddenly squealed with delight. She jumped up and down with excitement. "Thanks for giving me the heads up, Bambi. And yes, I'll act like I haven't heard a thing until the rest of the pledges cross over on Friday."

Baron turned to look at her again with a deductive smile on his face. Quickly putting two and two together, he'd come up with one correct answer – his wife had made it into her chosen sorority.

After a few more minutes of excited chatter, Aurelia concluded her conversation with Bambi and told Baron what he already knew. "I made it into the pink and reds. I'm officially a Kappa now. Well, at least I will be on Friday." She put her bottle of water on the counter beside the refrigerator along with her cell phone and purse.

"I heard." Baron grinned, turning the food down on low

so that it could simmer while they talked. "I'm so proud of you, baby. Very proud indeed."

"Thanks. I never would have tried to join a sorority had it not been for you. Now I'll finally have another thing that I've always wanted – sisters," Aurelia said with glossy eyes.

Despite their current discord, Baron embraced his wife. It pleased him when she didn't pull away. Although he wanted to do so much more than just hug her, he kept things simple out of respect for her feelings.

It was Aurelia who boldly took things to the next level.

Blame it on all the alcohol she had with Crystal at the club. Blame it on her raging libido. Whatever was to blame, Aurelia couldn't resist trying to get in a kiss when Baron wrapped his arms around her. She moaned with pleasure when he greedily dove into that unexpected kiss and feasted upon her tongue like it was his last meal.

Did he taste the bananas she ate a while ago? The whipped cream? The scotch? All the other things she consumed during Crystal's instruction?

Aurelia moaned again when Baron's equally greedy fingers grabbed hefty handfuls of her bottom and pulled her closer to his hardened desire. Oh how she missed those large hands of his. Oh how she missed his everything.

Responding with equal fervor, Aurelia kissed him back just as ravenously. She pressed herself all the more closer to him. Even started to grind against him.

Baron moaned this time. Known for taking full advantage of a situation, he sent both of his hands inside her pants. One in the back, the other in the front. Within seconds he was touching her in places that had been neglected for far too long.

Aurelia gasped as two of his exploring fingers boldly entered her woman's gate. Her core instantly clenched and spasmed with need. The rivers of her passion began to overflow their banks.

"Ooo...baby. You're drenched," Baron muttered against her mouth as he continued to skillfully prime her pump.

Aurelia sagged against the fridge behind her as her knees grew weak, as the trembles begin in her body in full force. She forgot about how quickly this man could make her pop. About how masterful he was with his hands. About how her button of pleasure just needed his slightest touch to open up the floodgates.

"Don't you need more than this, baby?" Baron whispered, supporting her back with his right hand while the left continued its sensual assignment. "Let me give you more than this, Ree-Ree," he pleaded, before diving in for another deep kiss.

"Yes," she panted out, unable to refuse him anything in this heated moment.

At her word of consent, Baron temporarily paused their kiss. His hands went into overdrive in his need to undress them both, to make something more happen. Within a few short minutes, Aurelia's clothes were a forgotten pile on the floor. The only things that remained were her heels.

As for Baron's clothes. It had taken all of ten seconds to remove the white t-shirt and gray gym shorts from his body.

Capturing Aurelia's mouth again moments later, Baron ravished it good before sending his lips down to suckle a taut peak. His hands reached farther down to roam her lower curves, her slopes, and her valleys.

Aurelia moaned and arched towards his hungry lips. Her fingers grabbed thick handfuls of his hair and pressed him closer. Her hips moved in time with his skillful fingers.

Baron feasted until he felt her trembles return. Then he swiftly and gently turned Aurelia around to face the fridge behind her. "Look over your shoulder at me, baby. I want to see those pretty eyes when I take you," he requested huskily at her left ear as he held her tenderly about the waist.

Aurelia did as he asked, loving the feel of his hard frame behind her. She gasped and moaned when he soon gave her even more things to feel and love. All just as rigid.

From the sound of Baron's deep guttural moan as he smoothly united them to the hilt, Aurelia knew he was about to take her hard. She wanted him to, which is why she braced her hands against the fridge and arched her lower body to him.

Bending almost to a squatting position, Baron surged upwards with vigor. His hips made a loud slapping sound against her bottom soon thereafter.

Aurelia squealed with delight at his aggression. "Yes," she panted out, urging him on in his possession.

Possession is the correct word to describe what Baron did to her up against that fridge. Each squat, each upward surge, and each intimate slap was meant to reclaim, to brand, and ultimately to please her. He talked through the whole process.

"That's right, baby. Keep looking at me like that," Baron said huskily.

Squat, surge, slap.

"Keep letting me see all that love in your eyes," he continued.

Squat, surge, slap.

"I need to see it. I need to know that I'm still the man of your heart," he said.

Squat, surge, slap.

Aurelia's mind was in a literal fog at his ardent words, his fervent actions…his scrumptious everything else. In just a short amount of time she went over the edge with a loud scream.

Baron soared over the edge soon thereafter.

Wait a minute. That wasn't fog in Aurelia's mind. That was smoke in her face. Real smoke!

And that loud shrill sound that continued to pierce the airwaves even now had not come out of either of their mouths. No, that high-pitched noise was from the kitchen's smoke detector.

Reality suddenly came crashing into the room like a Mac truck. Tonight's dinner was on fire!

By this time, flames were flaring up on both sides of the wok. The food inside was a charred mess. More smoke filled the air.

Why hadn't they noticed these things sooner?

Baron and Aurelia withdrew from each other at the same time. He rushed over to the fire extinguisher on a nearby wall. "Stay back, baby. I got this," he said, not wanting her in harm's way.

Aurelia stayed all the way back. In fact, she picked up her clothes and retreated to the kitchen exit near the rear stairwell. However, she did not officially leave the room until she made sure he had the fire under control and was no longer in danger of getting hurt himself. She even turned on the vent so that the smoke would clear out of the room faster.

After running full speed up the stairs, Aurelia stopped at the top landing to catch her breath. What are you doing, girl?! Do you just want to send the man the wrong message? she scolded herself as she leaned against the wall with heaving chest.

The answer to her first question was: Satisfying the needs of her body.

The answer to her second question was: No.

Aurelia didn't want Baron to think that he could get off so easily after causing her so much pain. She wanted him to suffer a bit longer so that he wouldn't be inclined to repeat his actions with Megan or any other woman.

Unfortunately, when he suffers, I do, too, Aurelia realized, missing his lips and hips already as she walked towards her favorite guestroom on shaky legs.

* * *

Downstairs, Baron dumped the devastated chicken and vegetables into the garbage with a smile. Was he happy about the ruined meal?

No.

Baron was pleased to no end to find his wife still so responsive to him. Still so willing to give herself to him. Yet the fact that Aurelia ran upstairs and closed the door to a guestroom and not the master suite told him that she was still not quite ready for full reconciliation.

Soon, I hope. Baron put the now empty wok into a sink of water before retrieving his clothes from the floor. Upon opening a few windows to let the remaining smoke out, he went to the nearest downstairs bathroom to take a quick shower...alone.

Afterwards, Baron cleaned the stove and the wok and started dinner all over again. Considering everything that happened tonight, he wasn't surprised in the least when Aurelia took her meal in the guestroom. He ate his meal in his office while working on a new formula that was going to enhance their times of intimacy even more in the future.

* * *

Aurelia woke up in a bad mood after a fitful night of sleep. First of all, it had taken her the longest time to even go to sleep last night. After that kitchen encounter with Baron, her body was still too fired up for slumber. It wanted more loving. Needed more loving.

Refusing to honor her body's demands, Aurelia got up in the middle of the night and took another shower. A cold one this time.

When she finally did nod off, she kept dreaming about Baron. About his lips. About his glistening chest. About him in a fireman's uniform with her begging him to please put her fire out.

Aurelia had to take another cold shower this morning just to keep from attacking Baron over breakfast. When the hot flashes returned by lunchtime, she decided that it was time to let bygones be bygones and just reconcile fully with her husband.

Baron is a quick learner, Aurelia reasoned as she exited her noon class. Surely he's learned his lesson by now, she hoped. She planned to find out tonight, despite the fact that she felt ill prepared to perform the extra special treats he was likely expecting with their full reconciliation.

Aurelia's lack of preparedness wasn't for lack of trying. She'd really put her all into that first session with Crystal in spite of how emotionally draining it had been. She'd cried. She'd gagged. She'd cried and gagged at the same time during several demonstrations.

It wasn't until Aurelia had had a couple of stiff drinks that she was finally able to relax enough to do what needed to be done. Now she wondered if she'd be able to get through the real live experience sober. Or would she have to get blitzed every time?

I'm not turning into an alcoholic for anybody, Aurelia thought determinedly, recalling how both sets of her grandparents had died as she made her way out of the science building to her car.

No lunch in the cafeteria with friends today. She had some errands to run in between classes and so would grab a bite to eat along the way.

Today was the day Aurelia collected her weekly mail from the P.O. Box she still had. She also had a 1pm appointment to finally show someone her vacant apartment. A man by the name of Lane Baker answered her rental ad via email two days ago and arranged to meet her at the site today.

Aurelia was glad she listened to Baron and kept the utilities on at her old place. Otherwise she would have had to deal with the inconvenient tasks of getting everything turned back on in time for today's showing.

Just then, Aurelia's cell phone rang.

It was Emile. From the rapid fire way she talked, Aurelia knew her mother was upset about something. When she discovered what that something was, she got upset, too.

Thankfully, everyone in the Bunting family was still relatively healthy and safe. However, the same couldn't be said for Aurelia's childhood home.

It seems that someone had been sabotaging the renovations on the Bunting house ever since they started. Supplies were being stolen from the shed that the contractors had erected on the property. Someone broke into the house last week and spray painted red letters on the sheetrock in the living room. And just last night, four windows were broken.

After last week's break-in, Baron arranged to have discreet security cameras posted around the house. With the help of those cameras, the Bunting family now knew who was sabotaging their renovations – jealous Jewell.

Emile was not only calling Aurelia to report that bad news, but to tell her of her plans to have Jewell arrested. Not right now, but after she'd gotten her kids off to school to spare them any unnecessary shame and embarrassment. Jewell's children were going to be embarrassed enough once the whole neighborhood learned of their mother's arrest.

"Don't call the police on Jewell at all, Mama," Aurelia said when her mother's tirade finally ended.

"H...huh?" Shock reverberated in Emile's voice. "I thought you be de first to seh 'off wid she head'."

Aurelia chuckled. "Maybe tomorrow. Today, I'm in the mood to show a bit of mercy to others."

"But if we let her off de hook, she prolly tink she kin keep it up. De house neva be finished den," Emile protested.

"I didn't say let her off the hook, Mama. No, I want Jewell to stay on the hook for a long time to come. I just don't want to get the police involved because of her kids." Aurelia thought about her own son and how he would feel if she was ever arrested. Then she mapped out a plan that would include sending Jewell a copy of the tape with a brief note telling her to stop the vandalism or else be persecuted to the fullest extent of the law.

"Yur daddy would be so proud of you, gal," Emily said once she heard the details of that plan. "Not many folks keen 'bout showing dat kinda mercy to an enemy. Not even me."

"Like I said before, I'm in a merciful mood today." Then after asking for updates about Trent, Aurelia concluded the call with her mother.

Two blocks down the road, Aurelia's mood suddenly changed. It became gloomy and full of fury as she parked in front of her old apartment building.

Standing in front of the building was none other than Cain Laker. Or rather Lane Baker. He changed his name soon after leaving California, which is the first thing he said after approaching Aurelia's car. The second thing was that he wanted her back.

When it rains it pours. Aurelia wasn't thinking about the weather either.

No, the weather in Alcove looked kissed by God today. It was her life that suddenly seemed cursed.

* * *

"I'm not coming back to you, Cain." Aurelia frowned up at him through her lowered car window.

"Lane," he corrected. "And why not? Because you're married now?"

Aurelia's eyes widened. "How...how..." She quickly checked her left hand to make sure she hadn't mistakenly left her wedding band on from yesterday.

"How did I know that?" Lane finished for her with a grin. "Surely you know that money can buy information."

Aurelia's frown returned. "That money would have been better spent taking care of your child. Have you settled things with Roxy yet?"

"I told you that baby's not mine."

"Have you had a DNA test to prove otherwise? And even if you have, it doesn't matter to me. Like you said before, I'm married now." Aurelia pressed the button to automatically raise her window again.

"But I don't think you're going to want to stay married to a man with mob connections," Lane rushed out in a lower tone.

"What?!" Aurelia paused the window mid-ascent. "Have you lost your mind? My husband's not—"

"Yes, he is. I have proof. Proof that pertains to that business he co-owns in Vegas." Lane produced a brown envelope from his blue jacket pocket. It had the words Client #4 written in the top right corner.

"Let me see that." Aurelia lowered the window and reached for the envelope, but he quickly snatched it back.

"You'll get it over dinner tonight."

"I'm not having dinner with you, Cain, Lane, whatever your new name is."

"You will if you want to know the truth about your wiseguy husband, if you want to protect him from public exposure." Lane smoothly slid the envelope back into his inner pocket. "I'll be at The Crowne around 6pm. Wear a pretty dress. The shorter and tighter, the better." Then he walked away from her car without uttering another word.

Dang.

Aurelia could say one thing for Cain/Lane, he knew her well enough to know that she couldn't stand an unsolved mystery. That she wouldn't rest until she knew what was in that envelope. That she wouldn't leave Baron until she had proof that the allegations against him were true. And that she obviously loved her husband enough to want to protect him from public exposure. Which meant she was going to be at that restaurant at 6pm.

How am I going to explain missing dinner to Baron. Aurelia started up her car. Bump the rest of her classes. She'd just have to make up any missed assignments later.

Instead of going back to school, Aurelia headed home. She needed a peaceful place to think things through. She needed time alone to weigh her options.

CHAPTER FORTY-TWO

Aurelia was relieved when she didn't have to explain anything to Baron or be faced with telling him a convenient lie. She found herself completely off the hook when he called to say that he was working late again tonight and for her to eat dinner without him since he was still pretty full from the big lunch he'd eaten with Count.

Count showed up in town earlier today to deliver the items they'd left in Bel Air and to apologize to Baron face-to-face about his part in that Megan situation. Over a large lunch at The Crowne, the two brothers had settled their differences and formally reconciled.

Afterwards, Count returned to Bel Air with a much lighter conscience. He still had yet to fully reconcile with Earl, although they were on speaking terms again because of their mother.

Aurelia was happy about Baron and Count's reconciliation. She was sad and worried that the reconciliation she had planned with Baron tonight might be put off indefinitely if what Cain/Lane said was true.

With her ex-boyfriend at the forefront of her mind now, Aurelia showered and changed into clothes and shoes that Baron hadn't bought her. She just couldn't wear something he paid for out to dinner with another man, not even lingerie. That in and of itself felt like cheating.

Tonight Aurelia wore a pair of rhinestone studded stilettos and a blue halter-styled dress that she'd kept from her pre-marriage days. The only kind of lingerie that could be worn with such a formfitting dress was a thong. And even that was from her pre-marriage days.

The dress Aurelia chose was not only tight, but short as

well per Cain/Lane's request. She hoped the plunging front and open back would sway him to give her what she came for in record time. The sooner she saw this proof he spoke of, the sooner she could deal with the implications of that proof.

Before leaving the house, Aurelia made sure to leave all of her rings at home. She also left Baron a note on the fridge. It simply indicated that she was eating out tonight and around what time she would be back.

For your sake, Baron, and for our marriage's sake, I hope Cain's claims are bogus, Aurelia thought as she got into her VW and headed for The Crowne.

* * *

"You look very sexy in that dress, Aurelia," Lane complimented after she was seated and their drink orders had been taken by Claude of all people, who was their waiter for the night.

"Cut the small talk, Cain, and let's get down to the business at hand." Aurelia noted Claude's disapproving frown as he walked away from their table.

Could this day get any worse? Now she was going to be interrogated and lectured at school tomorrow by a concerned friend.

"Lane," he corrected.

"Whatever," she retorted. "Now where's your proof?"

Lane retrieved the brown envelope from his red jacket pocket. "It is right here, sexy," he said, holding the envelope up with a smile. "But you don't get to see what's in it until after we're finished with our dinner." He smoothly slipped the envelope back into his pocket.

Aurelia scowled at him. She didn't appreciate being manipulated like this. She loved Baron too much to manipulate Lane in return with something he wanted – her body. Wearing this revealing dress was as far as she was going to go out of respect for her marriage. Even now she wondered if she'd gone too far already.

"Now back to that sexy dress," Lane continued. "What kind of thong do you have on underneath?"

Aurelia opened her mouth for a quick retort. When he suddenly flashed that envelope again, she bit back her intended retort and switched gears. It was then that she realized that Lane was smarter than she originally thought. And yet he was still not smart enough to realize that she would never reconcile with a man that blackmailed her. She could barely look at him now without feeling disgust.

"What kind do you think I have on?" Aurelia asked in an even tone.

Lane smiled in triumph and put the envelope back into his pocket. "I hope it's edible." He chuckled as he licked his lips. "Or is that part of your life still off limits?"

"It's still off limits."

"It won't be after tonight." Lane licked his lips again.

Aurelia's flesh crawled. This man was out of his mind if he thought she was going to do anything sexual with him tonight or any other night. Yet because she loved Baron and wanted to protect him from public exposure, she would flirt her Peter Cottontail off tonight.

All during dinner, Lane engaged in flirtatious banter with Aurelia. He talked about the good times they had in the past, especially those of a sexual nature. About how much he missed her, including how she challenged him to be smarter. And about how much he wanted her back.

Aurelia got a brief reprieve from Lane when he excused himself to the restroom. Unfortunately, that's when Claude decided to tear into her.

"Why are you having dinner with this creep, Aurelia?" Claude asked sternly, yet discreetly as he returned to the table with another basket of bread and an expensive wine bottle. "I thought you were so in love with some guy named Barry. Or was Cain actually Barry the whole time? Is that why no one has ever seen your mystery fiancé?"

"I can't explain everything now, Claude, but just know that there is a real Barry. In fact, I'm only having dinner with Cain tonight to protect Barry," Aurelia explained, also calling her ex-boyfriend by his real name.

"Protect Barry?" Claude bit back a curse. "Did you hook up with some drug dealer? I knew you were heavily into guys with money, but surely you didn't sink this low."

"Barry's not a drug dealer, all right," Aurelia said, hoping that that was not a source of Baron's money, as well.

"Well, what is he then?" Claude persisted, pretending to pour more red wine into Cain's glass on the other side of the small round table.

Aurelia took a deep breath and whispered, "Barry is a college professor. He's Professor Baron Weaver."

Claude's eyes bucked. The shock of her revelation caused

him to spilled wine on the linen tablecloth. Thankfully, the tablecloth was deep burgundy in color and wouldn't show the stain once it was dry.

"Please don't tell anyone, Claude," Aurelia petitioned as he quickly righted the wine bottle and mopped up the spill with a napkin.

"You don't have to worry about that with me. I don't snitch on friends." Claude gave her a sincere look that confirmed his heartfelt words. "But as your friend, I have to tell you that you're playing a dangerous game here, Aurelia. Besides the potential of this thing blowing up in your face at school, there's no guarantee that Cain won't expose Professor Weaver even after blackmailing you to have dinner with him tonight."

"Hmm…I hadn't thought about that." Aurelia frowned.

"Well you need to," Claude concluded and then walked away just as Lane headed back to the table.

* * *

"I'm willing to do almost anything to get you back, Aurelia," Lane said, after returning from a prolonged trip to the men's room. "Outside of violence, that is, since I can't afford to mess up my prettiness," he added, still considering himself to be a lover, not a fighter though he certainly had the bulk for the latter.

"I can see that," Aurelia replied, reminded of how conceited he was. The man still referred to himself as pretty for goodness sakes! "What I don't see is the evidence you promised to show me after dinner. I've eaten all I'm going to eat tonight and your plate is completely empty. So either hand over your proof or I'll consider this whole thing a bluff and walk out right now."

Lane moaned at her feistiness. "Still so full of fire, huh?" He chuckled and finally slid the envelope over to her.

Resisting the urge to snatch the envelope up and tear into it, Aurelia forced her right hand to casually lift it from the table. Using one of the clean steak knives near her plate, she carefully slit it open. For a second there, the hot Crucian blood in her actually incited the urge to slit Lane's throat instead for bringing all this extra drama in her life. Yet she quickly squashed that savage urge.

Once Aurelia had a chance to view the evidence she had to admit that it was pretty incriminating. Inside of the envelope were invoices to casinos with known mob connections. Those same invoices bore huge dollar figures and were signed off by Baron Weaver and his Vegas business partner, Gino Veneto, whom she had yet to meet in person.

All this time Aurelia thought that Baron's company in Vegas only dealt with the good casinos. All this time she thought he was so principled in every way.

I guess he's not as principled when it comes to how he makes his money, Aurelia mused as rage and a sense of betrayal settled into her soul.

"Now that you've seen all that, feast your pretty little eyes on this." Lane slid another envelope across the table towards her. A white one this time.

This new envelope contained all of Lane's contact information. It also contained a pre-nup agreement that guaranteed Aurelia a sizable amount if she came back to him. Another sizable amount if she actually married him within the year.

"You need to put this money towards your child instead of trying to woo me." Aurelia slid the white envelope back to him. She'd earned the right to keep the brown one by even showing up here tonight. "Besides, I would never deal with a deadbeat dad, especially when I have a child of my own," she added, ready to do what she could to turn Lane off to the max. She wanted him so repelled by her that he would never seek her out again.

As expected, Lane's eyes widened with shock at her revelation. "I told you that baby boy ain't mine. I can't have kids. Remember my medical condition? And what is this about you having a child?"

"I'm betting that Roxy's child is yours, despite your previous medical condition." Aurelia silently noted that he knew the sex of the baby. That meant that Lane was keeping up with Roxy's whereabouts, too. The little slickster!

"For one thing, there would have been no need to change your name if you didn't fear a paternity lawsuit," Aurelia continued. "You could have simply taken a DNA test, which I'm sure you haven't done by now, and proven that the child wasn't yours. Plus, I see that you're still functioning with only half a brain. A man that's really trying to assume a new identity and fly under the radar would have at least changed his appearance somewhat instead of trying to retain his 'prettiness'. He certainly wouldn't have taken me to a popular restaurant so that people could see us together, thereby facing exposure himself."

"Aurelia, what is this about you having a child?" Lane demanded to know, focusing on what he cared about the most in this intense moment. "Are you pregnant by this guy?"

Aurelia couldn't have gotten pregnant by him at any point during their year long relationship. She'd been a stickler for good birth control practices, despite Lane's claim of sterility. She hadn't wanted to end up like her Aunt Gladys, who had more children than she could properly take care of.

Plus, Aurelia didn't look anywhere near pregnant in any of the pictures his private investigator had taken since their breakup. She definitely didn't look pregnant tonight in that dress.

Could the P.I. have made a mistake? Murray had seemed rather distracted the last time he talked to him. But what man wouldn't be distracted after just burying his wife due to her untimely death?

"No, I'm not pregnant, but I was once upon a time. In fact, my little brother is actually the son that I bore out of wedlock as a teenager," Aurelia replied, continuing to use the truth to her advantage.

Lane's eyes stretched wider with shock. "I..."

"Clearly your P.I., or whoever else you used to spy on me, wasn't as thorough as they should have been," Aurelia continued. "Or maybe you were too dumb to tell them to research my past instead of just spying on the current affairs of my life. Even if I left Baron today, I could never go back to a man like you. I need an intellectual equal in a man, not someone straight off the short bus, you dingee." She stood to her feet with her purse and the brown envelope in hand.

"That's better than being a mobster!" Lane hissed out his retort, causing a few eyes to look their way at his harsh tone.

"You'll do well to remember what my husband allegedly is unless you want to end up swimming with the fishes," Aurelia whispered in his ear. She could only hope that playing on the sordid reputations of mobsters would seal his silence on the matter forever. Or at least until Baron got out of the racket because those were definitely his signatures on the invoices.

Fear instantly entered Lane's eyes. He stiffened in his seat.

"Goodbye, Cain," Aurelia concluded, calling him by his real name again before turning to walk away with her head held high.

Lane didn't dare follow her. He might be a slow thinker, but he was definitely no fool. No way would he intentionally expose a mobster.

Lane had basically shown Aurelia the truth about Baron in hopes that she would leave him on her own. He'd gambled on her hatred of all forms of organized crime and lost. It didn't look like Aurelia was any closer to leaving her husband than before; despite the proof she'd been given tonight.

On top of all that, Cain might have changed his name to Lane, but the man inside was still the same. He still didn't want the responsibility of a child. Not Aurelia's child, not even his own.

As of right now, Lane was going to forget that Aurelia and Baron Weaver even existed. If only it was as easy to forget about the child Roxy had borne.

* * *

On the way home, Aurelia stopped by Roxy's place. As expected, her ex-friend looked surprised to see her. Embarrassed, too.

Aurelia didn't know if Roxy's embarrassment stemmed from her having gained twenty pounds since they last saw each other, that tent-like floral housedress and unkempt ponytail she wore, or because she was still living at home with her mother in the projects. Probably all of the above.

"A…Aurelia, what are you doing here?" Roxy stammered out through the raggedy screen door.

"I'm here on a mission of mercy," Aurelia replied, pulling two things from her purse – a silver key ring and a piece of paper.

"A mission of mercy?" Roxy echoed, looking like she wasn't sure she liked the sound of that.

"Yes, here is the key to a place you and your son can live in rent-free until May. The address to that place is on the front of this paper. It's only an efficiency apartment, but it's decent and in a neighborhood slightly better than this one." Aurelia handed off the key ring and slip of paper in her hand.

Roxy received both gifts with eager hands. "That's what's up, girl," she said, too desperate for help to question Aurelia's motives. She really didn't have a need to. Roxy remembered how benevolent her ex-friend was. How Aurelia seldom gave gifts with strings attached. How any strings that did exist usually led to positive things.

"The name, address, and phone number on the back of that paper all belong to Cain, who goes by the name of Lane Baker now," Aurelia shared, despite the fact that she had yet to get a thank-you or any other display of gratitude for anything she'd ever done for Roxy. "I advise you to contact a lawyer immediately before your baby daddy leaves the country again and continues to try to shirk his responsibilities. To help you out even more, I put the name and number of a good attorney that specializes in family law on that paper, too. It's in the bottom right corner. Just tell him that Aurelia referred you and he'll waive any upfront fees."

"Thanks so much, Aurelia," Roxy said with thick emotion in her voice as she studied the front and back of the paper in her hands. Suddenly she look up with glistening eyes. "I'm really sorry for backstabbing you. I was just tryna up my status in life the only way I knew how."

"You can prove that you're truly sorry by doing every positive thing you can to make a better life for your child," Aurelia replied sternly, even though her eyes held forgiveness and understanding in them. "And, Roxy, please don't act like Bon Qui Qui from Mad TV when you talk to the attorney. Count Weaver is very serious about his job. If you want him to take you and your case just as seriously, you can't behave like some hoodrat."

"I'll be on my best behavior," Roxy vowed with tears streaming down her cheeks now.

"See that you do." Aurelia blinked back tears of her own. "Goodbye, Roxy." Then she turned and walked away. It was time to go home and deal with her own problems.

CHAPTER FORTY-THREE

Baron drove home as fast as the speed limits would allow him. His haste revolved around the phone call he got in his office a few minutes before getting off from work tonight. A call that he could recall every detail of even now as he quickly turned left at the green light and entered the neighborhood where he lived.

"Do you know where your wife is right now?" a male voice had asked Baron over the phone.

"Who is this?" Baron demanded, wishing he had caller ID at work.

"Somebody who knows where your wife is." The stranger chuckled. "That tight blue dress I asked her to wear tonight looks real tasty on her. Real tasty." He smacked his lips and chuckled again.

Baron literally saw red then. "Who is this?" he hissed through clenched teeth.

"The man who should have been Aurelia's husband, wiseguy," the stranger hissed back. "Now excuse me. I have some tight walls to go stretch out."

Then the line suddenly went dead.

Clenching the steering wheel as tightly as he'd held his office phone after that call, Baron found the same questions floating around in his mind now as they had at work.

Was Aurelia really cheating on him? Had she gone back on her commitment to make their marriage work? Even after their strong reconnection last night in the kitchen?

How was Baron supposed to keep an open mind in light of all this? How was he supposed to not assume the worst of his wife?

I'm trying, baby. I'm really trying hard to have faith in

347

you, Baron thought, right before he saw Aurelia enter their driveway from the opposite direction.

Now more questions arose.

Why was she driving her VW instead of her Cadillac? And was that a blue dress she had on?

Baron's eyes bucked a minute later when he saw how revealing that blue dress really was as Aurelia exited her vehicle. She 'is' cheating on me! he deduced hotly as jealousy fanned the flames of his temper.

So much for not jumping to the wrong conclusions. So much for not assuming the worst of his wife.

* * *

Baron's temper grew even hotter when Aurelia barely looked his way after spotting his vehicle pulling up behind her in the garage. When she stalked into the house and slammed the door, knowing he was right on her trail, his temper erupted.

"Where have you been?!" Baron demanded when he entered the house a few seconds later. "And with whom?" He slammed the door behind him, as well.

"I was at a restaurant with Cain tonight, if you must know the truth." Aurelia nailed him with a hard glare as they faced off in the kitchen. No burning food was on the stove to interrupt them tonight.

"Ca...Cain?" Baron stammered out, now knowing exactly who called his office. He was also astounded by his wife's honesty. It was so unexpected, so...so refreshing. Maybe she wasn't cheating on him after all.

"Yes, Cain. Or rather Lane, which is what he's calling himself these days."

"What were you doing with him?" Baron frowned as fear clawed his insides. Was she suddenly missing Cain's third leg? Or had the situation with Megan pushed her to return to a former lover as a backup plan?

"Certainly not cheating, if that's what you think," Aurelia replied, continuing down open and honest lane.

"I don't want to think that. But it's kinda hard not to when I get a phone call at work from some mystery man describing exactly what you have on now, asking me if I knew where you were, telling me he was going to stretch out your tight walls tonight," Baron said with flaring nostrils.

Aurelia's left brow rose. "So that's what Cain was up to during his long trip to the men's room. Why am I not surprised? Either way, his plan to get me back didn't work. Not only am I not a cheater, I'm not about to hook up with a man that doesn't want to be a father to his own child, much less mine."

Baron could have jumped up and clicked his heels together at her response. Yet doing so was too premature. After all, exactly what was she doing with Cain tonight? He decided to ask Aurelia as much again since he hadn't gotten a full answer before.

"If you didn't go there to cheat, why did you meet up with Cain tonight?" Baron inquired. "Especially since you agreed not to have lone meals or private meetings with any of your male friends."

"First of all, Cain is not my friend. Secondly, I went there to keep you from being exposed. Not just about our student/teacher relationship, but also about your alleged mob ties in Vegas," Aurelia shared with flaring nostrils of her own.

All color drained from Baron's face. That would explain that 'wiseguy' comment, he mused, feeling his face turned heat up in the cheek and neck areas.

"I can explain…" Baron began.

At his guilty reaction, Aurelia let out the first expletive she'd ever uttered in his presence. It was loud, harsh, and potent with anger. Neither of their mothers would approve of what she said.

"You betta start explaining tings quick or I'm outta here, mon. Tonight. For good!" she demanded, folding her arms across her chest.

Realizing the gravity of the moment, Baron asked Aurelia to have a seat at the kitchen island. Taking a seat beside her on the next stool, he took a deep breath and then did what his wife required – explained everything.

"During my early college years, Gino and I were roommates. We were very close friends, almost like brothers," Baron began. "One day Gino came to me and shared how his family was struggling to keep their heads above water after his father's stroke. About how he was in danger of having to leave school because of the mounting financial troubles at home."

"You were wealthy even back then, Baron. Why didn't you just help him out?" Aurelia asked.

"I did offer to help him out financially, to at least pay for his tuition so that he could stay in school. After all, it was our senior year in undergrad," Baron replied. "But Gino was too prideful. He didn't like owing anybody anything, especially not a friend. Instead he suggested that I add my brilliance to his and head to the Nevada casinos in order to build up a quick buck legally. So willing to help out my friend any way I could, I agreed to that weekend gambling trip. Plus, in my youthful arrogance, a part of me wanted to prove that I could outsmart the casino systems with my knowledge of probabilities."

"Like in the movie 21, huh?" Aurelia asked.

"Exactly," Baron replied. "Except that movie hadn't come out yet, so Gino was basing his suggestion on the late '70's MIT Blackjack Team that the movie 21 was inspired from."

"Always the teacher," Aurelia observed with an exasperated sigh and a shake of the head. Too bad she couldn't fully appreciate that history lesson right now in light of their current circumstances.

"Unfortunately," Baron replied, noting and understanding her irritation with him. "Anyway, like the MIT group, Gino and I hit the blackjack tables since they were one of the few games that could legally be beaten if a player was skillful enough."

Then he shared how they used various techniques to improve their odds. Techniques such as card counting, shuffle tracking and hole carding. He went on to share how they went to casino after casino stacking up winnings.

"I told Gino that we should stop after the fifth casino run, but he wouldn't listen," Baron continued. "Besides concern for his family, greed had taken over. We had over a million dollars apiece and he still wasn't satisfied." His eyes turned sad. "It was at the sixth casino that we got caught. Some scary-looking Italian guys accosted us in the elevator, took us up to a secret room, stripped us of our clothes, jewelry, and money, and then threatened our lives if we ever came back to their casino."

Aurelia gasped, realizing how close Baron came to being fish bait. "What did you do?" She sounded more concerned than angry now.

"Well, Gino started crying as all of his plans to help his family and stay in school unraveled before his very eyes. Unwilling to see my friend and his family remain destitute, I pushed past my own fears and negotiated a deal as calmly as I could, wearing nothing but my boxers and socks. I told our captors that in exchange for them letting us leave Vegas alive and letting us at least keep our winnings from other casinos, we would never gamble at their casino again. And that we would show them how we beat their system so that they'd know what to look for if anyone else tried it. That way, they'd be able to fix any kinks in their systems."

"Obviously they went for the idea," Aurelia deduced. "You're still alive, richer than ever, and you and Gino have a gaming security company in Vegas."

"Yes, they went for that idea in spades, no pun intended. They even introduced us to a few of their associates who needed our help as well. They all paid well for our services. Very well. By Monday morning, all of Gino's money worries were gone, he no longer wanted to be in school, and he wanted me to go into the gaming security business with him now that we had all these lucrative 'contacts'."

"Why did you? You certainly didn't need the money. You clearly wanted to complete your undergrad education," Aurelia said.

"Because without me, Gino's business would have failed no matter how much money he put behind it."

"How so? Is he a bad businessman?"

"Yes and no. Yes, Gino is a bad businessman due to his tendency to make rash decisions under pressure and his underlying greed. Gino is a good businessman when it comes to being an expert networker, his intelligence, and his ability to be very charismatic at times. Good at sizing people up, the casino owners quickly determined that I was a stabilizing force in Gino's life. A voice of reason, so to speak. Plus, they liked how great I functioned under pressure, my honesty, and my ability to look at the bigger picture."

"In short, they would only do business with Gino if you were on board in some way," Aurelia deduced.

"Exactly. So although I usually keep my distance from Vegas and all casinos as a whole, and although I basically let Gino handle the day-to-day operations of our business, the casino owners still count on me to be that voice of reason for him when it comes to major decision-making. I also sign off on all invoices over a certain dollar amount to keep Gino's greed in check."

"What do you get in exchange?" Aurelia asked.

"I get to be richer than my father and all of my brothers put together. I also get to keep my friend alive," Baron concluded in a solemn tone.

"Keep him alive?!" Aurelia exclaimed. "You mean to tell me that after all these years and after all the money Gino has made, he still doesn't have a handle on his greed? He still can't make sound decisions without you?"

"Afraid so, baby." Baron nodded. "Before I came to see you last December, I had to fly to Vegas to personally talk Gino out of expanding too fast overseas. Especially in areas that were simply too volatile to even sell bread in, much less gambling services. War torn areas."

"I see." Aurelia took a deep breath and blew it out. "Well, Baron, it seems that you have an additional dilemma on your hands. You can keep bailing your friend out and keep your mob ties, however legitimate your part is. Or you can teach your friend how to be a responsible businessman once and for all, sever all ties to the mob, and keep your wife."

Baron shot to his feet. "What do you do, Aurelia? Look for reasons to leave me? A little while ago it was about Megan. Now it's about Gino. What do you want from me, woman?!" he said, raising his voice.

"Peace of mind!" Aurelia stood to her feet as well. "I want to know that the man I'm married to is one, not a cheater. Two, not going to put me and my family in danger one day due to his questionable business ties. If you recall, one of the reasons I refused to marry Marshall was because I learned about his uncle's ties to organized crime."

"I'm nothing like Oliver Jean-Baptiste," Baron spat out through clenched teeth.

"No, you're not. And I don't want you to be either. Which is why I'm asking, no, begging you to get out while you still can, baby," Aurelia said calmly, draping her arms lovingly about his neck.

"How much time are you giving me to work all this stuff out with Gino?" Baron instantly calmed down, as well. It was amazing how the same woman could rile him up one minute and calm him down the next. This must be love.

"A month. Anything beyond that and I'm going to have to make some hard decisions about what's best for me and my family. Agreed?" Aurelia tenderly stroked the side of his face.

"Agreed," he whispered huskily.

"Good." Aurelia smiled. "Now if you'll excuse me, I'm going up to take a long relaxing soak in the tub. I need one after the extremely long and tiring day I've had." Then after placing a brief smack on her husband's mouth, she turned and headed for the rear staircase.

Baron frowned as he watched her walk away. That disappointing little smack hadn't been nearly enough to satisfy. And the sight of her shapely legs and enticing bottom in that skimpy dress had him thinking that it was time to take their relationship to the next level...tonight.

CHAPTER FORTY-FOUR

While Aurelia took her bath, Baron stayed downstairs and sliced up some fruit. After he filled a red ceramic bowl with various fruit chunks and individual pieces that had not required cutting, he covered the bowl with plastic wrap and put it in the refrigerator to chill until later. Upon cleaning up behind himself in the kitchen, he went upstairs to shower and...

Wait.

Baron's waiting officially ended around midnight. He'd given Aurelia enough time to take her bath and rest up for a couple of hours from her long day. Now it was time to wake her up for a nighttime feast.

But first he had to make a brief stop in the kitchen for his prepared bowl of fruit. He also had a portable stereo to retrieve from his office.

When Baron entered the guestroom that Aurelia occupied a few minutes later, he smiled wide for more reasons than one. First of all, the door was open, not closed like usual. Secondly, that blue dress she wore tonight had been crumbled up and stuffed in the trashcan by the closet.

Good riddance, Baron thought concerning that dress. He never wanted to see that garment again. Wanted to burn it in the fireplace across the room so that no one would ever be able to wear it again.

Yet what made Baron smile the widest in this moonlit guestroom were the skylights. They beamed directly down upon his wife in a most appealing way. A row of three beams were aligned from her neck to thighs as she lounged on her back in slumber. One beam of light was at her neck. The second at her navel. The third right between her thighs.

If that isn't an invitation, I don't know what is. Baron gently put the stereo on the nearest dresser. After pressing play, Like a Dream by Mykah Montgomery filled the airwaves in a soft and soothing manner.

Baron eased closer to the bed with the ceramic bowl of fruit in hand. His eyes bucked when he saw Aurelia's hips suddenly begin to move in slumber.

Was this woman that hot-blooded? Or was her body just that in tune with music?

Shrugging out of his robe a few feet away from the large bed, Baron allowed it to drop to the floor unnoticed. He didn't want or need a stitch of clothing on to do what he had planned next.

Putting the bowl on the nightstand, he settled down beside Aurelia on the bed. The magenta animal print chemise she wore covered more skin than that blue dress had.

"Wake up, beautiful," Baron leaned down to whisper into his dozing wife's right ear. He licked her lips a few seconds later to make sure she awakened.

Aurelia immediately stirred from her sleep. Instead of being startled, she smiled up at the man she'd just been dreaming about making love to. "Am I dreaming?"

"No, baby. This is real." Baron smiled down into her lovely face. "Now open wide. I brought you a little midnight snack."

Trusting her husband completely in that sexually charged moment, Aurelia opened her mouth to receive the small strawberry that he removed from a nearby bowl. She moaned as the sweet juices of that fruit hit her palette a few seconds later.

"That's good to you, huh, baby?" Baron asked huskily, watching her mouth move, loving how her dimples disappeared and reappeared as she chewed.

"Yes." Aurelia spoke around the fruit in her mouth.

"I came to taste your fruit tonight. Will you finally let me?" He made his intentions known upfront in word and deed as his free hand eased up her right leg.

"Yes." Aurelia nodded. She readily moved her legs apart for greater access.

Baron licked his lips and moaned at her consent. He briefly closed his eyes to savor the moment. Now he felt like he was dreaming.

"Will I have to return the favor tonight? I want to, but I

still don't think I'm ready to reciprocate just yet," Aurelia shared, being just as upfront and honest as he'd been.

Opening his eyes, Baron shook his head as he looked down at her. "No, baby. Tonight I just want to serve you." Then he leaned down to capture her lips even as his hand found her nub of delight and primed her body for what was to come.

When that long kiss was over, Baron kept his promise to Aurelia. He smoothly removed the chemise from her body and s-e-r-v-e-d her.

Using fruit as a sexual aid, Baron fed Aurelia various items from the bowl in between eating fruit off select areas of her body. Slices of melon were eaten from her melons. Grapes were eaten from her navel. A cherry was eaten from...

No, that cherry was literally devoured from the center of her sexuality.

Moaning loudly from his ravenous actions, Aurelia's island hips got in on the deal, turning the fire of their passion up even higher. Her whispers of 'yes' and 'more' made the moment that much hotter.

"That's right, beautiful. Dance for me," Baron encouraged, lifting his head slightly from her frame. When she complied with a fantastic slow rhythm, he dipped back down greedily for more hot chocolate.

Aurelia almost lost her mind when she heard him actually slurp from her cup.

Slurp!

The pace got steadily faster. The noise level in the room got steadily louder, exceeding the volume of the music in the background.

Unused to this kind of pleasure, this level of intensity, Aurelia threw her head back and screamed Baron's name at the top of her lungs. A violent shudder rocked her body. Her lips begged him to take her completely.

Ready to pop as well, Baron quickly withdrew from her body long enough to reposition himself above her. He became one with Aurelia just as she proceeded to go over the edge yet again. Who knew she was so multi-orgasmic?

Feeling the quivers of her release from the inside out, Baron went for broke again. This time in a different way as he hammered against her with sweet precision.

Aurelia hammered back...fervently, behaving like a sex-starved woman. She couldn't seem to get enough of him. Tried to give him as much of her as she could.

Baron didn't know if all that fervor was from what he'd just done to her or from the emotional rollercoaster they'd been on lately. Either way, her actions had him howling out his own pleasure at the top of his lungs a few short minutes later.

The whole thing was just so…so…liberating.

As Aurelia cascaded down from ecstasy, she cried. Yes, from their outstanding lovemaking tonight. But mostly she cried from the realization of what they stood to lose if Baron didn't dissolve certain business ties.

"Please work this thing out with Gino, baby. I don't want to lose another man that I love," Aurelia sobbed as she clung to his glistening frame. "Daddy's gone. Marshall, too. I even had to leave Trent behind for a season. Please don't make me leave you, too. I want to stay with you forever."

"I want you to stay with me forever, too, baby. Don't worry. I'll dissolve my partnership with Gino within the allotted time. I promise," Baron whispered, gently kissing her tears away.

Then rolling them onto their sides, he continued to hold Aurelia close until her tears ceased. Baron remained in the guestroom all night. No more sleeping alone for either of them.

* * *

The next morning, Aurelia was very silent over breakfast. Not only was she still processing her feelings about last night, she was literally hoarse from screaming with ecstasy. She kept looking at Baron across the breakfast nook, particularly at his mouth, as he ate his usual morning orange slices and read the business section of the newspaper.

What was once a normal breakfast routine, now had Aurelia shifting uncomfortably in her seat. Those lips. Those beautiful, lethal lips.

When Baron's lips enveloped another orange wedge, Aurelia fanned herself with the entertainment portion of the morning paper to cool her hot skin. She shifted in her seat again.

"Is something wrong, baby?" Baron looked at her with a raised left brow.

"No." Aurelia forced her gaze upon her plate, stopped fanning, and stilled her body in her chair.

"You sure about that?" he persisted in a huskier tone. A knowing smile was upon his lips.

Aurelia's gaze shot back up to Baron's face, this time at his eyes. Was that mirth in those gorgeous blue-brown pools of his? Was he laughing at her?

Did he know...did he know that she was pheening for more of his love? That it was hard for her to concentrate on anything, even food, around him because she needed that love?

"I...I..."

"Are you suddenly shy, Ree-Ree?" Baron interrupted, using her island nickname at leisure. "Just tell me what you want, baby, and I'll give it to you. Gladly. Thoroughly."

Did he want her to break out in Meli'sa Morgan's rendition of Do Me Baby? Aurelia couldn't ask for what she really wanted. She couldn't ask for that. She just couldn't.

In reply to his question, Aurelia simply shook her head.

Besides, wouldn't it be selfish of her to do so? After all, she still hadn't reciprocated from last time. Again, Aurelia wanted to return the favor, but still felt unready. Plus, just the thought of Baron mentally comparing her feeble efforts with the expertise of his exes ushered anxiety into her soul.

Aurelia didn't want him disappointed in her in any way. She certainly didn't want him disappointed with that particular experience once it occurred. It would be like trying to cook a decent meal for him for the first time and failing all over again.

Even now Aurelia could remember the grimace upon Baron's face when he took that bite of jerk chicken she burned in St. Croix. The disappointment in his eyes had secretly crushed her spirits that day, though she played it off and brushed it aside at the time. That same disappointment later served to make her determined to be a better cook. Now she was.

In the same way, Aurelia wanted to present her new sexual skills to Baron when they were sharp enough to impress him. Thus the need for more private lessons with Crystal.

"I'm going to get dressed for school." Aurelia tried to avoid the subject altogether now as she rose to her feet.

Baron grinned knowingly again. "Just so you know, I prefer you to oranges any day."

At those words, a rebellious moan escaped Aurelia's lips.

She held onto a nearby counter to steady herself as a wave of hot desire slammed into her, making her knees wobbly.

Within seconds, Baron was behind her. One hand went about her waist in support. The other hand gravitated to her pulsating triangle like a magnet. "School and work can wait," he growled out.

Then Baron scooped Aurelia up in his arms and carried her to the dining room table in the next room. There he gave her what she couldn't ask for, what she needed, what her body demanded…and a whole lot more.

* * *

Aurelia went to school with her knees still on the wobbly side. She found it hard to concentrate all day. She kept daydreaming, kept remembering all the new things Baron had done to her over the last twenty-four hours.

By the end of the day, Aurelia knew that she'd lost her edge. The man had her mind gone.

Gone!

She felt like a drug addict, in need of another fix.

Aware that she needed to do something to even the playing field again or at least cause him to lose his mind, too, Aurelia got on her cell phone and called Crystal for another lesson. Today!

CHAPTER FORTY-FIVE

February

A strange dynamic played out in the Weaver house during the month of February. Although Baron and Aurelia shared the same bed now, continued to share meals, and enjoyed an active sex life, they were also arguing more often.

Blame it on the big red X's Aurelia kept adding to the kitchen calendar every day. Those X's served as constant reminders of Baron's need to dissolve his partnership with Gino. It was also a reminder that all was not right in their marriage no matter how much they made love.

Growing weary of the underlying tension between them, Baron arranged a trip to Vegas to see Gino two days before the end of the month. Trying to get his partner on the phone had proven fruitless after he made his initial dissolution request for an equitable split. Baron hoped that Gino would at least honor the face-to-face meeting they set up to resolve the issue once and for all.

Unfortunately for Baron, Gino wasn't able to make it to their meeting. He had last minute business out of town. He called Baron with the change in plans just as he landed in Vegas.

Thus Baron had to turn right back around and go home disappointed. As a result, he now had to face his wife and ask for more time on his promise. But first he was going to sex her up. Maybe then Aurelia would be more conducive to exercising a bit more patience with him.

I know exactly what will do the trick, too, Baron thought arrogantly, licking his lips greedily as he made his way home from the airport.

* * *

The very next day, Aurelia made one of the hardest decisions she ever had to make in her life. She left Baron.

Okay, maybe it was a coward's move to leave while the man was at work, but Aurelia simply didn't have the heart to leave while he was home. She also couldn't chance Baron changing her mind with his hugs, his kisses, his…everything. Thus she'd doubled back from school, quickly packed her necessities, called for a cab, and then went to a hotel since Roxy was now living in her old apartment.

Exactly why did Aurelia leave Baron today?

For several reasons. First of all, he failed to extract himself from that Vegas business in the time they agreed upon. Secondly, he seemed to give up trying to do so.

Thirdly, even before his face-to-face meeting with Gino fell through, Baron had grown increasingly irritable around the house. He accused Aurelia of nagging whenever she brought the subject up, which was not very often. She'd let her calendar marks speak for her over the last four weeks to keep from nagging him. Yet he'd still scowled about those.

Fourthly, Aurelia was no fool. She knew that remaining at home would lead to more sex with Baron. It had become just that hard to resist him now, especially with his increase in muscle mass. Just watching him lick his lips was enough to send her over the edge these days.

Aurelia knew that continuing to have sex with Baron would lead to even more slothfulness on his part when it came to dissolving his questionable business ties. The fact that he actually had the nerve to ask for two more weeks on his promise just last night proved that to her. The fact that he asked for that extension after he'd made sweet love to her for hours had infuriated Aurelia.

Why couldn't Baron have asked for that extension before sexing her up? Why did he have to act so manipulative? So Cain-like?

Instead of giving Baron an answer last night, Aurelia had exited the bed and gone to her favorite guestroom to sleep. The daggered look she gave him before she left the master suite was enough to keep him from following her or from saying another word on the subject.

Just in case Baron failed to understand the reason for her departure, Aurelia explained everything thoroughly in the letter she left him on the fridge today. She also wrote that she would not return until he emailed her copies of his partnership dissolution agreement. His signed dissolution agreement.

Aurelia took such drastic measures to keep from relenting on her stance this time. It was too important to their future happiness.

In the meantime, she would continue her weekly lessons with Crystal to sharpen up her skills since she had no interest in divorcing her husband. This way, Aurelia would be able to reciprocate Baron's affections accordingly when the time was right. That right time would occur after he took care of that delicate piece of business in Vegas.

* * *

Needless to say, Baron hit the roof when he arrived home and read Aurelia's letter. He immediately called her cell phone. "Where are you?" he demanded when she picked up the line.

"In a hotel," Aurelia replied evenly.

"Which one? I'm coming to pick you up and bring you back home," Baron said, quite aware that she'd left both of her cars in the garage. He thought she was next door visiting with Mrs. Applegate until he read her letter.

"I'm not coming back until you keep your promise." She stood firm in her decision.

Baron took a deep breath and blew it out. "That again."

"Yes, that again," Aurelia echoed irritably.

"I told you that our schedules were out of whack this last month. Gino and I simply couldn't get together to iron out all the wrinkles in the dissolution. Plus February is a short month."

Aurelia scoffed. "I know stalling techniques when I hear them, Baron. If the dissolution of this partnership was something important to either of you, it would have been done by now."

"I don't know about Gino, but this dissolution is very important to me. Not only did I get Count to draw up the necessary papers, I've gone to Vegas, and I've been calling Gino at least three times a day during this whole month. I just can't seem to track him down long enough to sign anything," Baron said, letting her know that he had not been as slack as she thought.

"Well, I suggest you put out an APB on your friend then. Because until I see those signed documents, I'm staying right where I am."

Click!

At the sound of that click, Baron let out a frustrated roar in the kitchen. Although he knew there was no use calling his wife's cell phone back since he was sure she'd turned it off by now, he did so anyway. When he got no answer, he retrieved a telephone book, sat down at the kitchen island, and began to call every hotel in town.

Once I find the right one, I'm going to get down on my hands and knees and beg her to come home, Baron thought, not feeling so arrogant now. He was even willing to sing Tank's Please Don't Go chorus until he was dry in the throat and hoarse. Anything, just anything to get his wife back.

"This woman is officially the smartest person I know," Baron said an hour and many phone calls later. He didn't know whether to be proud or irritated about the latest discovery concerning his wife.

It seems that no hotel or motel in town had an Aurelia or an Aurora staying within their walls. Which meant she'd clearly used an alias to reserve her suite, a new alias at that. Plus the fact that Aurelia didn't take a personal car meant that Baron couldn't cruise the hotel parking lots to find her that way either. That kind of detailed planning took some smarts.

Once again, calling Aurelia's friends was useless. None of them were supposed to know about their relationship. Even though Claude knew about them, it was highly unlikely that he knew where she was either. And it wasn't something that Aurelia would have told Bambi because of all the questions it would raise. One of which was, why are you at a hotel when you have an apartment?

Baron didn't dare call any of their relatives. They'd only want to know what he did to cause Aurelia to leave him this time. He didn't want to share that data with anyone. Nor was he prepared to field all the ensuing questions they would undoubtedly have if he did.

It was bad enough that Count knew. He'd scolded Baron repeatedly over the years for getting caught up in this kind of partnership in the first place. The scolding suddenly stopped when Baron asked Count to draw up those dissolution papers. It started back when those papers still hadn't been signed after a month's time.

Throwing his hands up in exasperation, Baron made his way up to his empty bedroom instead of starting on dinner.

He wasn't in the mood to eat. He wasn't in the mood to watch TV. He wasn't in the mood to do anything except call Gino…again.

Unfortunately, Baron only got his partner's voicemail…again. Too frustrated to sleep, he took a shower and then went downstairs to work in his office.

* * *

After abruptly ending that call with Baron, Aurelia started to have second thoughts about leaving him. Maybe it was the sound of his sexy voice that had her body humming even now. Maybe it was the fact that she just learned how hard her husband really had been trying to do right by her over the last month. Or maybe, just maybe, Aurelia finally realized that she was being just as controlling as Baron.

This continual running away, all these ultimatums, and even the X's on the calendar had all been her way of trying to control the situation with Baron. Of her need to limit the amount of pain and suffering their relationship caused her.

But didn't love come with a certain amount of pain and suffering? Shouldn't we at least be willing to suffer for and with those we loved? Even Jesus suffered for those He loved. At least that's what Aurelia had been told all her life and believed. Either way, it was a good example to follow.

And wasn't it unfair to give ultimatums to someone who was trying his hardest to work things out? Weren't ultimatums supposed to be given to those who were half-stepping or not trying at all? Baron was doing the best he could under the circumstances.

As for all this running away, Aurelia now saw that that was a sign of her immaturity. Why couldn't she have stayed and exercised more patience with such a diligent man? Better yet, stayed and helped him come up with viable solutions to his dilemma.

Who cares that she didn't help Baron get into this trouble in the first place? Wasn't it more important to help him get out of it? Isn't that what being an equal partner in marriage was all about?

Realizing the error of her ways, Aurelia quickly packed her things and made arrangements to check out of the hotel. Before she headed home, she showered and changed into a purple dress that she purchased from the hotel boutique just today.

That halter styled dress with its draped pendant mid-bust

accent, A- line skirt, and open back was supposed to be Aurelia's going home dress. Since she was officially going home tonight, there was no better time like the present to wear it.

CHAPTER FORTY-SIX

Aurelia arrived home around 11pm. She found Baron in his office asleep at his desk. His computer was still on. Graded papers were in messy piles to the left and right of his head. The portable stereo behind him was softly playing Lisa Fischer's How Can I Ease The Pain in the background. The music was courtesy of a local radio station's quiet storm hour.

Aurelia's breath hitched. She felt a tug on her heart at the sight of her adorable dozing husband. She also felt a stirring in her nether regions at the sight of his bare torso. Her core instantly clenched with need.

Without moving from the doorway, Aurelia already knew that Baron was not completely nude. That he likely had on a pair of silk boxers since he never took off all of his clothing unless he was about to bathe, make love, or go to bed.

Those boxers are about to disappear in a few short minutes, Aurelia thought determinedly. Then she quietly eased upstairs to get a special bag that she hid in the guestroom closet after her first lesson with Crystal. It was time to show Baron that she was in this marriage all the way with him.

* * *

"Bar-ronnnn," Aurelia sang from his office doorway a few minutes later. "Wake uuuup. I got something to telllll...youuuu," she continued to sing as she crossed the threshold with a large black bag in hand.

At the sound of his wife's voice, Baron stirred from his troubled slumber. "Ree-Ree, is that you, baby?" He rubbed the sleep from his eyes as he sat upright in his chair.

"You better believe it. I'm home for good this time. No

more running away like some silly little girl. No more giving you unfair ultimatums. No more trying to control you in any way. From now on, I act like the woman you deserve to be married to." Aurelia walked towards him with her most sensual strut.

"Do you really mean that?" Baron came wider awake the closer she got to him.

"Absolutely," Aurelia replied with sincerity, stopping just shy of his desk. "You like my dress?" She turned around slowly so that he could see it from all angles.

"Yes. You look so…so…beautiful," Baron stammered out after swallowing hard over the lump in his throat. That dress made Aurelia look like a true mestizo Latina, especially with that pink rose in her hair.

"Thanks. I bought this outfit with you in mind." Aurelia faced him again with a smile.

Baron swallowed hard again. "You did?" His body was already harder than dried cement.

"Oh, yes." Aurelia removed things off his desk and onto a nearby file cabinet as she spoke. "This is my coming home dress. Or rather my coming home for good dress."

Baron moaned. "Why are you clearing off my desk? Are we about to have makeup sex?" He licked his lips at that very thought. He retrieved a tic-tac from his right desk drawer and put it in his mouth just in case.

"Yes." Aurelia grinned over at him.

Baron stood to his feet at full attention…all over. "Come here." His eager hands reached for her across the expanse.

"No." Aurelia shook her head and moved farther out of range. "Have a seat back in your chair, freak boy. Freak girl is about to fulfill one of your greatest fantasies."

Moaning aloud, Baron literally ached with need and tingled with desire. Even so, he settled back down in his chair and awaited his wife's next move.

No more words were exchanged as Aurelia rounded the corner of Baron's desk with her bag. Her hips moved in time to Sade's The Sweetest Taboo as it played in the background.

Determined not to chicken out after her fancy speech and all that sensual buildup, Aurelia pushed her sudden case of nerves away at the same time that she boldly pushed Baron's chair back against the wall. Straddling his lap, she aggressively attacked his minty mouth to buy more time to build up her courage.

Aurelia's bag slid to the floor unnoticed as Baron responded in kind, pulling her tongue deep within his mouth. Moans vibrated in the back of their throats as they feasted upon each other.

When Baron's hands roamed her curves at will, Aurelia reluctantly brought the delicious kiss to an abrupt end. Now that her confidence was restored, she was determined not to get too distracted from her intended course.

"Don't go. Please," Baron lamented, reaching for her again as she stood to her feet. Surely she hadn't changed her mind at this point. If so, why?

Aurelia smiled. "I'm not going too far, baby. Just far enough to show you how willing I am to please you in every way. Tonight."

Baron let out a relieved sigh and relaxed again.

Meanwhile, Aurelia retrieved a small vinyl mat out of her large purse. When it was in the right place, she took a deep breath of courage, knelt upon it and went to work.

As Aaron Hall's I Miss You cued up on the stereo, Aurelia removed Baron's silk boxers and then pretended that he was one of the bananas she practiced on for weeks. She envisioned the round plums she practiced on, too.

Following Crystal's advice to the letter, a sense of power surged through Aurelia when she saw Baron's eyes roll in the back of his head at her first slow descent. He moaned aloud and tightly gripped the armrests of his chair as she ascended just as slowly, applying pressure in all the right places. She remembered to honor his crown with smooth reverential swirls.

Baron moaned again and opened his eyes to watch her work. He continued to moan as she repeated the same unhurried sequence over and over again.

"You're doing good, baby," Baron encouraged in a husky whisper as he watched her ascend yet again. "So good."

Ready to show him just how skilled she really was, Aurelia descended once more. This time she took him farther than Megan or any other woman ever had.

"Don't hurt yourself, baby. I know you're an overachiever, but you don't have to overextend yourself tonight," Baron whispered, moving back a bit out of consideration for her, even though he thoroughly enjoyed everything she'd done thus far.

Aurelia shook her head in protest and moved even closer,

determined to stay on course. She was going to put her stamp on this gorgeous man tonight. Show him how much of an overachiever she really could be.

"Are you sure..." Baron's voice trailed off as Aurelia exercised control over muscles he had no idea she even knew how to use. Violent shudders of liberation rocked his body. A loud roar erupted from his throat as he went over the edge with a look of awe in his eyes.

Intoxicated by Baron's strong reaction to her ministrations, Aurelia smoothly released him and just watched as he closed his eyes in deep ecstasy. Who knew that she would feel so accomplished afterwards?

Continuing to watch Baron go through the aftershocks of what she'd just done to him, Aurelia rose to her feet and sat upon his desk next to her bag. Reaching inside that bag, she retrieved a small silver flask that held a special concoction that Crystal recommended she use after the fact.

As Aurelia drank of the mixture, swirling it around in her mouth before swallowing, an even greater sense of accomplishment swelled in her chest. She'd finally gotten over the trauma Oliver Jean-Baptiste had caused. She'd finally evened the odds with Megan. And she'd finally reciprocated the kind of love her husband wanted and needed. Successfully.

It was a good night. A very good night.

When Baron finally returned to his right mind, he immediately reached for his wife. "Come here, beautiful." He pulled Aurelia into his lap for a succulent kiss that was potently mixed with alcohol and a few other things.

By the time that long kiss ended, they were both breathing raggedly. Heartfelt I-love-you's were exchanged.

"I figured those full soft lips would be lethal, able to bring a man to his knees. What you just did to me was...outstanding," Baron said, cupping her face tenderly in his hands. "No woman..." He paused to compose himself as emotion glistened in his eyes. "No woman has ever pleased me so thoroughly. How...how did you know exactly what to do? Especially since you've shied away from all my attempts to teach you over the last month."

"I know, and I'm sorry about that," Aurelia replied. "But the Gino, Oliver, and Megan situations had me too tense to let myself go in every way with you. Plus, I couldn't come to you half-stepping. I wanted my first time doing that with you to not only blow your mind, but to blow all of your exes out of your mind in the process. Thankfully, I was able to enlist the help of a neutral subject, namely Crystal from the club."

"Dingo's Crystal?" Baron's brows rose.

"Yes. Using bananas, plums, and a few other things, she taught me everything she knew on the subject. Judging from your reaction tonight, I'd say she taught me well."

Baron grinned, using both index fingers to trace her dimples. "Yes, she did. Very well. Remind me to send Crystal a big thank-you gift."

"I will." Aurelia grinned, too. "It'll be from the both of us since she refused to take any money I tried to give her for the lessons."

Smacking his lips and giving his tongue a quick suckle, Baron asked, "Why do I taste scotch, cinnamon, and honey on my tongue?"

Aurelia chuckled. "That's part of the mixture Crystal showed me how to make for afterwards since some men don't like kissing their women in the mouth post-fellatio."

"Ahh...I see." Baron nodded. "I also see the need for all the various properties in that mixture. Let's see, the scotch is the antiseptic. The cinnamon and honey are for flavor, right?"

Aurelia stared at her husband in awe. The brilliant man had not only just guessed each ingredient she'd put into the mixture, but the purposes of them all. With a greedy moan, she threw her arms about his neck and attacked his lips again.

Though taken slightly off guard, Baron dove into that kiss just as eagerly as he did the last one. His hands began to travel this time. They went...

Up Aurelia's shapely legs, which were devoid of stockings, freshly shaven, and shiny with body oil.

Under that sexy dress, which was about to be ripped off. Down to her sizzling core, which was about to be possessed. Past those...

Crotchless panties?

What?! Baron moaned deep within his throat at that unexpected discovery. He kissed her with even more fervor. His body hardened anew as it became clear to him that Aurelia had not only come into his office to give tonight. She'd come to receive as well.

Baron was ready to give her everything he had. "Get back on the desk," he whispered against her mouth.

"Yes," Aurelia purred out and then eagerly rose to her feet.

Within seconds of her settling upon the desk, Baron was inside of her. Deep inside.

Aurelia gasped and moaned as her body stretched to accommodate him. Was he suddenly larger? She knew he'd gain more muscle mass in other areas of his body, but when had his private dimensions changed?

After briefly capturing her lips again, Baron's hands relieved her of that dress and flung it away in lieu of ripping it off. At the sight of her beautiful brown globes, his mouth went to the left one. A hand went to the right. The other hand supported her back, holding her steady as his hips withdrew before surging forward in a slow counterclockwise motion.

Low, elongated moans spilled from Aurelia's lips as Baron continued that slow advance and retreat rhythm. Was it possible for a man to stroke a woman's mind away? To make her forget her own name?

Oh yes.

Before Baron was through with her tonight, Aurelia didn't know if she was Aurora, Aloe Vera, Allison, or any other names that began with an 'A'. What she did know for certain was that she was home to stay.

* * *

The next morning, Baron woke up feeling lighter than he had in weeks. He felt even better upon receiving a nice breakfast in bed from Aurelia and a special treat afterwards.

As Baron drove to work whistling, he thought about that special treat again. About how 4 was no longer his favorite number thanks to his creative wife.

Licking his lips now, Baron smiled in memory of the innovative and highly stimulating math game Aurelia played with him over breakfast. How as she fed him from the large platter of food they shared, she kept giving him basic math problems to solve.

What's $55 + 14$? What's $219 - 150$? What's 23×3? What's $138/2$?

Whether Aurelia used addition, subtraction, multiplication, or division, all of her math problems yielded the same solution – 69, which was now Baron's newest favorite number. He licked his lips again as he recalled what happened after that game was over.

During their post-breakfast joint shower, Aurelia helped Baron come up with another solution. A solution to a problem she hadn't created.

Aurelia basically told Baron to switch up his strategy with Gino since it was obvious that his partner was deliberately trying to avoid him, thereby avoiding the loss of his longtime crutch. After all, no one was that busy.

"Switch it up like how?" Baron asked as he washed her back.

"By playing up to his greed," Aurelia replied. Then she suggested that Baron have Count revamp the whole dissolution contract in Gino's favor and then leave a message on his partner's phone telling him about the change.

"I guarantee he'll suddenly be very available. He'll probably call you back within a day's time. That's if you're willing to sacrifice a few extra bucks to finally be free of him," Aurelia concluded.

"It's more like several million extra bucks, but I'm willing to sacrifice even that if it means keeping you. You're worth it, baby." Baron turned her around to face him.

"Oh, Baron," Aurelia purred and then attacked his lips right there in the shower. That act eventually led to so much more.

Baron moaned. His body swelled with desire as the details of that steamy shower scene came rushing to the forefront of his mind. He couldn't wait to see his wife again.

* * *

Missing his wife terribly by lunchtime, Baron decided to do something that he'd never done before – eat in AU's cafeteria. He knew he would find Aurelia there. If the food gave him indigestion, he would just have to live with it.

Whatever the cost, Baron needed to see his wife right now. He needed to be around her somehow.

When Baron entered the cafeteria and perused its menu items, he found the selection surprisingly full of healthy choices. He chose a large green salad, a baked chicken breast, and a bottle of spring water. After paying for his food, he found an empty booth and sat down. Now all he had to do was locate his wife.

Remembering what Aurelia wore this morning, Baron discreetly scanned the room for someone wearing a formfitting red linen jumpsuit with pink and red heels. He'd wanted her to wear another one of her dresses today, but since the jumpsuit showed a fair amount of her calves, he was satisfied with her choice of outfits.

Baron hadn't sentenced Aurelia to dresses only by any means. He just preferred them over trousers because of his desire to see her sexy legs every day. If the pants she wore showed some part of her legs, he was content.

Just then, Baron spotted the very legs in question. They were deliciously crossed as Aurelia sat at the end of a long table, laughing with some of her sorors and a few of their boyfriends. The sound of her laughter soothed his soul. Her everything else stirred his body.

Jealousy instantly replaced Baron's desire when he saw a male student named Fletcher Torrey stop to flirt with her. He immediately sized up the competition.

Tall, lanky, with mud-brown eyes and a beard area that looked like a Star Crunch due to poor shaving habits, Fletcher was anything but drop dead gorgeous. However, he was very charismatic, a good dresser, a star basketball player on AU's winning team, and a member of a top fraternity. Combine all those assets together and it was easy to see why he was so popular with the ladies.

Would Fletcher be popular with Aurelia?

After all they'd been through lately and overcome, and especially after what Aurelia did to him last night and this morning, Baron seriously doubted any man could take her from him now. His wife was all the way in their marriage now. She dove in with both feet just last night. And yet he waited with bated breath to have that theory confirmed.

"I told you once before, Fletcher, I already have a man," Aurelia said, promptly letting the basketball player down easy and causing her husband to breathe easier at the same time.

"I hope your man is worth all this faithfulness," Fletcher replied with disappointment.

Aurelia looked down at the ring on her right hand, smiled, looked up and said, "He is."

"You heard the woman. Now go away, Fletcher." Flora shooed her twin brother away from her place near Bambi and Claude.

Baron wanted to rush across the cafeteria and kissed Aurelia senseless. Instead he pulled out his cell phone and checked his messages to see if Gino had returned his early morning call yet. Sure enough his partner had call.

Aurelia was right about him, Baron thought, listening to

Gino's voicemail, which included the acceptance of the new terms of their dissolution and their new meeting time.

After that call, Baron contacted his travel agent to arrange the Vegas trip. He made arrangements for two since Aurelia was accompanying him this time.

Having promised to keep Aurelia abreast of every bit of progress he made towards resolving the Gino issue, Baron texted her with updates. He watched her nod with approval as she read his message a few seconds later. When she turned and actually smiled his way, an emotional lump gathered in his throat. His body grew cinderblock hard. Baron had no idea that she even knew he was in the room.

Aurelia had known her husband was in the cafeteria from the moment he walked in, though this was her first time looking his way. How could she not know Baron was around?

Some of her unattached sorors had swooned with lust at the very sight of him, even talked about some of the sensual things they wanted to do with him. Things that Aurelia had already done with Baron.

Plus, Claude had given her a secret look and a directing nod from his place beside Bambi. A nod that said, 'Your husband is that-a-way', since he'd been told most of the story about Aurelia and Baron by this time, though Bambi was still in the dark on the whole issue.

I luv U, was Baron's next text message.

Aurelia texted back, I luv U 2.

Lunch is good, but I wish I wuz feasting on U instead, Baron texted in return. It took everything in him to remain in his seat when he saw her breath hitch, her hands tremble on her cell phone, and a light shudder rock her body at his provocative text.

But Baron had to stay put…for both their sakes.

It took Aurelia several deep breaths, a few sips of her cold beverage, and a bit of shifting in her seat before she was able to text back. Her simple return message read, I wish I wuz feasting on U 2.

Those words had Baron in need of a few long swigs of his water and a few deep breaths. It was going to be on and popping again when they got home tonight.

CHAPTER FORTY-SEVEN

March

On Monday, the Weavers took off from work and school and took an early flight to Vegas. Baron's meeting with Gino was scheduled two hours before the company's official workday began and they didn't want to miss it.

After a brief introductory period, Aurelia remained in the plush reception area with Holly, the company's secretary. She'd come to work early for this very important meeting. Baron went with Gino to his private office in the back. The men had some long overdue business to discuss.

Baron remained quiet while his partner silently perused the contract. He saw surprise and then greed register upon Gino's face when he found the document just as one-sided as Baron claimed it would be over the phone. One-sided in Gino's favor.

The dissolution agreement basically gave Gino everything in the business with Baron only getting a cash settlement of just twenty percent of what the company was actually worth. All stock options had even been forfeited.

"Are you sure this woman is worth giving up so many millions?" Gino looked eager to sign his name on the documents in front of him. His right hand kept twitching.

"Yes," Baron said without hesitation. "You met Aurelia today. You saw how beautiful she is. She's even more beautiful on the inside."

Instead of responding to those comments, Gino called Holly into the room to witness all signatures and to notarize the necessary documents attached since she was also a notary public. Once the business was all his, Gino's face suddenly took on a smug look. He became extremely vocal in the worst way when he and Baron was alone again.

"Now that we are no longer partners, I guess I should be frank with you. I've wanted to fly solo for a long time. I'm thrilled that you will no longer be holding me back from expanding how I want, when I want, where I want," Gino said, sounding just as smug as he looked.

Baron's cheeks flamed red with ire. He mentally kicked himself for being dumb enough to actually think Gino was his friend. "Since we're being so honest here, I guess I should say that I never wanted to be your business partner in the first place. It was like babysitting a kid all these years."

Gino's cheeks flamed red now. "Well, this kid has officially grown up. When are you going to grow up and stop thinking that the best way to the top is the straight and narrow road. That being a do-gooder actually means something in this world. And that a black woman is an ideal life-mate for any man, no matter how beautiful she is."

"Why you ungrateful little smurf!" Baron roared. Before he knew it, he'd yanked the other man clear across the desk and slammed him to the floor. Hard!

"Get off me!" Gino shouted, struggling against his ex-partner's bulk as the man straddled him across his slender torso. Baron had always been thicker and taller than him, but when had he become so strong?

"I'll move when I'm good and ready, which is the same courtesy you extended to me this past month." Baron looked menacingly down at the man whose arms he had pinned to his sides with his knees.

"Get off me now or I'll have you and your whole family killed," Gino threatened through clenched teeth.

"And who's going to keep you and your family alive when Big Mink finds out what you've done?" Baron countered indifferently, calling the nickname of one of the most dangerous casino owners in Vegas.

Big Mink was also one of the most dangerous mobsters in North America. Fortunately Baron was a favorite of his.

Gino's face paled with fright at the mention of Big Mink, who only tolerated him. "Why you stinking wetbac—"

Baron's fist connected with his opponent's face before he could get the rest of that racial slur out of his mouth. No one would speak of his Hispanic roots in such a derogatory way in front of him. No one!

"I risked my life for you, compromised my integrity for

you for years, almost lost my wife over you, and then practically gave you the whole business." Baron squeezed Gino's throat with both hands now. "And this is the thanks I get?"

"I…I," Gino sputtered out, gasping for breath.

"Let him go, baby," Aurelia suddenly said from the doorway.

A fearful looking Holly was right behind her, biting her nails. The two women had come running down the long hallway when they heard yelling and a loud thud.

"Please let him go, Baron. We didn't come here for this. We came here to be free, remember?" Aurelia persuaded.

At the sound of his wife's voice, Baron loosened his grip on Gino's neck. "You have my wife to thank for this dose of mercy." He withdrew from his ex-partner/ex-friend. "If you don't learn how to think clearer under pressure, control your greed and your wayward tongue, I seriously doubt you'll be shown any mercy in the future by anyone." Baron rose to his feet.

"L…let me worry…about that," Gino gasped out, holding his neck as he sat upright on the floor.

"Oh, believe me, I will." Baron snatched his copies of the signed contracts from the desk. "Stay safe, Holly," he told his now former secretary as he took Aurelia by the hand and led her out of the building.

Holly followed the Weavers up front, leaving Gino behind to recover alone. Returning to her desk, she finished typing her letter of resignation with relish. She started on it soon after notarizing the dissolution papers of the Weaver/Veneto partnership.

Long ago, Holly promised herself that if the upstanding Baron Weaver ever left the company, she would, too. That day had finally come. Now it was time for her to make her exit before Gino got more than just himself killed.

* * *

On their flight home in the private jet Baron rented for the day, he told Aurelia everything that happened in Gino's office. Or rather the parts that she missed since she'd heard and seen the latter portion of their altercation for herself.

Aurelia wasn't surprised in the least to learn that Gino had been a closet racist all this time. "I could tell he didn't like black people from that limp handshake he gave me," she said from the luxury white leather seat beside her husband.

377

"Gino shook my hand as if he was afraid the blackness of my skin would somehow rub off on him."

Baron frowned. "I never picked up on his prejudice until today. I honestly don't know how I could have missed it. I mean, I roomed with him for almost four years in college." He paused for a moment in deep reflection. "Maybe I got thrown off by the fact that Gino befriended me first, even requested to be my roommate after that initial freshman year together. The fact that he actually used to date black women during our undergrad days must have also blinded me to his true colors."

"Baron, you always want to believe the best of everyone. That's one of the things I love about you. The downside to being that way is the potential of being taken advantage of until you discover a person's true colors." Aurelia tenderly stroked the left side of his face to calm him back down. "In Gino's case, I think he went after your friendship because you were rich, generous, and loyal to a fault. Plus, the fact that a Pee-Wee Herman looking guy like him could actually hang out with a walking magazine cover like you had to have benefited him on the social front."

"Count always said Gino was riding my social shirttails in college. Said he caught him looking at Megan the wrong way one time, too. But I didn't make a big deal of it. I'm used to other men coveting my women." Baron smiled and added, "I've never dated an ugly woman in my life."

Aurelia chuckled. "All right, Mr. Ego-Tripping," she teased, nudging him playfully in the side. "If you're so used to other men coveting your women, why do you flip out whenever one of them even cuts his eye at me the wrong way?"

"Because you're the first beautiful woman to ever have my whole heart. Not just 75% of it like Megan had, the whole hundred," Baron said with serious eyes. "This may sound sappy, but I want to build a house of love with you, baby."

"Oh, Baron." Aurelia smiled at him with glossy caramel pools. The kiss she gave him was succulent and long. Had the flight attendant not returned with their beverages two minutes later, it might have lasted even longer.

"Speaking of desperate women, I bet those were the only kinds of black girls Gino dated back in college," Aurelia said, picking the conversation back up where it dropped off as the lone flight attendant quietly left the room. "I seriously doubt he was ever in any real relationships with them. In fact, I suspect that those dates were actually one-nighters with loose women who didn't mind getting low for him." She took a sip from her orange juice filled flute before returning it to the table beside them.

Revelation flickered in Baron's eyes. "I think you're absolutely right about everything you just said. Especially the part about Gino not having real relationships with the black women he took out. As I recall, he never talked about having intercourse with any of them. Only about how he made them all fall to their knees before him."

"Which confirms my suspicions about that little weasel getting a perverted kick out of black women bowing before him." Aurelia's hands balled into fists at her sides. Her body stiffened in her seat. "A man like dat would really need ah gun pointed at meh head before I eva served him!"

"Calm it down, beautiful," Baron soothed, pulling her into his comforting embrace. He knew where her mind had gone just that fast. "You don't have a man like that, remember? Your man doesn't mind honoring and serving you in every way. Matter of fact, if you want, I'll honor and serve you right now," he whispered with a lick of his lips.

Aurelia immediately relaxed again. "We can't get busy here," she whispered back. "I know this is a private plane and all, but it's not that private. The flight attendant is right in the next room."

"This plane can be as private as we want it to be. All it'll take is a few dead presidents and we could be left alone for the remainder of the flight." Baron's eyes gleamed mischievously. "Are you game?"

Aurelia nodded eagerly. "I'm game."

Baron grinned, loving how liberated she had become in the sexual department. After he paid the flight attendant off, he returned to his seat and made sweet love to his wife. Slowly. Very slowly.

During that whole mile high tryst, Baron kept thinking about how sad it was for anyone to hate such delicious brown skin. About how fortunate he was to be given the opportunity to even love such a woman as Aurelia. And when he finally went over the edge, he looked upwards towards heaven in thanks.

CHAPTER FORTY-EIGHT

Baron had to work late the following Monday. Aurelia was on campus as well tonight. She had a sorority meeting for the big step show coming up in late March. They needed to plan their outfits and work a few more kinks out of their dance routine.

As the president of the forensics club, Aurelia also had to make out a requisition and have it approved for the field trip the club was scheduled to go on soon. That requisition required Baron's signature since he was the lead advisor.

I'll drop it by his office after the meeting, Aurelia thought, eager to see her husband again, though nothing sexual would happen between them when she did. Not only was she having major cramps tonight, but they agreed not to engage in any more sexual activity on campus.

Aurelia suddenly winced as pain shot through her lower abdomen.

Where's that Midol? She moaned, not feeling sexual tonight at all. Snatching her purse open right there in the Kappa sorority house foyer, she quickly took something for her pain.

* * *

On the other side of campus, Baron ambled back to his office after a long day of instruction. He'd been working late more frequently, subbing for several night professors who just needed some time off for vacations and other family issues. This extra workload had done wonders to help keep his mind off his dismal marital circumstances.

Thankfully everything at home is as right as rain now, Baron smiled as he closed his office door. He reminded himself to lock it, lest Rhoda drop by her own office again tonight and try to stop in next door to talk with him awhile.

The persistent woman usually tried dropping in for a chat first thing in the morning, on Baron's lunch break, and after his night classes. Did she not have a social life at all? And did she completely forget about his earlier rejection?

Unknown to Baron, Rhoda remembered his blunt rejection well. It stung her heart deeply the night it happened and for weeks afterwards. Over time the pain of that rejection eased and she started rebuilding her fantasy of having her very own knight in shining armor. Especially since he still seemed so available and didn't have a trace of the gay vibe.

Baron hadn't brought a woman to any of the faculty or campus gatherings since Jordin's appearance at the carnival. Nor had any female stopped by his office claiming to be his woman yet. Until one of those things happened, Rhoda was going to keep pursuing him.

To keep from downright ostracizing his colleague and creating a hostile work environment, Baron kept his office door closed as much as possible. He also kept it locked since Rhoda had a nasty habit of turning the doorknob after only one knock.

Ten minutes into grading papers, Baron got a phone call from Dean Paterson. That call was to inform him that one of AU's older professors had had a heart attack that very night. That unfortunate incident meant that the science department would need Baron's help with even more classes until a full-time replacement could be found.

"Will I need to take over all of Gustav's classes?" Baron asked his supervisor.

"No, just the ones that don't conflict with your current teaching schedule. And also the one that won't upset your personal/professional balance," Dean Paterson replied discreetly.

"Meaning, the class with my wife in it," Baron said, getting right to the point.

"Exactly. I have a few other professors in mind for that one, even though you would have been the best choice for the job otherwise. I'm waiting for each of them to get back in touch with me now. It's on a first-come, first-served basis since it is a senior level class and thus comes with more serious-minded students."

After being given a list of classes to choose from, Baron

got off the phone and returned to his stack of student papers. Twenty minutes later, there was a knock on his door.

Baron grimaced, assuming that it was Rhoda. When he reluctantly went to answer the door, he found someone else on the other side.

Aurelia.

"Good evening, Professor. I stopped by to get you to sign off on a requisition for the forensics club," Aurelia said, stating the purpose of her visit loud enough for any other professors in the vicinity to hear. Suddenly she winced in pain when another unrelenting cramp sliced through her lower body.

"What's wrong, ba...?" Baron's words trailed off when he suddenly remembered where they were. Instead, he opened the door wider and ushered her inside. Although he closed the door behind them, he failed to lock it in his preoccupation with his wife's well-being.

"Now tell me what's wrong, baby," he continued in a tender tone, pulling her gently towards him.

"It's just cramps." Aurelia gingerly rubbed the bottom of her stomach. "I took something for the pain, but it hasn't kicked in yet."

"How long ago did you take it?" Baron ran his hand soothingly up and down her back as he talked.

Aurelia looked down at her watch. "An hour and a half ago? Those pills should have worked long before now." She frowned.

"I agree, but since they haven't, don't take anything else. Wouldn't want you to over medicate yourself trying to escape your pain. Here's what I want you to do instead." Then Baron mapped out a natural plan of pain relief for her.

That plan included Aurelia going straight home to make cinnamon tea with a dash of ginger, taking a warm bath with candles and music playing in the background, and then laying on the bed with her eyes closed and her knees elevated as she practiced deep breathing.

"You do all that, you might not ever have to rely on pills for pain relief again," Baron concluded. "Now give me that requisition and a quick kiss, so you can be on your pretty little way."

"Yes, Dr. Weaver." Aurelia draped her arms about his neck as she tilted her lips to his.

Just then, a light knock sounded on Baron's office door.

"Baron, I bought you a healthy salad for dinner." Rhoda twisted the doorknob even as she spoke.

When that door swung open, Baron wanted to kick himself for not locking it again. He'd been so distracted with Aurelia that he forgot.

"I knew it!" Rhoda hissed with venom in her voice and eyes as she glared at the hugging couple across the room.

* * *

"Come all the way in and close the door, Rhoda," Baron ordered, immediately taking control of the situation as he withdrew from his wife.

Doing as she was told with her free hand, Rhoda nevertheless slammed the door in protest of what she'd seen tonight. Of her hopes being dashed once and for all concerning Baron.

"I knew you slept around for grades." Rhoda directed her anger towards Aurelia like most women did when they refused to acknowledge the man's role in a secret love affair. "You probably slept with Claude to get him to help you pass my class. Don't worry, Baron. Once I tell the dean about this little seductress, you won't have to worry about her trying to sue you for sexual harassment."

Baron's cheeks flamed red with ire. His eyes flashed fire. "First of all, watch how you talk about my wife! Secondly, Dean Paterson already knows about our nuptials," he replied, promptly coming to his wife's defense.

"Your wife?!" Rhoda's eyes bucked. The large salad container in her hands fell to the floor unnoticed.

"Yes," Baron replied, putting a possessive arm about Aurelia's small waist. "We got married in December, which is the same month I told Dean Paterson about us. In fact, he's the one that advised discretion until Aurelia graduates, even though I wanted to share my happiness with the whole world."

"I didn't..." Rhoda stammered out. "I didn't know."

"You weren't supposed to," Aurelia quipped, having lost what little respect she had left for her ex-professor. "As for the grade I got in your class, I earned it the honest way by studying hard, listening to instruction, and taking great notes. The same as I do in all of my classes, including the one I took from Baron."

Rhoda glared at Aurelia, incensed that she would be so disrespectful to a superior, even though that superior was disrespectful to her first. And to hear Aurelia freely refer to Baron by his given name as if it belonged on her tongue was infuriating. Not to mention how cozy she looked standing next to him.

"You owe me $9.50 for the salad," Rhoda told Baron for lack of anything else better to say.

"Here's a twenty. Keep the change." He pulled the stated bill from his wallet and handed it over.

"I will." Rhoda practically snatched the money from his hand. Then without another word to either of them, she turned around and stomped out of the office, slamming the door behind her.

Shaking her head at such childish behavior, Aurelia chuckled. "I see why she can't find or keep a good man. Desperation and immaturity are not only surefire male repellents, but they're also relationship killers."

"You got that right," Baron replied. Those were two additional reasons he resisted Megan for so long back in the day. She'd been too desperate to have him and had remained immature for years. When she finally grew up, she wrapped her desperation up in seduction. The latter is what helped to sway him eventually, but not anymore. Aurelia kept him good and satisfied in every way now. Even if she didn't, Baron still wouldn't go back to Megan.

"Anyway, I guess I better clean up that mess before it sets into the carpet too bad." Aurelia moved to do just that.

"No!" Baron protested in a stern tone. "I'll clean up the mess here. You go on home and look after yourself," he ordered, stopping her in her tracks.

"Yes, sir." She saluted with a smile.

Baron cracked a smile, as well. "Sorry about my tone. That woman just rubs me the wrong way. I didn't mean to take it out on you, baby."

"You're forgiven." Aurelia gave him a warm smack on the lips. Then after getting her requisition signed, she bid him farewell and headed home.

Baron stayed behind and got his office together. He opened the windows, allowing the room to air out from the strong smell of Italian dressing and garlic butter that saturated it. In doing so, he overheard Rhoda next door on her office phone. She was talking to Dean Paterson.

Was she calling the man at home to confirm Baron's secret marriage?

No, Rhoda was calling to confirm her availability for the Forensic 402 class the dean had asked her to teach earlier. The same class that Aurelia was in. The same class that Rhoda just got permission to teach.

Aurelia is definitely not going to like this, Baron thought, not too fond of Rhoda teaching his wife again either. Especially not after what happened tonight.

CHAPTER FORTY-NINE

Aurelia followed Baron's instructions to the letter. By the time he arrived home, she was lying in bed with her knees elevated and watching TV with a big smile on her face. An empty salad bowl, fork, and mug sat on a wooden tray on the nightstand beside the bed.

Aurelia looked so happy and content that Baron almost hated to wreck her mood with his bad news. But he had to. She had to be told about Rhoda.

"I got bad news, baby." Baron removed his jacket as he walked over to his closet.

"Bad news? What kind of bad news?" Aurelia sat upright with a worried frown now.

"Dr. Gustav Vinson, your forensics professor, had a heart attack tonight."

"Oh no!" Aurelia gasped. "Did he die?"

"Thankfully no, but as a result of his new health issues, Gustav won't be back to finish out this semester." Baron hung his jacket up in the closet and then bent to take off his shoes.

Aurelia sighed in relief.

"Unfortunately, Rhoda's going to be teaching that class until a permanent replacement is found," he continued, looking back at her with a grimace.

Aurelia groaned loudly. "I understand why you can't teach my class, but surely they could have found somebody, anybody else to teach it besides Rhoda Griffey."

"I agree." Baron let out a breath of frustration before turning to place his shoes on the proper shelf in the closet. "But the thing is, teaching that class was on a first-come, first-served basis. I heard Rhoda calling to confirm her availability before I left the office tonight. From the sound of her triumphant reply soon thereafter, I knew she'd won the opportunity to teach your class."

Aurelia's frown deepened. "There's no doubt in my mind that she's going to do everything in her power to flunk me so close to graduation, especially after tonight and despite all your good deeds towards her."

"I won't let her." Baron moved towards the bed.

"I don't see how you can stop her. Rhoda's the new sheriff in town in that classroom. What she says will be law until they find someone else, if they find someone else so close to graduation."

"I can stop her by tutoring you at home so that you're extra prepared in her class, by scrutinizing every bad grade she tries to give you, and if push comes to shove, by exposing her vendetta against you to the president of the university." Baron embraced her stiff frame. "I love you, Ree-Ree. As your husband, it's my job to protect you from those that try to do you harm in any way."

Aurelia instantly relaxed. "Oh, Baron," she purred, snuggling against him. She'd never felt so protected in all of her life. "I love you." She looked up into his eyes.

"I love you, too." Baron smiled down into her face. He gave her a tender kiss on the forehead before leaving the bed to remove the rest of his clothes. "By the way, how are you feeling now? You certainly looked pain free when I walked through the bedroom door tonight."

"I am pain free!" She chuckled, throwing her hands up in the air. "I don't know if it was the tea, the bath, or any of the other things I did tonight, but I haven't had any pain or any need for pain medicine in hours. Got any more great medical tips to share?"

"Tons, all of which I'll be glad to tell you about later." Baron laughed as he unbuttoned his shirt and removed it. "Right now I need to shower and eat whatever's left of that pasta salad in the fridge." He nodded pointedly towards her empty bowl on the nightstand.

Aurelia burst out laughing. "I only filled my bowl once tonight."

"Sure you did," Baron said, remembering how heartily she'd eaten the turkey bacon and pasta dish he cooked for dinner last night. She'd gone back for thirds.

"Next time cook more," Aurelia suggested with a chuckle.

"Or better yet, open up a restaurant in the mall or something. That way, I and everyone else can eat as much as we want of your delicious meals. That way, other health-conscious diners won't be faced with fixing their own meals every day or surrendering to the temptation of eating at some unhealthy fast food place."

Baron suddenly stopped short in his tracks, mere inches away from the laundry hamper. "Opening up a health-conscious restaurant in the mall is not a bad idea at all." He turned around to face his wife again. "I've been looking for more positive outlets for the cash settlement I received in that Vegas dissolution. I put 30% of it in church on Sunday. Now I need to figure out what to do with the rest."

Aurelia's eyes bucked. "I had no idea you'd given that much in Sunday's collection plate," she said, though she was very much aware of how many millions he'd gotten out of that Vegas settlement. Baron always kept her updated on his business portfolio, allowing her to see just how much his net worth increased or decreased on a weekly basis.

"No wonder the pastor called today to personally thank you for your donation," Aurelia added, reciting what she'd heard on the answering machine tonight.

"I'll be sure to call him back first thing tomorrow." Baron put his shirt and the rest of his clothing in the quality wicker hamper that Emile made and shipped to him as a thank-you gift.

"Mama and Roxy called today, too," Aurelia said, reclining back on her various pillows to relax and enjoy the view of the beautiful naked man across the room. Watching Baron was more enjoyable than watching TV or looking at the mural of the northern lights that had been painted on the bedroom's south wall during her renovations to her new home.

"Mama called to say that she and Trent moved back into the family home without incident and that they love all the renovations to the house," Aurelia continued, forcing her mind back on the subject at hand. "She also said that business at the Bunting Basket-Making Company is booming. Uncle Sam is now making deliveries three times a week for the shop."

Baron smiled. "That's great news," he said, closing the closet door. He suspected that his in-laws would do well in business all along. The Buntings were good, hardworking people of integrity. They just needed somebody to give them a helping hand as they fought their way out of poverty. He was glad to have been one of those somebodies.

"It really is great news. If business continues to boom, you should have your original investment back by the end of the year." Aurelia looked downright proud of her family as well.

"No rush," Baron said unconcerned about that investment as he headed for the tall dresser on the north wall with his watch in hand. "I know your family is good for it." He recalled how many checks his in-laws had sent him in repayment thus far.

Emile even offered to repay him for the renovations to the Bunting house and for her new car. As expected, Baron refused those offers. He wanted those things to be gifts to his wife's family. That same day he cancelled Aurelia's loans to him and to all of her outside lenders, giving her the gift of debt freedom as a belated wedding present. He wanted his wife free in every way.

"By the way, did you say Roxy called, too?" Baron closed the long multi-chambered box that held all of his jewelry. "How did she get our new number?" The Weavers had gotten their home number changed to an unlisted one right after Megan called. Earl was the only relative that hadn't been given the new number for obvious reasons.

"Roxy called my cell," Aurelia explained. "She basically called to let me know that she and her son are going to be moving out of the apartment soon. It seems that Count finally caught up with her baby daddy, arranged for a court ordered paternity test, and then secured an impressive child support package for Roxy when the test revealed that Cain really was the father. Now she'll be able to raise her son anywhere she wants, send him to private school, and to the college of his choice."

"More great news." Baron chuckled and added, "I expected no less from my brother's efforts. Count is like a hound dog when it comes to deadbeat dads. He can sniff them out quick. Then when he finds them, he pounces and drags them back to the state of accountability. You know that's how he met Jenny, don't you?"

Aurelia laughed. "Yes. Jenny told me all about how Count tracked down her and her sister's deadbeat dad. About how she went to his law office to get back child support for

Arlynn, who was fifteen at the time and how Count not only got back payments for her little sister, but for her, too, even though Jenny was twenty-five at the time. She says that's when she fell in love with your brother. I don't blame her. I'd fall in love with a man that went the extra mile for me, too."

"Isn't that what you did?" Baron headed to the bathroom now. "Didn't you fall in love with a man willing to go the extra mile for you, too?"

"Yes, I did," Aurelia replied, licking her lips as she raked her gaze over his bare muscular frame.

Baron stopped in his tracks again. "I can't handle you looking at me like that, baby," he said huskily even as his body swelled with desire under her hot gaze. "Not this time of the month."

Aurelia chuckled. "Only one part of me is on restriction right now. The other parts are still working just fine." She smacked her lips.

Baron moaned, surprised and yet thrilled that she would even offer such a treat during a time when she definitely didn't have to. "We'll pick this particular conversation back up after my shower," he said, squeezing out some of the ache.

"Fine with me." Aurelia grinned. "Now back to the subject of Roxy's call. She said something about how I'm probably not going to be able to find anyone else to rent out the apartment on account of the building's new ownership. Roxy said the new owner is kicking everybody out soon, so that he can tear the building down and make room for a parking lot."

"I'm doing no such thing!" Baron protested as his passion flew away as if it had wings.

Aurelia's eyes bucked again. "Y...you own that building?"

He took a deep breath and blew it out before speaking. "Baby, I own a lot of things you don't know about," Baron finally replied, realizing that it was time to tell her exactly which businesses were under the umbrella of the parent companies that she'd seen in his portfolio. His shower and dinner would just have to wait.

* * *

Aurelia listened in silence as Baron got out his laptop and then pulled up a long list of businesses he either outright owned or were invested in. Halfway down the list, she began to notice a pattern with his business holdings, particularly the newly acquired ones. They were all connected with people whom he'd had some dealings with, good or bad. Mostly bad.

Baron owned 25% of the television station where Jordin worked, 25% of Cain's music store franchise, 25% of the restaurant where Claude worked, and even 25% of the trucking company that Megan inherited from her deceased husband.

Baron outright owned the apartment building Aurelia used to stay in and a third of the businesses that supplied the Jean-Baptiste scuba business. He even owned stock in the boats Oliver leased for that business.

"Okay, before you show me the true identity of another business that you own or partially own, please explain why you even have certain businesses, particularly the ones associated with our enemies, a guy you thought was a rival, and a building I used to live in," Aurelia said, looking at him now instead of the computer screen.

Baron took a deep breath and blew it out. "Count says I'm a crazy control freak for owning any part of my enemies' businesses. I say I'm only protecting me and mine. This way, if my enemies get too far out of line again one day, I can use my various ownerships to quickly snap them back in their rightful places."

"You would have used your clout at the restaurant to get Claude fired if he and I had turned out to be a couple after all, wouldn't you?" Aurelia said, asking that hard question after a moment of silence.

"Yes," Baron admitted, meeting her gaze head-on.

"Would you have had me put out on the street had I truly left you and gone back to my old apartment after that Bel Air trip?" she said, asking another hard question.

"No, but I might have raised your rent so that you would need me again," Baron replied honestly.

"You are a control freak!" Aurelia raged, springing up from the bed.

"Yes, a control freak who has learned his lesson about trying to control his woman," Baron admitted, closing the laptop. "I wouldn't dare try to force you to come back to me or to stay with me now. I want you here by your own will, of your own accord."

As Aurelia stared into his sincere eyes, all of her anger fizzled into nothingness. Even the tension in her shoulders left.

"Are you here of your own accord, Ree-Ree?" he asked in a semi- whisper.

"Yes," Aurelia replied, being just as honest as him. "But if you're no longer trying to control me, then why are you kicking all those people out of my old building? Some of whom are too old to suddenly be homeless." She paced the floor in front of him.

"I'm not kicking anyone out on the streets," Baron replied. "Each and every tenant in that apartment building will be given an equitable relocation stipend by me and offered subsidized housing in other parts of town by the city of Alcove."

Aurelia stopped pacing to gawk at him. "Really?"

"Yes, really. Nor am I going to tear down the building and turn it into a parking lot like Roxy said. I wouldn't dare do that to a place with such historical value." Then Baron summed up the research he'd done on Aurelia's old apartment building. He shared how it used to be a grand hotel back in the '40's and had even housed a U.S. president once when he was passing through town.

"By me purchasing that apartment building with the express intent of restoring it to its former glory, the city of Alcove has agreed to help pay for the more costly renovations and to start revitalizing the surrounding neighborhood to add even more value to that part of town," Baron continued. "When it's done, they're going to put the restored hotel among Alcove's historic listings and offer tours to and within it. But only on certain floors since most of the upper rooms will be rented out to overnight guests."

"So you're about to become an hotelier?" Aurelia actually looked impressed. She certainly didn't look or sound mad anymore. She even returned to her seat beside him on the bed.

"Maybe not after what Roxy told you." Baron frowned. "I told the city officials that I would back off this deal if my image as an honorable property owner was put at stake as a result of their faulty handling of the PR surrounding the relocation process. I don't want or need any publicity at all right now, especially any negative publicity for obvious reasons."

"Well, since the residents aren't talking about picketing or formally protesting just yet, I think your realty company should send out a letter to all of the tenants explaining your intentions for the property and your intentions towards them," Aurelia suggested, putting her arms about his bare torso. "Include an 800 number they can call to get more information and that ought to solve your negative PR problem."

"That's a great idea, baby. I'll get on that ASAP," Baron replied. "One last thing we need to talk about before I take my shower."

"Is it more bad news?" Aurelia frowned. She'd had her fill of bad news today.

"It all depends on how you look at it," he said. Then Baron told her about the trust fund that he established for Trent back in December. About him padding that trust fund with the earnings he received from the Jean-Baptiste empire. About how this was his way of getting Trent at least some of his rightful inheritance.

"But if you think I should dissolve those associations, too, on account of who Oliver is connected to, I will," Baron concluded, putting the ball firmly in her court.

Aurelia was silent for a long moment as she pondered the matter further. "Actually I don't think you should dissolve those associations at all," she finally said.

Baron's left brow rose. "How is this setup any different from what I had with Gino?"

"Well, for one thing, you are not in direct partnership with Oliver like you were with Gino. Your name is not on any incorporation papers or on any loans connected to him. Which means if Oliver angers his questionable associates, they are not going to come after you. That would be like killing the local grocer because he sold a loaf of bread to a hungry gangster. Secondly, I was never against the honest money you made from the casinos, but rather against the danger involved from doing business with certain casino owners. Since your company couldn't seem to do one without the other in Vegas, it seemed best to just sever your ties there altogether."

Baron lifted his left brow even higher in surprise. "Are you trying to tell me that you're actually all right with my business dealings in the V.I.?" He wanted to be clear on the matter.

"I'm fine with them just as long as you keep yourself on the supplier side of the equation and not directly involved with Oliver in any way." Aurelia shuddered. "The man still gives me the creeps to this day."

Baron put his arms around her and gave her a comforting squeeze. "You need fear him no more. Not only am I here to protect you and yours, but from what I researched, Oliver is too busy with his own troubles to try to pick a fight with us. His companies are financially strapped from mismanagement and he is battling serious illness in his body. According to my research, Oliver returned to the islands in December to try to salvage the business holdings he still has left there and to recover from a bout with prostate cancer. Both seem to be touch and go at the moment."

"Wow! You really have been on top of your game with this man."

"I had to be for you and Trent," Baron replied. "By the way, I named my Virgin Island based investment company Wehpen, which sounds like the word 'weapon', but is simply nephew spelled backwards."

"Nuff respect!" Aurelia said with glossy eyes, so proud of her brilliant husband.

Baron simply chuckled, rose from the bed and returned his laptop to the closet. Then he went to finally take his shower. A long thorough one in light of that special treat Aurelia hinted at earlier.

When Baron reentered the bedroom, he found a tray of food waiting for him, his favorite beverage, and the television turned to his favorite channel.

Did he also find his wife waiting to give him a special treat? No, Aurelia was sound asleep on her side of the bed.

Baron smiled, falling in love with her all over again. He could care less about that special treat now. He already had everything he needed.

CHAPTER FIFTY

The next day, Aurelia went to school with a light heart, despite the fact that she was going to be in Rhoda's class again. Blame it on the great breakfast in bed she'd gotten this morning, the red rose beside her pillow, and all the kisses from her attentive husband.

After feigning surprise like the rest of her peers when they learned of Professor Vinson's health crisis and their need for a substitute teacher, Aurelia quickly went into benevolent mode by organizing the usual class fundraiser. She hadn't gotten two words out of her mouth before she was interrupted by Rhoda.

"Actually, I will be taking up all donations for Professor Vinson." Rhoda gave Aurelia a daggered look that caused many eyebrows to rise around the room for more reasons than one.

Every student in that class knew that Professor Griffey was a moody person. Sometimey even – sometimes she was cordial to students, sometimes she wasn't. However, none of them had ever seen her behave benevolently towards anyone, not even her colleagues. Nor had they ever seen Rhoda glare so viciously at a student the way she glared at Aurelia right now.

Completely aware of the real reason for Rhoda's disdain, Aurelia decided to pick her battles wisely. "Actually, I think that's a great idea, Professor Griffey. I have a lot on my plate right now anyway. Do we need to give you our donations now? Or should we bring them to your office before the end of the day?"

Rhoda's cheeks grew crimson. Frustration flashed in her eyes. She didn't expect Aurelia to relinquish control of the fundraising so quickly. She expected more of a fight. Had even wanted it so that she could exercise the seniority that she had in this classroom.

"Give them to me before the end of class." Rhoda scowled; determined to keep Aurelia from coming anywhere near her office...and subsequently near Baron's, too. "Great! Now I have even more work to do," she mumbled underneath her breath as she turned to write on the board behind her.

Rhoda had no one to blame for her extra workload but herself. It was her own fault for volunteering to oversee Professor Vinson's donations when Aurelia was more than happy to do so. Plus, she didn't have to teach this class. There had been at least three other professors willing to cover for Gustav.

And yet Rhoda didn't blame herself for one bit of her current anger, frustration, disappointment, and unhappiness. She blamed Aurelia for them all.

* * *

As expected, donations from Aurelia's classmates were at an all-time low that day. The total of Professor Vinson's benevolent fund barely amounted to twenty-five dollars. Had it not been for Aurelia's twenty, it would have only reached the grand total of five bucks.

Blame it on Rhoda's offensive attitude and the fact that the students just didn't trust her with anything beyond teaching them what they needed to learn in this course. Some of them were starting to have their doubts about that based on how lazy she acted today.

After writing out a few notes on the board, Rhoda returned to her desk and proceeded to read a fashion magazine right there in front of them. She even had a pink highlighter, using it to circle the outfits she would buy next on each page.

When Claude asked Rhoda to review their previous assignment, she looked peeved to be interrupted and then reluctantly went over the material. Yet the last ten minutes of class, she seemed quite eager, too eager to talk about some big test she was preparing for them on Friday.

Sensing that they were not going to get much help from Rhoda, many students grouped up after class for an impromptu meeting. Some came to complain and vent their anger. Most tried to come up with viable solutions to pass this required course.

"I say we petition the dean for Professor Weaver to teach the class instead," Bambi suggested, immediately getting a lot of support for that suggestion.

"He's a better teacher than the nutty professor anyway," Damon Penn ranted, offering even more support for that idea. Everyone knew that he wasn't too fond of female professors anyway.

"I think we should form a study group instead," Claude suggested, after sharing a knowing look with a silent Aurelia. They both knew that she would have to drop the class and end up graduating later than expected if Baron replaced Rhoda. Especially since it was too late in the term to take the class at another college.

"I agree with Claude." Aurelia quickly jumped on board that suggestion. "Professor Weaver is already teaching additional classes at night. It wouldn't be fair to overload him like that. Besides, we're a pretty smart group. We can handle Professor Griffey all on our own."

"Maybe you can, Miss A Student. But what about us C students, who are barely squeaking by as it is?" Damon argued.

"That's simple. Those with better grasps of the information will help those who are struggling with the material," Claude said, coming to Aurelia's defense against their disgruntled male peer, who was known to be envious of all women smarter than him.

"I agree." Bambi leaned her support to her boyfriend and friend/business partner/soror. "I also think we should have our first meeting tonight in light of this big test we're about to have on Friday. A test that none of us know how to study for just yet. Is 6pm at the student center a good time and place for everybody?"

Always the peacemaker, Aurelia mused concerning Bambi, who was very close to becoming her best friend ever. If only she didn't have to keep so many secrets from her.

Aurelia hadn't even given Claude permission to tell Bambi yet. Her reasoning was that the less people that knew about her and Baron, the less chance of that knowledge being leaked out, even accidentally.

As soon as the coast is clear, she's going to be the first one I tell, Aurelia vowed, putting Bambi at the top of her 'do-tell' list. Then she went to her car to call her husband.

* * *

Baron frowned when he learned that his wife was going to be late coming home tonight and why. However, he was flattered when he learned that the students had actually been thinking about petitioning the dean for him to replace their lazy instructor.

"The only plausible solution is your study group since your peers are not open to petitioning for one of the other science professors to replace Rhoda," Baron said, packing his briefcase with additional textbooks and other instructional items for his next class. "I would stop by and offer my input on the material, if not for the fact that it might cause conflict in my department. That would be all the incentive Rhoda needed to go to the dean and accuse me of interfering with her class. Or worse, try to take my direct interference out on you. And I definitely can't have that. I'm two steps away from confronting her about how she treated you in class today as it is." Even now he glared at the wall that separated his office from Rhoda's.

Aurelia blew out a frustrated breath. "We really could have used your input, too."

"You'll still have it, but it'll be indirectly given." Baron chuckled mischievously. "I'm going to tutor you at home. Then I want you to take what you learn and tutor your classmates."

"Do you really think I'm up for that task? I'm not a teacher like you, baby. I've never even tutored anyone before."

"Sure you have. Trent and our next door neighbor are proof of that. The way you insist on checking his homework every night via computer screams of a teacher's heart. And the way you broke down what the problem was with Mrs. Applegate's pepper plants was instruction at its finest."

"I was just being motherly and neighborly," Aurelia insisted.

"Yeah, right." Baron scoffed with a chuckle. "But seriously though, it wouldn't be like you to keep all the tips I'm going to give you to yourself. Which means you were going to end up sharing them with your classmates anyway whether I suggested it or not."

Aurelia smiled. "You know me so well, dear husband."

"Learning even more every day, dear wife." Baron checked his watch. Then realizing they only had seven minutes to get to their next class, he closed his briefcase and prepared to end their call. "Now give me a quick phone kiss and get your sexy self to class. I don't need you getting on the bad side of yet another instructor," he teased.

Aurelia sucked her teeth, reluctant to end their call. "I'm going. I'm going."

Baron chuckled again. "As for Gustav, just buy him a really nice gift of your own and take it up to the hospital to offset the crappy one Rhoda is sure to buy him," he suggested, addressing the last minute item on his heart.

"Good idea." Aurelia made a mental note to do that on her lunch hour. Then after blowing her husband a quick kiss through the phone, she finally concluded their call and headed to her next class.

* * *

Rhoda was not a happy camper when all the students in her forensics class started making A's. Every last one, including students that used to struggle in her class. Students like Damon Penn, who now had a healthier respect for the female intellect thanks to Aurelia's tutelage.

Rhoda hated that her students had grouped up and were now helping each other pass her class. She hated that Aurelia had the highest grade of them all. That really burned her.

Rhoda grew even more miserable when she attended the school's annual Greek step show in late March and saw Aurelia excel in yet another way. In a way that suggested that Baron was a very satisfied married man.

It all started when Aurelia's sorority got their turn in the spotlight for today's competitive event. To the tune of Ciara's Oh, the Kappa ladies came out from between the stands wearing pink and red baseball caps, pink midriff hoodies, red jean shorts, pink sneakers with pink and red socks. All of the ladies except for one, that is.

Aurelia was driven into the large arena a minute later on the hood of a pink 1969 Pontiac Grand Prix. She wasn't positioned as a beauty queen by any means on that vehicle. No, she was sitting on the hood of that slow moving car mimicking the moves of her sorors from the waist up. That in and of itself was enough to make the crowd go wild.

Bambi, the driver of the car, parked and got out. Then she joined the rest of the ladies in pink and red as they gathered around the pink vehicle to finish their routine. Every move was perfectly timed. Every step was on point.

Bambi danced as if she had never had an accident. No wonder Claude was one of the loudest cheerers in the stands.

Rhoda looked around and saw other sororities green with envy at the ingenuity and skill of Aurelia's group. The fraternities were cheering like mad, spurred on mostly by lust for the dancing ladies. Their cheers grew to a loud roar when the breakdown portion of the song came and Aurelia went to work on the hood of that car, surpassing even Ciara's video moves. The other ladies in pink and red backed her up by doing similar moves at ground level.

By the time that routine ended, it was clear who today's winners would be.

As expected, the Kappas won the step show this year, which meant all victory benefits would belong to them for a change and not the Deltas or one of the other Greek associations. Those benefits included the winners being honored with an after-party at a local hotel the Greeks had a contract with, a block of rooms for the winners at that hotel, food, and beverages.

Thinking about all the hedonistic things she'd heard about those after-parties, Rhoda made her way over to a sunglass-wearing Baron. He'd watched his wife perform from the first row bleachers, licking his lips the whole time though the rest of him was the picture of impartiality.

"You know she's probably going to be bombarded with indecent proposals at that party tonight," Rhoda leaned forward to whisper in Baron's ear after settling down behind him on the bleachers. "Especially after the way she danced on that car," she added, unaware of Dean Paterson's disapproving frown two rows behind her.

Baron's mouth went into a straight line at Rhoda's words. "Sounds like jealousy to me," he replied discreetly, yet bluntly. Then he rose from his seat and exited the arena, leaving Rhoda to stew in her jealous ire.

Although Baron knew what his colleague was trying to do with that jealous whisper, he also knew that she spoke truth. Men were going to be coming out the woodwork trying to get at Aurelia tonight.

Baron couldn't blame them. He understood the male psyche. He didn't have to like it though.

* * *

Had Baron known that one of Aurelia's former strip club clients was in the audience today, he might have been less understanding about the male psyche. He might have turned outright violent again, like he'd been in Gino's office.

Dr. William Johansson came out to the step show today. Yes, to support Bambi, who was his favorite patient to date and also the niece of his receptionist. But he also came to get another glimpse of Aurelia in action.

Although William called off the private investigator months ago and respected her marriage, he couldn't resist the opportunity to see Aurelia dancing again. He wasn't disappointed. She'd been outstanding today, performing better for free than she ever did for money.

Baron Weaver is one lucky man, William thought, rising to his feet.

Suddenly someone bumped him from the left.

"Sorry," Rhoda said emotionally, stumbling a bit as she blinked rapidly to clear away the tears that had temporarily blinded her.

"Are you all right, Miss?" William asked with concern, holding her steady, lest she fall.

"I…I am now." Rhoda looked up into the eyes of a new opportunity. "My name is Rhoda and you are?"

"William. Dr. William Johansson." He smiled with a depth of attraction that hadn't besieged him since Aurelia.

On the other side of the arena, Mai Ly frowned. The hope in her heart dropped and fragmented like a piece of broken china as she watched with horror as her boss made a love connection with someone other than her.

* * *

"You're spending the night at the hotel?!" Baron asked with flaring nostrils, repeating what he'd just been told by his lingerie clad wife.

"Yes." Aurelia walked over to the blue jeans and long-sleeved pink and red shirt she laid out on the bedroom chaise before her shower. "My sorors are all sleeping over at the hotel," she continued, dressing as she talked. "Since they are unaware of my marriage, I had to say yes. I couldn't tell them that I had to be home with my husband tonight. Or that my fictional fiancé Barry was suddenly back in town, was too good to come to the party like their boyfriends, and wanted me to spend such an important victory night alone with him instead. If I did that, they'd think you were less of a sweetheart than I said you were."

"I see," Baron said in a much calmer tone, though his

mind was working a mile a minute to formulate another win/win plan. "In that case, enjoy your night of sisterhood."

Aurelia turned to smile at the lounging man on the bed. "Thanks for being so understanding, baby."

"No problem. But do me one favor. Wear a skirt tonight. A flared one." Baron secretly made that request for more reasons than one. "I don't want so much attention on your rear end. It was bad enough watching so many guys gawk at it while you were on that car today."

"I can do that," Aurelia consented, willing to grant him that favor for being so amicable about her impromptu sleepover. "By the way, did you gawk at it while I was on that car?" she flirted, switching her hips over to her closet for a skirt and a pair of pink boots.

"Yes, I did." Baron grinned, watching her bottom now.

"Good, because I was dancing with you in mind."

Baron moaned with need. Now he really couldn't wait to put his secret plan in action. Unfortunately, that plan was going to mean the end of something Aurelia held dear.

* * *

Thankful that Aurelia had left her winners' guest passes at home on the dresser; Baron was able to get into the party without showing his college ID. The disguise he wore insured that he would not be recognized otherwise. The basics of that disguise consisted of a brown wig, black leather skullcap, black leather jacket, black t-shirt, and a pair of black jeans and matching boots. Dark shades, a fake tattoo, a newly trimmed goatee, and a thicker accent completed Baron's look.

That's right. His goatee had been tampered with all in the name of love.

What used to be a full goatee had been trimmed down to just a thin strip of hair starting from his bottom lip to his chin. Even that was colored with temporary brown dye to match the wig on his head. To the undiscerning eye, Baron looked like Damian Chapa from Blood In, Blood Out, except with longer hair and a goatee. He definitely didn't look like a distinguished college professor.

The lengths a man has to go to just to be seen in public with his wife, he thought, trying not to be resentful of the ongoing inconveniences of his marriage.

Baron longed for the days when he could ride in the same car with Aurelia without wearing shades or some other kind of disguise, go to the grocery store with her, or take in a movie at a local theater without worrying about someone recognizing them. The only people that knew about them in Alcove were Dean Paterson, Liam, Jordin, Claude, Rhoda, and their immediate neighbors. Unfortunately, that was the way it was going to stay for a little while longer.

As soon as Baron crossed the threshold of the crowded party, he smelled alcohol on the breath of the person nearest to his right. That was one reason the Greeks always held their parties away from college property. This way they could be free to indulge in alcohol.

Baron was just relieved that they did so responsibly. Even now he could see the bartenders carding people just to make sure they were old enough to drink. No wonder there hadn't been any drunken incidents involving AU students.

Baron could recall his own college days where fraternity and sorority underage drinking had landed many students in trouble. Gino had been one of those students. Twice. Each time Baron had bailed him out. Not anymore.

Now where is that wife of mine? Baron pushed all thoughts of his ex-friend out of his mind as he scanned the room for Aurelia. After all, she was his whole reason for being here. The only reason he dressed up in the biker's costume he wore at last year's country club talent contest.

Suddenly jealousy sliced through Baron as he spotted Aurelia dancing to a fast song with none other than Fletcher Torrey. That pesky little fella just won't leave her alone, he thought, immediately heading in that direction.

CHAPTER FIFTY-ONE

"One more dance, Aurelia." Fletcher reached for her hand as the fast song came to an end.

"No." Aurelia shook her head and discreetly freed her right hand from his grasp. "I told you all my slow dances belong to my man."

"But your man ain't here tonight. I am. Surely you don't want to let this Keith Washington song go to waste." Fletcher smiled, laying the charm on thick as he reached for her hand again.

"Oh, but her man is here tonight," Baron interrupted with a thick Latin accent as he swiftly nabbed Aurelia's hand first.

"Bar...ry?" Aurelia stammered out with wide eyes. Her gaze instantly went to his mouth. She'd know those pink lips from anywhere. But what happened to his goatee?

"Si, mami. Your papi's here." Baron briefly lowered his glasses a bit with his free hand so that she could see his eyes and get any remaining proof she needed. "Let's have a go around, shall we?" He pulled her close as Kissing You cued up in earnest.

"Is this your man, Aurelia?" Fletcher asked, speaking to her, though he looked irritably at the man readjusting his shades. A brief flash of fear entered his eyes at the menacing tattoo on the back of the Hispanic man's right hand.

"Oh yes." Aurelia draped her arms about her husband's waist, despite her ire about his altered goatee and risky arrival. "Clearly Barry could make it to the party after all."

"Yes, and I'm ready to party with you all night." Baron bent down to capture her lips in a searing kiss that caused Fletcher to throw his hands up in defeat and walk away in search of another conquest.

Aurelia was a little wobbly after that long succulent kiss, but lingering ire gave her the strength to stay on her feet. "What are you doing here? Are you trying to blow our cover? Or is this about a lack of trust in me?" she whispered breathlessly in Baron's ear as they swayed to the slow ballad.

"I trust you just fine. I'm simply here trying to keep the vultures away," Baron whispered back. "And to send a clear message to everyone that you…" He paused to kiss the right side of her neck. "Are…" He kissed the left side. "Definitely…" He kissed the right side again. "Taken," Baron concluded and then licked a trail up to her earlobe.

Aurelia moaned with pleasure. All remaining ire ebbed away like water down a drain. Turning her head to the side, she engaged him in another long kiss.

When the kiss was over, Aurelia placed her head on Baron's shoulder and sighed. "I love you, baby. Great costume, by the way. I almost didn't recognize you myself. But did you have to take a hatchet to your precious goatee?" she said, still talking discreetly.

Baron withdrew a bit to grin down into her face. "Desperate times call for desperate measures. Just so you know, the rest of the goatee has to go, too. Since it's now established that your fiancé has this kind of goatee, I have to return to the clean shaven professor they first knew me to be just to throw everybody off even more. But don't worry. I'll grow it back come winter. And for the record, I love you, too."

"Too bad that biker theme doesn't go with Barry's businessman persona that I told my friends about." Aurelia chuckled, starting to find the whole thing funny.

"If they ask, just tell them that I'm a businessman with a love for motorcycles and a fetish for leather," Baron teased.

Aurelia laughed. "I just might do that. Did you come on the motorcycle tonight?"

"Yes, and so will you," Baron flirted, playing on words.

Aurelia moaned again, blushed, too, as excited heat rushed up to her cheeks and then down to her nether regions. "Is that why you told me to wear a skirt tonight?"

"Yes." Baron grinned. "I needed easy access." He reached down to cup her bottom through the blue jean material.

Aurelia moaned and pressed herself closer to him. "Where are we going when we leave here?"

"Home and you're driving us there."

"You're going to let me drive the hog?" Aurelia asked with excited eyes. Baron hardly ever let anyone drive his motorcycle. Not even Count.

"Yes, and I want you to take the long way, too. I even brought a jacket and helmet along for you to wear," he said, referring to the items he stashed in the bike's storage compartment.

Aurelia squealed with delight and attacked his lips again. That dance soon became a prelude to intimacy as they sizzled together on the dance floor.

* * *

"Wow! Aurelia is really going at it with that guy in the leather jacket," Bambi said, watching them from her table across the room. "I wonder if that's her fiancé."

"I'm sure that's her man." Claude refused to outright lie to his woman. "Aurelia wouldn't be hugging and kissing on anyone else but him."

"I can't wait to finally meet Barry," Bambi said excitedly. "As soon as they're done dancing, I'm waving them over for long overdue introductions."

This ought to be very interesting. Claude hoped that all of these secrets didn't blow up in Aurelia and Baron's faces tonight or any other night.

* * *

When they continued to kiss and dance provocatively slow, even on subsequent fast songs, Baron knew that it was time to make their exit. His body was in an uproar. By the way Aurelia purred in his ear, it was obvious that her body was in an uproar, too. They both had to take several deep breaths or they were never going to make it out of the room without tearing each other's clothes off.

"Uh-oh, Bambi is waving us over," Aurelia said, unable to miss all that hand movement from across the room. The girl was standing up and waving both hands in the air.

"No problem. I came prepared for that, as well. I even put a fake tattoo on the back of my hand in case I needed to engage in any handshakes during introductions." Baron showed her the skull and crossbones tattoo on his right hand.

"Great! Now dey gone tink I'm engaged to ah devil-worshipper." Aurelia frowned at the menacing tattoo as they made their way across the room to the table where Bambi,

Claude, and a few other sorors were.

Baron chuckled. "Calm down, baby." He placed a soothing hand at the small of her back and proceeded to stroke her tension away. "That tat is only there to intimidate the guys. Since most men know how painful it is to get one on the hand, how tough you have to be to go through that kind of agony, the fact that I have a tattoo there garners a certain level of respect all by itself. It certainly helped to drive Fletcher away. As for the ladies, I promise to be extra charming with them."

"Don't be too charming. There's enough women crushing on the real you. I don't need more crushing on your alter ego, too." Aurelia relaxed enough to laugh as well now. Inside she prayed that all went well as she prepared to formally introduce Baron to her friends and sorors.

* * *

The introductions went better than Aurelia expected. No one recognized Baron as their professor from school. Only Claude knew who he really was.

However, Bambi did stare at Baron extra-long and hard. She was curious as to what Aurelia could possibly see in the leather clad man, who looked nothing like the businessman that she expected. Bambi also wondered why Aurelia's fiancé looked so familiar, especially when he smiled.

"Barry and I want a little private time together," Aurelia told Bambi after the introductions were over. "I'll be back by the time our 3am sleepover begins."

"You're leaving the hotel? Why not just use one of the rooms upstairs? Ours is definitely empty right now," Bambi suggested, referring to the room she and Aurelia would share tonight.

Aurelia shook her head. "No, thanks. I prefer to do some things in my own bed," she replied, instantly recalling how very un-private that hotel room had been in Cabo. "Plus, Bar...ry's letting me drive the hog for the first time tonight. I can't pass up a chance like that," she added, quickly recovering from her near slipup.

"Suit yourself." Bambi shrugged. "And be safe out there...in every way," she added, admonishing safe sex and travel. Especially after that horrific car accident she had.

"We will," Baron said reassuringly in that same thick Latin accent. Then after a round of goodbyes, he led his wife to the nearest elevator.

"I thought we were leaving the hotel." Aurelia looked puzzled. They'd passed by so many exits.

"We are. But first you need to go to your room to retrieve your purse," Baron replied. "And remove your underwear," he whispered with a wide grin.

"Got it," Aurelia replied, quickly deducing the reason for this detour. Her purse not only held her cell phone, but also her identification. Her updated driver's license in particular declared that she was now Mrs. Aurelia Weaver. They couldn't run the risk of anyone seeing that during her long absence. The removal of underwear was for obvious reasons.

"I see now this is going to be a night to remember," Aurelia added with a wide grin of her own.

"You better believe it, baby." Baron reached down to give her bottom an avid squeeze of promise.

* * *

After settling upon Baron on the motorcycle's long seat, Aurelia didn't know how Baron was going to pull off the adventure he had in mind tonight. She soon found out as they rode through the city streets towards their home.

At the first red light, Baron moved heatedly beneath her as he pretended to adjust his body on the seat. In the middle of traffic!

Stifling a moan, Aurelia looked nervously around to see if anyone could tell what they were doing. Yet despite her anxiety, she was highly turned on. The thrill of possibly getting caught proved to be more exhilarating than she thought.

When the light turned green, Aurelia sped off. Though not too fast as to draw undue attention their way.

Baron's hands took that as a signal to go, as well. His ten digits slowly traveled upwards to her globes, squeezing their fullness. His fingertips brushed across her taut peaks ever so lightly.

Aurelia did moan this time. She wavered a bit in the road as they continued to close the distance between them and home.

"You all right up there?" Baron whispered in the right side earpiece of her safety helmet.

"Y...yes. Just a little distracted, that's all," she replied breathlessly, immediately straightening up the front wheel.

"Only a little? I must not be doing my job right then." He chuckled huskily.

"Do you want us to crash?"

"We won't crash with you at the wheel. My beautiful wife is an excellent multi-tasker. She can do more than one thing at a time," Baron said confidently, putting emphasis on a certain word as he readjusted his lower body on the seat again.

"Mmm…baby," Aurelia whispered, clenching the handle bars even tighter as a powerful release continued to build in her body.

And so set the stage for their tryst on two wheels. Every red light was an opportunity for Baron to stroke Aurelia's drizzling core. Every bump in the road caused united moans of bliss. And whenever they covered a long stretch of road with no cars in front of them, he helped her hold the handle bar steady with one hand while actively massaging the bud of her pleasure with the other.

It was a miracle they didn't have a wreck. Especially when Aurelia went over the edge not once, but twice before they ever made it home. By the time they finally arrived at their destination, she was breathing hard and drenched with passion's dew. She was also ready for some conjugal aerobics.

Baron was ready, as well. As soon as the bike was parked in the garage, he pressed the button for the garage door to descend, removed both helmets from their heads, lifted Aurelia up from the motorcycle by the waist and carried her a few feet away to his car.

Before the garage door was completely lowered, Baron had the back of that skirt up again, Aurelia leaned against the car, and himself snugly behind her. Fortunately, their garage wasn't in plain view of the street. Even so, Mrs. Applegate could have seen down into their garage from her second floor window if she happened to look this way before the door closed. Thankfully she was already sound asleep.

Aurelia was beside herself with joy and awe as Baron made love to her fast and furious. She'd never seen him so unleashed before. Was it the disguise? Did he feel more like a tough guy now that he looked like one?

Whatever it was, Aurelia wasn't complaining. She loved seeing Baron so feral and untamed. Loved that he was making her glad to be a woman once again. As a result, Aurelia went over the edge for the third time that night, this time violently, causing her knees to give way.

Though Baron shuddered with a powerful release right after her, he was able to keep them both on their feet.

"I...love...you," Aurelia panted out, looking back over her shoulder at her wonderful husband.

"I...love you...too," Baron replied, just as breathless.

"I'm...so glad...you decided to...crash the party...tonight."

"Me...too."

When they finally could breathe normally again, they went upstairs to their bedroom for more fervent loving. Except this time they took things very, very slowly.

* * *

Two hours before daybreak, Baron donned his disguise again, got the motorcycle ready for use once more, and then took Aurelia back to the hotel. Since she never actually got to sleep over with her sorors, he wanted her to at least be there in time to eat breakfast with them.

Baron drove this time since Aurelia was still relatively sleepy from their nap. She clung to him the way a woman does when she's madly in love with a man. That did his heart good. Made him trust her even more and feel considerably less antsy about her returning to a hotel that was likely still full of testosterone driven college men.

"I'll see you at home later, okay?" Baron told Aurelia after giving her a long kiss goodbye at the front entrance of the hotel.

"Okay," she replied with stars still in her eyes from the night before.

Baron smiled. "Keep looking at me like that and I'm going to take you back home with me now."

Aurelia chuckled. "Keep making love to me like you did over the last twenty-four hours and you're going to end up with a soccer team. I'll be surprised if my birth control worked properly after the work out you gave me last night."

Baron's eyes shined brightly with emotion. "It wouldn't bother me none. I want lots of strong sons and beautiful daughters with you. I'm also ready to bring Trent to live with us, which is yet another reason I can't wait for you to graduate."

Aurelia's eyes instantly watered. "Oh, Baron." She threw her arms about his neck and gave him another succulent kiss.

When Aurelia and Baron finally separated, she went upstairs to make her apologies to her sorors for returning so late. As it turns out, they didn't miss her at all. They were all with their boyfriends, including Bambi, who was sound asleep in bed with Claude in the first room that Aurelia checked.

I could have stayed home, she mused after that stark reminder that love/lust sometimes trumped sisterhood.

After leaving a note to inform her sorors that she would meet them for brunch instead, Aurelia got in her car and headed back home. When she arrived there safe and sound, she found Baron fast asleep, tired from their long night of loving. Undressing quietly, she slipped under the covers and snuggled against him.

Baron moaned as their bodies made contact. "You decided to come back home, beautiful?" he asked sleepily, embracing her familiar frame.

"Yes. Let's just say that my sisters were all occupied with their own men." She chuckled, stifling a yawn.

"Would you like to be re-occupied with yours?" Baron sent a probing hand downward.

Aurelia moaned at his intimate touch, giving him all the answer he needed.

* * *

With the sun hiding behind clouds in Saturday's sky, Aurelia forsook eating anything at home in lieu of having that bountiful brunch with her sorors in a few hours. She did have a glass of orange juice though.

Baron ate his usual morning fruit. He also had a protein shake to help build his muscles. After eating, he worked on his muscles in a different way in his downstairs gym while Aurelia showered and got dressed in their bedroom. She was off from work and the soup kitchen this weekend and thus took longer than usual to get ready today.

When Baron was sure that Aurelia had left the house, he went upstairs to take a shower and do a few other things he'd added to his morning routine. One thing in particular he always did in secret. No use telling Aurelia about that. If he did, the unwanted questions would start. Then he'd be faced with revealing yet another insecurity.

Aurelia already knew about all of Baron's other insecurities. Did he have to tell her about this one, too? He was embarrassed enough about it alone.

With the shower music on full blast, Baron failed to hear Aurelia's car returning to the house a few minutes later. She'd forgotten to take her daily dose of Vitamin C. With the weather stuffy and humid today, she wanted to starve off any congestion that might try to arise in her sinuses.

Downstairs, Aurelia smiled when she heard Latin music coming from the top level of the house. There was no doubt in her mind that Baron was up there busting a few moves right now. Every time he heard his native music, he couldn't help but dance. The same way she was with almost any kind of music, especially soca music.

Wanting to catch him in the act, Aurelia quietly ascended the stairs two at a time. When she got to the open door of the master suite, she caught Baron in another act altogether.

It wasn't his legs moving fast to the lively Latin beat. It was his hands. His rapid fire hands.

"What are you doing to yourself?" Aurelia asked, her eyes wide with disbelief as she took in the shocking sight before her.

"I was just...I was..." Baron stammered out as his hands jerked upwards. Thick creamy lotion slid from his palms to his forearms and on to his elbows. Some dripped on the floor and landed in wide splats on the rug.

"You were demonstrating once again that I'm not enough for you," Aurelia finished for him as her eyes welled up with tears. "Why else would you be doing that just hours after we had some of the best sex of our lives? What are you, some kind of sex addict?"

"No." Baron shook his head. "It's not what you think at all."

"Well, explain it to me, Professor." Aurelia blinked her eyes free and folded her arms angrily across her chest. "Help me not jump to the wrong conclusions after what I just saw."

Baron hung his head, took a deep breath, and then bravely met her gaze again. "First of all, I'm not a sex addict, nor am I dissatisfied with our sex life in the least. You please me tremendously. Always have and even more so lately. Secondly, all I was doing just now was applying a new enhancing cream that I created for men who wanted to be larger. It has to be applied vigorously to get deep down into the pores."

Aurelia's eyes bucked again, before returning to normal in realization. No wonder he seemed bigger down there. He was bigger!

"Why would you want to be larger?" Aurelia put her

hands on her hips now. "You're big enough. If you get any bigger, you're going to split me in two. I can barely handle you now."

"I created this natural enhancing cream and started drinking protein shakes soon after hearing about Cain's third leg," Baron confessed with flaming red cheeks. "I didn't want him to best me at anything or on any level, so I did what I could to even the odds. Much like you did when it came to Megan." He reached for a nearby towel and wiped his hands clean with frustrated swipes.

"Oh, baby." Aurelia shook her head at him as she moved closer to his nude frame. She had no idea that her comment about Cain's manhood would crawl up in Baron's mind and fester. "As of today, I want you to know that I'm thoroughly satisfied with what you were blessed with genetically." She cupped both sides of his face with her hands.

"Are you sure?" Baron stopped his current task and searched her eyes for truth.

"I'm very sure." She smiled reassuringly, stroking his cheeks tenderly. "Besides, Cain had himself surgically altered to get that way. It later cost him a testicle when infection set in during his recovery."

"Really?" Baron's eyes bucked now.

"Yes, really. So please stop treating yourself like a guinea pig. Instead have that cream thoroughly tested in some kind of double-blind study. Then if all goes well, market it to those less fortunate than you, those who could greatly benefit from such a product. Because you, Baron Weaver, definitely don't need any kind of male enhancement to please me. Never did. You can also stop exercising and protein-shaking it so much since I'm quite satisfied with your normal physique as well."

Baron smiled and let out a deep breath of relief. "You have no idea how much I needed to hear that. As for testing and marketing my cream, I think that's an excellent suggestion, though it's made from all natural ingredients, is water soluble, and has proven very safe for me. There have been no adverse side effects, except for an increase in hair follicles over the applied area. I'm sure with further research I could eliminate that side effect altogether and keep my shaving above my neck."

Aurelia's eyes bucked again. "You mean to tell me you've been shaving..." She had to pause when the giggles began.

"...down there?"

Baron chuckled, as well. "Yes, but only the overgrowth." He nodded. "And it hasn't been fun either. I don't know how women do that on a regular basis. It's such a hassle. If I was a woman, I'd live in the jungle and my man would just have to like it."

Aurelia's giggles exploded into full guffaws at those words. She laughed so hard that she had to lean on Baron for support.

He laughed hard, too...at himself mostly for being so vain and insecure. He'd try harder from now on to rest in their love and all the security a faithful marriage brings.

One good thing came out of all this. Baron now had another viable way to increase his growing fortune. Their growing fortune.

CHAPTER FIFTY-TWO

April

Today was Aurelia's twenty-third birthday. She received tons of expensive gifts from her in-laws, custom-made gifts from her family, and playful gifts from her friends and sorors. From Baron she received breakfast in bed, a large bouquet of roses, and a sizable check.

Another woman might have deemed that check as unromantic. But not Aurelia. She thought that check was one of the most romantic things Baron could have ever done for her. For with it he was helping to make yet another one of her dreams come true, which definitely put her in the mood for love.

Now Aurelia had enough money to not only expand her product line, she also had enough to launch that line on a grander scale. Now even more people would be given the opportunity to buy Aurora's Whispers as well as her new additions – Aurora's Caresses, which was her scented lotion and Aurora's Kisses, which was her flavored lip gloss and lip balm.

Aurelia was also going to add two male fragrances to her product line. They were Feral Knight and Latin Lover, both inspired by her handsome husband. She'd already given Baron prototypes of the fragrances and had even gotten Bambi's help to add those scents to soaps for men.

Keeping with the tradition of all her other birthdays, Aurelia had pulled innocent pranks on people all day, everyone except for Baron that is. She would not violate that promise she made to him early in their marriage.

The telemarketer that called their home this morning had gotten Aurelia's best British accent. Another had gotten her best French accent during a telephone survey this afternoon.

Both times Baron sat in the background and laughed to his heart's content while Aurelia struggled to remain in character on the phone. Yet the prank she had on deck right now was one that he practically begged to participate in, especially after he saw how much thought she'd put into it. How well she'd mapped it out.

"You ready to go inside?" Aurelia asked as they sat parked outside of a Burger King.

"I'm more than ready," Baron replied with mischievous eyes that matched his wife's. He was even willing to forgo his aversion to fast food for this impressive prank.

"Let's go then, partner." Aurelia readjusted her dark shades. Then after briefly straightening her McDonald's hat and shirt, she exited the VW.

Baron exited the driver's seat in another McDonald's uniform. Both had been found and purchased by Aurelia at a local thrift store.

The Weavers weren't in their local area now though. They were two cities away from Alcove, the way Aurelia planned it so that no one would recognize them. The dark glasses they wore provided even more anonymity.

"After you, senora." Baron held the door open for his wife as they prepared to shock a few Burger King employees today.

* * *

After ordering two burgers, fries, apple pies, and two large drinks, Aurelia and Baron sat at a booth and proceeded to devour their meal. Devour, as in having their faces only inches away from the table at any given time, shoving fry after fry into their mouths, smacking and chewing nosily, licking ketchup from their fingers, and doing a whole lot of loud moaning.

As one could imagine, all eyes were on Aurelia and Baron's table. Even the manager of the store had been summoned to the front to see these two McDonald's 'employees' act like they hadn't eaten in days or worse, months.

"I think it's time for us to go," Baron suddenly whispered to Aurelia when he saw someone pull out a cell phone and point it their way. "Otherwise we're going to be on all kinds of video sharing sites before the night is over."

"I think you're right," Aurelia replied, fully aware that a

video would increase the chances of someone recognizing them from Alcove, despite the dark glasses they had on.

"Don't forget to leave the extra napkins and condiment packets in the restaurant," Baron said, reminding her that she was a rich woman now. Rich women didn't need condiment packets from restaurants. They left them for those that did.

"I won't forget." Aurelia smiled at that reminder. Though it had been her life goal to achieve the level of prosperity that she currently had with Baron, she still found herself buying Ramen noodles at the grocery store and still thought it was a sin to throw out leftovers.

On their way out the door, the grinning restaurant manager said, "Come again!"

Not making any promises they couldn't keep, Aurelia and Baron simply smiled at the manager and waved goodbye. When they got inside their car, they burst out laughing. The laughter continued all the way home as they recounted the various expressions people had worn as they looked at them feasting away.

"Hands down I think the guy with the coke bottle glasses was the best," Aurelia said as Baron pulled into the driveway of their home.

"I agree." He chuckled, pressing the garage remote from inside the car. "The way he kept taking them off and cleaning them just to make sure he was seeing correctly had me about to break character several times."

"Me, too." Aurelia giggled. "This is the best birthday ever." She sighed in contentment.

Baron smiled over at her before gliding the car into the open garage. "I'm glad you had a great birthday, baby. My last birthday was the best one I ever had, too." He chuckled and then added in a more somber tone, "Except for the part where you snuck out of the house and sped away into the night."

"Oh, yeah, I forgot about that." Aurelia reached over to run suggestive fingers across his right thigh. "I won't sneak away tonight…or ever again for that matter," she whispered as the garage door descended closed behind them.

Baron moaned at her touch. "I'm about to make you scream my name, woman." He slammed the car in park, unbuckled their seatbelts and literally feasted upon her.

* * *

After a shower, a light salad, and a long nap, Aurelia was

417

up again and ready to enjoy the last hour of her birthday…intimately. But there was a slight glitch in her plans. Baron was beside her still dozing. All that greasy food had sent him into a deeper sleep than usual.

Deciding to just let him sleep through the night, Aurelia got up from the bed and made her way across the hall to her dance studio. She needed to burn off her excess energy somehow.

We probably have too much sex anyway, she thought, though she wondered if there was such a thing as too much sex, especially for newlyweds.

In any case, Aurelia put on some jazz and slowly stretched out her nude body, breathing deeply as she did. When she was done warming up, she positioned herself in the middle of the room and started to dance.

Aurelia did not dance like she had in the strip clubs. No, she danced like she had in ballet school so long ago.

With her eyes closed, Aurelia gracefully performed a string of French terms, most of which began with the letter P. She moved effortlessly through petit sauts, piqués, pliés, pirouettes, and plenty of pointe work as Cassandra Wilson sang Time After Time as only she could.

Aurelia's eyes remained closed even as she lapsed into a continual sequence of fouetté en tournant, skillfully remaining in place the whole time. At the end of her set, she heard loud clapping coming from behind her. Her eyes snapped open. Her head snapped around to see Baron standing in the doorway.

A wide smile was upon his face. His eyes shined with emotion. His equally nude body showed every chiseled muscle to perfection. He was rigid all over.

"You truly are a great dancer, baby." Baron came farther into the room with one hand open, the other closed. "You could have made it big had you stuck with it."

Aurelia chuckled. "So Dingo and Crystal told me."

Baron shook his head. "I'm not talking about that kind of dancing. I think you could have made it big as a ballet dancer."

"My mother always wanted me to. I wanted to use my brain to make it big instead." Aurelia walked over to the stereo.

"You'll hear no complaints from me." Baron licked his lips at her swaying hips and jiggling bottom.

"That's good to know." Aurelia bent down to turned the stereo off.

Baron inhaled sharply and licked his lips again at that delicious view. "Leave that on," he requested concerning the music as both of his hands. "I was hoping we could play some naked limbo for the remaining minutes of your birthday. Are you game?" He held up a long red ribbon that had been confiscated from the bouquet of flowers he'd given her earlier.

Aurelia turned eyes lit with adventure his way. "Oh, I'm definitely game."

CHAPTER FIFTY-THREE

For spring break, Baron and Aurelia went to visit with her family for three days. They had lots of island fun this time. Not like their last visit, which was mostly spent handling family business.

Baron and Aurelia even got to see Trent score the winning points in a soccer game. That was much better than just looking at pictures and videos of him playing. Plus they got to cheer for him with the rest of the Bunting family, including Trent's tutor – Locke Moore.

The Weavers also got a glimpse of how life would be with just them and Trent in the house since he stayed at their island home during their whole visit. The fact that his room at the new house was decorated exactly like the one at the Bunting home and the fact that he'd already lived in both houses helped a lot with any mental or emotional adjustments.

Over the course of those three days, Aurelia realized how much she missed being up close and personal in Trent's everyday life. How much she missed St. Croix as a whole. She also realized that her mother was in love with Locke. She decided to bring that last thing up to Baron on the plane ride back to California.

"Were you serious about Trent coming to live with us soon?" Aurelia asked from beside him in the first-class section of the large aircraft.

"Absolutely. Why?" Baron pulled trail mix out of a plastic container that he'd packed in her carryon bag in lieu of eating the salty airline nuts that had been offered them.

"Because after watching my mother practically sop Trent's tutor up with a biscuit over the last few days, I'm thinking that it's past time for her to be released from her widowhood and also from her life as a full-time caregiver." As Aurelia spoke, she considerately passed him a bottle of spring water from a nearby airline tray to have with his snack.

"I agree." Baron received the water with a grateful nod. "When do you want him to come? After spring break is over or after you graduate like we originally planned?" He poured a handful of trail mix into his mouth and chewed while he waited for her reply.

"After I graduate," Aurelia said after a bit of thought. "That'll give me a few extra weeks to get his new room together. It'll also give Trent a little bit more time to spend with his new teammates."

"Are you going to tell him the truth about his paternity before or after we move him clear across the country?" Baron asked, trying to cover all bases.

"Before. Maybe that way he'll understand better why he's being uprooted from the only mother he's ever known," she said, speaking her hopes aloud.

"Sounds good to me. I personally can't wait for Trent to meet all of his cousins on my side of the family." Baron looked excited just talking about it.

"Speaking of your brother's kids, one in particular. Do you think Earl Jr. is going to like the present we picked out for his birthday? I know Earl Sr. is going to like that Rolex we got him for his special day. After all, what man doesn't like a Rolex?" Aurelia said, secretly dreading going to that two-part birthday party on Friday afternoon. Nor was she too enthused about attending breakfast with all the Weaver wives at the country club on Friday morning. Quite honestly, she'd rather be at work and at the soup kitchen this weekend instead of in Bel Air.

But Aurelia couldn't back out of this upcoming trip to Bel Air. This trip was Baron's way of trying to rebuild bridges with his family after that awful Megan incident. The extra prodding she got from her mother-in-law concerning her attendance at their monthly breakfast helped with Aurelia's decision to make the dreaded trip. If only she hadn't agreed to sleepover at Earl Sr.'s house as well after Friday's party. But even that was keeping with a Weaver family tradition.

Incidentally, Earl Sr.'s birthday was actually the day after his son's birthday. Yet since all of the family was scheduled to be present for Earl Jr.'s party anyway, they decided to have

2222222

two parties in one on that day.

Aurelia could take comfort in the fact that at least she and Baron would be leaving Earl's house early in the morning for their first camping trip together. A trip that Marquess had been given an invitation to, but still remained undecided about.

Upon taking a long swig of his drink, Baron said, "Earl Jr. is an outdoor man like Marquess and I. Which means he's going to love the new tent we got for him. Trent sure loved his."

"Yes, he did. Perhaps Trent and Earl Jr. will become the best of friends when they finally meet. They already have at least one thing in common," Aurelia said, trying to put her best attitude forward.

Baron smiled. "I'd love it if they did."

But will Earl Sr. love our sons' closeness? Aurelia kept that thought to herself.

* * *

At the Weaver wives' breakfast, which was founded and orchestrated by Ana Maria as a way to promote bonding among her daughters-in-law, Aurelia found herself surprisingly having the time of her life. Who knew that Sasha, Meadow, and Jenny could be so much fun?

Aurelia suspected that the current lighthearted tone at breakfast was because of the original Mrs. Weaver's presence. Ana Maria was simply a joy to be around and was the peacekeeper among the wives. The fact that their mother-in-law was a devout catholic was added motivation for the ladies to make a special effort to get along.

Aurelia was surprised to see Marquess' ex-wife in attendance. Despite their divorce, Fran still claimed the Weaver family as her own. When she remembered that Fran didn't have living parents or close relatives and couldn't have kids due to infertility issues, she understood better why the woman kept the Weaver name and continued to participate in certain Weaver family events even after her divorce.

It warmed Aurelia's heart to see the Weaver women still behaving so accepting of Fran. She saw no reason to be estranged either. Fran hadn't done a thing to her. If anything she thought the woman should be pitied for all the stuff Marquess took her through over the years.

It didn't take Aurelia long to realize that Sasha didn't pity Fran at all, though she was still civil to her. Something must

422

have happen between them, she thought, noting how Sasha kept narrowing her eyes at Fran everytime she opened her mouth, as if nothing she said could be trusted.

Aurelia also noticed the daggered looks Sasha set Meadow's way when she thought no one was looking. She sent similiar looks towards Megan during Aurelia's last visit to Bel Air, though those looks were more overt.

Sasha must be Meadow's friendnemy, she thought, reminded of her past relationship with Roxy. Roxy had been her friend on the outside, but her enemy on the inside. That disturbing mixture had forfeited her right to be Aurelia's friend on any level.

As long as she doesn't cross me, I'm good, Aurelia decided concerning Sasha, who sat on the other side of the table.

* * *

People in glass houses can't afford to throw rocks, Sasha thought as Fran opened her mouth yet again to gossip about one of her neighbors.

Just shut up already! Her thoughts grew increasingly heated towards her ex-sister-in-law whom she personaly knew wasn't as innocent or as victimized as she seemed.

Sasha knew things about Fran that no one else in the family did. She recently decided to share those things with her younger cousin. This way Paula would have a more competitive edge over Fran, who was starting to have second thoughts about her divorce after realizing all the non-monetary items she'd lost in the deal. Priceless items such as the close knit Weaver family.

But why would Paula even need that secret information when she'd been dodging her feelings for Marquess for years?

Because she finally stopped dodging and decided to face up to her feelings. Because Paula was tired of running from true happiness out of fear. Because ever since his divorce, Marquess had taken himself off the dating field completely and seemed like a changed man. A truly changed man.

Because...because... Paula just loved him.

The fact that Sasha still owed Paula for being the first to finance her socialite lifestyle and wanted to finally pay Fran back for betraying her to Duke is what prompted her to invite her cousin to today's breakfast. In fact, Sasha expected Paula to arrive at any moment.

And suddenly there she was.

* * *

As Paula approached the Weaver table, she immediately felt all eyes on her. Everyone smiled in polite greeting. Everyone except for Fran. The redhead outright frowned at her.

Paula smirked at her enemy's frown. She squared her shoulders. She'd taken down tougher opponents than Fran plenty of times.

Drama alert! Fasten your seatbelts. This is about to be a bumpy ride, Paula thought wittily, feeling adrenaline rush through her veins as she mentally prepared herself for battle.

* * *

"What is she...?"

"I hope you ladies don't mind my cousin joining us," Sasha said, interrupting Fran midsentence. "Paula and I are going shopping for our mothers today. Since all the best shops are on this side of town, I thought it would be a good idea for her to meet me here for breakfast."

"Paula's always welcome. She's like family," Ana Maria said graciously.

Fran turned her frown to Meadow, who gave her a 'just-play-it-cool' look in return.

One of Aurelia's brows rose as if she sensed the rising tension at the table.

Jenny simply shook her head knowingly and then turned her attention to the gourmet styled hash browns on her plate.

With each step Paula took towards them, Fran's frown etched deeper and deeper into her face. She had full knowledge of Paula's history with Marquess. He'd told her about their brief tryst before their marriage. Fran, in turn, had told Meadow.

Although Marquess also claimed that he had no lingering feelings for Paula, Fran had seen smothering desire in his eyes every time the other woman was around. In fact, Paula was the only woman that Marquess ever openly lusted for in front of Fran. He hid all of his other indiscretions well and had done them in private.

Fran's only consolation had been the fact that Paula wasn't the type to have an affair with a married man. Well, Marquess wasn't married now. Hadn't been for months.

Had they hooked up again? What was really behind Paula's sudden appearance at a private gathering for Weaver wives?

Fran thought Marquess had opted for celibacy after his herpes diagnosis. A diagnosis that she was never supposed to know about. And yet she did.

Fran discovered the truth about Marquess' medical condition while searching through the files in Duke's private home office one day when she was supposed to be there visiting Sasha. Although she eventually got caught by the lady of the house, Fran quickly appealed to Sasha's misguided sense of retribution with a barrage of potent questions.

Those questions were: Aren't you tired of cheating men getting off scot-free for their infidelities? Don't you think Marquess deserves to pay dearly for all he put me through? If the shoe were on the other foot, wouldn't you want more ammunition to gain a better settlement in your own divorce proceedings?

Those questions were enough to secure Sasha's support and her silence. Now Fran wondered if she decided to change her mind. If so, why?

"Good morning ladies," Paula said pleasantly, taking the empty chair that Sasha signaled for a waiter to bring.

Everyone responded accordingly. Everyone except for Fran. She fidgeted in her seat, feeling as if she was sitting on pins and needles.

"Since I already know everyone else here, you must be Professor's wife," Paula said, turning her attention to Aurelia after her breakfast order had been taken.

"Yes, I am," Aurelia replied. "Nice to meet you."

"Nice to meet you, too." Paula smiled warmly. "I'm glad to finally match a face to the name. And what a gorgeous face it is, too. Sasha wasn't lying about your beauty."

Aurelia smiled. "Thanks a lot. I appreciate the compliments from each of you," she replied, expressing her gratitude.

"They simply told the truth, sweetie. You are quite beautiful," Ana Maria interjected. "All of my daughters-in-law are," she added, extending that compliment to them all like the great diplomat that she was.

Fran smiled, pleased that her rival hadn't been included in that group. She completely ignored the fact that she was officially no longer a part of that group either.

"Yes, they are," Paula agreed politely. "Your sons have excellent taste in women, Mother Weaver. Speaking of your sons, I need to text your third oldest now." She pulled out her cell phone even as she spoke. "Marquess is supposed to help me with an upcoming case and I need to send him a reminder."

"Don't you dare contact my husband!" Fran suddenly blurted out, causing everyone's eyes to go to her, including those of a few people at surrounding tables.

Surprise rested on the faces of almost everyone. Very few people knew that the docile redhead had so much fire in her. Fran simply didn't care what they knew at this point.

"I was of the understanding that you two were no longer married. Besides, this is just business," Paula said calmly, before continuing with her text message just as calmly.

"It's never just business with the two of you," Fran said, resenting how calm her rival was.

Paula paused and looked at her again. "I have never cheated with your husband. Never! You, on the other hand, have cheated on him several times." Again her voice was extremely calm.

"You got it wrong. Marquess constantly cheated on me," Fran said, speaking about things that were common knowledge among them. Yet her hands suddenly trembled on her glass. Her eyes darted anxiously at Sasha. She avoided Ana Maria and Meadow's eyes altogether.

"Yes, he did," Paula agreed. "But Marquess wasn't the only cheater in your marriage, was he? Or should I subpoena a few of the club's busboys just to prove my point? Maybe it'll help Marquess get back some of that money you stole from him in the divorce settlement by portraying yourself as an innocent victim," she said in rapid fire session, before calmly returning to her message and pressing send.

Fran gasped at the word 'busboys'. She sent a menacing look at Sasha, whom she now knew had betrayed her. "I'm not the only one who cheated on her husband at this table."

"Good Lord!" Ana Maria exclaimed, looking horrified by this sudden bad turn of events.

Aurelia and Jenny just looked on with silent interest as even more drama played out in front of them.

"No, you're not," Sasha told Fran. "But you're the only one that kept your infidelities a secret from your husband. I, on the other hand, came clean with Duke. He knows all about my one time affair, forgave me for it, and married me again anyway. You not only tried to hide your indiscretions from everyone, but also tried to make us think that Marquess alone was the bad guy. I don't think even Meadow knows about your secret affairs. But you know for a fact that I know. Our favorite busboys were roommates that summer, remember? I saw you coming out of that second bedroom myself the one and only night I was there."

"Good Lord!" Ana Maria exclaimed again.

"For the record, I never cheated on Earl," Meadow said, speaking her peace on the matter before things went any further.

"I never cheated on my husband either," Aurelia and Jenny echoed simultaneously.

Ana Maria sighed in relief. At least some of her daughters-in-laws were faithful. It was bad enough that three of her sons were cheaters or at least had been since Duke, Earl, and Marquess weren't currently cheating with anyone…for different reasons, of course.

Interestingly enough, the wives that were faithful were those that went to church on a regular basis either by themselves, with their husbands, and/or any children they had. Aurelia and Jenny were the only two daughters-in-law that kept their husbands in church nearly every Sunday.

"You should have cheated on Earl," Fran told Meadow. "He's had more affairs than Duke and Marquess put together."

"Enough!" Ana Maria shouted, bringing an abrupt end to the horrid discussion.

By this time, everyone in the large dining room stopped eating and talking in order to better listen to the women argue and air out their dirty laundry. When their voices had lowered, so had the music thanks to the club's staff that likely wanted to hear more clearly in the back.

"You heard the lady. Enough!" Meadow said louder, using her power at the club to gain the eye of the manager so that he could assist her in diverting attention from this particular table.

The manager met Meadow's hard gaze and immediately got his staff moving again. Soon the music was turned back up. People started minding their own business again. Or at least were pretending to.

"Fran, although I will always love you as a daughter, I do not approve of instigators. As a result, this will be the last family function I invite you to, though you may still call me at home when and if the need arises," Ana Maria said gently with stern, yet sorrowful eyes.

"But I didn't start it, Mother Weaver. She did," Fran said childishly, pointing accusingly at Paula.

"As I recall, you're the one that attacked Paula at the mere mention of Marquess. Whom you are no longer married to, I might add," Ana Maria replied. "Now if you wish to reconcile with my son, then you need to talk to him about that, not take out your frustrations on Paula."

"Marquess won't take me back even if I begged him to or gave all of his money back," Fran said, returning to the timid demeanor that everyone usually associated with her. A demeanor that everyone now knew was all an act.

"Because of the infidelities?" Ana Maria prompted, clearly not falling for her innocent act this time.

"No." Fran shook her head. "Because Marquess was never in love with me. He cared for me, yes. But he only married me because he couldn't have Paula."

"Is this true, Paula?" Ana Maria turned to the Rosario Dawson look-alike at the table.

"I honestly don't know," Paula replied quietly. "What I do know is that Marquess and I have always had an unexplainable bond. Whenever he looks at me, I feel loved, though he has never declared it."

"Do you love him?" Ana Maria asked.

"Yes," Paula readily admitted.

"Even with his herpes diagnosis?" Fran asked, testing to see if her rival had been told everything by Sasha.

"Yes." Paula frowned disapprovingly at Fran. "Although I would not have put his medical history out in the street like you just did."

"Good Lord!" Ana Maria gasped in shock. Her eyes welled up with tears. Assuming the worst about her son's illness, she got up from her seat and rushed to the ladies room, lest she burst out in heartrending sobs in front of everyone.

"Now look what you did." Sasha scowled at Fran.

"I'll go see about her and explain that it's not as bad as she thinks," Aurelia quickly volunteered as she rose to follow their mother-in-law.

"I'll come with you." Jenny rose too, looking just as eager to leave the drama behind.

Only Meadow, Paula, Sasha, and Fran remained at the

table. But that was more than enough to keep the drama going for a little while longer.

* * *

"Tell me why, Sasha." Fran said through clenched teeth.

"Why what?" Sasha replied, though she could guess what her ex-sister-in-law wanted to know.

"Why did you betray me today?" Fran asked. Her right hand clenched a steak knife. Was she planning on using it as a weapon?

"My cousin is not answering a thing until you put that knife down," Paula intervened with flashing eyes. "And I mean put it down slowly unless you want me to pull out my weapon." She patted a hard bulge in the black designer purse she casually lifted upon the table.

Fran glared at Paula.

"You better do as she says. Remember my cousin is way more streetwise than me and she's known for hanging out at gun ranges," Sasha reminded her.

At those words, Fran slowly returned the knife to the table. "Are you going to answer me or what?" she demanded of Sasha.

"I was only paying you back for telling Duke who got his hot little waitress fired," Sasha replied nonchalantly.

"I only did that to get him to keep quiet about the time he saw me kissing an intern in the hospital parking lot," Fran replied, as if that poor excuse was enough to justify betraying a friend.

Sasha shook her head at that lame excuse. She was glad their friendship was over for sure now. "The second reason I betrayed you is because I truly believe that my cousin is the best woman for Marquess. Unlike you, Paula loves him beyond his money, social status, and family ties. Even if Marquess was broke, living in the ghetto, and orphaned, she would still want to be with him. Can you say the same, Fran?"

Fran stared at her for the longest time. Finally she said, "No, I can't." Then she got up and headed for the nearest exit. She didn't issue a word of apology to anyone for anything that she had done. She didn't even say goodbye to Meadow.

"Good riddance," Paula said, speaking for them all.

Even Meadow agreed with that statement as evident by her adamant nod.

429

* * *

In the ladies room, Aurelia and Jenny worked together to reassure their mother-in-law that what Marquess had was highly treatable. That he could go on to live a full life and even increase the number of her grandchildren if he so chooses.

"He can?" Ana Maria asked, always happy to hear about more grandchildren.

"Most definitely," Aurelia replied.

"Speaking of grandchildren," Jenny began with a wide smile on her face. "Count and I are about to give you one more very soon."

"Really?" Ana Maria grinned with excited eyes that no longer shined with tears.

"Yes, really," Jenny confirmed, rubbing her hand over her still flat belly. "In about seven months to be exact. I was going to announce it over breakfast, but never got the chance to for obvious reasons."

"That's great news, Jenny!" Aurelia grinned.

"It's definitely news too good to keep to ourselves." Ana Maria grabbed both of their hands and headed for the door. "Most of the club just heard our woes. We might as well let them hear our joys, too. Come on, girls. It's time to show these people that nothing can keep the Weavers down for long."

And that's exactly what they did, too.

After telling the other ladies at their table Jenny and Count's good news, Ana Maria had Meadow to get the manager to announce it over the loud speaker, along with the message that everyone's breakfast was on the Weaver family today. Upon making a toast to Jenny, the Weaver women and Paula then proceeded to enjoy their own breakfast to the full. A freshly cooked breakfast at that.

What a family! Aurelia smiled wide with that thought as she dove into her piping hot meal with vigor. She couldn't wait to tell Baron everything that happened today. Being a Weaver was like being in a real life soap opera. Who knew rich folks could be so entertaining?

CHAPTER FIFTY-FOUR

Baron was right. Earl Jr. absolutely loved his new tent. He wanted to set it up in the backyard immediately after opening the box it came in. Aurelia went outside to help them while everyone else stayed inside for the family-only party.

Earl Sr. liked his present, as well. In fact, he put the watch on right after graciously thanking them for his gift. Earl also claimed that he would wear it for the second two-part celebration he and his son were having at the country club tomorrow. An event that would include all of their rich friends and associates.

Aurelia didn't know if Earl was lying or not about wearing his new Rolex tomorrow. She did know that she was thrilled to be excused from that event on account of her and Baron's Saturday camping trip.

In light of everything that happened at the Weaver wives' breakfast, it was no surprise that Marquess suddenly decided to go camping with Baron and Aurelia after all. Aurelia couldn't blame him for not wanting to subject himself to curious eyes now that his secret was all the way out. Had she been in his place, she probably would have opted out of that country club event, as well.

What Aurelia found refreshing was the fact that Marquess still had the love and support of his family. She noticed how he seemed almost relieved that they finally knew his secret. He definitely laughed more than she'd ever seen him. Who wouldn't in the presence of such unconditional love?

While Aurelia continued to help Baron and Earl Jr. outside with the tent, an unexpected guest showed up at Earl and Meadow's house. That guest was none other than Paula. She came with Sasha, Duke, and their kids.

Marquess was thrilled to see Paula today. Now that she was here, he definitely wouldn't partake of any alcohol. Though he'd been looking forward to having a drink once his parents left with all the children for their traditional grandparents/grandkids birthday sleepover, he now looked forward to spending a little quality time with Paula instead. That's if everything he heard about her earlier reaction to his diagnosis was true.

Like a magnet, Marquess and Paula's eyes found each other across the room and held. They exchanged smiles and started walking towards each other.

Paula, dressed casually in blue jeans, a yellow t-shirt, and sneakers, met Marquess near the brick fireplace. He was dressed in a green t-shirt, cargo shorts, and sandals on account of today's warm weather.

"Hi," they said in unison, causing them both to laugh.

"What brings you by today?" Marquess asked Paula after their chuckles subsided somewhat.

"Like you don't know." She grinned. "But in case you don't, you're my main reason for being here, handsome. Not the gifts I brought," Paula clarified just as bluntly as usual.

"I was hoping you'd say that." Marquess grinned, too, as his dark and gloomy world suddenly got even brighter.

No big surprise there. Paula always had a way of making him forget his misery. This time Marquess hoped his misery was gone forever.

* * *

A half hour after Paula's arrival, another unexpected guest showed up at Earl and Meadow's home. This time it was Megan. She came bearing gifts for the birthday boys.

Earl Jr. was given an expensive personalized go-cart. Earl Sr. was given a pair of gold cufflinks, a chance to see Megan's surgically enhanced figure and meet her new man. That new man was a handsome black man that used to be her chauffer.

"I'm sure Earl Jr. is going to love his go-cart," Earl said, feeling extremely irritated for more reasons than one.

"Earl, go tear our son away from the tent his Uncle Baron and Aunt Aurelia got him. In the meantime, Megan, come help me introduce your new man to the rest of the family," Meadow said with an amused smirk.

Megan bristled at that reference to Aurelia's status in the Weaver family. Yet she quickly recovered and followed her cousin.

Her plastic surgeon should be fired for putting that much silicone above pencil thin legs, Earl thought as he watched Megan walk away with inferior butt implants where a tight firm bottom used to be. Why did she do that to herself?

Megan's implants were already starting to shift out of place due to basic things such as sitting, walking, and bending. The fact that she was an avid jogger didn't help her situation at all. Did she not receive pre-surgery counseling? Did no one tell her that that level of enhancement was a bad idea for her small frame?

If she was going to do something like this, why didn't she come to me? Earl mused, though he already knew the answer to his question.

Megan didn't come to him because she knew he would have advised her not to have the surgery at all. A plastic surgeon had to be an artist to get a buttock implantation just right.

Megan's surgeon was obviously no artist, Earl thought, finally heading outside.

"Earl Jr., come inside for a moment. Megan just stopped by with another present for you. It's a go-cart. It even has your name painted on it and everything," Earl said, upon entering the backyard area.

"Aww, Dad, do I have to go?" Earl Jr. whined, pausing from his tent-erecting task. "We aren't even done fixing up the tent yet."

"Yes, young man. When someone gives you a gift, the least you can do is come see it," Earl scolded.

"And say thank you, too," Baron added, supporting Earl's parenting efforts, despite the fact that he would've never received such support in return and the fact that they were barely on speaking terms again.

"Okay," Earl Jr. reluctantly acquiesced upon his uncle's prompting. "Do you and Aunt Aurelia want to see my newest present, too?"

"We'll see it later. Right now we want to finish setting up your tent," Baron replied, speaking for him and his wife. "Go enjoy your go-cart, nephew."

Earl figured they would decline that invite, especially after all the trouble Megan had caused them. Thus he and his son went back into the house alone.

* * *

"Thanks for buying us some time. I'm not in the mood

for Megan's shenanigans today," Aurelia told Baron once they were alone in the backyard. "I don't want to be tempted to keep my promise to her."

"What promise?" he asked with a lifted right brow.

"My promise to punch her purple and relieve her of a few patches of hair the next time I see her."

"Oh really?" He chuckled.

"Yes, really. But for Earl Jr. and your parents' sakes, I'm going to suppress my savage urges and remain civil. Now if Megan pushes me too far today, I can't be responsible for my corresponding actions. And there will be corresponding actions," Aurelia said, feeling her nostrils flare with ire.

"Calm down, beautiful," Baron replied more seriously. "Now let's both put Megan out of our minds and get back to finishing this tent. Agreed?"

"Agreed." Aurelia nodded, quickly reining in her temper.

It only took Baron and Aurelia all of ten minutes to finish with the tent. Yet because they were unwilling to go inside with Megan still on the premises, they went to the fence at the rear of Earl and Meadow's oceanfront backyard and looked out over the sea for a while.

"Mmm…"Aurelia said, closing her eyes to take in a deep breath. "Sometimes I really miss the smell of the sea. It reminds me of home."

"Home as in St. Croix?" Baron wrapped his arms about her from behind.

"Yes." Aurelia turned her head sideways to look at him. "No disrespect to our home in Alcove, of course."

"None taken. My mother still calls Mexico home. Probably always will since she was born and raised there. She continues to visit as often as she can. It helps that California isn't that far away. It must be very frustrating to have so much land and part of an ocean separating you from your homeland."

"Yes, it is." She turned back to face the sea again with sadness tugging at her soul.

"Tell you what. How about we go to the islands one month out of every summer, one weekend out of every month, and as many holidays as we can manage between our two families," Baron suggested. "Would you like that, baby?" He gently trailed the left side of her face with his right hand.

"I would love that." Aurelia closed her eyes again, relishing his touch this time. She opened her eyes, looked back at him, and added, "I love you even more for suggesting that win/win solution."

"I love you, too," Baron whispered, leaning closer to engage her in one of their famous succulent kisses.

They soon became oblivious to where they were as that kiss deepened and their hips got in on the action. A slow grind ensued, rekindling and stroking embers from their pre-breakfast tryst that was sure to lead to a volcanic night of lovemaking later on.

"Oh, look. The newlyweds haven't quite gotten off their honeymoon yet," said a female voice from behind them.

Without looking around, Aurelia already knew who that voice belonged to.

Megan.

When she and Baron turned around, they were surprised to find Megan looking a lot differently than before. She had gained at least eight pounds. Most of them landed like a 747 in her rear end.

Can you say butt job?

Baron looked like he didn't know whether to laugh, be angry, or feel pity for his ex-flame. She'd clearly gotten plastic surgery to compete with Aurelia's curves. Curves that Megan deemed fat once upon a time. Turns out that was just jealousy.

Aurelia noticed the same things, but she also noticed that Megan didn't come alone. Her rival came with a date this time. A dreadlock-wearing date that Aurelia knew from St. Croix – Kingston Miller.

Kingston was one of Jewell's older brothers. He was also the first boy to ever kiss Aurelia's lips.

* * *

"Hello and goodbye," Baron told Megan, ready to bring their newest encounter to a swift end.

"Don't be so hasty, Professor," Megan replied. "At least stay long enough for me to give you and your wife an overdue apology."

Both of Baron's eyebrows rose in surprise at the mention of an apology. Aurelia looked equally surprised. Neither had expected that from Megan.

"In that case, state your peace," Baron prompted, ready to get even that over with.

"I just want to say that I'm sorry for trying to break you two up. After realizing how much you love one another, I decided to move on with my life," Megan said in a rush, as if she needed to get it out quick before she changed her mind. Then she turned to the handsome man next to her and added in a normal pace, "In moving on, I started dating Kingston, the new love of my life."

At the formal mention of his name, Kingston spoke up, revealing a thick island accent. "Nice to meet yah, mon." He briefly shook Baron's hand. "Ree-Ree, what it be, gal?!" He addressed Aurelia now as he boldly gave her a warm embrace.

Baron fought not to frown at such familiarity with his wife. Kingston's easy use of Aurelia's island nickname was one thing. To actually wrap his arms around her was something else altogether. The war of his frown intensified.

Baron quietly listened to the Virgin Island natives talk well into the house for the lighting of the cake, through the cake and ice cream distribution, and into the dining room where Kingston and Megan followed him and Aurelia. Why couldn't they have gone into the living room, kitchen, or den like the other partygoers?

While Baron silently moved his cake from side to side on his plate, he learned that Kingston was Jewell's second oldest brother. Same mother, different fathers. That Kingston and Aurelia used to play together as children. That Kingston was the first boy to ever kiss Aurelia.

"So you taught Aurelia how to kiss?" Megan said, looking very intrigued by that bit of information as the couples sat across from each other at Earl and Meadow's dining room table.

Baron was irritated by that same information. His irritation lessened considerably when Aurelia sat in his lap.

Kingston chuckled. "It be more like Ree-Ree taught me. She was always head of de game. Old for her age, if yah know what I mean."

"She was one of the fast girls, huh?" Megan instigated, looking too pleased by that notion.

"No, dat be meh sista Jewell," Kingston clarified. "Baby sista was quick to lift her skirts. Still is. Whereas Ree-Ree just knew tings on ah grown folks' level."

"Right," Aurelia agreed with Kingston's assessments. "I've always been intellectually mature for my age."

"That you are." Baron smiled, gently tucking a curl behind her left ear.

Aurelia returned that smile and gave him a brief smack on the lips. "I've also always been very, very curious," she said, forking up a piece of cake from his plate to feed to him. "At thirteen, I decided it was time to learn how to kiss. After reading up about it, I asked Kingston to be my guinea pig. He was fifteen at the time and I figured he'd had enough experience by then to not only tell if I was bad at kissing, but to also show me how I could be better."

"She ended up showing me ah ting or two." Kingston laughed. "After dat, I was set on making Ree-Ree meh gurlfriend."

"Did you?" Megan frowned at the sight of Aurelia licking icing off of Baron's bottom lip.

"No. Mr. Bunting blocked dat," Kingston replied somberly. "He didn't tink I was good enough for his little princess."

"You weren't as long as you were a part of that gang. My daddy didn't want me mixed up with guys involved in any form of organized crime. I didn't want to be mixed up with guys like that either." Aurelia briefly cut her eyes at Baron when she said that last part.

Baron nodded silently. He'd gotten her point loud and clear. Fortunately he was no longer even remotely involved with organized crime. Not even with his V.I. businesses. He made sure of that.

"You're not still gang affiliated, are you?" Megan asked Kingston in a whisper, looking disturbed and slightly aroused by this new information.

Kingston laughed at her expression. "No. Back den I was just anotha fatherless boy confused 'bout what it meant to be ah real man. When I heard all de great tings people said 'bout Mr. Bunting at his funeral, I knew den dat I needed to change. Dat's when I quit de gang, re-enrolled in high school, and finally completed meh diploma. I had to work and save up awhile before I could go off to college though. I finally did. I'm still in school now. Should have meh engineering degree in anotha year."

"Good for you, Kingston." Aurelia smiled with approval.

"Yes, very good," Baron agreed. "Where are you matriculating?"

"You can talk about that later. Right now I want to dance," Megan interrupted, grabbing her date by the hand before heading to the next room where other couples were dancing.

* * *

On the dance floor, Megan draped her arms about Kingston's thick neck and put her lips close to his right ear. "I'm not paying you to bond with Baron. I'm paying you to bond with Aurelia," she hissed in a whisper.

"When yah hired me for dis extra service, I didn't know de Virgin Islander would be Ree-Ree," Kingston hissed back. "And she looks anyting but unhappy if yah ask me."

"She's faking it. She's just with Baron for the money like I said," Megan lied. "Besides, don't you want to see what else your little island princess has learned beyond kissing? Don't you want to finally prove that you are good enough to have her? That you've actually become better than her considering her days as a stripper," she subtly suggested. "There's another five grand in it for you if you finish the job. And I'm sure you need that for your tuition," she added, trying to sweeten the deal even more.

Kingston was silent for a long while. "I'll finish de job," he finally replied, putting his education above his integrity, dignity, and since of island loyalty. He just hoped that Aurelia would understand his motives once this was all over. After all, didn't she put her education above everything else once upon a time?

* * *

Exactly how homesick is she? Baron thought when talk of the Virgin Islands continued even after the kiddie portion of the party ended.

"When was de last time yah been to ah hometown carnival?" Kingston asked Aurelia, keeping their conversation going.

"At least two years ago. Although Baron and I were in St. Croix this past December, we didn't make it to the Christmas carnival," Aurelia replied from her place beside Baron on the elegant beige and green couch in Earl and Meadow's living room.

Other couples were fellowshipping in various areas of the large house. Some were drinking. Others were dancing. Yet they all kept a watchful eye on Baron's group in the northeast corner of the room, as if they were waiting for drama to erupt between them.

Kingston's eyes lit up at Aurelia's response. "I was dere in December, too. But I stayed wid meh brothas in St. Thomas 'cause yah know meh mutha and sista crazy women." He chuckled. "Had I known yah was dere, I would've invited yah to catch de ferry from St. Thomas wid me and pop in to de Old Year's Night party in Jost. You know some of de best parties be held dere. "

"Old Year's Night?" Megan prompted, urging the discussion on from her place beside Kingston on the solid green couch opposite the newlyweds.

"Yeah. Dat's just anotha way of saying New Year's Eve where we from," Kingston explained.

"I see. Did you know that, Professor?" Megan asked of Baron.

"Yes, I did,"he replied through a tight mouth. "I also know that you need a passport to enter the small island of Jost since it is in the British Virgin Islands, not those in U.S. territory, which is just one reason Aurelia and I didn't go." Baron turned to Kingston and added, "The fact that my wife and I were on our honeymoon back in December was the main reason we didn't go to any island events. I barely wanted to share her with relatives, much less a multitude of strangers."

Megan bristled at the word 'wife' and the possessive message it carried. She smiled when Kingston didn't let any of that deter him.

"In dat case, maybe yah be able to make it to de carnival St. Thomas be having early May," Kingston replied. "Dere be ah parade, food booths, and lots of good music."

"What kind of music, Kingston? Reggae?" Megan asked, once again keeping the V.I. conversation going.

"Some Reggae, yeah. But mostly Soca and Calypso 'cause dey be more original to our islands," Kingston replied. "Ree-Ree prefers Soca as I recall." He smiled over at his childhood neighbor and winked.

"Yes, I do enjoy Soca more," Aurelia confirmed, frowning at that wink as she gave Kingston a stern 'don't-go-there' look. "Would you like something to drink, baby?" she turned toask Baron.

"Yes." Baron forced a smile her way, though he could feel his cheeks blazing with ire. "Thanks, beautiful."

"Any time." Aurelia ran a caressing hand across his left cheek. "I'll be right back." She leaned in close to his left ear to whisper, "Relax, baby. You have nothing to worry about here. I only want you, remember?" Then she withdrew slightly to give him a reassuring smile and a sweet smack on the lips.

"All right." Baron gave her a real smile this time. His body relaxed somewhat, though his guard was still up.

"I tink I get ah drink, too." Kingston started after Aurelia as she made her way towards the kitchen.

Baron immediately lost the battle of his frown, forcing his lips into an upside down U now. Then when Megan actually got up and sat beside him seconds later, he outright scowled.

What next?

* * *

"It seems our significant others have a lot in common," Megan told Baron once they were alone. "But then again, so do we."

"Commonalities do not guarantee a successful relationship," Baron replied evenly, trying to rein in his emotions. "Haven't you heard that opposites attract?"

"Yes, I have. But have you also heard that it takes two to tango? Meaning, you should have no fear of Kingston taking your woman if she doesn't want to be taken. Does Aurelia want to be taken?" Megan said.

"Who says I have fear of anything?" Baron countered, avoiding her questions by asking one of his own.

"Those flaring nostrils of yours," Megan replied knowingly. "You forgot how well I know you, Professor."

"It seems that I don't know you at all, Megan," Baron said, after taking in a deep breath to ventilate his temper. "The Megan I used to know wanted a man all to herself. The old Megan wouldn't be with a man who even thought about taking on another woman. But then again, the old Megan cheated on me, so perhaps I never really knew you at all."

"Admittedly I have changed," Megan replied, ignoring his reference to her cheating. "The new me thinks it's selfish for a woman to want to keep a man all to herself. The new me likes being in an open relationship like the one Kingston and I have. It helps me keep my options open." She looked Baron up and down with open interest as she spoke.

Baron scowled at her in response. "I see now that your apology was just as fake as that holiday ham you let them shoot into your behind," he said, causing Megan's face to turn beet juice red. "I also see that you brought Kingston here today to try to tempt my wife since it's clear that you will never be able to tempt me. Well, it's not going to work.

440

Aurelia loves me."

"I'm sure she does. But how much? And surely you know that anyone can be tempted. Case and point." Megan nodded to the left as Kingston engaged a drink-holding Aurelia in an island dance demonstration per Earl's request as soca music was cued up on the karaoke system.

What?! Baron raged inwardly as Kingston started to dance entirely too close behind his wife. He rose from his seat with balled fists. It was time to put his boxing expertise to good use...on Kingston's face.

Across the room, Count gave him a 'handle-your-business' nod.

CHAPTER FIFTY-FIVE

Suddenly pimp slapped by his conscience, Kingston promptly backed up a respectable distance away from Aurelia. In fact, a whole other person could fit between them now.

Although Kingston had been ready to take on Aurelia's angry husband, even though he was clearly outnumbered by so many Weaver men, he suddenly couldn't handle the guilt of betraying another islander. An innocent one at that.

So what if Aurelia lowered her standards and danced for money once upon a time. That didn't warrant Kingston lowering his standards to the point of betrayal. Especially to someone who had never done anything wrong to him. Matter of fact, Aurelia had only done right things to Kingston.

She was the one to sneak him plates of her mother's delicious cooking when his own mother refused to lift a hand to even put groceries in the house. This was despite the fact that the Buntings were almost as poor as the Millers.

Aurelia was the one to talk her father into letting Kingston work with him a couple of summers just to earn money for school clothes, despite his gang ties. She understood how important appearances were during those crucial high school years. How a guy didn't stand a chance of getting the cutest girls if he didn't dress impressively.

And hadn't Kingston been Aurelia's main advocate with his sister over the years? How many times had he scolded Jewell for being so jealous of another islander? How many times had he talked about how islanders should stick together, regardless of blood ties?

"Megan, I quit!" Kingston suddenly shouted above the

music, setting off a chain of events in the process.

Baron instantly stopped short in his tracks a mere twenty-five feet away, Aurelia stopped dancing, the music was turned down, and all eyes looked from the dreadlock-wearing man to the red-faced blonde in the northeast corner of the room and then back again.

Springing to her feet, Megan glared at Kingston from across the room. "No, consider yourself fired!" she retorted, confirming what everyone suspected all along – she'd hired her limo driver to be her escort for this event. There was no romantic relationship between them at all.

How pathetic!

"I actually consider mehself free," Kingston replied, having the last word as Megan stomped towards the kitchen, looking like she needed a stiff drink. He hoped she called a cab, too, since he was taking the rental car they arrived in. It was reserved in his name, even though her money had been used.

"I wanna formally apologize to everybody for coming here under false pretenses," Kingston continued, glancing around the room at the frowning faces. "I owe yah de biggest apology, Ree-Ree," he added, settling his sincere gaze upon Aurelia. "Dis no way for islanders to behave. I truly sorry for tryna scam yah and for shaming our homeland. Please forgive me."

Aurelia's eyes welled up with glistening emotion. "I forgive you."

* * *

While the V.I. natives continued to settle their differences across the room, Baron detoured to the nearest bathroom. He needed to splash some cold water on his hot face…fast!

It was either do that or play dentist and snatch a few teeth out of Earl's mouth. Especially since it was obvious that he was still helping Megan in some way. Why else had she been allowed to linger so long?

Yet since they all promised their mother not to get physical with one another again after that Count and Earl altercation, Baron knew he couldn't submit to his violent urges no matter how much he wanted to. However, that motherly promise didn't stop him from coming up with another way to give Earl some long overdue payback.

When splashing water on his face and getting a bit of covert payback hadn't lowered his ire enough to behave civilly towards Earl, Baron went outside to get some fresh air.

* * *

After walking Kingston out to his black rental Porsche, Aurelia went back inside and sought her husband out. Unfortunately, Baron was nowhere to be found in the house. She learned this after checking every room.

Aurelia finally located him outside in the backyard. He was watching the sun set in the western sky.

"Kingston's gone," she said, coming up behind him at the fence.

"Good." Baron turned to face her. "Is Megan still here?"

"Unfortunately, yes." Aurelia frowned. "I saw her in the kitchen throwing back shots with Earl when I went in there looking for you." It had taken everything in her to keep from punching Megan purple right then and there. At the time, finding Baron had been more important than exacting revenge on her enemy.

Baron also frowned. "Frick and Frack seemed determined to break us up," he said of Earl and Megan. "If you want, we can go to a hotel tonight instead of staying here for this traditional sibling birthday sleepover."

Aurelia shook her head. "The only place we're going is back inside to show Megan, Earl, and everyone else that our marriage is unbreakable." She tugged him towards the house as a great idea formed in her mind.

* * *

When Baron and Aurelia came back inside, all eyes were on them. Megan's in particular. She followed Earl from the kitchen when Meadow complained about him neglecting the rest of their guests.

Megan never did call a cab. Earl volunteered to take her home later after the party, giving her the opportunity to cause even more trouble.

"Marquess, can you put on some Shakira for us?" Aurelia asked the brother-in-law who was now in charge of the music.

"Which tune?" Marquess asked. "Paula will only dance on the slow ones."

"La Tortura," Aurelia requested, causing a collective gasp to resonate around the room. Megan's gasp was the loudest one of all.

Everyone there knew that La Tortura was Baron and

Megan's special song. How they performed it during a talent show at the country club the very first year they were officially a couple. How Baron and Megan lip-synched to that song and performed the dance movements of Shakira and her guitar-playing singing partner, Alejandro. How their performance was so good that they actually won first-place that night.

Aurelia deliberately chose that song to send Megan a message.

That message: Not only am I going to keep Baron, but I am the better woman for him in every way...even on your special song.

Although Baron didn't know that Aurelia was going to choose that particular song to put their marital solidarity on display, he immediately saw the brilliance in that selection. It was his wife's way of annihilating any remaining hope Megan had of reconciling with him.

Baron was in complete agreement with Aurelia's plan, even though it was probably going to devastate his ex-fiancée. Megan had no one to blame for her imminent pain but herself. She started this chaos. The newlywed Weavers were about to end it.

As the music cued up, Baron readily moved to the stirring beat with his wife. Others joined them on the dance floor. Paula remained seated, but she did snuggle against Marquess, which had him grinning from ear to ear.

Pulling from her Aurora days, Aurelia put on quite a show as she moved her hips exactly like Shakira. Except she moved her hips against Baron. Against his front, sides, and back as she circled him with suggestive dances. Dances that made other men temporarily envy her husband. Dances that made other women temporarily envy Aurelia or at least want to permanently emulate her.

Baron enjoyed every last one of his wife's provocative moves. He pulsated with need from the beginning of the song to the end.

"Think we got our message across?" Aurelia whispered in his right ear, draping her arms about his neck as a slow song cued up.

"Yes," Baron whispered back, reaching down to squeeze her closer to his hardened desire.

Aurelia moaned. "How many licks does it take to get to the center of your lollipop?" she flirted huskily.

"I don't know." Baron moaned out, highly turned on by her suggestive words.

Instead of saying another word, Aurelia acted. Lowering her body in time with her exploring hands, she caressed a trail from his neck down to his hips.

Baron sucked air through his teeth as Aurelia's head lined up perfectly with his pelvic area a few seconds later. What was she about to do next? And in front of so many people!

Baron wanted Aurelia to be sexually liberated, but not that liberated. Had he created a sensual monster? Turned her all the way out?

"Want to go upstairs and find out how many licks it takes?" Aurelia looked up at him with a mischievous gleam in her eyes.

"Aye!" Baron nearly shouted in affirmation, pulling her up for a long greedy kiss.

Just as the newlyweds were about to go upstairs to the guest bedroom they shared, Megan suddenly charged Aurelia like a mad bull. That's when everybody knew...

It was about to be a what – girlfight!

* * *

Enraged that her hopes had been dashed, that her latest plan to get Baron back had failed miserably, and that Aurelia had obviously become sexually liberated in the bedroom, Megan responded the only way she could think of right now – violently.

Unfortunately for Megan, Aurelia had the reflexes of a cat. "Dis heifer done lost she mind," the V.I. native said, smoothly moving out of her enemy's way. Her equally quick hands grabbed fistfuls of Megan's hair and slung her up against the nearest wall, knocking the wind out of her.

Everybody winced at the loud impact.

"I'll pay for the wall, sister-in-law," Baron told Meadow over his shoulder after seeing the wide crack Aurelia had made in the wall with Megan's body.

"Don't worry about it," Meadow replied gleefully, sipping her martini with relish.

Everybody suddenly winced again when Aurelia barely gave Megan time to catch her breath before sending a fist to her left eye. "Dis is whatcha wanted, right?"

Another fist to the same eye.

"I told you I gone give you someting to remember me by."

Another fist to the eye.

"Professor, don't just stand there watching. Stop the fight!" Earl shouted from across the room.

"He better not," Count inserted sternly. "Megan's been a thorn in our sister-in-law's flesh for months now. It's time for Aurelia to take her out."

The rest of the onlookers immediately voiced their agreement with Count.

"But she's going to kill her, if this keeps up," Earl protested even as Aurelia continued to punch Megan in the face, now switching hands to work on the other eye.

"I'll break it up…in a minute," Baron said, revealing no desire to break up this fight any time soon. Megan had this beat down coming for a long time. He wanted her to get every drop of it.

"If you won't stop it, I will." Earl headed towards the fight.

"Try it and see what happens to you." Baron turned to glare at his older brother. "Not even that promise to Mama is going to stop me from taking you down in your own house, if you interfere with my wife's right to defend herself."

Earl stopped in his tracks.

"You want her, Earl? Here she go!" Aurelia said, slinging Megan across the floor by the hair. Well, most of it anyway. Thick cords of blonde hair were still wrapped around some of her fingers.

"Meadow…help!" Megan cried from on her knees. No use calling for Earl. He was too scared of his youngest brother to move another inch.

Meadow took another sip of her martini, allowing Aurelia to kick Megan a few times in the ribs before finally intervening. "New sister-in- law, can you please show my cousin some mercy? You know, if you have time in your schedule and all."

"Sure, anyting for you, sister-in-law." Aurelia gave Megan one last kick before walking away with sweat streaming down her face. Her pink shirt was soaked in the T-zone and her blue jeans were a little bit more worse for wear. Beating heifers down was hard work!

* * *

As Earl drove a sniffling, bruised, and double black-eyed Megan home, he hid a satisfied smile. Despite how concerned he seemed about her back at his house, he was pleased that Megan's plan hadn't worked tonight. Pleased that Baron's marriage was strong enough to resist temptation.

Earl was even starting to like Aurelia. He definitely admired her chutzpah - her ability to rise above whatever adversity was thrown at her.

And who knew Aurelia could fight like that? Earl was almost afraid of her himself.

"Don't forget to keep ice packs up to your eyes all night. Don't try that raw steak remedy since that could be harmful to your health on account of the hostile bacteria factor," Earl medically advised Megan, continuing to feign concern even as his attraction to her grew less and less.

"Don't you think I need to go to the hospital and get checked out instead?" She held two ice packs up to her eyes even now. "Maybe even have them file a police report?"

"I can take you to the ER if you want me to, but keep in mind that you're the one that's going to end up in jail, not my sister-in-law," Earl replied.

Megan snatched the ice packs down from her eyes and glared at him through swollen lids. "Aurelia beat me mercilessly. I didn't get a lick in edgewise. How am I going to end up in jail instead of her?"

"Because you started the fight by charging Aurelia. And you did it in front of a whole room full of witnesses, two of which are esteemed lawyers in the area."

Megan winced at his words. "Oh." She winced again when she returned the ice packs to her swollen baby blues.

"So no hospital, right?" Earl prompted as he approached a red light.

"No hospital," Megan replied, sounding like the defeated foe that she was.

* * *

Back at Earl and Meadow's house, Baron scooped Aurelia up into his arms and carried her upstairs for a soothing soak in the tub. Everyone else stayed downstairs to help Meadow get the house back in order.

"You're so quiet," Aurelia said after ten silent minutes.

Baron hadn't said a word since they came upstairs. He was quiet even now as he sat in the large tub behind her, carefully trimming the nails she'd broken in tonight's fight.

"You're not mad at me for putting some cheese on Megan's grits, are you?"

Baron chuckled at that word picture she just painted. "No, I'm not mad about that at all." He finally released her hands now that he was done with his task. "I'm angry that it even came to violence at all. All of this could have been avoided had Megan truly moved on with her life, had Earl stopped being so jealous-hearted and interfering." He put the nail clipper in the green plastic tray beside the tub and leaned back from his upright position, bringing her with him.

"Yes, that would have definitely kept the peace." Aurelia grew silent and reflective for a moment as she relaxed against his wet hairy chest. Looking back at him a few seconds later, she posed a hard question. "Do you think Earl and Megan have something going on besides trying to sabotage our marriage? The jealous way he looked at her earlier today when she was with Kingston made me think he was attracted to her."

"That particular brother has been attracted to all of our women at one time or the other. I think Earl got fixated on Megan, not just because she refused to fall at his feet in adoration, but because she was mine – his favorite brother to be jealous of," Baron analyzed, revealing his knowledge of Earl's not-so-secret crush on Megan. "Given the opportunity, I think he would have slept with her even when she and I were together. However, since Megan always seemed so into me, I never put much stock in his ability to follow through on his attraction."

"Maybe he thinks he has a better chance with Megan now, given the fact that you're married to me now." Aurelia faced forward again.

"Happily married at that." Baron kissed the top of her head. "As for Earl's chances with Megan now, I still think they are slim to none. Why else would she try so hard to get me back, despite the fact that it's utterly futile?"

"I know dat's right!" Aurelia agreed with her accent dipped deep in ire. That same ire caused her body to stiffen like a cedar tree against him.

Baron chuckled. "Calm it down, island beauty. You know you have me lock, stock, and barrel." He kissed the top of her head once more, causing her to instantly relax again in every way. "Now although I hate Earl's continual partnership with Megan, I'm hoping that it is a sign that he's finally giving up hope of having her for himself. Such a union would literally tear our family apart."

"Especially since there are kids involved. Not to mention what it would do to Meadow and also to your brotherhood," Aurelia said.

"Don't forget that it would absolutely devastate my mother," Baron replied, revealing who he was most concerned about if Earl and Megan ever became a couple. "A year ago such a thing would have devastated me, too. Now I could care less who Megan was intimate with."

"Let's hope that that never happens for everybody's sake," Aurelia said. "I personally would not want Megan as a sister-in-law." She chuckled.

"Me, either." Baron laughed. "Now let's wash up before the water gets too cold or we turn into a couple of California raisins in here."

* * *

After their long soak in the tub, Baron dried them both off and then carried Aurelia to the guestroom's bed. He made slow love to her. He'd never been more gentler. He was especially gentle with her bruised knuckles.

Spooning in Baron's arms on the bed a half hour later, Aurelia told him something surprising. "Since graduation is only a few weeks away now, I've decided to forgo the birth control shot that I was scheduled to get on Monday and just start our family early. Not only am I ready to have your babies, I figure Trent will be more conducive to coming to California if he knew that he was needed as a big brother here."

Baron's eyes widened. "Are you serious?!" He turned her around in his arms.

"Yes." Aurelia grinned.

"Let's start working on our baby right now." Baron grinned, too, shifting their positions so that he was above her.

Aurelia chuckled. "But it's still too soon to conceive, Baron. The last dose of birth control is probably still floating around in my system."

"Consider this practice then," he replied huskily, preparing to join them again.

"Yes," Aurelia whispered, arching towards him with a willing heart and body.

* * *

A few doors down the hallway other couples were making love in their rooms. All except for two. Earl and Meadow were sleeping, too tired after their long day and still too emotionally distant from each other to spark a romantic fire even if they had a match.

Marquess and Paula weren't making love just yet. But they were making out heavily in his room. It was just a matter of time now. Just a matter of time before they both finally got what they wanted.

CHAPTER FIFTY-SIX

After bidding the campers a warm goodbye, Earl went upstairs to take a shower. Meadow was done with her bath by now, so he would have the whole master suite to himself while she cooked breakfast for their remaining guests.

A part of Earl wished that he and Meadow were still in the shower-together stage. But they left that stage a long time ago. He was solely to blame for that. What woman wanted to shower with a man that constantly cheated on her?

Yet in Earl's defense, he was not currently cheating on Meadow with anyone. Unfortunately, the motivation for his recent faithfulness was fueled by Megan's reappearance in his life. Now...now even that was changing.

To be perfectly honest, Earl found himself changing as a whole. For one thing, he no longer disliked Aurelia at all. No longer felt the need to. So what if she was black. So what if she had been a stripper. Aurelia made Baron happy and that was all that really mattered, right?

When was the last time I was happy? Earl asked himself as he lathered up his body in the shower a few minutes later.

No ready answer came for that question. It had been just that long ago since he'd felt any real joy. Matter of fact, Earl hadn't felt any real joy since his last child was born.

I need to see what I can to do change that, he thought, squeezing shampoo into his hair next.

Ten seconds into the shampoo process, Earl's scalp began to tingle. A lot!

Did Meadow make a mistake and order the medicated version of his favorite shampoo again? Surely she knew how much his thick black locks meant to him. Everybody did.

When his scalp actually started to burn, Earl knew that

452

Meadow hadn't ordered the wrong shampoo. That his shampoo had been tampered with by none other than…

"Pro-fes-sor!" Earl shouted, turning the water up higher as he quickly rinsed the tainted product out of his hair.

But it was already too late. Every strand of hair on his head was now completely white. How was Earl going to go to the country club party looking like this?

* * *

Marquess was silent in the back seat during the whole ride to the campsite. His disposition soured throughout the day as he watched Baron and Aurelia have tons of fun together out in the wild.

Seeing how happy his brother was made Marquess think of Paula again. About how badly he reacted when she took off her shoes last night in his bedroom. How he actually fled from the room and sought out a drink to curtail his shock.

How was Marquess supposed to react upon discovering that the woman he thought was so perfect only had one foot?

One foot!

Marquess didn't stick around long enough to find out why Paula was missing a foot. Now he wished he had. Now he wished he'd done a lot of things differently last night.

I need a drink. Marquess longed for that secret flask he hid in his sleeping bag.

Although he promised Baron he wouldn't drink during their camping trips, misery had him ready to break that promise big time. Marquess might have been able to keep that promise if he hadn't grown so dependent upon alcohol and thus carried some with him at all times for those just-in-case moments. This was one of those moments.

"I'm going to make it an early night," Marquess said, interrupting his companions as they smooched with their mouths and held kosher hot dogs over the campfire using long wooded skewers.

"But you haven't eaten anything all day," Baron said, upon freeing his lips from his wife. "At least eat one of these hot dogs that you insist on bringing every time."

"I could put some of that fish we caught today over the fire," Aurelia volunteered. Not only had she helped catch her share of seafood, she'd done her part to clean them for later consumption.

"No thanks. I just don't have much of an appetite today."

Marquess threw his hot dog laden skewer into the fire and rose to his feet.

"If you're still not up to things tomorrow, we can cut our weekend short and just head on back home," Baron said, despite the fact that he and Aurelia were having the time of their lives on this camping trip.

However, sometimes sacrifices had to be made on behalf of a hurting loved one. Marquess definitely looked like he was hurting right now, even though Baron had no idea why. No one did.

The last anyone knew, Marquess and Paula were on good terms. Certainly good enough terms to share a bedroom last night. No one had any reason to suspect that things had turned bad between them again since they were all preoccupied with their own relationships last night, Paula was gone by this morning, and Marquess was silent night on the issue even now.

"No need to cut the weekend short. I'm sure I'll be fine in the morning," Marquess concluded over his left shoulder as he hurried to his tent in search of his constant companion.

* * *

The next morning, Marquess looked even worse than the day before. His eyes were bloodshot red. No razor had touched his face. Fresh stubble littered his upper lip, chin, and jawline.

Now Baron knew something was wrong.

Marquess was usually a stickler for making sure he shaved every day, even in the wild. Baron was the one to let his beard and mustache grow at the slightest incentive.

"You look horrible today. Are you not feeling well? Or have you snuck alcohol on this trip after all?" Baron asked while they got their hiking gear together.

It was the perfect time to have this conversation since Aurelia was washing out their breakfast utensils in the river. That task would help them avoid drawing curious animals and the wrong kind of insects to their campsite while they were away.

At those words, Marquess was careful to keep a safe distance away from his brother, lest Baron smell the alcohol on his breath, despite the abundance of mouthwash he'd gargled with earlier. "I'm feeling fine. And, no, I have not snuck alcohol on this trip," he lied. "The sounds of you and Aurelia having sex into the wee hours of the morning kept

454

me awake last night. I barely got any sleep because of you two."

Baron grinned sheepishly. "Sorry about that. Ever since Aurelia told me that she's ready to start a family, I've been trying to sow as much seed as I can even though she probably won't be able to conceive until another month or so."

Marquess' left eye twitched at that happy news. A frown graced his lips. A slight tremor rippled through his hands. "I'll be right back. I forgot something in my tent." He dropped the thick rope in his hands.

Baron frowned with disappointment. He'd wanted his brother to be happy about his good news. Yet ever since he married Aurelia, the most he'd gotten from Marquess was jealousy, brooding, and condescension stemming from her former occupation.

What he hadn't gotten from this particular brother was racism. Earl held the market on that negative trait and even he was starting to warm towards Aurelia. Their eldest sibling even gave her a fond hug before they left yesterday morning, though by now Earl was probably more than a bit hot with Baron for bleaching his hair white with that tainted shampoo.

This is going to be the last camping trip with Marquess for a while, Baron decided, truly ready to pack up their gear and go home now. He just didn't like the way things were going. Didn't have a good feeling about this camping trip anymore.

"I finished the washing up. I got my camera in my hands. My survival kit in my backpack, complete with bottled water. I'm now ready to go experience more of nature and capture a few happy memories to share with our children," Aurelia said excitedly, interrupting her husband from his troubling thoughts.

Baron smiled at her enthusiasm. It made him push his feelings of foreboding to the back of his mind.

"You'll do better to put your camera in your backpack, too," Marquess inserted from behind them. "Hiking often requires the use of both hands." He spoke from experience as an avid hiker and amateur photographer.

"He's right." Baron confirmed, noting how his brother was suddenly in a much better mood. Maybe this camping trip might work out after all. Maybe.

* * *

Instead of taking the trail that led directly to the Sandhill peak, they took the trail that looped around to the north because it had more scenic views. Amateur photographers loved plenty of those. Some even went professional when they captured a certain scenic view just right and found a buyer for the photo.

"I can't wait to take a picture from the peak." Aurelia stepped up her pace on the narrowed path, despite the humidity and her sore muscles from Friday's fight.

"Slow down, beautiful, and let me go first. I'll feel much better if you are sandwiched between me and Marquess on the peak," Baron said, trying to practice caution.

"No, let me go first. I need to be in the left hand corner to get the picture I want." Marquess jogged past them towards the peak.

"Whoa!" Baron dodged out of the way of his brother's swinging backpack. The whiff of alcohol that attacked his nostrils told him that Marquess had indeed brought liquor on this trip. How much, he didn't know.

Unfortunately, Aurelia didn't get out of Marquess' way in enough time though she tried to. She avoided his body, but the backpack hit her left shoulder hard, throwing her completely off balance.

"Nooooo!" Baron screamed as Aurelia lost her footing and fell backwards towards a protruding boulder on the path. Although he ran as fast as he could, he did not make it to her before she hit the hard rock.

The loud cracking sound that ensued told Baron that she'd broken a bone. Judging by the location of the hit, Aurelia's scream of pain, and the way she clenched at her lower stomach, her pelvic bone had been broken.

CHAPTER FIFTY-SEVEN

Baron blasted Marquess for causing Aurelia's accident the whole way down the peak and all the way to the hospital. He also scolded him for drinking on their trip, which likely contributed to the accident.

Marquess kept apologizing to Baron, to Aurelia, and anyone else that would listen to him. He couldn't say 'I'm sorry' enough. His tears of repentance flowed freely.

Seeing how distraught, how guilt-ridden, how so very sorry he was, Aurelia nodded her forgiveness through her pain. She'd never seen a grown man so devastated before. Never heard one sob like that before either. How could she not forgive Marquess?

In contrast, Baron was like a stone wall. He refused to listen to anything his brother had to say. He didn't want an apology. He wanted Marquess banished from his life forever. But his brother stubbornly refused to leave his side without learning the extent of Aurelia's injuries.

Things got even worse when the doctors checked Aurelia out and discovered that the damage to her pelvic bone might complicate future pregnancies. That's when Baron flew at Marquess and slugged him, cursing him out in English, Spanish, and Italian. That fight went from the visitor's waiting room out to the hallway.

Marquess sobbed out more apologies and outright refused to fight back. His guilt wouldn't let him lift a hand in his own defense. He deemed himself worthy of every blow. Security had to be called to get Baron off of him.

"I'm so sorry, Professor. It really was an accident," Marquess said when the blows finally ended.

"An accident caused by your stupid drinking," Baron

retorted, struggling to get free from the two burly security guards that held his arms.

"I'll get some help. I promise. I'll go to an AA meeting right now." Marquess continued to sob in the hallway, uncaring who heard him or saw him in this humbled state.

"Who gives a flip?!" Baron fired back, struggling to get free again. "You can drink yourself to death for all I care. As far as I'm concerned, what you did today killed our brotherhood. I only have three brothers now and one of them is hanging on by a thread."

Devastated all the more by his brother's words, Marquess turned and stalked down the hall towards the nearest exit. He had to get out of here. Had to get away from the vivid reminders of what he'd done to Baron and Aurelia.

Poor Aurelia, Marquess lamented as another load of guilt settled upon his shoulders. I'm so sorry, precious little sister-in-law, he thought, finally and truly embracing her place in his life. If only it hadn't taken something so devastating to bring that miracle to pass.

* * *

At the other end of the long hall was a silently watching Paula. She'd been at the hospital visiting a client when she happened upon the Weaver brothers' fight.

Forgoing her appointment, she followed Marquess on foot out of the hospital, down the street, and into the front door of a local bar.

So much for his promise to go to an AA meeting today. So much for his promise to get some help. And yet help was exactly what Marquess was about to get whether he liked it or not.

* * *

When Paula walked into the bar, she immediately heard Keyshia Cole and Monica's duet entitled Trust playing in the background. How fitting, she thought, convinced that Marquess needed someone that he could trust not to hurt him in his vulnerable emotional state. She deemed herself that person.

"Fancy meeting you here," Paula said from behind Marquess' stool. As she spoke, she waved the bartender off with her right hand and a firm shake of the head.

Marquess instantly stiffened in his seat. "Pa...Paula?" He didn't dare turn around. He didn't want her of all people to see him this way. And yet it seemed unavoidable now.

"Yes, it's me." She sat on the empty stool beside him. "And in case you're wondering what I'm doing here, just know that I followed you from the hospital."

"You followed me?" Marquess finally turned to look at her.

"Yes." Paula fought not to wince at the bruising on his cheeks and that big goose egg on his forehead left there by Baron's powerful blows. Thankfully Marquess didn't have a glass jaw like Earl or he would have had to be examined at the hospital today, too. "After I saw what happened between you and your brother in the hallway, I followed you to make sure you were okay," she added, also fighting the urge to touch his injured face just to make sure he was physically okay for herself.

Marquess stared straight ahead again. "As you can see I'm fine." He took another long swig of his drink, uncaring that she was present now. No more putting up a front for anyone.

"I disagree, counselor. I think you haven't been fine for a long time," Paula argued, being just as blunt as ever. "I think you became considerably less fine when I gave you the shock of your life Friday night." She giggled.

Giggled!

At that joyous sound, Marquess' gaze snapped her way in wonder. He couldn't believe she wasn't mad about Friday night. Couldn't believe she was actually laughing about it.

"I'm sorry about the way I reacted, Paula. You caught me off guard. I wasn't prepared for that kind of…revelation."

Before Paula could respond to that statement, the bartender approached them again.

"Want a refill?" the burly man asked, more concerned about making another sale than about the abject misery of the bruised Latino he hoped to served again.

"No," Paula intervened. "He has somewhere he needs to be." She threw a few large bills on the counter to make the bartender go away for good.

"No, I don't," Marquess protested, reluctant to move from his stool of misery.

"Yes, you do. Now come on." Paula tugged firmly on his arm until he got up from the stool and followed her out the door.

* * *

"Exactly where do I need to be?" Marquess asked once

they were outside the bar.

"My place, so that I can do what I should have done Friday night." Paula tugged on his arm again, urging him to follow her to a nearby parking deck where she'd left her car.

"Which is?" Marquess prompted as they made their way across the street.

"Which is to explain how I lost my foot. Then find out if you're willing to accept me as I am, imperfections and all, the same way I'm willing to accept you."

"I'm more than willing to accept you as you are, Paula. I love you. If I haven't learned anything else from my youngest brother it's to stop caring about what society thinks about me and the woman I love. I would have told you that Friday night, but by the time I came back up to my room, you were gone," Marquess said, letting her know where he stood on the matter now…before she presented her explanation.

Paula stopped on the sidewalk and just looked at him with open mouth. "Now I wish I would have waited a little bit longer in that room. But after fifteen minutes, I figured you wanted nothing else to do with me. It was only after hours of shedding crocodile tears that I realized that you might have just been in shock. My presentation was kind of blunt," she said, referring to how she yanked her shoe off that night in the heat of passion. Then threw it and the fake foot across the room in an effort to shed her jeans faster.

"Yes, your presentation did leave something to be desired." Marquess chuckled, laughing at the situation now himself. Nothing about it had been funny Friday night. "Now is this the action of a man who wants nothing else to do with you?" He snatched her to him and then ravished her mouth. "I want everything else to do with you, woman," he said when that long heated kiss finally ended. "Everything."

"Fake foot and all?" Paula panted out.

"You better believe it, babe." Marquess gave her bottom a squeeze before releasing her. "In fact, I'm ready to make you my wife right now, then go to your place, and put months of celibacy behind me." The fact that he was currently outbreak free and doing well on his meds assured that he could do everything he just said.

Paula smiled. "I want to marry you, too. And I definitely love you, but first things first. Instead of eloping right now, let's hit up an AA meeting instead." She tugged on his hand again as she led the way into the parking deck.

"Are you sure?" Marquess replied, though he was willing to follow her anywhere.

"Yes. No time like the present to start picking up the pieces of your life. Besides, I'd much rather marry a man that actually took the first step to sobriety than a man with promises to do so."

"I agree." Marquess nodded. "By the way, I know Fran told you about my diagnosis, but who told her? Up until Friday only two of my brothers knew," he said, failing to mention Dingo and Raven since he was pretty sure they hadn't told his ex-wife.

"Actually Fran didn't tell me at all. Sasha did," Paula replied. "As for who told either of them, blame it on your medical records."

Then she shared how Fran sought to gain more bargaining power during their divorce by snooping in Duke's home office where he kept all family medical files. About how Sasha caught Fran in the act, but remained quiet because she was mad with all cheaters at the time. All male cheaters, that is, since they both had done their own share of cheating, too, by that time.

"I hope you're not too mad at my cousin. She meant well." Paula turned left to the section of the parking deck where her gray Lexus was located.

"I don't blame Sasha for keeping her mouth closed or for opening it when she did. Nor do I blame Fran for cheating. I was a rotten husband to her," Marquess admitted remorsefully.

"Yes, you were," Paula agreed. "Hopefully you learned your lesson about being unfaithful. In case you haven't, then know that I will not marry you today or any other day. But I will still take you to your first AA meeting. In other words, Paula don't share. And if I ever find out that I am sharing my man, I have a little peacemaker in my purse that will quickly restore order to the situation." She patted her purse.

Marquess smiled at her feistiness. "Believe me, I've learned my lesson well. No need to pull out the weaponry." He chuckled and then turned gravely serious again. "The fact that you're willing to even take a chance on me, especially after all you now know about me, is enough motivation to stay true to you for the rest of our lives. Plus, had you been my wife in the very beginning, I seriously doubt if I would have ever strayed. You are still the best lover I've had to date,

Paula. I want no other. I never really did after you."

"Can I have that in writing, counselor?" Paula teased as she disabled the alarm on her car with the press of a button on her gold key ring.

"Of course, counselor," Marquess replied in a serious tone that revealed how much he wanted to build her faith and trust in him...in them.

"I'm about to kiss you senseless." Paula gave him a ravenous look.

"I'm ready, babe. Been ready," Marquess said, licking his lips already.

* * *

On the ride to the AA meeting, Paula shared how she lost her right foot at the age of eight in a train accident. How the train operators near her childhood neighborhood refused to blow their horns because they didn't care about the lives of the people in that poor part of town.

"Fortunately, I had an outspoken mother, who wrote every newspaper in the state to get the word out about my accident," Paula continued. "She also called every lawyer in the phone book until one was willing to take our case. That lawsuit led to a large monetary settlement for my family and improved conditions in our old neighborhood. It also led to my discovering what I was put on this earth to do."

"Which is to improve the living conditions of the poor," Marquess deduced, familiar with the kinds of cases she specialized in.

"Right on the mark." Paula smiled briefly before turning solemn. "Yet while I sought to improve the lives of others, I failed to pay attention to my own personal happiness. Quite frankly, I never thought I would have any personal happiness because of my foot. I didn't think a man could love me with that kind of imperfection. Nor did I want to give him the chance to. Which is why I disciplined myself to walk normally and why I wear boots in the summertime, heels that come up to my ankles, or high-topped sneakers. It's also why I kept my sexual encounters few and strictly on a one-night-stand basis over the years."

"And why you kept your shoes on the whole time," Marquess added, recalling their own one-night-stand.

"Exactly," Paula replied. "Matter of fact, my shoes usually don't come off until I'm in my own bed alone. I even forbid my relatives to say anything about my foot, lest they risk being cut off financially since me and Mama still control most of the family's money. Even relatives that are prone to tell secrets like Sasha know to keep their mouths shut."

"Wow. Now that explains a lot," Marquess said, remembering how highly Paula's family esteemed her and her mother. They were treated like queens, no one dared cross them, or said a negative word about them. All this time he thought such deference was because Paula was an expert shooter. Now it appears as if it had been motivated mostly by money.

"Your abuse of alcohol explains a lot about you, too," Paula said, smoothly switching the subject onto him. "For one thing, it tells me that you've grown bitter and depressed about your diagnosis and divorce. That instead of facing your problems head-on, you want to numb out and act like they don't exist."

"True."

"Although I certainly understand your desire to numb out, I'm not about to sit by and watch you try to drown your sorrows about your diagnosis or rinse away your guilt concerning Fran, Baron, and Aurelia with alcohol," Paula said in a firm tone.

At that blunt reminder of his most recent cause for guilt, Marquess' eyes grew shiny with emotion. "Professor is never going to forgive me for what I did. Because of me, he and Aurelia may never be able to have kids." He clasped his hands together as he stared straight ahead.

"I pray that isn't the case. But even if it is, I think you owe it to them to straighten up your life. Show Baron and Aurelia, show everybody for that matter, that something good came out of today's unfortunate accident," Paula advocated. "As your wife, I'll be by your side every step of the way."

"I'll do my best," Marquess promised through a tight throat.

"I know you will. You always do," Paula replied as she parked on the side of a church that held local AA meetings. "As your colleague, I'm glad to see you taking this step to get your life back on track. God knows I didn't want to see another brilliant lawyer drink himself into an early grave. Who else is going to make sure that big businesses respect our environment? The world needs your kind of expertise in the courtroom, Marquess." Paula put a comforting hand on his left cheek, careful not to touch the bruise there. "I need you, baby," she endeared, caressing a line from his cheek to his strong chin.

Marquess' eyes closed at her soft touch. It had been so long since a woman gave him such tender affection. Too long since a woman uttered an endearment to him.

Opening his tormented eyes, Marquess stared at her for the longest time. "I need you, too, babe."

"You better." Paula grinned teasingly and then removed her hand from his face to put her keys back in her purse.

"Before we go inside to officially deal with my drinking problem. I need to double check something with you."

"Double check on."

Marquess swallowed hard and then asked, "Are you absolutely sure you're willing to marry a man with herpes?"

Paula gave him a tender smile. "I'm very sure. Based on all the literature I read about the disease, it is far from being a death sentence. Not only is herpes highly treatable and avoidable these days, it won't stop us from having a rewarding sex life or even children, which I definitely want."

"I can't wait to have all of the above with you." Marquess smiled in relief. "But like you said, first things first." He star up at the stained glass picture of Jesus on one of the church's windows.

Then after taking a deep breath, Marquess exited the car and went inside to finally face and get rid of his demons. When the AA meeting was over, he and Paula went to the other side of the church and eloped. After exchanging their heartfelt vows, they went to her place and made slow and extremely careful love until night turned into day again.

At the crack of dawn, they collaborated in yet another way by drafting a heartfelt letter to Baron and Aurelia. Just like the sun was ushering in a new day in this part of the world, they hoped their letter would usher in a new day in the Weaver family. A day of forgiveness.

CHAPTER FIFTY-EIGHT

While Marquess and Paula worked through existing problems, Baron and Aurelia found themselves faced with new problems. First of all, they had to find the best doctor to set Aurelia's pelvic bone back in place correctly to increase her chances of a successful future pregnancy. That doctor turned out to be none other than Dr. William Johansson.

Baron almost let his jealousy get the best of him again when Aurelia told him about William's connection to her. However, they consented to William's assistance after Duke gave the man glowing recommendations. Thankfully Aurelia was not yet pregnant, which meant that was one less thing to complicate matters.

Secondly, Ana Maria had a fit about her boys fighting among themselves again. She scolded Baron for not keeping his promise to her. He got another scolding when she learned how unforgiving he remained towards his brother, who truly was repentant about his actions.

When nothing Ana Maria said to Baron could sway him to forgive Marquess, she left the hospital in tears. That was another sad day for the Weaver family.

Thirdly, with Aurelia's accident, they had no choice but to tell everyone about their secret marriage and about her secret son. Especially with Emile and Trent being flown to California and with Aurelia and Baron having to miss so many days from school. The same number of days from school.

To make matters worse, her weekend job was now history in light of this accident. Liam was saddened by Aurelia's unexpected departure, but he understood it. He was also relieved that her condition was stable and extremely happy

465

that she and Baron could finally openly enjoy their marriage wherever they were.

The Weaver family handled the Trent situation well. By now they were used to unexpected secrets revealing themselves at the most inopportune time.

With Ana Maria leading the way, the whole family readily embraced Aurelia's son and her mother into their fold. The two of them were even staying at the main Weaver residence with Baron's parents. Having Emile and Trent around kept Ana Maria from getting depressed about the lingering discord among her children.

As expected, Trent also had to be told about his true paternity. Under the watchful eyes of Baron, Aurelia and Emile broke the news to the lad gingerly the first day he arrived in California. To everyone's great pleasure, he took the news well, too.

Trent shocked them by claiming to have already known the truth in his heart. He recalled how Aurelia had always been more motherly than sisterly to him. How when he was sick, she was the one that stayed up to cuddle him, read to him, and administer medicine during his recovery. How his grandmother only did those things when his real mother wasn't around.

Trent's only complaint was that he never got to know yet another father. After all, his grandfather died before he was born, too.

At the other end of the spectrum, Aurelia's instructors and classmates were beyond shocked to hear of her nuptials. Dean Paterson was the one to break the news to the instructors and to the president of the college, telling them only what they needed to know.

Baron broke the news to Aurelia's peers, namely to Bambi since Claude already knew. Everyone else learned through sheer campus gossip. Gossip that Rhoda spearheaded among her students and colleagues to try to make Aurelia and Baron look bad. Thankfully no one was told about Aurelia's history as a stripper or how she and Baron met. Otherwise that would have added even more fuel to the fire.

As expected, Bambi was upset to learn that she'd been kept in the dark all this time by Aurelia and Claude. However, since she was a peacemaker at heart, she was quick to forgive them.

"Your secret relationship definitely explained a lot," Claude told Baron as the professor sat by Aurelia's hospital bed like a dutiful husband on that rainy Thursday night. "All those sizzling looks you sent Aurelia's way when you thought no one was watching. The way you were harder on her than anyone else in your class. I knew something had to be up."

"Don't forget the fact that Barry had the same nose, mouth, and smile as our favorite instructor," Bambi piped in from the chair beside Claude. "By the way, that was a bold move showing up at our sorority party, Professor." She laughed.

Baron chuckled, the first smile he'd cracked in days. He hadn't even smiled when he read Marquess' sincere letter of apology. He simply grunted out that his brother ought to be sorry for what he'd done. Now the professor was smiling and looking like his old self again.

"And here I thought I was hiding my feelings and my true identity well," Baron said. "Guess I'm not as smart as I think, huh?" He chuckled again. "And yes, I was rather hard on Aurelia. Mostly out of my desire to make her the best student she could be, but sometimes out of jealousy."

"Jealousy?" Claude's left brow rose.

"Yes. Keep in mind, that Aurelia and I weren't yet a couple when you guys were in my class. Which means I had to silently watch men hit on her constantly, including you, Claude. Matter of fact, we almost didn't become a couple at all because of you," Baron shared.

"Because of me?" Claude's right brow rose now.

"Yes, like Bambi, Baron thought you and I had something going on beyond friendship," Aurelia interjected from the bed.

"At the time, I wished there was more beyond friendship between us," Claude confessed. "Now I'm happier than I could have ever imagined with Bambi. I can't believe I almost let her slip by." He leaned over to give his beautiful girlfriend a warm kiss on the cheek.

"You definitely would have been a fool to let her get away," Aurelia replied. "Speaking of fools, is Professor Griffey still giving you guys a hard time in class? She acted downright looney when I called to ask for my missing assignments. I thought I was going to have to call the dean just to get Looney Tunes to release them."

"Griffey is still the nutty professor. Even loonier now

that her newest boyfriend dumped her," Bambi revealed, sharing the latest campus news.

"I'm not surprised. Crazy is kind of hard for anyone to deal with," Aurelia replied. She didn't haved any sympathy for that particular professor since Rhoda never had any sympathy for her.

* * *

Aurelia had no idea how close to the truth she was concerning Rhoda. Right now the woman in question was sitting in her office drawing daggers through Aurelia's picture. Not the picture that was in the yearbook. No, this picture was confiscated from William's house last weekend.

Late Saturday night after another satisfying tryst at her now ex-boyfriend's house, Rhoda found herself unable to sleep. While William continued to doze, she went exploring in his house. Actually she went straight to his home office to see if it was locked the way it usually was whenever she visited. That was her first mistake.

Fearful that William was having an affair and keeping the evidence of that affair locked away in his office; Rhoda snuck his keys from the dresser and went into that forbidden room. That was her second mistake.

Within a few short minutes, Rhoda discovered a porn collection that went back decades. That didn't shock her too much. She knew that a lot of men were avid porn collectors. No, what shocked her was the file she found on Aurelia Bunting-Weaver.

As expected, Rhoda confronted William immediately. She also did it dramatically, waking him from his slumber with a bucket of cold water to the face, which he didn't appreciate at all. That was her third mistake.

After that the mistakes kept piling on thick. They lasted well until daybreak.

Rhoda accused William of being a stalker, which he wasn't. At least not in the violent sense. He'd only wanted to know if Aurelia was dating anyone and how serious it was. As soon as he found out, he called the P.I. off the case. Plus, that was months ago.

William told Rhoda that he had no idea what had been going on in Aurelia's life lately. That he'd been too wrapped up in their relationship to even care.

Unwilling to believe his claims, Rhoda then accused William of still being interested in Aurelia, which he wasn't.

The man hadn't thought about the ex-stripper since he and Rhoda became a couple. He hadn't even been to any strip clubs since they got together.

What finally proved to be the deal breaker was when William got that emergency call about Aurelia's accident early Sunday morning and Rhoda forbid him to help the injured woman. It was then that he saw just how insanely jealous she could be. How cold and callus her heart was towards someone in need, despite the fact that she'd been the recipient of a few good deeds in her own life. Good deeds by Aurelia's husband.

Where was the gratitude? The compassion for another human being in need?

As a result of Rhoda's unwillingness to put aside her personal feelings for the greater good, William promptly broke up with her. He didn't let her tears and begging sway him.

"You cost me too much this time," Rhoda said, shedding new tears as she put another dagger on Aurelia's picture. "And I know just how to make you pay."

* * *

On the island of St. John, Oliver Jean-Baptise returned to his home a defeated man. He'd just been told that he was cancer free, only to be further told that the treatments had so damaged his kidneys that he was now going to need dialysis. They even put him on a transplant waiting list.

A waiting list! Oliver seethed, deeming himself too important to go on anyone's waiting list. Plus, he was tired of suffering in general. He was ready to be healthy again.

I'll have to find my own donor. One from my own bloodline. Oliver instantly thought about Trent as he puffed on one of his expensive Cuban cigars.

Oh, yes, he'd known about the lad's true paternity for years. Although Oliver was initially incensed about Aurelia's direct disobedience to his orders, he pretended ignorance as long as she kept quiet about their connection and didn't come asking him for more money.

Now I think it's time for a little family reunion. Oliver grinned wickedly, walking over to Marshall's stately blue urn to dump another round of cigar ashes into it.

* * *

All the way in Florida a mentally challenged, twenty-six-year-old man with amber eyes threw his video game down on the den floor, and said, "I want to see Aurelia!" Usually in the best of spirits, Pierre acted beyond agitated today.

His guardian, neurologist Dr. Julian Gilman, aka Client #1, immediately tried to calm him down. "You saw her in March, remember? She's doing fine," he said comfortingly, referring to the last quarterly update he'd gotten from the P.I. he had on retainer.

"I want to see Aurelia face to face," Pierre insisted, letting it be known that pictures would no longer suffice.

Julian took a deep breath and exhaled. He'd known this day would come ever since he faked Marshall 'Pierre' Jean-Baptiste's death to save his life and then worked with him for years to regain some of his memory.

The only things Pierre remembered so far from his past were his parents, select childhood memories and of course, Aurelia. He knew who she was by sight and could recall deep affection for her, though those memories stopped just shy of that affection being consummated.

Pierre did not, or rather could not, seem to remember his uncle or his unfortunate accident. Nor did he remember to what degree his uncle was involved in that accident.

Julian didn't know how Pierre's accident happened either. But he did know that Oliver was directly responsible for it. He gathered that much when he overheard what the man muttered over his nephew's still body after requesting that they pull the plug on the teenager's life support.

Oliver basically said that he was glad his nephew was out the way. That if Marshall had lingered on much longer or else recovered, he might have had to cause a more gruesome 'accident' to occur. That he couldn't wait to be rid of him once and for all.

Drying his hands in the adjoining bathroom at the time, Julian had cringed upon hearing those malicious words. He waited quietly until Oliver left before exiting the bathroom. Imagine his surprise when he found the teenager breathing on his own again and his eyes struggling to open.

Julian wanted to scream to the rooftops that Marshall was alive. Alive! But doing so meant future harm to the teenager, perhaps even true death.

That's when Julian made the pivotal decision to save Marshall's life. It was as if fate was on his side that night. Everything he did to sneak the teenager out of the hospital worked.

Putting Marshall in a wheelchair and wheeling him to the nearest elevator without being seen had worked. Taking him to his car had worked, also without being seen. Falsifying all necessary documents had worked and even using a John Doe replacement body for the cremation procedures had also worked.

Julian then took Marshall to his home and tended to him around the clock. The fact that he had been scheduled to take his vacation anyway during that time proved to be most beneficial for his righteous mission. Unfortunately, Julian's girlfriend at the time had not appreciated him canceling their plans and thus dumped him. But that was a sacrifice he was willing to make to save an innocent life.

Making a wise decision to call Marshall by his middle name Pierre from now on, Julian took him off the island via private jet. He had to put colored contacts in Pierre's eyes, allow his beard to grow, and dye his hair to keep the teenager from being recognized. That transition had also been miraculously seamless.

Slowly but surely, Pierre recovered under Julian's care. Now he was healthy and fit, but with the mind of a ten-year-old due to brain trauma from his accident. As for Julian's lovelife, well, after he moved to Florida, he fell in love and married a wonderful woman named Gisele, who treated Pierre as if he was their very own son.

"I want to see Aurelia!" Pierre persisted, shaking his guardian from his deep thoughts.

"I'll take you to see her sometime within the next two weeks or so," Julian consented.

"You promise?" Pierre asked with hopeful eyes.

"I promise." Julian smiled comfortingly.

Pierre instantly calmed down and returned to his video game, revealing just how much he trusted his guardian.

As Julian walked back into the kitchen where his pregnant wife was cooking dinner, he took several deep breaths to calm down, as well. He knew that taking Pierre to see Aurelia would expose the young man's true identity and perhaps put him at risk again.

Could Aurelia be trusted with the truth? Did she still love Pierre enough to protect him from harm?

I guess we'll just have to find out. Julian picked up the phone and called Murray Underwood.

* * *

After talking to Julian, Murray hung up the phone with finality in his heart. This was the last assignment he was going to take concerning Baron and Aurelia Weaver. If he didn't need the money to pay the last of his wife's funeral expenses, he would have turned down Julian's request tonight.

Murray had already turned down another request to gather more information about Aurelia. That request had come from Oliver Jean- Baptiste. It had been quickly declined, despite Murray's money troubles, because that request was made with the evilest of intentions. He'd heard the malice in Oliver's voice. Had been chilled to the bone by the coldness of it.

Julian's request had been more reconciliatory, purer in motive and nature. Even so, Murray had reluctantly agreed to honor that request. The Weaver case had hit too close to home.

When Murray dipped into Baron's past and discovered that he was the man that his illegitimate daughter was insanely in love with, he knew that he had to back off. Especially after then checking into Megan's activities, past and present, and uncovering all kinds of atrocities.

Murray did not approve of his daughter's desperate quest to get an unattainable man. In fact, her desperation appalled him. That was pretty hard to do for a man that had lived through the Vietnam War, represented a slew of shady clients, and suffered the loss of his beloved wife and all the children she miscarried over the years.

Murray also knew that Megan would not approve of him either. For one thing, he was broke. He'd blown most of his earnings on booze and gambling for years. He didn't clean up his act until after his wife became ill, which required him to then drain all of their savings for her care. He even had to refinance their house.

Secondly, Murray also refused to acknowledge Megan as his child after impregnating her mother during a secret affair they had while he was stationed in California. Such rejection and abandonment caused Megan's mother to quickly find a replacement father. That man happened to be Clay Griswold, who was ten years older than her at the time.

Murray could have taken custody of Megan after her parents died in a car accident. All it would have taken was a simple paternity test. But he didn't. He didn't want to upset his wife by bringing an outside child into their home. He didn't want to rub his ability to produce a child without her in her face.

What daughter would be proud of a father with that much baggage? No, it was better to just let Megan be. Let her continue to think she was a Griswold, a name that she was clearly very proud of. That much was evident by the fact that she quickly dropped her husband's last name soon after his death and reclaimed her maiden name.

So it was settled then. Murray would never contact Megan. Not for money. Not for anything.

After I close this case, I'm moving to Canada, Murray decided, ready to leave behind his life in the U.S. and everything connected to that life…for good.

CHAPTER FIFTY-NINE

After calling Megan with the latest updates about Aurelia and Baron, Earl returned his cell phone to his pocket. Suddenly an unexpected emotion rose from the graveyard of his dead conscience – guilt.

There was guilt present for disliking Aurelia with no just cause. Guilt for betraying his brother, despite the lingering ire he felt about being rendered prematurely gray by Baron. Yet the most guilt stemmed from how Earl had treated his wife over the years.

Meadow didn't deserve to be cheated on. Never did. Despite how haughty she was in society, she'd always been a dutiful wife to him, a good mother to their children, and a great in-law to his relatives. She'd also been so faithful to Earl. That much was confirmed during that eye-opening breakfast the Weaver women recently had.

All this time Earl thought that Sasha and Fran had been the faithful ones. That it was Meadow who'd strayed in silent retaliation of his infidelities. And yet it had not been her. Not even once.

Ready to finally do right by his wife, Earl left his study and went downstairs to seek Meadow out. It was just them in the house since their kids were over to Grandma and Grandpa Weaver's home visiting with Trent. Grandpa Griswold had taken them over there after they finished visiting with him earlier in the day.

Earl found Meadow in their home gym. "Can we talk?" he asked, interrupting her yoga routine.

"Sure." Meadow smoothly moved out of her current position.

As his wife untwined her long legs on the red floor mat

she sat on, Earl felt something he hadn't felt for her in a long time – hot desire. He'd forgotten how sexy Meadow was in her own right. How limber she was, able to get in any sexual position a man could ever want.

For the life of him, Earl suddenly couldn't remember why he ever preferred Megan over Meadow. Why he'd risked so much, put so much at stake for someone that he wasn't really attracted to anymore. Especially after Megan went and jacked up her body with unnecessary butt implants.

"What was it you wanted to talk about?" Meadow asked, interrupting his deep ponderings.

"Oh…right." Earl swallowed hard, took a deep breath of courage, and then settled down on the floor beside her. "I wanted to officially apologize for being an adulterer. I'm sorry for hurting you with my cheating ways and for constantly disrespecting our vows over the years." When she remained silent, he took another deep breath and continued. "I also wanted to thank you for not divorcing me because of my infidelities. For loving me enough to remain my faithful wife."

"You never had to worry about me cheating or divorcing you, Earl," Meadow stated in a nonchalant tone.

His eyes bucked. "Why is that?" Even his own mother had grown tired of a cheating husband and left him.

"Because although I do still love you, I love the power that I have in this town more," Meadow explained in that same matter-of-fact tone. "I'm not stupid enough to give up that power by becoming a divorcee. Not when being the dutiful wife of a cheating husband gets me the sympathy vote as well as admiration for how nobly I'm handling it all."

"I see," Earl replied, starting to understand his wife a whole lot better now. Starting to wish he'd thought to come to her sooner about a few other things. "What will being the wife of a now faithful husband do for your balance of power?"

"It will show all my enemies that I was the better woman after all. Is that what you're proposing now?" A triumphant gleam came into Meadow's eyes.

"Yes." Earl smiled. "I'm ready to be faithful to you. I'm ready to be the second half of a power couple."

"I'm ready for you to be both, too." Meadow smiled.

Earl released a loud sigh of relief. Then after another deep breath of courage, he said, "There is more that I have to tell you. This way we can both be prepared and already have a plan in place to do some major damage control when certain things hit the fan."

"Don't tell me you got some tramp out there pregnant!" Meadow semi-shouted as her whole body stiffened on the mat.

"I've never gotten anyone pregnant, but you, Meadow. I've always been very careful about stuff like that. I only want children from my wife," Earl quickly reassured her.

Meadow instantly relaxed again. Some of the tension returned to her body when he went on to tell her about his deal with Megan. About how her cousin was actually the private investor he'd been working with to address their indebtedness in exchange for help with the sabotage of Baron's marriage.

"Everybody knew you were helping Megan," Meadow said. "We thought it was because you deemed her better for Baron than Aurelia."

Earl scoffed. "We all know that that isn't true. Aurelia's the best thing that could have ever happened to my brother, despite her race or background."

"I couldn't have said it better myself," Meadow agreed. Though she liked Aurelia from the beginning, the V.I. native quickly became her favorite sister-in-law after she beat Megan down.

Meadow almost hated to have her wall repaired after that incident. She'd wanted to keep that large crack for sentimental reasons. However, since she cared too much about what future houseguests would think, she simply took a picture of that crack and proceeded with the necessary repairs. Not a day has gone by since then that Meadow hadn't looked at that picture in her wallet.

"Although I told myself that I didn't care if Professor ostracized me for feeding Megan facts about his life, I now realize that I actually do care. A lot, despite the fact that it's going to take another two weeks to safely dye my hair back to its original color. I don't want Professor to disown me like he did Marquess, especially when he finds out why I really betrayed him to Megan," Earl continued with glistening eyes of remorse.

"He probably will disown you, too. But knowing how much Professor loves his family, I'm sure he will prove forgiving of both of you over time," Meadow replied softly, rubbing his large right hand in comfort just as softly.

"You really think so?" Earl asked with hopeful eyes.

"I know so." She smiled reassuringly, before turning very serious all of a sudden. "Now back to the subject of Megan. By any chance did you also help her because you were secretly in love with her? Wanted her for yourself?"

Earl's eyes suddenly grew even more remorseful. "I thought I was in love with her. Now I see that it was all just one big infatuation, one big case of wanting something forbidden. I don't even like Megan these days. Her desperation to get Professor back has become downright repulsive in light of her recent plastic surgery and the actual hiring of an escort."

"Have you ever had sex with my cousin?" Meadow asked, continuing with the hard questions.

Earl swallowed and took another deep breath before answering. "Ye—"

Slap!

"I knew it!" Meadow shouted, raising her hand to slap him again on the other cheek. Twice.

Slap! Slap!

"I'm sorry." Earl said the only thing he could at an awkward time like this.

"I know that, too," Meadow snapped with flashing eyes. "You are going to pay for that particular indiscretion, Earl Weaver, but not now. No, not now. Revenge against you right now would be counterproductive to the revenge I plan on taking out on my cousin soon."

"Don't you think we should focus on getting out of Megan's pocket first?" Earl rubbed his hands across both of his stinging cheeks. "After all, she does have the ability to bankrupt us."

"We'll get out of her pockets all right...after we've drained them dry," Meadow said with a malicious gleam in her eyes that surprisingly had Earl harder than concrete. "I propose we—"

Meadow didn't get to finish her statements until much later. Her mouth had been otherwise occupied from the word 'we'.

Highly turned on by all that fire in her eyes, Earl had attacked Meadow with his kisses, his hands, his everything. He didn't let her go until they were both spent and sated on the floor.

Meadow gave as good as she got during that spontaneous romp, proving that everything Earl ever wanted had been right under his nose the whole time. That she really was superior to Megan in all the ways that mattered.

* * *

While Aurelia slept, Baron decided to go down to the hospital cafeteria for a snack. He didn't want to eat hospital food, but since he wasn't about to leave this building until his wife did, he had to eat something.

Had Baron not upset his mother so badly, he might have had home cooked food brought to him every day. Although Ana Maria offered that particular service to him, despite their current estrangement, Baron refused it. He knew that that service would come with more scolding, tears, and pleas of reconciliation. Since he couldn't have one without the other, he declined everything.

Fortunately for Baron, Count and Jenny went to his Alcove home and packed him and Aurelia several suitcases of clothes. Unfortunately, neither of them were very good cooks. Sasha was an excellent cook, but she prepared her food with a lot of heavy ingredients. Though her meals were rich and delicious, they usually took Baron's system a long time to digest them, which is why he only ate a small amount each time.

In contrast, Aurelia devoured the food Sasha brought and politely asked for more. When Duke found out she was straying from her hospital diet, he immediately put a stop to it. Since Aurelia was still recuperating from her surgery, he didn't want her to consume anything that would overtax her body in any way. Not even his wife's scrumptious food.

Halfway down the hallway, Baron's appetite suddenly left him as his eyes happened upon a dark sunglass-wearing woman coming out of one of the elevators. In spite of the bouquet of flowers in her hands, in spite of that contrite expression upon her face, he knew that Megan only came here today to gloat.

"What are you doing here?" Baron asked when they were within normal speaking distance of one another.

"I'm here to offer my condolences to you and your wife," Megan replied. "I heard about Aurelia's unfortunate accident."

"From Earl, no doubt. Your own personal spy in the Weaver family," Baron said, keeping his guard up.

"Earl knows how much I still care for you. That's the only reason he keeps me in the loop," Megan said.

"I doubt that, but in any case, my wife and I are fine. You can leave now."

"Fine, Professor?" Megan said with a raised left brow. "From what I heard, Aurelia might not be fine for a while." Her voice lowered discreetly. "Just so you know, I'm more than willing to be a stand-in until she gets better. In fact, if it turns out that she really can't have any more kids, I'll even act as a surrogate mother…as long as the baby is conceived the regular way, of course." She chuckled huskily and then licked her collagen enhanced ruby-red lips the way he used to like once upon a time.

"Surrogate mother?!" Baron roared, uncaring who overheard him and definitely not caring about Megan's weak attempt at seduction. "My child will never be nestled in your body. I'll grow my offspring in a test tube at home before I ever let that happen." He took in a deep breath to ventilate his temper before adding in a lower tone, "As for being my stand-in of any kind, please get a clue, Megan. Some dignity, too, while you're at it. I don't want you anymore. Haven't for a long time. Will never want you again." Then he turned around and stalked back to his wife's room.

Megan wanted to burst out in tears and run down the hallway to the nearest exit, but she refrained. Using the techniques she'd learned in etiquette classes, she held her head high and walked calmly to the nearest stairwell. Briskly, but nevertheless very calmly.

As Megan quickly closed the distance between her and that exit door, she was suddenly very thankful for the dark glasses on her face once again. Not only did they hide the remnants of her black eyes, they also hid her identity from onlookers. She wanted no one to associate Megan Griswold with the ultimate rejection that just occurred in that hospital foyer.

Professor didn't really mean what he just said, Megan told herself, dropping the flowers into the trashcan she passed by. But in case he does, it's time for Earl to really earn his keep, she decided, pulling out her cell phone.
* * *
Megan got the shock of her life when she talked to Earl. Instead of her leaning on him to betray his brother even more; he leaned on her to cancel all of the loans he owed her

and to give him a sizable parting gift for his pain and suffering.

"Your pain and suffering?! What?!" Megan exclaimed. "Do you want me to tell your wife about us?" she threatened, leaving Baron out of the equation this time.

"Feel free to. She's right here." Earl handed the phone off to Meadow, who was lying in the crook of his arms after another vigorous round of lovemaking. This time in their bedroom.

"Hello, cousin," Meadow greeted pleasantly. "And before you ask, yes, I know all about your little torrid affair with my husband."

Megan gasped in shock at that familiar voice. At the fact that Meadow really did know about them.

"I also know how you've been blackmailing Earl to betray his brother for the longest time," Meadow continued. "Now I want you to know a few things. One, I am not leaving my husband. Two, you are going to cancel his loans to you and issue him that one-time cash settlement he asked for."

"I will not!" Megan seethed.

"Yes, you will," Meadow persisted calmly. "You will, if you want even a sliver of a chance to have a future with Professor. In exchange for cooperating with us, we will keep our mouths closed forever about your affair with Earl. We will also continue to give you insider information about Professor and Aurelia for the next year."

Megan's eyes bucked. She couldn't believe how much her plan had backfired on her. The very thing she tried to blackmail Earl about was now being used against her. Again!

Oh, yes. Megan's bluff had finally been called out.

If she agreed to this new plan, Earl would retain his marriage, all the social benefits that came with that marriage, a debt cancellation of all his loans, and enough money to start over with. Megan would receive very little in return, almost no guarantees.

"If I tell Professor first, I won't have to pay you anything and Earl would come out on the losing end," Megan countered, trying to regain ground with another bluff.

Meadow scoffed. "I figured you'd say that. But need I remind you of how family-oriented Baron Weaver is? Yes, he would be very upset with Earl once the truth came out. Shoot, he's upset with him now. But Professor would be quicker to forgive a repentant brother than he ever would an ex-fiancée. Especially when he starts to miss adorable Earl Jr. too much," she replied, showing that she was not against using her children to her advantage. She used them to get things from her father all the time.

"You're low, cousin," Megan hissed in defeat, wishing they weren't kin in that heated moment.

"You're lower, you slithering snake," Meadow retorted. "Be at our lawyer's office first thing in the morning prepared to sign on the dotted line." Then she hung up the phone in her cousin's face.

At that loud click, Megan yanked her cell phone from her right ear and just stared at it in silence. Tears rolled down her hot cheeks. Her knees grew weak, causing her to have to sit down on the stairs, lest she fall down.

"How could my life have come to this?" Megan lamented just as Fran came up the stairwell from the opposite direction, ten minutes early for her annual physical.

* * *

"Do you think she's going to go for it?" Earl asked his wife as he pulled her closer to him.

"She better if she knows what's good for her," Meadows replied, showing no mercy for her cousin.

"I have to be honest here. I don't feel comfortable with us continuing to betray Professor for another year. I feel bad enough for betraying him this long." Earl frowned. "In fact, I wish you'd left that insider info part out of the deal altogether."

"First of all, Megan needed some kind of incentive to cooperate with us. Her desperation to reconcile with your brother couldn't have worked better in our favor. In fact, the more desperate she became through all of this, the more blackmail-able she became, as well. Secondly, the insider info I plan on telling Megan will be stuff like what they planted in their garden this year. How many times they got their car tuned up. Stuff like that." Meadow smiled up into his face.

Earl burst out laughing. "Oh, I love you." He squeezed her closer.

"Don't start in with the love talk again yet. I still have to get my revenge on you," Meadow told him, pulling slightly away.

"Based on what I've heard so far, you're not leaving me, you're not going to cheat on me, and you're not going to rat me out to my family. What other kind of revenge will you exact upon me?" Earl frowned.

"Financial revenge. Tomorrow morning, our lawyers will have a few additional papers for us to sign. One will be the dissolution of that pre-nup agreement you had me signed. This will enable me to get half of everything you own in case you ever decide to divorce me instead. The other document will assign one half of Megan's cash settlement over to me for my pain and suffering," Meadow explained.

"I accept my punishment," Earl readily agreed, loving her a little bit more for logically meting out his punishment instead of doing so emotionally.

"The other half we will use to start investing in some of the companies your father is involved in," Meadow continued. "If we're going to be a true powerhouse couple in this area, we need to behave more responsibly with our finances."

"You have my full agreement. Now can I tell you how much I love you?"

"Yes." Meadow smiled.

"I love you." Earl leaned down to plant a kiss on her forehead. "I love you." He planted another kiss on her eyelids. "I love you," he concluded and then planted a final kiss on her nose.

Meadow moaned, relishing his love and attention. She lifted her lips to him, demanding one more kiss. A deep one this time.

This particular Weaver marriage might not have gotten to this point in the most positive of ways, but they were both satisfied with where they were as a couple now. Very satisfied.

CHAPTER SIXTY

Aurelia surprised the doctors with her rapid recovery. She was able to go home in under two weeks' time, although she would be on bed rest for weeks and it would be months before she could resume all of her normal activities.

The day Aurelia was released from the hospital; Baron had a rented Winnebago ready to take her, Emile, and Trent back to Alcove. He wanted them to be as comfortable as possible on the journey home.

Before they left Bel Air, Baron made sure to apologize to his mother per his wife's request. He went a step further and promised to at least think about forgiving Marquess and Earl. That seemed to be enough to ease Ana Maria's heart for the time being.

Count and Jenny followed the Winnebago to Alcove. While Jenny drove their car, Count drove Baron's. That was his mission on this trip – to make sure his brother's Porsche made it home safely. Jenny's mission was to help turn the den into an attractive downstairs bedroom for Aurelia and Baron. Both trunks were full of bedding, curtains, and even a few throw rugs.

Meadow used her clout on the hospital board to have all the necessary medical equipment waiting for Aurelia when she got home. Claude and Bambi had been given a key to the house to let the delivery men in to set up that equipment in the appropriate room. They also let furniture deliverers in to set up the new bed, dresser, and nightstand Baron ordered for the makeshift bedroom.

Fortunately, everyone and everything made it to Alcove safely. Count and Jenny spent the night. They would remain until the next evening.

Early the next morning, Baron left Aurelia in their relatives' capable hands. He had classes to teach today. He also had to personally arrange modified exams for his wife with her instructors.

Baron found 99% of his colleagues very cooperative and conducive to the idea of modified exams for Aurelia. The same percentage of peers and students were also very respectful and even approving of their marriage, despite the ugly rumors that abounded around campus for almost two weeks now.

The Weavers' individual upright reputations helped decrease the sting of the gossip considerably. So did the fact that they were actually married instead of just having a sordid student/teacher affair. But what swayed popular opinion in their favor the most was the main source of those awful rumors – Rhoda.

The whole campus knew what Baron had done to help Rhoda. To then hear her turn around and talk so disparagingly about him and his wife reeked of disloyalty, ungratefulness, and outright jealousy. Thus people soon turned a deaf ear to the rumors. They even deemed the majority of them as lies.

Saving Rhoda for last, although she was right next door to his office, Baron waited until an hour before his workday ended to request a modified exam for Aurelia. When he entered her cluttered office, he made his request short and to the point. "I came to request a computerized modified exam for my wife. All of her other instructors have consented to this arrangement. I'd like to know if you would, too."

"No," Rhoda replied smugly from her desk chair. "I'm not giving Aurelia a modified exam on the computer or anywhere else."

Baron stiffened in his seat. He'd expected some resistance to his request. Had even mentally prepared for it. Yet when he heard Rhoda's reasons for denying his wife that modified exam, he lost it.

"Rhoda, have you lost your mind?!" Baron roared from his seat across from her desk.

"If your wife wants to pass my class, she has to come take my exam in my class," Rhoda stubbornly insisted. "Like I said before, I do not trust Aurelia not to cheat. For all I know you might even take the exam for her."

Baron looked at her as if she really had lost her mind.

"You really are insane to even insinuate that I would help a student cheat, including my wife, and especially with a qualified moderator present. If you want to be sure that Aurelia doesn't cheat, feel free to come to our house with the moderator while she takes the test."

"I have no desire to visit your home. Nor do I have time in my busy schedule to baby-sit one student," Rhoda replied dismissively.

"Graduation is just two weeks away, Rhoda," Baron said calmly, now trying to appeal to her sense of compassion. "Surely you know how important this class is for Aurelia's completion requirements. Since she probably won't be cleared by the doctor to resume full activity within that time frame, most reasonable instructors would at least allow such a student to qualify for graduation in a case like this. And if you won't do it for those reasons, do it as a favor to me for helping you out when you needed it."

"For your sake, I'm willing to give your wife an Incomplete. Then she can take my exam when she's well enough to come back to school," Rhoda said, showing very little compassion. In fact, she smirked at the notion of prolonging Aurelia's graduation date. So much for her returning Baron's favor.

"Professor Griffey, may I speak to you for a moment?" Dean Paterson suddenly said from the open doorway behind them. "Alone," he added with a frown as he entered the office more fully.

"I...I, yes," Rhoda stumbled out, wondering how long he'd been there. Just last week he reprimanded her for starting yet another rumor about Aurelia around campus. How much trouble was she in for what she'd just done?

Baron silently nodded to their supervisor, then got up and walked out without another word, closing the door behind him. He could only hope and pray that Dean Paterson was going to deal with Rhoda accordingly.

If things didn't turn out equitably in this situation, Baron was going to make a trip upstairs to the president's office. And it was not going to be pretty. Matter of fact, the sizable endowment that he had slated for AU students from the Virgin Islands might even be yanked and given to another school.

I'm sure Kingston's school could use more scholarship money, Baron mused as he entered his own office seconds later. Maybe I'll do that either way, he thought, recalling the man's integrity.

Why not reward such admirable traits in a person? Why not make someone else's dream come true? Wasn't that part of the responsibilities and privileges of being rich?

* * *

After Dean Paterson finished with Rhoda, he went next door to talk with Baron. Once the office door was closed, he revealed that Aurelia would be allowed to take all of her exams at home with an authorized moderator as planned. He also shared that Rhoda had been put on administrative leave effective immediately. Which meant that she would not be around to give any of her exams. Another instructor would take over those duties.

"May I ask what prompted your decision to relieve Rhoda of her duties?" Baron inquired.

"An increase in student complaints and a phone call I received today from Rhoda's ex-boyfriend," Dean Paterson replied. "It seems that she recently discovered a previous crush he'd had on your wife, assumed the worse, and spoke of revenge. He wanted to warn me in case Rhoda did something stupid. Combine that with a most disturbing picture that one of our custodians found in Rhoda's trashcan and I had no choice but to relieve her of her duties."

"Her ex-boyfriend wouldn't happen to be a man by the name of Cain Laker or Lane Baker, would he?" Baron asked.

"No, I believe he said his name was Dr. William Johansson."

Baron chuckled and shook his head in wonder. "Amazing."

"Do you know this man?"

"Yes, and he obviously is a better man than I thought. You're a pretty decent fellow, too, Dean Paterson." Baron rose to his feet and leaned forward to shake his supervisor's hand. "Thanks for everything."

"You're welcome," Dean Paterson replied, rising to return that hearty handshake before releasing it. "Just take good care of Aurora and continue to make her happy."

"Aurora?" Baron's left brow lifted at his wife's former stage name. He plopped down in his seat again, unable to stand after that unexpected revelation.

Dean Paterson grinned sheepishly. "You're not the only one that encountered Aurelia during her days as an exotic dancer. A few out-of-town colleagues and I visited a club she worked for a couple of years back. She left quite an impression on all of us. I don't know about the rest of my companions, but that incredible stage act made me want to go home and spend some quality time with my wife. When I did, my marriage, which had been strained prior to that time, became stronger as a result."

"Yes," Baron said, unable to think of anything else to say in that awkward moment. He simply nodded farewell to the departing administrator, who'd given him quite a shock today in more ways than one. He was equally surprised at himself for not getting jealous about that last revelation. It felt good to be growing in a healthy way in that particular area of his life.

The whole ride home Baron wondered if he should tell Aurelia everything that happened today. Every single thing.

Would she be grateful or embarrassed by William and Dean Paterson's intervention? How would she feel about the dean being one of her many fans? And did most men instinctively want to help and protect Aurelia? Men with purer motives, that is.

If she's mostly grateful for their intervention, we'll stay in California after she recovers. If she's mostly embarrassed, we'll find a home in the V.I. where no one knows her as an exotic dancer, Baron finally decided, unwilling to keep any more secrets from his wife. He and Aurelia had come too far for that.

CHAPTER SIXTY-ONE

Mrs. Applegate had been a frequent visitor at the Weaver home ever since she learned about Aurelia's unfortunate accident. She'd grown fond of Jenny, Count, Emile and Trent in the short time they'd been there. She'd actually done more visiting with them than Aurelia over the last two hours on account of her need to study for upcoming exams.

So taken with the Weaver relatives, Mrs. Applegate gave Count and Jenny affectionate hugs before they left three hours ago. She gave Trent a pint of ice cream that she brought from a special ice cream parlor that catered to diabetics. Like him, Mrs. Applegate had to carefully watch her blood glucose levels as well.

Now the elderly woman prepared to leave again. This time to tend to her garden, though she did not leave without giving Emile more business for her shop.

"See you later, Mrs. Applegate," Aurelia said, bidding her neighbor farewell from her new bed as the woman passed through the den.

"Goodbye, sweetie." Mrs. Applegate smiled. "And, Emile, please take your time on those orders I placed today," she said, now addressing the woman who'd walked her to the side entrance of the house that led to the Weaver's garage and also to the Applegate house next door. "I know you have to divide your time between looking after your daughter and grandson, and keeping your basket business going."

"Tank you for being so understanding, Mrs. Applegate. However, I don't tink meh sista and I will have any problem filling yur order in ah timely manner," Emile replied, just as Baron entered the house from the side entrance.

"You're welcome. Oh looky here. The handsome man of

the house is home," Mrs. Applegate said as she turned to greet the man in question. "Hello, Baron. Goodbye, Baron."

Baron smiled fondly at her. "Hello and goodbye to you, too, Mrs. Applegate." After waving farewell to their neighbor and closing the door behind her, he turned to his mother-in-law and wife. "Hello, beautiful ladies."

"Hola, senor," Emile and Aurelia echoed simultaneously. That was fast becoming their normal greeting to him these days.

Baron chuckled at their united reply, loving their readiness to embrace his Spanish roots. Before long, they were all going to be fluent with each other's cultures. "Mama Emile, do you mind if I spoke to my wife alone?"

"No problem, mon. I need to check on Trent anyway," Emile replied. "Eva since he got dat new video game you bought him; all he wanna do is stay in his room. We be out back gettin' some fresh ayer and playing horseshoe if you need us."

"Thank you, Mama Emile." Baron gave her a warm smile of gratitude. That smile plummeted into a frown as soon as his mother-in- law left the room.

"What's wrong?" Aurelia closed the textbook in her lap to give him her complete attention.

Baron took in a deep breath and exhaled slowly through his mouth. Then he joined her on the large bed and shared everything that happened today at work. He left nothing out.

* * *

As Aurelia listened to Baron's recitation of today's events, she realized that her days as a stripper would forever haunt her in this part of the world. Maybe even in the whole state of California depending on where her customers had hailed from.

What made the situation even worse was the fact that Aurelia couldn't remember every man she'd given a lap dance to in those dark clubs or at private parties. She couldn't guarantee that they wouldn't remember her.

Part of bringing in the big bucks was to be unforgettable on and off stage. Aurelia had done some unforgettable things over the years with her limber body.

When Baron suggested that they relocate to the V.I. after she was able to travel long distances again and after he fulfilled the summer school requirement of his contract, Aurelia jumped on the idea. Living in the Virgin Islands would not only give her a chance to finish raising Trent in familiar surroundings, but also return to a place that she loved.

"Now that that's settled, get back to work, young lady," Baron playfully scolded as he pointed to the textbook in her lap.

"Yes, Professor. I gon' go finish read," Aurelia said, deliberately thickening up her accent as she flipped her book open again.

Baron chuckled. "If you need me, I'll be upstairs taking a shower." He gave her a kiss on the forehead before getting up from the bed.

"What's wrong with the bathrooms downstairs?" Aurelia asked.

"They're too small. I like being able to have more elbow room when I bathe." He stretched out his elbows in illustration as he headed for the stairs.

"Makes sense to me." Aurelia chuckled. Then she finally went back to reading her textbook.

Baron had barely made it to the top of the stairs when the house phone rang. "I'll get it!" he semi-yelled to his wife. "Hello?" he said into the receiver seconds later, using his normal voice now.

"Good evening, my name is Dr. Julian Gilman," the male caller began. "I'm calling on behalf of Marshall Pierre Jean-Baptiste, who is deeply concerned about Aurelia and now wants to see her again."

Baron's eyes bucked. "But Marshall's…"

"Not dead," Julian finished for him.

* * *

While Baron struggled to get over his shock, Julian quickly summarized how he saved Pierre's life, how his charge was doing these days, and why he thought it was important for Pierre's mental well-being to see Aurelia now.

To provide proof of his story, Julian had Baron go to his computer and look at an email he just sent to his school email account. That email contained pictures of Pierre from the time he entered his care until now.

Although Pierre looked like a younger version of his uncle, those amber eyes were all the proof Baron needed. It was like looking into Trent's eyes. Which meant everything Julian said was true. Marshall Pierre Jean-Baptiste really was alive.

"Let me talk to my wife about all this, then I'll get back to you," Baron said once he had enough pertinent details.

"Do you know how soon you'll be getting back in touch? Pierre is becoming rather agitated with each passing day. I think he senses that all is not well with Aurelia. Based on what my P.I. shared about her recent accident, all is definitely not well with her on a physical level," Julian said, revealing his thoroughness. "Or has some miracle occurred that I'm not aware of?"

"My wife is definitely making a miraculous recovery, but she's not completely out of the woods just yet," Baron replied. "In any case, how about I put her on the phone and let you tell her what you just told me. As a physician, I trust that you know how to break the news to her as gently as possible considering her own delicate condition."

"Of course," Julian agreed. "And for the record, I'm not sure if it's such a good idea to have their son around at the time," he said, revealing that he knew about Trent, too. "Pierre can only handle so much at one time. Maybe he'll be ready to meet Trent on a subsequent visit if the first one goes well."

"I agree." Baron walked with the cordless phone back downstairs. He brought his laptop, too. He had a feeling Aurelia was also going to need proof of this interesting new development in their lives.

* * *

Baron watched Aurelia's face anxiously as she listened to Julian's account of Pierre's miraculous survival and then actually saw pictures of him on the computer. He held her as she trembled and cried happy tears that her son's father was alive, sad tears that his brilliant mind had been reduced to that of a child's, and angry tears at who'd done this horrific thing to Pierre in the first place.

The phone call ended on a satisfactory note that included a future meeting time for Pierre to visit Aurelia. The laptop had been turned off and put on the nightstand a long time ago to avoid Emile and Trent from accidentally seeing the pictures on the screen. Fortunately, they were still outside in the backyard. They were playing miniature golf now, yet another thing that Baron had installed while they were still in Bel Air.

"Okay, I officially hate Oliver Jean-Baptiste!" Aurelia said. "Before I just had a strong distaste for him and a few pockets of fear. Now I just hate him! And yet I know I have to forgive him in order not to hinder my own progress."

Ever since Ana Maria told her that unforgiveness could prolong a person's healing and personal growth, Aurelia made a point of forgiving everyone that ever wronged her. Which meant she was going to forgive Oliver just like she had Rhoda less than an hour ago. She wasn't about to let them hold up her life in any way, shape, form, or fashion. Not anymore.

Baron continued to hold her close. "I don't like him much myself. I can't imagine ever doing such a thing to any of my relatives. Not even the ones I'm not too fond of at the moment," he added, thinking of Marquess and Earl now. For some reason he suddenly wasn't as mad with them as before. Maybe because Pierre was a testament to how detrimental family conflicts really could get if left unresolved.

"I wouldn't either." Aurelia wiped her eyes with tissue from the floral box on the nightstand. "Oh, Baron, how am I going to concentrate on my studies after this? I suddenly feel so overwhelmed by life." She let out an exasperated sigh.

"I'll help you, study-buddy." Baron picked up her textbook and opened it to a bookmarked page.

Aurelia's eyes immediately lit up with encouragement. "With you as my study partner, I'm going to get all A's now for sure."

"You were going to get those anyway," Baron replied with solid confidence that gave her even more encouragement. His shower would just have to wait. Thankfully, Emile was here to see about Trent and dinner tonight, making those two less things for them to worry about.

CHAPTER SIXTY-TWO

May

Thanks to a joint effort by the Weaver women and the Weaver men that were still talking to each other, a surprise intervention was planned to help Baron start the process of reconciliation between him, Marquess, and Earl. Uncle Miguel was there for moral and spiritual support.

Nicolas was also there, not only as the patriarch of the family, but to help keep peace and order. All the boys deeply respected him. They wouldn't dare disobey him, at least not to his face.

The intervention occurred at Baron's home. Aurelia made sure that she, Emile, and Trent were otherwise occupied when their 'unexpected' guests arrived. She was in the den with the door closed studying. Her mother and son were at a local park, scheduled to take in dinner and a movie afterwards so that the brothers would have even more uninterrupted time to work out their problems.

"What are you two doing here?" Baron seethed when he saw Marquess and Earl file into his home behind their father and uncle. Count and Duke brought up the rear.

"They're here to formally apologize for what they've done," Uncle Miguel answered for his penitent nephews.

"And receive some forgiveness, too," Nicolas inserted, looking pointedly at his youngest son.

"I don't know about that, Dad." Baron shot his father a frown.

"Oh, forgiveness is going to take place in this house today," Nicolas replied firmly, returning that frown. "Want to know why?"

"Why?" Baron was almost afraid to ask. He'd never seen

his father so angry or so red-faced before.

"Because I can't have my family in tatters just because you and your brothers don't know how to get along. And I definitely can't keep waiting for you to work it out on your own while watching this division tear your mother apart day by day. My woman will have peace of mind even if I have to hogtie all of you down to do it. Now everyone have a seat and let's begin this blasted reconciliation!" Nicolas asserted lividly and very, very loudly.

At those sharply spoken words from their usual easygoing father, the Weaver brothers scrambled to have a seat in the living room. Even Uncle Miguel sat down quickly.

"Earl, you start since you're the oldest offender," Nicolas ordered from his seat by the fireplace.

Earl nodded, took a deep breath, and began. "Professor, I want to apologize for all of my corrupt dealings with Megan and for being such a bonehead about Aurelia," he said without disclosing what those particular dealings were.

Though he'd been advised by their uncle/priest to come all the way clean, Earl decided to keep things general until Baron specifically asked for details. Why prolong and deepen the division in their family by listing every sin he ever committed with Megan? Especially when he was sorry for them all?

"Yes, you were a bonehead," Baron agreed. "And a few other things that I won't say in front of our elders." He scowled at his apologetic brother.

"True," Earl admitted somberly. "But back to my apology. I now realize that Aurelia really is a great woman, worthy of my highest respect and admiration, which I plan to give her from now on. I also realize that any hatred I felt towards her skin color was a direct reflection of my hatred towards my own. As of today, I am stopping all my skin bleaching treatments and will allow my complexion to get as dark as it wants, when it wants. If I learned nothing else from your wife, it was to love the skin I'm in whether anyone else ever does."

"Do you forgive him?" Uncle Miguel prompted, looking at Baron. He knew what it had taken for Earl to come here and publicly own up to any of his wrongdoing, however general.

Baron stared at Earl for the longest time in silence, trying to gauge his sincerity. Finally he said, "Yes, I forgive you. Just don't let it happen again."

"It won't." Earl breathed a sigh of relief and smiled. Now he could finally relax in his seat.

"Very good, boys." Nicolas nodded, blinking back tears in his eyes. "You're up on deck next, Marquess. Have at it, son."

At their father's prompting, a glossy-eyed Marquess took a deep breath and began his own heartfelt apology. "I didn't mean…to cause Aurelia…or you…any pain that day," he said, stumbling over his words, despite the fact that he was such an eloquent lawyer in the courtroom. "I pray every night that…that…she'll heal fast…and…be able to have a house full of strong kids for you." His voice broke on a sob. Tears came down his cheeks in droves, causing the tension in the room to grow.

"Try to pull it together, son. Either way, keep it moving," Nicolas gently prodded again as his own eyes refilled with glistening emotion.

Marquess nodded and sniffed back his tears. Then after taking a deep breath, he squared his shoulders and pressed forward in a surprisingly steadier voice. "As a result of my…deepest sorrow for all the pain I've ever caused you, I have decided not to impregnate my wife until you are able to impregnate yours. If that means Paula and I never have any biological children, then so be it. I could never be happy bearing kids knowing that I robbed you of yours."

Baron struggled with his composure from the beginning of that emotional apology until now. To see Marquess so repentant, so broken up about all the pain he caused, and so willing to make restitution at the risk of great personal sacrifice was heartrending.

"I forgive you, man," Baron finally said, blinking back tears of his own. "I forgive everybody who ever did me wrong."

"On that happy note, let us all have a word of prayer." Uncle Miguel beamed with joy as he stood to his feet.

After they prayed, the men visited with Aurelia for a while and then did what they usually did whenever they got together. They emptied the fridge and cupboard of snacks, watched boxing on TV and told jokes to see who could make their father laugh the hardest.

Baron won the joke contest this year. He had them all rolling with laughter after sharing what he and Aurelia did for her birthday prank.

Before his relatives left to make that long trip back to Bel Air, Baron surprised them by telling them about his enhancing cream for men. He shared what the test results were so far in the ongoing double-blind study, how promising the product was for men from all walks of life, and about the big pharmaceutical company that wanted in on the deal after his PR department pitched the cream to them.

"Since we're all on one accord now, I didn't think it was right to sign anything without first giving the men in my family a chance to participate in what is about to be another very lucrative business venture for me," Baron concluded.

A brief moment of silence lingered over his relatives as they looked around the room at one another. Suddenly they all started talking at once. Most had questions. All were pulling out their checkbooks...even Uncle Miguel, which made Nicolas laugh all over again.

Baron answered all of their questions, printed out copies of his research from the computer and distributed it among them. When everyone's curiosity was satisfied, he drafted up equitable contracts with the help of his two lawyer brothers. After all preliminary legalities had been seen to, he filed away their checks to be deposited in a joint business account later.

As Baron walked his brothers out to their parents' roomy teal-colored SUV that had been used for this trip, he pulled Marquess to the side for a private last-minute chat. "Look, man. I don't want you and Paula to wait for Aurelia's body to heal completely before starting your family. You've waited long enough to even be together as it is. Matter of fact, I order you to go home and work on your first baby tonight."

Marquess smiled. "Now that's an order I don't mind filling." He gave Baron a warm bear hug.

The rest of the men paused from various places in the front yard and just smiled at the hugging brothers. This trip had definitely been a great investment of their time and money.

When the Weaver wives learned the details of that joyous Alcove reconciliation and about the lucrative business deal they just signed up for, all of the Weaver husbands got kisses. All but one got a lot more than that.

No worries about Baron though. With Aurelia young, healthy, and quickly on the mend, he would have his night of romance soon enough.

* * *

As expected, Aurelia aced all of her exams. She was now officially eligible to graduate from Alcove University. And she did so…with honors.

On a bright sunny day, Aurelia rode her motor chair across the stage to receive her degree. The crowd cheered loudly for her, especially her sorors.

Aurelia's whole V.I. family was there, including Trent's tutor/Emile's new beau – Locke Moore. All of her closest in-laws were there, too, making the day even more special.

Non-family members included Mrs. Applegate, Dingo, Crystal, Six-Eight, and even William, all of whom Baron personally invited via telephone to make sure they would be present for his wife's special day. It was a given that Claude and Bambi were there since they were graduating also.

After the graduation ceremony, the Weaver group reconvened to The Crowne for a reception that Baron organized on Aurelia's behalf. He surprised and thrilled her by seating Dingo and Crystal at the table of honor with them. Had it not been for them, Baron and Aurelia never would have met.

Baron gave Aurelia an additional surprise when he made a toast to Crystal, crediting her with helping to make his marriage stronger and for being such a good friend to his wife. Crystal's eyes watered at that toast. In response she shared how inspirational Aurelia and Baron's love was to her and Dingo's relationship that they finally decided to get married, too. In fact, they were going to elope that very night.

Aurelia wanted to attend that ceremony, but physically couldn't. She'd already taxed her strength enough for today. The fact that she had a noon meeting with Pierre and his guardian tomorrow gave her added incentive to get to bed early tonight. Aurelia was going to need as much strength as she could muster for that encounter.

Thankfully, Duke and Sasha were taking Trent back to his home tonight for a kiddie sleepover that they planned for all the Weaver grandchildren. Thus the youngster would not be present when his biological father arrived tomorrow. The fact that Duke was a doctor and quite familiar with juvenile diabetes added to Aurelia's peace of mind about the sleepover.

As for Emile, she was flying back to the islands in the

morning with Locke and the Bunting family. However, she would return to Alcove in two weeks. Sooner, if needed.

* * *

Megan heard all about Aurelia's graduation from Meadow. She heard about the kind of shoes, dress, and jewelry Aurelia wore. Even the brand name of the motor chair she rode to receive her degree.

Megan heard nothing about whether or not Aurelia was going to make a full recovery. Nothing about if or how Baron's sexual needs were being met these days.

Meadow and Earl claimed to be ignorant of those things. They claimed that even though Baron forgave Earl, he restricted him from knowing too many personal details about him and Aurelia.

Since that explanation seemed feasible, Megan couldn't put up too much of an argument. Even so, she was pretty sure that she was being given the run around by her cousin and cousin-in-law.

To cope with her disappointment, Megan invited Fran to Vegas with her for the weekend. They'd become the best of friends after running into each other in the hospital stairwell.

Megan originally hoped their friendship would yield some juicy gossip about her cousin. Anything to regain an advantage over Meadow. Or at least enough dirt to get some of her money back.

So far Fran hadn't proven to be anything other than a great party and shopping companion. Somebody to help keep away the loneliness.

I wonder what Gino is up to. Megan was ready to ease a different kind of loneliness now.

Although she was starting to realize that reconciliation with Baron was just a hopeless dream, she couldn't help wanting to take one last dig at him by sleeping with his best friend from college. Unfortunately for her, he didn't seem to care about her or Gino at this point.

CHAPTER SIXTY-THREE

Baron looked out the bay window and saw Julian's blue rental sedan pull up in front of their house. He turned to his wife and asked, "Are you ready?"

"As ready as I'll ever be." Aurelia closed her eyes to take in another deep breath. "My heart is beating a mile a minute."

"You'll do fine." Baron walked over to the long sofa she sat on and gave her a comforting hug. "Just remember to call him Pierre, okay?" he reminded, giving her one last squeeze before going to open the front door.

"Okay." Aurelia nodded.

The introductions were awkward to say the least. But what else could they be under the circumstances?

The second Pierre saw Aurelia, he rushed to give her a big hug and a rose. The rose he unknowingly crushed in the bear hug.

Baron wanted to say, 'Don't hug her so tightly,' but he kept quiet. Especially since Aurelia didn't seem to mind the super tight squeeze from the burly man.

"Pierre hugs people he likes," Julian explained to Baron as he took a seat in one of the living room chairs. "He doesn't mean any harm."

"Pierre loves Aurelia," Pierre corrected, talking about himself in the third person as he gave her another bear hug.

"Aurelia loves Pierre, too," she said, struggling not to cry at the very sight of him, even more so at the way he communicated these days.

Though Pierre looked almost exactly the same, he acted so childlike. The Pierre of today was a cross between Forrest Gump and the Waterboy. Realizing that harsh reality suddenly made Aurelia very sad.

"Don't cry," Pierre soothed, withdrawing a bit to cup her face tenderly in his large hands. "I need you to be happy, not sad."

"I am happy." Aurelia met his amber eyes that were so like their son's. "These are happy tears."

Pierre gave her a knowing look. "Not all of them are happy tears."

"Most of them are." Aurelia smiled, forgetting how well Pierre used to be able to read her emotions. That had been yet another thing she'd loved about him.

Pierre smiled. "Yes, most of them." He leaned to kiss her on the right cheek.

Like Julian, Baron silently watched Aurelia and Pierre's interaction from a nearby chair. The smile on the doctor's face showed his approval. Yet Baron found himself fighting not to frown. A part of him wondered if Pierre recalled vowing to woo Aurelia until his dying day. If he was trying to pick up where he left off.

Although Pierre's hugs and kisses were basically nonsexual, Baron didn't like seeing another man so familiar with his wife. Nor sitting so close to her. When Aurelia declared that she still had love for Pierre, it cut him deep. Real deep.

Realizing that his feelings were selfish considering the state of Pierre's mind, Baron fought harder not to be jealous, strove harder to be understanding. He had to be a man about all this. Not some insecure little boy. As a result, the professor would rise to this occasion just like he had in every other area of his life.

"Would anyone like anything to eat or drink?" Baron scolded himself for forgetting his manners today. Everything just happened so fast. So many feelings had been invoked at one time that he'd forgotten to be hospitable with food and beverages.

"No, thanks," Julian replied.

"I'm not thirsty." Pierre didn't bother to look at Baron. He simply could not tear his eyes away from Aurelia. He kept playing in her hair, gently tracing the angles of her face, and kissing her cheeks right at the places of her dimples.

"I'd like some orange juice please." Aurelia sent a reassuring smile her husband's way.

Baron smiled in return as he rose to his feet. He was

pleased that at least she hadn't forgotten about him in the presence of her ex-fiancé.

Pierre looked to the recipient of Aurelia's smile and frowned. That frown left when Baron left the room. It quickly returned when the Latino man reentered the room with Aurelia's drink in hand a few minutes later.

"Leave the room!" Pierre suddenly demanded.

"What?!" Baron looked from Pierre to Julian with questioning eyes.

"Leave the room! I don't want you around Aurelia anymore!" Pierre said forcefully.

"Pierre, Baron lives here. He takes care of Aurelia. He has to be around her," Julian soothed, wisely leaving out the fact that Baron was Aurelia's rightful husband.

"But if he stays, he might take her away from me," Pierre whined like a child. "I don't want to lose Aurelia again. I don't want to." He stomped his large feet on the carpeted floor in a semi-tantrum.

"I'll leave," Baron quickly volunteered upon noting the concern in Aurelia's eyes.

"I'm sorry," Julian apologized to their host. "Pierre is a bit territorial over his favorite things. And Aurelia is definitely among his favorites. If it's any consolation, it took him a while to warm up to my wife Gisele when we were dating."

"I understand," Baron replied. He turned around and headed for his office.

"Thanks, Baron," Aurelia told her considerate husband as he left the room.

Baron simply nodded in return and kept walking.

Pierre sighed in relief and immediately relaxed again once his perceived competition was gone. Then he turned a happy smile to Aurelia and began chatting happily away with her about all the new drawings he'd done lately. They even spoke for a time in French.

* * *

Baron entered his office, but kept the door open. In his desk chair, he took in a deep breath and blew it out slowly through his mouth.

Just when he thought his life was finally starting to calm down again, this happens. Although Baron couldn't blame Pierre for feeling territorial over Aurelia considering their past, it bugged him that he couldn't do anything about it.

That he shouldn't do anything about it. After all, even though Pierre looked like a man, he was still just a big kid on the inside.

A big kid with a kid, Baron thought, reminded of Trent in that pivotal moment.

And just that quickly, his irritation returned. Yet for another reason this time. A less selfish reason.

Baron now had to deal with the possibility of Pierre behaving just as territorially over Aurelia when he finally got to meet their son. He couldn't allow Trent or any future Weaver children to be sentenced to another room whenever Pierre decided that he wanted to see Aurelia again and didn't want to share. Nor could he tell her that she couldn't see Pierre again. After all, the man was Trent's father.

What to do? What to do? Baron thought, working that brilliant mind of his overtime.

Suddenly the solution came to him like the dawn of a new day. He would suggest to Aurelia that she see Pierre on his own turf from now on. Once she was ready to travel long distances again, of course. That way, Baron and their children wouldn't feel like unwanted guests in their own home.

With his mind settled about that, the much calmer professor turned on his computer and proceeded to do some work. Although his jealousy was firmly and triumphantly in check, that didn't stop Baron from internally counting down the minutes to Pierre's departure.

* * *

An hour later, Aurelia appeared in the doorway of Baron's office on the electric scooter she used to get around on the first floor of the house. "I'm sorry about the way things went today, baby. I didn't know Marsh...Pierre was going to behave so possessively. Thanks again for handling it so well."

"It's not your fault or his that your relationship came to such a tragic end." Baron smiled, waving her into the room. "Although it would make my life easier if Pierre didn't still have so many amorous feelings for you, there's nothing either of us can do about it now. I just hope he doesn't react badly towards Trent when he finally meets him."

"Me, too, which is why I told Julian before they left today that the next visit will have to be after I've had a chance to heal completely and can fly to Florida to see them instead." Aurelia glided her way into the room on her traveling companion, which had been parked conveniently by the living room sofa for her. "I simply can't have my husband taking a backseat to my child's father in his own home. I also stated that I wouldn't be telling Trent about the survival of his father yet or bringing him to meet him until Julian had a chance to work with Pierre about the importance of sharing."

Baron literally grinned now. "Once again, we're on the same page." He got up from his seat, walked around to the front of his desk, and sat down on the edge of it. "I love you, you know that?" He folded his arms comfortably across his chest as he proudly watched her skillfully park her scooter sideways in front of him.

The woman was quite the trooper. Nothing kept Aurelia down for very long.

"I love you, too. You and those beautiful biceps." She licked her lips as she stared hungrily at his bulging muscles in the short-sleeved beige polo shirt he wore. "Let me show you how much." She reached for the zipper of his cargo shorts with quick hands.

"Whoa!" Baron stilled her hands on his shorts. "But the doctors said—"

"That I can't have regular sex," Aurelia finished for him. "They said nothing about other forms of sexual activity." She yanked his zipper down.

Baron was about to say something more in protest, but his mind went completely blank for a few highly pleasurable minutes. He didn't have another rational thought until Aurelia had satisfied him as only she could. Even then, all he could think to say was, "Thank you."

CHAPTER SIXTY-FOUR

June - July

Over that long hot summer, Aurelia did everything she could to cooperate with her healing. She ate well, rested, and even kept her physical activities down to a minimal, only increasing them with her physical therapist's approval. That last thing was the hardest part of all.

An active person by nature, Aurelia had to rely on mental activity to keep from going stir crazy in her bedroom, which was now in the master suite again. Having Trent there for the summer helped also. He was very instrumental in helping her in the garden. He definitely earned the title of 'King Weed Puller'.

Whenever Emile was in town, she helped with the household cooking, cleaning, and ironing. She also helped with Trent, although Aurelia never wanted a break from him unless it was time for her and Baron to be alone.

At night, Aurelia had to find other things to occupy her time. Baron helped her with those. Oh yes, he helped her a lot, showing her all kinds of creative ways they could please each other until the coast was clear for her to resume regular sexual activities.

Aurelia was finally cleared for those regular sexual activities the day before Independence Day. Fortunately, she and Baron would have the whole house to themselves tonight.

Emile was in the V.I. checking on things with their personal and commercial properties, and getting reacquainted with her beau. Trent had a backyard camping sleepover/adventure with Earl Jr. in Bel Air. He'd been personally picked up by Earl and Meadow yesterday.

With Baron out running last minute errands for their own trip to Bel Air tomorrow, Aurelia chose that time to get herself prepared for their night of loving. First was the shower to trim everything that needed trimming. Then was the long soak in the tub with her favorite bath oils.

Afterwards, Aurelia patted her body dry, applied custom made lotion to it and then put on her skimpiest bikini. Next she retrieved their portable stereo, her favorite mixed CD, and went outside to the solarium to lounge and catch some evening rays while she waited for her husband to come home.

* * *

Baron arrived home right before sunset after crossing the last three errands off his to-do list. Those errands included getting new tires for his car, a tune up, and groceries for the pasta dishes that he and Aurelia planned to fix in the morning and take with them tomorrow. Thos pasta dishes were served on the regular at his new restaurant in the Alcove mall.

Although Baron was somewhat tired after his long day, he wasn't about to let that stop him from celebrating his wife's good news. Their good news since Aurelia being able to resume full sexual activity was beneficial to both of them.

As a result of that good news, Baron failed to put the groceries up right away like he usually would. No, this time he put all the perishable items inside the fridge without even taking them out of their bags. The nonperishable things he simply left on the countertops. As randy as he was right now, the food was fortunate to make it inside the house at all.

Rushing upstairs, Baron looked for Aurelia in the bedroom where he thought she would be waiting for him. Disappointment tried to attack him when he saw the empty bed. It quickly flew away when he noticed the handwritten sign on the sliding doors that led to the solarium.

The sign read: I'm waiting near the fountain.

Baron moaned and headed in that direction. Suddenly recalling how he had to help the mechanic change one of the tires in the hot sun, he detoured to the bathroom. That was the quickest shower he'd ever taken, but he was thorough enough to accomplish his purposes.

I'm fresh and now ready to get dirty all over again, Baron thought as he dried his body with swift hands. Real dirty.

* * *

A small smile graced Aurelia's lips when she heard Baron's car pull up outside. That smile grew when she heard running water coming from the master suite's bathroom. Her smile turned into a full grin a few minutes later when she heard the sliding doors to the solarium opening.

It was about to go down now!

Yet Aurelia didn't move a muscle from her spot. She remained in the comfortable stomach side down lounging position on the chaise. She wanted Baron to see her in this position. Wanted her back, bottom, and freshly shaved calves to be the first things he saw when he came outside.

When Aurelia heard him moan a few seconds later, she knew he had gotten a good eyeful of everything she had on display. Then and only then did she lift her head from the cushioned pillow and look at him. "Clearly you like what you see," she flirted.

"Yes," Baron replied huskily, quickly closing the distance between them with long strides. In the background Howard Hewett's Can You Feel Me played on the portable stereo near the chaise.

"I like what I see, too." Aurelia loved how the western sun rays glistened on the water droplets that fell from his wet hair and slid down his hard hairy chest. "Very much so." She licked her lips.

Baron moaned with need as the front of his black silk boxers tented even more.

It was a good thing they had high banisters and tall foliage surrounding the solarium. No need to show the neighbors all that exquisiteness…or what was about to happen next.

Hovering above her now, Baron remained motionless for a few moments as he just stared at Aurelia's delicious brown frame in silence. He kept licking his lips while drinking in her beauty. He loved the sensual curves of her body. Her slopes. Her valleys. Her everything.

Although Aurelia's body had gone through many changes over the last year, one couldn't tell it by looking at her now. Her hard work with the physical therapist and the time she spent in her dance studio over the summer had paid off. She looked just as fit and trim now as the night he met her.

"You're so beautiful," Baron whispered, ready to spring into action as he undid the back and sides of her festive red, white, and blue thong bikini.

"So are you," Aurelia replied as he peeled the swimsuit

pieces from her body and cast them aside. She moaned when he lowered his lips upon her body and licked a hot trail all the way up her left side.

Baron's trail covered her…

Calf.

Thigh.

Chocolate bon-bon.

Back.

Shoulder.

He paused briefly at a few places to suckle in his ascent. After planting a brief kiss on her waiting lips, Baron dipped lower and started up the right side, covering the same key areas. By the time he finally made it up to her lips again, Aurelia was panting with need.

"Please, baby. Get this." She arched her lower body towards him as he continued to hover over her frame from behind.

"I thought you'd never ask." He smiled, using swift hands to remove his boxers and join them. They both moaned as he filled her to completion at a snail's pace. "Baby, what did the doctors do to you? I didn't expect you to be so…" He sucked air through his teeth and moaned.

"Tight?" Aurelia finished for him as her snug cove continued to adjust to his substantial presence.

"Yes, almost virginal." Baron moaned again and continued to advance, inch by delectable inch.

"Are you complaining?" Aurelia grinned back at him.

"No." He grinned in return. "I've always wanted to deflower you."

"Well, deflower away then." She shifted upon her knees and arched her lower body even closer to him in invitation.

Moaning at her eagerness, Baron finally joined them to the hilt. Then he proceeded to honor her request with slow circular motions that were meant to get her thoroughly reacquainted with the full act of lovemaking.

Aurelia's hips followed his instinctively. Her movements were timid at first as she slowly inched her way back into the groove of love.

"You're doing good, baby. So good," Baron encouraged hoarsely at her left ear.

"Are you sure?" Aurelia clenched the top edge of the chaise for support and became bolder in her circular rotations, dipping at the end. She'd been practicing that move all afternoon in and out of her dance studio.

"Oh, yes." He moaned out. Grabbing the sides of the chaise to help ground him, he withdrew just enough to surge forward and hit her special spot with a circular grind at the end.

Aurelia sucked air through her teeth, moaned, and immediately bucked against him.

"Aye," Baron moaned out, allowing that Spanish expression to roll off his tongue at her aggression. "Keep it slow, baby. I don't want you to overdo it," he cautioned, despite the fact that he enjoyed all that extra fervor.

"No lectures right now, Professor." Aurelia sent him a playful scolding look over her left shoulder. "Right now I need you to trust me to know my body's limitations and then help me give it what it needs."

"What does it need, beautiful?" he asked, willing to meet any need she had.

"It needs some ketchup bottle love, baby. Fast. Hard." She thrust against him with force already.

Baron smiled at her metaphor. Nodding in understanding, he surged into her at the right time, hitting the right spot, and using the right amount of pressure to wake up the bottom of her core from its long sleep and get her fruit juices flowing freely again.

They flowed all right…like flood waters.

Aurelia's body shuddered violently as wave after wave of ecstasy seized her. Her hips ceased moving. She trembled as the waves crashed over her, causing her toes to curl. Her mouth was open, but she was too speechless to say a word. All she could do was close her lips and just moan.

Baron kept up that vigorous pace until his own body trembled with release. Throwing his head back, he closed his eyes as his essence poured into her. He bit his bottom lip to keep from crying out.

Maintaining their connection, he shifted their bodies to a spooning position on the wide chaise while they endeavored to catch their breaths. "That was great, beautiful," Baron said after an awe-filled moment of silence. "Better than ever before."

"Yes, it was." Aurelia sighed with contentment. "Who knew sex could get even better between us? I thought we had reached our pinnacle months ago." She chuckled.

"My father says that sex is like good wine – it gets better

with age." Baron chuckled, too.

"I do believe you're right." She sighed with contentment again. "By the way, you better enjoy this position while you still can, because in a few short months, it's going to be nothing but missionary style for a while."

Baron's eyes bucked. "What exactly are you trying to tell me here?" He turned her face to his.

Aurelia grinned at his shocked reaction. "I'm trying to tell you that while you were at the front desk signing off on some insurance forms earlier today, the doctors were marveling about how my pelvic bone was strong enough to support a pregnancy now. However, they recommended that I wait another three months just to be on the safe side. Which means by October I can get off all birth control and we can finally start expanding our family."

"I think we just got our very first miracle." Baron looked even more awestruck now.

"Oh, I think we've had many more than that." Aurelia chuckled. "As I reflect on our whole relationship, I see that it took miracle after miracle to not only get us together, but to also keep us together."

"So this is probably more like miracle number 2,000, huh?" Baron laughed as well, holding her even closer to him.

"More like 12,000 if you count the little miracles, too. For instance, every time I cook a decent meal that you and Trent actually like is yet another miracle."

Baron burst out laughing. "You've come a long way, baby. So what if one meal out of the week is a flop. One out of seven ain't bad at all. It used to be seven out of seven."

"So true." Aurelia snickered. "It's a good thing you didn't marry me for my cooking."

"A part of me did marry you for your cooking. Your bedroom cooking." Baron chuckled, kissing the side of her damp neck as You by Raheem Devaughn played in the background. "I like every meal you serve me in the bedroom. They're always delicious and piping hot."

"Oh, Baron," Aurelia purred. She let out another sigh of contentment as a nice breeze wafted over their bodies, cooling them down further. "By the way, when did the stars come out? Were we at it that long?"

Baron just laughed and planted another kiss on her neck. Then before any wayward mosquitoes could descend and ruin this special moment, he finally disengaged them, picked

Aurelia up in his arms and carried her to their bedroom for more snuggling and of course, more loving.

CHAPTER SIXTY-FIVE

September

After rethinking a few things, Aurelia and Baron decided that it would be better to remain in California for a few more years. That decision was made back in August after Emile married Locke and it became time for Trent to attend regular school.

With Aurelia's name on the boy's birth certificate, they simply couldn't enroll him in a V.I. school where the wrong kind of attention would be cast their way. They especially didn't want to draw any attention from Pierre's uncle, who was now living full-time in the Virgin Islands again.

However, the Weavers did relocate nevertheless. They moved to a place where only two people knew them – Count and Jenny. That place was Irvine, California. They chose Irvine because of its good schools, job opportunities, prime real estate, low crime rates, and the fact that there were at least two relatives nearby. Count and Jenny even lived in the same neighborhood.

The fact that Irvine was farther away from Bel Air than Alcove was an added incentive. There was little chance of running into Megan there.

They later learned that Megan left the whole state of California over the summer. She moved to Vegas after deciding to become roommates with Fran and a steady girlfriend to Gino.

Sadly, Fran and Megan ended up losing nearly all of their money by overdoing things at the casinos, shopping malls and boutiques, spas, and in numerous other self-indulgent activities. Fran went and found a job when most of her money dried up.

In contrast, Megan unknowingly sold her deceased husband's trucking business to Baron, or rather to the Wehpen Company. With those funds she continued to overindulge herself. She and Fran ceased to be close friends when their lifestyles became polar opposites. Their split could be blamed solely on Megan, who no longer wanted to be friends with a boring nine-to-fiver.

Meanwhile, the Weavers continued to grow their finances. All of their businesses were in the black and they just rented their old home to Mrs. Applegate's son. Doing so enabled their former neighbor to have her grandchildren around more often and also kinship nearby in case of emergency since she was getting up in age. This arrangement also allowed Mrs. Applegate to keep her daughter-in-law from taking over her house since the two women still clashed on occasion.

Claude and Bambi, who were now married, moved into one of the condos Baron owned in Alcove. The first six months of rent were given to them free as a wedding present. That was the most expensive wedding gift the newlyweds had gotten to date.

As for Aurelia and Baron's new house, they loved it even better than the old one, although it had two less bathrooms. They celebrated Trent's 6th birthday there, inviting family and friends from near and far.

Trent loved his new school. Baron loved his new job. Instead of being one of many professors in Alcove University's science department, Dr. Weaver was now head of the whole science department at Irvine Fuller University, a school that rivaled most Ivy League colleges in terms of quality of education.

With her priorities so much different these days, Aurelia decided not to obtain a new job right away. Getting things settled with her health and family came first. Not to forget the fact that she was still overseeing a perfume company that now had its own lab, ten regular employees, two delivery drivers, and a warehouse.

On top of all that, with her plans to become pregnant in another month, Aurelia had to be more selective about finding a forensic job that was family-friendly. A job that would allow her to work flexible hours like her perfume business.

Because she was about to expand her family, Aurelia also

decided to visit Pierre while she still could. She didn't know how he would react to the sight of her soon-to-be pregnant frame. As of yet he did not remember that she'd ever been pregnant by him and thus didn't realize that she had actually had that child by now.

When Pierre accidentally saw a picture of Aurelia and Trent in her wallet, which had fallen out of her purse, she found herself reluctantly telling him a half-truth to protect his delicate mind. She basically told him that Trent was known in the V.I. as her brother. She did not tell him that in California the lad was known as her son. That, in fact, he was their son.

These days, Baron worked hard to legally make Trent his son, too. He brought up the adoption possibility last month to Aurelia and a visiting Emile. Both women agreed to let Trent make the final decision on the matter.

Today was the day that Baron and Aurelia planned to make that pivotal suggestion to Trent. They both hoped he would be conducive to the idea.

* * *

"You look nervous, Mama Ree. Why?" Trent asked, noticing how much Aurelia fidgeted beside Baron on the brown sectional sofa of their new home. In the background soft Latin music played from the house's intricate intercom and stereo system.

Reminded of and relishing the new title he'd bestowed upon her lately, Aurelia immediately relaxed. "I'm nervous because Baron and I have a big question to ask you. Before we tell you what it is, we want you to know that you can say no, although we hope you say yes."

"All right. What is it?" Trent looked from her to Baron. There was no trace of his accent anywhere.

Aurelia had been working on toning his island tongue down for months for two main reasons. One, she wanted Trent to be better understood stateside. Two, she was trying to avoid playground ridicule from his peers, who were still too young to appreciate the differences in others. So far so good, although Trent did tend to return to his accent when excited or upset. Like mother, like son.

"We wanted to know if you would let me adopt you," Baron said after taking a deep breath of courage to calm his nerves. Who knew that this would mean so much to him? "In other words, I'd like to make you my official son. An official Weaver man."

Trent's eyes bucked. "I would like dat ah whole heap!" He grinned excitedly, immediately putting both adults further at ease. "I just hope meh birth daddy won't be too upset 'bout it up in heaven," he added in a more somber tone.

It was at that moment that Aurelia realized that it was time to tell her son more pieces of the truth concerning his paternity. She took a deep breath of courage of her own, blew it out, and then came out with the hard stuff. "Trent, your birth father is not in heaven yet. We thought he was, but found out just recently that he was still alive."

"He's alive?!" Trent's eyes bucked wider. A smile briefly touched his lips before drooping into an angry frown. "Why he no see me yet? Don't he wanna see me?"

"Well, right now your birth father is not emotionally or mentally able to handle seeing you…at least not as his son," Aurelia replied gingerly.

Then she went on to explain that Pierre had had a very bad accident while she was pregnant, suffered some brain damage, and as a result, was not able to deal with even the knowledge of a son right now. She also shared how during her last trip to Florida, Pierre did see him via photo, but how she ended up having to stretch the truth again by claiming that the child on the picture was only her little brother so as not to upset the mentally challenged man.

"I still wanna meet him," Trent decided with a firm shake of the head. "Even if he kin only know me as yur brotha."

"Are you sure about that, son?" Baron looked outright proud of the brave lad, who was a strong trooper just like his mother.

"Yep." Trent nodded. "In the meantime, I still want to be an official Weaver man since I know you want me around and can handle me being your son," he added to Baron in a much looser accent.

Both adults smiled. Rendered speechless, Aurelia's eyes welled up with tears. Happy tears.

"We'll make the arrangements for Pierre to come meet you as soon as possible," Baron replied, finally ready to invite the other man into their home again. Hopefully Pierre was ready to share this time.

* * *

Around 2am, Baron received a most disturbing call. It was from Big Mink of all people. No need to ask how the

Italian man got his number or even knew where he was now. Big Mink had connections all over the world. Some of them were deadly connections.

"I called to see if you wanted to collect on those favors I still owe you," Big Mink said in Italian, not even bothering to identify himself before getting to the point of his unexpected call.

Baron instantly became wide awake at the sound of the other man's voice. He could never forget that distinctive voice, which was a cross between gruff and raspy. Very Marlon Brando-ish.

"Sir, why would I need to collect on them now, if ever?" Baron asked in Italian, speaking low as he eased out of bed.

"Because doing so could save the lives of a few of your loved ones."

"I'm listening." Baron headed for the bathroom for more privacy.

There he listened very carefully as Big Mink revealed Oliver's plan to take out Aurelia's whole family just to gain guardianship of Trent. How the man really didn't want the boy out of love or out of a need to share what was left of the Jean-Baptiste empire. After all, the reason Oliver never had any children or got married was because he didn't want to share his fortune with anyone. The wicked man only wanted Trent so that he could harvest his organs.

"Over my dead body!" Baron raged loudly, thankful that the bathroom door was still closed, lest he awakened his wife.

Big Mink smiled, taking great pleasure in the younger man's loyalty to his family. Loyalty was one of the top admirable and even sought after traits in organized crime. "I figured you'd say that, which is why I'm giving you the power to make it over Oliver's dead body instead. All I need is your word and he's a goner just like Gino."

"Gino's dead?" Baron exclaimed, speaking in English this time. In his heart he wasn't too surprised by that dreadful news. His ex-friend just didn't have do-right in him anymore. Hadn't for a long time.

"He had it coming for a while now. Plus, he owed a lot of people a whole lot of money."

"Why didn't you call me sooner so that I could use at least one of my favors to save him, sir?" Baron replied in Italian now that he was somewhat calmer.

"For the very reason you just stated," Big Mink replied. "I couldn't allow Gino to be saved this time, not even by you, Professor. Like I said before, he owed a lot of people a whole lot of money. When they came to collect it, he only had half, even after emptying out the bank account of that Bel Air blonde he was seeing. You know, the same blonde you were going to marry once upon a time."

Baron shook his head in disgust. This was getting worse and worse. "Is Megan dead, too?" he had to ask, speaking in English once again.

"No. She was spared because she had no clue who Gino really was or what he was really up to. I made sure of that. Right now she thinks he just stole her money and skipped town. That's what she needs to keep thinking, because she's never getting that money back," Big Mink said with emphasis.

"I understand, sir." Baron returned to Italian again as his body relaxed in relief. Although he didn't like Megan anymore, he still didn't want her dead. "Now back to Oliver. Since I don't think I can live with a man's death over my head, I propose that he be told to back off of me and my family forever."

"Some people need more than talking to."

"Not if the right people talked to them, sir," Baron countered in a respectful tone. "Besides, if Oliver is as sick as you say, he won't be here much longer anyway. Just let him die of natural causes."

Big Mink chuckled. "All right. It'll be as you ask," he finally consented. "By the way, I'm proud of how you've been keeping your nose clean all this time. Have a good life, Professor."

"Thank you, sir…for everything. You have a good life, too," Baron replied as the phone call concluded. Inwardly he knew that no trace of this call would ever appear on his phone bill or Big Mink's. That was just how well connected the Italian man was.

When Baron finally opened the bathroom door seconds later, he encountered none other than Aurelia.

Dang.

I wonder how long she's been listening?

* * *

"I may not know Italian, but I heard enough English in your conversation just now to know that somebody's dead.

Who is it? Megan, Gino, Oliver? All three?" Aurelia asked, not bothering to pretend like she hadn't been eavesdropping a few seconds ago.

"Gino's greed finally killed him. Megan is still alive, but she's now broke. Oliver, well, have a seat on the bed so I can tell you what the deal is with him," Baron replied, ready to tell his number one confidant everything. Everything except for Big Mink's name and true identity, that is. No use getting them all killed.

Aurelia listened in shocked silence as he shared the basic details of his conversation with a man that he refused to even mention by name. A man that had the power to kill others at whim. A man who just pledged to protect Aurelia's whole family simply because of Baron's uprightness. She'd never loved her husband more than right now.

"Say something, baby," Baron gently prompted when she remained silent a full thirty seconds after he finished his summation.

"I'm too full to seh much of anyting right now." Aurelia blinked by tears. "So let me show you how much I appreciate having such a wonderful man of compassion and integrity in my life," she said with a looser accent.

Before Baron could respond, Aurelia attacked his lips and proceeded to make love to him with ferocity and with an intensity that he never even knew she possessed. Talk about passion!

Afterwards the Weavers did something even more amazing together. Something that they'd never done after sex before – they prayed.

Before her eyes closed in slumber again, Aurelia wanted to personally thank God once again for bringing Baron into her and her family's lives. She didn't realize until tonight just how much of a godsend her husband really was. Or that his mob ties would actually help her family instead of hurt them.

After Baron added his own words of gratitude to that prayer, they both said a united 'amen'. Then they snuggled together in bed until sleep descended again.

CHAPTER SIXTY-SIX

On the Saturday that Pierre was scheduled to meet Trent, everything that could go wrong did. It was a rainy day in Irvine, Aurelia was coming down with a cold, and the batteries in both cars went dead at the same time. The VW was currently on loan to an out-of-town classic car museum and it was raining too hard to use the motorcycle. Thus even those forms of transportation had been cut off from them.

Yet the Weavers refused to reschedule today's meeting. It meant too much to Trent. To all of them.

To try to turn this tide of seemingly bad luck, Baron called Count and asked him for a ride to get the necessary new car batteries. Jenny came over to look after Aurelia while the men were gone. The pregnant woman had to wear a surgical mask for obvious reasons. She gave Trent a mask as well.

Together they pampered Aurelia with lots of TLC and Vitamin C, which she stopped taking while on all the other medication she'd been given over the summer. Now she saw how unwise that was. The congestion in her sinuses seemed like it was trying to make up for lost time today.

"I think I want to be a doctor, Mama Ree," Trent told Aurelia after successfully taking her temperature again.

"You can be my doctor any time," Aurelia encouraged. "I feel better already thanks to you and Aunt Jenny." She smiled from him to her radiant sister-in-law.

"That's Nurse Aunt Jenny to you, senora," Jenny protested playfully.

Aurelia and Trent laughed. By the time Baron and Count returned, the patient was well on her way to recovery.

* * *

518

"What's taking them so long to get here?" Trent asked his mother as they waited in the living room for Pierre and Julian to arrive.

Baron had gone to the airport to pick Pierre and Julian up almost an hour ago. Although the new arrivals could have taken a taxi or rental car, Julian thought that thirty-minute drive to the Weaver house would get Pierre used to having Baron around. Thus making it easier to be around him for the remainder of their visit.

Incidentally, Gisele would not be accompanying them on this visit either. She only recently had her baby and was still resting at home.

"It's a stormy day, Trent. Baron had to drive slower than usual to the airport," Aurelia explained. "Plus, there was that flight delay because of the storm and he had two flat tires while he was there," she added, reminding him of his stepfather's latest text message.

"Oh." Trent nodded, comprehending his mother's explanation perfectly. Although his face grew calmer, he still continued to fidget in his seat near the door. Blame it on nervous energy.

Just then the doorbell rang.

"I get it!" Trent leapt up from his seat. "It's probably dem right now."

Before Aurelia could remind him that Baron wouldn't be ringing the doorbell to the house since he had a key, Trent had flung the door open to reveal…

Oliver Jean-Baptiste?

"Go to your room, Trent," Aurelia ordered when the gray-haired man boldly stepped into her home without being asked.

"But…"

"Now!" Aurelia cut off her son's protest. She had to get him away from Oliver.

The frail-looking man might have lost a lot of weight, but the evil in his heart would undoubtedly give him enough strength to do harm to someone. It had certainly caused him to become brave enough to defy a direct order from Baron's powerful mobster friend. If someone was destined to get hurt today, Aurelia was determined that it would not be her son.

Fortunately, Trent quickly moved away from the door. He even left the room, but he did not go to his bedroom as

Aurelia requested. He simply could not leave his mother completely alone with the wicked-looking man. Why oh why did he ever open that door?

"No need to get yourself all upset." Oliver shut the door behind him. "I come in peace." As usual, his voice was devoid of an island accent since he considered that manner of speaking beneath him and a major hindrance to him in international business.

"Says de spider to de fly, huh?" Aurelia retorted. "However, dis time I believe you'll find me ah lot more defiant den dat particular insect." She rose to her feet and got in a self-defense boxing stance Baron taught her during one of their joint workouts.

Oliver threw his head back and laughed. Even that sounded wicked. "You always were a spitfire. Definitely too spirited for my timid nephew. And you still got the sexiest pair of lips I've ever seen on a woman," he said, deliberately trying to stir up old memories. Wicked memories.

At the mention of his nephew, Aurelia remembered that Pierre was on his way to her house right now. Did Oliver know that? If so, how did he know that? Either way, Aurelia had to get rid of him quick!

"What do you want, Oliver? Why are you here?" Aurelia asked, cutting to the chase. Being around him made her flesh crawl.

"I'm here to collect on a debt," Oliver replied casually, just as casually sitting down in a nearby chair.

Aurelia heard a few of his bones pop in protest as he sat down, reminding her that he had become a very old man in just six short years. Undoubtedly evil had rotted his bones and aged him prematurely. Seeing Oliver so frail caused any remaining fear of him to dissipate in her heart.

"I don't owe you anyting, mon," Aurelia said with rising ire.

"Oh, yes, you do," Oliver insisted. "You owe me big for taking my money and not holding up to your end of the deal. You kept that child against my express wishes. Then you used my money to take care of him. I'm here for my repayment."

"Dis little surprise visit is 'bout money?" Aurelia walked over to her purse, which was hanging on a nearby wall hook. "I be glad to write you ah check so you kin be on yur merry little way."

"Keep your check. I don't want it." He waved his right hand dismissively.

"What do you want then?" Aurelia asked warily, although she was pretty sure she already knew what he really wanted today.

"I want one of Trent's kidneys as my repayment," Oliver replied bluntly, confirming her suspicions. "The doctors tell me I need one very badly, preferably from a close blood relative. That boy is the closest living relative I have, which means one of his kidneys rightfully belongs to me."

"No!" Aurelia shouted, incensed by his arrogance. "You not gonna use meh son for parts. Besides, Trent had surgery just last December. His body can't take anotha invasive procedure so soon. Den dere's his diabetes to consider—"

"That boy looked healthy as an ox to me." Oliver quickly dismissed her concerns for Trent's health. Only his own health mattered. "Plus, he's young. Children are resilient. He'll be just fine after the surgery."

"No," Aurelia persisted. "I'll give yur money back wid interest, but not one of meh son's kidneys." She didn't care how healthy Trent was right now or about the fact that a healthier diet had resulted in him having to take less medication these days. Oliver was not going to use her son's body for parts and that was that!

Oliver rose to his feet. "Don't make me get angry, Aurelia. You wouldn't like me when I'm angry."

"I don't like you now. Never did. And who you 'posed to be now, mon? David Banner from de Incredible Hulk?" She quipped at that unoriginal line he just sprouted. "Now once and for all, de answer is no!"

"I see you want to do this the hard way." Oliver yanked a small gun from his right jacket pocket and pointed it at her.

"What be yur plans now, Oliver? To kill me and kidnap meh son in order to harvest his organs?" Aurelia said, more shocked than afraid at the insanity of Oliver's intent.

Did mental illness run in the Jean-Baptiste family? The kind that had not been triggered by accident? If so, hopefully that trait skipped Trent's genes, the same way her father's diabetes trait had skipped hers.

"If you had only cooperated with me, you could've joined us on the private jet that I have waiting for us at the airport, been there for your son at the hospital, and returned home with him once everything was over, all safe and sound. But no, you just had to be difficult!" Oliver waved the gun menacingly at her. "Now call the boy back downstairs."

"You won't get away wid dis. Baron and his very powerful associates will make sure of dat," Aurelia replied, stalling for time.

Like Oliver, she knew that Trent wouldn't come back downstairs unless she asked him to. She also knew that the frail man probably didn't have the stamina to go hunting the boy down in the large house. There were just too many places to hide.

Oliver scoffed. "I've gotten away with much more than that, little lady. As for your husband and his associates, they're going to have to find me first. By the time they find out what I've done, I'll be long out of the country and in hiding."

"Baron be here any minute now. He won't let you make it to dat jet."

Oliver laughed in derision. "You really think that husband of yours is Superman, don't you? He might have been able to rescue you and your family out of poverty, but unless he can fly, I seriously doubt he'll be able to stop me in time. Not after I paid some local street punk to slash both of his front tires to give me a good head-start out of town," he said, solving the mystery of Baron's sudden flat tires. He still didn't let on that he hired a P.I. to find her and Trent, a new one since his old P.I. refused to have anything more to do with him. "Now call the boy downstairs real nice-like."

"Did you pay some local island punk to murda Marshall so dat you could snatch his inheritance and keep it for yurself?" Aurelia did her best to keep him talking. The longer she did, the longer Trent would be safe and the quicker Baron would be home to rescue them. If only there was a way to get a warning message to her husband.

"Stop wasting time, Aurelia. Either call Trent down here or I shoot you now and go up there to get him myself." Oliver looked like climbing stairs was the last thing he wanted to do.

Suddenly, a loud blast of Latin music blared from the house's intercom system.

Seeing that as an opportunity to make a hasty escape, Aurelia took off for the hallway, leaving her purse and the startled old man behind. She had to get up those stairs, into Trent's room, where there was a phone and plenty of golf clubs, baseball bats, and even a few heavy horseshoes. Any kind of weapon would do since there were no guns in the house.

"Wha de…" Aurelia started when she saw Trent already in the hallway with his cell phone in hand. The boy had been working on a plan of his own the whole time.

Beaming proudly at her brilliant son, Aurelia pointed to the stairs, silently letting him know what her plan was. She counted on them being younger, healthier, and faster than Oliver to make it up to Trent's room in time to even the odds a bit.

Would they make it?

CHAPTER SIXTY-SEVEN

Aurelia and Trent made it to his room with more than enough time to spare. Oliver was just approaching the bottom of the stairwell when Aurelia slammed the bedroom door closed and quickly locked it behind them.

If only she wasn't battling a cold. Then maybe she wouldn't be so winded right now. Wouldn't be coughing so noisily.

It was a good thing the music's volume was turned up so high. Otherwise Oliver would know exactly which bedroom they were in within the large house from Aurelia's loud coughing alone.

"I texted Daddy Baron and told him 'bout de evil man wid eyes like mine," Trent whispered, showing how smart and strong he was as he pushed his large wooden toy box in front of the bedroom door. "He texted back dat he be coming home right away and bringing de police wid him. He told me to turn de music up real loud so we could have ah good chance to get upstairs."

"Brilliant," Aurelia wheezed out, so glad that she taught Trent how to read and write early in life. So glad that they'd bought him that cell phone, despite his young age. "Nuff respect, son," she added, still trying to inhale deep enough to steady her breathing. Aurelia also did her best to muffle any subsequent coughs, though she was pretty sure Oliver couldn't hear her over the loud music.

"Dat wasn't all Daddy Baron said. He told me to tell you dat he loves us both and for us to get under my bed and wait for help to come." As Trent spoke, he stacked crates of baseballs and basketballs on top of the closed toy box. He moved even faster when the music suddenly cut off. All that could be heard now was the heavy downpour outside.

Realizing that Oliver had found a way to disable the intercom system, Aurelia went over to her son's closet in search of specific weapons. Time was of the essence now for sure.

"Did Baron also tell you to push the toy box up against the door, too?" she asked, after finally getting a good deep breath into her lungs. Now her whisper really did sound like a whisper instead of a congested wheeze. Her accent had also loosened again. Blame it on the peace Aurelia felt knowing that her husband was aware of their plight and was coming to help.

"Yeah." Trent nodded. "But de stacking was all meh idea."

"Smart boy." Aurelia swiftly pulled two bats and two golf clubs out of the closet. "Here, son. If by some evil design the demons in that wicked old man make him strong enough to get through a locked door, a heavy toy box, and crates of balls, I want you to hit a homerun with his knees. I'll knock his block off." She handed over a bat and a golf club.

"We not gettin' under de bed?"

"No." Aurelia shook her head. "We've hid from this man long enough. Now stand on the far left side of the toy box while I stand on the right side nearest to the door. We're about to play some baseball today."

As Trent received the weapons his mother handed him, a look of sheer admiration entered his eyes. Aurelia's courage inspired him to be just as courageous. They would make it through this new trial just like all the others…somehow.

To make sure they did, Trent pulled on a few silent prayers that his Grandma Ana Maria taught all the Weaver grandchildren. It couldn't hurt to get a Higher Power involved, could it? They needed all the help they could get right now.

* * *

"I'm going to shoot you in front of your boy just for making me climb those stairs in my condition," Oliver wheezed angrily from the top landing of the stairs. "Don't you know that I am a sick man?" he said, kicking the first unlocked bedroom door open.

Aurelia bit back a retort. Now was not the time for a sharp tongue. Now was the time for silence.

Suddenly a myriad of lights shone from below. Yes, the

outdoor lighting of the house had come on by this time due to the lateness of the hour as day prepared to turn into night. But some of those lights belonged to cars.

Those car lights belonged to Baron's Porsche and several police vehicles. One cop car was in front of the Weaver vehicle, which contained Baron, Julian, and Pierre. Two more were right behind it.

"Give it up, Mr. Jean-Baptiste. We have the house surrounded," a no-nonsense sounding officer spoke through a bullhorn. His voice could be heard clearly above the rain, which was starting to get lighter now.

Oliver cursed. "Now look what you did, tramp!" he accused Aurelia two bedrooms away. The fact that the police were here and he'd been addressed by name meant that somehow the word had leaked out about him and his intentions.

Again Aurelia remained silent. She put a finger up to her lips and shook her head to caution Trent to remain silent, as well. His face had gotten red with rage at that unflattering name she'd been called. The boy definitely had that Bunting temper. Both of them had gotten that trait from her father, who'd been a sweet man until riled up by some injustice.

"Mr. Jean-Baptiste, it is in your best interest to surrender your weapon to us and come out peacefully," the officer outside said, speaking directly to the sick man again.

Oliver entered the bedroom of the door he'd kicked in, tiptoed over to a window, stood beside it and carefully slid it up, leaving the vertical blinds intact. "I'll surrender peacefully when this tramp in here agrees to give me the kidney I need," he shouted down to the authorities.

"If you're sick, Mr. Jean-Baptiste, we can get you some help at one of our fine local hospitals," the officer said.

"Unless they have a kidney from one of my close relatives handy, going there won't do me a lick of good," Oliver replied.

"You're doing it all wrong!" a frustrated and very familiar voice suddenly said from below. "My uncle responds better to blackmail than negotiation. Isn't that right, Uncle Oliver?" Pierre said, exiting the car with Julian and Baron.

"Frenchie?" Oliver choked out, straining to see who was talking through the slits in the blinds. It sounded like his nephew's voice, but yet so childlike.

"Yes, Uncle Oliver, it's me," Pierre shouted up in that

same childlike voice. "They call me Pierre now though ever since my brain stopped working good. Anyway, I need you to let Aurelia and Trent go. If you don't, I'll tell these nice policemen here all of your secrets, including the ones about me and my parents." He spoke of things that he started to remember as soon as he heard his uncle's angry voice. Highly incriminating things.

Oliver didn't know how his nephew had survived this long, but upon seeing Julian standing next to Pierre, he quickly realized who helped him recover. Who also kept him hidden all these years.

Oliver also realized that he was about to lose everything. The businesses, the houses, and the remaining trust fund money. Everything.

For if his nephew was alive and past the age of twenty-one, everything had to go to Pierre as determined in his brother's will.

What was the use of having a new kidney now?

Julian would undoubtedly remain Pierre's guardian once the whole truth came out, which meant that Oliver would be penniless. Not only that, he would spend his remaining years in jail for trying to murder his nephew and actually murdering Pierre's parents. The latter was something Pierre discovered long ago and tried to blackmail his uncle with when he sought Oliver's approval of his marriage to Aurelia.

Was it even necessary to bring up the mob? Big Mink had warned Oliver to leave Baron and his family alone, including all in-laws. Although Oliver cancelled any hits on them and had intended to just borrow Trent for a while, he knew that that excuse wouldn't jive with Big Mink. He knew he'd signed a guaranteed death warrant on himself by coming here today.

Oliver didn't want to live in a world where he was among the poor anyway. But he also didn't want to die in prison. He definitely didn't want to end up as fish bait after some mob hit. Thus Oliver would take his destiny into his own hands today. Yet before he killed himself, he intended to send a few other people to the grave before him.

"Mr. Jean-Baptiste, are you still there?" an officer prompted when he'd been silent for too long.

In reply, Oliver aimed at Julian and squeezed the trigger, hitting the man in the chest. Before everyone else could take cover, he pointed the gun at Pierre.

Suddenly another squeezing occurred. This time in Oliver's chest.

"Aaughhh…" he uttered in pain, clenching at his chest with one hand, still holding the gun with the other. The gun went off again right before Oliver fell to the floor in a heap.

* * *

Oh, God! Please let my loved ones be all right, Aurelia prayed two rooms away, wishing she was more spiritual like her mother-in-law after hearing those shots down the hall. Maybe then she'd have the reassurance that her prayer would go through.

Suddenly there was a loud ruckus downstairs. The front door had been pushed against the wall upon being unlocked by Baron's key. Multiple pairs of feet met carpet and then the staircase itself.

Shortly thereafter there were sounds of feet running down the hall. Some of them entered the room where Oliver was. Some kept coming closer to Trent's room.

"Is dat de police coming for us, Mama Ree?" Trent asked excitedly.

"I think so, baby," Aurelia replied. "But let's wait a few more minutes before removing our barricades just in case."

Soon there was a female officer at Trent's bedroom door. "Mrs. Weaver, it's safe for you and your son to come out now."

"Please be all right," Baron could be heard whispering on the other side of the door.

In the distance, the sound of an ambulance coming nearer to the house was also heard. The rain had all but stopped now.

"Dr. Weaver, I thought we told you to stay outside," the officer scolded.

"I stayed outside long enough," Baron argued. "Now speak up in there, Ree-Ree! Trent! Tell me that you're all right."

"We're both fine!" Aurelia shouted as she and Trent worked together to remove their barricades.

When the door finally opened, there was Baron standing with enormous relief on his face. He snatched Aurelia and Trent into each of his arms and hugged them tightly. "Are you really all right?" He withdrew a bit to look at them both, one at a time. "That old fool didn't hurt you, did he?"

"No, we're fine thanks to Trent, who did everything you

told him to do and then some." Aurelia moved closer to her husband again. She squeezed her son closer, too. Their son.

"Good boy," Baron told his stepson.

"Ah de man, huh?" Trent smiled up at his stepfather with glossy eyes.

Baron smiled down at him with equally glossy eyes. "Yes, you de man."

"I hate to break up this tender moment, Dr. Weaver, but we need to take your family downstairs and let them get officially checked out," the female officer gently reminded him with shiny eyes of her own.

"Of course," Baron said, allowing the officer to lead the way downstairs.

"Is Pierre all right?" Aurelia asked as they descended the stairs in single file on the right side of the wide stairwell to allow for authorized traffic on the opposite side. "We heard gunshots."

"Physically, Pierre is fine," Baron assured her. "Emotionally, he is distraught because Oliver shot Julian. The paramedics are with both of them now. They might need your help calming Pierre down though."

"I'll do what I can." Aurelia nodded. "By the way, where is Oliver? Did someone shoot him in return?" She didn't really want the man dead, just out of their lives for good.

"He's being worked on by paramedics upstairs," the officer with them replied. "It looks like he had a heart attack, causing that second shot to go wild. You'll probably need to re-plaster and repaint that bedroom wall after we retrieve the bullet from it."

"If that evil man dies in our house, we're moving out and letting somebody else deal with that wall," Aurelia said firmly, receiving nods of confirmation from Baron and Trent.

None of them wanted to live in a place where the likes of Oliver Jean-Baptiste had died. It was going to be hard enough living here after he tried to terrorize Aurelia and Trent in their own home. So far the chair Oliver sat on would be thrown out, the carpet he walked on would be replaced, and all the walls would be repainted. Those things had already been put on Aurelia's mental to-do list.

"In any case, we're going to sleep at Count's house tonight anyway," Baron said, spotting his brother through the open door ahead.

Count was among the crowd of concerned people now gathered a distance in front of the house. But that's the way it should be. Relatives should always be somewhere around in times of trouble.

* * *

Fortunately, Oliver did not die at the Weaver home. He died hours later at the hospital. No one grieved for him, not even Pierre.

The young man was too busy grieving over his current guardian, who fortunately did not die. The bullet went straight through Julian's body without damaging any vital organs.

Hallelujah!

Aurelia proved to be a great comfort for Pierre, even more so than Gisele who was flown in via private jet thanks to Baron. While the doctors worked on Julian, Aurelia kept Pierre calm by speaking riddles to him in French. He answered every one of them correctly. While the police questioned Pierre about his uncle's many secrets, she kept him calm by simply holding his hand.

A silent Baron sat nearby, looking on with approval. Trent had been entrusted into the hands of Count and Jenny soon after he was checked out by competent ER physicians. They took him home with them upon leaving the hospital.

During the course of the night, it amazed Aurelia that her former beau could remember almost everything about his past now except for their times of intimacy, her pregnancy, and their forfeited nuptials. It was as if Pierre's mind was deliberately protecting him from that which he was still unable to handle.

But why?

Why was it easier for Pierre to remember and handle all the wickedness of his evil uncle and not his intimate relationship with the woman he once intended to marry? At this point Aurelia really didn't want him to remember those things. It would only complicate matters. They all had enough on their plates right now as it was.

Another thing that amazed Aurelia today was the fact that her cold symptoms had all but disappeared while her adrenaline was at its highest. Yet as soon as she and Baron settled into a guest bedroom of Count and Jenny's house, every symptom tried to return with a vengeance. There was lots of nausea and vomiting this time.

Baron ended up having to take Aurelia back to the hospital. There it was confirmed that she was pregnant.

Pregnant!

And it wasn't even October yet.

It seems that some of the medications Aurelia took during the summer had weakened the effects of her birth control. Because she'd answered in the negative when the ER doctors asked her the pregnancy question earlier, no pregnancy test had been administered then. Every possible test had been conducted this time around.

Now the Weavers had even more reason to move forward with their lives. And they would as sure as the sun would rise tomorrow and set in the western sky.

EPILOGUE

Three Years Later

Aurelia and Baron had a beautiful little girl eight months after that Oliver incident. They named her Baroness Ana Emile Weaver and she was completely diabetes-free. As of this writing, Aurelia was pregnant again. With another son this time.

Although the Weavers still lived in California, they continued to spend their summers, select holidays, and monthly weekend visits in the Virgin Islands. Doing so gave them a chance to enjoy Aurelia and Trent's homeland as well as visit with their island relatives, who were all still prospering due to their profitable basket-weaving business and the real estate holdings they now owned.

With that prosperity came better health care. Now Aurelia's uncle had his diabetes and high blood pressure under control. Because Uncle Sam was physically stronger now, he helped out in the shop more days out of the week and managed all Bunting rental properties.

People on the island finally know that Aurelia is Trent's real mother. They also know that Pierre is the biological father, despite the fact that Trent still bears the Weaver last name. The truth finally came out when Julian and his family relocated to St. John to live year round in Pierre's childhood home, which was just one of many properties the young man inherited after Oliver's death.

Actually the truth about Trent's true paternity didn't have any choice but to come out when it did. The day Pierre happened to see a pregnant Aurelia walking along a beach in St. Croix, memories of their intimacy came flooding back in and he became confused.

A part of Pierre's brain thought she was pregnant with his child. The other part knew that she couldn't be because the time frames didn't add up. There was no way Aurelia could still be pregnant with his child after all these years. It didn't make sense.

Pierre was devastated to learn that Aurelia was actually pregnant with Baron's second child, her third, and that she was married to the Latino man. Had been for years now.

Ironically, the only thing that appeased Pierre was the knowledge that at least Trent was still his and that he could spend as much time as he liked with him. Especially during the summer months. To please him even more, Aurelia added Pierre's middle name to Trent's. Now the boy was legally and officially named Trenton Pierre Bunting Weaver.

It didn't take long for Trent and Pierre to become the best of friends. Although Pierre will probably never be mentally able to handle being a father, he sure knew how to be a great playmate. He also knew how to keep a promise.

After Pierre vividly remembered telling Aurelia that he would take care of their child, he had Julian to arrange for Trent to have half of the Jean-Baptiste inheritance right now. Aurelia put those funds in the trust that Baron established for their son a long time ago.

Since her oldest child was financially taken care of for the rest of his natural life, Aurelia took the money she earned from her perfume business and put it into trust funds for her younger kids, including the one on the way. Baron doubled her contribution every month from his share of the profits from his successful natural enhancing cream for men. Now all of their children were trust fund babies.

Trent was still doing well in school. He was a positive influence on his classmates and even on his birthfather. Because of him, Pierre returned to his previous stance of tolerating Baron's presence and even speaking civilly to him, though the other man couldn't touch Aurelia or Trent while he was around.

Baron respected Pierre's feelings. He'd made his peace with the situation long ago. He knew he would probably feel the same way if he were in Pierre's shoes.

Baron was also very understanding about the fact that Aurelia still occasionally saved ketchup and mustard packs from the fast food restaurants she visited, still bought Ramen noodles, and still thought it was a sin to throw out leftovers.

Life had taught him that it sometimes took a while for a person's poverty mentality to leave, despite an abundance of present riches.

As for the rest of Baron's family, his parents were still alive and well. Nicolas and Ana Maria continued to dote on their grandchildren and pray daily for even more of them to love.

Count and Jenny were still happy and fruitful. They were up to their third child as of this writing. Now they have two girls and one boy.

Marquess and Paula have been equally fruitful. Although they still had to practice certain precautions, their marital bed continued to be very fulfilling and productive. In fact, it has produced two strong sons thus far.

Earl's black hair, darker complexion, and finances were completely restored by this time. So was his marriage to Meadow. Together they were a force to be reckoned with in Bel Air. As a result of Earl's new pride in his heritage, it was now chic to be Hispanic at their country club.

Duke and Sasha still have a strong marriage. They moved to Beverly Hills and became a power couple of their own there. They even had one more child, another son.

With the reduction of infidelity among the ranks of the Weavers, there was also a decrease in schism among the brothers. Baron and Earl were closer than they've ever been thanks to the tight relationship of their eldest sons. He and Marquess were camping regularly together again, but on a bi-monthly basis due to their busy schedules. They even brought their wives and children on occasion. However, the more risky hiking was left to the men for obvious reasons.

As for the Weavers' friends and associates, Dingo and Crystal got out of the adult entertainment business altogether after they were married. Now they provided regular entertainment such as singers, musicians, dance troupes, and comedians to hotels all over California and Nevada. They even serviced the historic hotel Baron restored in Alcove.

Six-Eight took ownership of the strip club after Dingo and Crystal left. He rehired Raven, who'd gone to nursing school after her diagnosis, to help keep better track of the medical records of the girls and to provide monthly seminars at the club about the importance of safe sex. Raven regularly conducted some of those same seminars on college campuses in the local area.

Cain, which was the moniker he returned to, finally decided to become a part of his son's life. He figured why not get to know the person who was receiving so much of his money. That decision led to Cain not only falling in love with fatherhood, but also with Roxy, who had become quite a classy lady by this time. He married her on their son's third birthday. They all lived together in his Alcove home.

Kingston finally finished college thanks to the Weaver scholarship that he received at the beginning of his senior year. After graduation, he returned home to the Virgin Islands and married a wonderful woman from St. Thomas.

Jewell straightened up her act after the Buntings caught her red-handed on film. Now she actually lived in Aurelia's childhood home with her children. The Buntings couldn't have asked for a better tenant. Jewell always paid her rent on time and took good care of their property.

Claude went on to medical school while Bambi immersed herself into managing the day-to-day operations of the rising perfume dynasty that she and Aurelia owned. Although the Greenmans were still waiting to start their family, they were thrilled to be the godparents of Baron and Aurelia's kids.

Rhoda was still manless and childless. However, she was able to find another teaching position on the east coast. Although she would have loved to take more revenge on Baron, Aurelia, and even William, she recently set her sights on a new man and thus was quite willing to just hate her California enemies for the rest of her life.

Jordin no longer hated Aurelia and Baron. After her boss assigned her to do a piece on how the Weavers had positively impacted the city of Alcove, economically and otherwise, she realized that they were people to be admired, not loathed. People to be emulated, not envied. Because of her new positive outlook on life, Jordin was now happily engaged to the handsome new sportscaster at the station.

Dr. William Johansson was also happily engaged now. After Mai Ly followed her niece's example and finally declared her interest to the man she wanted instead of waiting for him to make the first move, they started dating. The rest, as they say, was history.

After Gino's betrayal and disappearance, Megan left Vegas an even bitterer woman than before. Had she only followed Fran's example and made herself useful to society by finding a job, she might have met and fallen in love with another upstanding guy like Baron and gotten married by now.

Fran was deliriously happy these days. She was going to be even happier in three months. That's when the surrogate mother she and her new husband hired to carry their embryos gave birth to their twins – a son and a daughter.

Upon leaving Vegas, Megan sold her Bel Air home, which was all she had left of any substantial value, and moved to Canada to start a new life. Ironically, she moved across the street from a mature, blue-eyed man named Murray Underwood. Murray was fast becoming a positive father figure to her. Megan needed someone in that role ever since her Uncle Ford became so proud and engrossed in his own daughter's life.

If only Murray's positive influence on Megan's life had been present before she left the states. Then maybe she wouldn't have sent Baron an inflammatory letter about her and Earl.

Although Baron suspected that that letter might have held some semblance of truth in it, it was largely disregarded as falsehood.

Why?

It was too imbalanced. Megan blamed Earl for starting their illicit affair, accused him of blackmailing her for money without provocation, and claimed that he tried to sabotage Baron's marriage all on his own. As a result of her refusal to shoulder any blame or present a more balanced view of her dealings with Earl, Baron deemed Megan's letter the bitter ramblings of an equally bitter woman.

On top of all that, Baron had already forgiven his brother for dealing with Megan on any level. Why revisit the past and all of its pain again? It was better to just keep moving forward.

That's exactly what Baron and Aurelia did, too. They moved forward into their happily ever after.

The End

www.ingramcontent.com/pod-product-compliance
Lightning Source LLC
Chambersburg PA
CBHW071335020726
47502CB00001B/100

9 780099 123 4 004

LETTER TO READERS

At first I was going to make my usual closing comments in paragraph form in this section. At the last minute, I decided to put them in bulleted form instead and entitle them 'Morals Of This Story', because if nothing else *The Professor* was a long fable full of important lessons to be learned and applied to real life...for those whose hearts are open to it.

Morals Of This Story:

- Never start a relationship off with sex. Take the time to really get to know a person before becoming intimate with them. If you don't, you can very well open your life up to minor things such has uncomfortable situations (Baron and Aurelia), to major things such as disease (Marquess and Raven) and unplanned pregnancies (Cain and Roxy).

- Know that everyone has secrets. Never crucify someone for theirs when you know you have some of your own. Especially if your secrets are even worse.

- Lies will get too heavy to carry after a while. So why not just tell the truth from the start?

- One lie usually leads to another. The only way to stop them is to just be truthful.

- Be careful who you tell your truths to. Everybody can't handle certain types of sensitive information.

- Husbands and wives should talk about the hard things (i.e. sensitive topics) in their relationships if they want to avoid those very things tearing them apart later.

- You really do reap what you sow. Megan and Rhoda sowed destruction into the lives of others and they reaped the very same thing in their own lives.

Thanks for reading along with me!
- Suprina Frazier/Mi'Chelle Dodson